MOUNTAIN STANDARD TIME

BY PAUL HORGAN

NOVELS

The Fault of Angels

No Quarter Given

Main Line West

A Lamp on the Plains

Far From Cibola

The Habit of Empire

The Common Heart

Give Me Possession

A Distant Trumpet

Mountain Standard Time (*a collected volume
containing Main Line West, Far From Cibola, and The
Common Heart, with a Foreword and three Afterwords
by the author*)

SHORTER FICTION

The Return of the Weed

Figures in a Landscape

The Devil in the Desert

One Red Rose For Christmas

The Saintmaker's Christmas Eve

Humble Powers

HISTORY AND BELLES-LETTRES

Men of Arms (*juvenile*)

From the Royal City

New Mexico's Own Chronicle (*with Maurice Garland Fulton*)

Biographical Introductions to Volumes I and II of

Diary and Letters of Josiah Gregg (*edited by Maurice Garland Fulton*)

Great River: The Rio Grande in North American History

The Centuries of Santa Fe

Rome Eternal

Citizen of New Salem

Conquistadors

Mountain Standard Time

MAIN LINE WEST
FAR FROM CIBOLA
THE COMMON HEART

by Paul Horgan

INTRODUCTION BY D. W. BROGAN

FARRAR, STRAUS AND CUDAHY · NEW YORK

Contents

Introduction

by D. W. Brogan

"I have never been in Europe. But I imagine life is very local and intense there, wherever it may be. I think *we* are essentially *at home* in an idea, a climate of belief. . . . I mean, if we are at home in the idea of being Americans, it is related much more to why this country was born than it is to where we live."

In this statement from *The Common Heart,* Mr. Paul Horgan underlines the special character of his approach to the American novel. In one way, he is very much a regional novelist, whether the region is upstate New York, notably the city of Rochester on the edge of the Great Lakes, or New Mexico, western Kansas and Colorado, the region of "the High Plains" and of the Rocky Mountains. Mr. Horgan admirably conveys, as readers of this collection will speedily learn, the atmosphere of the High Plains and of the Rockies, and sets it off against the more settled life, the more stable society of New York State. In this sense, he is as much a regional novelist as he is a very distinguished regional historian.

But in another and deeper sense he is concerned with a highly mobile society, with personal problems and personal changes. His dilemmas, his tragic situations are set in a landscape that is vividly evoked. But the real theme is the human dilemma, not the physical background in which his often tragic story is set.

As is indicated in the title of one of the novels reprinted here, *Main Line West,* the human situation is developed in a society that is perhaps too mobile for its own good. The sound of the railway train in the night, the horse-and-buggy crossing the empty and almost featureless landscape of Kansas, the car taking characters to the edge

of the ancient society of the Indians, all underline the loneliness aris-
ing from mobility. Men and women meet, more or less accidentally,
in a society always on the move, and such centers of stability as they
have are provided less by society than by their own cravings. They
are most of them, in many ways, exiles, thinking of remote towns
and villages in Michigan or New York or California, and not given
much support by the society they live in.

Mr. Horgan is, indeed, as his historical work shows, a devotedly
patriotic citizen of New Mexico and of the whole Rocky Mountain
area. He succeeds in setting the mobility of his American characters
against the impressive and ancient landscape, linking human destiny
with the great river, the "Rio Bravo del Norte" or, as we call it, the
Rio Grande. The ancient Indian pueblos, often abandoned, recall a
society that did have its own stability, its own habitual way of life
which it neither wished to change nor could change. The Spanish
settlers in New Mexico had brought their own form of stability to the
nearly empty land. The old Mexican gentleman who had known
Cavour and who lived long enough to see New Mexico transformed
by the coming of the car and the plane, for all his knowledge of Europe and for all his ironical contemplation of the vicissitudes of
human fortune, still belonged to a society more stable than that of the
Yanquis.

When the American invaders came into this Mexican territory over
a century ago, they brought with them a new way of life. Yet they had
not created a satisfactory adjustment to the New Mexico of the Indians and of the Mexicans. The Spaniards who had come north from
old Mexico at the end of the sixteenth century were better able to ad-
just themselves to the new land than the *Yanquis* were. They brought
with them a highly organized and traditional religion which could
absorb and did absorb a great deal of the old Indian culture. The
simple evangelical gospel teaching of *Main Line West* seems curiously
rootless compared with the religious culture imported by the Spaniards
and imposed on the Indians who took as much of it as they wanted
and no more. The Americans who come from the east and the west
are still not quite at home in the ancient land. They have imported
with them the new technological urban society.

The period that Mr. Horgan deals with, the time of the First World
War, of the Great Depression, and of the eve of the Second World
War, saw the transformation of all the Rocky Mountain states, and
especially of New Mexico, to a degree that no one could foresee forty
years ago. Mr. Horgan cannot have foreseen that the minor village of
Los Alamos, near Santa Fe, would become one of the most famous—

or notorious—spots in the world, the cradle of the atomic bomb. The Albuquerque that he describes has multiplied its population five times since then, and is no longer the comparatively tranquil small town that Mr. Horgan brings to life with such mastery. But the coming of the atom bomb, the coming of industry to New Mexico, to Colorado has not altered one of the basic conditions of human life as it is described here. The violence of the natural environment appears in all the novels. The misery of drought, the overwhelming violence of the great storms, the dependence of rural life on an unchangeable and often inhospitable natural setting is part of the human condition. And if the doctor hero of *The Common Heart* conveys to us his devotion to his native state, makes plausible his abandoning Rochester and its far more sophisticated society for what was then the small frontier town of Albuquerque, Mr. Horgan does not hide from us the ugly side of this frontier. *Far From Cibola* reminds us of what we may easily forget, of the desperate misery of the depression in rural America, especially desperate in a region where nature's favors were fitfully bestowed. Poverty, violence, savage racial brutality are all part of the picture. It was in pursuit of the mythical "seven cities of Cibola" that the sixteenth century Spaniards had wandered aimlessly over the desert and over the prairie, and the El Dorado of the wandering Spaniards of the sixteenth century was no more remote from reality than the vision of a bountiful America which was betrayed in the depth of the Great Depression.

The strong streak of violence and intolerance which is part of the American national inheritance is shown to us in *Main Line West,* whose heroine is a victim not only of that traditional American figure, the traveling salesman, or of a naïve and limited religion, but of the savage intolerance of American patriotism. Cibola, in whatever form it was conceived, was remote enough from the ugly realities of frontier life.

But it would be very unjust both to America and to Mr. Horgan to end on a note of mere despair. The Albuquerque of *The Common Heart,* full of the pangs and pains of the human situation, yet gave to those inhabitants who were capable of accepting the gift, love and the possibility of a useful and comforting life. It is revealed in the innocent happiness of the nuns at the hospital and of the boy who can find in the prospect of being a doctor, of healing and saving, compensation for the pangs of crossed love. No one will accuse Mr. Horgan of being a deliberately cheerful writer, but there is happiness in achievement in all of these books as well as a candid assessment of the weaknesses of American society.

And despite the disclaimer of a regionalist approach in literature, the background is as important as the human society which is dwarfed by the fantastic landscape. No one who knows New Mexico at all can fail to be moved by the evocation of the great river, of the mesas, of the astonishing mountains, of the astonishing sky. Perhaps this is a world in which people of northern Europe stock will never feel at home; but it is one that Mr. Horgan makes intelligible to us. It is a magnificent backcloth against which his movingly human characters live and love and die.

Foreword

The zone of Mountain Standard Time reaches in the American southwest from western Kansas to the California line and embraces, from Canada in the north to the Mexican border in the south, the great spine of the continent, the Rocky Mountains.

In a diversity of character greater than that of the other time zones in the nation, it includes the great prairies of Kansas; the plains of eastern Colorado, eastern New Mexico, and West Texas; the continental upsweep of the land into the flanks and pinnacles of the Rockies; and finally the high mesalands of New Mexico and Arizona with their buttes and canyons.

In such a land of great visible distance and openness of light, Nature seems to stand forth direct under abstract passions of vast acts of weather. And so too in that country human passions seem to show forth in direct power and effect, through the variety of people in its immense neighborhoods.

It is the land of the prairie farmer. If his world is flat, so too may be his spirit, his voice, his private containment within a human horizon of drought-like shrewdness, all of which must affect his family and they in turn their society. It is the land of the little caboose-red railroad towns some of which grew into wayside cities along the transcontinental rail systems—cities laid out in grids reaching at right angles to the tracks in magic alleys of neon light if seen at night, and two-to-four storey perspectives of drably colored commercial fronts if by day. The land of the cattle or sheep ranchers, and the farmer of irrigated fields, who come to town once or twice a week for gossip and supplies and connection with a world otherwise lost to them where they live and work hidden in the open plains. Land of any town with forty houses set about an intersection of two state highways which cross like a plus sign in the flat wilderness. Of windmills at far intervals calling the water of life out of the earth on which rain falls so scarcely. Of mountains always visible either close to or far off. The Great River rising in the Continental Divide in Colorado and flowing down through all of New Mexico and then turning southeastward to make a vein, in places containing only dust or gravel, which ends at the Gulf of Mexico. Land where the voice of the wandering evangelist uses all the accents of the people who hear him—echoes of the south, and the prairie midland, and the Plains Texan, and the town settlers from anywhere else. If the evangelist's effect can be called regional, it is suggestive of a civilization delayed for a few generations in arriving at an expression of life which to be civilized must represent the highest collective style of its component people rather than the average, or the lowest.

Above all it is the land whose human history, traceable for tens of centuries, seems of all histories which compose the nation's character, the most immediately recoverable in its environment, and yet the most alight with the quality of legend—just as its landscape, made of hard mountains and cruel distances, seems touched with fantasy. When trail-makers from the east first saw the Rocky Mountains shining on the far horizon, they thought they were seeing clouds.

In those land spaces of the southwest, great as they are, a person stands in relief like an earth feature, small, perhaps, but strongly lighted and as strongly shadowed.

In something of the image of this, I saw the people of the novels in the present volume when I first unfolded their stories; and because the main action of many of their lives, and the climactic episodes of all three books, occur in their part of the country (to which I have belonged for much of my own life), I have gathered them here under the enclosing title of *Mountain Standard Time*, under which their hours are reckoned.

P.H.

CENTER FOR ADVANCED STUDIES,
WESLEYAN UNIVERSITY.

MAIN
LINE
WEST

To my Brother Edward Horgan

Contents

Book III   THE SPIRIT

Book IV THE POWER

Book V THE SON

Book I • THE FATHER

I · NEW TIME

Of origins, which grow and change and mean all ways in life, people, living in the flat outland countries of America, might say, as of a storm coming on the horizon, "A cloud no bigger'n a man's hand." From such a little cloud, coming like a drifting pearl over the almost watery line where the horizon laps remotely upon the sky, the whole day might draw a new temper; the cloud increasing and the sun raying from behind it fanwise; the blackness growing and hanging low, darkling shadows into the windy bend of wheatfields, silvering the golden crop as the day changes; and driving people indoors before the menace of the sky, which does not yet show whether it is to be cyclone or torrent. It is in Kansas, where the colors of the land become toylike as the darkness grows. Faded red barns become rich plum color; the trees bunched in land hollows at the flowing together of hills show candy green as the sky blackens; the wheat bends and breaks its whispering surf against fences; over the flat country the telegraph wires run beside the railroad, and a far freight train travels like a child's toy, taking in its path the whole outland dream of restlessness, movement, the travel as of storms to nourish new places and destroy old ones, a nostalgia in the outlanders for the places they've dreamed of, but never seen, but which have become part of their experience by the vitality of imagination. . . .

It is what the people have—imagination and consequent restlessness. The symbols of it (in the early 1900's when this story begins with the little cloud) are the white wooden church where emotion can bind everybody together, and the tracks that run from coast to coast, going by with life, mysteriously hinting of splendid places elsewhere, from which the train has come, and exciting places yonder, to which the train is going, pausing here only to change engines and breathe a spell, then running on secure through the heavy storm which has gathered out of the sky, and with a boom of wind has struck on the wide Kansas lands and finally driven kernels of rain on roof and window. The rain comes like assuagement on the lonesome earth.

II · THROUGH THE RAIN

There was a buggy driving along a road that ran between two wheat-fields. The rain was like a curtain blowing in the faces of the horse and his driver. They couldn't see more than a few feet ahead or to the side, but from the whipping folds of the curtain in their faces, they began to shiver with cold. The horse seemed frightened, but he kept clopping ahead, his head bobbing in obedience. The driver pulled his coat collar up and huddled into himself, and let the reins hang loose, knowing the horse was a better guide than he was in such blind weather as this afternoon's.

It was now chilly, where it had been hot. The dust was gone out of the air. The man could breathe. He felt cheered by the miniature strife he was having with the elements, and as he was a man always to enjoy his own notions of well-being, he examined with almost physical pleasure the minor hazards he was facing and overcoming. He felt sure his sample-cases in back, and under the buggy seat, were securely packed and his goods were not wetting. For the rest, it wasn't far from dusk, and he had set out from Athens anticipating a nice easy starlight drive over to Freola, where he would put up at the New Kansan Hotel. Now he would hardly make it by midnight. Or even later. He might have to sleep out on the road.

The horse stumbled, and he leaned out to see the road, and saw that it was running into the sunflowered ditches in little chocolate rivers. It was slippery. The rain combed his skin and flashed through his black mustache. He laughed out loud and ducked in again under his swinging buggy top, and began to sing a song, out of appreciation of the fact that life was made up of all sorts of experiences, and this was simply another one which he could later tell amusingly, a traveling salesman who was affably fitted for any situation. The song he sang was obscene but cheerful. He idly remembered the girl who had taught it to him in Mississippi eight months ago. He had a clipping of it in his wallet, where he kept so many things of interest, and into which he was always dipping for some proof of the statements he delighted people with.

The rain seemed to whistle into a new direction and to lose power; he peered ahead; it was a wide-storm, that he could see, and might settle down into a steady drizzle all night. He suddenly needed comforting; he reached into his vest pocket and pulled out his cigar-holder, which he put empty between his teeth. This was a hint in taste of well-being once more. Then he saw a house down on the right, and he resolved to pull into the yard and ask if he might stay and dry out a little. He couldn't see himself being refused, for he knew by experience that he was successful with people; they liked his red face and his merry small blue eyes; the elegance with which he dressed, the care his mustache got with its curled tips, the fact that he was always willing to do more than his share to entertain, and if he was the guest, to pay for hospitality with flattery and charm; and if it were strangers he encountered, they always yielded to his gay little dignities, such as the way he squinted his eyes and cocked his head before introducing himself, a well-groomed and barbered man of middle twenties, a little short and stocky, but easy and humorous. Strangers liked how he drew out his wallet with a sort of expert confidence and reliability, and with a touch of irony in the grace of his gesture handed over his card, which read, "Mr. Daniel Milford," in real engraving, thick-and-thin with little flourishes, purely ornamental, like the chirps of a bird in graceful flight.

III · THE PLACE

One of the Kinneyman children, the girl Retha, watched the stranger's buggy turn in at the gate and come up the graveled road to the house. The rain was blowing down the window glass like silk, and went like stain into all the little dry dusty crannies of the white wooden window frame set in cement made to look like stone blocks. The dust was wetted and released from its stifling cracks, and the wet wood made a sweet scent for the air; the greens turned darker in the window box, and Retha, with her face flattened on the pane watching, was excited by the rain and its freshness in the world even before she saw the man get out and start running to the shallow porch. He skidded on the wet scattered grass which now stood muddy. The sky was timeless, not like afternoon any more, nor yet like night; but like wet gray paper.

There was stamping on the porch and then a polite twirl of the bell-key at the front door.

Retha pulled at her flat yellow hair and yanked her plaid apron tighter across her new young breasts. She knew the rest of the family would be gathered in the dining-room, waiting, watching, by the time she got to the door. She went to the door properly, and opened it, ready to blush. The man was very wet, and she was outraged to see that he looked merry. She half closed the door and backed into the hall a pace.

"You-you see," he said, with the smiling stammer he had, "I've gotten sort of *wet*. —I wondered if you people'd mind if I came in to dry out a little?"

"I don't know!" said Retha in a gasp of childish bewilderment, and then blushed like a woman, so that Dan Milford looked sharplier at her, and his eyes twinkled from the freshness of her face and flesh, sunlight inside a ripening plum, sweet and tart. In such matters he often felt his mouth water. He knew how to conceal it, too.

The hall was deep and dark, and the dining-room showed cavernous in dusk beyond, a gray light losing itself in a mirrored sideboard where stood orange glass dishes and vases. Out of this cave where figures seemed to shift there came a slow-walking woman, with her head on one side and her apron pulled up. She was not old but she was gnarled. She was early wrecked by the uses a woman can be put to; the exhaustion of violence was in her face as she came near the open door, and she smiled with a suspicious sociability. Milford repeated his own charming introduction for her, and she drew her daughter away behind her.

"It *does* look ' might never let up, don't it:" said Mrs. Kinneyman, debating whether or not to let him in. She heard whispers of interest from the other children in the dining-room. The life of the house seemed all tentative, a matter of lurkings and private conclusions, shyness like shame, and yet human desire winning through wry caution. They all wanted to see more of the man. They made ghostly little noises in the dining-room, and Mrs. Kinneyman at last stepped back, and said:

"Well, you might's well. . . . Lloyd, you take the horse and the gentleman's buggy down t' the barn."

Milford came in. The door shutting after him was like the end of a journey. He said,

"I hope you'll let-let me introduce myself, I have my card," and he pulled out his wallet and gave over the card.

"Oh, well . . ." said Mrs. Kinneyman, taking it, in a hopeless way of admitting the elegance of the stranger. "My name's Mrs. Shide Kinneyman. Thiz my daughter Retha, and you saw Lloyd, that's my boy. Then Mr. Kinneyman, he must be down ' the barn. —Let me take your coat. We have a fire in the range, I'm baking today."

They made him reluctantly at home in the front room. The rain darkened the day still more, and he had a sense of the house resuming its life which he had interrupted. The smaller children, three of them, two girls and a baby boy, came down the hall toward the door of the front room, and like a little school of fish floating in strange currents of opinion through the dark air of the hallway, they eddied near, and then flipped away, and came to gaze; to suspect; to venture; to tail away; and peek; and at last come into his range, to see the large watch that whacked off the minutes in a sharp tick. Milford felt better after the children decided to know him; and having always to taste the approval of people, he began to work hard at winning these infants.

All the time he was estimating the Kinneymans from the room. It was a dark room, with green-and-red wall paper, and the furniture was heavy oak. A hanging oil-lamp had a shade of rose-and-milky glass with a design of little bluish bubbles around the edge. The carpet was worn and moldy, but it still showed four white swans breasting a tide of scuffed roses in green banks. In one corner stood a harmonium with red velvet glowing through its scrolled walnut face. The white buttons of the various stops looked inviting and pure in the dim dark room. Pools of limited light lay on the floor from the front windows where there were stiff lace curtains.

Yet it was a room with life in it; there lingered a whole complicated chord of smells, all the pungencies that had been cooked in the kitchen were part of the fabric in the room. The keys of the harmonium showed little stains of use in the cracks. The house itself seemed like a ruin of use, much like Mrs. Kinneyman, who was worn with child-bearing, cooking, adoring the Lord, appeasing her husband, and catering to all the acts of creation which the large farm lived on, with its people, its land, its animals. Yet a cloud of doubtfulness in the atmosphere was just as noticeable as all the evidence of life.

Milford was always curious about people; and in terms of his own nature, he liked to think them out. He said to himself, while the children played silently with his watch, and examined his ruby ring, and stared at his kindly face,

"They must be strait-laced; yes, they have all the same wants and urges people have anywhere, but they are ashamed of them, and how do I know? Well, that girl who opened the door for me, yellow and pink like primroses, she is dying to be tickled and kissed and hotted up, and she's scared to death of it; but she feels her beauty, and it wants to tell her things to do, but do you think she can do them? or even imagine herself? —I wish she was about three years older, I'd have me a time."

He stuck his jaw out slowly in a private grin of taste.

"And the mother. That poor old wreck? She's not so old. You can almost see her *husband,* from looking at *her.* I bet he hates her. I bet she hates him. I bet they don't even *know* it. And that kid Lloyd, that boy, he's about sixteen, with a head of hair like corn silk. He'll get away, a boy on a farm, shucks; he'll know everything there is to know right now. Only he's got to pretend, and act ashamed like the rest of the family, or they'd *know* about him. They'd find him out. —Go to it, kiddo."

IV · IRMA

Presently the dusk was arrived.

Mrs. Kinneyman came in and said his coat was dry, might-nigh.

"How far's Freola?" he asked.

"—Land, you going to Freola?"

There was a faded humor in her voice, which was dry, a scratching of dry leaves together.

"I was headed there, I always put up at the New Kansan there.

". . . I make Athens my headquarters now, in this territory. . . ."

"Almost twenty miles to Freola, road'll be wet all right."

"Yes, well, you-you've been very kind. I think I might better be——"

"Well, now, you might wait a minute, I can ask Mr. Kinneyman. . . ."

"No, oh, really——"

"—No, I can . . ."

They were talking about his staying all night, without mentioning it.

She started back to the kitchen, and he followed her, expostulating cordially, and winking at the children who trooped with him. Retha he found staring at him at moments and then tossing the thoughts of him out of her eyes by a lift of her head. Her brother Lloyd who looked like her, except for his plume of cornsilk white hair, blushed and grinned at Milford about his sister's funny, wicked dreams. He grabbed his sister, as they went into the dining-room after Mrs. Kinneyman, and twisted her arm expertly. She panted but would not cry out before a stranger, and the boy looked for approval from Milford for his lazy prowess.

"Lloyd, let her down, and go find your pa," said Mrs. Kinneyman.

He wanted desperately to have the man think he too was a man, and to answer his clear blue-eyed look of inquiry with some experienced approval. He let go of Retha, and suddenly ashamed was glad of the chance to run out to the barn.

"No, please, never mind, Mrs. Kinneyman," said Milford.

But she was in her province, the kitchen, and she tossed her head in the wan citrous light of the two oil-lamps. She said to the girl standing at the oven,

"Irma, turn around, and meet the gentleman, you wasn't fixing to meet him in the kitchen, but there he is."

"Oh, I'm s-sorry," said Milford.

She turned around and stared at him with tempestuous eyes. They were black and burning deep with annoyance.

"How ' do," she said, and turned back to the stove.

"It's Mr. Milford, Irma. —My sister, Irma, Miss Irma Gruvers," explained Mrs. Kinneyman to Daniel.

He saw that the woman was relishing with more and more warmth the chance to be social, to recall, out of the times of her courting, what it was you said to strangers who seemed t'be nice folks; and how to make the young folks feel to home; and what fun it was, instead of misery, to cook for a party, to feed people out of pleasure instead of duty. Mrs. Kinneyman's gray back-sloping face was a little flushed at the cheek bones. Her crooked gold-rimmed glasses glistened and her eyes shone, remote little lamps that were glowing once more before it was too late. Her gnarled fingers and bent bones had some rebirth of spirit in them. The children felt it, and suddenly moved to her, taken by love for their mother because she seemed like some one they had always imagined but never seen so clearly.

Milford nodded, and turned around and went back to the front room to wait for supper.

He hoped they'd leave him alone, to think:

The girl at the stove was tall, and her hair was black. It was frowning over her brow in damp curly lines, and her eyes when she'd looked around seemed deep in dark luster. She stood like a fine filly, he thought, admiring horses and women with the same inarticulate subjection to physical beauty; and he was practiced in his estimates; and in the second he had seen her he saw something about her that had him touched off inside, and expectant, as if some one had lit a fuse and he could see the spark burning closer and closer with the exciting force of its message and the tremble of contact that it must at last produce.

"Irma Gruvers, and she's the sister of that poor Kinneyman woman! She's as dark as the rest of them are blond, or . . . or gray. I guess she lives here with the family. Well, you never know where you're going to find it. They may say beauty is cheap, like all the other things in the world you can't buy but have to have. . . . I never saw anyone like her in my life. There's not a touch of paint on her face, and I never saw a mouth like that without it. And those hot eyes up in those burning cheeks!"

He heard some one coming down the dim hallway and he sat up in the oak-and-black-leather armchair where he had been dreaming. What if it were she!

But it was Lloyd, coming back from the barn.

"Pa is coming right up. —But I figger you'll stay, because I told him Ma wanted you to, and so he said, all right, unharness the horse, then. So I did. It sure is rainin'."

"That's fi-fine, Lloyd. You people are mighty nice to-to take in a stranger like this. —It's a big family, too, all you children and then Miss Gruvers, is that the name?"

"Yep. My aunt Irma. —She sure is crazy," he said affectionately.

"What: what ' you mean?"

Milford laughed engagingly, burning at the inroads he could make on her biography.

"Oh, you know, I mean, she plays the organ all the time, and sings, and she goes to the prayer-meetings. And joke? She jokes all the time! —Say, ' she get mad at you, say, look out!"

He laughed. This suggestion of Irma's temper and spirit made Milford grin and nod, a little desperately. He said to himself,

"Don't be such a fool! You hardly know her! Don't think you'll get anywhere with a girl like that, these respectable farm folks are the cagiest in the world, and if it got to anything serious, you'd never feel like facing the girls back home, and all the other places, they'd kid you to death. —There's that boy, sitting there and telling about her and he hardly knows she's a woman!"

Lloyd was squirming his long legs out in front of him, and cracking the knuckles of his velvety tan hands and just talking because he was fascinated by the visitor. The boy's white silk hair slid over his face and as he talked he watched Milford to see what he could learn about growing up like that, to be some one else and a man free on the world: these wants showed through his cornflower-blue eyes like love he didn't know about.

"And so she was mad at you because you saw her in the kitchen and she didn't have a chance to get fixed up. I kidded her! *Say,* I kidded her! After I came back from the barn."

At the word barn Lloyd blushed, remembering the things he had seen in barns, the hot seedy twilight in the barns and the bed of hay, where boys and girls lost themselves and found each other.

Then they heard the back door slam, and Lloyd said,

"There's Pa."

Milford readied himself to please the farmer, and make it clear, with a joke between men, how you doggoned sure enough got fooled sometimes by the weather.

V · THE HAPPY EVENING

Halfway through supper Irma forgave Daniel Milford for catching her in the kitchen by the stove, hot and sweaty, as she said. There was a new merriment going around the table, and Mr. Kinneyman sat bent immense and bony over his plate, looking up through his eyebrows at the strange party going on in his house. He was a light-haired man with small, hot-looking blue eyes in his tanned face. His face and hands, all of the flesh of him that showed, had creases like miniature gullies in the skin. His face was savagely gouged, like the land after the passage of a fast-running rain that makes temporary rivers which plow the ground and leave sun-baked veins of rut afterward. The man was gouged by the secret life of inarticulate passion he had; a thing that showed most frankly when he was at work. There he was a giant of endeavor, and he could free his voice, hooting at his team; and he was like a slow windmill with his arms, signaling orders to hands at the end of the field; but away from such things, he had nothing to say, no feelings that he knew how to show. He never knew he suffered in other than bodily ways; but it showed in the gullies of his cheeks.

He ate without comment.

His yellow-to-brown mustache quivered and preened over his mouth like a sparrow's wing shaking off dust.

Now the family was complete. And complete, it was annihilated. Alone, Retha had been desperately voluptuous, without knowing it. Here she was a sulky child. Lloyd was now a stony-faced bully, watching for sly chances to nip his younger sisters and brother, who wondered every day at the forbidding calm of the family table. Mrs. Kinneyman was silent; she chewed her food in odd little spasms, as if seeking a tooth that wouldn't hurt. Her only social comment was to smile with a cracking face whenever Daniel looked her way, and nod; having forgotten long since that this was not the life she once knew, and that what children learn from early atmospheres trails them like a cloud ever after.

But Irma and Daniel made it actually a merry party, between the two of them.

The others thought those two understood one another at once. Irma saw him as a wit, a man whose main delight in life was a good time, and what that meant, she could only decide in her own terms; so that the most innocent conclusions were all she drew. She was torturing Daniel unconsciously by what he knew would be wanton tricks in anyone else. If any of the girls he knew in the cities he made had gone on half so brightly and hotly as Irma, he would have known what they were after, and given it to them.

Not that she was ever immodest; her gestures were simply frank, and she was so used to her own vitality and beauty, he decided, that she never paid them any heed, or used them, beyond admitting that she felt wonderfully well and felt like singing hymns.

This is what they did after supper. They all moved into the front room. Mr. Kinneyman hesitated in the doorway and his little eyes burned dryly with a discouraging expression. The children looked at each other and exchanged the meaning of a sigh. His wife looked up from her place by the table under the hanging lamp.

"Well, Shide?" she asked.

"Oh, leave him be, Frisbie," said Irma, turning from the harmonium a moment. "He don't like the music. . . ."

At that Shide Kinneyman made a click in his throat, and turned away into the dark hall. They heard him go shambling down toward the kitchen.

"Hya! Pa's got insulted, now," giggled Retha.

"I did not," said Irma. "I just said he didn't like the music."

"Go on, sing," said her sister Frisbie Kinneyman placidly. The children thought again that their mother was impish and charming tonight. She had a little faded grin that they didn't know very well; she seemed not to care for the moment what stark mood Pa would be in for days or weeks after this. She began to rock gently, and the light from overhead in the rose-glass oil-lamp painted her in strong dark shadows with mellow glow on her dim hair, her glasses, her aproned breast, the rooty knuckles of her hands resting on the rocker arms.

Outside the eaves were dripping and the evening was banked in a misty air.

"Like to be a hot summer," said Irma, turning the pages of the hymnal on the lectern. Daniel stood beside her and stared down the cleft of her back that began to show below her nape; it glistened with a touchable softness. He looked at the curl of her ear and followed it forward to where the hair rose from her temples and dwelled backward in a black wing. Her turning eye let him alone; he watched breath and thoughtless impulse use her red mouth in little quirks of expression.

"The traveling salesman and the farmer's daughter," he said to himself ironically. "I've got to get out of this, or *into* it, one. . . ."

The organ began to maunder and then change into a familiar hymn which Irma sang. The children sang. Mrs. Kinneyman amazed them by lifting a thready voice out of her heart and letting it waver around the tune like steam from a teakettle veiling its own wan whistle.

They got warm and eager over the hymns, and used the Lord enthusiastically.

It was an hour before they stopped singing and settled down to talk.

"Mind if I smoke?" asked Daniel.

Mrs. Kinneyman looked around for authority; then said,

"Why, *no:* I guess if you want to, you can, this time!"

They all tittered at this, and when he lighted his cigar in his holder, it seemed daring even to him.

"Well, th-this has been the nicest evening I've had in a long time," he said.

"Pleased to've had you," said Mrs. Kinneyman.

"Mister, you *cert*ainly can *sing!*" said Irma. "I never heard those hymns so fine, you must be a regular church-going Christian to put so much into all those hymns!"

It was what she wanted him to be.

"I certainly am," he said, with the right amount of manly humor in it. "I tell *you* you should never lose the religion God gave you at your mother's knee!"

"No, sir!"

Irma gazed on him with the frank pleasure of a child. She must be about twenty, or more, he thought. He suddenly had a desperate wave of pity and annoyance for the distance between them. He resolved that he must put out of his head the wants she reminded him of so poignantly; unless there was just a chance that she wasn't really like the rest of the family and so hopelessly removed from "life" as they seemed to be.

He said to himself, while listening to Mrs. Kinneyman's wandering story of how come Irma came to live with them,

"I could come back in a few days from Freola and see if it's just as bad as it is now. And at my age! You'd think I was that boy Lloyd there, getting so hot and itchy over a farm girl with a Christian soprano voice and million-dollar eyes!"

But the real voluptuary in him was also a realist. He saw that if he was to know his desires taken, then he must proceed in her way, on her terms; and even this ceased being a dull prospect when he imagined the kindling delights of pretended innocence, so that they might discover together, as it were, the things he was aching to love into her. That was his first thought of the word love; he turned from staring at Mrs. Kinneyman and stared at

Irma. He felt a little pale. He was glad Mrs. Kinneyman went on contentedly ruminating over the history of her own girlhood and Irma's, because he was incapable of saying anything; trying to recover himself from the commitment he was making before it was too late and before it might show either as frightening desire in his eyes, whereat Irma would shrink, or as a proposal of marriage, at which she might possibly leap. In either event, he would be the loser.

"—so she came here to live, ever since, and we're just s'glad to have her," said Mrs. Kinneyman. "She was the youngest, and she's quite a lot younger than I am. Mr. Kinneyman says folks always take her for our datter. I always think that's s'funny. So she and I're just the last ones of our family together, the way they scatter . . ."

Retha had fallen asleep. This recalled the mother to her real world, and she stood up, and gathered the other children in for bedding.

"—*was* s'late," she apologized, with a happy smile. To have forgotten time! She took the family away. As he left last, Lloyd stopped a second and turned to look at Daniel and Irma staying together. His young eyes were big and questing, mirrors of what he would want to do. They smiled him out, and Irma laughed at him and called him a great big puppy. He went at last into the dark hallway, aching to celebrate the stinging richness of his blood in this damp night, while the eaves dripped and the flat lands were veiled in mist that would not rise, as the burden of the boy's curiosity would not rise from his choking heart.

They listened till they heard his last step gone upstairs. They were sitting on the settle of oak and black leather. It was so quiet now that they could hear the windy breathing of Mr. Kinneyman. He had gone to bed with his door open, down the hall on the same floor. The house had no secrets between its people; the walls were thin, and the ceilings so high that all sounds echoed and grew as they traveled.

"Yet if I do," thought Daniel, "I'll probably never have another chance to try. It's too soon."

They sat talking. He told her about his life and his job, and she asked clever questions, and didn't notice that his voice quivered breathily now and then. She was glad to learn that he did a nice business as salesman for the Seneca General Store Supply Company.

And she asked, with honest curiosity, but nothing else,

"Are you married?"

"Ma-married!"

He laughed a little sickly, seeing himself quite possibly doomed, already.

"I've lived twenty-six years and courted a lot of girls, but none of 'em would ever ha-have me yet!"

"Oh, *you:* expect me to believe that?"

"Why not?"

"I guess you've had plenty chances ' get married, if you wanted."

"No, honestly. I just don't seem to appeal to the girls I-I l-*like,* and the ones I don't, why, I can't shake off to beat the dickens!"

"Oh, go on!"

"No, honestly!"

He was ready to stand up and walk around to keep control of himself. He was delighted and furious, both. He was treading the very ground he was afraid of, and it felt sweet to his step. He knew they were sounding like a pair of fumbling children. He only hoped it would stay on that plane of innocence if it weren't going to go any farther.

"No, that's the truth," he said, facing her urgently, at which she recoiled a little, and gazed at his eyes and mouth in a sort of darkling wonder that crumpled him up inside. "No, I m-mean, there was a girl in Emporia I used to know, and I proposed to her, and you know what she did?"

"Yes, I know what she did," said Irma, teasingly.

"Well, what:"

"She says to herself, a man that travels is only half a man around the house, am I going to mar'man like that? —Isn't that what she said?"

The whole tale being a lie, he was delighted to add this to it.

"Now how did you know that:" he marveled, holding out his hand to shake hers, as if in congratulation.

She gave her hand; and at his touch, she couldn't conceal a little gasp. It was the last straw. It betrayed that she was as excited as he was. This hadn't occurred to him. He began to swell in his heart and held on to her hand and he saw a blush come traveling over her white, white skin and gather around her eyes which darkened and seemed misty, so that he saw plain as day that she was touched; that she too had been parrying with childish words and retreating behind them into the amorous and womanly feelings he had despaired of bringing alive in her.

She pulled her hand away and turned her head.

He was on her like a lion, with his hands at her hands, and his mouth near her cheek not to speak but to tell dumbly what he wanted.

She smiled; she turned her cheek farther.

The stair creaked in the hall.

They untouched.

"That lamp chimney *is* smoking," she said, and arose, and he sickened slightly at the losing of that intensity. The stair creaked again and steps seemed softly to withdraw. She turned and looked wisely at him from the dumb-show of adjusting the wick. She nodded. In her nod there was an innocent kind of acceptance of what they both thought of . . . it was Lloyd, on the steps, burned out of his bed by the suspicion he had and needed to satisfy in envy. Then she nodded again, with emphasis, as if to say,

"Well we're up now, time to go to bed."

He reached for her, and tried for her waist.

His face implored like a little boy's.

She wanted to laugh him tenderly awake from his desires; but she knew the vanity of little boys thwarted at play, and she took him seriously by grasping his hand and shaking it.

"Good night, Mr. Milford, I did enjoy the singing. —It seems so few men are good Christians, and you *must* be, or you couldn't sing 'em like that. . . ."

He wanted to hush her and kiss her silent from these educational ideas. But she had possession of herself now, and said,

"Frisbie fixed the room across the hall for you, the downstairs front bedroom. I'll be going up now. Lloyd'll call you for breakfast. —Good night."

"Good night. —Listen!" He said the last word in a whisper. But she didn't wait.

She went to the stairs and into the darkness of the upstairs hall, as far from his reach as she would have been miles off through the soaking countryside.

He stood thinking that if he could only kid himself a little, or laugh over it, or regard it as something to tell the girls when he got home next time, it wouldn't be so bad. But he only felt miserable and pathetically happy, seeing desire as ruinous, a force before which he was helpless.

VI · FROM THE HEART

He left for Freola the next morning early in the robin's-egg blue light of the new washed sky. There had been a heavy breakfast in the cavernous dining-room where the sun never seemed to have entered, and the house was wreathed in the smells of farm cooking. The heat had already climbed into the day with the sunrise; the sounds of summer drudgery came already from the fields and from the cicadas in the grass. They would sing and sing until the sun rode past the zenith.

He could not find a moment alone with Irma.

He grinned to cover his exasperation, and nodded at her over something the children did, hoping that she would see it as a nod from the heart, meaning what he had stirred alive in them both last night. He tried to wax confident on her gaze—to say to himself,

"She knows, and I know; she knows that if I come back, what I'm coming for."

The farmer, Mr. Kinneyman, went to the barn in silence after breakfast. Cramping his shiny, cracked fingers together in a dusty claw, he shook hands with Dan Milford, saying nothing, but sidelonging him with his bleak gaze, that yet had some fire of suspicion in it, a pale blue shaft of misunderstanding that never satisfied him with what it saw, or ever spoke clearly to anyone else, as it went through his sandy eyebrows drawn down.

His wife was cordial.

"Well," she said, and stopped.

"Well, I-I don't know how to—" started Dan.

"Well, just s'glad," resumed Mrs. Kinneyman at the same moment, so that their voices blurred each other, and made a tangle of friendly absurdity. They both stopped and laughed. Irma was with them. She smiled in a secret drollery.

"Now, next time you go by, don't wait for th' rain to stop you," declared Mrs. Kinneyman, in a spurt of daring, which she tried to support by a look of appeal at Irma.

"I-I was ho-hoping you'd say something like that," laughed Daniel. He held out his hand. Mrs. Kinneyman took it with a shy grace, suddenly like her daughter Retha, her head on one side, and her love for human affairs dimly showing. Daniel was warmed by the geniality of the one who confers fortune. He turned to Irma.

"And Miss Irma, I n-never can say thank you enough . . ."

"And-what-for?" she demanded in brisk mockery. Her black eyes burned with light like ice, and humor, and her red mouth was teasing in a crooked smile. He looked at her and thought, "What for!" and said,

"Well, that wonderful cooking, and . . . the music last night, *last night.*"

He emphasized it a little.

"Oh: the food; that's all a man ever——"

They laughed again, and heard Lloyd coming around from the barn with the horse and buggy.

VII · THE TEMPTRESS

Presently Daniel was trotting along toward Freola, asking himself what in the world made her so different from all the other girls he ever knew, and why he should be so taken by her. He grinned at the image of himself, infatuated with a farm girl, and then he shrugged, and thought,

"Oh, well, what's that got to do with it?"

In the afternoon he saw Freola lying on the yellow horizon.

He spent three days there at the New Kansan Hotel, doing business, and uneasily evading the engagements he had made with the cigar-counter girl on his last trip. She was a red-haired girl with skin so pale it seemed sometimes almost greenish, and her eyes were lashed by sandy fringes that irritated him as much as they interested him. She was the only woman in Freola who concerned herself with activities of the mind; and to find this passionate intellectual selling cigars in the hotel lobby, which was made of pressed metal panels and pillars painted white and green, and lighted by gas chandeliers, was always amusing to him when he "blew into town." He came from the cities; he was smart in his clothes and tastes; she thought of him as her type; and they had for a few years celebrated his visits with daytimes spent in sly looks across the lobby, or humorously innocent banter in loud voices, and with nighttimes spent in making love and drinking whisky. Her name was Maude. She drawled when she spoke, and liked to make her remarks impressive by half-lidding her eyes.

"The old she-devils," she would say during a midnight gossip with Daniel in the frank state of their casual enjoyment. "If they knew I smoked these cigarettes! would they be on my trail! This town is so buttoned up the devils are all mixed up with the Christians. —I read a book by Robert W. Ingersoll last week and got caught."

Daniel was amused by her, and always played up to her lazy pose of omniscience, of sophistication that was really pathetic for its hardness and barrenness of feeling.

But on this trip, he avoided Maude; saw her scornful calculations across the lobby, and nodded; and in the evening on Friday, elaborately idling toward the stairs with a yawn and a stretch, as if he were dead tired and going up to a good night's sleep, he felt her look in his back like a mocking prod, and he shook himself in anger, and turned around. There she was, looking at him like a cat, with her gray eyes, her red hair and the purse of her slowly moving lips.

He went over.

She put her hands up to her head and stroked the forward pompadour in fashion. Her sleeves were huge. Her corset curved her body. He knew how her white breasts lay in the top of the corset like pale fruit in a pink china dish.

"Say, haven't you been a little obvious?"

"Hello, Maude! —No, just busy. —I'm dead."

"I was just so sure you had gone decent on me!"

It was in her low suggestive voice, reminding him of her ways at love, when with an evil wit she would say things to him that made her almost sexless and abstract in passion. She had a kind of perversity that matched her pose as an "advanced" woman, full of daring, a woman who would rather seduce than be seduced, and whose body had amorous imagination of its own, regardless, seemingly, of will.

"I haven't been here so long," said Dan.

"Long enough to make a hellcat out of me—if I cared."

"Give me three of those Barnum panatelas."

She got the cigars out for him, and looked keenly at him.

"Perhaps you've *fallen* at last."

He flushed with anger.

"Say, look at you," she said softly. "Who says I'm not a bright girl! —Will you tell me all about it?"

He couldn't help laughing, recalling all the other confidences they had exchanged about their past lovers. Perhaps she could tell him: she *was* clever, annoyingly so: perhaps she could tell him what Irma might like; a woman of that sort was new to him.

"Can you come on upstairs when you're done here?"

She nodded. Her eyes flashed, and watered a trifle. He saw it as a response to amorous suggestion. Laughing at her, he nodded, and turned to go upstairs, to his room at the end of the corridor, where the gas burned dimly, and the carpeted floor creaked. The New Kansan Hotel was twenty-four years old in this time of the early 1900's.

VIII · HEADING BACK

Maude tried to make Irma sound like a fool.

Everything he told her she would chuckle at, and contrast with her own traits.

He was presently bored with that, and decided that it had been a mistake to talk about Irma at all. He felt that it was an indignity for her. Then he was alarmed because he had never felt so about any other woman.

"—and so I think you've met your downfall at last," said Maude. "You don't know, my God, how these farming people hold on to their virtue, as they call it! —Or if once it's gone, how they hoot and yell about sin, for the rest of their days! I know 'em! Don't they think I'm eternally damned because I read Ingersoll and try to improve my intellect and broaden out? Those old hellcats at the church socials, look at them; they were all girls once, and if ever any one of 'em had any fun, they've spent their lives being sorry for it, and also hating their husbands for not knowing how to give 'em any *more* fun. —No, Danny, you lay off. —I'm just saving you a lotta time."

"—You want another drink?"

"Sure. I'll drown your sorrows."

"I have no sorrows—yet."

"Well, when they come, they'll age you fast enough. —How old is she? Aren't you too old for her?"

"I'm about five-six years older, I guess."

"The Fascinating Stranger, starring Mr. Daniel Milford, a little comedy of the haymow. Here's how, Dan!"

They drank together.

They tried to mock his abstraction away.

Maude was more and more scornful. Her tongue bit him with words and challenged his vanity, and in her hardest ways became as unlike the spirit of Freola as she could; and it only tired him, and he felt none of the indulgent pity for her that he'd known before, the poor girl with superior possibilities, caught in the bigoted town and seeking courageous ways out through having a scandalous mind. . . .

The next day at ten o'clock he sent for his horse and buggy and headed back the way he'd come.

IX · LOVE AND VANITY

For weeks he tried to reason with himself.

His drumming trips took him away and they brought him back. Every time, he drove out to Kinneyman's. The summer advanced. There were smoky silver hazes in the early mornings over the exhaling landscape. Life seemed especially vivid to Daniel. He decided, from every way he had ever heard about, that this time he was lost and doomed, because before if he had been attracted by a girl and got nowhere with her, he'd just been able to laugh it off in a drunken spree with "one of the girls" in any town he happened to be in. He now saw his old life changing and perhaps slipping away from him . . . a life of trains, of hotels, of sample-rooms, the masculine privilege of poolrooms at evening, and later in the night, the sociability and easiness of prostitutes, "the girls," as he always designated them, among whom he had many real friends. They respected him because he was kind and generous; because in his desire to be attractive, he was always out to entertain them, instead of the other way around, because he was a "rolling stone," and never complicated their lives, but always came back in a month, or six, or a year, breezy and red-cheeked, saying he'd just "blown into" town, and was feeling *right*. . . .

In a helpless sort of study, he watched himself progressing with his courtship.

He was clever with the Kinneymans.

He knew how to be whatever the other wanted of him. With Mr. Shide Kinneyman, he was taciturn and quizzical, and given to making piously bitter remarks about women. It always made a great success with Shide.

"You-you need 'em, but by God you can n-never trust 'em," declared Daniel.

"Hish-sh-sh," said Shide, a watery ghost of a laugh in agreement. He squinted at Daniel, and wondered how come he kept coming back to call and visit.

With Lloyd, Daniel was genial and confidential, making the boy feel that any day now he'd take him over to Freola with him and . . . and they'd make a night of it, with likker and "the girls" and cigars and the like, vague but excruciating, manhood indulgence.

". . . How old *are* you, then:" asked Daniel, looking Lloyd over.

"I'm going on eighteen, next year," said Lloyd defiantly.

"You're pretty well developed. Let me feel your muscle."

Lloyd cocked his arm and stuck up his chest. He quivered with the desire and exertion of proving himself, holding his body tautly displayed and hungering for approval.

"Yes, you've g-got a good build. —One of these days we'll have to see."

He winked. Lloyd blushed and grinned.

He charmed Retha by looking at her as if she were a woman and teasing her as if she were a little girl. This gave the burgeoning child a safe happiness.

". . . All right, then," said Daniel, "I'll just *bet* you: I'll c-come back here Hallowe'en and I'll bet you I'll b-beat you ducking for apples!"

Retha almost slid off her chair in a squirm of pleasure at the blue snap of his eyes and the fondness in his cheerful face.

He dried dishes for Mrs. Kinneyman and went into long harangues about his travels and various cities, knowing she would never ask for it, but giving her what she most wanted, some glimpse, however meagre, of the world beyond, and he told her what he could in the slightly daring tone of a man who is dissipated and wants people to think that has a certain value.

"—That was one evening at the Cliff House in San Francisco, Mrs. K.," he said. "I saw her come in and take a table near the windows with this man; you could look right down on the breakers coming in on the rocks below; well, sir, you'd n-never believe the dress she had on; wasn't *a stitch of c-cloth on her whole back!* And when she looked around, who do you suppose it was?"

Mrs. Kinneyman gasped softly at her dishpan, and looked up, unable to ask. He went on,

"Lillian Russell! —Her hair was yellow, silvery you know, when the light—say, just about the color of yours!"

She took it and believed it.

And Irma.

Now at last he knew his rôle with Irma.

The fall was crusting the pumpkins in early morning and the groves of trees over the hill quivered blue in the twilights of dawn and dusk. He had come and gone many times. He had done with the family all the things they did in society . . . church, a barn dance, a drive to town for a revival meeting which was held under a great tree with kerosene lanterns hung on the lowest branches, an ice-cream social at the home of the editor of the *Freola Weekly Star-Gazette;* and everywhere people liked him, because he was each time what they wanted him to be. Everyone thought it especially interesting when he thought of something he had in his wallet, and pulled it out, thumbed through the clippings, papers, and notes, and found what he wanted, and read it aloud, stowing it away again during friendly laughter.

But Irma alone continued to look at him without tribute to his charm.

He had started off wrong, he decided.

In one of his midsummer visits, in the evening, he had asked her to show him the farm; and they had set out to walk in the high twilight. The air was hot but not sticky, and as they walked it got a little darker, a falling as of a hush in which their hearts might soon be heard. Or so he felt. They went on past the windmill to the barn, and looked through its wide door into the rich depths of the interior, and in the darkness with the faint filter of some atmospheric essence out of the silvery sky about the moon, the barn's inside seemed alive, as if the darkness there might be made of a great density of black smoke, turning in slow eddies. They went on past the barn and came to the pig-sty, where the stench made their stomachs gulp, and the pigs came moincking obscenely as if they were to be fed by the two figures who watched for a moment. They could hear the hard tap of the pigs' hoofs on the firm ground and the suck and gutch of the hoofs in the stinking muddy ground near the center trough. In the moonlight, the pigs were monsters of gluttony and filth.

"Look, please, let's go on," said Daniel.

They walked on into the field nearest the sty, which stood in corn. The rows were as high as their heads, and walking by them they were faintly dazzled by the spiny gleam of moonlight on the corn leaves.

"Our place runs on through this field, and down the hill and over t'that next pasture, where the trees stand," said Irma.

Her voice was soft, and it had a little quiver; in a moment Dan was prickling with excitement and he took her arm and said,

"Let's walk down there, where the trees are. . . ."

She nodded and they went on.

He now and then caught a deep breath.

By a curious silent harmony they said nothing to each other. They seemed to feel that the night was so eloquent of tenderness and generosity, the silent stir of the air and the cooling moon, the darkness like a soft garment enfolding secrecies with peace and sanction. . . .

At the grove of trees there was dense shadow. Here they stood and gazed about them; and then they sat on a grassy slope in the heavy rich dark; and then Daniel was lying and his arms tried for Irma, and she came to lie in his grasp, trembling and resistant. In the dark he could know her face better than ever, remembering her eyes and the white skin and the scarlet mouth; the bloom of plumpness to her cheeks and throat; he kissed and kissed her, dimly feeling that she was struggling to be away from him, but his heart was blown full of the summer night, and he lost thought in touch.

But she twisted free in a moment. She stood up. She sounded as if she were weeping, and he came up beside her and whispered. His voice broke from the whisper into sound, and in the black grove, it sounded like some night bird talking, natural to the place and terrifying, too.

He embraced her again, this time gently and to soothe her. He felt her rage of response and denial.

"I love you, honey."

"—Let go, Dan."

"Honey, we ' been a l-long time . . ."

He was pleading.

He sounded now without the breeziness she had seen in him everywhere else. His sudden sincerity almost touched her to love him and let him; but she shook her head and came away from him, and started back up the slope toward the cornfield. He followed. He was angry. He took her roughly and squeezed her arms; and had she turned to struggle, or snatched her arms away, he would have stormed her with his body and drunkened them both with lust and ended their time forever. But she simply walked on, letting his angry touch stay; and then he cooled and his want changed to shame, and in silence they walked through the rows of corn that pattered their leaves together as they brushed them with their shoulders.

They were calm when they reached the house.

Irma seemed even sorrowful, and when she told him good night, she was so gentle that it whipped him alive again, and bound him closer than ever to her. In her eyes was a kind of inquiry, estimating him, a reservation about him that maddened him as much as her desirability. He wanted to turn that distant light out in her eyes; he wanted to prove to her, a good innocent girl, what he had shown so many girls in cities all over the country. His vanity entered the struggle, and as soon as it did, he began to lose.

X · THE PROMISE

On his succeeding visits he had exciting and foolish times dealing in terms of innocence with his passionate desires, which were simply turned back on him by Irma's genuine goodness. It had never struck her in her whole life as a possible thing that she might think of love and a man aside from marriage. This was a thing her sister dreamed about, and sometimes consciously mused over with realistic resignation. But not Irma; she was sincerely good. The more Daniel came up against this quality, the more he found it hard to believe; but she resisted him in the midst of passionate moments when they were alone, and evidently did it without any trouble. It was simpler for her to behave according to what she had been taught to believe than according to what she felt.

It was August before he began to try reasoning himself out of his fantastic trouble.

"Can you see me:" he said to himself. "A rolling stone like me; marrying her? or any other girl? but especially a girl from the country and taking her on my rounds? The whole thing's ridiculous. —That's all she's waiting for. You can tell by the way the Kinneymans act, too. The family has come to regard me as a member, a son-in-law. —I got myself in fine, didn't I: getting them all to like me, one by one: and now look at them. Look at me!"

He went over and over the ground in his thoughts. If Irma was ruled by her reason and decency, then he was mastered by his feelings, which became tempestuous at times, and he would cynically look at himself, and jeer. He had a sort of extraneous realism that came along with his passion, and he saw just where he would be heading, yet going ahead anyway. He was careful to tell himself that he was not in love, really; that once he had her, the thing wouldn't last, anyway; excusing his little conscience with the belief that Irma wouldn't know anyway what it was all about. . . .

One time in early October after supper one evening they were all still sitting at the Kinneyman dining-room table. The children had been playing a wishing game aloud. Lloyd wished for a career as a prize-fighter, with diamond-and-ruby championship belts, trunks with the American flag stitched on the right thigh, oiled hair, a breast full of cigars, and privately, two girls, wearing black silk stockings up, up, up under their many skirts and petticoats and ruffles, and letting him find the garters; Retha wanted a baseball bat and a corset; the little girls wanted dollies; the baby boy was inarticulate; and in the dreamy pause in which the youngsters all saw their desires in midair, Irma said:

"Well, all I want, some day I want a rose garden and a harp."

There was a bewildered silence at this. Shide Kinneyman pished out his hateful laugh like a sandy whisper. The children thought it was the worst waste in the world not to really *wish* when you were wishing.

Daniel heaved a sigh. It was the end. He didn't know why this should do it, or if the time was come, anyway; but after supper, he took her out the front yard and across the road and they sat in the tall grass that smelled sweet and chill; and he took her hand to work it longingly in his.

"Irma, I want you to marry me?"

Silence.

The night was crisp. She shivered.

He said, "I'll promise you that rose garden and that harp, honey?"

"Why, yes, Daniel," she said, before she began to weep.

He hugged her and dwelled on her lips and hushed her. She pushed him a moment later, and said,

"—I'm through my cryin' now. —I thought you never *would* ask me!"

He went cold for a second at this.

He had the sensations of a loser, and he concluded that he always thought more cleverly than he acted. But now in any case he had a certain peace, like a stone that wouldn't roll any more.

XI · THE TROTH

Of the wedding what most of them remembered for years afterward, and forebodingly, was that for the first time they smelled likker on Dan Milford's breath. They couldn't really believe it at first; he had shown them the perfect likeness of a manly Christian; and even now, in his wedding clothes, with his hair brilliantly brushed, his face merry and pink, his white waistcoat, and the tapering cut of his black suit, they simply couldn't believe it of him. But it was too late; there was no time for warning. Irma was ready and she married him in her dress of pleated muslin with a lacy veil down the back.

"She needn't come back here for takin' in," declared Shide Kinneyman, foreseeing the lot of the drunkard's wife.

Mrs. Kinneyman was heartsick, for she honestly believed the devil dwelled in the rum bottle; and also she had come to love Daniel in a friendly way, and she felt betrayed.

There was a large crowd. The marriage was done in the living-room where the harmonium was. They stood up without much bother and had their vows woven together by the minister of their church in town. It was in October. Outside there was a buggy waiting. In the hall was Daniel's silk hat, which Lloyd wore secretly into the dining-room and back, and Daniel's new cane, of brown wood with a bone handle carved to represent a dog's head with saw-teeth and green glass eyes. When the short ceremony was over, the guests had cider and maple cake while Irma went to change her gown. Daniel stood among the men guests; and at a moment showed his bottle and winked inquiries as to who wanted a drink. There was an embarrassed and fumbling response, but several young men had a swig, yowing in answer to the hot whisky scorch in their mouths. Shide Kinneyman saw the indulgence and like the very person of his place and time, he laid down judgment, a judgment that would matter, not because it was wise, but because it represented almost a unanimous opinion of that people, while his eyes reddened and dried hotly, and his breath clattered dryly in his throat, full of hatred and dustily comforted by the promise of vengeance that must always overtake the sinner.

Irma came back, blushing in her broadcloth tailored suit, with a straw hat with cloth roses on it sitting far forward over her black hair and sparkling face. Daniel cheered up; the whisky widened his prowess; he lost his trapped feeling, and marveled openly at her beauty and his fortune. He went to meet her and took her arm. She left him to kiss her family all good-by. She began to weep laughingly, and Lloyd jeered sadly at her and Retha wept. Frisbie, her sister, no longer knew how to kiss anyone, or touch the feeling of her heart upon another person; so she only laid her wrecked hands on Irma's forearms primly, and from the tumult of her happiness, relief, and hope, the fierce want that her young sister should know a life of rich tenderness, she said, after clearing her throat:

"Well, see you come back whenever you can, Irma. . . . Well, good-by. . . ."

Now the crowd closed after them as they went through the front door to the shining buggy out in the yard.

And as if by signal, an obsession for vicarious indulgence visited the crowd; they clambered to the buggy and the strong young men held the wheels; they gathered at the four wheels and lifted them off the ground, laughing wildly, while the horse reared in fright, and Dan stood with the whip and the reins, and Irma looked in imploring shame at her friends who were sporting so with her.

"You know what ' give her for me, Dan," cried some young man.

The crowd laughed eagerly, and let the buggy down. Dan cracked the whip, and the horse plunged. He made a getaway toward the gate, and the young men began to run after. The fever was extending to the women, and the joke of connubial coupling hiked up their feelings. They too wanted to repeat the time of wedding; they wanted to mock the ones who were just approaching it; they wanted to help the young men in the cruel impromptu ceremony.

Dan's buggy was turning into the road. One of the women in the yard screamed,

"Let's follow them!" and a wave of shrill delight broke over the guests. They ran toward their wagons and buggies in the side yard.

The day was warm and the road was dusty under the blue-and-yellow October sky.

Now that curious chase set out. The wagons and carriages and buggies turned into the road after Dan and Irma. Irma turned and saw them through the dust of their own buggy.

"They're coming after us, Dan!" she cried, half humorously and half angrily.

He flushed. He stood and whipped his horse. They were heading for Athens, the first town east of the Kinneyman farm. The railroad ran there.

"God damn 'em!" he said.

She winced; and looked to see if she could tell by his face whether or not he had been drinking again. He was scowling fiercely, yet he was grinning, and she felt safer and easier.

They could hear catcalls from the chasing procession, cries as if from beasts in heat, joyously full of announcement and anticipation.

"I'll outrun 'em," said Dan, standing and whipping the horse again. He suddenly laughed, and taken by the heat of the tradition, he reached and roughly armed Irma's waist in a series of hugs. "Look ' see if they're gaining, honey!"

She turned. The dust was beamed in sunlight. She could see the rocking buggies, and in the leading one one of the boys of Athens stood whipping his black felt hat over the horse's rump while his girl drove. They were not gaining; but they were near enough to smell the quarry and press the chase, whose object nobody could state.

"They're not gaining," said Irma.

"—I didn't figure we'd make the drive this fast," gasped Daniel. "But now ' we reach Athens maybe we can get the earlier train, she goes east at twelve-twenty!"

Far ahead they could see the trees on the horizon where Athens was. They galloped between the yellow fields of fall, where the corn was shocked and stacks of hay stood still, and the great racks worked from field to barn.

This was what saved them.

They saw a huge rack-wagon coming slowly off the field toward a gate on to the road. Daniel leaned and beat his horse to get by before the rack should turn into the road and block his way. The rack saw him coming; it didn't slow its measured pace for a moment, but slowly came to the gate, and as he passed, it went turning into the road, blocking it with an immense load of dusty sweet hay. The chasing buggies slowed down; but it took the rack a long time to turn and head west on the road; and when it was moving in a straight line, the other buggies couldn't pass it with speed, for the road was only ordinarily wide, and the mow on the rack overhung it lavishly on both sides. By the time the leading buggies were free of the delay, Dan and Irma had a safe lead. The cries of the wedding guests faded into the dusty warm day. Dan let his horse trot a while; but as they neared Athens they heard a faint sound blown down the flat country by the breeze; it was a train whistle; and leaping to the whip, Dan said,

"That's the twelve-twenty," and the horse began to gallop again and soon they rocked into the shady streets of Athens and across town to the depot.

They made it.

He gave the horse and buggy over to the care of the station master to return to the livery stable; and with Irma and their bags, he was ready for the train. She came in in a few minutes. Now for the first time Irma felt married and committed; and she gasped and wanted to ask him a dozen different things; but there was no time; he armed her to the train and into the nearest car. A Negro in sweat-softened rags handed their bags up after them. They looked down on the gray weathered station platform and the boards began to move slowly past. They watched the gray station with its wooden Gothic windows and rooftree of scroll-sawed Gothic ornaments go by. They saw the shaded dirt streets of Athens appear after the depot was gone; the outlying shacks and huts; the farming country begin; and along a distant road leading into town over the flat land, a miniature buggy tearing on, the horse bobbing at a gallop, the driver standing up, in a white dress; and beside her, a youth in black whipping his hat through the air, and Irma and Dan laughed at this as anyone would laugh at some one who was too late but didn't know it.

XII · THE PAST

Their honeymoon was months long, because Dan took her every-where his job led. They were happy in very different ways. He was like a lion, or a cock; genial and proud of her and the marriage he had resisted for so long. Her chaste temperament excited him as no artful mistress could have. She seemed to get prettier every day; and he glossier and more substantial-looking. As a pair, they always drew eyes in hotels and trains. But it was in such places only that Irma disappointed him. He was used to the lavish ease in manner of more worldly girls, and her shyness in the presence of heavy dignitaries like hotel head waiters, train conductors, and the scattered minor personages whom Dan knew in various towns, always made him impatient.

"Now, look, why don't you t-talk right up to them? Last night you h-had a grand chance to make a hit with Judge Carberry, and all you did was grin at him and then look at m-me!"

"I know, Dan, honey; —I get so scared and funny with those important folks. . . ."

"Well, they *are* important, and they may be able to d-do some-thing for me some day; and you could help out by playing up a little. . . ."

He would smile kindly at her and reflect in clear moments like this that for him to marry a country girl was the damnedest per-formance you ever heard of. But at other times, alone with him, she was all that he could want. She was high-spirited and had no shyness with him but only a warm and healthy desire which she revealed to him in frank yet not wanton ways. It was an endless delight to him to strike wonder and passion alive in her through making love. He used to love watching her dress, and in his hale masculine way, he had a genuine taste in matters relating to her clothes, and with his clean pink hands, he would help her dress, and tie her veil, and kiss her through it. Her long black lashes stuck out through the veil and tickled his cheek until he felt little electric voltages threading in his skin, in the roof of his mouth; and time and again he would make them stay in their hotel bedroom, instead of going on downstairs to dinner, which they would forget to order.

His trip with her became a kind of exhibition tour. He showed Irma off to his old companions, though she never knew it. Several times he had run into the girls and told them about Irma, and now as he blew into town with his bride, he would see them in lobbies and bars where he went for his cocktails. He described Irma, and said that if they were in the lobby that night at seven-thirty, he'd come down with her on the way to dine in the dining-room, and they could see her. Later, tomorrow, some other time, they could tell him what they thought of her. He'd really like to know. They waved their ruches and calculatingly drifted their heads a little, making the paradise feathers on their hats waft gently. They looked at him through sceptical eyes, and bit their mouths in amusement.

"Who ever thought you'd do a thing like that:" was what he'd hear. "You're a rolling stone if I ever saw one . . . whataya going to do with a wife and family?"

"There's not going to be any family," he said, hurriedly. "That's one thing sure. Yes, I can take Irma around with me, but God help us, if she has a baby, we can't take a kid along, and I can't settle down, that's all there is to it. . . ."

He got involved with that idea and began to put it clearly to Irma.

"See? —I'd have to leave you home somewheres, and go out on the road alone, and I don't want to do that, you can s-see that, can't you, honey:"

She was heartfully in love with him.

She took his warning about having a child in a dumb submissiveness. It hurt her, because she loved children, and they seemed so well to fit into the future which would include also a rose garden and a harp, which he had promised her. But Daniel was a new force in her life, and she quickly learned to be obedient to him, and to rely on him for the smallest decision. This sometimes annoyed him, and he'd get his trapped feeling again, when he saw her wanting to do something, or go somewhere, but waiting, with her large black eyes softly wooing his with love which he didn't want, at the moment.

"Well, go on, what d'you w-want this time:"

"Oh, I'm sorry, honey, I just wanted to go down to the lobby and get some lemon drops," or something equally trivial.

"G-go ahead, then."

They lived in hotels everywhere. It made it easy for Daniel to leave her and go out alone when he had "a deal on," or something to do which would only "tire my honey out."

He often went off to get a drink. She had timidly complained once about his likker habit.

"Your likker habit is going t'be hard to break, some day, honey," she said.

"Who said I was ever going to break it!" he roared, in a flush of rage; and then said he was sorry, and kissed her.

He could get out that way and meet his old friends. They'd go and loll in one of the green velvet booths of a saloon somewhere, and in that vat-soured air, Dan inhaled an old familiar ease, and began to know that Irma was one thing in his life, and this was another, and the two would never rhyme, and he thought himself lucky to have both.

"Well, did you see her when we passed you by tonight?" he asked his friends.

They were two young women, plumed and pompadoured, with high stiff collars, and broadcloth suits tailored to mold their breasts and narrow their waists. They had interesting habits which he remembered and recognized with a sense of fun. One of them would lean back and raise her bust as if to free a fold of skin from the clasp of her corset. The other had a little way, almost French, he thought it, of brushing an imaginary mist from before her eyes. They were heavily scented. They were his idea of what a woman ought to be. Irma always seemed just a farm girl to him.

"Yes, we saw her. Sure. She's a right sweet-looking girl."

"—She looks about as much like the wife of the snappiest gent between here and Chicago as, as Mrs. McKinley does!"

"However in the world didja do it, Dan?"

"Yes, tell us: I said to Clara, I said, Clara, what got him *that* time!"

He grinned and shrugged. He couldn't easily put into words the feeling he had for Irma. He didn't himself know how much vanity, desire, and an older propriety than either had led him to take a wife. He liked to hear the slightly spiteful remarks of these women. They spiced his relation with them, and Irma too.

"Well, I must say, you girls don't seem to take very kindly to Mrs. Milford!"

"Well, all I remember is the way you always used to talk. You said ' woman didn't breathe who could take you and tie you down. Said ' easiest thing in the world to get fed up on one girl. Said you were too smart."

He felt a turn of irritation. It had to be hidden.

"Go on," he said. "Who says I'm tied down?"

"Oh, no, not at all," they jeered.

"N-no, really, everything is just the s-same, only I have a lot more fun!"

"Yes, how long will it last!"

They were probing with indifference and expertness into the fibers of doubt. He felt angry. His face turned redder. They watched him, and exchanged glances. By God, they didn't know what they were talking about!

"Listen here!" he said huskily. "First place, I'll always do just as I damn please! Second place, Mrs. Milford is a lady, and you girls just don't know anything about that!"

"Oh, is that so, the idea! She's not's attractive as all that!"

"Well, I'm sorry, you know what I m-mean. . . ."

They were jealous and scornful. That tickled him. He knew they liked him; women always did. They'd calculate him and there was welcome in the resultant glance they gave him. The very things that made him think well enough of himself to dress as richly as he did, made him take for granted the attentions of all sorts of women, without his ever deciding that he owed them something in return, something of his heart, the tenderness which when a man gives it is always a little unexpected, and because of that, winning and exquisite.

"Well, all I say is, a man like you that's always on the move, he ain't got any business setting up a *family*."

"I t-told you before there isn't going to be any family."

"Well, leave that off; you're still on the go, go, go, all the time. —That'd be a hell of a life for anybody but a girl who was cuh-razy about a fellow."

"Well, she is," he said. "She says she likes to travel: with me:"

"Well, who wouldn't:" —with the teasing resentfulness which as a tribute he loved to wring out of women. "Is that a new ring you got on? Let me see it."

He held forward his hand. He was wearing a deep gold ring with claws holding a large stone the color of burgundy wine in sunlight.

"That's elegant."

"I got it in Chicago on our way back from Niagara Falls. —That was very interesting. The F-falls, I mean. We went under them in a little boat. Now the next thing I want to s-see is California. They s-say a lot of people are heading out there. The place is bound to build up."

"Leave it be. You got a fine business right around here, all this

territory, there aren't many young fellas your age doing as good as
you are, Dan; you know that. —I certn'y like your ring."

"Ye', I know, but travel is comfortable, the accommodations are
fine, you'd be a back number if you didn't get around, I'm like that
anyway, minute I blow in one town I'm ready to light out for another. . . ."

That's the way it always was with America.

The whole country had always been restless, moving from place to
place, growing and taking and looking still farther ahead, to see if
there are other places to be seeded and then left . . . as if the roots
took too long to grasp and rear and bear, as if the planter had to do
and be gone. Looking always for a country of content, people concluded that the next move would surely reveal its valleys to them.
Sometimes they went and came back, with the emotions of return
making them happy and discovering to them the strange news that
here, at home, after all, was the content they were looking for. They
traveled nowadays on trains, and the people responded in their actions to the meaning of the railroads in their lives, about which they
never stopped to think, but which symbolized so much of far worlds
to the horizon-lost farm, and all things divided by distance. It was the
first mighty machine to hold the imaginations of child and man both.
The people took to it, with folk lore resulting. Its systems were so
far-reaching and so well run that people began to think railroads almost a natural force, and the cry of the train whistles could mean
anything they had a mood for; it could mean sorrow that had no
meaning except rootless pity, a response as to music; it could mean
the proof of other life and dim comfort to a lonesome place on the
plains; or ambition, or memory of other days; or invitation; and
lightin' out. . . .

They were a proof that there was much to do and you had to hustle
to get it all done. You had to keep busy if you wanted to get ahead.

The railroads ran all day and all night.

Something that never stopped was especially American.

The trains kept coming and going, and every one of them carried
people who went because they had things to do which couldn't've
been so well done without the trains. They were a proof of energy, of
life itself, to the nation. And like anything that looked right for what
it did, they were beautiful——sadness and power all mixed up with
the blessing of nourishment, as the outland country shipped their
crops to the cities, and the trains from the cities went past, leaving
their brief sign of smoke, that died in the air like a man's imaginative

thoughts when there was no one to listen to them and use them for anything.

XIII · HOTEL BEDROOMS

She got used to the sight of strange towns from hotel bedrooms. She thought some towns looked more lonesome than others, but those were always times when Dan had gone out angry. His humor was changing toward her, and she fancied that it began the time she asked him why he never took her out in the evenings with him any more. It was the first hint that he might be guilty of hurting Irma; and the kind of thing he thought of as sporting life suddenly looked sordid to him, yet desirable even so; and he defended his movements with shouts of rage, banging his hands down on the dresser where he was using the mirror to tie his tie.

"—If your popular friends could see you now," she said, furious at him for the first time.

"What: you!"

"—Oh, *my* yes; everybody thinks he's just the grandest thing in the world, never a cross word, and just so polite, and this and that, with a smile for everyone, and the attentions to all the ladies, and a-singing hymns when they're the thing to do, and getting drunk when you're out so's that'll be what people want you to do. . . ."

He had the vanity which dared to realize the fact when it was presented; but it also realized the danger of truth. He turned dark red, and his mouth twitched. He raised his big hand ready to hit her. Then he felt a cool wave of superiority break over him and he shrugged and laughed, sincerely; and turned back to the mirror with his tie, feeling that after all, if this was the way she was going to behave, then he need have no sense of duty toward her any longer. He was the most attractive man in his wandering little world of salesmen, lobbies, saloons, expensive restaurants, and Pullman cars. His cheerful face was known everywhere. He was all things to all men and women. It nourished him more than food.

So he would leave Irma in the evenings.

They didn't quarrel stridently again for some time; and when he left her, he did make a gay pretense of having business, which would only bore her. And there were times when he came back without the climate of drink about him and with a familiar coaxing tone in his words, so that she thought the old times were restored, and they made love, and slept and awoke without thought or opinion saving only that of the blood appeased.

He was continuing to have the two sides to his life.

She filled her hours by sitting in her bedroom with newspapers, and sewing, and having conversation with the chambermaids. They told her what to do and where to go for amusement. She went to take walks to the park which a chambermaid remembered passionately; and she went to a vaudeville on the same recommendation. From the floor housekeeper she found out which department store to roam in, and collect samples from, which she would finger desirously in the evening when she was left alone. She got bits of cloth and in her mind made plans about using them in furnishing a house, curtains, chairs, bedspreads. She would read the paper, and perhaps go downstairs in the elevator, which was controlled by a cable that passed through the elevator car and was pulled up or down for stop or go; and after taking a look around the lobby, she would retire upstairs again, to sit between the heavy lace curtains at the window and look out upon Main Street; Dan always insisted on having a hotel room in the front of the building. She would watch the crowds come and go, and see the lights start up in the falling dusk, first the gas street lamps lighted with kerosene tapers; and then the theatres, with their wiry gold elecric light, and the street cars coming like slow chariots in the distance; and now and then a fire engine coming by with a wind of sparks trailing it and three gray horses galloping and great red wheels skidding as they swayed across the car tracks.

Now and then she went to prayer-meetings in the various towns. But she was a stranger, and had no need to be busy meeting people when she was going to move on in the next few days anyway.

XIV · SOMEONE SHE KNEW

One night in a large city in Texas he came home to the hotel late. He was scowling. There was an idea in the back of his head, and when she spoke to him he grunted at her with scorn in his voice. He undressed partly, and then turned to face her. She was in bed with the covers pulled modestly to her breast. He stared at her with his eyes screwed up, barely nodding his head in calculations.

"It never occurred to me before," he said.

"What:"

"—What do you do with your time when I'm away from the hotel, doing business and making a living, so we can t-travel around the country in luxury and put up at the best hotels and make a big noise as if we were millionaires?"

His own voice deepened his grievance. He was for the first time gripped by the idea of jealousy. He had never dreamed that she would do as he did in escaping from their wedding bonds. But this evening he had been sitting with some old friends, one of whom had seen him with Irma the day before. And she had declared that he was a fool to go trotting around after other girls, with a wife like that, who was probably already sick to death of being left alone night after night, while her husband was out making hay in the hayloft; did he suppose she stayed home like a good girl, just waiting for him? Didn't she like a good time as much as he did? Then you could bet she was getting it, with somebody else. . . .

It was an opinion that reflected more about the speaker of it than the subject of it; and at first it made Dan laugh with alcoholic indulgence, and say that his wife, by G-god, was better trained than that, and anyway she wasn't that type of a woman, and it was a different story, besides, because a man could do things a woman simply couldn't.

But they drank some more and the pitch of the argument was raised with the lowering of the glasses, and what could have slipped past as an idle and unworthy suspicion became an obsession, born of his own guilt, the drinks, and what he regarded as worldly wisdom and an understanding of human nature on the part of his old friend, who after all had seen a lot of men in her time, and knew 'em like a book, and women too, for she spoke as a woman.

Irma listened to his pouting accusation and in all innocence answered him with her bleak truth.

"I—I stay up here, mostly, and read, and sew on that fancy quilt I'm making. Why? —Oh, maybe sometimes I go down and take a walk, you can't stay cooped up all the time . . ."

He pulled at his trousers and got them off. He kicked off his shoes. He didn't care how he appeared to Irma. He thought she was being cleverly evasive.

"Oh, so that's a-all, is it? How do *I* know? —Listen here, Irma

Milford, if I ever catch you even *look*ing at another man, I'll k-kill him, and may k-ill you, too!"

She sat straight up. She bolted up in bed and looked like a small girl who is scared out of her wits by something she can't understand. Her whole flesh quivered in protest. She thought Dan looked like a stranger in this idea, and she couldn't say a thing.

"Hear me?" he said.

He looked narrowly at her. The likker was waning, and instead of a golden eloquence he now tasted in his mouth the stale clothy flavor of folly after drink.

"Well, am I to believe it's true, if you s-sit there and say nothing?" But he was no longer drunkened and righteous.

She turned suddenly and fell to her pillow and began to weep. She had cried alone plenty of times; but he had never seen her weep since those days which seemed to have happened so long ago in the country between Athens and Freola. In the gassy light of the hotel bedroom, he suddenly became aware of the forlorn and wandering character of the life he had put her into, and her shaking bones under her nightgown as she sobbed pulled him down from his exalted nonsense with a pathetic bump. Here she was in a new aspect, and it touched him. He was in his pajamas now, tying the string around his belly, which had fattened noticeably in the past months. He lumbered over to the bed and sat on it, and his weight rolled her a little toward him. She resisted this, and tried to hunch away from him. She was trying to stop crying by hiding her face in the pillow. He saw the nape of her neck damp with glistening sweat where her marvelous black hair began to grow. He bent over and kissed her there. At the touch of his lips, she stiffened and lay rigid, holding her breath. He laid his hand on her back, gently. Slowly she rolled over and looked up at him. She seemed to be looking for some one she knew, who was gone, and every stranger who resembled him was a new pang and a vanished hope.

"I'm s-sorry, honey," he murmured.

He wooed her again.

It seemed to end her loneliness against her will now.

XV · MIND MADE UP

They were moving west, gradually.

In El Paso, one time, he came home and without thinking about it, walked up the stairs to their room on the second floor. He turned down the corridor, and when he came to the elevator, he saw the door open, and the Negro elevator boy leaning there and talking with a grin to Irma.

Once they were in their room, he raged at her and appalled her by the violence of his imagination in the things he accused her of indulging in with the elevator man. She was feeling a little ill and every day she feared more and more to tell him why. She had been standing in her room in a little tempest of nerves, and she went out to take the elevator downstairs just for diversion, and the big black boy who ran it looked so cheerful that he improved her spirits right away. She didn't pause to think how strange it was for her to find comradeship in the company of a Negro servant; she was simply grateful for the boy's innocent happiness that played alive through his person in every way. They told each other trifles, like how far they had traveled, and the worst storm they ever saw, and about the climate of El Paso . . . five minutes, a few words.

"—I know th-those niggers! —Can't fool me!" roared Dan. "Damn black buck! Been having him up here? Go crazy over a white woman any time! What ' you mean!"

"Dan!"

"I'm going ' report him! Daring to talk to a guest! —Here, where's my coat!"

"Dan!"

"Well, what:"

"You're drunk! Sit down! —Do you know what you said? Oh, Lord, I hope you'll not remember when you wake up!"

He remembered.

He knew it was all foolish, and that its only importance was how it betrayed the irritation and wreckage of the marriage. He hated her now for being right; it seemed to him that in some curious and subtle fashion, he, who always used to be perfectly right, was now always in the wrong, with her, at least. Away, he was still sure of himself and charming. He was able to be honest elsewhere. Here, he constantly paid the price of his dishonesty.

She managed to get him to take a nap. When she was alone because he slept, she dared show her feelings to herself.

What would they have said back home?

What would Shide Kinneyman think? Whatever it was, it would represent the opinion of her homeland, the opinion that all her life she would have to face and satisfy if she were to know the simple content of the native. She hadn't been able to write her sister, Frisbie Kinneyman, for months. Now she wanted to write and tell her sister that she was expecting a baby. But that seemed unfair without letting Dan know it first. She had invented many ways of telling him, so that he would receive the news as a blessing instead of a bore.

When he awoke in half an hour, he was weak and shaken, and he felt pathetic. He sat up and his head ached. He saw her sitting there watching him. Frowning to cover his remote sensation of tenderness, he went to her and told her he was sorry what he'd said was so bad. He lighted a cigarette and went past her to the window and stared out. His attitude told of how he wanted to recover for them the untroublesome habit of temper in which they lived and dealt with each other. It had something to do with shame and self-respect, and if he made the official amends here, he would have no questioning guilt behind his charm when he went out later and saw his friends and business acquaintances. They would never suspect that he had behaved obscenely to his wife and bitterly accused her of things he shouldn't even have thought about anyone. He squared his shoulders. He reflected that it was fine to be big about your mistakes and clear them up right away. He felt renewed.

"Well, we'll be going on tomorrow. —There's a ch-chance for some new territory out in California. The office has written me to go out and l-look it over. There're lots of new towns out there, opening up, the railroads are taking and putting in spur lines, great fruit country and lots of traffic."

He was serene and he always sounded wise about matters of this kind.

"—Do you think we'll ever live out there?"

"How'd I know: —I heard of a little town, Coronilla, name, the S.P. has just run the railroad in there. Might be a chance to sell supplies on a big scale at first."

"Are we going there?"

"Look around, might s-see a chance to invest in some real estate, too. Not a bad thing to do; growing town, California's great place, wonderful climate they say."

"—Dan!"

He turned to look at her.

She sat down on the bed as if at the impact of his glance.

"Well?"

"Maybe they'd have you live out there, I mean the company, and run all the business out there for them? Stay there instead of moving around?"

"Say, wh-what on earth are you talking about:"

"—That time in Dallas, three months ago?"

He stared. She said,

"Well, that's it, Dan. —I'm going to . . ."

He saw it in her face. It made him shut her words off with a gesture; it astonished him with such fury that he couldn't speak, and this saved them both from a renewal of their ingenious quarreling, in which they wounded each other with terrible aptness. The pause was long enough to let his mind see and rearrange and decide; it was the thing that made him such an excellent business man, that capacity for making decisions with the certainty of a thing already past, because he could see the whole train of future events so clearly projected by his thought. He now kept his silence a moment longer, and saw in detail what he would do; how this news of Irma's would affect them; and his conclusion reached, after all these months of irritation and responsibility, he felt like taking a deep breath, full of confidence. He was almost a new man, he told himself; the only thing that had been making it so difficult was the fact that he hadn't been able to make up his mind.

He went over and took Irma in his arms and patted her back.

"Well, well, well. How long ' you been keeping this secret?"

His mildness made her feel faint with relief. She sobbed dryly once or twice, and then her natural robustness of spirit came back, that she had lost for so long, and she laughed and hugged him.

"Maybe California is the answer a-after all. We'll see."

"Well, Dan, whatever you decide. . . . It seems I never *can* decide for myself."

He nodded at her.

He reflected that it was amazing how much gentler he felt toward her now that he had his plans made for them. That had been the trouble all along, indecision.

XVI · LOOK AROUND

Their trip to California was gay and happy.

They marveled over the new landscape in Arizona and he bought her paper cornucopias full of grapes on the train. It seemed to her that a promise of new life attended this move they were making, and her eagerness made her very pretty, full of courage and enthusiasm for beginning life all over in another place, starting from scratch among strange people whom she would have to win.

Their train got into Coronilla one evening at seven o'clock.

They had crossed a wide flat land, covered with tawny grass. Far beyond rose dim mountain slopes. The little town lay alone in the plain, but it had a busy character, and seemed to be already rooted like other growths of the fertile flats. There was one long street, with cafés, a bank, a hotel, and stores. Stretching out from this were other streets that reached the open country in straight lines and sooner than the perspective would show. There were a few trees standing by the tracks, around the newly built station and tool-houses and water-tank. In the clear evening, the town showed its lights, a tiny capital in this kingdom of plain and mountain and sky, already the center of force and dominion over the land.

They took a hack to the hotel two blocks away and there Dan said,

"We'll stay here until we can look around and find something better for a 1-little more permanent arrangement."

Her heart settled within her.

XVII · THE SOWER

This was new territory; in the next few days Dan covered it in his usual style. He left Irma at the hotel and went to call on the leading business men of the place. He spent a cordial hour with the banker, in the red brick and white cement bank that stood on the central corner of Coronilla. This interview was a source of satisfaction on both sides. Dan was pleased by the attentiveness of the banker, who read the clippings pulled out of his wallet with pleasure, and said that he was very glad men of substance and an eye to the future were hearing of Coronilla, and thinking of investing capital here. Dan inquired about real estate. The banker sent him to his friend up the block.

With this man, Dan took a slightly different tone, that of the sobersides who knows the value of a dollar, slightly less the indulgent capitalist he had been with the banker. The real estate man showed him some fine property right here along Central Avenue; and Dan took an option on a building which contained a café run by a Chinaman, above which there were rooms for rent. The Chinaman paid a very low rent, but he could be thrown out, the real estate man said, and something more profitable put in.

"We'll see," said Dan.

He met the doctor of the town on the street, and in a few moments' conversation managed to use a few medical terms offhandedly, and in quiet decency, said,

"We'll be needing you ourselves, before long, Doctor. My wife is——"

The blunt shaggy doctor grunted with interest.

"Population growing," he declared, with humor.

"I'll want my wife to meet all you f-fine people," Daniel said. "She's at the hotel."

Everyone thought he was a "live wire," and the charm and ease with which he roamed the town gave him very soon a certain status as a local personage. When in a few days he took up his option on the café property, and it was announced in the Coronilla weekly paper, he was regarded as a leading citizen. He paid seven hundred dollars for the property as it stood. He had the bill of sale made over in his wife's name, as a "little surprise," and then they moved into the rooms over the café to live.

But when he disappeared a while later, without a word to anyone, everyone was ready with suspicious talk, saying that he was too good to be true, and that you could always tell that kind from the way they dressed, rather loud, with flashy jewelry, and the like, to think he would go off and leave his young wife who was expecting a baby! They couldn't imagine what made him do it, except that he must be bad all through; not knowing that what he did was the finish of his carefully arranged plan, which in all its details had occurred to him in the hotel bedroom in El Paso on hearing of the promised birth of his child, whom he thought of as a son, though without eagerness or anything but the habitual propriety that made his a vain life in so many ways.

Book II · THE MOTHER

XVIII · THE LIVING

His birth long later might have been thought of as a mean coming; at the time, there was so much tumult in the souls of the mother and the infant, and in the hour, the place of the event, and in the uncertain future, that there were no opinions, but only feelings.

Irma was impressive, with her white skin and black hair, and her dark eyes had deep coals of vitality in them; they glowed with suffering, or simply with meditation, for she was thoughtful and her feelings that arose in her heart found their ways to her mind in a pleasantly clear way; she seemed to understand that destiny had seized her; and as its servant, or victim, she knew also that she had little to say about her life except that she had to live it. She was suddenly a woman. The people who knew her in Coronilla noticed the change. They thought her now a personality, in her lonely responsibility, instead of an ornamental adjunct to her husband. For the glories and shapely ways of the future, she warmed her head with thoughts of her baby. It was to be a son.

His father was gone. She didn't know where he had gone, or anything except that he had left one night to talk business with the section superintendent of the railroad and see if he couldn't place a few dozen lanterns for sample use by the building gangs of the railroad and he had never come back to Irma after that. Simply walked out, affably. On that evening, a clear green California evening while the level brown land for miles around turned cool under the sky that seemed to have both desert and sea in it, she heard the night freight pull out, and even went to the window of her room over the little restaurant to see the train go black and proud across the skyline, leaving its thin long rub of dying smoke on the pale air that darkened so rapidly as she looked.

There could have been no other way for him to leave. The freight conductor confirmed this on his next return to town. But long later when she gave up hope, she would think of him as being perfectly at home in the caboose of the train, with the trainmen; laughing so modestly through his heavy brown mustache and cocking his eyes and hooking his thumbs under his belt. He was almost thirty, and she could describe him from head to foot, dressed or undressed; and in passionate moments of deprivation and bitterness, she would think it a good idea to have the law on him; to bring him back; make him pay for his fancies, as she said to herself, and yield her the security she felt he owed.

But he had disappeared as cleverly as he did everything else. She wrote his company, and they replied that he had resigned by letter some months ago, and they had no trace of him.

He had left her with no money; but the ownership of the property was something, and her despair was of a kind to make her seek ways to overcome it. She thought she ought to be busy. She ate several times in the Chinaman's café downstairs, where there were almost no customers. It was a smelly and miserable place, a high room with a smoky green ceiling and walls. A few tables were set out in the front of the room, and behind them, a wooden counter cut across the space, dividing it from the kitchen behind. The kitchen was a shadowy place of blackened zinc smoke hood and stove pipes and a brown pine cabinet with a broken glass door in which dishes were kept. The proprietor was named K'ang-Hsui. She told him one day that she was going to work there; it was her property, and if he didn't like it he could get out. Before he had time to answer she had them both busy scrubbing the place out.

She couldn't get him to talk to her; he accepted what she did without expression on his nutty little face. His eyes sometimes looked evil, but she had no way of discovering that his sense of astonishment and outrage was so great that he was weeks finding words for his opinion. But then trade picked up, and Irma's cooking became popular. She divided the money of the first week, and paid him more than he had ever earned in two weeks before. He loved money. He began to accept Irma inwardly as well as outwardly. He liked to smell the dollar bills in his possession, and taste the coins and spit appreciatively.

She had her son in November, when the sunshine was obscure through a chill air, and afternoon was falling toward dusk full of winter. She was attended by Doctor McBride and a woman she knew whose husband was an undertaker in the little town. In a sense, any birth was a community event, just like any death; and Mrs. Milford was well thought of by everyone. Since her husband had left her, she'd been courageous and quiet about it, going to work like that in a restaurant, the one where first he had taken her to eat when they came to town last year to settle, the one over which they'd taken rooms to live, whose windows looked down the main street of the little railroad town, so hot in summer, so bleak in winter, so easy for a man to go away from.

The bedroom was full of the café odors from downstairs, and the light at the window was wan, like a headache. She was crying and not noticing it. They were tears of exhaustion, and she had no will to shut out the memories that clamored in her head, and made her long for places in the past where she had been loved and secure, and long for pictures in the future that would make so much up to her for what she was having now. She remembered Kansas, where she came from, and to which she was always going to return, the farm, the white church, the red sand blowing and the hot summer moons riding dusty in the sky. For the future, she saw her son, who was so near to life now; and the idea of her duty and her escape from loneliness made her cry harder, with happiness and a kind of ecstasy in her pain, so that she heaved up in bed, and sobbed against her drawn-up knees, shaking her head with its heavy black hair falling forward from her white nape, when the doctor came and rubbed her shoulder with the back of his hairy hand, and murmured.

"Never mind," she mumbled.

He continued to soothe her, and exchange professional looks with the midwife who stood in the corner by the window pillowing her arms on her aproned belly.

The wall paper was pale yellow with blue bows arranged in a pattern of vines. The furniture was brown, except the bed, which was of brass. From outdoors came sounds dimly describing the street—horses and their hoofs, their whickering breaths, the shuffle of feet on the board sidewalks, and the cough of the only automobile in town, which at this hour every day drew up to the red brick and cement bank on the next corner to call for the president. The placid declarations of evening outside; over on the tracks an engine working; fat hissing remotely down in the café as supper was moving. Knowing these by habit, Irma could ignore them; yet they managed to intrude into her especially bright consciousness and feed her mind with more thoughts to race there between the queer strikings of pain with every breath and movement of bone.

"We'll be all right," the doctor said, tapping her into silence for a second.

In the white nightgown on the big bed with white counterpane, and her pale skin showing down her back and arms, she looked classic, shadowed with her streaming hair and the gather of darkness in the room.

"They all have to do it," thought the doctor, in a sort of explanation and excuse for his feeling of excitement and concern; the admiration he felt for the large woman in labor.

The midwife was rocking herself slightly on her heels, in a haze of spiritual content; delivering her own children all over again in recognition of the attitudes in her friend Irma.

And Irma herself was in a sense the victim of the moment, estranged by its great pain from the familiar place she was in; bearing not only the child of her love, but also the way to the future, the design of her whole life from then on; visible consequence and living hope. She was already full of love.

"I know he will be great and good and fine," she mourned, but the others in the room heard no words, only a sound like a weeping dove, or a prairie owl such as lived on the brown lands hereabout and filled the still air with a mild sober fluting. "Oh dear Lord: oh God: oh fine," she thought and said, in the same throb of breath and voice that was meaningless to those who listened. Night was coming full outside across the plains, and in the room, the doctor went to light the gas, turning it up high for a sure catch of the match, and then squeaking the cock back until the big butterfly of orange-and-blue flame was quivering above the jet, and flipping with a little noise.

Irma fell whimpering back to the pillow and her eyes spoke for her, and the doctor came forward motioning to the other woman.

"The woman is smiling, I do believe," said the doctor to himself as he bent over Irma, and spoke to her. She was smiling, and the saliva was whipping to her lips and drying there. A vagrant fancy crossed her mind and then took reality in a gleam of her eyes, and she clutched at the doctor and asked him,

"Am I going to die?"

XIX · DANNY

Then it became a night of portents.

That only one person saw them was enough. It was Irma Milford, lying in a feeling of pathetic sweet repose, with the born baby at her side insinuating himself upon the world, the world of her ribs and breast, her curved arm; she could feel his astonishing liveliness and know a pang for the furious refusal he had to see the world before him, with his little face featured with tiny symbols of likeness, tightened and closed and wrinkled.

Such portents as these:

At eleven-thirty an engine over on the tracks busted open a steam-cock and let a trundling issue of white escape from its boilers; and the sound was so near, and so long, that the whole town heard it, either awake or momentarily divided in sleep. Irma heard it, and she thought vaguely that steam escaping from a railroad engine meant something in the future for them both; going away, always traveling; Daniel had gone; when she could afford it, the two of them left would go back to Kansas. The steam changed in her wandering weak thought to the hiss of rivers in flood and the swipe of wind past the steeple of the white church in Kansas. Under the hissing steam sounded a low booming throb like a pulse. The curtain of air was just so dense that night as to make this throb carry and vibrate in Irma's bones as it never again might do. She was shaken with resolve and the resolve became belief, as so often in people the funneled time of long ago is delivered and repeated, race to person.

Another portent was the curious light in the east. Lights in the east! As a little child she had known what magic and religion lived in them! Looking up at the high ceiling of her bedroom where she lay awake and willful of so much, she could see from the corner of her eye how a reflection lingered on the window glass and touched the lace curtains and flickered in the black depth of the quiet sky. When she would turn her head to see the eastern lights, they would vanish; but let her look back at the high ceiling and in the corner of her eye she would perceive the odd light.

She delicately touched the baby.

He was there.

He lived, and she thought dear Lord, fine and good and clean.

She began to weep with a protective impulse. For how many years would she have to remain strong and tender about him? She could do it. And at last she would be able to sit down; she would lean back in her chair and rock all afternoon, the afternoon of her whole life, while he became the strong one, and tenderly repaid her for this night and those past weeks and the coming years of struggling.

At two o'clock the alarm clock went off below in the restaurant. It bleeded its tiny fury in a high yang until someone got up and fumbled and shut it off, and there was a stirring of life down there in the back room.

The sound awoke Irma from the exhausted and mindful sleep she had found, and she stirred, and the baby gasped and began to suck the air and to choke; finally to cry in dim long yelps.

"Hush, Danny," she said.

How naturally it happened! she thought then. His name was Daniel Milford Junior, for though he might never know his father, still this was his son; and could be loved for his difference rather than his likeness.

The movement downstairs continued.

Then she remembered.

It was K'ang-Hsui, the Chinese cook, getting ready to go hunt for quail, and her mind sought the morning at the window, searching for light; and when the Chinaman went out of the back door downstairs, bent on hunting, Irma was glad she had been awakened; she was so feverishly active lying there that she thought how dear it would be to her child some day when he was big enough to be given a gun and granted the hunt, when the day would be making its way out of the east and perhaps a damp wind would be blowing before it, bringing rainy scent and a drive of birds.

In the dark high room above the café with the light so faintly coming back from the street outside, she stirred and looked around. She knew this was where they would live. This was where everything had happened. It was a place she loved now. Breathing deeply and falling drowsy, she devoutly sheltered their souls with a prayer out of an old hymnal that she was accustomed to look into now and then. The old black book lay on the square table in the corner. On the table was a peach-colored linen cloth embroidered in silken colors patterned as pussy willows. By the table was a rocking-chair, light cherry brown, with a leather seat, and brass tacks, and a carved headboard showing a woman's profile. A trunk stood across a locked doorway that once had led to an adjacent room. It was a tin trunk stamped to resemble canvas. It had a rounded lid. The big brass bed filled the center of the room. A wardrobe built out in a corner of the room was shielded with striped curtains of loosely woven braids . . . a former portière. There was a stand with china basin and pitcher in the opposite corner. Under the gas jet on the wall near the door to the hall was an oval mirror framed in gold. On the floor was a mottled carpet with a large and irregular stain in one corner . . . dark brown on dark green. The floor boards were painted light brown. In the corner by the door leaned Mr. Milford's cane with the dog's-head handle carved out of bone. It had eyes of green glass, and the dog seemed to be always smiling, showing his teeth smartly.

XX · THE LASTING MARK

Habit had nothing to do with opinion, she found. She was still fully knowing about her husband, and from time to time, alone, at work, or suckling her child, she would let her thoughts drift into conversational words, knowing the answers in her own mind, of course, but somehow finding peace and strength in talking to him.

"Dan, maybe after all you'll be back?

"But you'd at least write to me, then. I don't know why you shouldn't write. I know time does fly, it seems to me I hardly ever get a thing done, but I do work hard, and try to make up my mind and do the right thing when time comes for it . . .

"Yet when I *am* working, and keeping my baby, it seems the time never does pass; that's because you get tired and lonesome, everything looks wrong to you.

"Worst time I have is to make up my mind.

"You always did that for me. Remember?

"Now I wonder:

"You reckon I better stay right here and let the baby get big and strong and me work for him and make a little money, riding herd on that Chinaman downstairs, or you reckon I ought ' take little Danny back to Kansas right now with me? —You *know* I can't do that. You *know* I can't face Frisbie and Shide and the children, *now*. . . . You know ' they'd say? You just *bet* you do! —I think, and you think, I'd better stay right here, then. Later on, Danny grows up, and I've got a

little money saved so I can go back and be inde*pen*dent, why, then
we'll see. Oh, we'll go. That's home. . . ."

So he was still a force in her life.

That he should remain so had more to do with her simple goodness
than with his talents. He was trivial, and he had come up against
some one kind and virtuous and it was the finer qualities in their
union that bore the lasting mark of it.

XXI · DANCE OF DUST

It was only by watching her child that she managed to have a sense
of how time built life as it went on; the struggle of the little boy to
exist by her side and grow farther from her every day, in curious
little ways that she hardly saw, but only felt.

She went back to work in the café downstairs as soon as she was
able; and left the baby upstairs. For three years he had an upstairs
life. People became humorously used to her running up the back
steps with a great bustling clatter to see how the boy was; and when
she'd come down, pink-cheeked and industrious, going to work again
with exaggerated zeal, her black eyes dotting with light, they all felt
pleased at her frank concerns. She worked behind the counter and
among the tables, some days in a frantic state of fatigue and irritation
which she would conquer by smiling hardly, frowning and talking
half aloud to herself in wry rebuke for her clumsiness or her general
despair at running a restaurant with a Chinaman for cook, and keeping her child alive so desperately and wanting to go home to Kansas
so badly she couldn't even mention it. On other days she would be
genuinely serene; and the world would open before her with its blessings, until she could hardly count them. She would idly dream about
her baby and see every customer who came and paid her for meals
as a direct benefactor of the little son Daniel Milford had begot and
gone away from.

No one ever asked questions any more about Mr. Milford. Only
lately had Irma taken all his clothes from the wardrobe hung with
the striped curtain, rolled them up, tied them with saved string, and
sent them down to the Salvation Army on the corner four blocks

over, there by the tank where the engines stopped on the tracks to
pick up water.

All that was left of him was the dog-headed cane; and that, because it was a somehow handsome and luxurious article, a vestige
from a former life of gentleman's pursuits, canes, polished hats, little
genteel trips on excursion boats, epochal rides in somebody's gasoline
automobile, some business connection of Dan's . . . that cane was
retained and because a symbol held more power than what it stood
for, Irma began to cherish it, and plan for the time when her son
would carry it, along about in 1920, ten or fifteen years from now.
The cane was a sort of wand that showed her the future . . . Dan
Junior a fine young man, with his black hair, and herself with her
hair still black, and her white skin and people inquiring if she might
perhaps be his sister? and were they on the way to, to, to some place:
like Chicago or New York, which she'd always wanted to visit. . . .

There was something that touched everybody about the way she
recognized her job and did it.

She seemed to say, with her laboring body, and her profound dark
eyes, that she was strong, and that as long as she had to, she would
work, and raise the child; and when he was in his turn strong, and
ready, then they would go, he would lead her from then on.

She told the baby all such things when they were alone upstairs,
sitting by the window, looking out the lace-curtained glass. She would
hum to him, and let his wet straying little fingers fumble across her
face and mouth and in her hair. His head was large and it rocked on
his fat shoulders and his gaze wove witlessly around the dark brown
room; she would watch for enlightenment to strike into his eyes;
obscure terrors would strike her, thinking he was "slow," that he
might never speak, that the vacuity of his spirit might never be filled
by the world, as wonderfully as his little body was being filled by
shapely life. And at night she would often awake in a start and listen
for his breath; fearing him suddenly dead; she would arise in her
nightgown with her heavy hair falling forward and bend over the
crib made from a painted packing-box. Holding her hair away from
her face, she would silently beseech the sleeping baby for some proof
of life; she was seeking so much more than his own life . . . it was
a dream-like fulfillment again of the short joys she had known, and
a prediction of the great future, which made the sober present bear-
able, in terms of sacrifice and faith. The infant perhaps would stir;
stick his lips together with his tongue, and lick like a puppy, not
awakening; breathe in little gasps and then lapse again into silence;
and Irma would know the filling ache of gratitude and hope in her

throat; and return to bed, to fall asleep, shutting out the fears and the wan lights reflected off Central Avenue downstairs, and too exhausted by the love she had to give out to remember her loneliness and abandonment.

It was often suggested to her by men, agreeable men who traveled on business, or came in with the new business brought by the railroad, that she end her solitude; and she'd impatiently say to herself, "Pshaw!" and if they persisted, she would turn on them with a strident fury half made of a lickety-split humor, and say in a high voice,

"Don' you know better ' come in here and talk thataway t'me? I'm married woman, and I'll always be married woman, taking care of my baby, you go 'long with your fancy ideas, I know too much about men already and I don' need t'find out any more! —Here's your hot-cakes."

They would mourn the fact, and continue to admire her, for her staunch handsomeness, and the great capability of her ways with food and service and people's personalities. After a time she became accepted as a really virtuous woman; her life seemed a little happier then, with that pressure taken off, that male approach that she distrusted and could imagine herself welcoming too easily again.

They might all have been K'ang-Hsui, so far as interesting her was concerned.

She would give him orders in a friendly brisk way and run upstairs to see the baby; and come down again, and find the Chinaman wrong or careless; and fling out her great virtue at him in a mock-harridan tirade; at which he would grow green under his skin, and his tongue would dry, and though he labored at the stove, he would make elaborate murderous designs with his hands; shaking pepper into a soup, he would be thinking of her eyes; carving spareribs he would be deliciously avenging himself on the person of his employer; dark furies, these would last only until she spoke next time to him, as indifferently and agreeably as if she had never scolded, or he had never killed her fifty times.

K'ang-Hsui was forty-six years old. He was tiny, and his face had the color and the texture of a shelled almond. Perhaps a third of his daily life was known to Irma and the public of the café. For all of them, he was simply a Chinaman who kept very clean and cooked everybody's meals from habit as they wanted them; and had thus a certain established place and value in the little town. He would grin, and they'd think him almost as nice as an American; in excitement, over anything at all, his jaws would puff out mysteriously like the jaws of a horned toad or lizard such as dustily sparkled along the boarded walks in town in hot weather; and then people would reflect that you never could know an Oriental.

They were all sure he smoked opium. At first it had been fascinating to consider; but its truth and its apparent lack of effect upon K'ang-Hsui limited the thrills and finally killed them.

But even now, people would occasionally say to Irma,

"I'sh'd think you'd hate to have your baby left around where that Chinaman is."

She would pantomime rolling up her sleeves, and the wielding of a meat-cleaver, and grimly imitating a man's threat, reply that so much's a finger; just a finger of his on that baby of hers, and he'd see: h'h!

There was never any issue about it.

K'ang-Hsui was most discreet about the child and the apartment upstairs.

For three years the baby never left the room except with Irma. He grew and napped and ate and began to talk up there, and when she'd have time, she'd take him out walking.

For the next two years, he had a back-yard existence. Suddenly whole domains were opened to him there, after the brown and limited universe upstairs. All day long he would play in that new place of gray weathered fences, piled boxes, strange cans, the lean-to where K'ang-Hsui lived, attached to the kitchen, and the arterial alley where life streamed past, made of animals, boys, papers blown in the wind, and the dance of dust in sunlight.

XXII · THE CANE

In a somnolent afternoon, the café was empty, and the baby had awakened from his nap but lately. Irma was peeling vegetables at the counter, and her voice was drifting in a wail of thoughtlessness among the dim mid-afternoon sounds of things stewing on the stove, and wood being chopped across the alley out back and down a little ways, by the laundry; and a tap-tap of a sound of little Dan at play in the back yard. "We're *all* right," she kept thinking, between the idle musical phrases of her song. "We're all *right,* m'baby's a strong healthy little codger, and I'm a strong woman, and I'm making a living, ain't I? I'm keeping body and soul together, for two of us, ain't

I? You just bet your life I am.—It won't be long now: he's four years old, and give me eight-ten more years, I can do it, I can stay here, and make out all right, I'll manage, just leave me alone, t'go m'own way, I'm saving a little money every year, we're a-goin' home before I get s'old I can't have any pleasure, and little Danny grows up s'much he won't be able to get used to Kansas and the way folks are there. —Imagine that: in two years he'll have to be going to school: well I declare. —If I keep my health, and keep my customers, just ain't nothing goin' stop me. —We're *all* right, Danny:"

She stopped this reverie which confessed so much of her misery because it protested so valiantly to herself, and raised her head sharply, and listened. It was so quiet! Where was the baby?

She'd heard him come downstairs a while ago, and she hadn't turned around to watch him coming, but lowered her head and smiled into her pan of parings with such delight and love rising in her heart and bringing a swallow to her throat that she didn't want the baby to see her so. She knew in her mind how he looked, flushed and pudgy from sleep, coming down one step at a time, clutching the rickety banisters as he went.

He had gone out to the yard.

But it was quiet now.

What might he be doing? Crossing the kitchen to the screen door which was the color of dust—dusty screen and faded wood—she went out full of exact and terrible imaginings.

Danny was not in the yard. She ran to the alley. It was deserted. The afternoon sunlight stood wan shadows on the weathered wooden fences. The wood-chopping up back of the laundry had even ceased. She turned and said: "Now, I'll just keep calm; I'll find him:" and went back to peer among the piled packing-cases and cans that had accumulated there for two or three years.

Then she saw the door of K'ang-Hsui's lean-to partly open.

She went to it and knocked.

Silence.

And she recalled absurd fragments of fear as to what Chinamen did to babies; and wringing the door open with a fury that made her scratch her hand on a loose edge of screen, she went in and found them.

In the middle of the small floor stood Danny, unexcited and interested in the strange room he was in for the first time. Facing him standing by the wretched bed of gray blankets and mouse-furry rolls of dust gathered for years, was K'ang-Hsui, quivering in silence. In his hands he held the dog-headed cane, clasping it on his breast. He waited for Irma as his fathers always waited for fate, and shook his head.

He fondled the cane.

He clearly wanted it.

Danny ran and grabbed Irma's leg and skirt, happy and mindful of some game or other they all might play.

She touched the child's head and then passionately picked him up and hugged him from the brink of the horrors she had imagined.

"Give me that cane!" she commanded.

K'ang-Hsui handed it over silently.

She raised it for a blow and she felt suddenly sick from the smell of the room and the dog's teeth K'ang-Hsui showed and the wet sound of his breath slaking through his flat little nostrils. He was puffing out at the jaws. He didn't move. He waited for her to strike him, but his eyes were full of terror and death that would follow. He seemed to get smaller. The room was dim and it stank. . . . It was charged with ugly and stinking feelings now; Irma trembled and it shook Danny, who turned and looked at K'ang.

"Ah!" screamed Danny, and began to cry and kick Irma's body in terror at the sight of the Chinaman's face.

Irma lowered the cane.

"What do you mean, K'ang-Hsui!" she began to say, but he licked his mouth and shut up his teeth and gravely interrupted:

"Danny bling stick. I look at it. —No no no, no steal! Look at! *No steal!*"

She swallowed the ill effort of her throat to choke out the horrid airs of the room and of anger.

"What you mean having my baby in here!"

He hissed again, a puffy, snakish, and glittering intuition of what accusations her thoughts were making; but he neatly achieved innocence by palming his hands upward and saying that Danny had come in all by himself to play, bringing the dog-headed cane with the green glass eyes.

The baby was still crying; he felt the atmosphere; the stridencies between two people he'd become very used to in harmony.

"Hush-a-baby!" said Irma, and then stared with snapping black eyes lidded down to a keen look at K'ang. He stared back, and began to smile-close, smile-close his mouth, and duck a little in a bow; some courtesy to follow a quarrel with. His mind was eagerly busy with a dream-design of how to murder her again; but he smiled, and in a second, she said,

"If I ever catch m'baby in here again, I'll . . ."

She went out of the lean-to and let the screen door hiss and slap to with opinion. Outside, the baby stopped crying and shook his sobs off gradually.

She took him in with her and sent him upstairs with the cane to wipe his face on the towel hanging on the lower door of the wash-stand; and went back to her work. Her fears went down slowly; after all, she had never had any reason to suspect K'ang-Hsui of any wrong or theft or anything but an aloof, almost a shy, cuteness with the baby. He wasn't the kind of Chinaman who made sausages out of little babies. —If she'd been a minute later, though, she thought: "He'd'a had that cane packed away and I never *would*'a found it!"

Half an hour later, she heard a scuffle out in back, and the grunt and twang of the screen door of the lean-to; and went to see K'ang-Hsui hauling his tin trunk across the door sill, wearing his gray Sun-day hat, his brown overcoat, and carrying under one arm a brown-paper bundle.

"Why, K'ang-Hsui, where you goin':"

He disdained answer. He got almost professionally busy with his trunk-moving.

"Now looka here, you good-for-nothin' cook you," said Irma, with droll exasperation and a chuckling humor, "you can't let me down like this now! *Go* awn! put your trunk back there and come in here t'get supper!"

He was now undecided; he turned around and sat down on the trunk looking at her.

He was sober and his mouth was in a childish pout. She wanted to laugh at him, but she knew that'd have been fatal.

"*Sure*, I lost m'temper!" she told him. "*Sure,* I might'-nigh wal-loped you over the head with m'cane! But I *did*n't, did I? —You got t'get supper!"

He regarded the ground and hugged his ribs.

"Pooh!" said Irma. "I been lots madder than that at you; and you never kicked up fuss like this!"

Dismissing it as if all were now settled, she turned and went back to the kitchen humming a snatch of a tune.

In a little while she didn't look up or give any sign; but she knew K'ang-Hsui was back at the stove being very quiet about his move-ments at first, but when supper really got going, he banged pots and oven doors and it was a sort of conversation with Irma, who had many private speculations about the childishness of men, no matter what their color.

XXIII · FOOD

Young Danny never questioned the conditions of his life so long as he was lost all day long in the intensities of play, when the back yard and the mean complicated delights of trash and alley and tumbleweed blown became his dominion. He missed Irma when she had to go downstreet shopping; he was enraged with her when she failed to indulge his fancies, most of which had to do with food, the earliest simple symptom of a life feeding itself on that of the world which would nourish it: food in the fat pretty face of the little boy, and almost a kind of thought in his stomach, ravenous and imaginative before eating, reflective after.

Irma was busy in the café from six in the morning until nine at night.

What he needed she would do for him as she could, running up the stairs and washing him, or stooling him, or dressing him, or handing him something to play with out of the tin trunk with the curved lid.

The dog's-head cane was nowhere to be seen.

He curiously began to look for it one day, and didn't find it. That night he asked where it was, and she told him "Never you mind: I know; I got it safe," and from then on, though he never was sharply aware of it, he would speculate from time to time as to the cane's hiding-place. He couldn't imagine what to do with it if he found it; but the day of K'ang-Hsui and the cane was the first time he'd ever been scared of anything real, and fascinated.

XXIV · THE INHERITANCE

Irma sent him to school when he was five.

He was shocked into pity for himself and a kind of numbness in the mind.

How strange this was, to be among other small beings, and to be resisted if you demanded something they particularly prized as their own!

He would howl on his way home from school, and his face wetting and his nose jellying forth over his mouth would be patted by the wind carrying lines of dust; and dirty, hideous, glorious in his inner importance, he would arrive at the alley fence back of the café and there linger, bawling, until Irma came out. She would come rapidly, like a stalking picture of worry, and hum an angry tune. He would never be able to tell her what was wrong; she would shake him and demand to know:

"Do th'treat m'baby mean: what is it! Tell mumma!"

The groan of sympathy in her voice pierced him like sweet pains, and his shrieks would double, and his abandon become most bitter. All she could do was shrug and think that she'd better pick him up—heavy and getting big, for a boy his age—and carry him in the house, as she always called the café and its sleeping-room above, and give him a piece of pie and let him take off his long stockings, that she sent him to school in so's he'd look nice alongside the other children, the banker's little boy, the railroad-station agent's children, Doctor McBride's youngest, and the few others.

But at night she would worry still over this strange sorrow that fell on her child, and made him ugly, sick, and mean.

Such thoughts could only let her think of another, and at that she would roll her face blank and quiet in the pillow and try to erase big Dan out of her dark sheeted mind; for needing him, she would see what he would do for them, how everything could be solved by his presence, how happiness always dwelt where he was. Another strain of her thinking blamed him accurately for many things, for being a drinker, for lying to her many times, for remaining cheerful about misfortunes that were his own fault, for pretending always to be rich when he was never anything but poor, for dressing like a cheap actor, yet so becomingly; for liking the world where gaiety was *bought;* for being, almost, a character out of the songs and ballads of the time, the start of the twentieth century: a swaggering Charlie who traditionally left behind him a trailing chorus of sad wimmin gladly dishonored and gladlier left.

"Never coming back, now. Are you, Dan: it's been too long, hasn't it: I made up m'mind to that long ago, but it's funny how it keeps coming back t'me, and I have to say over and over, never coming back, so's I'll believe it at last. . . ."

XXV · THE WORLD

But young Danny suddenly got over his sickening woes, and began to find something busy going on in his brain, a thing that began to exercise and develop a mind, which took him out of his body instead of kept him in it with signals of hunger, heat, cold, bowels, and sleepiness.

He no longer came home yelling his inchoate protest that the world was outrageous and that he, Daniel Milford Junior, must refuse to be its victim. That had been all feeling.

Now came mind, and later, whatever it was to be, could begin to crack and settle, character.

He was now a little less plump, and his hair was coal black, like Irma's, and he had blue eyes, and his cheeks were pale but not ill-looking. He had a precisely carved mouth, raised forward in a child's pout. When he went, he usually went slowly; not traveling what he touched, but rather the ways of his imagination, some far country, with a familiar population, where he was king.

In school his book of geography fetched him best; and he began to imagine things about maps, learning the names of places and rivers, mountains, seas, the continents. Then he would travel, and take everywhere the knowledge he had, but seeing them newly, the crates and the sheds of the back yard as palaces in China; the long rickety steps going up to the bedroom as a flight of princesses; the alley, and its dogs humble or suspicious, loping obliquely following trails of scent in the air, and its traffic of carts and wagons, and Negro migrations through hot afternoons with dangle of bones and kick of shoe in the dust, the alley was the great streets of the world in one.

The rug upstairs in the bedroom had a stain on it, an irregular spill of dark brown on dark green. It resembled a new continent on a map.

There in the evenings Dan would lie down with cardboard and scissors and make seaports, walls, ships that moved in the shadow of his desire before the currents of a wind Irma tried to fathom when she'd find him so.

If she disturbed him, he would be cross.

She was closed away from him.

When she would chant, "We're *all* right, Danny," he would look up at her gravely, busy with something else, and she would see that he took her for granted; their being all right needn't be mentioned, since it was her place to see that they were; his placid disinterest was so like his father's private security that it would make her cross in her turn; and one night she went in a heavy sag of exhaustion across the room from the door, having just come up from the restaurant; walking to bed as if it were her last walk; she stumbled on the edge of the carpet and knocked down Danny's seaport, not even knowing it, and fell on the bed stupidly knowing he was still up, and must be put to bed himself. Her eyes were shut and her hands lying down on her brows, fingers curling upward and trembling a little.

Then the bed began to thump and shake.

Danny, in a passion which coaled in his eyes and dried his voice, was beating at the brass rods of the bedstead, shaking them, kicking, hating with his whole body.

She woke herself to motion and looked. Where it came from, she didn't know, but an icy new energy had her, and she got up. She reeled from the flow of anger to her mind, but she went straight to him and seized him with her hands raw and red from washing below, and as they touched him, their two angers, the mother's and the child's, fused something like love, so that a great fury of feeling was loose between them.

She heaved herself to sit on the bed, and clutched her boy hotly. His arms and legs flew and struck her, she felt her bones heat with pain under his strikes; but she pinned him on her lap and spanked him thoroughly. At the first blow she felt his hatred turn calm and sorrowful; and she began to weep for what she was doing; but doing it, she could not now stop, and striking him, she struck the harder for the suffering it really gave her, the release of her life without feeling, her body dread with fatigue, her loneliness, and the child's loneliness which he solaced elsewhere, in ways that had no concern of her.

XXVI · LOVE AND PLAY

He found a friend.

All year in the schoolyard the doctor's son, Tom McBride, had glared at him from around corners, among groups of children, and then suddenly looked off each time in a sour scorn. Danny tried to ignore him and expressed this by scowling, as he thought, to himself. It was a profound world, the schoolyard, where the children rehearsed the acts which later would be not mimic but the very meaningful motions of their later lives . . . love and play, the use of earth for creation, as the children here created from sand and gravel whole systems of river and mountain and house; strife and gain, as here the children strove and robbed each with the other, bearing prizes and injuries afterward; crime, the seizure of destruction as a fury upon the little souls; goodness, some child hearing within some curious pang of will to give, and going then with dirty hands and sand-colored face to present his treasure, whatever it might be of the sticky jewels in pants pockets, or some little girl breathing hotly like a puppy running to kiss some one, a donation calling for no answer, pure and filling in itself.

One morning during recess Tom McBride set his little face in a pug of feeling that made him look like a small bulldog. His lower teeth showed where he had his mouth screwed up and his chin sticking out. He looked ready to cry but he had his fists clenched and his legs tensed in their brown corduroy pants. He was watching Danny Milford across the yard. Danny was hanging on the low wooden fence of the yard with his elbows, his back to the fence, his belly curving out, his head hanging back across the fence, to see how the world looked upside-down this morning: it always looked brand new, upside-down, with new colors and shapes, all amazingly suggestive of the right-side-up yet far finer.

Around the corner of the low brick-and-wood school building the teacher strolled.

In a moment the bell would ring.

Tom hissed through his large and doggish teeth and jumped up from the ground. When he landed, he began to run for Danny. He had his head down and his fists charged the air and beat his way. An imp of fury had him, and made him faster than he could have been, and meaner than anyone expected. He butted Danny in the belly with all his force. It knocked them both down. Danny was astonished not having seen this coming. He was sick, from the shock to his stomach. He began to cry. Leaping in agony and trying to catch his breath, he saw Tom McBride standing before him suddenly finished with what he had done. Danny shrieked. He weakly threw himself on Tom and began to claw at his face with his fingers. Tom backed up but hardly defended himself. The teacher came running. They were obliged to come at noon to her desk and stand while she made a little sermon;

then she required them to shake hands. They did this without looking at each other.

They managed to leave the room separately.

The next day Danny opened his desk where he kept things so neatly and lovingly. In the middle of the little clear space at the center of the desk was a new penknife. He examined it with a lump of anguish and delight under his heart.

He opened all the blades and tried them and closed them in various sequences, trying out every combination of arrangements. He tried out which pocket it felt best in. It was white and it gleamed with nickel.

He didn't wonder where it came from until these more abstract pleasures had been tasted.

He looked around at the other children. They were all busy, dreaming or reading.

Presently he saw Tom McBride, hunching and scowling yet eager, back in the corner at his own desk. Tom nodded and grinned under his scowl and pushed his fingers into his nose and hitched in his seat. Danny held up the knife and pointed at it and then at Tom and then at himself. Tom nodded. Danny blushed and felt a shiver of something strange travel his bowels and his very sitting bones. Then the teacher closed a drawer of her desk with a bright neatness and smiled and began with, "Well, children:"

XXVII · WHAT LIFE BROUGHT

"Tom this, and Tom that, Tom-Tom-Tom," said Irma, bustling between the stove, the counter, the ice-box, the tables out front.

It was angry pride and secret lonesomeness. She gladly had her boy with the doctor's son; folks might think it funny; but she thought it quite right, even though she *did* have to work in a restaurant with smelly old kitchen and a monkey of a Chinaman. It wasn't any more'n right and proper that Irma Milford's baby should spend his time with the nicest children in town, anywhere!

The boys were about the same age, and in the next year or two or three, they grew more than in such a period ever before.

Irma would regard them changing from time to time, and compute Danny's growth along with the savings account she had in the red brick and white stone bank down on the corner; and firmly nod her head at the way her plans were working out. The rates of growth in both her possessions were about parallel. When the time came, they could go, all right.

Now a new world opened out before Danny.

He was no longer alone. He found himself changing from the shyness of himself among others of his kind, and he found Tom McBride willing to take him everywhere and show him everything of that double world which looks entirely different to children and to their elders.

He found that Tom was just as excited and stimulated by Danny's private world of the maps, the uses of magic, the value of speculation as Danny was by Tom's actual world.

That suggested the difference between the two. Danny wandered off from his harassed home into dreams; Tom found entire satisfaction in the physical ways of life, and simply widened his knowledge of them whenever he could.

Further, Tom had wisdoms that Dan eagerly shared. They would steal illustrated books out of Doctor McBride's office in the afternoons and go out with them to the barn behind the doctor's house, and there laugh in whispers about the immodesties they found in the pictures. They were like monkeys in their excitements, unashamed and unaware of any meaning in what they did, but simply gratified.

They decided to have a secret society, limited to themselves. The most they did with the idea was discuss exquisite and incredible initiations which new members would have to undergo, rites of obscenity and feats of strength, perhaps even the smoking of a cigar.

"Where would we get the cigar?"

"We could steal it," said Tom.

They both looked and shivered at each other.

Soberly they came down out of the barn loft, and impressed by their consciences with what they had even thought of, they said good-by, and Danny went home.

With some fierce intuition, that night Irma cuddled him as she told him it was time to go to bed. She suddenly ached with longing and with devices in her head and heart for Danny grown up. He was a handsome small boy, large-headed and nearly nine years old. She made him look into her eyes, and tell her if he was sure, certain, swearin'-true that he was a good boy and would be a good man. There was nothing of sin on his soul that could have done more than exasperate her briefly, and make her scold him; but now challenged so, he blushed and stammered; he lost his saliva and his eyes turned wild as if light were going inward and revealing him utterly. He thought of the kind of misdemeanor he and every boy he knew had done now or then . . . little depredations, little lies, foolish lusts and misunderstood compulsions; and she saw these thought-changes happen in him, and she shook him hardly by the shoulders, kneading his slight bones and soft flesh with her large working finger.

"Daniel Milford Junior! Have you done anything you can't tell mother about!"

He gulped and remembered that terrible thing about perhaps stealing a cigar.

She looked fierce and hot. Her black eyes danced and snapped. Feebly he clutched at the one hope he saw, which was that they had not yet actually stolen the cigar, and maybe might not ever do so. He felt wretched. He wished she wouldn't do things like this. It was time to meet them. He dropped his head, and shook it, for "no," and murmured *"uh,* uh." She took his chin and lifted his face.

"I'm glad. You're *sure?"*

He looked up, clear-eyed to her pleasure, and wounded her with delight in the way he said,

"I ain't done anything."

"That's right," she said, nodding firmly. "Don't say ain't, just because I fergit now and then when I'm working hard, and haven't time for the fancies and the rights of this and that. But I don't want my baby-boy t'get habit of speaking wrongly."

She had recovered their feelings for them, in this brisk little tirade, full of humorous complaint. Now she made him stand up from his chair, and she shoo'd him to bed, laughing, waving her hands after him, and turning back to the table to waste a little time; for he was growing and she believed he hated to have her watch him undress and get into his long sleeping gown; therefore she sat at the table and looked across the room away from him out the window, where the nightly town lay revealed, and made her think, "Now I *wonder* what ever made me come here in the first place, and what ever made me stay on here in the second place!", but the answers were unknown to her, and she shook her head at herself for wondering and for being satisfied to go on taking what life brought her.

XXVIII · GOOD AND EVIL

Danny spent only his times for sleeping at home any more. School had him most of the week; but after school, he was loud and active among the boys who fought wars on the edges of town, wide dirt streets that straggled suddenly and turned into brown plains widening to the flat horizon. They fought wars with sticks and wooden rifles and stones, and much silent oratory of gesture, defiance that welled from deeper than they knew.

With Tom, Danny wandered all the places of the town and its sources.

They began to go down to the tracks and hang around the trainmen and watch the engines switching up and down in the late afternoon. Sometimes they wanted to see the night freight go out, and would stay until after dark, shaken to their frames by the voom and fuss of steam as the engine lingered.

They would always regard the engine with awe, trying to realize that this up close was the same locomotive that from across the plain looked like a shining new toy. Seen nearly, the engine had only the poetry of immense utility about it, unlovely and crude in its details, with warts of steamy sweat on its iron hide, oozing rust from its throbbing plates, leaking water with violence in some places and in others, with slovenly drips; the plates crazily bolted and loosely jointed, that whined and sang when the engine rocked along the track.

The freight went out usually between eight and nine. When it was gone, the darkness closed in after its brilliant headlight and the wind of sparks from the firedoor, and the two boys would think "Gee!" and hurry home more or less dreading the corner where they would separate and go on alone.

They noticed presently that a fat and rugged old brakeman would swing his lantern at them and peer at them as if to scare them away; shake his gray head at them and wobble his loose toothless cheeks.

They began to hide, on their evening expeditions to the tracks, so he wouldn't see them. They thought of him as Mr. Dogface, for he did have the drooping and earnest cheeks, jaws, lips, even nose, of a hound, the hound's brooding pessimism in his pale eyes.

"Duck, hey, there's Dogface."

"Orright, Mr. Dogface, I see you."

They edged around between the baggage truck and the end wall of the station and watched the old brakeman come heavily shambling down the platform in his grease-velvety overalls. It was still light enough to see without the lantern. He was shaking his head and musing.

The boys crouched.

"Mr. Dogface, what's he want:"

They believed he wanted to have them arrested, among other things. They thought perhaps he might want to kidnap them. Perhaps he had a sawmill where he privately sawed young boys up for dog meat.

He came closer and they cowered behind the truck. They averted their faces. Appallingly, he stopped by them as if his progress was dreadfully designed to bring them together. They squeezed their eyes shut. They heard him whistle in his lungs as he breathed, a fascinating musical chord produced by asthma.

"Hey, you, you two kids, there, now:" he said.

They crouched lower and covered their faces.

"Now, there, you kids," he sighed in a thick voice. "Get up, I ain't goin' to hurt you. Come on."

They looked up. He was waggling his loose old face at them and standing humorously with his great belly pushed out and his head forward.

"Come on."

He nodded.

They got up and stood before him.

"Praise the Lord," he remarked, reminiscently, and then said, "C'mere, now: listen to me:"

He led them to the edge of the walk. The tracks gleamed off darkening in the evening distance.

"Oh Lord, guide these children," he said, putting his hands on their shoulders. "Stay away from these here railroad yards, now, you two kids. Iddn't any place for a pair of youngsters. Praise the Lord. The Lord don't want little children hanging around places like this, where they can get hurt, or tempted, or led away, astray, Glory, Glory!"

He was emotional. His eyes were mysteriously fiery. The boys were completely bewildered.

"What?" said Tom.

"Just my bounden duty," said Mr. Dogface, "I am a good man, I have confessed Jesus, Jesus saves, let him save you, my little man. —Stay away off'n here. There's bad men that come here sometimes.

Down there by the water-tank, where the trees is, those tramps and hoboes, they stay there days at a time, sometimes. No telling *what* they might do, see a pair of tykes like you all hanging around. *Yes, Jesus!* Oh, oh."

The boys' imaginations began to gleam. They looked down the tracks toward the red water-tank where it stood among heavy trees. There was a smoky pull of firelight against the dusk, a camp fire. Their hearts smote them with peril and interest.

"You mean down there, Mr. Do—, down there the tramps come and camp? Where the fire is?"

Mr. Dogface sighed and shaggily nodded his head. He was alight with the wonder of God and the power of religion, the zeal of the saved, the doubt of old age that youth can ever find its way.

"And they're *bad* men: I mean *bad,* un*ree*-generate, and drowned in the *seas* of sin? oh, sinners, you stay away from here . . ."

His voice rose in the calm evening by the peaceful freight train and took on a hymnal tone, and the boys thought more than ever of the old hound, dewlapped and moanin' at the night sky. Their excitement was a warm thing in their veins.

"Gee, yes, we will stay away, thanks, Mister."

"I guess my family would feel pretty terrible if I got kidnapped by tramps, or something."

Mr. Dogface nodded with closed eyes. His heart knew the peace of duty done.

"Shoo: go'n now, go'n: oh, praise *Him!*"

They stumbled away from him, amazed and eager. He made religious noises as they drew away and they forgot that they used to imagine him dangerous, a menace to them; and not knowing the eating fire of inspiration as it might visit an empty old man with the warming glow of belief, and make him innocent again, and want to share the Lamb, they chuckled and skipped and trotted with their shoulders hunched against the falling chill, and said,

"Mr. Dogface! He's crazy as a bat!" and as soon as they were out of his sight, way past the freight house, they took to the shadows of tool-houses and trees and without having exchanged a word about it, began creeping down toward the tank past which the bonfire showed brightlier now, and the night was coming mysterious, and danger dwelt in the place and men they had been warned about.

The early night was quiet. They crept through bushes and trod the cindery earth like Indians. Presently the red tank loomed just above them, dark on the darkening sky. There were several big trees; two small tool-houses and a clear space of ground covered with grass and sloping like a small hill down on the far side to an irrigation ditch that sometimes had water in it to feed cattle that waited in the pen over across the tracks.

The boys now went down on their stomachs. They crawled with elbow and knee slowly forward until they could see the whole intimate little clearing, where the fire flipped and cracked. There was a can standing in the outer coals of the fire and steam arose from it. On an upended wooden box was a black jacket. But no one was visible. Only the fire lived.

They hardly dared whisper. Wind flittering through the leaves in the profuse trees over them made them shiver and look at each other, so much it sounded like whispering and hints of danger. They wanted to see some tramps, and watch what they did. If they didn't know they were being watched, the tramps would no doubt be terrible, and talk, and make horrible plans. —Then all the more dangerous to overhear such, because if the tramps caught them and knew they knew their secrets, why, then, why, something quite fearful and inexact would occur.

The ground began to thunder as the boys lay on it, near the tracks. The night freight was starting to move out. They craned back across their flat shoulders and saw the lemon-yellow beam of light come quivering along the way and race ahead of the engine in the shining steel tracks. The engine fumed and ground its way. Far, far back along the line the couplings jerked and rang and the squealing train was yanked along into increasing speed. The smoke tasted in the mouths of Tom and Danny where they lay as it went by. The firedoor flung a tiny hell at them and a mesh of sparks. The earth trembled and shook them. They could not hear anything but the train. It rollicked past above their very heads. They clenched their teeth and fists and squinted to resist the thundering sustained shock so near. But they didn't dare move off until all was quiet and they could free themselves safely from their fatal and secret point.

A change in the timbre of the tracks told them the end of the train was coming up. They opened their eyes and scrounged around and sure enough, there was the caboose, lighted up like a country church. Far gone was the engine, and fading was the clamor.

The evening was about to hush again.

On the rear platform of the caboose stood a heavy bellying figure. They recognized Mr. Dogface. He was clutching his lantern. His head was raised to the receding sky over the town. As he passed, the boys heard a stentorian moan of music, and saw the old man's head turn upward with conviction. The brakeman was singing a hymn. The bumpety banging wheels almost drowned him out, but not quite.

The boys felt somehow guilty, seeing him go on so, and they themselves right here where he prayed them not to be!

The fire had died down suddenly during that passage of the train. Where should they be: but home:

Down the track they saw a figure coming dimly out of the dark, and without further subtleties, they turned and ran back toward the station on the slippery cinders of the trackside.

XXIX · IN THE GROVE

The next Saturday, Danny and Tom took their lunches in boxes and set out to spend the day courting danger.

It was an early spring day, and the air was golden and cool.

They walked far to the westward until the town was opened behind them in a flat looking cut-out of irregular shapes and heights. Then they started to follow the irrigation ditch that led toward town and kept their eyes on the tall heads of the trees they were aiming at. Across the flat land they could see miniature railroad cars and the little dust-red tank and dark sweeps of shadow dropped by the great trees interrupting the sun.

They talked as they went. They stopped now and then to look at bird tracks in the muddy sides of the ditch they followed. Sometimes the water would have made a dark and velvety mud; and at that, they would kneel down and sink their hands into it, squeezing the mud, slapping it on the dry caked earth above it, and model shapes and surfaces; then kick their work into lumps, and walk on. The grasses were yellow still from winter's ways, and brittle.

"That Chinaman tried to steal me once, when I was very little," said Danny.

"Who, K'ang-Hsui?"

"Yep. He did."

"Holy Gee."

"My ma found me in his room."

"I bet she give him dickens."

"She might-near killed him."

"He sure is a funny one. —Does he ever talk? I never heard him talk."

"Funny! —He talks when he has to. Most-time he talks his own langwidge to himself, I don't know what he says."

"He must be old."

"He sure is old."

"I bet he's dirty."

"He smells funny."

"My papa says all Chinamen smoke opiun."

"So does K'ang-Hsui. It's what makes him smell funny."

"Papa says they have to have it after a while."

Danny nodded.

"Papa says they'll steal and kill and lie and everything, only to get it."

"I know," said Dan, "drug fiend."

Tom looked at him in surprise, respectful.

"That's it. Where'd you hear that?"

"I read it in the *Examiner*. They had a long article about it, this girl, she was a *big* lady, though, married her husband, and he was rich. But he didn't know she was a drug fiend, and they went on a trip, and she couldn't get at her drug and finally she told him. It had her picture with diamonds on."

"What did he do:"

"Oh, he said she must stop it."

"You can't stop it, you lie and steal and everything, my papa says."

"No, she didn't stop it. —They had a fight and he killed her."

"Oh."

They walked, satisfied, for a while. The town was getting brighter and darker, realer, as they approached.

"Gee, I hope K'ang-Hsui keeps on getting his opiun."

"Why?"

"So he won't fight and steal and lie and kill to get it."

"Oh."

"You know what?"

"What," said Tom.

"—About K'ang-Hsui? —It's very funny."

Danny skipped and kicked a clod of dirt. It was an embarrassed gesture.

"No, what," asked Tom.

"Well, I don't think he ever goes to the bathroom."

"No!"

Tom stood still and his eyes bulged. Then he giggled and slapped his hip, and laughed aloud, and declared this was not possible. He was a doctor's son and knew what had to be; and so discussing this they walked nearer and nearer the town, engrossed in their argument, relishing it the more because it had no solution and because it dealt with a subject they considered tremendously funny.

But suddenly Tom halted and whispered,

"Fsss! we better go carefully now."

They were near the cattle loading pen to which the irrigation ditch led; and after it passed the white pen, the waterway went on past the grove of trees by the tank, and under the railroad embankment trestle, and was lost on the other side in a small swampy hollow of thick grasses and gaseous mud and damp banks.

The boys got to their bellies and began to advance along the ditch-side crawling. They were on an expedition. There might be some tramps camping by the trees. They thought they could see a column of smoke rising into the treetops in the still morning. They put their lunch-boxes on the ground behind a little clump of tall grass and new shoots of poplar root that showed gray twigs and pale green leaves. Then they moved forward until they were in reach of the cattle-pen. Running and scrambling, they climbed to the top rail of the corral and peered across the distance to the shady grove by the tank.

There was somebody there.

Now that they were here and the enemy in sight, Tom and Danny were empty of plans. What did they want to do, anyway? They wanted to see how close they could come to what they regarded as danger, and still not be caught. Anything that made the old brakeman the other night so full of holy sounds and all, must be pretty bad. They were at an age when anything bad was exciting and promising. They had the projects of adults in their small tough bodies.

They saw figures, three, no two: two men moving around in the grove among the blue shadows and the smoky shafts of sunlight that filtered through. They weren't trainmen, because they were in clothes that had different colors, light upper and dark lower; no gray dark overalls.

"There are some," said Danny.

"What'll we do:"

"We better get down before they see us."

"Yep."

They slid down to the ground.

"What d'you guess they're doing:"

"I don't know."

"Let's see."

"How we go:"

"Look, we get in the ditch and walk squatting over, like this, see, and when we get there we can watch them and listen to them, see what they do."

They started down the ditch again. Here the ditch was wider and deeper; it had dry sides, and only a trickle of water drying along the bottom. The boys trod where the sides rounded and sloped to the bottom. By crouching, they kept out of sight. Presently they were embraced, in the ditch, by the shade of the grove. It was slippery and harder to walk here, because the water collected in a little deep that made a pool. There was less dry sloping ditch-side to walk on. But by clutching at the bank and the tough clay-held weeds and grasses, they managed to stay hidden and safe, not more than twenty feet from the shaded center of the camp, where a small fire exhaled, and the two men sat now, one reading a newspaper, the other scraping mud off his left shoe with a bark-covered twig. They were silent. So were the boys.

Both of the men were old, to them; one as old as Mr. Dogface. The other tramp was as young as the clerk in the station office, about twenty-six. The older man was heavy and reading his paper, his hands trembled very slowly, so that it seemed as if he might be deliberately shaking his hands so; except that the regular pulse of the shake lasted too evenly and long for that. He had a red face and gray whiskers days in need of shaving. He moved his mouth as he read. He was sitting on a log. The young man jabbed and scraped at the mud of his shoes in short angry movements. He was scowling. He had a heavy face, but young-looking, under black hair. He looked big, sitting.

The boys watched so long in silence and the men kept doing the same thing for so long that whole hours of silent time seemed to have passed when the young tramp threw down his twig and stretched savagely, throwing his arms and dodging with his head and making short grunts. It was an animal gesture; the boys cowered down a little and gazed wideningly. The young man rolled over on his belly and lay scowling up at the fat companion who went on reading his sedately trembling paper.

"Yah, what're you going to do, now," asked the young man. His voice was resonant and hard.

The old man blurted a small scornful laugh and ignored him, and turned a page of the paper with an air of great interest, literacy and even elegance.

The boys watched fascinated while the young tramp's face turned a deep brown red with annoyance, and his almost white eyes of pale blue flinted down to edges of light as he stared. He rolled a little side to side on his elbows, propping himself, and he seemed to grind his body against the earth in futile anger. He was a big fellow. His hands, closing against his biceps as he had his arms crossed to lean on his elbows, were big and brown.

"I said, what'ch going to do: wake up, you old bastard."

"Mind yourself," replied the other man, in a wet hissing of loose lip and mild character. "Sspeak ssweeter if you have to sspeak at all."

He flipped his paper again and raised his head to look down on the print as if he were wearing glasses.

"Oh, —!" This was an oath.

The young one drew himself to a crouch on his knees and then arose in a slow muscular test, bracing out his chest and vainly watching his body demonstrate in exercise. He wore a blue denim shirt and black corduroy trousers and heavy shoes.

"My feet hurt me. I'm going to wash my socks."

He left the fat one sitting on the log and turned his back and leaned down to unlace his shoes. He took off the shoes and set them preciously on the grass. Then he took off his socks and shook them out.

He rolled up his trousers legs.

Walking toward the ditch where the water was collected in a little pool, and looked up at from below, he seemed like a giant, and his dark hair fell down across his eyes and made him look like a great boy, scowling and ugly inside.

Danny jabbed Tom's thigh with his thumb, as if to say, "Hey, lookit him coming, what can we:"—and there wasn't time to finish the thought.

The young man had begun scrambling down the bank and sliding when he saw the two boys, and he grabbed at the sliding dirt under him and swore startled.

The boys stood up.

And he rested there on his tight hams, sitting and staring at them. His small light eyes were kindling over them as if in premonition of thought. His face got pleasanter. He began to grin, and showed his teeth, little even teeth, so little that they seemed merely edges of white under the gums. His lips were thick but well marked. The boys had their hearts drumming like wings in their shirts. Danny was half grinning in sick surprise at being found; when Tom hiccuped and said, "C'mon!" and started to run.

"Oh, no, no, you don't! —Hey, wait a minute!" said the young man, and threw himself swiftly after Tom and grasped him before his movement was hardly on. Danny stood scared moveless.

"You let go, you let me go," said Tom in a hoarse desperate tone.

"Sure, Spike, when I'm ready," said the tramp, and with one heave, hoisted Tom up on the bank edge and then followed him with Danny. He trundled them forward before the fat old man sitting on the log.

"Look who's here, Fat," he said.

The fat man looked up and at the boys and then sighed.

"You're after trouble, are you, Oscar: they'd have the police right on you if you took anything from them."

"Oh, no, they wouldn't, would they:" said Oscar, bearing his huge thumbs into the boys' arms until they howled from pain. "Would you?"

"No, let go, hey, no! Cut it out," they squealed.

"Sit down, then, and tell Fat you'll be glad to stay awhile. —Never mind, Fat won't hurt you, I'll see to that!"

This was heavy humor.

The boys squatted on one knee, alert and white and not really sure if there was anything fearful in their state.

"Now turn out your pockets," said Oscar.

Fat had resumed with the paper, from behind which he now and then gave over an almost matronly glance of mild concern, estimating, while the boys laid on the ground their treasures. Oscar watched with heavying temper.

"All that crap! What else you got? What could I do with that crap? —Here, I'll take this."

He leaned down and took Danny's white penknife that Tom had given him. Danny spontaneously reached for it and Oscar closed it in his veined fist.

"Oh, you won't let me have this?"

His voice was gently ringing and its mock politeness, the taunting style of his words, made him a puzzle to the boys. He looked like a great guy, big and strong and young, maybe he was kidding.

"Why, sure, *I* want it," said Danny about the knife. "*He* gave it to me."

"Well, isn't that sweet. —Now what else have we here for the good of the lodge? —Look here, Fat, here's all of a nickel. —What a fine meal we can get on a nickel!"

He swept his hand over the pile of buttons, spools, glass marbles, rubber bands, a champagne cork, a glass jewel off the end of a hatpin, and folded bits of paper with lore written down, a broken lead soldier, two rusty keys to nothing, and the rest of the pocket collection, and scattered the objects widely and lost.

"You:"

He took Danny's arms and crossed them and began to bend them against each other. His smile got larger and darker and there was a gracious muscular ease in the way he did it that made him seem happy at his craft, while Danny began to cry silently, with tears falling past his white face, and the pain made him breathless and without voice. Tom could hear little gusts like "H', h', h'," in Danny's throat, and Oscar held the arms at their most painful, and said,

"Now, see if we can't think of some way to supply Oscar and poor old Fat here with some dinner. It's almost dinner time."

Tom leaped up and began to beat on Oscar's back.

"Yes, yes, let him go, I've got it right here, over there, I'll get our lunch-boxes. Please, mister, let him *go!*"

"So you can both run away!"

Oscar laughed indulgently and tightened the bending of the small arms and Dan cried and his voice caught on and he screamed briefly.

"No, I'll hold on to little brother here while you go and *come back* with the lunch-boxes. Then we'll see, if we like the lunch, why, we'll see."

Tom ran as hard as he could and brought the two lunch-packages back, and dumped them on Oscar's lap.

"Enough?" Oscar asked Danny, and Danny, coughing against the run of tears and nose, nodded, and was let go.

Fat leaned down from his log, to see what the food was.

"Well, it's about time you came to," said Oscar.

Fat sighed, and smiled at the boys, as if to say he was helpless, and so far as he was concerned, he was their friend.

He stooped over and the blood rushed to his head turning him fatter still and turkey-colored. He reached into the first opened lunch-box for a hard-boiled egg he saw. Oscar made a fist and knocked the fat old brown and white hand aside.

"Hold your water, there, Fat. If they ain't two of them eggs, I get *this* one:"

"There's one in my box too," said Dan.

Fat glanced at him gratefully. He rubbed his heavily folded belly that showed with the folds of his shirt and he rubbed his bristling jaw. Oscar found the other egg and let Fat almost take it, almost, al—: taunting him by offering and withdrawing it just before grasp, until the babyish ease of the prank bored him and he picked up the egg and tossed it, saying,

"Oh, all right, you old sow belly, have it:" throwing it past Fat so that it lit on the ground and cracked and moistly took in dirt. Fat preserved a curious dignity at that, went and got his egg, broke away the shell, and cleaned it on his shirt. Knowing he was helpless, he knew it would be silly to be even angry, since he couldn't support his anger. He bit the egg; his eyes suddenly watered as the taste flowed into him and he gulped with pleasure.

"Look, we got to go," said Tom.

He tried to make his pug face appealing and polite; but it was white and scared, and desperate; just as would inspire Oscar. In silent waggery he reached over and took Tom's ear and began pulling it on and up till the boy yelled. Then he dropped him, and took another bite of his sandwich, and advised neither of them to even *want* to get away. Oscar and Fat ate ravenously and like dogs, watching each other, thinking possibly if the one finished early, he would have the other's food; a live wish in Fat's eye, but not in his arm; while the boys watched them and felt too hollow for hunger.

Fat actually, at one point, waved his sandwich at Dan and said, "Have a bite?" but withdrew it to finish himself, for Oscar was eyeing it.

Oscar sat belching pleasurably.

XXX · THE THIEF

The noon was hot and still.

It could hardly seem that a block away was the station, and the street, and town, just over the tracks there lay home and safety.

The laundry had a whistle that blew for noon. When it sounded now, so familiar and unaware and cheerful, it harried the boys, and Tom had an ill lump in his throat, and Danny dragged his palms across his face to hide his stinging eyes.

They had both before in their lives seen deliberate cruelty; but never before had they been the victims of it.

"Ever see this one?" said Oscar suddenly and hit Tom on the chest and then as he looked down, hit him on the chin, and as it threw his head back, hit him in the belly, and as his head came over in a crouch of pain, pushed his head down till his back cracked.

Tom came out of it and consulted Danny with his white pug face, huge-eyed and staring with torture, but lipped firmly against despair.

"Now we ought to make our plans," said Oscar.

He rolled himself over by the log and got comfortable, spreading his legs and pulling his pants out of his crotch and caressing and then crossing his legs.

"How long we figger stay here, Fat?"

"We go out tonight. —I gotta get to Memphis."

"Tonight. Night freight go out, don't it:"

The boys nodded.

"Figger we need some money. Now how we going to get it?"

"I haven't got any, I swear I ain't got a dime," said Tom.

"Nor no more have I," said Danny.

"I wonder," said Oscar. He picked in his teeth with a dried grass and looked at them with his white eyes. He showed his deep gums above his short teeth.

"You better let these kidz go, Oscar, I'm telling you," said Fat. He nodded ominously. "Plenty trouble get into, police ever hear about it. Never would believe anything you'd say. —You kidz better go," he added with a sudden flabby decisiveness.

The children were up like kittens, then, straining to be gone, yet turning their pointed faces at Oscar as they moved delicately to their haunches for going. Fat was trying to get between them and Oscar; but his musty, sagging fat body was unwieldy, and there was the milk of terror in his wet eyes, for Oscar was getting to his feet with a lunging poise and coming on them.

"Now Oscar," cried Fat huskily, flapping his hands at the boys to run while they could. "Sstay where you are, I know what I'm doing:"

Oscar savored the physical control he had; he flexed his big arms, and came strolling upon Fat. The boys were trying to fly; but this long second hypnotized them; and it was over in another wink. Oscar opened out his hand and slapped Fat on the face. The noise of it cracked like dry wood and Fat fell down, slobbering. Then Oscar stood still a moment, and looked at the boys. They tried to be sturdy; they squared their chicken-boned shoulders at him; Fat was heaping himself together on the ground in a mound of dignity and resignation. He was trembling his fingers on his stinging mouth and his paralyzed nose. But he croaked,

"You'll be ssorry, Oscar!"

Oscar spat at the ground; he was like a snake who hissed spit and poison and had to do it because that was his destiny, mindless and without opinion, but evil from construction. He reached forward and picked the boys up and threw them back across the clearing and they lit on the ground near the log and the ashy camp fire where the smoke was thickening and drifting as the fire died in the hot quiet noontime.

The boys had the shifting hope and desire of captives; they kept looking around; seeing the sights of their everyday world, places they knew, ways they'd walked; and desperately tried to find the way back to them now, and knew that until Oscar chose to let them go, they could not go. They had a fearful faith in Fat still, and kept looking at him with their white small faces; but he now said nothing, but only blinked at them like an old tired cow, and ruminatively moved his jaw around to relieve the cracking ache it had since the blow.

Oscar lay down on the ground and seemed to relax into comfort. He crossed his legs at the ankles, and squirmed and flopped himself on the dirt until he seemed ready to go to sleep. He had his forearms crossed on his forehead and his eyes shut.

There was a long hot silence.

The town simmered in the drowsy noon of spring.

Fat was rocking himself a little on his haunches. His resignation was monstrous; he was complacent to the cruelest and the foulest treatment, which he confused lazily with fate. Near sixty, he was master of a philosophy that let him be in rags and corruption and without responsibility. And he had done what he could.

The pause was too full of mystery and foreboding to last.

"Look, why can't we go! —Let us go!"

Oscar luxuriated in this, which he had been waiting for. He pretended to be sleeping, and he drowsily grunted, "Uh?", at which the boys both began to make breathless and brave demands to be released. He humorously "awoke" and rolled up on one elbow and side to look at them.

"I keep you here because I can't be bothered letting you go," he declared. "I have plans for you."

He smiled. The blood flushed to his heavy face and made his smile dark.

"I can use you. In different ways."

"—Oh, shuckss," said Fat, in a kissing sort of lisp, pouting and scared.

"Shutup, Fat."

The boys were pledging with resolve. They could feel it as they sat side by side, touching at shoulder and elbow and knee. They seemed to hum in their bones with the same need and intention, to run when they could; to run and gasp and fight their way back across the tracks; they would get up and simply start to run with bursting hearts and pray they would be free.

Oscar squinted at them, and nodded, as if his intuitions were also a power over them.

"Anybody who might happen to think they could get away, well, just forget it," he said.

Their hearts sank.

They felt like little boys again.

Their mouths dried.

They fell victims to their own imaginations, and saw the terrors of slow death by torture, and the grief at home when they should be missed.

"Now this is the idea," said Oscar. He sat up and crossed his legs and began to talk. He said he needed some money. One of the boys would go in and get him some money in town; he didn't care how; just get it, that's all; the other boy would be kept here until his buddy with the money returned; then if it seemed like enough money, he'd let them go,

"—*may*be."

They began to protest.

"We haven't got any money, that nickel was all I had, gee, I can't get any money!"

Oscar laughed agreeably and took a foot of each boy and began turning it until they rolled to their faces in the earth with compliance to pain.

"That's my answer," said Oscar.

It was Tom who had to stay, and Danny who had to go.

Everybody understood that any attempts to bring back the police or anybody's parents, or anything like that, would result in awful terrors. They all listened to the idea that even after he was gone, Oscar didn't want to hear any talk about making complaints; or else he would have to come back and finish up this job.

It was two o'clock by the time Danny was coming up the alley back of the café, cold and sticky with sweat and fear. He couldn't talk to Irma; he would begin to cry and fall down to hide it and to stop talking; and she would come to him and comfort him, and pat his hiccuping sobs into quiet and make him tell her what it was; and then what would happen to Tom? And what would become of him? Oscar would destroy them both, as promised. He wished he'd been the one to stay behind there in the mild grove of great trees that glistened in the afternoon light and the peace of the tracks, where no trains came till evening.

He would have to steal the money.

He knew where the cash drawer was along the backside of the counter.

Tears began to tickle into his eyes as he thought of robbing his mother.

He began to consider how she spent her life. He never before had thought it pitiful or difficult to work so hard for the money that went into the cash drawer that had a cupcake pan in it for the change and different coins.

He was in the back alley now, looking through a wide crack in the fence. He saw the kitchen screen door. About now Irma would go upstairs for a little while, as she did every afternoon. He would have to get rid of K'ang-Hsui if he was to steal successfully. It was all quiet.

He waited.

Presently he saw Irma appear passing the kitchen door. She had on her hat and coat. She passed the door again, inside there; and then he saw her shadowy form retreat up the café and go out the door on Central Avenue. She was gone. With a gust of despair in his breath he crossed the back yard and entered the kitchen. It was empty. K'ang-Hsui was not there.

Danny went to the cash drawer and opened it.

It was empty of everything but a few pennies and some dimes. The halves and quarters and bills were gone. He knew Irma had got them and gone to the bank. She had turned that way on the walk.

Now he really knew panic.

There was nothing else he could do.

But K'ang-Hsui might be in his room.

He went to the back yard and the brittle door of the lean-to, and went in.

K'ang-Hsui was lying on the bed, on his side, his knees drawn up, his arms folded on his monkey breast, his little bony face grimaced in sleep.

"K'ang!" called Danny.

Instantly the little yellow eyes opened and like a lizard's eyes steadily gazed. The little man's body didn't move at all, or his lips, only his eyes awoke and gazed.

"K'ang-Hsui, I have to talk to you, I have to get—listen, K'ang, will you loand me some money, five dollars, I'll get it back, honest."

The steady dark little eyes closed again. Motionless. No breathing, no word.

He had retired into his lizard's world. Danny could not reach him. "Listen K'ang!"

He went and shook the little body. It didn't respond with look or movement.

Danny was sobbing.

He pinched and twisted the Chinaman's arm, and begged for a loan. He began promising extravagantly. He begged K'ang to take anything he had, or something, he'd sell anything he had, but he had to get some money.

"I'll sell you my watch, upstairs, that I got for my birthday, it has seven jewels!"

There was a change in K'ang. He was not tense against the shaking. He smacked his dry mouth once and then rolled over on his back.

"Sell?" he said with his eyes still shut.

"Yes, oh, yes, K'ang!"

"No watch; no: no want. Buy cane."

"What: what cane:"

"Dog cane."

Danny had to remember.

K'ang lay quiet waiting.

"Oh, yes, I remember now, Mamma had a cane a long time ago, with a dog head."

"Ya, ya," said K'ang nodding violently.

"But it's gone! —She put it away!"

"Look-find."

"Will you buy it for money?"

"Buy for money. Go-see."

"Oh, I will. Wait here, you wait, I'll get it, I'll look everywhere! —You got to give me a lot of money for it, I *got* to have it, about five dollars, I'll hurry!"

Danny ran out and in the back door and up the stairs to the bedroom above. He was hollow with dread and force toward finding the dog's-head cane.

Upstairs he rummaged in everything he could; he looked under the bed, and behind the trunk, and in the wardrobe, back of the clothes that hung there; there was no sign of the cane. How long? It was years ago that he was excited and bothered one afternoon about the cane. How should he remember even what it looked like? He sat on the edge of the bed and for a little interval, he was blank; his terror and his fatigue, the exhaustion of his imagination, let him sit there on the big bed witlessly, trembling slightly, and staring at nothing.

A sound awoke him.

He looked around at the door.

It was K'ang-Hsui, standing in the doorway grinning. He held a cigar-box against his hollow stomach, and as Danny looked around, he rattled the box which clanked with the sound of coins. K'ang-Hsui licked his mouth and lips with a dry clacking sound, and nodded. His eyes were like black marbles lying in dust, dark and gleaming and sharp, with light. He was excited. His breath caught the air faintly, sounding like a little dog.

"Catchee?" he asked.

"—I don't know where else to look, I can't find it."

"Look-see:"

He pointed to the top of the wardrobe, the slat-built lid from which the striped cloth curtains hung.

"No I didn't:"

Danny ran and placed the straight chair with the brass-tacked leather seat against the wall in that corner and climbed up. He found packages on top, tied in yellowed newspaper. There was a long wide cardboard box. There was a long bundle wrapped in an old piece of dark cloth that was silvery with dust. He touched it. He lifted it. This was it.

He climbed down and K'ang-Hsui made a take for the wrapped cane, but Danny cried,

"No, my money!"

"Come-give."

"—We better go downstairs," whispered Danny, suddenly scared of Irma's coming home.

They went down the stairs and into the yard and lean-to. K'ang-Hsui closed the screen door and the wood door of his room, and the light was mysterious and local, by the little dirty window. He sat on the bed and set his cigar-box of money on his lap and reached across it for the cane.

"Five dollars!" said Danny with a sinking heart. This was too much money.

"Tlee dollar!"

Danny unwrapped the cane.

He had forgotten how fine it was, the green eyes of the dog, the long bone jaw carved in a slender open smile of sharp little teeth that felt pleasant on the flesh of the hand, the brown-stained carving of hairs on the dog's skull. The cane had assumed a terrible importance now, one of that succession of trifles that seemed in childhood to be the very stuff of life.

Danny began to think of what Irma would do. He remembered what might be happening to Tom, over the tracks.

"Hurry, K'ang! —Don't you want it?"

"Tlee dollar ten tsent!"

He touched the cane and Danny suddenly wondered why K'ang wanted it; yes, it was a nice cane, but that wasn't very much of anything to own at best. But he saw how eager K'ang was; he couldn't know how in K'ang's soul that lived beyond time, there was a slow flow of desire and will that drifted between sense and dreams as a river passed through day and night. For seven years or more he had wanted the cane, some matter of private honor, some subtlety of vengeance upon Irma, some crafty delight in the ingenious carving of the bone.

They tempted each other and whispered and Danny felt increasingly the temper of evil and sin within him; he had stolen and was selling and he would lie afterward; he felt oddly grown-up; the world of childhood was gone; it was a world of whispers, dark ratty corners like this one; strange powerful cruelties like Oscar's, and innocent sunlight, that he lived in today.

Three dollars and sixty-nine cents was what K'ang finally said.

At any further whispered urge, he simply shut his eyes and set his dusty face. He shook his head. He rattled his cigar box.

Someone went by whistling in the alley.

It reminded Danny that he might be discovered.

"Yes, yes, all right! Give me the money!"

He threw the cane on K'ang-Hsui's lap and had to wait while K'ang unwrapped and rewrapped the stick in its dark cloth and sheathed it down in his bed on the far edge among the blankets where the slightest stir freed rolls of dust that drifted into the air and settled again.

Then he began to count his money.

He picked up a dollar bill, and two halves, and gave them over. Then he reached for the bill and took it back, substituting a silver dollar. He picked up a handful of pennies and counted out nine, saving back the shiny ones and adding to the dirty ones a collection of dimes and nickels, each selected after comparison with the other money in the box.

"Oh, hurry, K'ang!"

"K'ang hurry."

It was finally done.

Dispirited, Danny took his money and tied it in his handkerchief and put it inside his shirt. Then he went carefully into the yard and the alley and peered back through the fence to be sure he was not seen. And now he was hungry; he would go back to the kitchen and take a doughnut from the wire cage where they were kept. Yet if he delayed, Tom might suffer. Yet if he went hungry, he might be sick. He went down the alley.

He thought,

"Perhaps some one will see me, and think maybe I look peculiar, and follow me."

He was certain the terror and guilt on his heart must show on his face.

"If they follow me they will see where I am going and they will save Tom too. Then they will kill Oscar and I will make them let Fat go free."

He walked down the street and turned the corner and was on the street leading to the tracks, three blocks from the station.

XXXI · THE DUTIFUL

The air was floating-full of the sunny releases of the day, mild little stirs from the growing leaves and grasses of spring, the acid waft of weeds and the glistening hang of dust above the dirt streets. Presently the sun would start its faster fall, and the air would chill, and shadows and distance would move in the eye with a blue hazy change to night. The nights would still be cold at this time of year.

No one saw him.

He went alone. His teeth were clenched against the rebellion of his whole self, his heart, his stomach, against his skin as he walked.

Now he could see the trees of the tank-grove separate from the buildings lying this side of it.

It looked perfectly still, there. What if they were gone! He began to run a few steps. But he was too tired and hungry to do it long. At last he reached the tracks and started up the near embankment, the low cindery hill. His misery rose into his mouth and he could not help the sore pity of his return to the scene of fright and torture.

He stumbled over the tracks, down the other side, and into the grove clearing, where he stood waiting for them to speak.

And they did.

"Hi, Danny," cried Tom. His face was rivered with dried dusty marks. But he waved and grinned at Danny.

Oscar sat on the log. Fat was asleep against a tree over at the edge of the grove.

"You're just in time," said Oscar. "Your friend here has been lonesome. He has been crying for you. —I can't see why. —I haven't done anything, have I now:"

He smiled narrowly at Tom as if to influence him to agreement.

"No, you haven't."

"Oh, I haven't, eh," said Oscar, "you don't call that anything: well, I'll give you something to remember!"

"No, no, wait, yes, it was something, it was awful, mister, don't, don't, don't!"

Tom whimpered on his breath and rubbed his left arm where it still hurt from Oscar's twistings.

"All right, you," said Oscar to Danny. "Give it to me."

Danny opened his shirt and pulled forth the knotted handkerchief. He held it out. Oscar took it.

He was silent and apprehensive while Oscar opened the handkerchief and counted the money. He actually hadn't expected so much; he frowned and spat to hide his satisfaction. It was going to be fun, with this money, when they got to the next town, he and Fat; only Fat needn't have a dime of it, the old sow belly.

He looked sharply up, thinking to dismiss the boys now that they had served him.

But he thought (and they could see his thought run back of his whitish narrow eyes, the thick mouthed discussion he made silently with himself. They drew together and watched with pinched and staring faces, certain that new horrors were being planned),

"If I let them go, they will get somebody after me and this money, that kid stole this money, they'd find out. I'll keep them here. We go out on the night freight."

He looked up and said,

"You think that's enough money, do you! Well, I'll show you different! —You're going to work for me."

"When can we *go?*"

"When I'm good and ready, see? —And if either of you say a word, any time, about me, or what you did today, I'll come back, and I'll kick the hell out of you! Hear? I'll take the both of you somewhere where nobody ever'll hear of you again, and I'll show you what's what!"

Fat stirred and awoke a little, and murmured that he'd like to be allowed to sleep. Oscar swore obscenely at him. Then he set the boys busy washing his socks in the pool in the ditch, where he had discovered them so long ago this morning.

He made them wash everything he had in his roll of possessions.

The sun was falling.

He built a fire and made them hold his clothes there to dry. The smoke wavered and fanned into their faces and into their clothes. As the dusk began to glimmer across the light their spirits fell sorely, and they felt abandoned and lost.

Fat awoke and added twigs and leaves to the fire and shivered toward the flame, chilled in his shapeless soul. He hummed a little tune. He seemed to welcome evening and the firelight and sight of children puttering at their woeful tasks.

Oscar sat sprawled hugely against the log, dreaming of the wild party he was going to have on his money when he got somewhere. As his spirits rose, he felt hot-blooded, and his face turned dark with flush and his pale eyes reddened and watered and he told over to himself what he would do when he got a woman again and what he had done in the past and what women had made known to him of himself, and of how that knowledge of his power, his hugeness, his might, was what he had to express more and more, and live for, and have proved to him over and over again, else he dimly feel himself defeated, a creature powerless and wild.

"Yai-hee!" he suddenly yelled, and stirred his rump and his great legs with lust. He jumped up and picked the boys away from the fire where they were waving his two shirts. He knocked their heads together and crushed their arms in his grasps. Then he saw Fat leaning over to gather a few more fagots for the fire, and he made a running skip and kicked him and tumbled him to the ground.

And now he was calmer, a little appeased.

He came back and told the boys they were to be free after the night freight pulled out.

"Fat and I are taking freight tonight. When we're gone, we're *gone*. You can go home then. I'll be *on* my way!"

The boys nodded and shivered.

They had very little to think about anything.

"Yes, sir! *On* my way! And am I going to get my ashes hauled when I hit town! Yai-hee!"

Fat came into the firelight that now fluttered in the increasing dark. He was silent and he was hurt; but he made no protest. He added his scrapings of bark and twig to the fire and sighed heavily, sitting down a little away and alone.

The boys didn't stir until the relief engine that would take the night freight out came idling up the track and crossing the horizon in their vision where evening lingered in the lower sky and night already possessed the earth.

Then they knew hope.

But they could not be sure.

Oscar repacked his roll.

Fat pulled his possessions out of his pockets and seemed to be counting them, to be sure his packing was all done too.

From far down the line they could hear the freight train whistle as it drew near town from the other side, coming along the dark evening plain letting blue smoke out against the blue darkness.

"When we get the train, you stay here and kick the fire out," said Oscar. "Then you can go home."

"Ssay, why don't you give him back his knife, Oscar, that kid . . ." said Fat.

Oscar broke wind with his lips and tongue. It clearly expressed derision for the idea.

"Now what are you going to tell when you get back home, you babies?" asked Oscar in his whining burlesque of a gentle tone.

"Nothing," said the boys in tired chorus.

"And what will happen to you if you *do* say anything?" said Oscar, tasting the sugar of menace in his mouth.

"You'll do something to us."

"You'll come back and hurt us."

Fat sighed, almost in apology for the idiot dramatics of his friend.

"That's right," Oscar nodded. His big face nodding in the firelight was like some Hallowe'en monster, for it looked largely jovial, unreal, a mask of candle-lighted grinning, with the firelight on it.

"Because you never *will* meet any bigger bozo than I am," declared Oscar. "I can afford to make threats, I can; because I can back 'em up! See?"

"Yes sir."

"You *better* see!"

And even the boys were no longer impressed. This was the monotony of the bully, who never knows when to stop. They were tired and sick with hunger and the day-long presence of dread in their bellies.

The freight whistled closer.

Presently its lime-yellow beam showed far down the track, and they dumbly watched it pull closer and shake its white plumes, cloudy in that dustless air, and stop at the station.

Then there was loading, and backing, and breaking and coupling; the relief engine switched the cars and then backed to its position.

"Well, good-by, you babies," said Oscar.

He ambled over to them and they stood up, peering at his face with wrinkled monkey looks of wonder and courage. He grasped their throats and pushed his thumbs on their windpipes. They choked and gagged. They kicked at him and pushed with their tingling hands. He finally dropped them, and laughed. Then he said,

"Remember, now," as a warning, and when the engine bell began to roll around, making complete circles and hooping in its carriage, and the steam began to sunder the still night, he turned and said,

"Come on, Fat, we got to catch this number," and just like that, without any more fuss, they walked out of the clearing, and up the track a little way where the engine always began to feel the grade as it led out of town, and there they waited, in the shadow of the cindery embankment.

The boys crouched by the fire, staring, to be sure if he came back that they would see him.

They couldn't believe they were free.

But now came the train, as they had watched it several nights ago.

It rolled and quivered up the track as if in great bony pain, and it took the grade with a hiss and a spin of its engine wheels while metal sparks went blue at the darkness, and the chimes of the car wheels rang and spun against the ear; and the wooden walls of the cars creaked, and the couplers chanted. The train rolled by.

The headlight and the steam behind it made a traveling cloud of light way up at the front of the passing train.

Against that light, cloudy white and yellow, the boys saw two figures rise and catch at the iron ladders of cars midway in the train. The figures merged with the shadow at once; but they were gone; moving away. They were gone.

"Well, holy gee!" said Danny.

He sounded sore-throated.

They stayed crouching at the fireside. The cars made a cindery wind that blew the smoke awry.

The singing, creaking train was almost gone.

Here came the caboose. All its windows were warm with the light of lanterns. On the back platform a lantern showed hanging by the hand. It rose in an arc and fell again. Blazing like a country church, the caboose went by, and on the platform at the train's end, Mr. Dogface, the brakeman, once again stood there intoning his soul into the night, baying with great hound moans the name of the Lord.

It was like a mysterious visitation of a defied prophet. The boys cowered and shook.

They stared after the train as it withdrew into the darkness. In a few seconds they could hear no more of the pious and hollow trumpeting from the old man but they could see his lantern swing with the energy of the music, and it made their hearts come into their mouths for what he had told them and what had come true.

"Come on!" whispered Tom.

They stood and stamped the fire.

The smoke ate into their clothes.

Soon it was all dark and quiet.

They grasped each other's hands and climbed over the tracks and down the other side, and went running up the straight street whose corner three blocks over hit Central.

XXXII · WILDERNESS

When Danny got home, he lingered in the yard for a moment to see: it was nearly ten o'clock. Yet there sat Irma, up at the counter, leaning her face on her hand. She was waiting. He could see her there as he approached the door.

She looked up when he made a scratching sound in opening the screen door. She looked around, and stared at him quietly while he went to stand before her.

The café was empty. It had cold smells of food in it, long-fried edibles.

"C'mere," she said.

He walked over and felt the surge of pity in his heart for some nameless condition of life that moved him deeply.

"Give me m'money that you stole," she said, holding out her hand. Her voice was cold and thin. It told the child, even, of the suffering in pride and betrayal she had gone through. He shook his head and opened his mouth, stricken at her knowledge.

"Y'stole my cane, and sold it, and got money for it, and you owe me the money; —not to say, where've you been all day, and all night, leaving me here t'worry and slave and tear my heart out worrying!"

"—I haven't any money," he said.

She energetically reached forward, took him in her arms, shook him, and then turned him down on her knee. Her relief at his homecoming, and her fury with the terms of her life, and with his dishonesty, shook her into rage. She took up a wooden paddle for mixing batter and began to spank him. After a few strokes which he received with gasps, she threw down the paddle and pushed him from her knees and covered her face with her hands and wept.

The wood smoke smell of the fire of the day lingered in Danny's clothes, his corduroy pants, his flannel shirt. He noticed it now, the sharp dead smell.

He rubbed his fingers on his face, and nose, as if to make his senses forget.

"Oh, Lord, oh, Lord," sighed Irma through her tears. He had never seen his mother cry before.

She suddenly became a human being to him. He could see that her grief was over him. She hadn't even finished his spanking. He said,

"How did you know? About the cane? —I can't tell you!" he added, in awful respect for Oscar and his threats.

There was silence while her weeping abated. Presently she could look up and not into his eyes, but at his person. She talked in hushed and hesitant words.

"I came home this afternoon, and went upstairs. You left a chair over by the wardrobe, and I looked on top t'see what you was doing. I saw the cane was missing. —K'ang tried to steal it once before, years ago, when you was but a baby. —So I went right down and I marched right in, and asked him, and made him give it back, and I paid him what he give you for it. —It's the only thing I've got left of your papa."

She suddenly dropped her face into the crook of her arm, to hide the confusion of grief, memory, and bewilderment in her eyes. He tried to pull her arm away and look at her face; but she would not let him. She turned away.

"It's all wrong," she murmured against her sleeve; "I'm no kind of a mother to you, and I've lost m'baby, he's gone wicked; I've tried m'best, for years and years, I kept saying we're all right, everything's all right! —But it isn't. I'm tired out, and I'm lonesome, and I've let you *run,* and go *bad,* and *steal,* and *lie,* and worry your mother t'death. —I figger just pick up and go. That's all there is t'do. —I been hoping and praying t'go home t'Kansas all these years: I don't know. . . ."

This was so wretched and strange, coming from Irma, that Danny had again the new feeling of her being a woman: more than his mother; a creature who perhaps did not exist for his sole convenience, after all. Her vague despair and her mumbled words acquainted him with what went on within her, a thing he never suspected before.

He could not make her feel him or look at him; finally she went upstairs and he followed her, and then a light seemed to strike across her thoughts, and she seized his hands and rubbed them in an agony of emotion; then raising her hands to the high stained plaster ceiling beneath which she had borne him, she called upon the Lord to listen to a woman who worked so hard and was so tired she never had the time t'go t'church, and to look upon her now, and upon her baby, who stood in a wilderness of sin and misery, Lord; oh, my soul. . . .

"I'm hungry," he said.

"Hungry?"

"They wouldn't let me eat all day."

"They—? Never mind. Come on."

She energetically hurried him downstairs and soon he was eating, while she watched him and tried to break open in thought the mystery which he dared not confess.

XXXIII · TIMES START OVER

"It's all changed, now. I wonder what you'd think, but you're so long gone away I don't guess you'd know your wife and the baby and that's the little baby you never saw.

"I don't know.

"M'boy got in' trouble someways, Dan, and I don't know what 'tis, and can't make him tell me, and he just goes *on,* he looks like a dog, or a scared rabbit, or maybe he looks like a pony that's afraid of being broke. . . . It all happened on that Saturday. He was gone all day. He stole from me, and he lied, I *think;* —I wish you's here! It takes a man t'deal with a growing boy, Dan.

"You know how some times just seem to start everything over?

Well, that's how it is now. —Like when you showed up from Athens that day. Lord land alive! —Never going to forget it?

"But I always heard Frisbie say no trouble ever came separate, she said you could just sit down to make up your mind more was coming. So here we are.

"Oh, I *raised* him, all right.

"I cooked and fed him and sent him t'school and watched over him when he was sick and tied up his finger when it got hurt and petted him when he got picked on over to the school and saw he was respectable with clothes and took his bath and kept himself nice and sweet and ready for anything that might come along! I did all that, Dan. But that's not it.

"No, it needs some one else. It needs some other place. You think I better go back home? There's Frisbie and Shide, and the other little ones, they'd be a little older but Danny wouldn't mind . . . I could be a mother to him there. That's what's all wrong. I'm *no* kind of a *friend* to him, take care of his inners!

"Lord, Dan? I haven't written to Frisbie and Shide for so long? Well, I've been ashamed. I didn't know what to —how to —But I'll just have to tell them. . . .

"I tried and tried to get Danny t'talk t'me. . . .

"He just won't. Did he go stealin', reckon?

"Maybe it's that Tom McBride!

"Trouble, trouble, Dan!"

XXXIV · TO PRAY

It was a curious thing, but everything went into change, some of it wrong, as they thought, some of it right; since that one Saturday in spring.

Irma was sure Danny was a bad boy.

Danny was sure he was unjustly treated, and became sullen and secret. He looked in upon his woes until they repaid him by seeming rich and pitiful and inspiring.

K'ang-Hsui was feeding a worm in his soul, a miserable hungry worm that ate farther and farther into his pride, so that more and more he sought the dreams of his pipe.

Both Tom and Danny were forbidden by their parents to see each other, each faction regarding the other's child as the leader who led its own astray. The boys would meet, nowadays, in elaborately secret places, after school, and on Saturdays, and compare bitterly what life was doing to them.

But one day Tom came with a pugnacious set to his mouth and a scared look in his eyes. He met Danny in the back of the Baptist church, which stood on a sandy corner where four very young trees reared hopefully.

They sat down in the shadow of the gray board church with its black tar-paper roof.

"Well, I got sick of it, and I told them," said Tom.

"Who: what:" said Dan.

"My papa and mamma. I told them what we did that day, and where we were. I told them you had to go home and steal to get me free."

Danny leaped to his feet and danced around.

"Oh, you shouldn't, you got us . . ."

"What could he do:" demanded Tom. He threw his head back and squinted like Doctor McBride, quoting him. "That hobo probably won't ever come here again. How'd he find out we told?"

"*We* told? *you* told," said Dan bitterly.

"Well, anyhow, you can go home and tell Mrs. Milford, now."

The awful pact had been broken.

Dan felt let down. Tom was scornful of any further chicken-heartedness.

The friends parted with reservations.

When he reached home for supper, he was in a somber mood of doubt about everyone. He luxuriated once more in the pleasures of the martyred, and answered Irma's incidental questions with shortness and irritation.

It was prayer-meeting night, and after she was through with her supper hour, she went upstairs and dressed herself for going down-street.

When she came down, she looked for him, but he was gone. But she would pray for him, if she hadn't forgotten how, since the days back home when the way to meet people and entertain them and raise your spirits and theirs together was by meeting them in God, the singing of hymns, the rocking of a whole congregation in the champ and oh-yes of the heart giving outward and making its owner known to God and man. . . . That was the old days back in Kansas.

Now she would try to bring back what she could to save her boy.

When she got home he was already asleep in bed, and she forbore to wake him, but she leaned over him and tried to flood him with the radiation of her happiness. It had come back! the spirit! and she had sung and closed her eyes and been one again with people.

They had been so kind; the preacher made reference to her in his sermon, seeing her there again, after so many years, how long? since Danny was a baby? ten years almost? ten years that she had spent in desperate labor for the living of her child and herself; and at first content in his willing babyhood, the sweet abjection of his powerless life, she had sought nothing else of life or spirit. But she could not give all to her work any more; she could not know Danny as the image of her dreams, for he was growing up, and his divergence from her thought of him was a strange and cruel kind of robbery.

But tonight she had learned her answer.

In the gray board church rising rudely from the sandy corner of the street, she had heard the voices call; they all called her, they clapped their hands and cried her name with that of the Lord; their feet began to stamp when she raised her arms and closed her eyes and nodded her head; they drummed on her soul with every energy they could make; and she had felt them take her to them, and she had felt how the soul does rise in answer to such a call.

While the preacher held out his hands and called "yes, yes," and the people in the church for the prayer-meeting cried and baaed and whimpered like so many clean white lambs trotting their way through dust and distance to the green pastures, Irma arose and went down to the front and told them that she was once again alive with Jesus.

"*Oh,* my!" they cried, with their palms up and their eyes shut.

She told them a sinner reclaimed was the crown of glory.

"Yes, praise!"

"I come home."

"Home with Him!"

"I'm a poor woman. I work and I slave and I hope for m'baby."

"Amen."

"I worry and I try and I fall down and I get up and keep on a-goin'."

"Yes, Lord."

"But I *know:*"

"Ye-e-e-es!"

"I *know* there isn't anything like the glory of the feeling of the peace of God in your heart and knowin' He walks with you and guides you and makes you love your man across the street and your woman next door and your baby upstairs in bed all warm and safe, and your friend over in the next county and everybody you ever heard of and all mankind!"

Her voice rose to a singing ringing shout, and it pierced them and made them shiver when they cried as a response to her strength that poured from her like a deep river,

"Yow! Praise His name!"

What was she doing to them?

All the time she talked, or chanted to them, her heart rose higher and freer, and she felt the tears of gratitude form in her eyes and stay there to make them shine, not fall to make her bleary. She had known this high energy and certainty as a younger woman, back home, but she never in her life could have seen herself as she was now, standing in front of a whole churchful of people and leading their hearts to the Lord. But why hadn't she the right to have changed in these fifteen years? What a difference there was between her two selves, in that time! The girl would have been even a little ashamed of the woman who now exhorted and smote with the blow of the Righteous. And the woman could say with a sad understanding, to the girl, "What you judge is the unknown before you; how can you suspect the winding of life's course until you have followed it?"

At the end of the prayer-meeting, when she was back in her seat again and modestly sitting with eyelids lowered across the excited and stinging liveliness of her eye, the people came to talk to her, and look upon her with surprise and envy. And the preacher came to take her hand and squeeze it, to tell her that she was gifted with tongues and possessed the message of the Spirit, and that she must come often to give it to them.

If everything seemed awry with her life and Danny's, then somehow, here was the answer.

She went to sleep upon a sea of vague speculations and possibilities. Some certainty was growing in her, and she felt as if she would never again have doubts, desperate and lonesome, about anything.

XXXVI · THE BULLIES

Days went by in safety.

Dan was at last able to admit that Tom, by telling his parents about Oscar, hadn't turned the furies loose. No evil had come in vengeance.

The boys became good friends again, and attuned by a certain wild energy to the same gestures, they began to play with the knowledge they'd learned on the terrible Saturday. As soon as school was recessed, they met in the yard and strolled around waiting for victims; whom they would seize and torture; twisting arms and pulling ears upward, and releasing but not freeing the bewildered children who could not believe that Dan and Tom were so ornery.

The two boys said,

"Oh, so you've had enough, hey?

"*I'll* show you something to cry about!

"I have *plans* for you.

"It does not suit me to let you go yet.

"—Maybe *this* will give you something to remember!"

They were intoxicated with the power of the bully, who conceives himself tremendous and great, and so long as the self-image lasts, can somehow impose it upon others.

And they were thickening and lengthening in their bodies. They were shaken and sickened and inflamed by whatever they saw, thought and dreamed of, turned loose in a fancy of desire in a world strangely clear and new to them, and their excitements had no laying in any one occupation. It was not enough that they run and game until they were ready to drop exhausted at twilight on the playfield while the light fell away and the scented evening glistened and darkened in shadow between the small houses of the town; they had to chase their playmates and hurt them if they could; they had to break windows and cut the wire that held the joints of school room chairs together; they had to eat until they were thick with bowels; bending together they had to exchange obscene words and fluting laughter behind fences and in barns, and so bring alive in hollow craving the feelings and calls of manhood; they were animals wild in the home pack, running with laughing fangs and mimic fury.

All this had its shocking aspect to the adult world of law.

Dan was punished at school for making a younger boy cry; he and Tom were found with a girl their age touching in sin; the boys smelled of smoking; they were overheard planning to hop a freight, ride to the next town, rob the hardware store, and disappear forever.

Reports went from school and various other places in town, back to the boys' parents. Doctor McBride stopped in to see Irma Milford as he was going by one day, and saw her moving around in the café.

"Those scallawags of ours," he said. "Beats me, what to do with them."

"What have y'heard!" demanded Irma, with her face white and her dark eyes firing.

"—Nothing much new, but I dinno. —You knew about that day in the early spring, when they were both away all day and half the night?"

"I couldn't get Danny t'tell me one word, he said he couldn't and fell t'cryin'. . . ."

"My Tom finally told me. He was scairt to the pink, but he told me. —They were both held captive by a couple of tramps down by the tank, there, by the tracks. They got hurt and scairt both."

"My *land?*"

"Your Danny had to come back to town and get some money to give those bums, and then they wouldn't let the boys go till the train went out that night. Said if they told, they'd come back and kill them. Said better not mention a word, or they'd know what they'd get. . . ."

Irma smiled and shook her head. Her voice got high and breathless, like a child ready to cry.

"I couldn't make him tell me," she said. "He got the money, he sold his papa's cane to my Chinaman here. I bought the cane back. I ain't had the heart since to even *look* at Danny, he was lying to me, I thought, and I was so hurt. —Now listen to that: *he was afraid t'tell me!*"

The stout old doctor nodded.

"They kept my Tom there while Danny came to get the ransom money."

"Land *alive!*"

"—They're a pair, all right."

"It's my own fault," she declared.

"Oh, come:"

"I should've believed m'baby. Now he's gone bad, and running around raising cain because his own mother didn't have faith in him, that's all it is, I been a mighty poor mamma, Doctor . . ."

"Shucks! you had a hard job t'do, Mrs. Milford. Now don't you go gettin' spoilt, bad enough with those two wild Indians of ours. —I keep missing my cigars. —Teacher wrote home and said they bully all the smaller children. I whaled ' tar out of Tom for that. Said he was going t'run away. Says he don't have to stand for that kind of treatment. Says he figgered he'd go get drunk. —I got so mad I just grabbed him again and whaled him all over again."

The doctor looked shamedly at his hairy knuckles:

"—Maybe I been too busy myself to help m'boy."

They stared at each other.

They were closer to each other than he could have been with his wife, or she with: with whom? She had no one. But as parents of the boys who grew struggling with their own wills into identity and separateness, they allowed the suffering of their hearts to show to each other; and in this exchange, they found a little relief, some strength, and a humorous wisdom about such things as the nuisance of beloved ones, the helplessness of love in the face of youth, and the necessity for high resolves.

"—Praise God," murmured Irma while an idea touched her in start.

"Now don't you worry, Mrs. Milford," said the doctor, regarding her and thinking what a handsome and earnest woman she was. "I'll always do what I can to help you with Danny. —He's not really bad. Nor is my Tom. —Lord, I wish I had no more on my conscience than what they have, or ever *will* have!"

She shook her head, refusing his enthusiastic optimism.

He went on out, then, and left her to her changing horizon. It was opening up in her thoughts. It lifted her something like a song, and it reclaimed Danny for her, and it came at last after all these years as the answer to what she had wanted to do ever since she came here: and that was, go away.

XXXVII · "TIME'LL COME"

When Danny came home in the dusk about six o'clock and passed through the kitchen area on his way upstairs, he said "Hello, mom," and Irma ducked her head at him and turned her face away; she was working between the stove and the customers at the counter, and her hands flew faster at their work, her face darkened with effort and excitement, and the sweat gathered under the delicate hair at her temples. She walked between K'ang-Hsui at his chopping board, his sink, his stove, to the public, as she always called the eaters; and she nervously looked out the front of the café to see if anyone else were coming in who would have to be served. But in a time, she had everybody established, and telling K'ang what to do for a moment, she left the kitchen and trotted upstairs to the room.

When she came in and closed the door, her speech sank back into her heart.

It was time to talk and offer Danny a new life, and she was powerless.

He sat on the bed tying the laces of his best shoes which he had just put on. He whistled gently and didn't look around to her.

She was hot and untidy from work, and guilty in her feelings about her son. But her resolve was taken, and she came forward to sit beside him and touch his back in a caress with her hand.

He squirmed a little from it.

"Say, listen, Danny:"

He nodded.

"—You know momma well enough t'let her say anything to you she wants to, now don't you:"

"Y'a."

She took his chin with her fingers and turned his round face toward her.

"—Honey, we're going away."

"What for:"

He was surly. The affection in her tone made his grievances of the past weeks kindle freshly, and in his pity for himself, there was also love and pity for her, so strong, that he didn't want to show it.

" 'Cause I been no kind of a mother to you here! 'Cause I thought you were wicked and a thief and 'cause I didn't know you stole your papa's cane t'save Tommy McBride from those hoboes! —I know it all! I know it ain't s'much by itself, but I know it means *something,* and I can see this is no way for a boy to live, and I have to see to spend more time with my baby! I've failed you! But no longer!"

She was passionate and enclosed him with her arms. He fought her embrace and felt a hot surge of ruefulness in his throat and his eyes. His furies and cruelties seemed shameful now.

"Guess I just had to wait for a real excuse to pick up m'tracks and make for home. Well, when your baby gets to going the wrong road, it don't seem like you'd need much more of an excuse to light out and find the right one for him!"

"—I'm all right, mom," he said; and then sighed with a catch of breath and fell to her breast sobbing.

"Hush, now; no ten-year-old boy has to cry like that!"

Her hands worried tenderly through his hair, and the articulateness of her instinct told her as no words of hers or his could have how much lonesomeness and fury he had hidden and shown by the terms of his growing ways. She came near crying herself; but the busy noises downstairs, the cry of K'ang-Hsui's voice echoing an order, kept her thoughtful of the work she had to go on with.

"Wh-at are we going to do, then?" asked Dan.

"—I don't just exactly know. But you can bet your life we're going t'leave here! —I've wanted to do it ever since you's born!"

He mastered himself and got sturdily to his feet. He sucked at his running nose and scratched his legs. He smiled at her.

"Now you get washed and come down for your supper. —Don't tell anybody yet. Time'll come."

She nodded at him and went back to the kitchen.

XXXVIII · DEDICATION

The next Wednesday night for prayer-meeting was an early summer night, with a white radiance lingering in the western sky, and filtering in through the white frosted-glass windows of the church, where Irma and Danny sat together listening to the Scripture reading.

It was the Reverend Marcus up there in the plaster and stained lath stage who read with his heavy voice fluting and trembling with sounds that sometimes were elegant and sometimes foreboding.

The twilight faded slowly in the church.

Presently a glow of pale golden light washed on the window from the dying day. People stirred. It came time for a hymn, and they arose to sing it each conceiving himself as no longer mean with daily traffick, now at peace with body and soul, and dimly yawning within, anticipating the excitements of worship that grew out of the people when they gathered, by common donation of spirit, no one man or woman able to give all the divine juice that was needed; but each responding to some current until it crackled in their souls and struck like lightning out of a cloud and made them shout and stamp, and weep; groan with the happy burden of the saved, whose name was forgetfulness.

On that evening, when the day was darkened finally, and the wiry yellow electric lights were turned on up by the piano and the preacher's stand, Irma rose to the feeling, the trundling music of hymns, and came down the aisle of brown wooden chairs, nodding her head emphatically and wavering her fists in the air with womanly defiance. She stood before the Reverend Marcus and declared,

"Yes sir!"

then she faced the congregation who knew the time had come for their hearts to be in their mouths, for Irma always somehow brought balm to them in their piety which remained confused until someone ordered it.

"I'm not fit:" she stated.

"Oh, Lord," they moaned.

"I'm not fit t'be a mother."

"Praise!"

"M'child was delivered unto me out of the *grand*ness of God's heart!"

"Amen!"

"And what I do:"

"Sister?"

"I play him false. Oh Lord, have mercy!"

"—Mercy!"

She folded her hands before her face and felt them quiver with power and remote tingling as if they were touched with magic, not like her red wrinkled fingers at all. She opened her arms wide then, and embraced the people and took them with her out of the town, out of the church, the sandy streets, the flat plain, the outland world where they lived, and by the bursting knowledge in her heart of God's goodness and human sin, and the triumph that attended the meeting of these, she took the people with her into another country.

She talked and sang for half an hour.

Danny was at first squirming with the strange feeling of it, his mother there in the public eye, carrying on so; but as he saw how the people moved with her, and dwelled on her words and breathed with her and spoke rhythmically with their bodies in response, he was taken too; and when she called him to come to her, he arose and without shyness went to her down the brown-wooden-chair aisle, and into her touch. She turned him around, and said to him that he must tell the people of God, God's children, what he had done that was wicked: for then he would be clean again.

"Tell them how you lied in your heart!" she said, "And why; how you did it to save a companion from danger! How your mother wouldn't leave you be but deviled you and drove you darker into the ways of sin, oh my Lord!"

"The Lamb liveth!"

The bodies were bent and the faces were hidden and the hands quivered shading the eyes; the voices rang into the bleak rafters of the plaster church, and the sounds of protest, divinity, unworthiness and salvation rose over the people and brushed through the strings of the upright piano and made them clamor faintly; the four hanging electric lamps quivered their filaments in vibration; the pale windows shuddered when feet stamped; the plaster walls hardened sounds and gave them back: so that the whole building entered into the work of spirit which because it came from people's dim and tyrannical needs, was allied with the divine.

"They shall wal-l-k always!" wailed Mr. Marcus, kneeling on one knee on the little stage behind Irma.

From between his fingers he glimpsed the congregation; he saw that they were moved and rapt as never before. He saw them heave and subside under Irma's sway. He shook his head keenly and knew her work was cut out for her, if she would but heed. If he were but an unmarried walker in the Way: he thought, how far they two could go together!

He was a tall and many-folded man, his face and neck, hands and arms showing as deeply rivered by courses of weathered skin as the bark of an old tree, and of the same gray-brown. From his long neck issued his deep nobly-whimpering voice, rolling with hawkings and thunders. His hair was gray and it fell forward like a gaunt boy's above his gloomy bird's eyes. He wore a long black coat and a pair of striped working trousers, for he worked a farm near town.

Before he could realize how selflessly he was doing it, he was on his feet and waving his long arms like branches at the congregation, across the heads of Irma and Danny.

"I say unto ye that this sister must take the staff and go her into the vineyards to labor!" he called, with a rattle of wind and wet in his throat.

"Amen!" cried the people, rising.

"Many times now we have listened to her read us the Word and carry us the Message, praise His name!"

"Alleluia!"

"Our hearts is touched. The Holy Spirit moves us when she speaks."

"*Say,* say."

"It is for them that toil to know the road, and take it!"

"Lord!"

She turned and looked at him. His remote eyes were cloudy with shadow and sharp in points of furious light. He hardly saw her. He was weaving his great black arms together, blowing in the wind of conviction. His knees were bent and he shook his brow locks. In a moment she ceased to be astonished.

XXXIX · "AND I WILL LISTEN"

"So now I know, Dan.

"You should've seen it. There was that church, just packed tight, and I felt the Spirit, so I went down, and I began t'talk, and talked and talked, I prayed like I never prayed before. I had Danny there with me, and I showed him to the people. We sang hymns and Danny sang, I heard his voice. It was like your voice singing hymns. I'll have him to sing hymns whenever we hold meeting.

"That's what I'm up to.

"Reverend Marcus says he knows the thing to do.

"Says I can make a success of it.

"Never saw a woman he says who can *get* 'em up and *make* 'em stomp like I can, and *mean* it, he says.

"I'm going off and travel around holding revival meetings.

"I'll be taking Danny along and we'll be together all the time. —Maybe I'll get famous and have my own piano-player, and my song soloist, and sometimes they have a trombone choir, land alive, music like that makes your heart come to God so easy you wonder how you never did it before!

"—Some day maybe in some city Dan there you'll be, and seeing my name on the church, or if we afford it, maybe seeing it on some advertisement billboard somewhere, why you'll walk right in and say to yourself, 'That's Irma, the same one,' and pray? the people'll be praying and me leading them, and all things belong to God and to

God all things are possible, so in the praying and the people there, you'll get down on your own knees maybe, and be lifted up then and cry out to God that here you are! And I will listen, and see you! And then it will all be over and everything will be right again, Dan?

"Oh, Lordy!

"Got to be practical, too. . . .

"Sell café to K'ang-Hsui. I got a nice business built up, and I own the business, you saw t'that, I wonder why you always did that, Dan? Giving me that real estate —Anyway, sell out to K'ang and have enough money to start out with on the trail. Work m'way east to home, and drop in on Shide and Frisbie Kinneyman like nothing at all was unusual about a famous woman evangelist calling on the home folks some week.

"—I haven't written to them yet. . . .

"But if I am a success, I can do that, plenty time for that later.

"Now I've made up m'mind, talking it out this way."

XL · THE DEAL

The news that Mrs. Milford was leaving to Toil (—in the Vineyard) went around town quickly; and now for the last few days her customers came in and ate and drank under her influence, a little awed, and regretful that so good a cook and so friendly a waitress was leaving them.

"What've you done with the *café?*" they would ask.

"Sold it. My Chinaman bought me out. He'll go *right* on."

They would look at K'ang-Hsui, and his returning grin of proud ingratiation half disgusted them and half consoled them. After all, they'd eaten his cooking for ten years, why not continue?

Irma had summoned him a few mornings ago to talk business. It was a painful interview, for she found suddenly that the pots and pans, the bread-board, the pale-green oil-cloth on the counter, the 1904 calendar which she had kept because it was richly embossed with pink and green roses touched up with diamond dust, had come to mean something like symbols for security and honest fatigue after work to her; and her doubts arose; and she saw herself giving over a way she had made for herself to go out in the world without any assurance but that which came from the Reverend Marcus and, presumably, through him, God. But she resolved at least to get what she could for the place; and the deal transpired in the back yard on a packing-box.

That morning K'ang-Hsui was less like a lizard than like a mouse; gray and a little fusty in odor; little black eyes ready to warn his secret character of the white woman's greed or thievery; he held his little hands together like dusty paws and hunched his shoulders listening. She told him she was leaving; that he had to buy the place and carry on. She knew he had money.

"P'k!" he said, like a mouse, and darted off in his mind to quivering caution.

"Oh, you know you've told me so," she persisted. "Naturally I don't have any *i*dea how much, but we sh'd be able to make a deal here, now."

He closed his eyes and told over his past misfortunes at her hands, and listened to himself while she waited for him to speak. Every time he recalled an outrage, he saw the future, his own independence, his own restaurant, his mastership. He could live upstairs in the room. There were excellent places up there to hide what he owned. —If he refused, she would sell it to some one else, and he would still be a slave.

"Missee stay here," he said, opening his eyes and nodding. Then he went to his lean-to and presently came back with four cigar-boxes wrapped in a piece of dirty black silk. She knew they must hold money.

It took him an hour to agree on a price; and another forty minutes to decide which bills and coins to give her, enduring minute agonies which he piteously revealed in his sick grin when it came to choosing between a clean five-dollar bill or five mussy ones, and so on. But at last it was done.

She gathered the cash in her apron and went inside.

She said she was going to leave in a day or two. She went to the bank with her fortune and with her savings, found that she had five hundred and seventy dollars. After ten years! she thought. It wasn't much.

That evening she worked again. When K'ang-Hsui saw her come down at five o'clock to start supper, he was violently thrown from his dreamy happiness into a dry toadlike anger. He thought she was done! He was master here! He had paid his money!

He said nothing. He breathed through his teeth and his cheeks worked like a toad's. But he cooked supper, while his mind worked luxuriously through a scheme to be very nice to her and then when she would least suspect it, he would turn and kill her in six different ways. But after supper she jokingly said she guessed he owed her wages for working for him t'night; but she'd not make him pay, and his heart cleared of the jealousy there, and he thought her very generous. She spent half an hour helping him clean up; giving him suggestions in the habitual form of orders; and at last held out her hand to shake his; which doubled him up with pains of shyness and embarrassment crossing his arms on his stomach; until at last he did touch her hand with his cool fingers and titter like a field-mouse, when she went up stairs, he watching her, and alternately lifting his each foot in ceremonious arcs, farewell.

XLI · CHILDREN TO THE FUTURE

Danny and Tom met to say good-by a night later.

They toiled down through the town streets kicking up sand and pressing downward with their fists in their pockets. They walked over toward the station. A switch engine was breathing steamily at rest down the track.

"Well, I'll write to you," said Dan.

"Sure. I'll write to *you,* too."

They were strangely remote from one another. They behaved like boys who have just met under the worst possible adult urgings.

"Where do you think you will be?" asked Tom.

"We're going to Kansas. My mamma used to live there."

"Yes, but I thought you were going all over, the way they *do.*"

"Yes, well, maybe we will be. I guess we're going first to Cloudfield, where Mom is going to preach and have prayer-meetings."

"That's it," said Tom. "That's what I mean. My poppa said she was a 'vangelist now."

"Reverend Marcus says so, too. —I'll get to travel all the time."

"That old Reverend Marcus," said Tom.

"Yes, but he got Mom this week at Cloudfield. He wrote to some people over there, he used to live there. He told them my Mom was the best 'vangelist."

"Gee, I don't see what you want to *go* for," murmured Tom.

They were by the tracks now, staring at the engine. It was dark, and the fires in her box glimmered in a thread of live light; if they'd squinted their eyes at it, and so misted the things they looked at, they'd have thought the fires lived along some far horizon, camp fires, an army bivouacked, or grass running with flame down from the foothills.

They fell silent.

Then Tom giggled, derisively.

"You'll have to go to church all day," he chanted.

"Will not!"

"Oh, yes. *Oh,* yes."

"—I'll be on trains, and see everything."

This brought another silence.

"Maybe you'll see Oscar, somewhere," whispered Tom.

"Gee, maybe."

"Oh boy, I hope I get to grow as big as that when I'm grown up."

"—What do you figger you want to be:"

This was a dreamy and a favorite topic; they had done it all before; but each time it was the same, and new.

"*I* know," started Tom. But Danny spoke in a rush.

"*I* want to be a millionaire, and have all that money, I will give six million to my Mom, and then I will dress in old clothes and go around the country, they won't know that I am as rich as all that, and when they say move on, old tramp, why then I will tell them who I am, and hand them a thousand dollars to have anything I want. 'All right,' I said, 'you think you're so smart, I guess I can *buy* that old café of yours, not just a cup of coffee,' I said. I said, 'Here, I'll take the whole place, I happen to have ten thousand dollars right here in my dirty old pocket,' I said, 'that'll fool you, I guess.' —What do you *think:*" he asked Tom.

Tom nodded indifferently. It was his turn.

"I just found out," he said. "I want to be an undertaker."

"What!"

"Poppa took me down yesterday to Mr. Graum's, and I saw everything. —There was a dead man there. He was naked." Tom giggled.

"Gee!"

"They have everything there, and you fix 'them' all up. —And there was a beautiful room, chapel, *he* said, with a painting of Christ Jesus, kneeling there. It was all dark around it, and they had one light going, and it made a great big diamond star in the sky show up like a light. That's where they have the funer'ls. —Poppa said I could go sometime when they had one. —Mr. Graum is a very nice man."

"Gee, I wouldn't like that," said Dan with a wince.

"Oh yes you would. It's just like being a doctor, only they're dead."

"Well, but gosh, you won't make any money!"

"You make money, somebody is always dying."

"—Yes, that's so. —But I don't know . . ."

"You always were scared-cat," said Tom amiably.

"Heck, no."

"Heck, yes."

"Heck, no."

The future was no more significant, or more doubtful, than the darkness beyond the softly breathing engine on the track before them.

They turned back toward home.

When they reached Central Avenue, and their ways divided, they shook hands loosely with hot and damp paws, and said to each other, "See you again sometime," and each went his way feeling for the other some pity, a little impatience at something too easily given up, and a secret belief that for going away: or staying: each would some day be very sorry . . .

Book III · THE SPIRIT

XLII · THE TRAVELERS

The week at Cloudfield was a moaning success.

Irma and Danny stayed with the family of the local rector, a friend of the Reverend Marcus; and it was a new power she had to bring strangers into her spiritual arms and soothe them and make them good in the eyes of the Lord.

She came to have confidence in her voice when she led hymns, and it now began to rise in strong melody that had an unwavering, clear, calm tone to it, something like a loud bell that never died away but was changed to another pitch or cut silent.

She taught Danny some hymns, and he began to sing at the meetings.

He had been somehow drawn into the excitement and delight of public show without any shyness; and she got him a new suit of blue serge, and black stockings, and patent-leather slippers; and a Buster Brown collar, so that when he rose and joined his hands like a praying angel before his serious bowed head, he could hear people in the congregation rustle and murmur, how sweet he was, what a handsome little boy, and then his pure voice would start, and they would reveal on their faces the envy and love they had for a child already abroad on the Lord's errand.

Danny by now was a good-looking child, with his black hair and his pale brown face, his blue eyes, the brooding curve of his largening mouth. He was getting tall for his age, too; resembling a miniature man, which would give Irma new qualms about him, for there was war in Europe, and its news kept waving over America, in this first season of the evangelism trail for her and Danny. She could imagine him as a soldier.

They moved on from Cloudfield, California, to another town farther south, where the Cloudfield minister had connections. From there she went on in the same system until she was on her way eastward to Kansas. It took her many months to get there during which she gained more and more assurance. Something she had which made people loosen their tight heart strings. She grew prettier. Her face filled out a little. She was freer to remember womanly graces and use them, now that she no longer sweated ten hours a day over a hot range.

She became a clever traveler.

She showed Danny his country.

He would stare out of hot day-coach windows at Arizona, New Mexico, Colorado, Texas, Oklahoma—— the country of Mountain Standard Time—— wondering in the endless dusty afternoons of late summer why he ever thought it would be fun to be traveling all the while; until he would fall asleep, to awake at dusk when the train was choofling along through a magic light, and he would be interested in the shadows of day meeting those of night outside.

When they reached Kansas, she had a week of revival meetings in a town far from her home town; and she looked around to see where she might settle. But where was that brilliant, brighter-than-life world she had remembered tenderly all this time? It was as disappointing as a reality, after you have learned its image from a post-card, an experience she and Danny had had several times already in their travels.

It might even have been another country, that old Kansas which she had left, and had longed to return to.

Suppose things were as different at Athens and Freola?

Now seeing her countrymen again, she thought she saw in the light eyes of the men what Shide Kinneyman would look at her with in his heart, she a woman abandoned by her no'count husband and with a child who'd never seen his pa, and making her own living by being prominent, this in itself would be suspicious. Frisbie would look at her with the eyes of the women who lived remotely in this sunny wide land and who had seen another hope of life fail. Irma remembered the girlhood charms she had recited against the future in her heart. She used to agree with Frisbie's plans for this time which turned out to be so different.

XLIII · NOT HOMEWARD

"I can't make it, Dan.

"I didn't write, and I can't go back and *tell* them everything. . . .

"Take Frisbie.

"She hasn't had much life. She always wanted me t'have it. I remember when you came and was coming after me every week, she used to say I should go, just go on and get out, and see what there was in the world. She said *she* knew. She said the world was what you took of it. Said she'd do it different if she had it t'do over again. When we got engaged, she nigh cried from happiness, and said she wasn't sorry to lose me, I'd be a famous city lady sometime living with my husband so rich in a house so fine. She used to whisper to me right in front of Shide, to get out, and go with you even if I never even heard so much's a word about a wedding ring. . . .

"Or take Shide, then.

"Well, you know Shide just's well as I do.

"He could be mean to me, and I wouldn't care. But he'd like as not take it out on Danny. He'd find ways to show Danny that a boy isn't much who hasn't got a papa ever since before he was born, when his papa ran away!

"*Uh*-uh.

"I'm just going on and do my work, and maybe some day long time later when I am sure-'nough famous, then they'll hear about me and that'll be different. But I can't crawl home this way, Dan. I thought everything would be the same, anyway. Yes, well, it never is. . . ."

XLIV · ALIEN RETURN

But even this way, it was pleasant. She was Sister Milford, and she frequented the best tables and beds in each town. Almost invariably, the pastor in one town knew a near-by one whose church was yawning for her coming. She was granted a sum out of each collection. She showed returns in conversions and renewals and heightened spirits in all the congregations she visited. She preached at random.

But more and more an eloquent message rose from her heart as the months went on and the war in Europe grew in fury.

She preached on peace.

She knelt down with the congregation and embroidered the name of President Wilson with heavenly garlands, for that he keepeth us out of massacre and bloodshed, Lord: and at that point would come the baa of the lambs behind her, happy and witless, hardly hearing what she prayed, so sincerely did she utter it that the mere sound was enough to uplift the penitent soul. . . .

Yet when the meetings were over and she was free to be a woman again, laughing and keen with her new friends everywhere, she would see that they were merely people; nothing was special about them; they were citizens of that country whither her heart had journeyed so often in the years of her exile and labor; and they were just folks like herself, or anybody.

After a time of puzzling, she shrugged her soul, and made up her mind that the older you got, the less you had to expect anything but disappointment in this life; there was time for the Glory-Glory after you was dead and gone. . . .

One evening at Newton, Kansas, she was strolling in the twilight with Danny before time to go to the tent where she was to meet her flock.

They heard a whistle from a train, and the sound wound through the evening whose sky was like water pale from light coming a deep way, and the train approaching seemed a messenger, it was even a thread leading how many destinies away into other worlds: she grasped Danny's hand and they hurried down to the station a block or so away to see the train arrive.

Again she saw it coming, and it brought her pangs, that return of her past, when as a girl she would come with the young people in her home town and see the trains go back and forth over outland America. She used to have a peaceful longing to go.

She would have a loving envy for the people she saw on the train, looking out the windows at Kansas, and coming *from* somewhere else and going *to* somewhere else. The simple idea of going, being on the move, pickin' up and lightin' out . . . it was enough in the old times to smother her heart with the tight embrace of ambition and faith.

The trains would go by, carrying America from place to place.

Now in evening at Newton, she watched the ten-minute wait of the train, and everything about it looked to her as if the passengers were striving through their lives, as she strove through hers; they were no longer a fortunate and idle and blessed people, but people who went where they did and did as they did because they had to, just like her.

And that was enough to make her think of the great change since the old days.

It made her decide that she must have changed. If that could be, others might have too.

The engine began to roll its bell. She grasped Danny's hand tight-lier as the steam sang and the train started west. There was an obscure excitement about it.

Then they watched it darken into the distance and the remote sailing away of the lights, green and red, at the end of the last car, until they were brushed out by the smoke horizon of night.

They went back to town.

The town was awake now in the early evening. A confectionery down the street had its doors open and a pianola was playing an elaborate concert arrangement of military airs, both German and Allied.

The street was paved.

The corn was pushed out into the country.

—But that was another thing.

The corn used to grow in lots right in town, and the dust from the dirt streets would rise and linger and then settle down on the corn, making the broad ribboned leaves look silvery in the sunlight. A horse going by used to kick up a sweet-smelling, stifling little haze. The buggy wheels rang and rasped on the pebbly dirt and pulled a tiny wake of sand up as they rolled. The country was in the town and the town was in the country.

That was what she carried off with her long ago, pictures of that pastoral quality, which now she searched for in vain. She was exasperated by the things that were missing, the way people used to sing in the evenings, the buggies squealing down lanes between fields, not because there was a particular virtue in such things, but because they were the things she knew when she was happiest; and she had expected them to greet her on her return. Coronilla, California, had never had them. That was why she wanted them so much here . . . but she could not even enumerate them to herself. All she knew was that the new paved little towns, and the moving pictures that kept everybody at night, the automobiles that coughed and flanged along the streets and made tempests of dust in the country, the reaching west of the idea of the Eastern cities, until every town was hell-bent on being a metropolis, all these were strange to her, for they had grown behind her back. She felt dispossessed in her own home, the alien return of the traveler was her lot.

She would talk to Danny about the old times. He would listen, and think her strangely happy. But he never saw her pictures.

Whatever image he would have of the world would always be somewhat confused with Coronilla, California, which Irma didn't know. It would be a picture of a population and a character in which those early elements would filter and stain and control him. At times he'd be as happy as she in recalling the early past. At other times, he would know her sense of loss and drift, and never know exactly why.

Their lives were like the vine which grows close on the earth; wandering far from its root, and striking into new sunlight and shade and fastening upon other growing things which when the root is cut will keep the vine striving forward.

XLV · BROODING HEAT

As they traveled, he had to be kept amused. She tried reading to him from her Bible, which she studied and memorized and from which she developed a great source of eloquence, having at tongue for any occasion in her work, a high reference and a passionate moral. But Danny would fall asleep on trains listening to the Bible, and from time to time he began to go up and down the cars to collect the newspapers and magazines which other travelers had thrown down.

They were full of the war.

He made a collection of great figures in the war, cut them out of papers and magazines, and filed them in a big school tablet of rough gray paper lined in blue which he carried with him in his suitcase.

How he would pore over these generals and kings!

He dramatized himself in their uniforms and their gorgeous lace-like fronts of medals and decorations. He was devoted to the Kaiser, and had more pictures of him than anyone else, for he felt that the

Kaiser had more style than his enemies. Danny would twirl his imaginary mustaches in secret and lift his head.

Irma watched this with misgivings.

It helped her sermons to grow more and more like sieges against the stolidity of the people. She preached about peace. She would declare that what was peace: why, peace was God's goodness in the heart of a man.

"Amen."

"Is there any peace like the peace of a heart that lifteth up to Him?"

"Lord!"

"Sinner has a war in his soul. He has a war in his heart. Good and evil fighting over him."

"Bless the Lord!"

"God Ammighty is going to win that fight and end the war in the soul *of* the sinner!"

"Yes, yes."

"Oh-h-h-h, we can't win our peace without God's help, and all things without peace is wicked! —War's wicked! Killing's wicked! Thou shalt not kill, it says. Don't you s'pose it *means* it?"

"Praise!"

They watched her rise in the course of an hour to an almost sobbing strength and fury. Her face turned white and her black eyes flashed and then at times would hold a gleam that seemed really to be a steady light, a glow like fire in opals, or the furnace light in a dog's eye when the light strikes it just right. Her hair dampened at the skull and seemed darker. She used her arms as if they were played by a wind. They were long and gaunt gestures, without conscious grace; but her conviction made them moving. Her voice grew hoarse and to speak became such an effort that she'd try to yell to produce an audible word. She'd close her eyes and cry out. Their souls were pierced. They hardly heard what she talked about, what obsession of her own heart she was trying to share with them. Standing in her white starched dress with her eyes closed under the rich calcium light that made deep green shadows in the reaches of the assembly and over her expression as she moved, caverning her eyes now, now carving with darkness at her temples and the bone of her quivering cheek, the furious apple of her fist, she led them in feeling, and it was all they asked. It was all they needed to join them with each other in waves of spirit that rose to the Lamb. They sobbed and called back to her at the rhythmic intervals her discourse created.

She ate her heart out preaching peace.

She was preaching against loneliness, the dim terror she felt every time her eager imagination showed her the many ways in which she could lose all she had, the only thing she had, which was Danny.

War was the most dreadful way of all, for he would be glad to go, if he were old enough, and the war lasted.

He glistened and dreamed over his war-lords.

She could see his mimic play even when he thought he was being secret in his thinking.

With the rest of America, she was hymning the President for keeping out of war.

But it was all people could talk about. The war was a hooded dream that pursued them like a cloud. It was as if they knew one day that they would have to fight in it.

All across the country there was a brooding heat, cloudy and electric, a time of charging that carried gaiety with it, and a new turn for society. The twentieth century seemed to be getting into its stride, with lots of money and a laughing strength. Like the cities the towns built theaters and office buildings. The villages paved their main streets. The towns had golf and country clubs and people from the city were entertained with their own citified pleasures. The pianola made a clanking music in anyone's living-room. Motor-cars ran alongside the transcontinental trains, as people took to touring. Success was a whole nation's birthright then, because whatever they did seemed to turn out so well.

The war was over the sea.

It was full of rapes and dreads, things to make Americans shudder, in the first years of it.

In high-school auditoriums speeches sounded forth, perhaps a wounded Canadian told his tale.

Appeals for Belgian relief became confused with pictures of dead babies and maimed women.

The mysterious seas of the earth were washing forever-deep the pale bodies of men lost in the tragic currents, and when a great ship went from the shore, no one could say when its smoke would be seen again, or its band play for the happy return.

In the cities, foreign-born people took to shadows and fences like the foxes who trot delicately out of the way of dogs, showing on their faces the pointed courageous grin of the wary and the suspect.

From here and there, men from abroad went back home to join their armies.

XLVI · TIME AS ENEMY

How it grew: no one could say: the belief of the world grew and it held that America must fight. War is a unanimous emotion, anyway; the seizure of a whole people with a single frenzy, and the delivery of that passion must follow for the people's satisfaction. Everybody at war wanted his neighbor in it.

"—If what I am doing is good, then to prove it you must do it too, and show me that I am right. If you don't do it too, then one of us must be wrong. It is not I, for I am fighting for a brave and beautiful thing. Therefore it must be you, and you are a coward since you will not. You are worse, a traitor, in fact, you are *against* me: I will persecute you!"

So it blew, that temper, across nations.

Irma Milford would dream strangely about the whole emotion like a wind or a wave that she felt but did not name, could not be exact about. After her evenings of ecstatic pleading for the value of peace, she would come home to whatever house or hotel they stayed in, and go to bed, and lie straight with exhaustion.

"Oh, Lord: I must sleep:"

But she would lie awake in dry sobs and feel herself racked by the vague fears she owned, and what wearied her more than anything was the fact that she couldn't pin down her conviction that war was coming; she could only feel it in the daily life she saw. It was as though her vibrant eloquence, the clear passage of some force from her soul that moved people when she arose and spoke before them, were conducting impressions to her, ideas that disturbed her and that perhaps only she out of many people could receive, though she couldn't deal with them.

The tense weeks fell after one another with speed.

One day everyone said, "The *Lusitania!*"

She had gone down with hundreds of Americans off the coast of Ireland, and the news rolled around America like a battle-cry. The papers began to push and speakers began to work and Congress thundered. Now that they were challenged, as they felt, the people didn't want to wait any more while the President wrote notes to the Kaiser. They didn't want to get their hearts to bursting with glory and cubbish daring and then be told to sit down there wasn't going to *be* any fight. The cheeky boys of America sparred with phantom enemies and knew their own power that they could feel as they moved, and in that they were each like their country.

There were months of hollow suspense.

Then the whistles blew and the bells rang. Clear-eyed and merry and innocently ready to kill, the great nation heaved to the march. We went to war laughing. (People always everywhere went to war laughing.) We said we'd be right back. (It never *is* going to take more than a minute to polish off that guy.) We had no hatred. (But hatred is a weapon and we were soon equipped with it.) We were doing a noble thing, we were punishing wickedness, and hated to do it, but now that we started, it was going to be thorough. (If what we believe is truth, then that was true.)

Love swept over the land.

Americans loved themselves and each other with intense and aching joy.

They were all going the same way to do the same thing. How deep and warm the burden of fellowship in men's hearts when they go forward together!

"It's a great war!"

All the old values of peace were forgotten and the new ones of war took their place, just as deeply and surely as if they were to last forever.

Danny tore up his pictures of the Kaiser and lost interest in his other generals and kings, because now he was seeing real soldiers every day, going past in troop-trains, walking the little city streets at evenings on leave from camps, seeing the effects of the inspiration of the country as they showed in youths delivering themselves, bone and heart, to die; girls showing themselves to soldiers, and obscurely obeying the desire of love to traffick with honor, hazard and death; mothers weeping for the first wounds, those of parting, and drying their eyes fiercely proud of their sons and of themselves for the passion of hatred they kept for the enemy, a strident and cold rage, more terrible in the woman than the man's muscular joy of combat was in him; churches organizing for Red Cross work, and clubs, and societies; and the old men staying home to exhort and support the soldiers, the old men with fire in their red eyes, and mimic tempests of valor under their shrinking ribs, where beat the pulse that would knock until all use was over.

Irma fell ill in late spring.

For several weeks she and Danny stayed in a cheap railroad hotel in southern Colorado, while the war rolled forward. Danny served her, and wondered what was her illness, and tried to encourage her by bringing his excitements to her bedside, the civilian furies of war, which he saw all day long.

But she would lick her mouth and the fever in her eyes glowed as she saw him obsessed and mighty with the joyous hunger of the war. And she felt him lost to her, and it was all she had in the world to lose, which was too much.

She would send him down to the street to play, so her feelings would not hang upon him and destroy the last belief she had, which was that he loved her.

Then she would consider her state, and conclude that she was simply broken down by exhaustion; that she never had taken a rest in all her life; and that now was her time. She would say that Danny was too young to be in danger of the war. But at the same time she would know that the war was a symbol for the things in life that could either take him away or destroy him.

Meantime, he was at the station watching the trains draw by.

All he saw of soldiering was as merry as a picnic. The troop-trains always stopped for a few minutes there at La Gata, Colorado, and the local canteen women went down the platform giving the boys things to eat and smoke and read. The train windows were crowded with the youths, scrambling like puppies over each other, and in the authority of their cause, they behaved again like schoolboys, freed from school; they were men freed from responsibility, and all of them seized the interim between: going to college or earning a living, and getting changed for life or death in a muddy battle: with larkish spirit. They said grinning and violent things to the girls, who would have slapped their faces four weeks ago, but who now had comebacks as full of invitation as the cracks were full of indifferent outrage. They already, the boys, had the soldier's indifference to the value of the very life they had just left. They felt a humorous pillage their simplest right as they crossed the country to war. Danny watched

them with longing and envy. How fine to be one of them! Some day
he would be. He would fight too.

The soldiers looking down would see his intense face lifted staring
at them; his eyes dark blue with excitement, his hair black, and his
expression full of awe and brat pugnacity; and it would amuse them,
and they would call out to him, "Hi, buddy! Join the parade!" and
throw him a piece of chocolate, at which he'd have splotches of red
blush over his face and he'd stand on one foot, speechless with dedication, while the soldiers laughed and the train creaked and pulled
out.

—What was wicked about this?

His mother was always saying how wicked it was to fight. He had
heard her sermons time and again. Lately they had not been in any
churches. But then she wasn't well. Still, it seemed as if the "calls"
hadn't come as they used to, only a few months ago.

The churches were lusting after blood, too.

When they awoke to war, they realized what Irma had been saying to them all along. It was not what they wanted to hear.

They wanted to be swung into step by a mighty God of vengeance
and dread. They wanted to know that on their side was the King of
Kings, and on nobody else's side. More, they not only wanted him on
their side, but in their own denomination.

In early summer the first troops were already fighting in France.
The casualties began to come home. Now the people had their cause
baptized in blood. Now it was a dedication, and like the forgetfulness
of lust, which veils all consequences and enchants the moment, there
appeared to be something ennobling about death in combat; even
the ones who lost their lovers and sons and brothers and fathers were
not horrified at the thing-making objectivity of death; they were
grieved and strengthened. The months passed through the spring, and
only one fortune prospered, that was the fortune of war, in people's
hearts, in the country's factories, in the temper of a citizenry, and in
the churches of God. That summer came in hotly, and in training-
camps, the drills went on, readying the next wave of men for the combat in which already many had died.

XLVIII · THE FORWARDED LETTER

Here at La Gata, where Irma lay sick in the railroad hotel, the minister of the church she knew came and said to her that perhaps it would be just as well if she devoted her time to getting well; and perhaps come back next year for a week of revival meetings. Right now, he declared, they were s'busy with war work, and auxiliary activities, he just didn't see *how* they could go through with the plans they had had for *her*. —Besides, he believed, some folks didn't see eye to eye with other folks about the war, and God Ammighty's great message for the American people.

His close little eyes squinted on her as in a smile, and his mouth which lay forward like a baboon's dryly smacked once or twice to take the place of a nod.

She knew what he meant They didn't want her. Nobody would want her from now on.

He was just about to leave when he remembered a letter in his coat pocket. He patted his coat, and pulled out the envelope.

"I was mighty like to go off and forget to give you this," he declared.

She took it, and he nodded at her with curiosity. She saw that the envelope had many forwardings on it, and that it had been addressed to her originally at Coronilla, California. It looked like a governmental communication. She put it under her pillow and waited for her visitor to go.

"The letter," he said, "it come from Brother Meak, over at Salinas. —I happened to write him you's here. He said you's over there a few months ago."

She nodded.

"Looks like it traveled a long way. California? You used to live in California?"

"Years ago. Almost nobody knows my address out there. . . ."

He glistened at the wretchedness in her voice. But she refused to look at the letter while he was there, and shrugging again, with thanks to goodness he'd had enough sense to turn her out of *his* church, anyhow, he went away.

Her imagination had told her already what the letter contained.

It flew like a shuttle between likelihoods and deductions. Her very blood seemed to tremble, yet she could see no shaking of her hand. The tears arose into her eyes and she was glad to be alone. She took up the letter and began to tear the envelope open slowly, begrudging every little scallop of white paper she made with her reluctant hands.

Her mind had flown in this wise:

"It's a government paper. —Now who else but Dan had my Coronilla address? What's he done: he's gone and joined the army. They've sent him overseas. He gave my name and my address, and he remembered. You remembered that much, didn't you, Dan? That you were my husband and the father of my baby? So you told them, like any man, they all, everybody, want some one to know when they're gone? Don't they: so you told them if ever you—why, they should tell me?"

She had the envelope open and the letter out. It was an official form and it told her with a curious kind of impartial compassion what she had already believed in her thought. Dan had been killed in action the night of June 21st.

—It called him sergeant.

He and five men had been on a reconnoitering party and at half past eleven at night, they were coming back to their trenches through a little meadow of wet gaseous earth. They were crawling. Their hands and knees slid in wavers on the mud, and it was a kind of strange swimming in semi-solid matter. A star shell went up near them. They couldn't stop moving quickly enough in the slippery mud. The shell bloomed in the green heaven for a long moment and only when it went out they had achieved stillness. They froze. They whispered, "Hold it!" A hundred yards away a low mound showed on the horizon which was now pale again close to the earth since the star shell was dark. From the low mound a brief premonitory click sounded, and then, blowing bullets like kernels along telegraphic fire spurts with mad ugly clatter, a machine-gun hosed them down into the sighing mud as if it played water upon paper flowers. Their bones were studded with impact, and they relaxed as their arms and legs blew brokenly in the prevailing stream of that bullet wind. It was a little storm, and like anything in a storm path, they bent before it, now gracefully, now resisting a moment, and then nodding back until the next flurry. Presently the idiot-talk of the gun was silent, and so were the sergeant and his five men. Another star shell went up and shed an exquisite light over them, as if it were a stage and the lamps must pick out beauty. There was another click in the machine-gun emplacement as the gunner disengaged, successful. The star went out.

After a time, the barest news of that went through all the various channels and reached its destination.

She lay into her bed and set her head down on her fists. She had an impulse to talk to Dan in one of her private musing thoughts; but he wouldn't be alive in her image any more, and the sense of her aloneness was something she couldn't afford to recognize any more. While he lived, there was always the chance; now dead, she was indeed abandoned.

She suddenly sat up and her eyes with tears in them were wild. She considered now that whatever she did must be on her own decision. She felt herself facing defeat that would perhaps kill her, if she let it seize her. With the tears pouring down her face, she told herself what in his lifetime she had reason but no will to say: that she must forget Dan now forever, and go on living. It was a moment of illness that was critical. Some odd strength, some realism, showed in her character at the moment, and in panting haste she stood up and cleared her eyes, patted her face with her sheet that she stood clutching to her breast with one hand. She saw herself across the room in the mirror.

"No sir!" she said.

It was as if the hardest blow of all were what she needed to make her rise again in her courage.

She dropped the sheet and pulled her black hair off her wet cheeks. Breathing on a little sound like "M-m-m-m," she went to the hotel dresser to find her purse. It was lying in the top drawer. She opened it to count her money. Her hands were trembling. She felt like calling out in protest at her weakness, the sick feelings of her heart and her fears. She saw her life and her son's as without chance; she had tried her best for him, and what happened: he fell into bad ways and she had discovered her sinfulness and neglect, and they had arisen and gone forth, and until this scourge had fallen on the world they had prospered. She counted the bills and the coins in her purse, and the ecstatic nervous fingering she did made her think of K'ang-Hsui back in California, fondling his money as he counted it out of his cigarboxes.

She had little enough money left.

All those months and years of railroad traveling, hotels, and the like; where did it go? She had no sense of having been extravagant. But the collections in her meetings came in handy now and then;

and always she had the idea of settling down somewhere, and then she could earn money again some way.

"We're *all* right," she mumbled as she put the purse back and covered it with her scarf in the drawer; and went back to her bed.

There she closed her eyes and made fists with her hands over her thinning breast. She ground her teeth and vowed that she would get well. She must go out and work again for Danny's sake. Surely there was somewhere a church, even a handful of people, who would hear her cries for goodness and peace? —It was now an obsession, and she could not possibly think of her work as an evangelist without now seeing it only as an opportunity to cry down the war.

She thought that she must get well so as to bring Danny in off the streets, or be with him when he did go out.

She thought,

"We have enough money t'last us for another few weeks. Tomorrow morning I'm going to get up, and put on m'clothes, and buy us some railroad tickets and clear out of this town. —I believe I know where I can find a pulpit. —There's nothing the matter with me!"

When Danny came home later she began to cry on seeing him. But she wouldn't tell him why. She never told him about the letter from the War Department. He had long ago forgotten whatever she'd told him about his father. Now he was frightened for a moment of her grief; then sulkied by it.

XLIX · THEY GO AGAIN

She arose the next morning and put on her clothes. She was almost blind from weakness and she could hardly stand. She felt sweat seep to the air from her body and make her feel hollow. Danny looked anxiously at her, and when he spoke to her, she bit her lips together and nodded at him.

By a cruel concentration she got their things together, and Danny ready, and themselves downstairs; she paid the bill at the desk, and they went across the gravel yard to the station. She bought two tickets for a town down the line to the west. Then they sat to wait for the train.

As they waited, an eastbound troop-train came charging through. It stopped for fifteen minutes.

The canteen girls swarmed down the platform and fed the soldiers, who struggled for the sunlight and the smiles outside the train windows, crowds of them in each window, pulling and shoving like young dogs in a pen. Danny jumped up and went to watch them, and walk by the train as he liked to do. Irma called after him; and he came back, troubled by the passionate light in her eyes, that were so dark and sunken.

"No sir, you don't! . . ." she said, with a breathy ferocity. "You stay by me, right here! —See what happens to you when you wander off and get mixed up with strangers, like those tramps back in Coronilla! —Doctor McBride, he told me——"

She fell speechless and troubled back against the waiting-room seat. Danny pondered in anger. He couldn't understand what she felt, or why.

"When can we go back home," he demanded, sulking and mischievous.

"Home! Y'call that home!" she said, looking at him with amazement. The tears gathered in her eyes, and she thought he was taunting her; but when she saw that he was serious, that he remembered Coronilla with longing, as she used to dwell on her memories of Kansas, she was tried again by the desperation that had hounded her for the past many days.

The troop-train on the tracks began to move away. There were cries of merriment and gaiety. The women waved and the soldiers winked and cawed, all in terms of the accepted slogans for love and bravery, courage, farewell and the future . . . the slang of emotion.

After the train was gone, the sunny quiet of mid-morning returned. Presently from the east, another train whistled and they got ready to take it.

L · THE FORGOTTEN WORD

The town down the line was far from Paradise. Irma had one or two connections there, and she called on them, trying to hide her illness, which was less troublesome now that she was resolved to be on her feet and doing. One minister told her the church had no time now for revivals, because the war-drives took everybody's spare energies, and maybe she'd care to help that way; though there were no collections or fees she could expect. Another elder she went to see suggested that she organize a series of Good-Time-Hymn meetings in the training-camp which was on a plain six miles out of town. He said the soldiers were fine clean Christian boys and they sure would miss their old-time religion and she sure could give it to them, if she but would. He had light-blue eyes set in milky little cups and his lean white bearded face wagged like a billy-goat's when he talked. She said she didn't think that was what she wanted to do. —The soldiers wouldn't have any offering-money.

Her elder drew himself up and thumbed his lapels. In his quavering old voice he trumpeted,

"Mercenary, eh! At a time like this, and a chance to give God's word to them heroes going t'die for us all!"

She wearily took herself away from him.

There was nowhere for her to preach.

They went from town to town, and the money fell lower and lower.

In their wanderings she seemed strangely to recover her spirits and health a little each week; but she was a different woman still, and forever, from the strong and eloquent mistress of the Word that had set out on this divinely inspired journey. She couldn't forswear the work and the words that had given her such release from that old life of loneliness and drudgery. Though there were no meetings to invite her to speak to them, she would now and then find a prayer-meeting and go in among the strange people of the town and simply attend them with her presence; now and then feeling the old fury rise in her and commend her to herself as one whose spirit still could do battle.

At times like that, she would watch for the moment during the prayer-meeting when a whispering pause fell over the company; then she would rise and begin to pray aloud; and the heads would come up and listen, and in no time she would have them crying amen to her, and giving her the beat of the hearts; and she would know herself again.

During such evenings, Danny was on the street, waiting for her. He would wander off, into the downtown of the small cities they passed through; and when he had the money, he went to the movies, shows given in long narrow theaters shaped like shoe-boxes. The darkness was perfumed and under the sweet smell of the atomized scent which the management squirted around, there was the smell of breathing bodies. The films were accompanied by music played from rolls by a mechanical organ. Sometimes there was an operator of the instrument who pulled ropes and produced the sounds of percussion instruments along with the flapping and groaning of the pipes.

The excitement of the evening always reached a pitch of revelation when the picture was cut off, and a dazzling white plane of light cut across the screen. Sometimes they would throw a lantern slide of an American flag on the screen, and then a man would get up and address the people. He was a Four-Minute Man, and he (and many like him) gave time and tongue to the work of exhorting the civilian populace to buy Liberty Bonds, back the war, do their bit. The terms of passion which he used were common to the whole people. He would raise his arm and utter the word "Crusade!" and all the hearts that listened would trundle faster; he would mention the boys who have gone to fight, and tears would come up in the packed and aching theater; this was the new evangelism. It moved Danny deeply.

Presently the speaker would retire and the people would feel but not know that their souls were bound together in beliefs and aims like those of another secular religion. The picture would come back to the screen, and the player-roll organ would hiss and thump again with its tunes of melancholy grandeur.

At her prayer-meeting Irma would stand and pray with her eyes shut. She would feel the excitement of her ideas working toward word, and when she would pray for the war to end, for peace, for the safety of all those men and refer to the whole thing as wicked and contrary to the laws of God, another excitement would arise, and counter her. The people would suddenly begin to hear what she was saying, and they would stir, and be silent, rather than droop and amen her with bleating accord.

She could always feel the change in their temper.

It saddened her. She would halt her prayer. She would look around. The faces were defiant and unwelcoming. They put her from them as a stranger, and would have none of her again.

One night in one of these meetings, they began to hiss and boo. She left them in proud silence.

But walking away, she declared to herself, "I am right, my heart is right! I know it!"

It was just another town to move on from, then. Moving, there was still plenty of time for reflection, and she was now and then unable to recognize herself, this wandering prophetess repudiated by

the people she came to with the Word . . . the same message that
had been received with such love and relief only a few months ago.

LI · HOPE

At last in Los Algodones, large town on the main line where they
spent a vacant week, Irma was given hope.

They were staying in another railroad hotel across from the long
sprawling station, and attached to the hotel was a little restaurant.
Her third day there as a guest she asked the manageress, a fat woman
with a black mustache and wet yellow eyes, if she couldn't work as a
waitress in return for her room and board and Danny's. The woman
smiled as if she were smelling something; Irma felt a menacing response in her.

"So, you can't pay me! —I've had yer kind before . . . I'll get the
police!"

"No, I can pay you. But I'm running short on money pretty soon.
I've got to make some somehow, I thought I'd just suggest it."

The woman was instantly mollified. She made a pretense of a
yawn and tidied her hair in social assurance.

"Well, excuse me, but so many of 'em come along. . . . Why, I
wouldn't know about hiring you. . . . What's yer regular line?"

"I preach the Word of God. I'm Irma Milford, the evangelist?"

"No, can't say's I do, but that don't prove anything." Here the
woman simpered her mouth into scrolls and cackled like a parrot.
"I ain't been to church in forty years. —So you're a Sister!"

She nodded, marveling, and considering.

At last she gave Irma work in return for her room and board.

One night she asked her if she knew there was a revival meeting
going on down near the Elks Club. She said there was a grett big
tint on that vacant lot on the corner past the Elks Club. When her
work was done after nine, Irma and Danny went walking to find it.

It was only seven blocks away. The tent was glowing a shallow
orange with its lights up inside the top, and the top was cut against
the sky over the river and clouded with the stirring lace of cottonwood trees. The sky was a deep turquoise black, with a line of pale
light at the ghostly horizon.

The tent was half-full, and its sides were rolled up and open.

Danny and Irma went in and sat down in the last row of folding chairs. There was straw on the ground. Up on the platform where the piano was, a middle-aged man was conferring in a soft voice with the piano-player, a thick young woman in a white dress and blue hair ribbon and blue socks. They leaned and talked in whispers, and the congregation waited patiently. It had the air of a lull in some professional proceedings. The man was tall and when he suddenly turned and looked, they saw that his left eye was missing, which gave his whole left face a smaller look, a speculative squeeze of the features. He was smiling and his sightless half looked hectic and gay.

"Well, now that takes care of almost every day," he announced.

The people nodded, but this made no sense to Irma.

"Tomorra night, I'll b'back with you again, then Thursday, Reverend Tatum will speak; Friday, Jo Clem Masters will give the talk, and Saturday, if I get back t'town in time, (I have to be gone all day Friday *and* Saturday, there's some business I have down the valley a ways) but's I say, I'll be with you again Sat'day night, and if I *don't,* why, Miss Mollie here, our little piano leader, will see that either Reverend Tatum or Sister Buckley will take charge. —Now for Sunday afternoon, that's still open, but I'm sure now none of you need t'worry, because I'll see we have *some* one to lead the meeting on that afternoon."

He turned and smiled down on Miss Mollie, who puffed forth a noisy sigh and a smile.

"Y'see?" he said. "How can we object to a little inconvenience and hardship when our regular inspiring leader has gone off to join the army?"

The women stirred in their chairs and murmured with sounds of praise. The man felt this and it spoke like success to him.

"Yes sir: did he delay? No sir; did he say, Oh, please Mr. Uncle Sam, I got to stay and preach the Word to my people and I cain't go fight old Kaiser Bill! Did he? No sir!"

He exchanged his half-withered glance with Miss Mollie.

"What he do? He up and git! —I saw him off on the train yesterday myself, and the last thing he said to me, was he shook my hand, we shook hands and he says, 'Brother Trainor, you carry on,' he says. 'You'll b'back, Brother Doxey,' I says. 'The Lord needs you in the Vineyard,' I says, and he laughed, and we shook hands, and he says the war was no respecter of persons, he says, 'But the Lord hath entered into my right arm,' he says, 'and I shall *smite'!*" —here the voice rose to a startling shout.

Voices murmured, awakened into response.

Irma felt her heart beat.

There was some homely and reassuring atmosphere about the tent: the bright acetylene flares up on the tent poles, the comfort of the people sitting face to face with some power that moved them in ways they could never question or explain; the shadows down the street that she could see out from beneath the tent, and the cars idling past on the pavement; the platform itself, with its charts and blackboards with texts and elementary pictures of Heaven and Hell. . . .

She sat until the meeting was over, and then went down, with Danny clinging to her hand, to see the one-eyed Brother Trainor, and seize him with advantage.

She waited on the outskirts of the small throng that gathered around him after the last hymn and the final blessing he had given them, straining with his single eye watering toward the tent-top, and twisting his half-face in small spasms of eloquent feeling, and swinging his arms upward, and shouting in a new voice like a breath blown across an empty bottle top, hollow and ringing; and when he was free of all except Miss Mollie, who sat like a lumpy little girl on the piano stool, she said,

"Brother Trainor? I'm Irma Milford."

"Yes, Sister? God's friend? I'm a-listenin'?"

"You don't know me, then: I'm a worker in the Evangelism of the Lord, Brother Trainor, I've been all over Arizona, Texas, Oklahoma, Colorado, and Kansas, the last few years when I left California, where I used to live."

"Now that's it," he said, with one of his consultant heaves back at Miss Mollie, and back to Irma again. "I figured I knew your name. Why certainly!"

"Y'see?" said Irma, suddenly very happy at his knowing who she was: the straw of the lost. "I heard you say how you didn't have anyone to handle your meeting for Sunday afternoon. —I could do it. I *want* to do it. —I could show you letters from half a *doz*en ministers, and church boards, where I held meetings. —This is my boy Dan, he sings on my platform."

"Well; Master Dan," said Brother Trainor, squatting and leaning to see him better. His eye turned in the side of his face, as if he were a bird who must twist his neck to see. "Well, sir: tell me about your precious mumma. —Can she preach? Can she sing? Hey?"

Here he cocked his face and its eye up at Irma, and winked it, to include her in the professional gaiety.

"Sure," said Danny in a low voice, trying to withdraw his look from the dead cavern of the lost eye, but he could not.

"She can, hey: well, sir, shall we give her a chance?"

He straightened up archly, and then with a brisk seriousness, he turned to the piano woman who wore the outward innocence of a girl.

"Miss Mollie, this'z Sister Milford, Sister, Miss Mollie: Miss Mollie plays all our hymns, and sings for us too. —She is nigh to heartbroken since our leader, Brother Doxey, left for training-camp."

"How-do," said the pianist. She put forth her hand to Irma. They shook. "Yes, he's gone, the draft got him, poor Edgar. But he would never be one not to go if they called."

She smiled brightly at them all, and sighed. Irma nodded, and figured that later she could tell her a thing or two about being deserted, willy-nilly.

"Well, now it's just fine. —Praise the Lord, let you but face the difficulty, and He will find a way. Here we had nobody to lead us Sunday afternoon, and along comes Sister Milford, who everybody has heard of. —We'll expect you at three o'clock Sunday. And will Master Dan sing for us?"

"Oh, yes," said Irma feeling for Danny's head and looking at Brother Trainor with almost a panic of gratitude. "—And m'usual collection?" she asked.

"How much:"

"Fifteen per cent?"

"Land alive, Sister, you must be pretty *good*. . . ."

"When I stay a week anywhere I get twenty."

"All right, but don't think it'll make you rich, fifteen per cent of *this* town's return to Jesus'd hardly keep a daog!"

He wheeled indignantly and peered at Miss Mollie, who pouted for him, and they nodded in joint professional outrage.

"Yes, well, good night. I'll be coming back, and *thank* you, mister, praise God for a real Christian!"

She took Danny from the tent and they walked back to their two-story hotel down by the station, where the sky above the tracks was alive with drifts of golden-lighted steam and smoke against the higher darkness.

LII · BIRD AND SNAKE

On Saturday afternoon after lunch, Brother Trainor appeared at the hotel and asked for Mrs. Milford. The proprietress was at her lobby counter. She had laid her bags of fat on the counter and was dozing wide awake while the glistening sweat rolled ticklingly into the creases of her neck, her breasts, her elbows.

"Upstairs. Number 27. —What ' you want?"

"Oo-hoo!" he chuckled in his reassuring bottle-top voice. "I'm Brother Trainor, and Sister Milford is on our staff of the evangelistic party down to Seventh and Gold streets. I have to see her."

The woman drooped her eyelids and shivered at a thought that crossed her sleepy mind, thinking that to be kissed with that one dead eye would make her sick. She squnched her fat shoulders together and tossed her head toward the stairs.

"Go on up."

He went by her and presently knocked at Number 27 with a gay little rhythm, shave-and-a-hair-cut, and put his head on one side whimsically. He was tall and rawboned and with his publicity instinct knew how to dispose himself so as to make this clumsy body winning and common and appealing, like an actor who thinks he can ape the humorous gangle of Abraham Lincoln.

Danny opened the door, and seeing who stood there in the dim hall where daylight filtered down its length from a single window at the end, he closed the door a little again.

"Hi, Buster. Is yo' mammy there?"

Danny nodded.

"Just you tell her ' let me in, son," he said, with a beady whisper of cajolement.

Danny shut the door and went to Irma on the bed.

"It's the revival man. He wants to come in."

"Then let him."

She sat up and touched her hair and then stood. She was dressed. Danny opened the door again. Brother Trainor walked by him, immense and strange in the room. He went to Irma and shook hands with her in silence. He shaggily nodded his tousled head and seemed to pour through his grin a wealth of unsayable glees that only the hoot for the Lord could express. She recoiled a little from him, and nodded.

"Sit down, Brother Trainor."

"Sister Milford, I will. —Sho', Dan, there, he wasn't goin' t'let me come in! An' it was really t'see *him* that I came!"

He turned and winked his live eye at Irma, and Danny said,

"What? What for!" very realistically, as if there could be no possible traffic between them.

"Well," said Brother Trainor, "Today's Saturday, ain't it?"

"Yes. . . ."

"War going on, iddn't there?"

"Um-hm. . . ."

"Got airoplanes, haven't they?"

"Yep!"

"Well: now I'm fixin' for you to see the best show you ever saw ' your life."

"Now that's nice, isn't that nice, Danny?"

"Yes, Mom."

"See?" said Brother Trainor. He reached out his huge hands and pulled Danny to him with the clumsy tender touch of the healer who is awed by his own gift. "Now looka here. This very afternoon out on the mesa up above town, there's goin' t'be a flying circus. You ever ben to the circus?"

"Sure, with clowns and animals, and so forth."

"Well, this circus is all in the *air!*"

"You mean airoplanes?"

"Sure do! They's a big party of French, and English and Belgian aviators goin' do stunts all over the sky and they're travelin' around the country to show us Americans how the war is in the air over there in France. They're helpin' to advertise the Liberty Loan drive too. —Now how'd you like t'see that?"

"Loop-the-loop!" said Danny. "I'd *like* to."

"Woo-hoo! I *though-h-h-t* so!" laughed Brother Trainor. "Well, then, here y'are. —Here's fifty cents. You take a jitney that runs up the hill out to the edge of the mesa and then you can walk to the airfield a little ways away and you'll see all that flyin' and get the thrill of *your* young life!"

"Can I Mum?"

"I guess so, Dan. —Be careful and don't talk to anyone. Mind you come right home when it's over."

"Sure."

"Lord bless it, what I'd give t'be a kid again!" mused Brother

Trainor pushing Danny with humorous despair and courage toward the door.

"Thank Brother," said Irma.

Danny looked at him.

He saw the big gouged face and the puckered eye-cup, like a trumpet-shaped flower which has withered and folded together in a purse of brown decay; he saw the large bony body sitting there hunched as if to reduce its size apologetically yet with annoying self-satisfaction; he hesitated as if he didn't want to go.

"—I wish I had the time t'see all those wonderful air aces show how they shoot down enemy planes!" sighed Brother Trainor, not to Dan, but to Irma. He sighed. "Lord keep us!" softly.

Dan ran impulsively back to kiss Irma on the cheek and then he ran out and closed the door and clattered down the stairs. The proprietress at her counter awoke enough to see him spin through the door and down the street toward the jitney stop; and her sweating thoughts closed her off in a doze again after she recognized the fact that the man had got rid of the child and was up there alone with that black-haired, white-faced woman with the snapping dark eyes.

The jitney was crowded. Dan had to hang on to the top struts and stand on the running board. It was a Ford, driven by a girl in a khaki uniform. Her face was freckled and powder and rouge couldn't hide that. She drove jerkily; but was content to be heroic, doing man's work at home during the war. The car ground up the long hill and presently leveled off at the edge of the mesa.

The afternoon was hazy with heat which arose from the plain and waved in the air and made the mountains beyond look now nearer and in focus, and now distant and fading. The ground was hot on the sole of a shoe, and dusty. The brittle sharp grass and weed that grew there made people slip as they walked, and their steps crushed the leaves and stirred off the dust; a wry smell with some vagrant sweetness in it came up from the trampling of the crowd that moved toward the airfield.

The ground was freckled tan. The air was silvery with heat. The mountains were violet gray rock. The sky was white arching into a deep and dusty blue.

At the hangar the crowd was gathered and staring at the dozen airplanes lined up on the scraped ground.

Officers in foreign uniforms stood near their planes and talked to a few of the prominent citizens who were there to see the show and make excellent example by buying Liberty Bonds at the table set up

for the purpose. There were blue French uniforms with brilliant spots
of ribbon and medal. There were gray-green Belgian and brown
British and Canadian. Danny wriggled through the crowd and stood
in front staring. The soldiers with their planes made him ache. The
men were young and a few of them had faces like boys. One or two
had mustaches like men. But he could see himself doing what they
did; and that he could not, was not old enough, was unknown, and
baffled by the delicate airships that stood waiting, made him sad and
eager. He wanted to run over and shake hands with the young
French officer with the blue eyes and the silvered mustache, because
the Frenchman, bored by the enthusiasm of a leading citizen talking
to him, had let his gaze rove and seeing Danny, had smiled at him
and blinked.

A motor ripped alive.

They craned to see. Down the line of ships a propeller was whirling
like a current of the silvery heat waves over the mesa.

Then another ship began, and another, until all twelve motors
burred together. The pilots put on their glasses and helmets. With
terrible unconcern they climbed into their ships. The ships were small
and frail-looking. Until they moved, they seemed made of sticks of
wood, and braidings of thread, and varnished cloth; machinery of
metal and rubber and flying scatter of oil; they seemed unlikely con-
structions for hazard or the mild emptiness of air. But when they
moved, one at a time forward into the taxi run, lifting their tails and
going from clatter to sing in the motors, and spinning across the
ground touching, touching, losing, rising, free! and lofting on a long
curve into the waving curtains of heat against the sky, they became
things of that element and not machines. They became part of sky-
life, as the animals of the mesa were part of its hot and dusty element of earth.

The planes were gone and tiny and silent far out toward the mountains. Then they wheeled and came back and their first sounding
again on the ear was a burr of noise. It was like rattlesnakes in the
sky, the long drone of menace that was so native to this place. The
drone deepened and its beads of sound heavied. The ships came over
and one after another dived up and looped and curved out again
straight. They climbed and were lost in the silver heat and then they
fell straight to the earth in a shriek of wind and power, and the
people could see the little black head that was the pilot leaning out
to look and their hearts came into their mouths for what they remembered of him in his uniform and for what any boy in uniform
was to them in their own terms, and for an instant they knew they

would die as he would die, crushed on the hot ground; but his motor screamed into a new pitch and the ship curved out in a long line that took him above the ground again, and again as he faded into the sky before his next stunt he sounded like a rattler strangely proper to the sky and to the heat and dust below.

The young Frenchman flew so close that they could see his face, laughing. He bowed amusingly to the people and then in a rapid spiral climbed and poised aloft a moment, as if to give them time to get ready for his trick. He then began to drift down crazily, the falling leaf, and as he dropped he let off a smoke bomb that printed his erratic wake on the sky in long white puffs. Some women began to scream. The crowd tightened. Immediately over the hangar the Frenchman righted himself and came out of it and flew by again, ironically bowing to the applause he could not hear but took for granted. They breathed easily again and turned to watch a sham battle between two Canadian and two British planes, which were weaving about one another in a shrieking droning pattern, tangled and over and over looking as if collision were about to happen.

Now and then planes came down to land.

The pilots would have a drink of ice-cold lemonade which was being sold by a couple of boys at their own stand erected for the purpose. They would drink and smoke a cigarette and wave their hands and be off again.

The show went on all afternoon. Cars kept coming out from town.

If so lightly these fliers used their lives, the people felt, who could say the war was not noble and fine!

In almost an agony of desire, Danny and all the other boys of the crowd stared at the sky where the flying snakes purred and swooped and struck in long lines of movement.

LIII · BROTHER TRAINOR

Neither could say at once what quivered just below the words they spoke.

The hotel room was dimly sultry. Its one window looked out across an inner yard, enclosed by two-story buildings, where iron fire-escape platforms and ladders scratched the sunlight into spider-web patterns.

The walls were of dusty brick or faded boards, giving back only heat, and no light. There lived cats and centipedes, and there lounged the workers of a laundry around the corner. The laundry gave out steam into the air and curious musical sighs from exhaust pipes, and remote clanging of machinery.

"But the boy'll b'happy. We needn't talk all day about him," said Brother Trainor. He was easing himself in the chair that creaked under him. He had his thumbs tucked into his suspender straps and his head on one side, smiling like a homely but trustworthy country lawyer with kindness making him a famous eye. Irma sat on the edge of the bed properly with her feet together and her hands folded in her lap. In the hot shadowy light she seemed strangely cool, her colors of black and white showing with a luminous purity in the close air.

"I've announced your program for tomorrow, already, so let's talk about *you*," declared the visitor. He leaned forward. Some big joint somewhere in him creaked.

"—I surely am grateful."

He chuckled.

"Reckon you could stop bein' so shy?"

She looked startled and sharp.

"Shy? Land, mister, if you'd been through what I been through ' nothing that could surprise you, or make you shy, one."

She challenged him with her look and a new hardness in her tone. It kindled him. He was delighted. He dropped his big head down between his shoulders and rubbed his fingers across his thick hair in a humorous kind of inner debate, some postponement, for enjoyment, of the thing that was coming. He murmured lovingly to himself. Then he looked up with a grin of shrewdness, and turned his head so only his real eye showed.

"Tryin' t'tell me you know life, eh?"

"Well:"

"Tryin' ' show me old man Trainor can't show *you* a thing or two, Miss Irma? Daggone if I don't believe she's got somethin' t'tell old Lancey Trainor that he'd sure admire t'hear! —Hyuck! Hyuck!"

She stood up against his wheedling laughter.

He stood up and looked down on her and enfolded her in the atmosphere he was exuding. He had a little movement of sound in his throat, a fraction of voice, and it rose and fell with his breath. He was in excited want, and though he sustained the masquerade of the genial benefactor and the trustworthy deacon, his hands were trembling, hugely, as he put them toward her, and his eye shone with a red energy that was like a chink of fire in a furnace seen through a firedoor. She felt all this as much as saw it. He stepped toward her and had his hands around her upper arms and he lifted her off the floor a little and set her down. She raged with a blinding strike in her nerves and it made her too weak to stand. She fell back to the bed and held to the ornamental brass of the foot of it.

"Looka here, Irma, honey," he said softly. He bent over her. There was something both frightening and pathetic in the rawboned burlesque of tenderness he made, as if, wanting to be exquisite and persuasive, his fumbling hands and clumsy frame and engine-like thighs must render him foolish and menacing instead.

"Brother Trainor, you get out of here, and leave me alone. —Sending my little Dan off!"

He sat down and ground his hands together as if to capture his desire and strangle it.

"*Sure,* I sent him off. —I tell *you,* I haven't slep' since that time you came down to the tent! I tell you, it's *bad!* Looka here, honey? I'm just old Lancey Trainor, and I ain't got much for looks, or I ain't got one of them dancin'-school pretty-ways to make over you with, and I'm just a big clumsy old ox of an overgrown kid doin' what I can for the Lord's work, and I know I'm human, and I know I'm a sinner, and I know I'll suffer the damned terrors for that I *lift* up my eyes not to Him, but to the lusts of the flesh, I know all that. I just cain't he'p it! —Irma honey, ain't you goin' to call me Lancey, and let me go to heaven with you?"

There stood tears in her eyes now.

He felt his mouth dry up and the tongue itch in his throat from dryness. Behind his plaintive speech there raged devices and designs, and ways of carrying them out; his hands trembled in his mind at what they wanted and would do; he saw her changed; he saw her naked; he welcomed the sign of emotion in her eye and schemed to take her grief and fright and change them into passion. He had done it before; he could do it again. He reached burning in his blood and when he touched her all his arch tendernesses vanished, and he threw into play the long bones and farmer's sinews that made him, and stormed her with kisses. She suddenly lay still and empty.

He kissed her with his eye shut and missing the response of her rage, he arose and looked. She was whiter than ever, and he thought she had fainted. But he saw that she was awake, and that her signs were those of illness.

She was in such a panic of physical revulsion that it made her sick.

In a curious sort of politeness she seemed to be looking at him with apology, some modesty that now took the place of her fright, and changed his feeling entirely. It was a long moment before he could speak. But she spoke first.

"Brother Trainor, you better go. —I feel like you should have known better ' come here and act like that. —I can't help it, you never even asked, I never gave you any encouragement!"

He stood away from the bed. He felt cold down his back. If she had continued to fight against him, or if she had yielded to him with enthusiasm, in either case he would have taken her. She had rebuffed him not with her mind, but with the sickening of her body. He disgusted her. He offended her. He recoiled in his thought from knowing himself so distasteful. Then he wanted to be even more distasteful. He fingered his face. His fingers strayed to his withered eye. He gulped and felt some tingle spread through his nerves, as if some poison were being released through him.

"Yah!" he said softly and thickly. "Not good enough for you! I make you sick and you sweat and turn pale and have to bite your teeth t'keep your stomach down, do you! My fault this eye o'mine ' gone? My fault ' clumsy old overgrown boy from Texas without chance in ' world t'make anything of himself? My fault you come along and swagger round struttin' and flumpin' and drivin' a man might-nigh crazy ' your fancy pretty ways?"

He was acting his self-pity now as he had acted before the winsome fellow. He saw himself as what he said, an overgrown boy, though he was too old to meet the draft age-limits. His hair was shot with gray. Yet he now actually did resemble a rueful and stupid child gathering temper for another display of bad judgment after it has once been rebuffed.

"I know I'm not handsome and fine and got my eye put out fightin' wharf-rats ' waterside of Galveston, and like that! Just ' same, ' human, ain't I? Got feelin's, ain't I? —Lord, for that the vanity of *this* Thy servant shall make him to *see* the light!"

He stood panting. His eye now looked religious, and it managed to bring a sense of shame up in Irma. She stood up. She thought of the tent, and tomorrow.

"—I don't know how you'll think of it now," she said. "I believe we ought to kneel down and pray and purify our hearts, and go the better on the Lord's errand. I believe we'd do our work tomorrow all the better."

Her innocence silenced him for a moment while he worked over her with his look. She didn't bear him no grudge. She behaved as if nothing had happened. She was still countin' on handlin' that revival tomorrow, just as if nothin' had happened. 'Sif he weren't put out and furious. 'Sif she hadn't a-made a fool of him. Why, any self-respectin' Christian girl after what she'd done woulda *died* before she'd have the nerve to think he'd let her go on with the revival after that. . . .

"Brother?"

She was appealing to him, yet she didn't seem to know it yet. He felt his blood begin to pound again and he knew the hope rising in his breast like a lump. Perhaps he had tried the wrong way, he thought. He could see how eager she was to go on with tomorrow's meeting. He could see that it was more than the collection she wanted. It was as emotional a need for her as what made him crafty now, and led him to say, "Glory, glory!" and seize her by the hand and turn her away from him toward the bed and kneel down, dragging her to her knees there in the middle of the room facing away from him and a little in front of him.

"Oh, glory," he sighed. His voice began to sound with the hooting tone that worship always brought alive in his throat. Yet he prayed softly. He saw Irma lift her head from time to time in saying "Amen!" and he bitterly knew she was congratulating herself on a good work in turning him from lust back into the path of virtue. At such reflection, his voice trembled, for he admitted that the path was intended to lead him back to his original goal. He prayed with passion, then; curiously, something in his voice made Irma recall the attitude he used toward Miss Mollie, the piano-player, and in an intuition, she knew how it stood between Brother Trainor and that other girl. She marveled at his headlong foolishness, for she had already seen in his posturings on the revival platform, how the largest thing in his life was satisfaction of his vanity, the solace of his person by the humorous pleasure people had of him in public, this repayment for his awkwardness and his eyelessness, this canon which at all costs had to be preserved. She thought again of his being an overgrown kid, and the whining self-love in his voice when he called himself that; and she knew again by intuition that he was the bullying sort of kid who would try to break that which he wanted and was denied, especially if there were anyone to watch his brave show.

"—yes, Lord. Thy sinner. Glory."

"Amen."

They stood up.

He challenged her with his eye, and slowly began to grin, without humor, but with calculation and foretaste.

"If tomorrow is a great success, we'll see," he said, making it

cryptic and significant by putting his jaw forward and nodding.
"—Ain't I the limit? Lettin' you come-along-and-do just 'sif nothing
had happened?"

"Well?"

"Well, eh: ' think I act s'kind to everybody who treats me mean?
—You sho treat me mean, honey:"

But he was not trying for tenderness. His quiet hard voice was
predicting. He had a picture of next time all finished in his mind.

"Then I'll see you tomorrow, Brother."

"Lancey:"

"Oh, all *right, Lancey,* tomorrow then at some before three? —I
made arrangements to be off work here at the hotel for tomorrow
afternoon and evening."

"Hot dog, tomorrow evenin'!"

He shook himself grotesquely, shambling his big frame like a big
horse. Then he turned to go. He hated to do it. She held the door
open. He knew now what it was: she was stronger than he was. She
had licked him, by God. He flushed and wiped a stinging away from
his eye. He nodded at her as if with a promise he would keep, perhaps to her displeasure or pain. She lifted her head higher and knew
herself in the right, whatever he meant by all his nonsense. All this
was exchanged in feelings and attitudes. They understood each other
perfectly. What their words said was,

"Well, then good-by, Sister," in a hearty tone so it could be heard
down the hallway and sound disarming and Christian.

"Good-by, Brother Trainor, everything will be fine."

"Yes, that's the way we'll handle it, then. —Hope the little ol' boy '
havin' good time watchin' airoplanes!"

He chuckled. She laughed.

When he reached the lobby, he was combed by the most sceptical
look the proprietress could release from her moist fat eyes. Something in the way he walked told her what she thought she knew. She
ticked her tongue with private disgust at such behavior. She made
her living out of what went on in her hotel rooms. She never ceased
to feel superior and virtuous by contrast, since fifteen years ago she
had quit the life of a prostitute.

It was late afternoon when Danny came back.

The planes had been down from the sky for a long time, but he had waited to see them cleaned, and the motors tested again, and the oil and gas checked, and the soldiers put on guard over them as a dramatic gesture toward possible and unlikely sabotage. He had seen the young officers get out of their ships and at once be swamped by crowds of people, young women and girls, thrilled and eager and ready to entertain them. The Liberty Bond sale went on at the table set up near the hangar. People came and subscribed. The young aviators signed their autographs for boys and girls who asked them. The crowd refused to go while the fliers were still there.

"Boy, haddi, ' hate to be up in one of them things and have a wing come off?"

"Sure can *fly,* can't they!"

"Boy, *I* say so!"

"Must be a great life!"

"How you mean?"

"Oh, fly around ' country and put on ' show and get to see everything and so forth."

"Risk your neck thataway day in-day out? No sir, not me, thank you!"

"Shucks, ain't no risk. . . ."

"No? You just *think* there isn't!"

"Yes, well it's still worth it."

"Huh?"

"Yeh, look there, all 'em girls and wimmin crowdin' up close and how-do-you-doin' and just waitin' for 'em, hot dog!"

"Yow! plenty fun ' all 'ose girls!"

"Shucks, you got to be aviator, and go flyin' round and wearin' uniform and talkin' Frinch, make a hit with girls like 'at. Boy, bet they get plenty drunk tonight, and have plenty fun!"

The fliers were moving to parked cars that waited by the hangar. They were chatting with the young girls of the town, young laughter and cheer.

Danny had heard the crowd talking.

He was sore and somber from the nervous thrills of the afternoon; and he saw the fliers as heroes, not as cheerful young bucks who when their ships were down safely, liked to go off with girls and get drunk. He resented the easy opinion of the idle talkers. He hated the girls for claiming the heroes so simply. He couldn't imagine the fliers drunk. He walked home in the fall of afternoon vaguely depressed and tired out by the perceptions of the day, which included a non-childish hint of beauty and courage somehow inescapably bound together with meaner realities; flight in the sky, and return to the earth, the living of the flesh, in which the soul dwelled.

When he climbed the stairs to room 27, and opened the door, Irma turned from the dresser where she was getting ready to go downstairs to work in the café, and at sight of him, she was overwhelmed with such relief and feelings of safety for them both, that she went down on her knees and held out her arms to him and rocked him in a tight embrace. He said,

"What is it, Mum! I'm all right, Mumma. Don't sound like that!"

"Ssh! honey!"

She couldn't speak. She would never tell him. He wouldn't really understand. But to hold him so purely and believe in this flesh of goodness and proof of life helped her forget the afternoon, and its menace, and the whole time of struggle that seemed to stretch back into the years through which she had never been able to afford giving up for a moment to despair or wrath.

LV · THE POSTERS ON SUNDAY AFTERNOON

Over the small city the scented heat of summer afternoon drifted on the idle wind. It carried little wafts of scent from the immense crowned cottonwoods that grew up and down the outlying streets, and along the river beyond town. The town lay between river and desert beyond which were mountains. It was, thus, full of strange clear lights and high airs that now and then dropped cooler on the Sunday-afternoon pavements and then again pressed hot and sweet into the breath and made sleep remembered, forgetfulness, the idleness of rest and dreaming.

Seeming to be in a murmuring daze, the whole city partook of Sunday afternoon for pleasure and quiet.

The streets sweltered and hissed under the tires of the cars that went by, people idly "out riding."

The store windows were black with reflection and, in spots, white with the depths of the sky and the quiet of the day. The most exciting things in view were on each corner, the recruiting posters for the army, the navy, and the marine corps. Little boys loitered near them sometimes, feeling their wills stiffen and strike out into a dreamy world of battle and triumph. The posters showed everyone's father and uncle, Uncle Sam, pointing his finger and saying "I want *you* for the United States Army!" They had battleships bashing through enemies' seas in a glory of smoke and prowess. There was a dying woman with a bloody breast holding her baby up to an American soldier and blessing him with her lithographic final smile as he leaned to take over the sacred charge, grinning like anybody's brother in the next block, an American genius for frank and funny young strength. There was a striding woman, heroic size, America's own national picture, walking over the ocean with a sailor in one arm and a soldier in the other, her robes flowing behind her and billowing, until she seemed like an angel of vengeance and beauty. There was a poster of a father marching away from his family; his little son was dressed in a newspaper cocked hat; their little dog had a toy rifle slung around his forequarters; the mother was in volunteer Red Cross worker's habit "—to the last one of us!"

But the town seemed oddly peaceful, riding by these challenging and pitiful shouts in paint and word. The great trees stirred and let their fragrance and released their little white wisps of pollen that flew on the strains of the wind, the hot wind off the sandhills over the river.

On Sunday afternoon there was a sleeping of the passions, as if there were no war. The morning papers had not said that any trooptrains would be going through that day. There would be no rushing mob at the station to see the boys.

Book IV • THE POWER

LVI · THE HEAT; THE DRUMS

Irma brought Danny to the tent beyond the Elks Club at a quarter of three in that afternoon. They walked, and were hot by the time they got there. The tent was already filling up. They went to the rear, where a canvased enclosure made a sort of dressing-room. In it, the heat was dry as if reflected off hot stones. The gold sunlight poured against the canvas walls and turned them apricot bronze. Miss Mollie and Brother Trainor were waiting inside. When Irma came in with Dan, they laughed, and rattled their folding chairs as they changed position suddenly, sitting side by side. Miss Mollie had on her blue hair ribbon again, and this she fetched up to smartness on top of her head. She was breathing warmly and she smiled into Irma's eyes with invitation of knowledge, woman to woman. Mr. Trainor winked his clear eye at Danny's, and the dead eye stayed appallingly open and mirthless.

"Well: 't's a hot one, all right, today is," he said. "You ready, Sister Milford? We're a-goin' to have a fine big meeting today, all for you:"

He estimated her, in her fine white dress, her thinned face so white and her black deep eyes, the blue-veined movement of her white hands. He thought her a fine woman; what else he thought seemed to burn like a crying want in his single eye. His voice quivered with desire under the Lord when he spoke to women.

"I'm ready. Whenever you say," said Irma. "My Dan is going to sing the opening piece, I expect you know it, to play it, Miss Mollie?"

She handed the pianist a sheet of music, entitled "Making the Grade for the Lord."

Miss Mollie nodded that she knew the piece, and hummed the first few bars with a lavish indifference.

The crowd in the tent sounded in the calm day like a flying quilt of bees coming as shade into some sunny meadow, and filling the air with soft drone of flight. A haze of white dust rose into the air of the tent as the people kicked, walked and shuffled. They steamed in the broiling heat which the orange-canvas top filtered down over them. Their faces were expectant and when the sweat ran, they peacefully wiped it away. Irma looked through the peephole across the platform at them.

They were almost all women.

She saw with a pang that women without men came to hear her speak, and she knew that the men were gone mostly because of the war; she felt in advance the wise words she could give them, the consolation, the sharing of the experience of lonesomeness, the lifting of these hearts with hers to God, because her heart would know what they suffered!

Presently Brother Trainor looked at the crowd and hawked with satisfaction in his throat.

"Better get moving, now, then," he said. He surveyed them all and nodded over each, and then led them out to the platform before the crowd which quickened and exuded want, desire, the empty vessels waiting to be filled. As he walked to view, Brother Trainor lifted his voice and it blew hollow and ringing like the puff across a bottle top again, and he said, sustaining it like a cry,

"Oyo, oyo, my friends, praise the Lord, praise, praise, praise-ee! Glory, glory *be!*", and laughing, too, like an actor of tremendous charm, who quaffs the personalities before him to get inspiration, and who gives himself back in every little way of his living, his look, his eye, the voice, the turn of head, the simple pride of body, all without shame and almost pure so.

In the sunny stifle of the tent, the women rose to him, and gusts of pleasure rewarded him from the packed tent, where the little dust haze made false distances, and seemed like an image of heat.

"Oyo, glory, sisters! I know. I-i-i-i-i *know:* why there's s'few men folks here today!"

The women gasped to hear it again.

"Where ' men? —Fightin', that's where!"

"God bless them!" cried some one.

"What fo'? Fightin' fo' what:" he demanded, and savagely bored into them with his eye. "For you, and you, and you, and me, and our babies, and by God, for our very *lifes!*"

A woman hiccuped in a sob. He located her by the sound, and leaned toward her direction.

"Yes, ma'am! Oyo. Oh, we shall pray for your bleeding heart, sister, and it shall be made whole, and the Lord shall enter in and ye shall have the *stringth* as of ten? Praise!"

The sobbing woman made a soft sound appropriate to the hot drifting afternoon of Sunday.

Nodding promisingly, Brother Trainor turned to Irma and called her forward.

"Now, ye faithful, I give you our teacher for today, one who goes the lingth and bridth of this land of ours carrying the Word, and seeding the Field. Sister Irma Milford, the leading lady evangelist of the West!"

He stepped back and aside with a dancing figure, and thrust Irma forward to her people. She stood slim and with a kind of troubled insecurity about her body, but her face was keen with resolve; and she smiled, looking down intimately at the near faces, as mother to mother, and said in a gentle voice,

"Reckon we all like to see our babies do good for us and everybody:"

She looked farther back to the middle rows, and raised her voice:

"You c'd guess till Doomsday, and never find a greater glory to God than a little child who praises His name!"

She encompassed the rear rows, and cried out, her voice ringing level like the tone of a bell caught and held, the old sound she hadn't heard herself make for so long that now it made her eyes hot with gratitude.

"Amen! if we listen to the heart of a child, we shall be humble in the sight of the Lord! and pleasing unto Him! —My baby boy is going to sing for us, and let us hear him, and know the inno*cence* of the pure in heart! —Danny!" she called, turning to him. He came from his slatted chair and with an actor's routine of long familiarity, he paused and looked up at her with eloquent appeal.

"Mumma, what shall I sing:"

"Your favorite hymn, son."

The women stirred and murmured at this public sweetness.

"I'll make the grade for the Lord, Mumma."

"—And so must we all," said Irma, turning suddenly to the crowd, and nodding.

Then she retired to her chair and Danny went to the piano where Miss Mollie sat waiting for him. Her enormous childish eyes were brooding openly on him, and she made womanly gestures to remind him of her, as he stood by her. Then she began to play, exaggerating her quality of small girlhood, in personality and gesture over the keys.

Danny faced the people and smiled shyly and then caught his first note with a little surprise, as if it came sooner than he had wanted. He patted his hands together and kept them so, and with an expressionless face and gravely open-eyed, he sang in a piercing but musical voice, "Making the Grade for the Lord."

He seemed like a small boy and at the same time like a little man. He was handsome. His black hair fell in a soft wave across his brow, and his blue eyes were large and liquid with the pathos of reverence as he heard himself sing. Irma had dressed him in his blue serge suit and his big white Buster Brown collar. His sturdy legs had socks and his shoes were large and shiny black. The women could see him as a son; and they could know him ahead of his time as a man and a lover. He had assurance without knowledge, and power so long as he stood doing the tricks of eloquence his travels with Irma had taught him. With these, he had boyish betrayals, sudden failures in poise, a scratch at his thigh, a wave at a fly around his head, a brief glance at Irma to see how he was doing; which endeared him the more to the listening mothers before him.

He felt the pull of his voice and personality at them; he was sorry to be done when he sang the last words; he had paid the words no heed, singing them merely as sounds. He had sung the whole song without variation in tone or expression. But something of him made it effective. When he was done, the women clapped. Miss Mollie pretended to be a little girl and looked at him like a hectic woman. He stared back at her without understanding and went back to his chair, but something held his eyes on Miss Mollie, at her piano, and her confusion between girl and adult struck him with its blend, and he began to blush while the hot afternoon tasted dusty in his nose, and secrecies of all kinds, from all his trivial little times as far back as he could remember, returned and increased his blushing torture that was so sweet at the same time, like a cut that hurts and itches and wants soothing and more hurting all at once. He almost lay in his chair with his head down and watching Miss Mollie, seeing her intensely, and grasping with his eye the round fall of her breast against her dress, a detail which he could see under her arm as she sat in front of him, half-facing away from him. —Suddenly he snapped his look away, and touched his face, as if the rise and fall of his thoughts were visible there, lustful and bewildered. He straightened up and tried to look saintly. He stole a look back at Miss Mollie. She was the same. But now in this redeemed second's time, he was changed, and he viewed her with indifference that held a little longing for that other feeling he had had and that was gone away.

Irma was down at the front of the platform now.

She was holding her Bible. She seemed to be getting acquainted with the throng by looking at them, and letting them see her.

He listened hazily to the sounds beyond the tent. One arrested him. It beat like an echo. It was a distant chord of drums, sounding in some street, echoing over the heated roofs, and it beat for the march, somewhere soldiers were marching. He moved elaborately off his chair and tiptoed down to the canvas room back of the platform and found his hat. He heard Irma begin to speak inside. Her voice rose like the happy sure voice he had known before, and not lately. Feeling that she was swinging into her sermon, and that he wouldn't be missed, he ducked out into the pressing sunlight and stood for a second, listening motionless so that even his own movements, the rub of cloth, the let of breath, would not veil what he wanted to hear; and now he caught it faintly, that beat, "B-r-r-rt, b-r-r-rt, b-r-t: b-r-t: b-r-t," and he began to run toward the drum's direction.

LVII · THE SILENCE

The canvas of the tent was pale hot gold with filtered sunlight. When they would close their eyes to pray and hear themselves in their hearts, the people in the tent saw bright red quivering waves go across their sight beneath their lids. They heard Irma's steady bell voice sing out over them and preach the lesson.

From the rear of the tent she looked large and pale, and her black eyes were like coals in her white face. Her being a woman was exciting to the audience, which was mostly women. They were used to men leading them in godly ways with trumpeting voices. But each could now see herself, and love the idea, that she too might arise and sway multitudes.

All they heard at first was the sound of Irma's voice; the words were so familiar that they heeded nothing but the slow beginning of their own blurting emotion; and they rocked on their chairs and called back to her with the devotional echoes of release which she was trying to bring out of them.

Brother Trainor sat in the hot shadow of the upstage tent wall and cocked his knee, watching Irma with a public smile of benediction, in which his blind eye figured like a whispered curse. He watched her as she worked, and saw the fine striving of her body in the conviction she tried to share. The afternoon was ripe for passion, of any kind; he was full of it, lechery and piety together, the one inspiriting him with an aching fury, the other filling him with bland authority which would turn his lust into command if he had a woman of his following. Miss Mollie was half asleep bolt upright by the piano; divided between petulance and excitement left from Brother Trainor's embraces before the meeting.

The listening women were hot and grieving toward God; there was so much for them to moan over, and thank God for! They would have been frightened if they'd realized how fast their feelings were rising, on this still Sunday afternoon, under the tented sunlight in the vacant lot behind the Elks Club.

"Who taught us how to live, then! Why, Jesus!"

"Oh yes!" murmured the women.

"Oyo," said Brother Trainor calmly, tipping back into the hot shadow in his folding chair.

"He gave unto His children the commandments by which they shalt live!"

"A-men."

"Now I'm ' poor woman."

"Praise His name!"

"I got nothing in my life *but* my life."

"Oyo."

"What ' going ' do with it?"

"Praise. . . ."

"Going ' live ' best life that I know how to!"

"Yes, Lord."

"Going ' let everybody else live! Going t' take care of my baby, and love you and you, and everybody and my neighbor, and let everybody else live!"

"Lord?"

"Try my best and save my own soul, if they let me! —You *say,* if *who* let you: ain't nobody going ' bother you ' living ' life according to Christ Jesus! —Oh-h-h-h-h, yes! What ' they doing right now? Killing and maiming and blowing everybody up and babies dying 'cause they ain't got milk, and boys dying 'cause they poisoned with gunpowder and men dying 'cause the whole world forget *'Thou shalt not kill'!*"

There was a sudden dusty silence.

No one echoed her feeling with a happy moan.

Her voice came flat against the tent roof and died out. It was so still that Irma as she caught her breath and streaked her hand across her sweating brow made a sound that everybody could hear. She swallowed in her dry throat. She was shaking and tears danced in her eyes.

"Suppose He didn't mean it when he gave unto Moses the tablets, and writ with a fiery finger, 'Thou shalt not kill'?"

She leaned out to them and nodded, wringing her fingers. The faces below her were lost to her in the gold dusty silence and the haze that stirring feet on the vacant lot floor had made to come up in the air.

"Well, He did mean it! —Why did He mean it? *So your baby boy and my baby boy, and our husbands, and our brothers and our cousins and our uncles and our boy friends and our lovers and our sweethearts and our downtown clerks and our farmer boys and our milkman and our preacher and our doctor and our fathers wouldn't take out and kill and get killt!*"

Brother Trainor narrowed his expert eye at the crowd and leaned a little forward. He was admiring Irma's passionate performance for itself, and it stirred him by the physical fervor she had, and the means she took of crying home her message . . . the swing of her arms, the stanching of her legs in her pose, the toss of her black-crowned head. She was sweating and he saw it and it made him tingle to think of. But he saw too what the women were thinking.

"Then it's wrong and it's got to stop and no matter who on earth says it is right, Our Lord and Saviour Christ Jesus the Nazarene says it's wrong in this book of His, and we must save our hearts by it!"

She whirled and picked up the Bible that lay on the preaching-stand and held it high in a pose of triumph.

"We must pray for peace! We must stop helping the war! We can't help murder!"

"*Say!*" said some one hotly in the rear of the tent.

It was a shrill and catlike sound, the first busting of opinion.

It released the women and they felt their notions slide into feeling.

Irma saw this change coming. She put down the Bible and fell to her knees. She put out her arms and began to pray. She was beautiful and in their eyes she seemed to undergo sacrifice for them, and Brother Trainor came down and knelt behind her flutily echoing her prayer in his blown quaver. She began to pray softly, and the near women saw that her face was streaming with tears from her closed eyes. Their hearts softened a little as they looked at her. But those farther back couldn't see this; and as she prayed that the nations might cease warring and America might save her sons, and that all here today might cleave unto God by not only desiring but acting for peace, they heard themselves menaced by this stranger in white; and their fastest beliefs challenged; and they hardened in their hearts again as they so often had in the past months when the war came home and touched them with death, terror, privation, pressure, even exaltation in knowing the country alive and at work as one being of which they were so passionately parts. . . .

She prayed really to herself.

They listened.

Brother Trainor put out his hand to touch her in warning, for he saw the temper gleaming like sweat over the faces of the women in the dusty sun shadow.

But he withdrew his hand thinking that she wouldn't know what he meant; and putting away the voluptuous chance, ready to mourn what might have been, he went inscrutably back to his chair upstage knowing before the crowd knew it the folly drifting alive among their challenged wills. He shook his head tenderly over Irma. Her face was now buried in her hands and her prayer went sobbing through them into the flat echoless tent. He could almost hear the impact it made against the anger of the women out there. Their laws were being scolded. He felt the emotion gather over them like a cloud. It fetched his risabilities, and again he thought of taking Irma away, touching her, and making her stop, but the public difficulty of explaining; and the importance of keeping the goodwill of the crowd for himself, in spite of his private hope toward Irma, kept him in his chair. He began to frown, and a lift like happiness or new youth occurred in his breast; he couldn't have said it, but the blood likeness between cruelty and love excited him. She had refused him yesterday.

How many other afternoons had she sobbed in prayer, and the people had cried with her, pure like little children, bleating in ravished happiness like the lambs in the greenest of fields? Now there was silence facing her. But not for long.

LVIII · THE LOVER; THE BELOVED

He ran part of the way and part of the way he tiptoed, so that he might hear better; and at last the drums sounded more loudly, and he turned a corner over on the north side of town to see them at last, a band of boys marching in the dust out toward the end of the unpaved street which ran right into open country, with no more road, or houses, or trees, or fences, but only the sandy green and brown of the mesa in a great plain that went far away to the misty blue mountains.

"Boys!" he thought in disgust, and he had seen soldiers marching in his mind, on hearing the drums. He had followed them by ear for half an hour, turning and skipping from block to block. The boys were in Boy Scout uniform, and their commander was a fat youth who marched majestically by the side of the ranks, his great flesh jellying at breast and rump and leg as he walked. He had little features embedded and twinkling in the great sphere of his head. He was scowling with martial fury and counting step in a piping voice full of intention if not effect. Danny ran until he was a few paces behind the troop, in which there were about twenty boys, and eight drums. Then he idled on the sidewalk watching them, feeling shy and tired now that his quest was ended. The drums still spoke, "B-r-r-t, b-r-r-t, b-r-t, b-r-t, b-r-t!" and now he could hear the buzzing twang of the snare strings under the drums, and the beat of the sticks seemed a little foolish, prosaic; no more, as in the echo over the streets where he had blindly followed them, a call to the blood and a trial of ambition.

At the end of the street the troop halted and the fat boy cried, "Fall out!"

The last house in the street was a white board house by the edge of the plain, and through a white picket fence the leader took one or two of his followers, and waved the rest away. They seemed to expect this, as if it were routine, and idled themselves off in various directions; while the fat scout sat on the steps and watched them go, tired and finished for the day with the duties of war.

He took in Danny in his gaze, and pointed him out to the other scouts on the front steps beside him. But they passed over the stranger and relaxed with their casual thoughts and there was nothing more for Danny there at the street's end, where the drums had lured him with all the intensity of childhood's pre-visions, and where their silence now left him with a child's equally intense feeling of loss when the vision fails and shame for credulity takes its place.

He turned to go back toward the busier streets of town. One of the home-going scouts was rattling at his drum, and alone, without the unison of its mates, the drum was an irritating toy in the hands of a baby, instead of a thing with a soul, a voice and a will.

In a few blocks' scuffish walking, Danny's spirits revived, and he thought he might not yet go back to the tent where the meeting would last till nearly five; but instead drift downtown and see what the movies had. He hurried then and began anticipating again: the yellow-headed girl sitting in the glass booth to sell tickets, the slick-haired high-school boy at the curtained door to receive them, the black and perfumed cavern of the theater, with the whinnying organ music that made you droop half asleep while your eyes stayed awake and watched the large happenings on the screen . . . a world unreal enough never to be disappointing.

He fumbled in his pocket as he trotted, and found his coins, on which he closed his fist. He ran on the shady side of the street beneath the great hooding cottonwoods. The sunlight was everywhere. It made the buildings look clean, so bright was it. The houses seemed asleep. As he neared downtown he saw more traffic, cars cruising through the afternoon. Presently he was on Central Avenue, walking west, right into the light of the sun. It was about four o'clock, and the sun was beginning to show its fall, leveling off great clear beams on red brick and white, window and gold sign, gray pavement and black poles and wires, the sunward edges of everything living in a liquid splendor of golden fire. The contrast now between light and shadow was deep. In the shadows everything was clear and yet veiled in daylight dusk with blue atmosphere, matching the feeling of heat with something like its image in air.

The movie shows had their electric signs going in front, pale and beating with light in this great late afternoon flood of light from the sky.

Danny passed up the first theater because he had seen the picture weeks ago in La Gata; at the next one he deliberated, but the posters in front seemed to be full of kissing, and that always gave him a baffled and disgusted feeling, especially when he felt himself pricking with curious interest over it; and he finally moved on to the next theater to see what they had before deciding about the kissing picture. As he crossed the street, he looked down it, to see what the confusion was about on the next corner over where he saw a crowd. They were glistening in the long sunlight of the next street and they showed up because the block between was in dancing gray shadow. He could hear the stir of voices, and they seemed to move slowly but together, turning down there in front of the red sandstone building on the corner, a tall building with a red tower that looked bright and rusty in the light. It had windows with rounded tops and great heavy arches of red stone over each; the doorway downstairs was deeply recessed in the red stone, and lay back under a whole series of heavy arches supported on squat red sandstone columns at the top of a flight of steps. He didn't know what the building was, or why the people clustered around it so. He wanted to see. He went trotting toward the light and the movement, which in its stir seemed so strange on Sunday afternoon. As he ran he caught the drift of flaming color from an American flag that hung over the doorway of the building on the shady corner, but which a hot lift of wind had taken alive into the sunlight.

Were they singing?

Their voices were high and sustained, and he couldn't understand what they were making with words. They were almost all women.

He stopped running and stood teetering on the curbstone across the street from the red stone building, which was labeled City Hall, as he saw by the carving over the door.

He was in sunlight, but the crowd was moving around into the shadow before the shady corner in which the doorway was. The women's arms were brandishing. They weren't singing. It turned his heart over with a tug to see that they were shrieking with anger.

"All right now! All right now!" he heard. They called it over and over.

He craned his neck, to see; then a man leaped up to the shady stone steps and began reaching for the halyards of the flag that leaned out over the crowd on its polished oaken pole. He made monkey gestures of grabbing at the rope, and called out in a hollow tone some sound of fury. He caught the rope. The crowd moved in a wave up the sidewalk, a thrust of achievement, as if it were their fury that had captured the flag halyards and brought the flag in toward the building where trembling hands arose to touch it and catch it, and bring it down.

Danny stood white with wonder.

Then there was another thrust from the crowd and some women were spilled stumbling up to the top step. Voices quavered. They echoed in the otherwise quiet street. They sounded like——

Now he knew what they sounded like.

"Mom!" he screamed, and slipped from the curbing and fell cracking his knee with a sound like a stick smashing on the pavement.

The women sounded like souls saving themselves, the oh-yes and amen of the Lord, and he knew it was the same congregation. He scrambled to his feet and danced in terror to see. He ran to the other corner and mounted a low pile of loose paving concrete scraps raked and piled there in the gutter.

He saw the top step where they had stood her.

They closed around her and the steps were full. Brother Trainor was beside her. He was holding the flag and seemed to be tempting the crowd with its folds which now spilled together merely cloth in his hands, the stars lost to sight, the stripes mingled and mean.

"Oyo!" he blew, *"Shall* I? *Shall* I?"

The women hissed and shrilled.

Irma stood facing them. Her hands were held by women on each side of her. Her face was whiter than her dress. Her hair was hanging hot and wet down her cheeks, pasted there by sweat. The black fronds of hair traced the bony swell and sink of her face. She looked deathly. Her eyes were shut and tears ran bitterly indifferent to her open mouth and breast. Danny began to weep. He shrieked to tell her he was there; but he gagged on his own breath and couldn't make sound. He grabbed himself at the crotch dancing and almost incontinent. The hundred women called and inspired each other. They didn't see the boy behind them.

Brother Trainor shook out the flag, and its beautiful weathered colors struck the women's eyes like answer to prayer.

"Make her kiss it!" some one squealed.

"Put it on her! We'll show her!"

Brother Trainor played infant in arms to the great mothering vengeful crowd. He consulted them with his dry eye and his shining one, and pantomimed putting the flag around some one invisibly before him, and the crowd called with agonized delight, and he laughed, "Spa-a-a-ah!" like one who should spit from overflow of well-being; and then he pantomimed making his unseen partner kiss the flag; giving the crowd an exquisite rehearsal of the pain they wooed of their fellow woman and victim. The women shrieked that was it. Delicately attuned to them, Brother Trainor moved slowly, so that they might share every quivering approach and making of this cruel folly.

Danny saw him touch Irma with mock respect, his fingers spread and insincerely graceful. He touched her with menacing gentleness until she opened her eyes and raised her head to look at him with hollow dread. She worked her mouth without sound, and seemed to be imploring the little favor of permission to stand sightless and thus alone in this world of hatred. But Brother Trainor lifted the flag like a merchant of fabulous goods, and with a bow, began to dress it about her. The women rustled and trilled.

Irma let her head fall down and she tried to raise her hands to cover her face, but the women with her stopped it; but Brother Trainor with the finesse of an artist motioned them to release her, and she put her free hands over her face, one at her eyes and the other across her mouth. The gorgeous flag fell about her tall fine bones like a heroic gown, and she might have been a poster of Columbia weeping.

That she should be clothed in that as in shame bent her heart in grief.

Danny knew the meaning of what they were doing.

He began to talk aloud and push against the crowd.

"I can tell them," he cried, fighting against the women's waists and legs to get through to Irma. "She loves the flag, she always made me have respect for it. They can't make it like that, not with her, let me come, I am coming Mumma, damn you old fat woman, let me by, let me by!"

In his fury he was a minor commotion. The women at first thoughtlessly let him pass; then he was recognized, and then lifted up and thrust forward, while they screamed that here was the rest of it, the brood, the nit, and their lyrical hatred dwelled on him as Brother Trainor leaned down to receive him on the upper step beside Irma.

"Oh, fine," said Brother Trainor. "Now we got everybody."

He held his arm over the street crowd for silence, while he looked down at Danny in question.

"Now *you* can tell us, my fine boy, how come your mother been German spy?"

There was a shrieking roar at this new idea. Brother Trainor winked his wet eye at the women in thanks for the applause.

"She's not! —Mom," he cried, and turned to her, pulling at her hand to see her face. But she could not uncover, and the sound of his voice and his touch on her seemed the last ignominy she could have expected. Now she sobbed and they heard her. They laughed in conquest. She bent low and would have fallen to her knees in the grayed flag but they caught her up and Danny put his arms around her waist. He couldn't stop to think why they were doing this to her; only they were making her suffer and shaming her in public; and in his mouth he had the stifling want to kill them and he wanted to spit and vomit at them.

"Take your dirty old flag!" he screamed.

Again there was silence in the street. Then it trembled to break, and crash into fury when Brother Trainor released it by bashing his fist against Danny's cheek with stern zeal.

"See? *She* taught him that!" cried some one.

"Poor child! 'Tain't *his* fault!"

Brother Trainor caught this and concurred gravely; he reached across and struck Irma and the crowd sucked its breath.

"The flag! The flag!" they called.

"Lord God forgive us that she touch it!" droned Brother Trainor in his strong hooting voice. He leaned down and picked up a trailing fold of the flag and put his flattened hand on it in blessing, a sacrificial moment; then he brought it enticingly near Irma's hidden face, withdrew it as if he could hardly stand the kiss they were calling for to meet the old cloth with weather in it, and at last he shuddered theatrically and roughly forced the flag fold into Irma's grasp and stepped back to shrug and resign and succumb to sudden weakness and a grief too large to bear. He waved to the crowd to finish the work.

He used them like a lover; playing their desires alive in them, and then letting them discharge feelings.

They hissed and gathered together and forced against the steps. Danny tried to kick against them. They were almost to the top step when one woman turned around and cried,

"Stay back, stay down, you won't be able to *see* her if you come all up!" and the women fell back.

Irma opened her eyes and ruefully looked at the flag on her body. She touched it as if to make a secret touch of understanding with the flag and what it stood for to her, something which this mob could not know or believe; and when they screamed to her to kiss it, the flag they said she was a traitress to,

"Traitress! Spy!" they called, she took up a little space of the cloth modestly and brought it between her thumbs to her salty mouth to kiss it. Her lips touched it. The pity of the moment shocked everyone. The women gasped and then fought down their shame. They began with foul words for her. They yelled for another kiss on the flag.

Other people were collecting, drawn by the commotion. Among them was a tall thin man in a trainman's blue uniform. He heard them cry "traitress!" and his sallow face flushed. He bit at his small mustache and mist gathered from his eyes on his large glasses. The emotion sank into him at once.

Then some one found the concrete fragments piled like stones in the gutter across the street, standing in a heap with a wooden rail and a red lantern as guards.

The first stone-like missile flew. It struck the arch over the door, and Brother Trainor winced and ducked. He whitened, turned to admonish, but thought better of it, and with a sick smirk, hopped down from the steps, as if to join his followers at their play and see the fun. The other women on the top step went down too. The crowd backed. There was space now. But the paving hunks flew and struck, flat and now hollow-sounded, and again soundless, hitting the two bodies standing together. The woman and boy flinched into one another and were silent, unprotected outwardly, but within, blooded by something like courage, and dignity, some way of suffering a time that was insufferable.

They were hurt.

The trainman across the street stooped and then heaved, throwing a clod of concrete. It sailed heavily over the crowd and struck. He choked on his spit when he saw it strike Irma. His legs were loosening under him. He cried out, "There!" but no one heard him, not even himself.

There was blood on the flag now. Danny stared hotly and drily at the inhuman faces and hands that threw the stones. He hardly winced when the stones struck his shoulder, his neck, his crown, the knee that was already bleeding from the fall into the street five minutes ago.

And suddenly he was a little animal, with action and rage whipping him alive. There was room now before the steps, and he shook Irma, and cried to her to come with him. He began pulling at the flag. She stopped his hands, and unwound it, and held it before her on outstretched arms, with unconscious grandeur. They started down the steps, and the women fell back irresolutely, and when she wanted some one of them to take the flag, they would not, but hid their hands and dropped their stones. Danny took it then and folded it and flung it at them, over their tightly pressed bodies and their heads and shoulders together. It unfurled a little and draped them and the women it touched cuffed at it.

"Quick, mom," he whispered, and took Irma's hand.

He began to run with her stumbling after him.

The light was firing out in the sky now.

The street was dimming. Crowning the cottonwoods at the street corners where the west-lying ways let the long sunlight through, the falling sun made gold leafy domes against the white sky.

The afternoon was spent.

The women of the crowd saw the mother and son go in weary desperation down another block, and turn toward the railroad station five blocks away; a few cried out to follow; a few stones rose, and feebled along the walk when they fell; how long? they were trying to remember. When had this begun?

Irma and Danny turned the corner then, and were gone. They didn't see her fall, and Danny try to lift her, and at last help her to a vacant lot where a billboard stood, and lean her down in back of it to rest until after dark, when it would be cooler; it would be easier to find their way back to the railroad hotel in case anyone should still be on the prowl for them, a fainting woman and a boy in his last day of childhood.

LIX · AFTER DARK

They stayed there till dark was fallen, and still they were almost afraid to move. They lay in the lot behind the signboard that was set catty-corner by the sidewalk, and were silent. The dust of the ground smelled close and hot in their breathing. They smelled the wry sweetness of the weeds so close to the ground. As their feelings abated they searched their thoughts and were puzzled. What was it that fetched people against each other in hatred and wild cruelty? That they should stand and throw stones; scream treason and foul the flag with hatred; put up flesh and blood in the public square to be tortured. . . . Irma and Dan had lived this, and could not say why.

About eight o'clock they stirred.

The streets were dark but for the corner lamps and the cars cruising around in Sunday-evening aimlessness.

"We might go, Mom."

"We might go."

"Can you go?"

"—I don't know. —I can go."

She sounded so weak and helpless that he leaned over her and tried to see her face. But in the darkness he could not, and instead he patted her arm.

"Where do we go?" she asked.

He was too busy in thought to hear the bitterness of this.

"Why, back to the hotel, don't we, Mom?"

"—Perhaps *she* don't know, there, at the hotel."

"Know what:"

"Today."

"Oh, Mom: that isn't going to —Will they keep on doing it?"

"We have to go away. It isn't safe, here, Danny."

She sounded scared. This scared him. He began tugging at her sore arms.

"Gee, then come on, Mom. We got to go."

They heard walkers coming down the sidewalk. Standing dizzily, they held each other quiet until the footsteps had died down the street, and then they came slowly but with instinctive bravado out from behind the signboard like cats disguising their errand with assumptive simplicity.

They went toward First Street where the railroad hotel was. They had to stop and rest now and then. Under a street light they saw each other's blood, and dust; heartened by what must be done for the other, they went on their way. At First Street there was more traffic; and they waited in shadow until the street was empty for a moment; then they crossed and went into the hotel. In the brown and green lobby, the light was dim, and no one was behind the desk. They hastened across the floor to the stairs and began to go up.

In the hall near their room they met the proprietress. She peered and blew her fat-constricted breath in surprise; and reached up to the light cord which she pulled, bringing the filament of the globe up to its remotely singing high. They stood revealed.

"Land alive! What was it!"

"—A car wreck," said Irma. "We were riding out with friends. —We're all right, just need a little cleaning up."

"I should just think so! —Mebbe I should call a doctor!"

"Say, no, really!" cried Danny.

"No," said Irma. "—We're leaving tonight, if you have my bill now, I will pay it. —We have to go to California. Yes, we have to go back to California, don't we Danny?"

The tears suddenly stood in her eyes, and she seemed to feel happier, as if the starting-point of any quest must always be its end.

The landlady assumed a magnificent detachment from the matter of money and smiled down her face with her eyes closed and her lower teeth biting gently at her upper lip and mustache. She encircled her huge bosom with her fat little arms and sighed.

"I suppose I can have a statement for you," she said, and went off downstairs creaking the wooden steps with her great heaviness.

Once inside their room, Irma and Dan felt the aftertide of excitement and peril.

"Really, Mumma? Are we going back to California?"

"See what time the train is tonight," she said. She lay down on the bed and said to herself that she must not go to sleep. To stay awake meant holding on to her thought, the salvation and the escape. Who knew what would happen to that if she ever again fell asleep, and lost the world?

Dan washed his face and brushed the dust from his hair. He found a cut in his head which had dried with blood and hair. It brought back the whole day, and the need for secrecy and flight.

He turned to Irma and said he was ready. She got her puse from under the pillow where she had left it, and took out some money, concealing from him how little there was left beyond that.

"Get my ticket . . . to Los Angeles. And tell them you're half-fare, and get your own. And find out what time the train goes . . . the next train west. I'll b'ready."

She fell back. He stood irresolute.

"Are you all right, Mom?"

She waved him yes, and to go on.

"All right: —I'll be right back!"

He went down.

A few moments later he was on the station platform, running. He had all the emotions of the harassed, frantically sober, more so than if he had understood fully what sort of temper they had been up against in the afternoon. He was now afraid to be seen buying tickets, for fear some one might stop him and have at him again. The ticket agent was sour and gray in the face, like a man who detests the food that keeps him alive; and must yet have it. Dyspeptically, he examined Danny to see if he were half-fare age, and admitted it. He asked if they would take Pullman; he admitted there was a day-coach on the train that left at ten-fifteen. He made change with petulant fingering of the coins and bills, and handing it back to Danny, squinted at him with meaningless but terrible concern. Danny felt the look as a threat, and grabbed his tickets and money and marched out ready to be arrested yet daring 'em.

There was a light summer wind playing down the tracks.

The train stood already pointing west.

There was no engine on her yet, but the cars were lighted and a few men stood in working-clothes to help her off. It was early. It was a little past nine. He went back to help Irma pack in the hotel.

The concept of duty made him feel staunch. He began to think hotly, "I would come back and kill them all, I'd show them, they would be sorry for what they did," and in this mood of vengeance he burst in upon his mother and told her of it, thrusting the tickets and money on her bedside, and trumpeting bravely how he would reclaim her suffering by avenging it. He shouted and stamped. She took him sorely to her breast and hushed him, letting him squirm and finally turn quiet as the exhaustion which burned in him like a dying coal lost its red energy and turned to hot ash that ached in his blood.

Presently she asked what time the train was going, and he told her ten-fifteen. They arose to get ready.

LX · THE BROKEN NIGHT

It was hot in the train, and lifeless until the engine was coupled and sent the pulse of its power back through pipes and the quiver of air.

They had found their seats in the rear end of the car, and put their luggage under them, and sat down. Irma was by the window with the shade pulled down. It glistened with a thin diamond dust of smoke-grit. The lights in the domed ceiling of the car were quivering and bright, and they were reflected by the custard-yellow paint in steady strain. Under such lights sleep would be at first impossible, then sudden and hypnotic.

Danny sat on the aisle chair and clutched the printed envelope holding the tickets. He was staring down the car for the enemy. He would not be happy until the train moved. Every time there was a call outside, he relaxed thinking it was departure. But when they didn't move, he jerked stiff again and aching. His round face was white, his dark eyes staring blue and fixed at the end door of the car. The faces of the afternoon crowd were in his memory. He knew them all. He hated them all. They had hurt him. Why?

"Mom, why did they do it, what started it?" he asked softly. She didn't answer. He turned to look, and saw that she was dozing with her head against the window. She had bandaged her head with torn rags in the hotel room before they'd left, and she had her hand over her mouth as she sometimes used to have it in laughing. Even through this familiar pose she was looking unlike herself and strange. The bones stood clear under her skin making it shine hotly.

He let her rest.

A brakeman walked through the car from the forward end. His lantern was lighted. He wore thick cloth gloves that made his hands look like a scarecrow's. Danny half-handed over the tickets; but this was not the conductor. He grinned and blushed and settled again into his fever of watchfulness.

The car was filling with passengers.

The air warmed up as they entered.

The only ones that Danny saw with any memory were the ones who came and sat across the aisle. It was a family of Mexicans, a fat father, a little thin mother, and a girl about fifteen, two boys younger than that, another girl, and a small baby in arm. They heaved the chair backs and made two seats facing front and two facing back, and settled themselves there, talking in Spanish, disposing newspaper bundles, and their hats, and taking possession with intense personal concern. Then the father made them sit down properly, and standing, he surveyed the rest of the car, nodding for his own satisfaction as he recognized that everything was going to be comfortable and was proceeding in an orderly fashion. He glanced at last at Danny, and Irma, and the boy's white face made him grin kindly, which Danny didn't see.

Just then the car creaked.

The farewell cry arose on the platform.

The Mexican personage sat down and composed his family and himself for the departure. Danny leaned forward as if to make the train go, *go:*

And finally it did, pulling through the yards where lights swung against the darkness in slow curves as they passed, and the wind came in the unscreened open windows bringing the pleasurable cough of smoke with it, and the smells began to change, from hot cindery plush and the smell of lumber and buildings and gasoline from cars, to things of the country: green trees rustling in the night wind, marshes growing straight grass that arose a yard high and clattered in the breeze, the river with its brushed banks letting a damp strain into the wind. The sound of the engine breasting along through the darkness ahead came back through the open windows. People talking had to lean to each other and shout, and smile and nod, instead of answer, whenever it was polite and possible to do so. The car rocked and the lamps quivered; the red wiry plush of the seats glowed richly in the light from overhead, and showed black as soot in the deep shadows where the chair backs slanted under. Danny could see down the whole car and down the next car through the windows in the end doors. When the track curved and the train leaned to take it, the next car ahead swerved slowly, showing its side, and then straightened again, showing the aisle far up there.

There in the next car was the conductor blocking the aisle and taking tickets. He was coming this way. Danny fisted his tickets and waited. When that was over there was nothing more to be afraid of. He turned to smile reassuringly at Irma. She had put a newspaper over her head to keep out the light and was asleep. He nodded to himself with responsibility.

The conductor made a slow progress. Behind him was the brakeman, following him a shuffled step at a time.

Danny's heart began to beat.

It was a fearful response to authority. It brought alive nameless guilts in him, and unnecessary defiance covered by false ease.

The door opened at last, a wind whipped into the car, and the conductor pushed against the door's heavy spring. He was fairly tall and thin. From here the shine on his glasses now and then showed owlishly. He examined the tickets he took with two looks, one through his glasses, the other under the lenses, and seemed never to look at the passengers. He used his pencil and his punch, and the brakeman handled the stubs of the tickets. Danny watched him as he turned from side to side. The high lamps in the cream-colored dome of the car put long black shadows down the man's face under his cap, and it wasn't until he was dealing with the Mexicans, who were being highly cordial, that Danny recognized him.

The conductor smiled at the Mexican baby and twinkled his nickel-plated punch at it; his teeth showed below his small dark mustache. His teeth slanted inward like a rat's. He ducked his head in nervous cheer. He turned back to take the tickets on this side.

Danny held them up and slumped in his seat.

The conductor took the tickets and gave them his two looks, fare and half fare, and from the corner of his eye he was aware of a sleeping woman with a newspaper over her face, and a small boy. That was all he saw, beyond the green striped lengths of ticket he held.

Danny was ready to be struck and beaten.

But the conductor merely handed the stubs on to the brakeman for checking, and licked his thumb to pull out the seat check from his little pink pad, afterward leaning over Irma to stick the check in the window sill.

Danny was stupefied as much as cautious.

He remembered the crowd thickening that afternoon, and the man on the opposite curb in a trainman's uniform picking up a cement clod to throw. That began it all. He remembered the face with the snarl like an animal's smile, and the glasses, the mustache, the chin that was a bone sloping back to the neck in a long flat slide. Small and lame from the beating of the day, Danny yet felt stronger than the man, for he knew as a dog might know it that the man was a coward and went through life cheating himself with impostures, as today he had impersonated the patriot who is the first to lend his arm to the destruction of enemies.

The conductor didn't recognize Danny. He hardly saw him. He saw the tickets and that was all. At the rear door of the car just by the Milfords' seats, he turned and surveyed the car with a thin pompousness, and then went on into the next car back. Following, the brakeman paused and switched down the overhead lamps until only one globe in each fixture was burning. Then he too vanished, and the car was left in a pale twilight for the night.

Then Danny began to dream with his eyes open.

He dreamed that his pursuers were clever. Here they were, letting him get on a train and then when the train was running into the country, here they turned up on board. He awoke with a start and rubbed his eyes. The dream was harder than what really was, but he knew the conductor was real, and he began to scheme: what should they do? Get off at the next stop? But Irma was asleep, and they had paid all that money for tickets to California. What would happen when the conductor came by next time? If he threatened them, Danny said, I will fight him. I will throw him off the train. The train will rock along and come to a big curve and after that there will be a long bridge over a canyon, miles down, and a terrible river running down there. We will have a battle on the back platform, and we will be up and down and up and down, and at last when the train is halfway across the chasm, I will make one mighty effort and triumph will reward my efforts, for I will take the villain and I will choke him and trip him with my heel cleverly and he will fall off the fast-moving train to go hurtling to his well-deserved end far below in the roaring waters of that treacherous river.

It was a comforting lapse into dreams again, in the sight-idiom of the movie serials.

The motion of the train was a lullaby from a machine, rocking jerkily until bodies knew the rhythm and relaxed to it.

The sound of the train became other sounds between dozing and waking . . . a great waterfall, with wild country hooting and hushing it in its airy plunge, a thunder on rock to tremble in the heart with dim memories of what it took to become a man, and simple exaltations at the beauty of Nature . . . it became the veil of wind across a wide open space blowing a skyful of hissing sand . . . it became the rumble of buffalo in herds pounding Westward to vanish . . . it became steam and iron wheels again and the grind of couplings with sweet musical whine on the curves.

Danny didn't know how much of the night he was awake.

Now and then he was busy with thinking about the other people he saw down the car, he would see their faces lean out into the aisle and then their heads disappear and then their arms fall relaxed to the sides of the chairs. The Mexicans were all asleep. The fat father seemed to have grown beard since he got on the train. Relaxed, his heavy face trembled fleshily with the train's movement. He looked sad with his snapping black eyes shut and his heavy mouth rolling open.

Danny went to get a drink of water down the car at the other end. He went softly. He was convinced that he must be secret and careful, not attract attention, but stalk. The sleepers with their possessions gathered around them seemed open to attack, and he resolved not to sleep any more that night. They had no secrets, sleeping in public like this. He saw a young man and a girl asleep on the dusty red plush seats, and they were fast in a love-locked hold, their faces sweating with desire, and their legs mixed. The boy's mouth was open on the girl's cheek. Their bodies must have been uncomfortable. Their hearts were thumping and wanted no ease.

He got back to his seat and carefully lifted the newspaper that still covered Irma's face.

Her eyes were partly open and she was breathing very slowly. She stirred a little and he guiltily put the paper back, hoping she might not awaken, promising her protection silently.

Fresh strains of the country outside blew in on the wind with smoke. The engine was remote sometimes and again it sounded just ahead there.

He watched.

Once as he watched he slept with his eyes open again and when he awoke and started, he turned to see how Irma was; and found her wide-eyed and staring at him in the dim light. She was weeping silently, with a steady film of tears clouding her eyes and falling down her cheeks.

Before he awoke, she watched him a long time.

Her mind was talking.

"Oh, Dan: they came at me!

"The first I knew, they were out of their chairs and down to the platform, and they grabbed me and carried me out along the street, cryin' and yellin' and I didn't know they really were mad at me. . . . I couldn't figure what it was . . . then they began to yell about the war, I knew then, I talked too much truth. . . .

"Next time we meet I can tell you all of it.

"We're going to California now.

"Danny always wanted to go back, and you remember that's where he was born, after you went away. That's where you'll find us when you're ready."

The boy stirred in his sleep while she watched.

It seemed to bring her out of her bewildered daydream.

"What did I say, Dan?

"Oh, I know what I said!

"You'll never be ready to come back!

"I got a letter from the War Department and I remember now. Never talk to you any more, darling. Never listen to what I think you'd say to me when I ask you. Oh, but you can't hear me! Oh, but you know everything was forgiven years ago, long years ago. I've had my troubles. I've had my *good* times, too. I've had my griefs. Now they've killed you. —I was going to tell those women today how you got killed, wasn't going to mention your name."

The film of tears ran down over her eyes and out to her cheeks.

"Lord Jesus, let him hear me talking; this is my prayer, so he can hear. Lord lift up my husband and include him in the Light! Make it so's I can meet him when ' time comes! Provide for my son. Oh, Lord show him goodness and kindness in ' world, he ' seen plenty other. . . ."

Then Danny awoke.

He moved to speak, to touch her.

But she shut her eyes and seemed to sleep again at once, and though it frightened him, he did not touch her for reassurance, but let her sleep and went back on guard.

There was nothing to guard against. He was awake when dawn began to creep. He watched it for some time thinking it was a reflection of the dim lamplight overhead upon the glass of the window across the aisle. It seemed to change as the train changed direction.

But staring at it he suddenly saw it as the pallor of light coming up beyond the black rim, moving slowly and far off like the first skyward drift of a dust storm from behind foothills. The day took hold and pace.

And with it, the country showed . . . bald plains spotted with black-looking bushes, and far levels that now and then broke upon the horizon in stubby buttes and fell off again in long sweeps of line back to the level. Now and then a highway showed near the tracks. It was lined with telegraph poles and wires that dipped and rose at even intervals, now higher, now lower, as if to show the air-course of a bird that flew with the train and soared from invisible peak to peak.

This was day.

It came calmly, first cold light, then silver, then pale gold. The train was running westward. The rising sun threw its shadow ahead of it on the tracks. There seemed now no need for caution. At the first admission of this to himself, Danny fell asleep. The whispering world of the creaking car vanished with its night-lamps quivering above and throwing down tragic shadows upon faces and dreams. He drank at sleep like a young tree that drinks at rain on the cracked earth.

LXI · THE CONDUCTOR

Irma awoke when the day began to turn hot.

She could hardly move from stiffness and a stifling ripple in her breast, something as if her heart were skipping along wildly. Her head ached with a thick pressed feeling. She was strangely frightened.

Presently the conductor came along, looking at the window sills to tally the seat checks he had given out. He was freshly shaved and his jaws looked pale with powder and blue beard. He was beginning to sweat in the hot morning, wearing the thick blue cap on his head. He wore a shining black coat with gold buttons.

When he got to Irma he leaned across her, and was about to go on when she spoke. She wasn't aware of ever having seen him before.

"Is there a doctor back there in the other cars?" she said huskily.

"Not's I know of," said the conductor. His voice was nasal.

"What seems to be the —Say, you got on at Los Algodones last night, didn't you!"

He was dismayed to see her here. The blood had turned black on her bandages. The heave of his hand had hurt her. He had stoned her. She gazed at him and her black eyes were full of pleading and an innocent charm. It was clear that she didn't know him. He blushed. He remembered: so large a crowd. Nobody would ever have been able to say later who was there. He could have left it at that. But she was ill; she suffered. His legs wilted at the knee and he had to stanch them against the cast-iron chair end.

"O-ho!" he said.

"I got on last night, I've been in an accident, and I feel so bad . . ."

"Accident, eh! —I saw you."

He was baffled by sensations of incompetence. With all such cowardice, it had to be conquered at some one else's expense.

"You're the woman they caught ' German spy, and made her get up and kiss the flag yestdy ' City Hall steps. —I was there. —I saw you. . . !"

"Oh . . ."

"What ' doing on my train! I ' like to know!"

She turned her face away to the window.

There was nothing he could do to surprise her and she didn't care. The trifling skip in her breast took her breath away and let her mind slip thoughtlessly along. She almost forgot him standing there.

He felt that she had eluded him.

But he could see how sick she was. He glanced down at the boy beside her, asleep. His legs trembled again. He couldn't say to himself, "I have hurt these people, and wronged them from feelings of wretchedness in myself. I am in debt to them. I hoped I was rid of them and my folly yesterday, but they are here. They are haunting me."

He said to himself,

"—Everybody did it, yestdy. —Country at war, there's no time t'be careless. ' Cleverest of all of them are women sometimes. ' Can't help it if her boy got hurt. —Hell, maybe ' use him as camouflage! —Keep an eye on these two, ' any funny business, turn 'em over to special police along ' way."

His eyes burned virtuously behind their lenses. Irma seemed to have dozed hotly into sleep. The boy was asleep like a small cat, stretched and graceful to use every good that sleep could give.

With his valor restored, the conductor went on back into the train, busy with plans. The draft hadn't got him, and might never. He was hardly eligible with his bad eyes, and the curved lean spine that made him look from behind like a tall old man. His feet were flat and trudging. But he knew from everything that went on nowadays that there were ways and ways of fighting for your country. Maybe this was a chance for him, right here. Maybe he could "turn her over" when they got to Los Angeles. He vowed at every station to watch her so's she couldn't get off or slip the kid off with messages, more likely that, because she looked sick all right, but they were clever sometimes with *that,* too. . . .

He marveled comfortably at the idle chance that had led him to see what the shoutin' was about yesterday, and the discovery from bystanders in the crowd that there was a woman who insulted the flag, and was probably a German spy. . . . And here she was on his train, been there all night! He was in the war now. Those great invisible currents that swept the country together caught him up too, and he was endowed with strength from without. He conceived of himself as being clever, smart enough to be secret about it, and thus, useful to the government in devious ways. So often at times he had felt vaguely out of tune with his fellows, with the life of the towns he knew and lived in and went through, and so often had he made trudging and eager attempts to make himself of them, and thus know the delights of conformity, the brotherhood of a regular guy amongst others. Now the sight of soldiers embarking on troop-trains doing what he might not would no longer fill him with exasperation and longing. They would travel through cheering towns to battle. He, because he knew the value of chance and opportunity, would do battle no less than they.

Yes sir!

He saw a satisfactory memory of the poster which showed his enemy . . . a wild boar with little pig eyes and bloody snout and dripping fangs wearing a German soldier's helmet . . . facing the beast was a beautiful youth about to hurl a red, white and blue javelin into the ravening heart of the monster. . . .

In the forward car Irma felt the train slow down and she saw the outlying sheds and tie-piles of a railroad camp. She pushed the shade up to see out. The window was partly open.

The train creaked to a stop.

Laborers outside rested on their tools and gazed up at the train windows.

They were burning old ties by the track-side. The smoke, full of oil and tar with which the ties had been prepared against the weather, blew up along the cars and into the windows.

Danny stirred.

He fought the chair he lay in a second.

The smoke drifted into his head and made a dream of a camp fire, a fire in a little clearing by a railroad water-tank in a small town, a town long ago known, and there he was captive: there were Oscar and Fat again: there was Tommy McBride scared and refusing to cry: there was the smoke from the camp fire winding into his clothes and here came Oscar with his great hand held out and open in menace: "'Ah, 'oh," gasped Danny with hardly a sound, and awoke. He awoke and rubbed his eyes and sat up. The train was hot and the hot smoke from outside made him feel ill. The desert was baking under the oven-like sky. He looked at Irma, and his sleepiness cleared off from looking at her. She was so white. She looked at him so long a way away.

Their voices sounded flat and loud in the standing quiet train.

"Mom, what can I get for you."

"Nothing."

"Can't I get you an orange?"

"Nothing."

"Can I have one?"

"Take my purse——"

"You better eat something, Mom. Hh?"

"No."

The smoke drifted in from the tie-fire out on the ground. Danny leaned to see it. The dusty grape-red toolhouse stood back from the tracks under a cottonwood tree. The ground under it was black. The tree trunk was gray, and the leaves were sunny yellow. Beyond lay the Arizona plain, pale straw-colored and faint from heat.

"I wonder where we are."

"God knows, son."

He looked quickly at her. She was hardly able to speak. Her breath sounded in all her words.

At the forward door, the news butcher came in with a basket containing oranges, cherries in paper cornucopias, bars of chocolate, and bottles of ice-cold soda water colored like jewels and flavored with acids.

"Here he comes, Mamma. —I guess you better eat something. 'M going to buy you some chocolate."

"No."

She rolled her head against the seat back with her eyes shut.

He took her purse from her lap and opened it and got some coins. When the butcher was at hand, he bought an orange and a bar of

chocolate with almonds in it. The whole car was stirring for breakfast. Most of the people had their own boxes of food, which they ate
gravely, with careful manners; folding up their waxed paper and
bread crusts neatly; and eyeing each other as they ate with sober
pleasure. The Mexican family were more lively; the children reached
and grabbed and were smacked; the little boys sulked and were
teased by their father and then slapped again; the mother was sweating with heat and the suckling of her infant.

The train began to move.

The scorching land again began to wheel by in immensity of yellow
plain and white sky.

Irma touched her head with her finger tips and said "M'm . . ."
as if to chide some pain.

Danny was frightened again.

He tried to talk to her and comfort her, but could say nothing; he
patted her arm. Her arm was cold and roughened with chill. He had
to do something. He went down the car and into the next car forward. He saw the conductor sitting at the far end with his cap off. It
stopped Danny in his tracks for a moment; but knowing obscurely
that he could take any risks for what he had to do, he went on and
finally reached the conductor.

"Say, mister."

"Well, m'boy," said the conductor, not looking up from the newspaper in his lap, but seeing Danny from the corner of his lens.

"We've got to find a doctor or something, my mom is sick, back
there in the next car. . . ."

The conductor looked up now. He was relieved to see that the boy
seemed all right. He pursed his mouth and it stuck his small mustache
outward. He breathed deliberately through his mustache as if in estimate, and his eyes took on a look that acted the inner keenness he was
wooing.

"H'm. You think she is sick, eh?"

He snorted.

"Let me tell *you*, she ' all that's coming to her!"

His prowess in words gave him what he needed so badly. His face
flushed and he stood up seeing himself as a shrewd defender of the
right.

"All right," said Danny, white with fury. "I know *you*, too! I saw
you yesterday! Heaving rocks!"

The conductor took the boy's shoulders in a sharp grasp.

"Now, you calm down, if you know ' good for you. —Hold on,
now."

"You let go! —Damn you, old sissy coward, won't help a sick woman! I'll *go* and get a doctor, tell him whole story!"

He wrenched free of the conductor and began to run back down the car, while people craned after him, and then looked at each other with wonder.

The conductor followed and caught him on the platforms between the cars in the clamorous hot air.

"Ain't ' doctor on this train, I tell you! You listen ' me!"

He was shouting against the clangor of the train. He was converting his profound uneasiness into strength by trying to howl down the furious will of the boy who stood staring up at him with the pug face of passionate rage.

"She's sick! —You gotto help!"

"—'On't care what you say, ain't ' doctor on this train! Want me ' help *that?* Anybody insult ' flag deserves what ' get!"

Danny grasped the metal handrail that was fastened to the doorway of the vestibule and kicked the conductor at the shins. Then he was appalled by what he had done, and turned, heaved against the next door, and ran down the aisle to his own seat.

But the victory was his, and he slowly began to realize it. The man didn't follow; to put him off the train or arrest him or whip him. He gradually grew quieter and though he continued to stare down the car for the conductor to appear, it was almost chance that he saw him coming later, for he had turned to see Irma's sleeping face where her eyes were fallen into dark caves of shadow and her lids lay so pale and birdlike. The conductor passed through the car on his way aft, and he was humming a tune, and reading some train dispatches on yellow telegraph blanks. He never looked up from the papers, a busy man.

Something in his stride made the Mexicans stare at him; and after he had vanished, the fat father sat erect in his seat and put one hand with spread finger tips against his breast, and the other forward on his huge thigh, and closed his eyes, waggled his head, and silently smirked an opinion of the conductor's official airs. The children clattered like little parakeets with fun; and Danny laughed. The father awoke from his rôle and winked at Danny and his brown face smiled. He belched fundamentally, as if glad to be who he was. Danny felt less worried and lone.

There was now meaning between the aisles.

"La mamá, sick?" asked the man.

"Yes." Danny nodded.

"Que lástima. Is too bad. Ha?"

Danny nodded.

They all leaned to look.

Irma was quiet. The Mexicans could see how bad it was. They could do nothing to help. But their feelings lived directly through their eyes, the looks of compassion they gave her, and encouragement they gave Danny. The scrawny mother of the family, whose latest child played constantly at her depleted breast, moved her mouth in a hissing prayer and nodded her head at Danny through it, as if to give him both words and the efficacy of the prayer even as she said it.

They watched all day with him.

Hardly a word went back and forth, but when he turned, their eyes were always waiting for him, and their winks, their bright nods, their allowance for the claim of other creatures upon them.

LXII · ON THE MAIN LINE WEST

The train bangled on through the hot afternoon and seemed almost to become part of it, so furiously was the domed sky drawn by the sun into the very metal of the railroad coaches. The passengers could not remember ever having been cool. They slept and they awakened, and they trembled with the intimate squeaking life of the moving cars. The hot light of the sun showed dust against the windows, and new dust hotly furring the red plush seats, and cinders clinging anew to the window shades that were drawn down. The trundling sound of the train's movement was now so much part of the day that the passengers could detect new sounds as they occurred, and hear each other talking without much trouble any more. Since noon, the young man and his girl midway up the car had been singing songs, and he had been playing a ukulele. They had been timid at first, with their music, but the more he played and sang, the more an atmosphere of comradeship had gone through the car, and the people, with no greater converse than before, still had greater comfort among themselves, an easiness and sense of custom that were new. Everybody thought the young pair were cute and pitied them for their so evident desire to be alone and frankly loving; and watched them with cheerful caution to see them doze and embrace and wake up and doze again, and cover their laps with an opened newspaper that hid the passionate embraces of their hands.

The whole car, too, was concerned with the Mexicans, but in various ways. Some objected to the presence of greasers. Others thought of them with pity. Others watched the Mexican children playing in the aisle, so comfortable in the dirt, and nodded their heads at life in this guise.

Everyone knew too that there was a sick woman there in the right-hand rear corner, with her thirteen-year-old boy.

The brakeman had brought her a pillow from one of the Pullmans in the rear.

They would reach Los Angeles the next morning at nine forty-five.

In the hot tumult of the train there was a feeling like hypnosis, as if this state of torrid progress were unending, the ringing in the ears would never stop, Los Angeles would always beckon unachieved.

"Maybe you wouldn't want to grow up t'take care of an old woman."

It was Irma's voice, placid and gentle. It started Danny from the flushed doze he was in. He looked at her and his heart leaped for excitement and hope in her wakefulness.

"Hello, Mumma. —Can I get you some chocolate?"

"No, Danny."

"How do you feel:"

"Give me your hand."

"Do you feel better?"

"—The boys grow up and it's their time t'go out in the world and make life and make it for theirself."

She was smiling. He sank back immensely relieved.

"I always thought ' best thing I could do was raise you and wait till you got t'be a man, and then turn round and let you take care of me."

"I can take care of you right now, Mom."

"I know, Danny."

"—You had me scared, all day, lying there with your eyes closed. Gee!"

"Didn't want to scare you. I was just s'tired, I hadn't a calm bone in my whole body."

"Gee, it's hot, isn't it, Mother."

"—What time is it?"

"Is your watch in your purse?"

"Yes."

"—It's nearly three o'clock, twenty minutes *of*."

"Are you always going t'be my good boy?"

"Sure."

"—After all the hard work, it's too bad——"

"What? What d'you mean, Mumma. What's that? H'm? Tell me. What's too bad. H'm?"

She shrugged and closed her eyes.

She was still smiling, and he thought she was feeling much better. She was holding his fingers. Some tears came out through her dark lashes and rolled down her face. She said that small sound of pain again, "M'm . . ." with her brow gathered suddenly. Her smile opened and she tried to turn her head to look at him. But she lay there as still as she'd been all day, holding his fingers.

The Mexican father had been watching Danny all this time. Danny sat quietly. The fat man looked at Irma, and squinted and then said, in a whistling whisper,

"Oh, por Diós!"

and leaned to pluck at his wife. She peered with him, and crossed herself and thrust the striving baby off her breast for the older girl to hold. They looked at Danny again, and the sight of him, beginning to doze again from the heat and the song of the train and the somnolent ukulele down the aisle, turned their hearts over.

"Pobrecito," they said.

Then the woman went over to Danny and her husband heaved himself out of his seat and went shaking his head to find the conductor.

LXIII · THE MEXICAN

He was surprised to open his eyes and see and feel the Mexican woman untangling his fingers from Irma's. Then he turned to look at his mother, and as he looked he saw that she was dead.

He looked up at the woman standing before them both.

He looked down the car. The grinding noise of the car wheels rang in his ears. He began to have a quiver of breath under his voice, a little neigh like a pony's, and he looked back at the woman, shaking his head and feeling his eyes sting with heat and pain.

The woman had covered Irma with her long overcoat that had hung on the brass hook above the window.

The ukulele tunked on down the car and the drowsy idle talk went on around the young couple. Presently the far door opened and the Mexican father came back followed by the conductor. When Danny saw the conductor, his heart cleared and he knew what this was beside him, and he began to sob, mortally stricken by the humiliation of being in the power of this man; that his mother should be subject to the cold dispositions he would make; that his own aloneness should be touched off by the power in the hands of the enemy.

"Here, see, is too bad," declared the Mexican, pointing.

The conductor leaned over and looked, lifting the coat.

Danny threw himself head down into the lap of the Mexican woman. His crying sounded faintly above the train noise. The ukulele stopped. People looked back. A few of them came down the aisle, gathering curiously.

"Now, hush, youngster, wait a minute, wait a min-ute, there . . ." said the conductor leaning down to quiet Danny. He felt that this grief was an open accusation of himself. He had to seize the situation and control it calmly, with urbanity. His hands were trembling, and the vexation in his eyes made them water. The gathering people looked at him and down at the boy, and at the still figure under the coat. Everybody waited for him to do something. It seemed to him most necessary to get the child silent. Every time he touched Danny the sobs became shrieks.

"Now be sensible, you boy. ' Got to find out what ' do with you. . . . Listen to me:"

Danny broke from his touch, and the dry little grasp of the Mexican woman and ran to the door, and out to the platform. There he grabbed the handrail with both hands and held it hard, stopping his breath, and trying to quit his crying. All he wanted was to be alone and secret with what had happened to him. He wanted to kick and rage when he considered how she had died in public, with strangers and damn old fools all around, and the nasty music down the car, and the hot weather, and the black engine dust, and the whole violent thing that came from bad weather between people, temper and cruelty and the power to put death where life had been.

The door opened softly and he didn't turn around. He scrounged his eyes tight shut and gripped his hands on the railing begging in prayer to be alone and rich with his misery. A long time, it seemed, went by; and then a comfortable big hand came gently down on his shoulder, and the fingers patted him not irritably, or heavily, but

slowly, as if to coax his thoughts from bitterness and despair. Whoever it was didn't say anything, but waited; and at last Danny
turned around and the hand pivoted on his shoulder staying there;
and when he looked up it was the fat Mexican, with his stubbly
cheeks and heavily dramatic eyes, now softened into a quiet look of
respect. He didn't look sorrowful, or make sighs, or anything like
that; simply serious and respectful. It cleared Danny's head at once,
to be so regarded with sense and sympathy. The ache in his skull
slowed down its throbbing and he had an easy run of tears that didn't
heave his guts until he might stifle. In a few moments his eyes dried
up and he looked soberly back at the fat man who was lolling against
the vestibule wall. Now he fished out tobacco and paper and taking
away his hand from Danny's shoulder, he began to make a cigarette.

"You got ' papa?" he asked without any suggestion of inquisitive-
ness.

"No."

"—A brother? Or sister? *You* know: anyone else?"

Danny shook no.

" 'S too bad."

He smoked in silence.

The door opened again. It was the conductor.

"We get to Driscoll, Arizona, at four-ten," he declared. "I've
wired ahead. ' All be taken care of there."

The Mexican looked up at him.

"Put 'em off a train, eh?"

"Nothin' else t'do. —'Ey can take care of it at Driscoll. —You got
anybody t' wire to, boy?"

Danny turned away and felt the grief pushed back on him by the
man. The Mexican touched the conductor and shook his head, and
beckoned him inside a moment. There he told him Danny was alone;
had no one to find anywhere; and couldn't they not put them off at
Driscoll, but go on to Los Angeles, where somebody might take care
of the boy?

The conductor saw in this the way everybody would look at it.
He became strident, and shook his arms. He was thin-souled and
thick-skinned. He declared that there was no provision on the train
to take care of the dead. As for the kid, he'd wire ahead to Driscoll,
and the station agent would get the undertaker and meet the train,
and the like. Somebody'd feed the boy. —As for the woman, well,
might be ' as well out ' way . . .

The Mexican began to flush. His heavy cheeks trembled delicately.
He began to rumble. But there was no way he could express a re-

sponse to so cold a thing as the conductor's ways, and he went out to the platform again to stand with Danny and smoke. His wife sat beside the covered figure and held her infant and told her rosary for Irma. The other people in the car came to look, and pass on to stare through the glass of the door at Danny; some declaring that it gave them the willies; others talking of getting up a collection for the boy, and thus settling their consciences for being able to do nothing about the events of the dusty hot afternoon in the rolling train. The young couple put away the uke; and the girl was secretly and wildly stricken with a foretaste of death, if it should rob her of the flesh and heart she loved beside her; while he held her close and looked out the window at the wheeling horizon, yellow in the four-o'clock sun, and cursed in his mind because too he saw her dimly threatened.

Book V • THE SON

LXIV · DRISCOLL, ARIZONA

They could tell from the changing timbre of the wheels over track intersections and over the small bridges across arroyos when they neared Driscoll, slowing down. A few trees began to show by the tracks. There was a scattering of the usual shacks and buildings; dusty red; then a pavement of brick beside the train; and the creaking halt, the steel doors opening, and the day's frying heat pressing in.

Behind the station one wide sandy street stretched out to the rim of the desert beyond. Back of the street on each side were scattered a few houses, showing white screens of canvas on sleeping-porches. Around all these the pinkish earth lay baking. There was nothing but the quietest air over the town. Far off on the horizon a single pearl-round cloud hung radiant with reflected heat.

Here they took Irma off the train; there was a motor waiting with a glassy cabin and open doors in the rear. It was marked on each side, "Opper's Furniture Store," and below that, "Invalid Coach."

Mr. and Mrs. Opper were at the station, with a doctor. Danny saw them bring Irma out and lay her in the car. The Mexican gathered up all the bags by the vacated seat, and put them on the station platform, and then he helped Danny down the steps and took him to Mrs. Opper.

"Is the boy," he said.

"Oh, poor little man:" she said with refinement, and nodded understandingly, and the Mexican winced in despair at the professional grace the woman showed. She was short and plump, with nose glasses, and a discreet make-up on her face. She spoke slowly and her gestures were careful. She was about fifty, with brown-gray hair. Now a humorous sadness lay over her face, sad for the occasion, and yet dreamily sustaining "charm" with a faint smile. She took Danny's arm and drew him toward the coach.

The train hissed and its bell began to roll.

The Mexican fatly and quickly leaned forward and almost blinded by pity and a sense of powerlessness kissed Danny on the cheek. Then he trundled like a worried bear back to the train and climbed up the steps as it began to grind slowly ahead on its shining hot path to Los Angeles. When he reached the vestibule the brakeman closed the car door, and then he came to the glass to stare back; moved by the desolation of Driscoll, Arizona, where they were leaving a spent life and a new one drifting. He was aware of something behind him; he turned; it was the conductor, on tiptoe, peering across the Mexican's shoulder to see what last he could of the thing he had begun to share in twenty-four hours ago, secretly and yet of the public.

LXV · HOVERING IDEA

The night was almost as hot as the day. The desert returned the heat to the night sky which the daytime had baked there. The town of Driscoll was dark and still, early in the night. A few lights showed far back in the stores on Main Street, burglar guards; but aside from such ghostly effluvia, which seemed like some strange gassy breath of luminous earth in the stifling night, the darkness held fast.

The Oppers lived in rooms over their furniture store. Their building was the only two-story one in town. Below were the furniture showrooms, and the undertaking parlors in the rear. The back door was carefully locked tonight, as it always was on nights when there was an occupant of the refrigerated back room, where the shades were drawn and an electric fan blew against the hanging sheet that was kept moist by a slowly running faucet and hose.

It was a long time before Mr. and Mrs. Opper went to sleep. Their bed was hot and the sheets crept into little thicknesses that were uncomfortable. Their minds were busy with ingenuity needed to meet the sad situation in their charge. Lying in the dark they would talk a few moments and then be silent while thoughts kept them communicative until words came again. In the dark in their bed, they had the realest intimacy of spirit, for here they could not see

each other as they were after thirty years of married life; here lay not
two stout middle-aged people able to see in each other the daily light
of half-conscious disappointment at the final meagerness of their
life; here lay two explorers, a bride and groom, taking each other
lustily for granted, and seeing each other in mind still in the images
created by touch, instead of sight . . . the touch of hand and body
and the touch of mind in secret. To be so married was achievement
enough in a lifetime, and they would separately muse about it, yet
no more articulately than they felt the spending of their daytimes
as waste and failure; hovering idea, not sharp conviction.

They had given Danny a bed in the room formerly used by their
son Joseph, who had gone to war four months ago.

Mrs. Opper had sent him to war with calm charm; not asking
herself why he must go, or what it was she dreaded in silence; and
putting Danny in his bed, she felt her throat fill and watched him
until in a few minutes he was asleep sweating with the heat and
dream-strife against what he knew.

She sighed in bed now.

"He looks a little like Joseph," she murmured.

"Same blue eyes," said Mr. Opper.

"Poor little tyke."

"Did you ever:"

"No, sir, isn't the limit, things you hear about can happen right
in your own front yard."

"I talked to him, and talked to him, he don't seem to know a
soul. Said he used to live in Coronilla, California. Long time ago."

"—Was she very *bad?*"

"Doctor said ' must've been cerebral hemorrhage. Said ' came from
injuries, and ' said looked like heart too, somewhat. Bad condition
generally."

"I must say you did wonders, Joe."

"—It wasn't easy. Some bad injuries. Did you find a nice dress in
her baggage, Mother?"

"Yes. All white. —The little tyke says she was a lady preacher.
Evangelist."

"Irma Milford . . . seems I've heard the name, Mother. You ever
hear the name?"

"You know, I think I *have,* Joe, isn't that the limit, though!"

He stirred in wonderment.

They were silent.

There was a far and faint hum of water running.

"—I did go through some letters and things she had, but they didn't tell anything, Joe. She had sixteen dollars and some change in her purse, and that was all I could find. She maybe was going to Los An'les for some work. She looked like such a refined woman, too, didn't she."

"Sure does."

"Poor little tyke. I keep wondering what he will do."

"Yes, I know, Mother. Well, we'll have to see."

She lay smiling in the darkness. She knew how generous Joe was. She said to herself as she had said many times to other people, Mr. Opper is the most generous man you ever laid eyes on.

He was thinking that if it were daylight, he'd be embarrassed to have her see him right now, because in thinking about the young boy and what had happened to the things of his life, he was touched and softened; and at times like that he hated himself for the luxuriant images of grief that passed through his mind; just as he always felt wretched and moved at funerals, though he could perform his embalming preparations with objective skill and never a quiver. He always had to strengthen his will and speak to himself to recover from such seizures of sentiment; and now he thought passionately, "The boy is all of thirteen or fourteen; why, when I was his age, I was earning my own living, and developing my muscles working in a paper-mill in Pennsylvania, and a year later I set out on my own and I hiked out West to Ohio, I must of been only fourteen-fifteen, toughened me up, I'll never forget the experience, I wouldn't take a million dollars for it, teaches a boy to be self-reliant, if I had a youngster now I'd tell him to go and find some new country just being opened up, and dig in, and grow up with it."

But this saddened him again, for that was what he had done, finally, in Driscoll; and there were few ambitions possible any more in this town, which wasn't growing any more.

Mrs. Opper didn't need to see him; she suddenly felt drowsy and somehow decided that Joe was uneasy; she laid her hand lightly on his arm and composed herself. While he lay awake and again happy, she dozed off. Encouraged, he began to make plans for the morning. It would have to be in the morning, fairly early, before the heat of the day got started.

"Don't you think about eight o'clock, Mother?"

She came back obediently from the delicious roads of sleep and answered him a little thickly.

" 'M-*hm*. Fine."

"—Or would it be better nearer nine:"

She was fully awake again; recognized his habit of wanting to consider every objection to a plan before adopting it; and began to play her part in helping with disparagement in order to make the original plan the stronger if it could withstand such examination.

"Well, it might, Joe; eight's awfully early for services."

"Still, we laid Mr. Grangeworthy away at seven."

"Yes, but that was his wife, don't you remember? She had to get the eight-fourteen train for Holbrook? You remember, Joe."

"Yes, now's I recall it, I do, Mother."

"What about eight-thirty?"

"Well, sun gets so hot just about that time."

"That's so, isn't it the limit?"

"I guess eight's all right."

"Uh-*huh*. That way it'll give you time to be ready beforehand, and still leave you a full morning back here at the store, won't it:"

She made it sound like a piece of the cleverest planning on his part. He thought she understood things better than any woman he knew.

"Yes sir, Mother, we'll make it eight."

"Fine."

"—I only wish Joseph was here to help me:"

The familiar pang struck her; but she smiled in the darkness remembering the charm she had vowed never to lose, which gave her that vague smile all day long no matter what happened, so that most of the time she looked witless. It rhymed with one of her oftrepeated mental statements, which occurred to her at odd moments, *à propos* of nothing in particular: "After all, I've got my pride." Her pride now mobilized itself and made her heart beat at the absence of her son, the soldier, a youth in uniform lusting after life on the chanceful trail of death.

"Yes, I know, Father."

They were sobered for sleep. They drifted near the coast of sleep, and presently the waves came gently over them, the surf of night.

LXVI · UNDER THE SUN

The next morning Danny was almost sullen in his embarrassment. He vowed to weep no more. He still wanted to be alone. He was ashamed of the kindness of Mr. and Mrs. Opper. They looked with such pity on him. She asked him if he wanted some breakfast, and he said he did; and ate much more than he wanted to prove that he was feeling perfectly all right, and that his grief was none of their business; so little so, that he would convince them that he had none.

Somewhat before eight o'clock they all went in the small procession to the cemetery two miles out on the desert from Driscoll. There were many things about it that Danny didn't know . . . that the town council had agreed to pay the funeral expenses provided they came to under forty dollars; that the doctor had advised early burial; that the Oppers were taking care of the sixteen dollars in Irma's purse for him; and that the flowers on the coffin in the "Invalid Coach" had come from the little garden down by the tracks, back of the station, a plot of green grass and rambler roses maintained by the station agent's wife.

The day was already blinding yellow, and the hot sands stretching away in all directions were dappled here and there with greasewood bush. They drove on the highway for a mile and a half and then turned off on a lane with deep sandy ruts, and came beyond a little freckled hill to the cemetery gate, which was made of hunks of petrified wood cemented together, and topped by a scrolled arch of wrought iron with a design of grapes and leaves in vine. They drove in. The earlier graves were leveled by wind. There were crosses and stones, whitened by sun.

They stopped.

The deep sand thrown newly up on the earth was still a little damp and dark.

There was a minister from a church in Driscoll. With him they bowed their heads and their thoughts were alive like their hearts. As people do, they saved themselves from the time by seeing a severe grandeur in the desert, a tonic and gong-like wonder in the sun which gave life even though it burned, and at the end they turned back to town with some placid relief and invited work eagerly.

Danny had scowled and rather than weep he would have cursed. He hated saying good-by to his mother forever in the company of strangers. When he was back in his room at the Oppers' this overwhelmed him and he shut the door and went to the bed and fell across it burning with shame for the meanness and indignity of so much of Irma's life, and weeping for the chance he would never have of giving her what she had dreamed of having one day when he should be a man.

LXVII · GOOD NIGHT

All day the Oppers had kept very busy by pretense, so by the time night came there had been no chance to talk to Danny about his plans. He spent the day up in his room, dozing and waking, and going to the window to look out on Main Street. He could see down the three blocks to the tracks, and recognize in the frying sunlight what must be the ranks of red freight cars waiting. He saw the autos roll dustily up and down the street, and when afternoon came, some electric lights came on pallidly in the shallow theater lobby across the way, and a few people came up and bought tickets and went in to see the film, a war spectacle entitled "Intolerance." The white cracking paint of the lobby was a simmering background for many violent posters. He half-considered going to the show until he awoke fully from the hot drowsiness and remembered that this he must not do. It was only two days ago that he had planned to go to a show Sunday afternoon in Los Algodones.

He used to think in those years of growing up that if Irma died, what would he do: and lumps of despair would grow in his heart and throat. But now what grief he felt had nothing to do with himself, his precarious future, the animal needs which must be met. He kept thinking how unhappy she must have been; and of how she had looked standing with the flag draped over her in mockery; and he would flush in rage at the people who did it, and who had killed her.

Mrs. Opper put him to bed again that night, and in leaving him she said that they must "have a talk" in the morning. She said she was sure Dad Opper had something nice to tell him. She asked him if he wanted her to kiss him good night, and he said no, and coughed. She sighed and left him.

LXVIII · THE KINDLY

It had been on their minds all day. They had both weighed it, and turned it over, without speaking of it; for they knew that comfortably in bed in the hot intimate dark they would slowly sift it out into words, and see where they ended up with it.

"Well, Mother, I've been thinking it over."

"Yes, Joe?"

This was the first reference to the subject, yet she knew what it was.

"Of course, we have to look at it from all angles."

"That's true, that's so, isn't it, Joe:"

" 'Tisn't 'sif times were flush, and all that. Another mouth to feed, and all, I said to myself, before I come to any decision on this, I'll have to look into the proposition pretty carefully."

She smiled secretly at his familiar pretense of reaching decisions through reason; when she well enough knew that his actions were always spontaneous and emotionally derived.

"Of *course*, Dad."

A silence.

"I took him aside this afternoon, just before you went out to the Market, and I gave him his money, that sixteen dollars. I feel now maybe 'sif I should have held on to it, and let him have it more gradually. But ' course I didn't know then *what* my plans were going to be."

" 'N-hn?"

"I said, 'Now look here,' I said to myself . . . I began to think maybe a growing boy wouldn't be just what the doctor ordered, after all, it'd make a lot of extra work and trouble for you, around the house, Mother, and the like. Got to think of those things . . ."

"Oh, Dad, don't think of *me:* we have t'do whatever is best."

"Yes, well, I know," he persisted. "That's all well and good, but ' time he's grown boy you'll be putting out a lot of work for him, and I'll have to ante on the money side. —Pay him a little wages, and have him help around the place?"

He forgot that he was being critical of the plan, and his new enthusiasm warmed her.

"Now fine: that's just fine, Joe! You've *needed* a boy or someone to help, haven't you?"

They were trying to find excuses for the kindness that was working in them. They would be ashamed and shy about helping a homeless boy if they hadn't some excuse to offer their friends for doing it.

But it was an exquisite delight to defer deciding as long as possible.

"Well, we have to be sensible, about the whole thing," he declared.

They lay in silence for a time.

The familiar night noises of the little town drifted in the open windows where the lace curtains were pinned back for the night, to let a breeze enter should it spring up off the exhalant desert. Down on the tracks three blocks away a locomotive let steam.

"Did you lock up, Dad?"

"—I left ' back door open ' case a breeze came up, seems to me ' was mighty hot in the store today. I'd like to cool it off."

"Yes, but then did you hook the screen?"

"Oh, I hooked the screen all right."

A silence.

"He seems like a handy youngster, don't he?"

"Poor little tyke! Did you notice his eyes? He has such beautiful eyes! He's a right handsome little shaver."

"Well, I'll get him in in the morning, and tell him what we plan to do."

"Yes, that'll be fine, Dad."

She didn't know yet just what he intended, beyond keeping Danny to live with them. But this prospect was one that touched her and warmed her heart; she would be so much less lonely for her son Joe if she had some one to take care of. It would be like becoming a grandmother. She was sure they could make Danny happy, for their own Joe, she thought, had been one of the happiest youngsters she ever saw, but probably he got that from his father, who was one of the kindest men that ever lived, she remembered proudly.

Mr. Opper nodded his head on the pillow.

When it was time to go out in the fall to hunt quail he would take the boy along. In time he might buy him a gun of his own. It wouldn't do to spoil him. But there were a lot of ways a man could keep young, if he had some young person near him to go by. He would teach Danny to drive the car, and uncrate furniture, and perhaps get him a dog, it would have to be a hunting-dog, so they could take it out on the desert after quail. In November they could load up the car and go up north to one of the lakes and hunt ducks. Maybe the war would be over by then and Junior would be home.

Junior would be getting married before so many years . . . he would move away . . . he would have children of his own. . . .

"But you can just bet your bottom dollar he will have to earn what he gets," said Mr. Opper suddenly. "It'd be a bad thing for a boy to *give* him things, without having him learn the value of a dollar, make him self-reliant, I'll talk to him in the morning."

His wife had fallen asleep.

A little breeze actually had sprung up. He was glad he hadn't locked up.

LXIX · ROLL ALONG

Danny had few enough things to take with him. He had the sixteen dollars tied inside a handkerchief with knots around it which he set by biting them and pulling. He waited till everything was quiet, the faint burr of distant voices had died out in the room down the hall, and then he gathered his bundle which included Irma's Bible, her locket watch, and a clipping with her picture from the newspaper of Newton, Kansas, two years ago, and his best suit; and he went down the stairs to the rear of the Oppers' furniture store, where the night light was glowing in a mad little atmosphere of whirling bugs and moths.

He went to the screen door and unhooked it.

He might have been dreaming, for all the concern he had about going away without reason. But there was no reason to stay, so far as he knew; he was an embarrassment to the Oppers. He hated Driscoll, Arizona, and wanted to be as far from it as he could, forever. He had a good deal of money in his handkerchief, and all his life he had seen the trains roll by. . . .

He went down the dark shadowy alley behind the business houses of Main Street toward the tracks. He met no one. It must have been around midnight. The breeze played hotly down off the roofs to the dusty ground, making a little poignant stir that rose to be breathed.

There were work lights staring from the two ends of a switch locomotive. He came up to the tracks and stayed in the shadow of a low warehouse with a scarred wooden deck in front of it. The cars were switched back and forth. The engine was making up a train, picking up a car here at Driscoll and cutting it into a long line of cars that had arrived shortly after dark from the west and would head out east again tonight. He saw how the cars were yanked and assembled on the main line. If he got up and, when it looked safe, went up to the loading-deck and walked into the nearest box car which stood with its doors slid half back, he would be rolling out of Driscoll before morning.

This is what he did.

Once inside the car, the darkness was so boxed and fearful that he was frightened and moved to get off the train again and stay.

But he remembered the freckled hot ground of the graveyard, and this morning at eight o'clock there, and he tightened his jaws over a stinging growth of feeling; resolved about going, and when the engine was coupled, with a shattering jolt that caterpillared down through the train, he could hardly wait for the wheels to begin rolling. Wheels had no roots, and they could roll because of that. The wheels began to roll and when they pulled him along in the half-empty box car, they tore no roots from under him.

Afterword

This novel, flowing in a single stream of narrative carrying a central current of character, is something like a river which late in its career enters a narrows. As within the high rock walls of a canyon a river boils and tumbles, this story enters the scene of humiliation and torture of Irma Milford for the ideal folly which caused her to preach for peace instead of war, for life instead of death.

It was a scene drawn from an event which I witnessed as a boy of about fourteen in Albuquerque.

One Sunday afternoon during the first World War, I was idling along Gold Avenue on a bicycle. It was a hot summer day. I was vacant in mind and oppressed by the feeling of an eternal Sunday afternoon which the day seemed to bring to the small city where the streets were empty for the day of rest.

Or were they really empty?—for I heard strange commotions up the street ahead of me before I saw them, and then I saw a crowd, tightly packed, half running, and clustered in common movement about something or someone in their midst. Glad to be interested in anything that broke the baked stillness of Sunday afternoon in summer in New Mexico, I rode toward the scene.

All too soon I saw what was coming to pass. The throng—it was a mob, governed by the least charitable and civil of its gathered spirits—was dragging at its center a middle-aged man by a rope around his neck. He was sandy-haired, thin, red-eyed, pale with fear, hatred and rage. He was being forced to shamble along in a half-run to keep up with the pace of his captors, one of whom was a large citizen carrying a bundled-up American flag. I came close enough to hear the shouts of the crowd—"German spy! Traitor! Hang him!"—and I heard the man's breath puff out of his lungs and mouth as his body was pulled and turned by the mindless progress of his tormentors.

At the corner of Fourth Street and Gold Avenue in those days stood the old Commercial Club, a red sandstone building in the absurd Renaissance-Romanesque style imitated from Richardson in public buildings all across the land. A flight of stone steps led to a front door deeply caverned under a massive low arch supported by thick, short, brutal columns. The victim was trundled up to the top step and exposed to the crowd. Under blows he was made to face them. The large man with the flag shook it free and held it out as an incitement to the crowd.

"Make him kiss it!" someone shouted.

The suggestion swept the crowd and they roared approval. Sweating with fervor and virtue the large man improvised a ceremony. He turned to the victim and draped the flag over him. With one hand he held up a corner of its beautiful blue field with stars and with the other he forced the head of the tormented creature to bend to the flag and touch it with his dried and trembling mouth. At the consummation of the kiss, the crowd cried out in abstract glory, and demanded that it be done again, and again.

I was drained of the hot day until I felt cold. I believed I was in the presence of visible evil. With my teeth chattering I backed my wheel and turned and rode as fast as I could away from the sickening vision of a forced sacrifice.

I had no idea who the victim was or what he might have done to make other people scream "Traitor!" at him in the hysteria of their war feeling. I never knew what became of him in the end—except that there was not actually a lynching, for of that there was no subsequent news. The power of the many to abuse the one was all I saw.

It was one of the most dreadful, and most enlightening, sights of my life. When long afterward I came to give form to the lives of Irma Milford, and her husband, and her son, in their years, it returned to me with much force; and transforming its victim and circumstance, I used it as the emotional and physical climax of my story.

FAR
FROM
CIBOLA

To Philip Stevenson

Contents

I · UNTIL SUNDOWN

Far to the west, the mountain was shining like glass in colour and mystery upon the horizon. Smoke from morning fires vanished against the sky, pierced by the sunlight. In her kitchen, Ellen Rood laid wood in her stove. The children were in the yard, and their mother could hear the noises of their early work. Donald was hacking at wood with the huge axe that wobbled in his grasp. His sister Lena, with delicate childish movements, washed her hands and face in the tin dish that stood at the edge of the well. Mrs. Rood blew upon her fire, and though the smoke rolled back into her eyes, and sparks burned upward to sting her arms, she hardly noticed them. The children sounded happy, and in her own mind there was a strange content, for when the jobs of her household were going forward, she forgot the various halts in her life which made her experience. At least winter was over, and she would have no more strife with cold for many months. The summer would see Don grow a little more, and the farm let into their cupboards a little more food.

But behind such precarious comforts as these, Ellen Rood considered the promise she had made to Mr. Haystead in town yesterday. Everyone she knew was going to be in town this morning at ten o'clock. She had tried to avoid giving her promise to Haystead. Some pride held her back, perhaps it was Haystead's smiling fury, an expression like a threat, that had offended her love of independence. When he spoke of the Government relief, his small blue eyes went dry, and a little red. His big hands trembled on the wheel of his car. She knew that his family had suffered, and that he loved his children. It made her scornful to see a man shaken so by the common disasters of everyone she knew. But she had agreed to meet before the Courthouse at ten o'clock. There would be several trucks loaded with food, and a government agent to discuss the sale of crops with the men. Ellen's fire now roared up the adobe chimney.

The children were silent.

She called them, not looking for them through the window. She broke an egg into the coffee-pot. Grease exploded in little bubbles of heat in the bacon pan. Ellen said to herself that she was right to make up her own mind. She might go to the meeting, but she would do as she pleased after she got there.

The children hadn't come in. She went to the door. Her eyes were cooled by the light wind. Her breath grew longer in that burdened air of the morning. She called again. She stepped into the sunlight and walked past the house, walls of old adobe with a roof of hammered tin which her husband had made from waste cans a year before he died. A small shed faced her, with glass panes for its front. Here the chickens lived. Walking faster now, she heard a small commotion, a thrashing behind the shed, and Lena's voice chirping with a dry excitement. In a moment she saw Don standing on his bare toes, thrusting a pole at a snake that tried to coil in the shadow of the chicken house. Lena's hands were laid over her mouth. Both children were pale. The snake, a colour of the ground in shadow, flowed about the pole and retreated, thrusting away the loose dirt surface with a terrible constant strength. Ellen swallowed her breath. A sickness was in her tongue, and she stumbled forward running, her legs unsteady but her eye and her mind strong. She kept her voice quiet so the children wouldn't turn around. She took Lena by her bony little shoulders that shuddered from sympathy at her mother's touch.

"Get the axe, Lena," said Ellen. The little girl crying with a heart full of commotion turned and ran. Don's throat dried and contracted. Ellen heard him choke. She slid her arms over his brown thin arms until she could grasp the pole. Her fingers closed on Don's. She could feel his hard body beat against her own in their joint fight. It gave her a passionate anger. Stumbling together, inspired by her rage, they stepped into the sunlight, forcing the rattlesnake back. In the new light, the snake flashed and dripped with beads of light as if he were wet. The short grasses and the mild dust quivered upward under his lacing retreat. Donald's head was as high as Ellen's chin. His eyes were as sorrowful as her own. Her high cheekbones seemed to have a smile below them always, but her son's mouth, small and delicate, was stern. It resisted threats every day, from hunger and poverty, from natural pride put down by family grief; from private boyish terrors that he might die, and so leave his mother and sister without defense against the trials of living. On Ellen's face there was sweat. Her tongue dried against her teeth. The snake wrapped its golden dusky length against the pole. Lifting her arms, and Donald's, Ellen flung the snake twenty feet away, a streak that became part of the ground when it hit. Behind her Lena's hand pushed against her quivering flesh. Ellen reached back and took the axe.

"Don, stay back with sister," she said, and drew her fallen hair from her eyes and from the white corners of her mouth. She hefted the axe without feeling its weight, and started forward across the brief grasses, walking with a long pace, lunging jerkily like an old woman. In a little hollow of gypsum stone, white with pure sunlight, the snake rested ready, his arrow's head fixed. His rattles sang in the stillness, like a grasshopper in the weeds by the porch. Behind her Lena cried shrilly in her throat. The arrow's head moved slightly, side to side. The bright singing of the rattles loudened and stopped. The snake flew. It dustily struck the earth. In the confused shadow of her swinging skirt, where she stepped quickly, Ellen saw the dust-coloured body turn again into the coil. Panting out loud, sweating like a woman in labour, she grasped the axe handle with both hands as if it were the handle of a churn, and brought the rusty axe head heavily straight down. It was a thump that wounded the earth, a deep sound. The snake's rattles fluttered. The white belly turned up, and Ellen moved back again. She turned the axe in her hand and clove deep with it, cutting the snake behind its crushed head. A faint stench touched her nose, and entered her mouth, something that smelled damp and yet dusty, like mold, like a foul cistern, yet remote, as if it could be the imagined smell of an illness in herself.

She kicked loose dirt on the snake. The small rain of dust fell back where the body, bled of its smooth power, palpitated slowly to calm. Then she turned, dragging the axe behind her, and walked back to the children. Donald came forward on tiptoe.

"Is he dead?" he whispered.

Ellen took his hard thin shoulders and clutched them with her wet hands. She pressed her mouth shut. Tears rolled down to her lips. She shook the boy with a wild trembling strength. Lena was coming forward too. She began to cry again when she looked up and saw her mother's face, so worn, so familiar, assume the shape of a desperate smile now, while tears ran down its pale brown cheeks. The children understood that their mother was angry with them, and relieved, and fuller of love than she had ever been. The three members of the small, hungry family, three people abandoned by everything but their own ties, suffered a moment that lived as an influence forever after in their lives. The boy forgot it in time. But the weeping love of his mother, as a climax to courage, stayed like a picture with him always. The little girl knew self-pity and generosity, a throwing away of feeling to anyone who would take it.

"Come," said Ellen, turning the children toward the house. She took them to their breakfast. Entering the kitchen, she lifted the old yellow newspaper on top of the scarred sewing machine where she worked at times, and saw that her purse was lying there safe. The children laughed through the sucking breath of the lowering excitement. The purse was a black leather bag rubbed to a worn rust colour on the corners. It was a family joke, for Ellen referred to it as the "Black Maria," a phrase she had heard somewhere. Love of independence, and the agency of independence, these were shown the children forever by the frightened concern their mother had for her purse. It had rarely been a full purse. Now it was empty. Yet it accompanied her when she went to the village, and it rang in the mind like a nightmare when it was missing, with incident fears, pallid courage, and childish desire to make achievements to supplant the Black Maria.

The breakfast dishes cooked and murmured on the stove. Ellen agreed with Donald that the snake would not die until sundown; when he thought of that strange fact, his eyes troubled her. Lena shuddered, hating the snake and all mention of it. Her brother let thoughts drift in his mind like dust through fingers, a childhood feeling, which in words might give pictures of the damp hole where the snake lived underground; the gold tracks of its body through sharp grass in the dawn; the eye like a polished grain of sand caught in a drop of milk; the shift of those scales over one another as the body waved flat through the dust; the convulsion of the snake's body all day, the hot day, when the higher the sun rose the more lucent all shadows became, and smells from the desert were forced into the air, while insects made sounds like the air itself, and the snake turned hot and dead to the touch; until sundown, when the smallest grass could feel the cooler wind, and long rays of light bent upward on the horizon, and the dead snake would be at rest, no more treacherous and tried by life.

It was a land where men had to conquer trial and treachery always, the area of New Mexico that shared the plains country and the mountain country, and men deciding to live there chose the small valleys of reluctant rivers, and planted their trees, making a shade over their houses that was the only kind thing for miles around. It was the land of the Seven Golden Cities of Cibola, that had wooed the northward Spaniards so long ago. The natural mystery of plains giving back to the sky a second sunlight and of mountains drawing the horizon up to blue pinnacles dazzled men through three hundred years, and led them up the dry beds of creeks and over the heat lakes toward the Cities of Cibola, whose yellow gates they never found. Crossing the very plains and mountains where the terrible wealth was promised to be, they were always far from Cibola; their hope had no strength in it but greed; and legend was only a powerful mockery. What wealth they ever found in that land was created by man with the earth, and toiled for in obedience to the seasons; just as the human graces of shade trees and windmills had to be brought and planted before the land gave any comfort.

In this year, 1933, the marks of comfort were visible, once the town was in sight. The sky was blue in the slow-running irrigation ditches that dragged cool sandy mud from field to field. It was a cloudless April and the winter birds were joined by the mocking birds of spring, that sang all night long on fences and telegraph wires. In the early morning the air was scented with a sweet burdened wind.

II · SKYWARD

Living nearer to town than Mrs. Rood, the Larks still belonged to the country. Mr. Lark possessed a windmill that turned above his house and his turkey-run, shrilling and gong-like, a machine that drew upon the sky to bring water out of the ground. On windy nights, the fury of the turned fan and the complaint of the rudder chains woke Mrs. Lark and visited her for hours like pain. Her husband slept, immense and gaunt, while she held her hands on her breast, hoping to quiet the opinions of anger and disloyalty that arose there and made her heart thump. At such times she hated Lark; yet she could not hate him, for the length of their life together, and the vagaries of humour that kept him laughing or smiling into his old age. He dwelt upon memories, and that made her tender toward him; as a woman of labour and family long scattered, she knew the business of pushing the hours of the present to their fullest use. It was boyish of her seventy-year-old husband to be recalling, always, the circumstances of his boyhood, and the scandals of his early youth, the money he had brought West and lost, the feats of stamina he had performed on the range in winter through snow, or up the beds of dry rivers in the wry droughts of pitiless summers.

Yet Andrew Lark sometimes amazed her by conceiving a plan and executing it at once. In the light winds of the morning, in which his great metal flower turned and whined complacently, the idea struck him that if he greased the windmill, perhaps the next windy night would pass without the clatter that Nona Lark always complained of. He told her he was going up the ladder with a bucket of grease, and asked for his glasses.

"Now Andrew," she said, feeling short and helpless, wafting her glance across the pale blue sky over them, "you know you're too old to climb them rungs, that's thirty feet to the platform. You wait till Moses comes out next time. You just wait, now."

She saw him walk, the knobs of his joints pulling the tendons and releasing them jerkily. She knew from his hunched shoulder that he was smiling at her. His stubbornness was always irresponsible, a matter of laughter and sly slaps on her old thick buttocks if he chanced to pass her. She saw him go into one of the sheds that he kept so neat out in back. He emerged soon into the sunlight, wearing a wide straw hat and a rope slung across his blue shirt, that was thrust forward by the long bones of his great skeleton. To the rope was fastened a yellow pail full of grease and a stick.

"Andrew," she cried, hobbling forward; her face turned to a bright gold in the sunlight, deepened by parallel wrinkles, and toned by her freckles. "Now you stay away from them rungs."

Her cats gathered at her ankles with soft rubbings. Lark chuckled breathily and swinging his long arms that were heavy with bone instead of flesh, he passed her grinning. When she called him an old fool, he skipped, grotesquely, almost obscenely, with love of his own contrariness. At the foot of the gray weathered wooden windmill tower, he measured the height with a squint, and adjusted his bucket. He cleared his throat, and she thought angrily that he was about to begin one of his unbearably long monologues, drawing on all his past experience of windmills and their peculiarities. But he stood silent, putting his hands (they trembled, she feared) on the rung at his breast height. Then he started up.

His ascent against the blue broken pattern of sky that showed through the tower scaffold was an unbelievable movement to Nona Lark, standing below. His old legs that passed across the earth with rheumatic trouble, his arms that creaked in supporting a newspaper, were conducting him higher and higher. An absurd flow of pride touched Nona in the throat, and increased her fear. The silver wheel of the mill spun slowly above him, and he climbed to it without pause. Soon his arms were clawing through the square hatch cut in the platform below the wheel. He raised his head above it, and smelled the wind. The wheel, throwing incessant spokelike shadows over this higher world, whistled sedately by his very ear. Looking down, he saw Nona, and waved, as if he had gone on a far journey. A gray sickness crossed his eyes, at the changed colours of his wife, his farmyard, his roof, the bushes and tulips below there. The blood flew away from his sight and his mind. But only briefly. He recovered in time to see Nona wave back, and flop his hand at her whine of worry.

He drew forth his glasses, large black-rimmed circles, and set them on his nose. Then he crawled to the works of the wheel and the center rods, the chains, and the rudder that hummed as the wind shook its silver fin flatness. With his stick, he paddled purple and gold and black gobs of grease upon the bearings of the mill. Turning with the wind, a movement that took a skill of which he was proud, he saw the fan shaft eat the grease and pack it back into the unseen housing where it turned and went soft. He thickened the chains with plentiful greasing where the iron links chafed and squeaked. The wind was melodious in his ears. His zinc windmill with such sharp blades, twisted sailwise to own the wind, filled his heart with pride. Not for years had he been so close to it, for his boy Moses usually came up to fix anything that needed it. The mottled pale blue and silver blades charged and clanged softly as the wheel turned. That was a sweet noise, not one to keep anyone awake, a poor farmer's wife, whose old head was the scene of so many worries, real and invented. Andrew Lark deliberately avoided looking down at Nona, for that might suggest to her that he cared as much as a trotting mare's turd what he thought of her fears. He made a rich and hearty job of the greasing.

When he was done, and the fan turned, the chains quivered, without any metallic sound but only the sound of how the wind was taken and thrust by, he sat down safely beyond the turn of the bladed wheel and pulled out his newspaper from his trousers pocket. He leaned against a corner timber of the tower, and began to read. His incessant habit, it infuriated Nona now, for the unconcern it displayed. She threw her apron up to her face and flashed it down again. She turned back to the house, panting with anger at his absurdity. Once there, it struck her that he was up there to grease the thing as a favour to her, one she had begged to have done by Moses. In her parlor, troubled by the complexities of which her life was made, love mixed with exasperation, and gratitude with terror, she sat down on the ruby-coloured sofa of plush, and folded her hands against her lips, and sighed until she felt tears rise.

Through the cool dark doorway of the parlor, she could see beyond across the kitchen to the back door, screened. On the screen, haloed with sunlight, the three kittens leaned their forepaws high up, turning their heads sidewise and scratching dimly. The little one, mewing, pressed its pansy face on the screen. Nona left her sofa and went to the cats, thinking the little one was cute's a crab apple. She saw Lark walking toward the shed out in back. Her rising and falling from annoyance and tenderness and fright left her. She was suffused by an inner blush, some reference to their joint past, adventurous and successful. She knew how he felt about going up the mill. It was wonderful.

After breakfast he confessed that he had left his glasses up there on the platform. Her fury was so full at this that she couldn't speak. Her face flooded dark. He laughed. He flung his great flat hand against her breast in playful coarseness. He said he'd get Moses to come back from town with him in the afternoon. Moses would get them down for him. He wouldn't need them meantime. The silver zinnia hummed and flew slowly constant above the warming yard.

III · TO UNDERSTAND

On the farther edge of town, at the fork of the two roads that fed it, one leading to the railroad junction ten miles away and the other to the transcontinental highway that cut through the mountain, the long low shed of the cotton compress was a grape red in the early sunlight. The shed was so low that from a little distance it seemed to be part of the ground. In the good times, the trucks backed up to the delivery deck charging and ripping the air with exhausts, and the white and brown bales of cotton were rolled down the incline in a rich procession, while in the low tower above the shed the steam exhaust pipe blew like a gun, and the furious presses in the cool shadows of the building flung downward on the gray cotton with a wild grunt. Mexicans ran the machine, laboring half naked, deafened by the explosion of the exhaust and the echo like a low thunder in the eardrums, like a shocked blood, when the pressure was released and the baled cotton gorged forth to the waiting truck.

At the north end of the shed was an office, behind heavy doors. Here the clang and thunder and scream of the compress machine were slightly muffled. Yet when the plant was shut down, the silence was more difficult to stand than the boom of industry. No one stayed in the long red sheds but a Mexican caretaker, and the manager, and Heart DeLancy, his stenographer. But the manager was away, trying to save the business for his owners. The Mexican was surly from being underfed and indulgent of his humours which Heart thought obscene. She was sympathetic of his pennilessness, but the vigilance of her inner eye upon its own woes took all her emotions.

She was twenty-six years old. Her parents who had come here from Texas were dead, after raising her to her teens with intense propriety, naming her Heart out of sentiment for the love they'd had as bride and groom, and showing a long picture over the arc of years of how stubbornness must fail and turn weak when a man's hopes are time after time baffled by dry earth, disease upon cattle, the escape of the railroad through another town than this, and finally, most astonishing, old age and fatigue. Heart had worked for herself since she was seventeen. The results showed plain in her small brown eyes, which held a wry light, like some drift of fluid over unchangeable opinion. Her face was white, the skin drawn over the bones with a gentle firmness. Her slightly protuberant teeth showed always under her upper lip. When she laughed, it was a cold sound, yet her eyes danced, and a little flush took her cheeks. Her breastbone was prominent, her shoulders shallow. She was slow in her movements, even in her thoughts, but quick in her feelings, and full of desires, many of which she had happily fulfilled by her own enterprise.

The first of these was to be educated. Her Texan parents had both been full of intense but incommunicable opinions about life, the foundation of their experience, the trial at explaining their failure. Heart was convinced that education was the way to conquest of understanding. She had the usual schooling in county schools, and at seventeen, an orphan, had gone to take special work in a business college at Santa Fe. Here she worked as a waitress, supporting herself. Facts poured into her mind and were superimposed upon each other, warming her by their strange presence, and forgotten very soon. But the life she was leading brought her to the conception of another desire, one that she nursed until an inner gaiety arose whenever she considered it.

Seeing the tourists go through Santa Fe, in great cars, with clothes and accents from dim splendid places, she resolved to travel as much as she could her whole life long. She eavesdropped while her diners ate, listening to their tales, gossip, the fall of their speech, not intending to imitate, but desirous only of furthering the boundaries of her life, so bleak in its outline, yet so full of some inherited curiosity and fire at its core.

When she could typewrite and spell, when a little experience had shown her how to behave in an office, she returned to her home, and went to work for the cotton company. Her salary was good. The compress whistled clouds of released steam into the sunlight all day long, for months, years. The warehouse shed space was at a premium. The trucks rumbled off to the railroad ten miles away, bearing cargoes. Sometimes she rode to the junction, named Ramona, and watched the trains, saving her money in her bank account, and her feelings in her mind. At last she had enough money to board the train. She went alone to El Paso, and bought clothes. She went to California. The suffering light in her eyes was lost in her pleasure. She met people easily, talking with men as simply as with women. She spent her entire savings account in a month of investigation of the world. She came back poor, but content, and amazed by her own conversation, which drew authority from the facts she had observed, and sociability from the relaxation of her self-pity.

It was so in the good times.

Now the silence in the office at the north end of the raspberry red shed was a burden against her head. Heart was alone there. The cotton plants in the wide fields were withered and russet, from being unpicked. There was no one to buy cotton. There was nothing to bale. The engines and the steam were cold and silent. Her boss had cut her salary three times. Then he had stopped it altogether, for there were no letters to be written. Yet he had laughingly assured her that she was still the official secretary and left her her key to the office. Here she came daily, to sit before the typewriter, and compose letters to her friends whom she had met on her trip to California. She looked out of the window and could see ten miles eastward the brushed faint darkness above the horizon that lingered after the train went through Ramona. Between here and there was a tawny space of flat land, green only where artesian wells had been released, or irrigation ditches dug and willows planted. Out of the other window was the mountain, and the highway leading to it, people bounding on fat tires from coast to coast, able to assuage the restlessness that was American in so many of them as a people, and so individual in Heart.

She had been spoiled for the meagre design of her destiny, which was to live and die on the Southwestern plains, contributing what she could to the life of those small towns. Turned idle, her fingers unrented for the skill they had learned, she returned to her inner life, yet this time with no possibility of letting it purge itself in action and independence.

In town, opposite the Courthouse, was the newspaper office, with large plate glass windows reaching almost to the packed dirt sidewalk. Beyond the window was a linotype machine, which was operated by Rolf Kunkel. When she was successful, Heart had him call for her at the warehouse in the evening, and drive her home in his car. Other times, Rolf's shyness took on the quality of valour, a defiance, covered with blushes and contradicted by some watering of his pale blue eyes. He was nearly thirty, she thought. He was tall, and heavy at the shoulders and waist. His black hair grew in a formal series of waves to a peak over his left eye. She liked his large nose, and the biscuit of his chin, with the long cleft in it. She considered him handsome, and could imagine him in the clothes of a Californian. She was too crafty to investigate his mind, preferring the proofs of his value that she could detect in his body.

Day after day, idle in the office, she dreamed about Rolf. She passed a succession of plots through her mind each of which ended with his capture. At first she had thought in terms of marriage. Now, intense and lonely, without aim, her spirit straitened by poverty, she thought in dreamy terms of "illicit love." Rolf Kunkel went with no one else, she knew.

It was a morning like all the others, until the Mexican caretaker came up to the office door. She knew him by his walk, a step-drag, step-drag sound that betrayed his lame foot. She hated him, for he interrupted her empty bliss, and when he walked in she smelled the reek of his age and indifference, and was angry because he was smiling. She asked him what he wanted.

"Pues nada," he said, "nothing," and cuddled his old brown hands against his dirty vest, fluttering them against his belly as if they were captive birds. His smiling went on, and in his throat he made little moans of announcement and awareness. In a moment, Heart heard a car, and leaned to the window. Her pale cheeks reddened, which made the Mexican caper against the wall. Rolf Kunkel was out there. She watched him climb out of the car and come ambling heavily down the warehouse deck. His large face was sober, and she impatiently wondered what made him look so stupid. But when he saw her at the window, he grinned, and his blue eyes filled with shy cordiality, a mistiness, and she turned warmly away from irritation, to meet him, ignoring the Mexican's lecherous imaginings at this meeting.

IV · THE THREE SONS

If Mrs. Vosz went around saying that she had nothing left but her boys, then her husband, who was taciturn and opinionated at the same time, thought the same thing, but said nothing. The boys were triplets, seventeen years old, tall fellows, with yellow hair, and blue eyes that darkened with embarrassment or eagerness when they were filled with ambition or excitement. Their names were Richard, Joseph and Franz. It was a matter of delight to their mother when they left high school to help on the ranch, of their own free will. She took their hands in hers and wept upon their twisting knuckles, staring at them out of her weeping eyes with a claim upon them that was almost unbearable, for its intensity, the references it made to the amplitude of her donation to their living, and the dues which they must feed back to her in love. But Mr. Vosz, speaking calmly behind his curtain-like mustache, returned the boys to high school, and answered the fanciful fears of their mother with a rough tenderness in his touch upon her.

The high school was one of the few eminent marks made by man on the tawny land where the town stood. As the county seat, the town drew business traffic to the Courthouse, and boys and girls from surrounding ranches and villages to the high school. The Vosz triplets were popular in school, where their physical excellence, the thrice-repeated image of men growing out of clumsy sweating boys, whose hands were desirous and timid, whose minds dwelt upon the ripening of information with a secret and frantic intention, impressed the other students though they could not have said how. It was easy enough to admit that the triplets were magnificent athletes, which was true. The teachers sighed over them as much as the girls, for they were famous in their devotion to their mother. It was felt that anyone who was so good to his mother as any of the Vosz boys and was so clever in school, and so furious on the track field, must become a great man.

In the early mornings, Richard and Joseph would get up while a stratum of cool air still clung over the ground, and run a mile, pacing each other, their big chests lifted against the wind of their running, their legs rising and falling like harmonious parts of music. Franz, the other triplet, liked to sleep late. But his brothers got him up and dragged him out with them, making him practice with them for the track meet, which he disdained, knowing that he could do things with much greater ease than his brothers, and that he needed less practice, but only the desire like an inspiration to do anything, to do it brilliantly. Because he was so simply superior in the ease he had over his brothers, Mrs. Vosz often scolded the other two for picking on him. Their bland faces would laugh out at her, as if this were a malicious joke, not to be taken seriously. Franz would thrust his legs impatiently out before him as he sat down, and Mrs. Vosz, seeing how foolishly she had accused them, would begin to cry, begging that they not desert her in her poor fat old age, with her weak heart and her simple needs. This sentimental attack was even more difficult than her nagging. The triplets would crowd around her, stroking her bulging shoulders and back, making impatient sounds of consolation, while she let her head with its topknot of pale thin hair fall against the breast of one of them. If Mr. Vosz found such a stormy woe in progress, he whirled the boys away with his immense hand, and lifted his wife's chin on his wide thumb, looking into her eyes with a sad rebuke for her weakness. She would then control her heart that feared so many unnamable things, and let her love call out for acceptance by baking vast cakes and pies, pampering the boys and their father to excuse their memories of her tyrannical weakness.

But such moments had their weight afterward, when the triplets, abroad with boys and girls in exploration of fun and desire, would lose the sweet feelings of guilt they owned and find themselves hateful for the grief their mother would feel if she knew.

Such things as these didn't show in the pattern of the daily life which people saw of the Voszes. Mrs. Vosz went to her mid-week church parties in town, lamed by the weight her ankles carried, dressed in blue silk that billowed behind as she walked, nodding her head with its party hat that sat high on her faded hair. Mr. Vosz ran the ranch, though no one could sell cows at the price no one was paying. The sheep kept them alive, going at prices which a few years before would have been a rancher's joke. The boys went to school, working afternoons to get ready for the track meet. Richard was a hurdler. Joe ran the short dashes, and Franz ran the mile and did the high jump. The meet was to be held at the high school athletic field, on the edge of town, a sandy flat with a cinder track. Six schools in the region were entering teams.

But Franz still was too lazy to practice mornings. He could hear his brothers get up, and then the scratch of their spiked shoes in the ground outside his window as they practiced starts. He lay awake, with his eyes closed, then he slept suddenly again, until Dick and Joe dragged him out for breakfast. The sunlight was drifting slantwise across the stove where Mrs. Vosz was busy. The steam from the coffee pot turned a transparent gold in the light. The light bounded back from every clean corner of the room. The smell of breakfast, the virtuous smiles on the faces of his brothers, the unthought-of familiar shape of his mother, made Franz very happy, and he leaned far out upon the table in the kitchen, and thought of the track meet that afternoon; his stomach contracted pleasantly. It was a sensation that reminded him of the challenge to his stride, the fact that he would win, easily, and the simple chance that he might lose; the love for a physical game that kept him and his brothers so busy.

Mrs. Vosz brought the cereal bowls to the table. She set them down and watched the boys pour sugar and cream on. Their big hands, the hungry opening of their mouths, waved across her in a pitiful memory of their babyhood, and she passionately knew they were the same now as then, and that their hearts were untouched by the idea of love, and its consequences, which had drawn her own life down from girlhood to marriage, brief rapture and then devoted drudgery, with her mind losing everything but concern for her family, her body heavying, her fortunes lowering with those of her husband. It was some helpless devotion to life and acknowledgment of it that led her into the punishments she made on herself and the boys when she claimed them, over and over, to her own fidelity. After bearing a large family, now scattered into so many separate lives that touched her only incidentally, though she had given them birth, she had borne the triplets, a last terrible ordeal of her body, and a growing nourishment for her heart.

The boys finished their oatmeal. Their spoons scraped and they licked their mouths, looking to her with trust for the next food she had ready. Their eyes were laughing. She brought them their eggs and bacon and coffee, and then she said,

"I know you're good boys, I know it in my heart. A mother always knows."

She knew how they hated any tearfulness, or any of this business about love. Her words therefore sounded angry, for the control she threw into them. Franz slapped the table, and made a joke. They avoided the moment. They remembered times when they had not been good boys. It made them angry now to have such times brought up by what their mother had said. A certain mournfulness, an atmosphere of resentment, drifted over them in the kitchen. It was broken into open irritation when Mrs. Vosz said,

"How many of my boys are going to town with Papa and me?"

Joe laid down his fork, and said,

"Mumma, you know the meet's this afternoon."

The other two went on eating. But Franz looked up and saw the facile hurt expression on his mother's face.

"Mumma, you've known about it for weeks," he said. "We all three are in it. I'm running the mile."

"So you see, we can't," said Richard.

"What's happening in town anyway?" said Joe.

"Your father has to go to the Courthouse," said Mrs. Vosz. "Your track meet's not till the afternoon. We was going in the morning, and to lunch at the cafe, but I suppose it's too much to ask for a boy to be seen with his pa and ma."

There was a silence. The morning was recognized as hot, yet with stray tendrils of spring wind in it. The boys hated this sort of rebuke. Their silence, which was one of good judgment, seemed surly to their mother. She laid her plump hands with the smooth shiny filled skin on her bosom under her great rounded throat, and plucked in anxiety, irritation, at the loose flesh there.

"It's perfectly all right to get up before sunrise and get your breakfasts. I suppose I don't need any praise for that. Nor am I wanting praise." The strange churchy sound of the word praise took her emotions; it reminded her of God, God is love, and sorrowfully she began to weep. The boys knew it from her voice, for they were not looking at her. Their necks reddened. The intolerable justice of their debt, a debt of life and emotion, made them feel a little wild in their minds. But they went on eating, and their mother went on talking. "Oh no, you'd rather go off somewhere by yourselves or with them kids from school, God knows what you do with them, I pray so hard that you keep good and all, how do I know?" she cried, seeing the inevitable betrayal of her jealousies in the images of the triplets, who carried youth's burdens and needed to be rid of them, a need that contained fear and sweetness, a spending of youngness. "Every chance you get, you run away from us, you leave your home, God knows 'tain't much: your Papa has done the best he could:

and so've I, not that you care, with your track meets and all: what
is this crazy track meet: you ought to be on the ranch helping your
Papa instead of running to school with them girls. . . ."

Richard pushed his plate away and arose. He went to his mother
and touched her shoulder.

"Now, Mumma," he said.

She sobbed and refused his touch.

The other boys, with a heaviness in their hearts for the humiliation
of their spirits, and yet knowing a necessity of assuaging bitterness,
went to join Richard. They gathered around Mrs. Vosz and playfully
talked to her; they made jokes, and agreed that they were poor dumb
johns, and didn't deserve all she gave them. She admitted that her
heart was sore from things that she couldn't define, and that her
temper ran away with her. She kissed them all, and said she was
sorry for thinking mean things about them: she knew they were
good boys, in her heart, she said. They blushed. Franz, in confusion,
said that he would go to town with his father and mother, and after
lunch, he would go to the track meet. The other boys, he said, were
going to spend the morning at the field, practicing. He wouldn't need
the practice.

"I'll go with Poppa and Mumma," he said to Richard and Joe.
"You johns better get to work. I don't need the practice."

They all laughed together, and a new geniality came up. Mrs.
Vosz kissed Richard and Joe, forgiving them for not staying with
her. It was Franz, who did everything so easily, the handsomest, the
sweetest, she knew, it was he whom her secret heart loved as the son
of whom the three boys were the triple likeness.

V · INTENTIONS

Fat's Cafe was across from the Courthouse, and a couple of doors
down from the newspaper office. It was the place where occasional
transcontinental motorists stopped for lunches and suppers, and
where all five of the high school teachers went now and then for a
festive meal. In the good times, when the movies were showing twice
a week in the Imperial Theatre down the street, Fat had crowds for
supper. When the cotton compress was running, the truckdrivers and

the foremen, the visiting ranchers and farmers all came to eat with Fat. He composed affectionate little ads for the paper, "Fat's Cafe, The Lunch Grand," and "Elegance and Home-Cooking, Fat's Cafe," which brought his appearance and his voice before the reader's eye. Fat was the owner of a sad face with a fastidious expression. His flesh flowed in a widening line from his ears, the button of his chin, his buried jaws, down upon his breast and back. His arms were pink and delicately modelled, in spite of their grossness. His hands were small. With them, he worked over his hooded stove, and served his customers, smiling with his mouth, that never lighted his eyes in the same expression. His thoughts were always emphatic, but his voice was thin and high, a prayerful tenor that made him sound bewildered. His most constant thought about himself was that he needed to be hard. He would shriek at high school boys who tried to charge their cups of coffee and doughnuts. They would smile, and walk out, and later pay him, making him feel that some strength was missing somewhere in him. But the air of steam hooting softly above the range which he kept so well-shined always restored his happiness, and he forgot the necessity of being as sceptical, as narrow-eyed, and as "hard" as the men of the town whom he knew as a fellow citizen. His pride lay in his Cafe, in the accomplishment of every small order with as much elegance as he could put into his cooking and serving.

That was why he had a waitress; it was, he said to himself, why in such disastrous times as these he still employed a waitress, though the crowds were thinned down to the old level of his early days, when he had been sufficient to cook and serve too. Every morning at seven o'clock, Mrs. Rocker arrived, and she stayed until ten at night, leaving Fat to close up at twelve. She went home to her naked boarded house that had one room and three beds for herself, her husband and their six children. Fat had called for her once in his car, to take her to work. The sight of the bedclothes, the collapsing white enamel and brass beds, the hardened and shined and worn plaster of dirt on the floor, the happy, lousy children, the dogs and cats who slept and ate in the quilts and the dishes with the family, the smell of old lazy animals that filled the Rocker house, turned something in him to disgust and then pity. Mrs. Rocker had been so cheerful always, so unexcited about her way in life, that he'd assumed her to be well-taken-care-of. After that, he couldn't pick her up, and for weeks he struggled to be hard, and discharge her, for the place she came from must certainly threaten the cleanliness of his Cafe. But if she saw his sullen agonies of intention that failed to crystallize in act, she said nothing, but smiled at him all day long, rubbing the counter with rags, sweeping corners, pulling her hair out of her eyes, and laughing through her lips that shielded very few teeth. Fat remembered in despair the beautiful girls who waited table in El Paso, with their eyes painted blue and lashes black, their cheeks shading from high crimson on the bone to plaster white at the neck, their mouths rouged, their hair bleached. He often comforted his soul in bed with the scheme that he might one day marry such a person and bring her to his bed and his Cafe. In the meantime, Mrs. Rocker found things to do all day long in the Cafe, smiling with trust upon him, never questioning his rightness, and taking her small wages from him with an agonizing, flattering humility. She was simply dependent upon him: and too, her husband, the children, the cats, the bitch who trailed complacent dugs to feed the litter for whose mother the Rockers could spare a little out of even their own needs.

Yet as the months went past, and spring approached, with no better trade, the grocery stocking fewer dainties, the teachers staying home at their boarding house when the County passed up their salaries, Fat knew he must discharge Mrs. Rocker, for there was nothing to pay her with. He could do the work himself. It would be a relief. In the afternoons, when great dinners should have been mingling their rich fumes on his stove, with Fat himself tasting and planning, the stir of spoon in stinging messes, and deep content of filling up kettles with most edible stews, he had lately been sitting at the counter staring at newspaper pages, not reading, only watching pictures, while he grew drowsier and drowsier. The light changed and ebbed from his long narrow Cafe, while the polished light brown of the counter vanished way back in the room to shadow. The row of six tables opposite the counter receded like a darkening checkerboard. It would take a cup of coffee to wake Fat up at four o'clock. Waking from his unsleepy daze, he would see Mrs. Rocker beyond the stove sitting on the packing box which was her own domain and smiling at him, as if she were waiting for him to awaken and take her smile. Fat thought angrily that she looked at him like an old fool hound dog bitch. But he could say nothing.

In the morning he went out to the grocery, and returned with a number of extras. Good times or bad, there was no difference to Mrs. Rocker. But he knew that the track meet would bring a lot of visitors, and he must be ready for them. He could take in enough to give Mrs. Rocker a week's wages and tell her not to come back. He had just spent every dime he owned in cash, and still owed the grocery. The morning was brisk and sunny. Mrs. Rocker left the door open to smell the wind off the plains, while she scrubbed at the large mirror facing the counter. Her cleaning stroke left rubs of light soap. Fat dumped his provisions on the table beside the range, and got hotly to work. Every time he turned around, she was smiling at him in the mirror, clouded and turned witch-like through the soapy reflection. His fat hands flew, shaking the upper arms. His skill revived; his knife flashed in the steamy sunlight around the stove. His spice boxes of green and red with gold exposition labels flourished above the copper pot and the rubbed aluminum vat where the soup bone protruded, boiled blank of succulence.

Presently Mrs. Rocker moved back of the counter. To pass Fat she had to squeeze against the counter, and he had to tiptoe and lean over the stove. It made him blush with exasperation. Who wanted her here anyway? She was in the way! She bent under the counter to get her sugar sack to refill the bowls. Her buttocks touched Fat behind his leg. He turned, ready with a fury that he couldn't explain. But Mrs. Rocker, innocently straightening up, moved down the counter at her work. She poured the sugar into the glass bowls with hinged metal tops. Fat said to himself with the emphasis of his opinion, "God damn it!" and went on working. Pretty soon, the old mood came on him again, and the mixture of his vapours, the ingenuities of his baking and his precision, satisfaction at applying the knowledge he had found out for himself and turned to use, let him begin to sing. His voice, so short of speaking, was expressive in song, and an original melody he had sung for years at his work, over and over, without change, rose from him and vanished up the tin hood of the cooking range, a sound like a part of the morning.

Later, Mrs. Rocker came back from the front of the Cafe and showed him an empty catsup bottle. Her expression assumed openly that it must be filled, and that Fat, who had everything so excellent, would see to it at once. He looked at her toothless smile, the dancing, familiar content of her blue eyes. Unable to name it, and so argue it away, he saw again his obligation to her, which he must meet or admit failure. How could he tell her there was no money at last? You don't buy catsup for nothing. Maybe tonight if there was a crowd in, there would be money for that. Also, money to send Mrs. Rocker away with.

She set the bottle down and went back up the aisle behind the counter. He felt again the severe need to be hard. It was not his fault that the Rockers would starve together, the old man, the kids, the cats and dogs, anything else that lived in that shack. He turned back to his stove. A rattling noise from the front of the Cafe made him turn. He threw down his butcher knife and shrieked with all of his confusion, dividing his small voice with his unfamiliar vehemence, "Y' old fool, quit disturbing all that!"

Mrs. Rocker, who had been rearranging the Chesterfield cigarette cardboard displays, turned back to look at him, amazed and a little frightened. After staring at the sunlit window space, her eyes were dim until she was used to looking down the aisle of the Cafe. She saw, in a moment, that her fright was foolish. Fat was standing there, wiping his knife against his apron where it rounded across his stomach. He was smiling at her, his face was a heavy red, and the idea that he had sounded mad at her was lost in the new idea that he must have been joking, for he laughed a little before he turned to his meat block and began to slice chops.

In a few minutes the Sheriff came in for a cup of coffee. Mrs. Rocker served him, for that was her office; and when it was done, Fat strolled down the aisle and leaned on the counter where the Sheriff was, and the two men without speaking greeted each other by staring into each other's eyes, long and with unchanged looks on their faces, the Sheriff looking above his tilted cup and Fat leaning on his palm; neither having anything to say, yet mindful of the custom of sociability.

VI · COWARDS

In the road camp eight miles from town, Leo was awake when dawn began. He always woke up before sunrise, with a cold abandoned feeling in his stomach. He wrapped his thin arms around his chest, shivering at the fleshless articulation of himself, and watched the sky send reflections of light on the hazy brown earth. When the sun was up, the road camp would awaken. He would drink coffee, and thank the men for letting him sleep all night with them. Then he would start off again, walking on roadsides that had small stones in their dirt. When he stepped on a small stone, the jolt shocked by relay all the way up to his neck, and his head, a small head with white cheeks and reddish eyes, rolled with an ache. Cold and dismal though he felt the dawn to be, though it was early spring and an occasional smell full of sweetness and promise touched his nose, he closed his eyes and inched into his blanket, planning in his mind how warm and happy it would be if he could stay all day, sleeping in the blanket in the little tent. But this was a positive desire; his strength, physical force and private will, was all gone. He hardly possessed opinions any more, saving only that one which let him believe in his heart that life was altogether miserable, a thing that could just as well be denied and ended, in spite of the strange gripings in his stomach that made him beg food every day, or in his mind that kept him toiling toward California, on alien roads in the company of no people but other aimless paupers like himself.

The sun now showed, after silent trumpetings of gold rays above the waving line of hills. A blur of gold that looked wet as melted metal grew along the horizon. An intimate light turned the sunward edges of all things in a brief golden beauty, cactus bushes, small pebbles, the poles of the telegraph by the road, the small tents of the camp, the barred and chained bodies of the trucks, any growth. Then the light became suddenly equal, and shadows faded, while a returned chill smote the air that had been briefly warmed. Distant hollows in the ground lost their blue mists of broken light, and clumps of trees came out from obscurity, and the town eight miles away in the sharp early light had a clean toy-like look.

Leo was fogging his memories in a returned sleep when the boy in the tent with him sat up with an explosion of breath, and a yawn full of noise like the sound a dog made when yawning. Leo's nerves sickened tight at the disturbance. His tent-mate crawled out into the light and went to wash. He was greeted by a dog. There was one more moment of stillness in which the humming of messages on the roadside wires travelled clear, and then the camp seemed all at once to be awake and busy. Cooking smells drifted to Leo's nose. The mucus wept a little at this stimulus, and rolling his head with weak desire to arise, Leo felt the saliva run down his mouth and choke him. But he came to his crawling position, and left the tent. His feebleness made him seem old, though he was twenty-six. His smile of ingratiating thanks, of willingness to help with anything, made him look like a sneak, for a scar held one corner of his mouth down, and any pleasant expression turned to a sneer on his face, while in frown or repose his face had a thin starved dignity, under the bald rise of his round forehead that bulged and made his head so much too big for his neck and shoulders. The camp boss told him to sit down and wait for breakfast, impatiently, embarrassed by the weak murmur of Leo's voice, and the tragic affability he so hardly managed.

At last, holding a tin cup of coffee that burned his fingers, he knew a tide of courage run through his aching tripes, and he told the men eating with him that he was moving on to California that day. He had been, he said, without work for fifteen months. He did not add that he suffered from tuberculosis of the lungs.

"In California I know plenty of people. I have an uncle who is a lawyer. The climate will be easier on me, too, than the East."

He spoke with a precision of word and tone, making reference to his past, which included education, ambition, content, and no plan for such a present as he owned. He told them he would make it in another week at the outside. From New Mexico to the coast was an easy route. The coffee, having shocked him into well-being, now cooled in him, and indigestion returned, his mood faltered, and he grew silent, weakened. The men ate stolidly, silent except to comment on cars that went by on the road, a few in series, then none for a long time. Leo looked after the cars.

"Damn their souls," he said.

The camp boss looked at him curiously.

"I had a car once," Leo continued, a pale flush showing on his cheekbones. It was a weak whimper that he made, and the boss indifferently turned back to his food, easily certain of what to think of cranks who magnified their hard luck into a whole attitude toward everybody else. But Leo went on talking, his big head shaking on its poor neck, making the only protest he knew to make against the circumstances of the life that let him lower every day into helplessness. It was a murmur, almost impersonal because of the feebleness of its delivery, against the larger lives that survived while his own faded. Everything he said referred to money, and its absence from his pockets. The men let him talk, hardly listening any more than if they were listening to the crying of a cat. Nor did Leo expect them to listen, for he was talking to himself. It was a rehearsal of the thoughts that made him dream at night. He presently fell silent, knowing no conviction from his breakfast or his tirade.

The men got up. The cook watched them dump their dishes into the big tub for washing. They went to the trucks, and soon a wild firing of the exhausts sounded out. The trucks lined up on the road heading east. The boss told Leo he was sorry he couldn't offer a lift on the road but the trucks were all working in the opposite way. Leo said it was all right; he thanked the boss for the night's shelter and the breakfast. The affability in his eyes touched the older man, and as Leo turned to walk off to California, stumbling slightly on the rutty roadside, the boss had a feeling of pity and half-comprehension, which if he could have said it would have told that every scale in life had eagerness to exist, and that to see this eagerness defeated by forces beyond control was pitiable.

Walking slowly, Leo had travelled over a mile when a car pulled up beside him. It was already hot in the open country, and the sparse sweat that his body could produce showed on his face. The man in the car said that a man he knew, the road camp boss, had told him to pick up this guy. Leo got into the car, breathing through his mouth. He smiled his unalterable sneer, and settled back on the seat. The driver was a fellow about thirty-five or so, Leo thought, heavily tanned, and thickly built. He was smoking a pipe. His face was bland and almost merry. The car was an old coupe, travelling with loud winds of mechanical maladjustment. Yet it was cool in the car, and Leo felt a kindness toward the day that brought a sensation of strength with it.

His driver said he was coming down from his filling station in the hills to town, and could take Leo as far as that. He claimed to be always willing to give a guy a lift. He spoke with a Southern accent, and presently revealed that he was from Georgia, and in a rush of confidence that surprised Leo, he sketched his past with an assurance that it must be of interest to anyone. He'd been in the navy during the War, and after that had a job with a bank that didn't pay enough, and it was a raise to drive a long-haul freight truck in Alabama. That didn't last very long. The Texas oil fields looked good, and when they cut down, he drifted up to New Mexico and got a job helping in this filling station. He enjoyed talking about himself, contented with his past, and requiring little of the present. Leo thought him an enviable person, for the bodily strength he had, and because life to Leo had become the necessity of wanting what others had. Facts about Leo didn't interest the driver. He gave no time for any confession. The first interruption in his agreeable reminiscing was a blowout. The left rear tire gave out, and the rocking car slid on loose gravel for several yards before it was halted. The driver sat still for a moment, humorously nodding his head.

"Wul, Gawd da-yum!" he said.

Then he shrugged, and got out, lazily, stretching his arms after tucking his pipe away. He knocked the seat cushion out of place, and dragged out the oily dusted tools. Leo stood by him, wanting to help. The driver threw him a wrench to start loosening the nuts on the rim, while he himself jacked up the axle. Leo set the head of the wrench over a hexagonal nut, and threw the force of his body against the lever's force. Up his arms went pains with a fluid swiftness. He smiled and tried again. A little gray caked dirt fluttered to the

ground from the wrench head. He couldn't turn it. His chest began
to hurt. He coughed, slaking his dry mouth. In a moment, the driver
came around beside him, and then saw that nothing had been done,
he grasped Leo's arm with a lifting grab and set him aside, making a
disposal of such a puny wretch. Leo stood by. Rage boiled in his
throat. In a few twists of the wrench and an easy slide of muscles,
the driver had the nuts off the wheel, and the tire bouncing on the
ground as he leaned it against the running board. While he worked,
the driver whistled a tune. Now and then he looked at Leo, who
was sitting on the shady side of the car. He thought Leo was laughing
until he saw that it was shivering that made his head wobble and
his shoulders tremble. But there was nothing to shiver about, and
he ignored it, turning back to the new tire which he was screwing to
the wheel.

Leo was shivering from injustice. His arm was bruised where the
thin flesh had been rubbed against the bone by this man who had
set him aside like so much tumbleweed. In his heart was a need
to refuse further help from such a man. He stood up. The driver
began to let the jack down. The car settled on to the new tire and
the driver withdrew the jack. Leo watched the spare tire flatten down
almost as low as the punctured tire had been. He waited for the
driver to see this. He pointed it out to him, smiling with a timid return of friendliness. The scarred lip showed his teeth. It looked like
a sneer, a delight in this foolish hard luck. The driver looked at the
tire. He kicked it. He turned back to Leo and said, in a roar of
sudden exasperation,

"Well, wap off that Gawd da-yum smahl!"

He went to the front of the car and pulled out an old tire pump,
and set to work. It was slow going, and the tire rose imperceptibly.
Leo sat watching a Negro approaching them from down the road.
Making a small cloud of dust with his kicking feet and swinging his
hips from side to side as he walked, a mincing, muscular stride, the
Negro approached, and Leo could see that he was young, and of
medium height. His eyes were sleepy. He was smiling. In his hand he
carried an old stick. The driver didn't see him coming, but when the
Negro said,

"Mownin' boss,"

he turned, resting his fist on the pump handle.

"Whey you come f'om, nigga," said the driver, in an exaggerated
accent that Leo coupled with the fact that he was from Georgia.

"F'm down de road," said the Negro, leaning in a friendly way
against the rear of the car. "Havin' tah trouble?"

"Git a holt hah," said the driver, throwing the pump handle toward the Negro, who smiled like a pickaninny with candy and did nothing. The driver tightened his stance on his spread legs. He looked at the Negro waiting. The Negro laughed out merrily, full of sunshine and goodwill on the morning when the wind blew so gently and so freshly. He crossed his legs, standing with a certain natural elegance, a racial and physical ability to express his mood with every change of his body.

"Did'n yoh heah me, nigga?" said the driver. Leo saw that his face was a deep plum red. His own mouth turned dry, suddenly, when he saw that the driver was angry. The Negro closed his eyes and shook his head, shaggywise, spilling out the mood of comic happiness he held.

"No zah, boss," he said in a rich voice, hoarse with comedy. "Ah don' want pump no tahs . . . ," exploding into a hooting laugh that assumed universal amusement at the situation. Leo saw the red fade from the neck and head of the driver, and relaxed thinking that his anger was gone. But stooping quickly to the ground, the driver picked up in each hand a small stone that would fit the closed fist, and with a blast of breath from his nostrils, he bounded forward and hit the Negro twice, once with each fist, against the temple and on the jaw. The Negro's eyes fell open, and he choked on his laughter. He dropped his stick. He fell against the car and rubbed his head. In his hoarse voice, roughened first by amusement, he began to wail, making no words, but only doleful syllables. Before him stood the driver, boxing the air, and leaning and leaning with his body, and smiling with the simplest face of pleasure. There wasn't the slightest look of fury about him now. His merry eyes were lighted with fun. The rhythmic, slow spar of his hands had a gaiety in them that was full of grace. He turned his body at the waist, swinging rapidly. He waited for the Negro to recover his breath, and to lose his amazement of pain.

The Negro lowered his hands from his head, with his enormous fingers spread out. Leo thought it was like a monkey in a zoo lowering his paws from his puzzled head when he had a headache, a thing he couldn't explain or touch, some alien menace.

"Come ohn," said the driver. His voice was teasing and humorous. "Hit me: hit me, nigga."

He backed off as the Negro lunged forward on his feet. Blood was curling down the Negro's face from the cut temple. He shook his head. The driver poked out with one rapid arm, and cuffed the Negro's ear, a stinging and taunting hit. Leo sat down on the running board suddenly, too shaken to stand. He tasted the coffee from breakfast as it regurgitated into his throat. He swallowed with control. The Negro was weakened by astonishment. Leo clenched his mouth and hoped the Negro would hit the driver.

"Hit him!" screamed Leo suddenly.

"Ah'll hit 'im," said the driver, lazily looking at Leo with appreciation, and instantly thrust his fist into the Negro's belly. The whimpering stopped. The Negro took in a series of shocked little breaths through his mouth, making a sound. Then he skipped out from his position against the rear of the car, and dancing wildly on the road, he gave an appearance of having his tail erect, with his head up and his back curved in. His hands played across his front. The driver glowing with delight danced around as the Negro's eyes cleared and watched for an opening. It came, and the black hands drove to the pink jaw, that jerked away. It was the last blow the Negro landed.

"Oh, yeah?" said the driver, and clutching his stones till his palms sweated against them, he swung right and left against the Negro's head, his body; breaking the left ear and ripping teeth down into the bone with a remote crackling sound. He beat the Negro back to the side of the road. The stoned fists cracked against the black skull. They drove into the Negro's belly, rising up under the heart and the ribs. Leo saw the Negro stagger and fall into the ditch, and ran forward from horror. The driver leaped down into the low ditch beside the road and picked the Negro up. He stood him on his swaying legs, and knocked up the Negro's arms, making an insolent demand that the Negro defend himself, guard his body before the new attack. Blood ran down from the Negro's eye, looking pink upon the grayed flesh of the face. The driver grinned. His pink jaws were widened by the pleasure of his blows. The pain of the Negro's first blow on his face was something exciting and stirring, like the quickest delight imaginable. The Negro wandered in tiny circles, hardly standing. Along with the sedate and narrow welling of blood out from his lips came a whispered wail. The driver leaped once more. He drove one hand to the Negro's mouth, closing the fat lips and whitening them. He struck with a wet accurate sound at the jaw with the other hand. The Negro's eyes rolled upward, and the lids stayed open, and the eyes showed white. Bleeding slowly, the Negro fell to the ground in the ditch, where it was half shady. His breath wheezed with wetness. The driver threw down the small stones from his hands and spat on the ground. He looked cheerful. He stirred the Negro once with his foot, almost gently, and watched for any awakening. There was none.

Scratching himself in the crotch with an easing sensation of triumph, he went back to the car and slapped Leo on the shoulder.

"Ol' nigga get fresh wid me," he said with a certain tender simplicity. He laughed softly in his throat, and leaned down and picked up the brass tire pump. He bent his back up and down over the pump. The tire rose slowly again.

Leo went to the side of the ditch and looked in. Half in sunlight, the beaten man lay like a large baby, his knees bent, his forearms bent back and the hands lying with relaxed curled fingers above his shoulders. His head was rolled to one side, and the red and white issue from the mouth flowed slackly to the ground. The eyes looked dead. But threads of tortured reflex tightened in the body, and it quivered every few seconds, accompanied by a windy grunt from the working throat of the Negro.

Leo sat on the edge of the ditch and wept. He could taste his own illness in his mouth. He wept without ideas and forgetful of words. In his weeping were flashes like blindness that showed him how much he hated the driver and his acts. He felt hatred for himself, who had stood vomiting and helpless while the Negro had been beaten down to a ditch. He saw the body stir now, slowly, as if awakening from some hibernation. But it quieted again at once, with only the shocking quiver tightening and loosening in the torso and along the legs.

The driver threw down the pump and kicked the tire.

"'At's O.K.," he called to Leo. He unscrewed the pump hose from the tire valve, and threw the pump into the seat with the other tools. He replaced the seat cushion. Then he walked over to the ditch. He chuckled, and said as if he liked the Negro,

"Ol' nigga be 'bout an hou' comin' 'roun. . . ."

Leo set his wrists against his eyes to stop his weeping. He stood up.

"Time we got goin'," said the driver, and turned back to the car.

"You're going to leave him here?" said Leo.

The driver stopped. He laughed generously.

"Fo' Chras' sake!" he said, and then disdained further answer or comment. He clambered into the car and started the engine. He called to Leo to hurry. Looking again, Leo saw the Negro there, whose life slowed in the black body. Then taken by a strange panic in himself, Leo turned and ran to the car and clattered in beside the driver. They drove off. The wind cooled them. Nothing could cool the burning shame Leo felt, to be riding here now. The driver lighted his pipe and sighed, for his body was contented with the spend of violence it had made. He smiled dreamily. His mouth moved around the stem of his pipe as he talked.

"Ol' nigga," he said, with amusement. "He sho' made a mistake to git fresh wid me! Eh?"

He turned to Leo.

"He sure did," said Leo, loathing himself.

"Sure beat up on 'im, didn' I?"

"I'll say," said Leo.

"See 'im try to hit me?"

"Yeah," said Leo, and laughed. The droll pity in his voice satisfied the driver. Its cowardice set Leo trembling in his breast. He closed his eyes, looking inward upon himself. All he saw was a tired soul, begging sleep.

VII · UNDER THE WIND

The Courthouse stood in the hot sunlight, with shadows of the tall trees washing over its yellow brick front. The building was two stories high, rising toward a roof of chocolate coloured slate. In front was a tower that rose a third story, and ended bluntly, in a cluster of dormered windows. All the windows of the building were tall and narrow, with rounded tops. Their edges were trimmed in gray stone. The window woodwork and the doorways, the glimpse of cool hallway inside, were finished in dark varnish, brown with a glow of red beneath. The Courthouse rising from a country of dust had something of dust's colour in all its parts, except where the shadows waved like a cool wash across its front, in blue leaf echoes. The trees were great cottonwoods, planted forty years before, watered in their early sprouting by the ditch that used to flow from the river; grown in their middle years to be large enough for hangings after posses returned with human trophy; now stately, like patriarchs whose wisdom lives in their mere physical presence, after all sight and mind have been feebled.

On the thin scatterings of grass before the Courthouse, the crowd grew as the morning went on. Shortly after eight they had begun to assemble, leaving their cars, trucks and coupes and sedans, touring cars, around the corner and down the main street, parked in front of the newspaper office and Fat's Cafe, a line of various cars spreading as far as the garage at the point where Main Street became highway. They came with lunches wrapped in paper. They came with empty stomachs and fearful breasts. Their greetings were lively and happy, as the eddies in the crowd changed and distributed the individuals. Coming together for a common purpose, the people of the town and the country were easy in their meeting, like people who have for generations drawn comfort from the camp meetings and revivals of the plains. They made a texture of gossip, walking and glancing at the Courthouse under the trees. High in the yellow green boughs the wind turned coolly.

From the throng rose a sound, broken yet sustained and overlapped, like a murmur of bees, heard closely. They talked about the troubles that touched them all equally, in common. There was no money and since there was no money, often there was no food, and certainly no good clothes. As individuals talked, their private and separate prides appeared, and though they had come like everyone else to demand and receive help from the Government this morning, their eyes and their voices carried hints from the past, when the ranges were cropped by great roving herds of cows that moved like the mottled shadows of clouds over the tawny unchanging land, and money rolled into the bank in town; when the stock corrals at Ramona, painted white at the railroad side, were always full of the rich herds waiting to be pulled east to market; when there was a vast cotton market waiting to buy the white burst pods from the local fields; when oil was predicted between here and Ramona, and the drilling crews came, setting up derricks that worked all night, with great white lamps flaring so they could be seen for miles. . . . A past unmindful of hope, for the great plenty and occupation of its time.

Now in the morning that grew hotter as they waited, stirring uneasily because it was after ten and nothing was done yet, the gossip enlarged itself from mouth to mouth. It was true that the representatives of the Government had arrived from Ramona a little after eight, coming by the seven-forty-five train from the North. They were seen in the Courthouse, going over the files of the local emergency committee with the Sheriff. In the meantime, rumours grew. The Government had sent money in bags. There was food in boxes inside the Courthouse, held safe in the vault, where the gold was, in its bags, a safe enough place since the bank had failed. A thin girl with a prominent breastbone, and excited eyes with a wry light in them, moved forward through the crowd, holding by the hand a tall heavy man who grinned foolishly at being dragged along so. Her voice was shrill, telling anyone that it was time to get help from the Government, and that it was also easy, with the gold in the Courthouse vault that had been moved in during the night, for safety.

"Did you hear that?" exclaimed a heavy old woman who sat on a bench near the front steps of the Courthouse. "They brought gold in during the night, in the Courthouse, during the night, they was attacked during the day, so they brought it during the night."

The news roved and crackled through the people, several hundred of them.

The door of the Courthouse was open, and they could see the dark hallway running the whole depth of the building, a brown tunnel with cool light at its far end. Now and then a door would open in the corridor, and a clerk would walk across to another office. Each of these small events caused the crowd to stir and shift, pressing closer. The people in front thought the people behind were crowding them toward the building, leaving plenty of space back there near Main street. But the space near Main street was filling gradually, as more people came. Old men and women grew tired, and their limbs began to tremble. They sweated and wiped their faces. At the far edge of the crowd, a small man with a heavy head on a thin neck lifted himself on tiptoe and craned for a look at the Courthouse door. He could see nothing. Slowly, with heavy breathing, he began to slide his way through the crowd. His voice, begging passage, was high, a whine, like a cat's.

At the front of the throng, a little girl, tired of waiting, ran up the steps and into the door. The crowd laughed, seeing their own desires so frankly acted out for them. An inner door opened, and a strange man led the child back to the sunlight, smiling with an official frown at the crowd. He stepped back in the building and closed the doors. The little girl began to cry, from petulance. The crowd was silent, totally, in a hush like the air in the treetops. Then sounds broke, they let their opinions out, and the press of each person upon the next, the hot morning, the desperation of their needs came together and lifted the sounds of voices into a low menace. Suddenly the bodies were pushed together. A witless agreement made everyone surge toward the doorway. The old woman sitting on her bench near the steps was overturned. The bench broke down, and she cried out in distress. Her son was somewhere else in the crowd, and her husband had been talking to a tall old man under the far tree. The people stopped and helped the old woman to her feet. They set the bench up again. Someone cried out, "Stop pushing!" and the tension relaxed. They breathed apart again. Perplexity grew, wondering what in the world could be going on in the Courthouse. A youth, bright with eagerness, ran to the trunk of the tallest cottonwood, and clamping it with his arms and knees, he climbed up. He walked out on the heavy branches toward the windows in the front of the building. He laughingly peered down, and the crowd looked up at him, delighted with his audacity, the scheme for seeing what was going on inside. He sat down on the bough and swung his legs.

"Can't see a thing," he called.

The old woman on the broken bench looked up and saw her son. She cried out to him to come down. He laughed. He turned and ran back along the bough, balancing with his brown arms outstretched, running on his toes, his yellow head bent to avoid the small branches about him. The leaves shivered at the impact of his feet on the bough. When he came to the trunk, he reached up for a higher branch and swung on it with his hands. He turned his body in midswing, and hooked his legs over the branch. Then lazily he swung himself up to a sitting position there and sat looking down on the crowd which had forgotten him. He was panting; his pink breast rose and fell under his rough blue shirt. He was thoughtless and contented with muscular play.

Shortly before eleven, Do Miller drove into town from Ramona, where he had been to pick up a part for a car he was repairing in his High Way Garage. The street choked with cars surprised him, but he remembered the meeting, treating it mentally with great scepticism, having heard at Ramona that the Government people were coming down just to make a survey, and see what had to be done, and how to do it. He drove his service truck as near the Courthouse as he could, and then walked half a block to see what was going on. He saw the crowd, stirring in the heat of approaching noon. Nothing seemed to be going on. It was sure a big crowd. Most everybody in town was there. He recognized dozens of people. He laughed at the expression made by the backside view of the fat man on the outskirts of the crowd, who was dancing on tiptoe, with his dimpled arms raised, in airy efforts to grow tall enough and light enough to see through the crowd, or above it. Do Miller rubbed his forehead with the back of his hand, habitually mindful of the motor grease that might be on his fingers, and turned away. The spider gear he had got needed installation. So far as he could see, there was just a mob of people waiting there for nothing. Touched by his own vague approaches to philosophy, he swelled his chest. Then he felt sorry that so many people would be disappointed if the Government people really had nothing to give them. He drove his truck back to the High Way Garage and went to work.

In the cool stucco interior of his garage, after a while, he could hear the noise. He sat back on his heels, setting his wrists on his knees, to keep the greasy touch of his hands off. In the whole stillness of the day, with the town deserted in favour of the meeting, no cars moving, or bodies passing, the noise grew and expended itself without stopping. The crowd was yelling. Do walked to the open double doors of the garage and looked down the street. He could see nothing. But the sound was angrier, and his mind made sudden pictures for him of who was yelling, the people he knew so well. He couldn't picture Andrew Lark screaming at a blank building, or Mrs. Vosz or old Fat. Mrs. Rood, whose car he had sold for her for sixteen dollars, would not raise her voice like that. Mrs. Lark was a proper little old woman, with the most modest eyes he had ever seen, always downcast, except when she said something fooling, when they were raised for a sly look. He threw down his tools and stuck his pipe in his mouth. He started to walk back toward the Courthouse plaza. In his middle was a slightly sick feeling, for the unrecognizable sort of noise the crowd was making. He thought he could begin to hear words, the closer he got. But they just eluded his ear that would sort them out of the confusion. When he climbed on top of one of the battered trucks driven in by a farmer, he saw the waving arms, the shaking heads that roused the howls. He stood in the sunlight, which was almost straight above him, intense and palpable.

Suddenly the noise from the crowd lowered.

A softer sound, the panting of all the breaths, made an expectant pause. The door of the Courthouse shook in someone's grasp again, and then it opened. The double doors were thrown open. The crowd slacked off a little. Air spaces widened between the figures. On the stoop of the entrance, the Sheriff appeared. Someone called out his name, and he waved his arm, genially, yet his face was cross. He rested his hand on his hip and slouched one leg. His voice was hardly audible, yet it was firm and impatient.

"We are doin' the best we can in here. It wasn't our idea to have any mass meetin', anyway."

Someone called to him, "Cheer up, Sheriff!" and the crowd laughed, nervously. They didn't know what his words meant. He opened his mouth as if to speak again, but changed his mind, and looked across the faces once or twice, and then backed into the doorway, which he left open.

From the rear of the crowd down to the very front, wriggling his way and panting, touching people's necks with his wet cold hands to make them give way, Leo struggled forward. He was possessed by a desire to be a part of the crowd. When they murmured, now, at being abandoned again by the Sheriff, he lifted his voice with theirs, making no words, but only a dutiful meow of menace that was absent-minded, bent as he was on reaching the front row of the impatiently waiting people. He knew no one around him. The driver had left him at the edge of town, hours earlier. Leo wanted to be washed; he felt that some atonement must be done by him before he could be again a human being, after the events of the early morning on the roadside. He let himself into activity, instead of thought. He crawled against the resistant bodies of the crowd, trying to pass them and be one of them. His face was white and his eyes fired with exhaustion.

On the outside of the throng, Fat rose again on tiptoe, keeping his balance by lifting his arms. He could see nothing. But in a moment he heard a sigh go up, some greeting, and knew that the people were busy with something. He became suddenly angry at being so ineffectual. He felt, in a quick minute of recognition, the core of something hard in him at last. With a fury like pleasure, he began to beat his way forward, not caring for his neighbors, and determined to find out why nothing was done for a starving country.

Down on her bench, Mrs. Vosz settled her arms on her bosom. She looked up to the stoop, and nodded her head with a vague matriarchal dignity. In the doorway, pausing briefly, was a strange man, who smiled at the crowd, and then walked slowly forward to the top step. He was followed by the Sheriff and another man and a woman who was taller than any of the men. She was dressed in a bluc linen suit. She wore glasses and turned her head from side to side, smiling with her upper teeth exposed. The crowd made sounds of expectancy, and satisfaction. They turned to each other, saying, "Well, at last." The Sheriff lifted his hand, and indicating the first stranger, he said,

"This is Major Drew, and he will say a few words to you."

Drew smiled to the Sheriff, and bowed, with a platform courtesy that seemed out of place. He turned to the crowd, and raised his shoulders and dropped them, settling his arms behind his back like an orator. He lifted his neck out of its collar a little, and cleared his voice. He had a large pink head and raised eyebrows. When he talked, they couldn't hear his voice at the rear of the crowd. He said that he and Mr. Edwards and Miss Molton had made a preliminary survey of the needs in this county. So far as was possible, they had read every report of complaint and request filed in the Courthouse. Maybe he should explain, said Major Drew, that the Government, in these matters, always required a preliminary survey, which was to be followed by a routine relief agency, where food and clothing would be issued as needed. He hoped it would be possible to establish this agency here within a month. In the meantime, he wished to say that the interest exhibited in the work was very gratifying.

Major Drew paused and brought his hands around from resting on his rump. He folded them in front, and cracked the knuckles, stretching his arms downward.

Miss Molton glimmered with her glasses and her teeth at the crowd. The blood was pounding in her throat, and her mouth was dry. Her smile was a twist of strain on her face, for she watched the crowd, and their quietness was strangely terrifying. Major Drew looked at her for understanding. The crowd had listened, but said nothing, and seemed to understand nothing. They simply stood, waiting, in the dusty heat of noon, under a somewhat risen wind flying faster over the low buildings of the town.

Major Drew nodded his head paternally at the near members of the crowd, and began to speak again.

"We find that your conditions here are very uncomfortable, of course," he said. "It will be our aim to bring help as soon as we can. But I *will* say, I *must* say, that up in the northern counties, the suffering is far worse than yours here is. We have been working night and day, nigh-tan-dday, up there."

"When do we get ours!" cried a voice from the crowd.

The crowd let itself down with a noise like wind. Here it was, the question, at last. Many voices brought it up, now, and full of self-pity, some of the old people began to moan and weep, holding forth their thin arms where the bones showed against the skin like the stems in a leaf, waving their arms vaguely at the group on the steps. Major Drew stepped back a pace and then forward again, as if he had made a mistake to retreat. He extended his arms.

"Please, please," he said. "Let me explain."

The news travelled back through the crowd to the rear, which had not heard, that the relief agency was a lie. There was no help. They talked about investigating and reporting, and so on. As it passed from unminded mouth to angry ear, the news lost all reality, and became merely something to defy. Knowing hunger, and remembering a winter of sharp helplessness, the people heard rumours inside themselves as clearly as they did the words from the steps.

Miss Molton was talking now. Her voice was piercing, and every ear could hear. Her words trembled from the strain of her sincerity. Her tongue clove to her mouth from nervousness. It made her sound guilty, and the crowd hated her for her hesitations. She told them that when the relief station was opened, it would run as long as it was needed, with herself in charge. She said she was sorry that the news had leaked out that the officials would be here today, because they were not prepared for any meeting, or to give out any food. Or money. Whatever had brought them together, she was glad she had a chance now.

"I'm glad I have a chance now," she said, wringing her bony hands upon her breast, "because I want a chance to tell you all how much everybody understands how brave you all have been in these hard times and they have been hard, and they might go on being hard times for a little while longer, and, but, the idea is that we have all got to do our best for each other. So now that we understand the situation and all about how it is here, why, Major Drew and Mr. Edwards and myself, we are all going to see that things, your problems and things here, will be taken care of. As soon as possible. The very first minute."

She opened her mouth to say something again, but she had no saliva, and she swallowed painfully. A bright wetness stood in her eyes, from the strain of speaking against the will of the crowd, that now crept forward thoughtlessly, its faces strained and blanked by the effort to realize the fact that there was no relief about to be given out. There was no gold in the bags in the Courthouse vault, or trucks of food. Miss Molton coughed, and then turned abruptly back to Major Drew and Mr. Edwards.

The atmosphere over the plaza seemed to grow closer and hotter. A mood like the warming of the day ran over the heads. For a moment, a bated interval, there was nothing. And then on a wail, a woman's voice rose, screaming,

"We want money!"

"—Food!" declared another voice.

They had stood most of the morning, waiting.

Without a summons, they had gathered from all their places to come, and once together, to receive.

They awaited leadership. They stirred from foot to foot, imploring one another with blank eyes.

The wind, like something in that human weather before the building, sang dismally against the trees, and the air darkened a faint little as the fine dust of the surface was stirred and turned.

The voices were talking against one another, yet with the same burden behind them. The relief committee on the stoop could not be heard. They nodded, with pleading expressions on their faces.

They shook hands with the crowd in pantomime, and failed to believe that a temper was gathering into a unanimous strength. To look at them, the people were kind and honest, average. Already one or two at the outskirts were beginning to drift away toward the waiting cars. Miss Molton nodded to her companions, and they turned. They went into the building. The Sheriff stared at the way the crowd fell back upon itself as the doors swung shut. Then he heard the wave begin to rise.

The mob tightened instantly. Small eddies of people in parts of the crowd turned against itself. In one of them, Heart DeLancy began to shriek an address at her immediate neighbors. She worked until her arms were free of the pressing people, and then above her head she waved them like brands. Her words tumbled out in a shrill line, and Rolf Kunkel, standing behind her, pressing upon her in a public intimacy that flushed his veins, heard a mad eloquence stream from her. Heart was wild in his eyes. Her strength was amazing. As she turned to free her message of discontent and desire, she struck him on the shoulder with her arm, and the blow hurt with a dull energy. It enflamed him to see her staring at him and screaming, as if she hardly knew him, yet had to convince him. She was convincing others. The crowd settled close around her, waving their arms. They called out agreements with her. There was gold in the vault, and it might as well help lives now as later.

She turned and pointed to the door of the Courthouse. There was a low silence, while the crowd paused, and the voice of an old man rose up saying a prayer. Awed and happy, the crowd knew its strength. They began to sway slightly, and Mrs. Vosz's famous contralto voice was lifted in a line of song. Under the tallest cottonwood, Ellen Rood heard herself singing also, a pale troubled voice that came back to her ears with all the force of her despairs that she had never yet yielded to, as she was yielding now. The old man praying was Andrew Lark. Every sentence he spoke ended on a rising inflection. His eyes were closed, and he was trembling, transported out of himself.

It was a short pause, filled with the breath of exaltation. Heart cried out again. There were echoes. They began to push against the bodies of each other, and as they moved, together, their voices roared. They started across the sidewalk to the foot of the steps. Leo was turned and rolled like a log in the current, rubbed against the trunk of one of the great trees.

"Oh Lord?" declared Andrew Lark, "where Thy steps take us, so there shall we walk? Lord. Amen: amen? Oh, Thy steps, Lord? We shall walk in Thy ways? Glory?"

As she murmured a faint melody, vague and hopeful, Ellen Rood admitted a strange peacefulness to her breast. Her heart seemed to be overflowing with richness, for she was at one with the people around her, and she remembered the revival times when the bleak sorrows of her little family had been made to glow with some fine life in the flood of prayer. So she felt now, clasping and unclasping her fingers; her eyes stared and her voice trailed uncertainly in the wake of her joy. It was escape. She was forgetful of herself, her children, the dangers of the morning, and the emptiness of the future. The crowd around her were moving and tightening toward the Courthouse. She raised her arms and imitated the threatening gestures of those around her. Her face was changed. She would not have known herself.

Mrs. Vosz struggled to her feet as the crowd closed about the bench where she'd been sitting all morning. The fervour of old Andrew Lark's prayer had started her singing, and she could see his face, tilted back and free to the windy sunlight. The slyness was gone from his leathery wrinkles. His eyes were dropped half shut, and he prayed with his mouth slacked, biting no labial words, only letting his tongue articulate in his mouth. Except for the dim movement of the tongue, he looked like a man dead, whitened by sun and sightless. His voice continued with a curious power. Mrs. Vosz began to weep at the beauty of her singing, which rose and fell in a mournful strident sound, hollow of music but charged with meaning for the crowd.

Heart DeLancy was steady in her effort. So much in her was being fused to a purpose that her influence travelled through the crowd. At one point she saw Leo fixed upon her with his immense eyes, and in a recognition that belonged to the genius of the moment, she knew his hysterical strength, and she grasped his thin hand over the heads of those near, and burning with a power that depleted itself only in action, they cried out and charged forward, making shocks and impulses that bruited from body to body and mind to mind. They moved. The singing of the women, the prayers from the old men were submerged.

Do Miller had about decided to go back to the garage when he saw the crowd tighten and heard the praying voices rise. He laughed to himself, at the inappropriateness of the sounds. He was moved again by the peculiar feeling that people he knew well, every day, seemed now like strangers, as parts of the crowd. He saw little old Mrs. Lark biting her lips together with an expression like a taste of vinegar, and beating her fists against the air, as she shuffled forward with the mob. With a red face oiling itself in sweat, Fat, the proprietor of the Cafe, had beaten his way through the crowd and now stood looking with an expression of stern virtue over all the heads near him.

Do was simply conscious of the changes he saw.

There was a shock through the crowd, some physical tug like the pull that goes down the line in a freight train from car to car. The crowd started up the steps, and at the same moment a loose stone sailed through the air and wrecked a window in the left wing of the front door.

Do Miller jumped up again on the truck where he'd stood watching before.

The glass chimed to the stone stoop. Men began scrambling on the ground for loose dirt and rock to hurl. Heart found a brickbat and threw it. It struck the stone trim of a window and fell feebly. They engulfed the steps.

The doors opened quickly.

The Sheriff stepped out holding his gun. With his left arm he motioned the crowd back, frowning sickly. These were his townsmen. He raised his arm over the charging mass. He fired three shots in the air, at random, and a few clipped fresh leaves spiraled slowly down from the cottonwoods. The three shots broke the noise with silence. The people stopped.

When the silence was complete, the Sheriff said,

"I'm sorry to use a gun against all my friends. Now quit, and get home out of here. We've had it hard all year, and 'tain't any easier right now. But it's going to be, soon's possible. They ain't any gold in here, nor food, nor the like. We can manage for another two weeks. Now we got to hold on. Now break it up."

He watched in silence then until he saw the first falter in the crowd. The sound of his three shots, fired over their heads into the air, seemed still to echo. Someone sobbed once, with fright and fatigue. It made a sound suggestive of shame. The crowd loosened. Some shook their heads. They returned as if from a dream to the direction of their ways, the separate lives that had been so intensely merged and shared.

With a scowl of friendly approval, the Sheriff nodded, and turned back into the building, leaving the door open, the way unprotected, for he knew by feeling that the menace was relaxed. The people moved out to the street from under the shade of the great trees, breaking up into small groups for talk, reassuring one another, and divided between shame and indignation at having been fired upon. They found their cars. How much longer they would be able to buy or barter gasoline and so keep the ability to move from farm to town, they could not know.

From behind the Courthouse, they saw the Sheriff's car appear with the Government officials in it, heading toward Ramona to catch the afternoon train.

Mrs. Vosz stood by her bench waiting for Franz and Mr. Vosz to get her. She was weak from the excitement of the day, and the tears still rolled down her cheeks from the commotion that her singing, her yielding, had made in her. She saw the crowd thinning. They stirred the dust. The wind picked up the dust and made a dull gold haze in the air. She saw Mr. Vosz moving toward her slowly; his sober stride contracted her emotions. She knew how he hated fuss. She wiped her eyes with her shiny fat wrists, and pressed her bosom to find control. She began to smile for him, when someone screamed "Look!"

and she turned to see.

Among the branches of the tallest cottonwood there was a slow rustle. She saw two swinging legs appear below the bottom branch, and then the fall of a body, that rolled on the dust and fought against stillness by cramping its knees upward. She saw the face of her boy Franz smiling with absent-minded pain. On the white breast through the blue shirt she saw a well of scarlet. The remnant of the crowd closed about him. She fancied she heard him call her. Whenever she needed it most, strength came up in her. She gave the back of the bench a shove for impetus, and walked with a violent weighty stride to the shade of the tall tree. The people opened for her. She knelt down with gasps of effort for her immense fat legs and body. She gathered Franz delicately into her arms and tried for his pulse. She had no tears, and she knew from the blue veils of his eyelids, the whiteness of his mouth and the inertia of his body that he was badly hurt.

"It must have been the shot," said someone in the crowd. "He fired them into the trees."

Franz opened his eyes and with an ashamed gallantry at his succumbing, he nodded and smiled that this was so. They saw the flesh eaten from his palms by the bark of the tree, where he had clutched them to keep from falling at once. His face was scratched by twigs and little branches. The blood rolled out of his breast and sopped the handkerchief his mother was holding against him. Mr. Vosz was suddenly beside her. In a low voice she ordered him to back the car into the plaza. People drifted close shaking their heads, and a new resentment against the Sheriff arose. Trembling, Mr. Vosz got into his car. Franz was dying, he could see it. How could his mother bear up so! They lifted the boy into the car. Fat had run to his Cafe across the street for clean napkins. They made bandages. Mrs. Vosz saw in her mind a surge, a threat of all that this life would cost; she bent down to slake the wound, rigidly staring at the bullet hole with its pale blue bruised rim to keep herself conscious of what must be done. They drove slowly to the street. Mrs. Vosz called out to Fat to send the doctor out to their place at once. Ellen Rood got into the car with Mrs. Vosz. The boy breathed with a short, slack sound. He seemed to fall lower and lower against the two women who held him. He kept licking his white lips. In a voice that was stern, his mother spoke softly to him.

"Be still; we will get you home; everything will be all right."

Ellen Rood saw how frank and delicate was Mrs. Vosz's touch upon the pack bandages that had to be changed constantly.

The road lay ahead of them in a straight line of dust. Though their house was one of the nearest farmhouses to town, they could hardly see it for the stirred cloud of dust that drifted low on the land. Mr. Vosz gripped his steering wheel and asked a question, how Franz was, but his voice made no sound. Pictures returned to him of the times of crisis in his family. Always it was his querulous wife who turned with a heavy strength to meet emergency and trial. He was weak in adversity. He thanked God that he had something to do, such as driving, though the wind carried fine gritty dust into his eyes, and pitted his cheeks, and rattled faintly upon the faded surface of the car.

As they neared the house, Franz opened his eyes with a look of inquiry. His legs stiffened against the women's for a moment, a soft tremor that seemed to press for reassurance. He shook his head a little, as if to shake free some puzzling thought. Inspired by Mrs. Vosz's majestic and serene control, Ellen Rood said,

"There!"

to the boy, and at once began to weep. He shut his eyes again and the trembling pressure of his body was quieted. By a secret hysterical suggestion, Mrs. Vosz thought of the track meet where his brothers were running and jumping. Her hands on his shoulders heavied with a terrible resentment that Franz was wounded rather than one of the other boys. She inhaled sharply in rebuke for the thought. The three boys would all gather again at the high school field. They would! They would!

The events were slow in starting, and the contestants strayed over the center of the field, a grassy place which was enclosed by the running track. In the white sunlight, which was filtered by the haze of rising dust, the athletes made a pattern of brilliant color. Their trunks and jerseys were spots of orange, vermilion, yellow and magenta, and white, blue, green and maroon. Their bare arms and legs drew color from all these tints of cloth. The grassy plot was already green, and moving against that and upon the black cindery track, the boys' shapes and colors leaped to the eye. They pranced like horses, limbering their legs for the events. They knelt and practiced starts. Running backwards, they danced against the wind, serious and intent upon the science of preparing for races. The two Vosz triplets paced each other, grunting under their breaths. They were watching absently for their brother.

At one o'clock, the starter's pistol sounded, cracking down the wind, which was rising continually, making it hard for the runners to breathe comfortably. The spectators were ranged upon unpainted bleachers. They were mostly boys and girls from the competing schools in the district, though a number of people from town had come from the Courthouse meeting to watch the contests. They sat facing the mountain, which was disappearing from its base upward, as the plain let its surface into the air in a wind of dust. The sky at the horizon turned a gray white. Above, it shone blue and brilliant where the sun stood.

Richard Vosz was announced for the high hurdle event. He trotted to his place in line. At the sideline stood his brother Joseph, watching him. Dick scraped the cinder track with his cleated shoes once or twice, and spat on his finger tips, a gesture of confidence rather than utility. Joe nodded at him. The starter raised his stubby pistol. He glanced at a small crowd of spectators who were just arriving, having parked their cars at the gate. He glanced down at his stop watch, and cried, "on your mark" "set" and fired.

The boys leaped ahead. Excited, the new spectators ran forward to see the hurdle race. They leaned down the track. The hurdlers ran with their heads up, rising with legs spread like wings to take the hurdles. Joe heard his brother's name from one of the newcomers. He glanced, and the speaker turned, and saw him, staring with a peculiar reluctance. Joe looked back at the race again. He saw Dick, yellow head and green jersey above white trunks, take the last hurdle far down the straightaway, and breast the tape in a final lunge. He started to run down the trackside to Dick, when someone took his arm, and looked at him, again strangely, and said,

"Joe, did you know about Franz?"

"No, he's late. Where is he?"

"They took him home."

A sensational communication that ran through the people spread to the bleachers. They began to rattle down from the board seats, and cluster around Joe, watching his face to see what he would do. They felt sympathy, but their curiosity was more powerful. Joe looked at the faces around him, where obscure messages were implied. He was suddenly turned by suspense, like fear.

"What about him?" he demanded.

"He got shot."

Heart DeLancy leaned forward, and came between two people to speak to him. She put her hands on his arm, and mindful of how much he looked like his brothers, she was excited so that her voice quivered.

"He had an accident, Joe," she said, turning to see the proper understanding of her tact in Rolf Kunkel's face. Rolf nodded soberly at her, and Heart continued. "He was sitting in a tree before the Courthouse, and the Sheriff fired at the air, above the crowd, nobody knew Franz was up there in the tree. The bullet hit him, and he stayed there. He sat there, I mean he hung on until the crowd was pretty nearly gone. He fell out of the tree after that, and your mother was there. And your pa. They took him home."

Joe looked at her in a wild silence.

She said,

"I don't know how bad it is."

Joe felt her fingers on his arm, and saw the faces around him echoing his own expression of fright. Their eyes opened like his, and their mouths dropped. They had seen what they came to see. He flung Heart's hands away and turning, ran down the trackside to meet Dick, who was walking slowly back to the starter's line, pigeon-toed, breathing hard, flushed with his victory and modestly hanging his head with a heavy grace as he walked. He was listening to the poured praises of his schoolmates without acknowledging them. Joe ran up and struck him on the breast, a heavy blow.

"Dick," he said, choking on his dry throat, "we got to go. Franz is hurt bad."

Dick paused a second, then without asking details, he fell in beside his brother, and they ran to the gate, past the crowd, Dick pausing only to grab up his sweat suit. He struggled into the upper half of it as he ran. They started through the gate and down the road that led to town. But Joe stopped, and said,

"We can't run all the way. . . ."

"Here comes Rolf. We'll ask him."

Rolf and Heart were hurrying toward his car. They waved to the boys to wait, and climbed in. The engine started. Rolf backed and turned, and overtook the boys, flinging the rear door open for them to get in. Dick threw himself on the seat, and lifting his legs, pulled on his sweat pants.

Rolf drove to town, where Main Street was thronged. The crowd had broken into small groups. Men stood with men and women with women, among the cars, talking. They seemed to be excited. They shook their heads, and as each little group separated and went to its various cars, there was an attitude, common to all, that contained grief and anger. Rolf drove slowly through the crowded part of Main Street, and then crossing town headed out to the open country on the other side. Joe sat forward gripping his hands. Dick sat side-wise, listening with him to another telling of the story by Heart. There was bitterness mixed with her sympathy. She leaned over the back of the front seat to talk to the boys. Her excitement of the morning was gone. She remembered her actions with a detached shame, and flushing at her own hysteria among the crowd, she told how the people *had driven themselves* into a riot, and that Franz had gone up in the tree before any of it started. They had seen him run out on a limb and try to gaze into the Courthouse windows. He laughed and ran back and had climbed higher. They had forgotten him. The sheriff fired into the trees. She remembered seeing some leaves fall, and hearing the strike of the bullets among the thick branches. In some awed fashion, she made an eloquent story of the descent from the tree, until the brothers writhed from concern and excitement.

Rolf sat, large and troubled, driving. His big face with the weak blue eyes was puckered in an agony of sympathy. He swallowed several times, for the lump of sorrow in his neck. The dust, twisting into the car by its speed and the wind, got into his watering eyes. Ahead of them, the sand blew in thickening clouds. They could see nothing, and now found it difficult to hear Heart speaking, in the increased wind. They rode swiftly along in a void of blowing dirt, anxious and impatient. Dick suddenly leaned and hit Rolf on the back, and said,

"God damn, can't you hurry, Rolf?"

Rolf said nothing, too amazed that he should be abused at a time like this. Heart turned back to the front, knowing she must not look at the fear on the boys' faces. Rolf leaned over his wheel, and the stupid suggestion of him that his body made filled the boys with despair. But he stepped harder on the throttle, and the car, groaning and cracking as it bucked the wind, leaped a little as it took new speed, and the boys sat back, and sat at once forward again, watching for a first glimpse of their house far down the road, which was hazed by the blowing drift.

Now thicker, the sand rose high enough in the sky to obscure the sun, and the light turned yellow, softening everything, and bringing a sharp drop of temperature. Off the plain below the mountain, the wind rose and carried sand, pulling it in a great veil across miles of ground, so that the town could not see the mountain, and the spring morning disappeared with its freshness under the choking afternoon, that swept its new atmosphere across the whole valley, obscuring everything.

VIII · SUNDOWN AND AFTER

Closing the hidden afternoon, dusk found the wind dropped, and the horizons clear, and a stillness in the air that was welcome after the choking storm. Ellen Rood reached her home just before sunset. She was left there by the doctor, driving back to town from the Voszes'. As she entered her yard, she called out for the children; and presently they came, meeting her with excitement, confusing her with news of the day's events, none of which she heard, content to know the comfort they gave each other by being together.

The sun was vanishing on the edge of the plain, warming that black shelf of the world. Donald suddenly squeezed his mother's arm and holding his breath from regret, he turned and ran back of the house where the failing light lay even. Twenty feet past the chicken house, he stopped running, and walked on tiptoe, bent like an Indian. He went through the dusty open places he knew among the scrub bushes and grass. His eyes were fastened on the snake. The closer he came, the more strictly he knew that he was too late. He had missed it. The moment toward which he had been working all day was gone. The sun was gone, and the twilight turned softly dim. The snake lay quiet, never to quiver again, as he had seen it quiver at intervals in the hot morning, and shudder under the sweep of the windy afternoon.

But if he had missed watching the snake's sundown death, he need no longer be afraid to touch. He went closer, and turned the snake over with his foot. The wavy coils slid and changed so suddenly, with such a heavy fluid weight, that he jumped back, scared by an echo of life. Then he laughed hoarsely at himself, a catch of breath in his mouth, and toed the snake once more to prove that he was not afraid. There was no quiver. The sun was down. The old snake was really dead. He kicked a few scoops of dirt against the long body, and trotted back to the house, where the light of a lamp in the kitchen made him shiver with awareness of the evening's coolness. The green yellow flare of the gasoline lamp through the window was something that made him feel all of a sudden like a very little boy again, and at the same time, charged him with responsibility, like a man. He quickened his steps, running to the door, needing to be inside, where the yellow lamp shone with quiet clarity upon everything he knew and loved.

Ellen too possessed some feeling of restored security in her kitchen. She laid the Black Maria on the sewing machine and covered it with the newspaper properly. Then leaving her hat and coat, she bent down and pinned Lena's hair up on top of her head, making the little girl resemble a tiny adult. The child squealed with fun. The heaviness in her breast began to melt, Ellen thought. She felt tired and no longer desperate, or lonely. When Don came in, swaggering a trifle, she wanted to laugh out at him for his assumption of importance. She sent him for water, and began to gather the sparse ingredients of her family's supper.

Moving at her familiar concerns, her mind became pleasantly empty. The children helped her. They ate their supper without talking, though thought returned to Ellen when she watched the children eat, with hunger and satisfaction in every gesture of their spoons, their mouths, their licking tongues and working cheeks.

After supper, they turned the lamp a little higher, and gathered in front of the kitchen stove where vestiges of fire still bloomed through the velvet ashes. Lena lay in Ellen's arms and Donald sat by her feet, facing her, while she read aloud to them in halting voice that wavered now and then from fatigue. The story was from Grimm's fairy tales, an ancient copy on gray paper with rubbed binding of faded red. The world of swans and forests, deep and treasured obligations in the hearts of princes and swineherds, was a simple and real thing to Donald. His little sister always dozed, breathing like a puppy, with hot nose and petulant little sounds. Ellen read with a monotonous inflection, an expression something like the doleful and vague aimlessness that her singing in the crowd had that morning. But the story always filled her with feeling, and some transfer of that touched Donald.

The evening latened. It was fully dark outside now, and the strange day was ended. Lena lay sleeping behind the fairy book. Don rubbed his eyes to stay awake, and Ellen had briefly forgotten the ride of the afternoon, charging through the dust storm with the heavied body of Franz Vosz held by her and his mother. Ellen knew before Mrs. Vosz that the boy was dead. Waiting for her to discover it, Ellen wondered wildly what to do. The car jolted on, beating against the crossroad wind. Presently they saw the Vosz house through a rift in the dust cloud. Mrs. Vosz petted Franz to encourage him. She found out then.

Small red embers sifted down the grate of the stove. Ellen's voice fell away. Like her children, she seemed ready and willing to succumb to tiredness. Around her, for this moment, were all of the things that let her have peace, however humble they might be. The room was crowded with possessions, none of which had value, yet all of which were valuable to her for the impulse she had to gather them and hold them, some attempt to make up with profuseness what she lacked in worth. Her mind wearily and in content turned upon the troubles she faced, along with the rest of the people in the valley. But aside from a feeling that someone was responsible for her, and must help her, must help everyone in difficulty, she was happy. The kitchen was warm and the children were by her. The lamp faded gradually, as its air pressure in the gasoline bowl lessened. She saw with an intimate pleasure that a pot of beans was soaking on the floor beyond the sewing machine. It was a kind of happiness to feel tired, and to give in to it. She sat with her eyes closed. Her high cheekbones preserved the illusion of a smile on her worn face, though her mouth drooped. She forgot the Voszes.

IX · SOLACE

By sundown, Franz Vosz was properly arranged in death. He lay in the front room on an ancient sofa. His face astonished everyone with its difference: he looked hardly like himself, they thought, not perceiving the absence of beauty, the famous splendor which all the triplets had in almost equal measure. Now, with color fallen out of his cheeks, and his eyes shut, his mouth stiff against his teeth, it was possible to see that the boy's features were anything but distinguished, and that bereft of its character, his face and body, impersonal, should fail to echo the things in him that had been loved. All the evening people came to look at him in the parlor, and were shocked by this trickery of death. They would look at the ageless face, and then consult their memories, and then turn to see the surviving brothers, to recover some image of that dead boy that would be recognizable. It was Franz's memorial, that the eyes of the living should reject his dead likeness as faulty; and seek for some less real thing than the facts of his bone and still flesh, the architecture of his person, and demand as vestige any reminders of his spirit, made of laughter, loyalty, wit, strength, and easy vitality and rich temper.

His father remembered him best.

He remembered exactly the difference in this son from his other triplets, which was a sly, childish pleasure in excelling them at everything, and a modest refusal to do so very often. He remembered that Franz had been cleverer with people than his brothers, and that he had also been, so, more inclined to tell lies, and evade bothers, all with the greatest and most charming blandness. Mr. Vosz had wept, in silent spasms, when he had driven in to his own porch and been told by his wife that Franz died about three miles back. He had carried the boy in the house, concerned in his mind with stopping his sobs, a first concern of duty and self-consciousness. In the early evening, he received the people who came to call, unable to say anything, but he shook their hands, and suggested with an embarrassed wag of his head that they were to go in the front room and see the body. He was divided between thanks that people should be so kind as to bring sympathy, and resentment that his private grief was so exposed to anyone who might come.

Mrs. Vosz, on the contrary, though she would see nobody, lying inert on her great bed and swelling its shape with her shaking body, required Richard to report to her whenever anyone came, who it was, what they said, if they had messages for her; her mind trivially busy with the social aspect of death in the family, while her heart slowly grappled with the grief that sat there. Her fat hands were fretful, wandering to her lips, or her temples, holding handkerchiefs and pressing her heart. In her eyes, behind the tears that streamed ceaselessly like a veil to keep her from seeing too clearly, was a latent spark of comprehension, a little force that would grow with her memories until she would know the real size of her loss, a deprivation that was the greater for her years of wildly building up its meaning and value.

She heard cars come and go; the low voices of consolation, the shriek of some uncanny dog in the yard. She commanded her mind to invent tasks. Her hands travelled with her thoughts, and lying in tears upon her bed, she seemed more active and restless than if she'd been on her feet at housework. Finding things for Richard and Joe to do, her voice told them in hoarse groans. Behind all these devices of evasion moved images of Franz, of her three sons, whose epitome he was. She saw him run down the yard as a tiny child, with yellow hair, and trip, falling, returning to her with bleeding knees, and a little face ugly in rage, his tears mingling with the run of his nose; she remembered his boyish cruelties to dogs and chickens with a perverse tenderness; how he looked asleep when his brothers had carried his cot one summer dawn out to the yard and brought her to see the joke of his not awakening; she called back family scenes in which her favour for Franz was clear, like accusation; and at this a new weight fell on her heart, and she half-sat up in bed, calling for Richard and Joseph, who came at once, scared by the terror on her great face that was wet with grief. She put out her hands, and took theirs, staring at the boys with flooded eyes. They held her to a sitting position, and murmured to her, soothing her, knowing that she was wanting to speak to them through the suck of the sobs in her throat. They exchanged looks, adult in their intuition; perhaps this was something worse than sorrow? Mrs. Vosz dropped her head, and said, at last,

"My boys must hate me, but don't ever leave me, he is dead, and I love you both just as much. . . ."

They were astonished. They hushed her, speaking tenderly, and she refused their efforts to quiet her.

"Maybe I have been a bad mother; I loved Franz and petted him, and you boys used to know it. Papa always said he was my favorite;

oh Dick," she cried, "maybe I have been unfair? Joe? You won't leave me?"

The boys blushed with wretchedness. They read in her eyes the fear that she might be abandoned by everyone now. It was less remorse and love for them than it was a feeble and pitiful fright lest the two sons she had slighted now feel free of her. Her body, working in the bed with restlessness, her reddened face, touched them with some humble return to the time of their dependence upon her, and they promised with a moved enthusiasm never to leave her. They convinced her, and she fell back again to weep and deny the pictures her mind made for her.

She finally let them go to see who had just arrived, and who was leaving. Outside her door, the boys looked at each other with an emotional shyness. A feeling like shame took them both. They went in and looked at Franz, seeing with memory the neat bullet hole in his chest, dark, rimmed with blue that faded to the white flesh. The visitors made the proper clucking sentiments around them. Their father hung his head and shuffled his feet by the door. Andrew Lark, in the corner, rocked faintly in the walnut runner-rocker, and declared to anybody who neared him that Franz Vosz had been a fine lad and a proper; and the brothers stood knowing without thought or word what missing Franz would be like, all things from their birth having come to them equally and with the same meaning for all three, having grown up closer than together. They shivered within their best clothes. By staring long enough, they could imagine that Franz breathed.

Andrew Lark stirred and rose, slowly, when his wife told him they'd better be going. She was mindful of the proprieties, and they'd been there too long already. The old man paused again to look at Franz, and knew a recognition like joy flood his mind; he saw a self-image at the same age, and passing Mr. Vosz, at the conviction that Franz was a fine and proper boy, Lark was heartier than ever, in his ancient way, going out with his wife and feeling a curious exhilaration.

But as he was leaving, a car drove into the yard, and the Sheriff came to the porch, and Lark turned back to see.

The brothers held the door against the Sheriff, instantly speechless. Their minds cleared, and they saw how soft and silly they had been all their lives. Their grief found its true nobility in a masculine, animal rage. It was the man who had killed their brother. They began to growl and whisper promises of what revenge they would invent and commit. The Sheriff put his hands against the screen door, and said softly, "Now listen, boys; listen"; and the limited commotion brought their father to the door.

Vosz thrust the boys away and opened the door. He grasped the Sheriff by the arm in a painful grip. Without speaking, he brought the Sheriff into the front room, through the dwindling crowd of visitors. They stood by the old couch and they both looked down. Vosz was a reasonable man; he hated the man beside him, and he knew any blame was foolish. He watched the Sheriff, who looked at Franz. Perversely, Vosz was angered when the signs of genuine grief showed in the Sheriff's face, and he felt this to be some intrusion upon the privilege of those whose loss it was.

The boys had gone to their mother's room, furious with the news. Mrs. Vosz opened her mouth, a shape of outrage. Now Mr. Vosz came in and said the Sheriff wanted to see her, and here he was. There was a shuffle of feet at the bedroom door, as Vosz stood aside; and the Sheriff came in to stand at the foot of the immense bed and feel his tongue cleave to his dry mouth as he gazed at the mother of the boy he'd killed. The brothers stood at the head of the bed. Richard was in the near light of the lamp, and his body cut off much of the light on the figures in the room. But Mrs. Vosz, struggling against her pillows to sit erect, was bathed all down her left side by a gold flow of light, that spilled on cheek and loose bosom, and the white of the bedclothes. Dark shadows lost her other side and put shapes on the wall. The silence in the house was full. Mrs. Vosz stared, shaking her head with the slightest movement at the Sheriff. The tears ran silently down her face and into the hunched hollows of her neck. She seemed to be sexless and without age, in the beautiful strange light, and in the attitudes of astonished grief she held, an almost impersonal embodiment of emotion, and without being able to say it or imagine it in words, the Sheriff thought that for the first time in his life, he was looking at the face of suffering, and he felt a new sadness for the messes into which people got through no fault of their own. He looked at the brothers, who were pale in the lamplight with hunger for vengeance. Vosz stood beside him, saying nothing. The Sheriff said, hesitatingly,

"There's hardly nothing I can say, Mrs. Vosz. I *have* to say I'm sorry, and you know and I know and his father knows it was an accident. But we all know *that* don't help matters none. But I *want* to say that I'd trade places right now with that boy if it'd do the good of giving him back to you. I *swear* I mean it, ma'am?"

His voice was rusted with confusion, and his words coming slowly had the dignity of entire sincerity. He let his fingers rest on the foot of the bed. Mrs. Vosz closed her eyes and allowed her head to fall back so that her thick neck swelled out at the sides. The loose hair drifted down to her cheeks. She made no sound. The brothers leaned to her and put their arms against her back, to support her. The Sheriff was made mean in feeling, to be so ignored, and he spoke again, with pleading rough tones.

"I maybe was out of place to come here, ma'am? but so long as I didn't come to pay my respects, I figured it was worse than coming where I'd be mighty unwelcome."

She opened her eyes and stared at him again. Her lips drew in against her teeth, as if to make her silence more terrible, more accusatory than ever. No one in the room took his eyes off her. There was a groaning splendour of grief about her shapeless body and her blotched and quivering face. In the front room, the visitors were as still as the dead, their eyes glistening toward one another as they strained to hear the furies that must be loose in the bedroom.

"Anyway," said the Sheriff, moving back from the carved walnut of the bedstead, "I can't tell you how *I* feel, but I know how *you* feel, Mrs. Vosz? and I swear to God A'mighty that . . ."

He could not say what he would swear.

He was sorry? The word was too little. Guilt? But his crime was not a crime. Mrs. Vosz leaned forward a trifle, as if waiting, extracting, the full dues of his misery. Her eyes went sharp, behind the run of tears, and she fatly stirred in her bed to await the avowals that were so hard for the man to make. The Sheriff turned to Vosz and shrugged. He ran his thumb up and down the lapel of his coat. He turned back to Mrs. Vosz, and saw with a fresh eye the ugliness of her abandoned body, and his feelings rose up in him with resentment that she should so refuse his poor offer of sorrow; he shook his head at her, and dropped his look, while the tears blurted into his eyes and a sob lost his breath. Mrs. Vosz leaned sharply, to see these signals of feelings. He turned and left the room in the same appalling silence she had met him with. He was followed by Vosz, who saw him to the front door. The visitors had retired to the shadowy corners of the front room and they saw the departure through the hall doorway. The front door slammed, and the dogs on the porch whimpered. They heard the motor start, and saw the headlights switch on through the windows. The backing and turning car threw an arc of light across the windows, printing shadows of lace curtains upon the peering faces. The whine and settle of the changing gears receded. It was silent again.

But only briefly, for rising in a sob of lost control, they heard the voice of Mrs. Vosz break forth in a storm of volubility.

She was sitting up, clutching at the strong arms of Richard and Joe, pouring out an almost wordless fury of sound. They could recognize in her thickened speech references to the man who had just left; they could perceive snatches of pictures in it, as if memories suddenly showed amongst the rages in her mind, and demanded expression. They squeezed her arms and stroked her hair, calling her to be quiet. The tears ran from her eyes and the saliva poured from her lips. She sweated and strove with her hands to say what was in her heart.

The sounds of this fury came to the front room as something terrifying, and a few of the women tiptoed to the bedroom door, full of an awed courage that demanded a sight of such grief. What they saw made them feel either sick or hysterical. The two boys grew frightened and exchanged impassive looks that included the notion of flight; but they would have denied it, and they heard the voice of their mother change, taking on the noble and witless sonority of one who prayed at a camp meeting. She made the shapes of visions in the air with her hands, and her voice became solid over the caught gasps of the sobs, and her husband came into the room to see upon her stained and wretched face some light like the light of those who receive the Holy Spirit, and he knew that she had found occupation in the old assurances of her Baptism. Her voice rolled on, like the river of a sermon. He fell to his knees by the side of her bed and put his head on the bedclothes and began to weep. Her hand descended upon his skull, and he felt its vibrant obsession.

Richard and Joe suffered for the way their parents had let go. They started to withdraw. But the mother embraced them with her rich tide of wrath and redemption, making them kneel too, rising in some majesty of strength above the shames and the griefs of her men. The voice poured on, filling the air with threats and judgments, phrases of hatred and promises of peace, the blood of the Lamb and the fires of Hell, with amen and amen and alleluia.

In the front room, Andrew Lark once again brought his wife to the door. The evening was clear, and as they drove away, the harangue of sorrow and comfort was still going on.

X · SURVIVAL

From far down the road, Andrew watched for his mill, and when he saw it, sharply edged against the last sheets of light that faded down from the deepening sky, he felt an uprise again of the exhilaration that had possessed him back there as he had gazed upon the dead boy. Mrs. Lark rode beside him, her hands folded in her lap, her eyes working right and left, right and left, as she told over in sympathy the terrible meanings of the house they had come from. She could tell herself that everyone had their time; it was best to meet it without terror; but when a grief so monumental as Mrs. Vosz's got loose, it went extra deep into hearts that before had known few doubts.

They rode, the old couple, bouncing in unison as the old Ford bounced. It was an ancient car, with a spidery look to its thin axles, its steering gear, the supports for its windrattled top. If anything could make it look more precarious and tentative than it really was, it would be to see Andrew Lark, himself so ancient, driving the Ford at its fastest speed, an old engine of potential destruction, driven by an old man whose steps must surely be numbered.

Beside him, Nona was murmuring the slow words of one concerned with proper misery. He hardly heard her. He sat driving, his eyes fixed upon some point farther than the road, his sharp old mouth that bent in the middle with a look like a lion's snout grinning with content. When he turned into their own yard and brought the Ford to a creaking halt within its shed, he heard Nona sigh heavily and watched her walk across the yard with her rheumatic, rolling gait. By himself, he stood in the cool yard. The wind had dropped. Above him the mill hardly turned, and he was thoughtless of it. In the late dusk, he stood like some old tree. When he saw the lights from the lamps catch and increase from Nona's match, he cleared his throat, and brought himself out of the curious haze of joy that had possessed him at the Voszes', and went to the back door where the cats were clustered hungrily, mewing and climbing against one another, and purring when Andrew opened the door and let them through the shuffle of his feet.

He dropped his stiff black felt hat on the kitchen table, and went to the front room. There was his newspaper, all set right by Nona on the table. The lamp made a live world of a circle of light, cutting across the red plush of the sofa, dropping to the green and brown carpet, crossing the black boards of the floor, the seat of the gold cane chair, and the dusty black of the coal scuttle. He heard Nona talking to the cats. He sat back in the morris chair which had adopted his shape like a shell, the green corduroy cushions hollowed for the curve of his long back and the settle of his bony rump. He heard Nona begin setting supper ready. He admitted he was hungry.

He went when she called him, and sat with her at the kitchen table, and as the evening advanced with his silence continuing, she began to worry about him. He was looking at nothing, only smiling, as if for himself, eating his eggs and scraping his porridge spoon and wetting his chin in silence. To make up for this strange look of his, she began to chatter, lamenting that such things could happen as happened today; she spoke of the time her son Elbert had died, as a child of three, and she said she could feel for Mrs. Vosz; to lose a child not yet grown, hardly, was so sad; she heard Andrew chuckle, and raised her eyes to him. He seemed to be alive with pleasure, some happiness which dismayed her.

"Andrew:" she said, putting her freckled old hand to his arm, "what's got *in* you!"

He shook his head, and shoved his chair back, and returned to the parlor and his big chair. In the orange glass miniature of a top hat he found toothpicks, and took one, and began raking his bloodless gums with it. She came and peered through the door at him, ankled by her cats, and was alarmed to see him lying back with his eyes shut, smiling and working his toothpick. She saw the paper at his elbow, ignored; and the change from his habit of hastening to read after supper filled her breast with a breathless fright. She went in and picked up the paper, and laid it on his lap, speaking to him. He scrambled for the paper with his fingers, and didn't open his eyes, only nodding. She left him, troubled by strangeness. In the kitchen a new fear took her, and she remembered that he had left his glasses on the windmill platform that morning; that Moses was supposed to have come out that evening to bring them down, and that the events of the day had prevented their seeing Moses. She thought, If Lark goes up there at night . . . he'll fall . . . and she folded her hands for the fool she had been in reminding him of his paper, for he would need his glasses for that, and in his musing and smiling, he could sit forever without them.

She silently went to the back door, and walked to the foot of the windmill. Her face was hot with a wild courage, but she looked up at the clear towering lines of the timbers, and said to herself, with feelings like weeping, "I could never climb it." She put her hand on the low rung of the ladder, as if to test her strength. The mill softly keened above her, and she looked up at it, seeing its blades against the chilling sky where the stars were brightening against the darkness. She shivered; it would be another cold night, and embracing her shoulders, she went back to the kitchen. Andrew was motionless. She went to her work of clearing up, listening for the moment when he would sit up and clear his throat, and declare that he must get his glasses down from the platform.

But her fears were stretched over the whole evening.

He sat, content and silent, in his big chair. When she came to sit with him and do her sewing, he looked at her. His eyes were remote and milky with odd meanings, and she decided not to ask him what he was up to. He could not have told her. He only knew that an inner sensation of power and life possessed him. It had arrived in him in the late afternoon, when he had looked down at the dead Franz Vosz, and seen so young a man, with so appealing a face, with such a strong body, laid useless forever; while he, Andrew Lark, who would never see seventy again, was alive and could feel the blood flooding his veins; and the things he knew filling his mind; and the things he saw coming into his eyes. He had shaken his head over the dead. And then he had admitted to himself that he was proud to be alive. He had thought of himself at Franz's age, looking at the boy. The whole chain of things that had happened to him in his life began to come back to him. His memory was prodigious. He saw how fortunate everything had been. If there had been any deviation from the line of his history, how different everything might have been!

But it wasn't.

He was conscious of his old age. The only triumph of old age, which is survival, lived in him too. He sat and mused all evening, shaken and enlivened by the happy selfishness of his own thoughts. The boy was dead, and Andrew felt an unmalicious satisfaction in finding himself still living. He forgot his paper. Every time he looked at Nona, when she recurred in his chain of memories, he wondered why she looked so perplexed. He would chuckle at her, and she, still possessed by thoughts of grief and worry, would be shocked at his levity, not knowing how he was welling with contentment, a sense of integral being.

He thought once of mentioning what was in his mind to Nona. But he sensibly decided that she would never understand him, and he closed his mouth again, after frightening her by holding it open for speech for a long moment. He only shook his head at her fussy inquiries, and sank back into preoccupation with his content.

The cats came suddenly to life in the kitchen, and raced out from under the stove when the clock struck ten. The day was over, and Nona was relieved at last, for he would never climb the ladder now, it was too late to read. It was bedtime.

She went to the kitchen and let the cats out for the night. They paused on the doorstep while she held the screen door open. They tasted the night, turning their heads whose little faces were hooded by ears and neck. Then, with silent accord, they turned and became parts of the shadow along the house.

Andrew rose from his chair, obedient to his nightly ritual, reflecting that it was just such regularity of habit that had brought him this far and that would take him years and years farther. He guessed he hadn't missed a minute in years from getting ready for bed at ten o'clock. Nona, in the bedroom, moved against the area of the lamplight like a sleepy and comfortable shadow. He appreciated dimly the wide and the heavy bed where so much of his joy and content had come to pass.

The yard was cleaned by the wind of the day. In the chill moonlight, he looked around, as he had looked around every night for so long. He spread his legs and began to make his water, yawning sleepily. He made a little river on the swept ground. He shivered, feeling the cold strike into him, and anticipating the warmth of bed. Inside, Nona, hearing his nightly watering of the ground, shrugged with impatience, her delicacy offended, reminded by this of all the little things that a lifetime with Lark had never reconciled her to. But they vanished from her mind out of habit when he returned to the house, chuckling and peering at her sidewise, saying that he'd forgot to get his glasses down off the windmill. Nor had he missed them till now. Now what did she think of that!

He trundled by her, pulling at his shirt with little grunts. She thought with an almost shamefully girlish notion how foolish he was, how much doing-for he required, and, remembering the Voszes, how if his need of her should be broken by death, she would know nothing to do but wait.

He let himself into bed, which creaked. He held up on one elbow, listening intently. An idle night breeze was about, and he thought it might be enough to make the mill swing around and screech. But he nodded his head with satisfaction when all he could hear was a constant, airy w'anging from the metal blades that turned slowly, and the metal fin that strove always to be parallel with the wind.

The evening rush was over by the time Rolf and Heart pulled up at Fat's Cafe. The light from the restaurant streamed across a limited area of sidewalk, with a golden spill that suggested warmth after the sharp and coldening evening. They went into the Cafe and Fat waved at them with his bare arm, a figure of buoyant good feeling, addressing them as Folks, and piping in his oily voice. He came around from behind the counter himself instead of letting Mrs. Rocker take their order. They sat down at a table opposite the shining coffee urns, and looked up at Fat hungrily.

"I've had such a rush," said Fat, "don't know hardly what's left; but you can bet, you can just bet on it, I'm gonna feed you."

He cocked his eyes at them, looked at them shrewdly, a regard that made Heart drop her eyes and inwardly admit the embarrassment and the confusion in her breast. Rolf told Fat to bring them whatever he had that was *good,* and turned back to Heart.

She looked straight into his eyes, and pulled a blush from his veins. They were both breathless; when they started to speak to one another, their words had a catching pulse under them. She laid her hand against her breast, thinking that was where her desire lay; but it eluded her touch, and she stirred in her chair with the possession of her feelings. Rolf hung his head. They had been driving in the car ever since they left the Voszes'. Without saying much of anything, the two of them had arrived at their conclusion, and Rolf knew it was Heart's strength that she had excited him, and with caresses and no words, had proposed to him the things that would happen after their supper.

It was warm in Fat's Cafe. The steam rose and whispered above the hooded stove. Presently Mrs. Rocker came with the thick white bowls containing the soup, flanked by crackers, that always heralded Fat's "Club menus." She walked with exaggerated care, her miserable slippers creaking and yawning at her every step. She bit her un-toothed lips with a grin of pride and caution, and at last set the steaming soup down before them, and retired behind the counter to consult Fat with one of her willing looks that so enraged him.

But tonight he sang in his heart. He seemed beyond rage, for that was the sign of a weak man who was not master of his world, and therefore of his temper. Fat was hard tonight. He narrowed his small eyes, and squinted into his stew with pitiless and rocklike character. He turned to instruct Mrs. Rocker to set some celery on the table for the guests, and lifted his eyebrows at her in an elaborate threat which she failed to recognize as such. Hard? Tonight. He would fire Mrs. Rocker tonight. The crowd from the track meet had filled his cash register. "Mrs. Rocker," he thought, "here's your wages and a little over. Good-bye, git. Git out, Mrs. Rocker, I said. Go on, git now, I said. You old fool, can't have a smelly old woman like you round here no more, I said. Waagh! whoosh! I said, and don't try no cryin and weepin and caterwaulin, I said, on me, I said, it won't do you no good 'tall. I said, I put up long enough with your cussed foolery, and wastin time, and taking my wages week in and week out, I said. Go on, I said, git!——"

He sliced some bread, warmed and enriched by this mental achievement of a scene he was waiting for with relish. He sent her to the table with the bread, and then leaned on his immaculate counter to watch the diners. His fat arms and pink elbows flattened out on the light yellow wood. Feeling hard, serene, a master of all situations that might touch him, he prided himself tonight on a keen, even a relentless understanding of other people. They might have secrets from some, but not from him. His own secret was so well guarded that no one would ever know it: who had seen him? In all that crowd? Nobody. He had picked up a brick, a loosened brick from the edge of the walk in the Courthouse plaza, and in a moment of glorious inspiration, he had risen above the crowd and hurled the brick at the doors, smashing the window, creating a leadership in destruction that through no fault of his own had been put down. But he, Fat, was the single hero of the day's events, though nobody knew it but himself; which was enough. His private virtue flowed throughout his immense and dainty body, a masculine elixir.

Heart and Rolf ate their supper in half-silence, consulting one another with small sounds and quick glances. Their breath lay under their words like soft laughter, and Heart could hardly eat anything. Rolf consumed everything as it came before him. She watched him eat, feeling possessive of him already, and noticing with a strange intensity such things about him as might at other times have disgusted her, his clumsy table manners, chewing with his lips open, packing his food with his knife, ways that were un-Californian. But to her, a preciousness seemed to cover everything about him; and in his mind, as he inarticulately preserved the heat that had them both, was some tenderness that covered his resentment at having been so obviously trapped and excited by her.

Fat played his fingers along his mouth, leaning on his palm and watching them through drooped eyes. There was solicitude in his heart, as he made idle and lascivious dreams about the two young people. He felt like offering them congratulations, with sly winks and tribal pokes in the rib for Rolf, and a shared reference to their common valour as masculine achievers. But he only hummed his little tune, and stored up the interesting moments, imagining voluptuously what Rolf and Heart would do when they went away alone after supper; leaving him alone with Mrs. Rocker, who would then be canned with grandeur.

He looked around from the diners when he heard the front door open slowly. He left his chin resting in his palms, his elbows planted in rings of their own fat upon the counter. His eyes narrowed, with the keen feeling he had had since noon. The door closed slowly and respectfully after a thin shaking man who walked down the aisle between the tables and the counter. His large head was unsteady upon its small neck. He was smiling, his lip lifted off his teeth by a scar. In his hand he held a scrap of a hat. Fat watched him approach, saying nothing, only turning his head to keep his eyes on him. Heart looked up, but didn't recognize Leo, and forgot him.

"Excuse me, mister," said Leo, in a breathy whisper, shaded with an attempt at charm and culture, party manners, "is there anything you could spare me to eat? I'm broke, and pretty hungry, I can tell *you*."

Fat drummed his fingers against his teeth. A flush like a smile rose around his eyes. He said, with a lazy mildness,

"*Nuh*-uh,"

meaning no by it.

Leo stood. His constant sensation of quivering showed a little in the way he moved his arms in a motion of appeal, as from one man to another.

"I won't need very much," he said, looking around at Heart and Rolf, and then at Mrs. Rocker, with a smiling abandonment of pride and independence, a public resignation of his only birthright. "I'm hitch-hiking my way to California, where I have relatives; my uncle is a lawyer there, and once I get there I . . ."

"*Nuh*-uh," repeated Fat, yawning artificially behind his hands. Mrs. Rocker stared at Leo with compassion. Her hands worked under her apron.

"Once I get there," continued Leo, "I could probably send you some money for what I might maybe owe you. Boy, I'm *hungry*."

A hearty idiom like that, coming in Leo's faded voice, brought tears to Mrs. Rocker's eyes. She was astounded when Fat stood up suddenly, leaning across the counter, and bawled in his thin forced voice,

"Nothing here for panhandlers and handouts! Now git!"

Fat subsided back of the counter, and turned his back, inventing business with sweeping the crumbs off his meat block where he also cut bread.

Leo turned around. The scar was frankly part of a snarl now, and his smile showed dry as the lips stuck to his teeth. He shuffled down the aisle toward the door. There he paused, having a ridiculous trouble in getting the knob to turn and the latch to open. Heart and Rolf lifted their heads, and Mrs. Rocker encouraged the temper in her heart. Fat scraped the crumbs over and over into separate little mounds. At last the door opened and Leo went out. The door slammed after him. Mrs. Rocker saw him turn up his collar against the cold night and move off into the shadows. She looked at Fat. He refused to look at her. He was saying to himself, over and over, "That'll show them," not knowing whom he meant or what was to be shown, except that he was tired of being imposed on all his life by people, confusing his weakness which came from within with impositions which came from without.

Three minutes went silently by. Then Mrs. Rocker rolled off her apron and dashed to the door and into the street. She stared up the walk after Leo's direction. Fat turned and screamed to her, "You come back in here!" hating her for acting upon the impulse that he had denied. She moved out of sight. Everything changed for Fat. The image toppled. He said to Heart and Rolf,

"I'd have done it, only if I feed one, I feed all. God knows I hate to see anyone go hungry. . . ."

Heart shrugged, a sophisticated gesture that was unconscious; she was thinking of nothing but herself.

In a moment Mrs. Rocker came back. She was remembering Leo's smile, a vehicle for hatred. She said she couldn't find him. He'd disappeared. He sure had looked hungry. She looked at Fat, shyly, with a trusting simple smile. He scowled at her and then sighed. He went flabby and weak again. Everybody else did what he wanted to do, and should have done. There she stood, not even thinking badly of him because he had turned away a starving hitch-hiker! Her watery blue eyes never concealed any opinions. If she had been momentarily furious, needful of feeding Leo, it was all gone now. She watched

Fat for her instructions, and took every little idle movement or expression of his as a signal of some kind for her.

She went to get the dishes from the table, and prepare for dessert, which Fat set out on the counter: two pieces of pie, cherry pie, of his own make, with thick juice running slowly from the crust to the plates. He laid squares of cheese on each plate. But Heart suddenly stood up, and Rolf stood with her. They said they didn't want any dessert. She smiled. Able to conceal nothing, yet secure in their sphere of excitement, they left the Cafe. Fat put his pieces of pie back into the icebox. Mrs. Rocker performed her nightly tasks before closing-up. At last, when he stood waiting for her to get into her hat and coat, his pockets full of the money emptied from the cash register, he looked at her and dropped his look, knowing he would never fire her; she trusted him; she relied on him; she thought he was o.k., even after Leo; she made him sick of the sight of her. He held the door open, and she walked out. He locked it, testing the latch a time or two. He felt abandoned, knowing it was his cherished self that he had abandoned. Mrs. Rocker walked her way, opposite to his. He turned and ambled up Main Street. The few stores were dark. The money clinked and rustled in his pants pockets. He was lonely and lowered in his own eyes. There was only one way in which to regain himself, to lose himself. Thinking pitifully of the waitresses in El Paso, with their blue eyelids, their black lashes, the fiery rouge that bloomed on their cheekbones and faded to the neck in a powdery plaster white, their yellow hair, their amiable hips, he left Main Street and trudged through the dust and leaves of the back streets, walking under the great hooding cottonwoods that strained the cold starlight, and came to the faded green board house that sat low behind a rotting fence. The windows were heavily curtained. There was no sign of life. But he walked to the door and rapped. In a moment, with a final question of folly in his mind, he was admitted.

XII · CONVICTIONS

The darkness was pungent with the smell of printer's ink and rolls of newsprint, mixed with years of dirt swept into the corners of the newspaper offices. In the middle of the rear wall was a door that had a window in it. The glass was filmed with a pearly dust. Through this the faint moonlight filtered. There was no other light. Heart moved to the door and tested the key in the lock again, to be sure the door was fastened. She heard Rolf stir and breathe where she left him, sitting on the long bench that was covered with her coat. She felt again the loving clumsiness of their hands, meeting and offering expressions of what was inside their hearts. Standing in the moonlight away from him, she saw her fierceness go, and marvelled that his should survive, should even grow so that his embraces seemed to her shameful in looking back on them, though she had desired them and brought them to being.

He called her in a whisper to come back beside him.

She walked slowly over to the bench and sat down. They could see each other like shadows, in the dimly distributed moonlight. He was not replete yet, not content, though from the moment of their slipping into the dark printing room, using his key at the back door, her abandon had asked physical questions. Not seeing her in the dark, she seemed to him a stranger, losing the sharp diffidence, the resentment in her eyes. He had not expected such wild tendernesses as she gave him. But now they had been given, she was again changed; and sat beside him on the bench in propriety, some seriousness that perplexed him and inclined him to anger. After all: he thought: there can't be any airs or secrets any more now.

"What is it:" he said to her, setting his large fingers on her breast. She shook him away.

"Oh, I don't know," she said, in a wretched whisper.

"Aren't you glad?"

"You hurried me. . . . I couldn't think."

He sat away from her, wondering if she really thought that. The sound of a soft sob convinced him that she did. Compassion and pride bloomed in his breast. He leaned to her again, and this time his touch was delicate and mournful.

"I couldn't help myself," he murmured, relaxing finally from his lust, taken by the new emotion of being a slave to his passions. She sighed again, and in a throe of tenderness and weakness, put her head on his breast. She resigned herself. She felt that she had a right to be weary, for the months she had been in bringing Rolf to this night. He stroked her hair, richly confused by feelings of desire and protectiveness, warmed by one and inspired by the other. But nothing he could say, his murmurs about the joy it would be to have other nights, the fact that they were not lonely any more, could make her stop her faint distress.

"What is it:"

"What have I got to look forward to now:" she said.

"What do you mean?"

"You know, well enough. . . ."

"No, really I don't."

She pulled away from him.

"Well, I know . . . I know just what I mean to you now, after this."

He remembered that there had been no words of love exchanged.

"Oh, come on," he said. "You know you'll mean more than ever to me now."

"Oh, I know that," she said. "But in what way: any girl will know the same thing."

"Well, if you mean will I go looking around after other girls, you're just crazy."

". . . not what I mean."

"Then what:"

"You won't have any use for me but in one way, now," she said, feeling sincere in the ancient ritual.

"Oh:" he said, his voice hushed as he realized his obligation. He hotly thought that she had led him on, God knows she did that. All afternoon, talking and hinting, and working on him, with her hands, and then being silent, she certainly had led him on. Her voice cut against his secret accusations.

"What could I do, Rolf darling? You knew I couldn't fight against you, you knew that. The trouble is, I love you, if I hadn't loved you, it would have been easy to turn you down. You know that."

Here it was. In terror, he stated that he loved her. He said that was why he had done what he had done. She embraced him gently, and waited for the other avowals to follow. She shuddered against his breast, making whispered references to his powers, the fact that he was overmastering, and even dangerous. In the intimate darkness, surrounded by the familiar atmosphere of his job, printer's ink and the acrid scent of linotype metal, cooled, everything she said seemed likewise familiar and believable. Perhaps, no, certainly he was overmastering. It seemed to him intelligent and logical when he declared, later, that they would be married right away. He told her he wouldn't hear of any objections, there was too much nonsense nowadays about women and freedom.

Heart closed her eyes, clutching his large shoulders. She had known her advantage and used it. He was convinced, even if she was not. She knew how he would act the husband, and that she would spend her life preserving for them both the illusion that he was a delicate tower of strength, whose control was capricious and dangerous. He would believe this himself, for it was only human to drink in a heartening belief about yourself, she thought; she also thought, closing her lips upon him to deny it, that her various inner convictions of truth and plan would accompany her, disappointed, though happiness could live over that. Holding each other, delivered to one another, they sought terms in which to declare their shared lives.

XIII · CONVIVIALITY

Hazel brought Fat out of her room into the sitting room at the back of the house. She walked in front of him, sighing with a comfortable propriety, and closing her thin kimono about her loose body. He followed her, sorry for passion vanished so soon, and stepped through the portières in the doorway. Hazel threw herself on a chair and crossed her legs, waving Fat to a chair at the table where there were a bottle of whiskey and several glasses. Two men who were sitting at the table looked up at Fat in a moment of silence. He recognized one of them as Do Miller, and said hello.

"Hi, Fat," said Do.

Do turned back to his friend. Both Do and the other man were sitting at their ease, in their undershirts, with their belts loosened, their shoes off, and their shirts and coats hanging on the backs of their chairs. The stranger had a cigar which got in the way of his words. But he spoke in a continuous stream of interest in himself, and what he had done, and was going to do.

Fat poured a drink and listened. Hazel yawned, and lighted a cigarette, smiling at Fat through the tears of smoke and fatigue. He felt suddenly very fond of her, and saw her with new eyes, as if she were someone whom he'd met in somebody's home. Remembering his half hour with her, he blushed. He turned his nose into his whiskey glass to hide his feelings. The liquor was sharp, a cheap grade of white mule. It made him gasp for a second. But with Hazel and whiskey, he was full of comfort. He belched loudly, a surprising thing for Fat to do, and Hazel, knowing him in his Cafe, knowing his elegance, the daintiness of his ways, laughed aloud at him, and stood up, pushing her hair over her forehead with both hands.

"Great big boy," she said, in a teasing voice. She turned and ran her arms down across his shoulders from behind. But a rap at the door interrupted her, and she squeezed his breasts and left. Fat settled down to listen. The stranger turned from Do Miller, whom he had been tapping on the chest to punctuate his stories, and looked at Fat with a friendly smile, as if to include him in the audience. Fat smirked. He heard the front door open and close, and then the sound of walking down the hallway, and another door.

"I tell yoh 'baout dis mawnin?" said the stranger.

Do shook his head and drank from his glass.

"Baout dat nigga?"

"*Uh*-uh."

"Boy howdi!"

The stranger dropped his head and laughed weakly, flopping his hand at Do as if to defy him to think up anything better than what was coming.

"What nigger?" said Do.

"Dis mawnin: I was pumpin tah up, lost all the air outa my spah tah, and nis nigga came along. I reckoned he was one onnem hitchhikin niggas, and I figgad givem a rad to town. So I tolm get aholt onnat pump, pump up my tah for me."

Fat leaned out on the table, flattered by the way the man's eyes sought his every now and then, dividing his story between Fat and Do, seeking in vanity for the applause of both.

"Well, ol nigga stan nere, and tell me he won't pump no tah. I looked at im, I said get aholt. Nigga begin to grin and laugh, and said he didn want pump no tah. Boy! Bam! did I hit im! zowie! I hit im so fast on each side of his jaw, he didn know what's coming or goin. I backed im up against the car, and I hit im again, swingin low, and he begin to cry. He cr-y-y-y, just like a puppydog. I told im, nigga, I says, put up yoh hands. You hit me, I says. Come ohn, hit me, nigga! Should of seen 'at nigga *try*. . . . Hit me, I says. An' I let im have it again."

The man took his head in his hand, closing his eyes and wagging, voiceless with amused memory, and full of sociability. Do Miller grunted in his chair, a sound of appreciation, and slumped lower to be comfortable. The stranger looked at Fat with dancing eyes, and Fat winked at him, and slapped the table top with a crash of his fat paw, drawn into the world of men who destroyed insolent Negroes, and enjoying the membership.

The talker threw himself back against his chair again, and stretched out his legs, scratching his groin, a gesture of self-congratulation.

"So, nigga, he try to hit me. An nen I get sore, well, not sore, but it made me mad, to have at nigga try to hit me. So I backs im up towards de ditch, and boy! howdi! did I let im have it! I knocked him down wid one blow, and nen made im stand up again." He smiled with modesty, his red handsome face looking strangely younger. "After he stands up, I knocks im down inna ditch, an boy! he's inna ditch for good! Knocked im out pretty as you please! He was a young nigga, musta been baout tweny-tweny-one. He had a good build on im too. Be a good nigga, if someone just teach him his lesson or two. Like I did."

He chuckled affectionately. Do splashed some more white mule in their three glasses, and they drank together, full of a common excellence, a power that made them enjoy one another, and that gave them a common point of view. Fat was flooded by sensations of ease and ability. Clearing his throat, a test of his thin tubular voice, he leaned forward and with exaggerated caution, began to tell a dirty joke. Do and his friend leaned forward to catch it. Fat knew they liked him. Their eyes and mouths echoed his own expressions as he told the story. They hung on his lips. When he finished, telling the end through laughter that he tried to control, they all threw back their heads and barked and coughed with amusement. They had found their common tongue. They sat drinking and smoking, solemnly rotating their turns to tell jokes. Each one was finished with the same raking laughter. Fat kept thinking, It does a man good to let go now and then.

Presently the portières were held up and a new girl came in. Her face was chalk white, with rouge spots on the cheekbones and blue shadows on the eyes, and a bowed mouth whose painted outline left the natural one. She had a bony nose, that looked as if it had once been broken, and that gave her face the look of a parrot, when she rolled her eyes and shook her yellow hair. Fat had never seen her before, but had heard there was a new girl at Hazel's.

She walked to the back of the stranger's chair, and leaned down over his shoulder. Fat watched her with a quiver of envy and admiration. She reminded him of the waitresses in El Paso. Her voice sounded now, a smothered sound as if her broken nose interfered with her speech.

"What're you doing?" she said, rolling her eyes at each of them in turn.

"Telling stories," said Do. "Do you know any good ones?"

"I know plenny bad ones," she said, and squawked. "But I never tell them to gennamen."

She uttered this with tones of refinement. The stranger smiled up at her, and she patted his cheek. It was like a little passage between married people.

"Where's Hazel?" she said, with a restless sound in her voice.

"Somebody came in, she went back there with him," said Fat.

"I can't see it," said the new girl.

"See what?" said Do.

"Hazel: can you? How any man could *look* at her, she so *ordinary* looking, I said to myself when I *come* here, My God, do you have to work under the same roof with *that!* She's so ordinary looking!"

Fat was startled. But, unable to make an opinion for himself, he began to view Hazel in his mind from this new angle. All he could remember was her general friendliness, a thing that always appealed to him. But he would never feel the same about Hazel again, having heard a doubt expressed about her. The new girl seemed somehow superior now, and he leaned forward to get her eye, and began to tell her the first story he had told the men. She listened to him, shifting her gaze from his eye to eye, breathing with her mouth open, waiting with short breaths and widened nose for the point of the story, an image of appreciation and encouragement. Fat blushed with content. His voice rose. When they all lost themselves in new laughter, he lay back in his chair drunk and reassured.

XIV · TO CALIFORNIA

The moon rode high, unharried by the wind and the cold that played along the ground. The road banked with the hills, far, far in the distance, and rose invisibly toward the mountain passes. The mountain itself was a shadow against the lighter shadow of the night sky, and Leo looked ahead now and then, trying to set his gaze steadily upon the dense and inscrutable darkness where the mountain opened and the road entered, a place where his steps must eventually carry him, though he murmured to himself in a little high moan that he felt so tired and hungry. . . .

It was the shocking coldness of the night that made him begin to wonder at his decision to take to the road, trusting for some kind of hitch to carry him nearer California. The afternoon had been whipped by wind and blown sand. But the morning, with its heat, had told of spring. Tonight there was an edge like winter in the air. He leaned into the direction he was taking, and breathed against his turned-up coat collar, making a warm mist of spittle. His hands were folded inside his shirt on his breast, and the fingers moved constantly, crawling over one another on his bony arch. His lips moved to the tune of the thoughts that rolled in his mind. (He had the conviction that he was striding firmly toward the mountains; that he would walk into the dawn somewhere beyond the dark canyons of black pine; that his promised land of California awaited him with warmth and money, kindness, a job, security. It was the place where his uncle lived, and all the movie women, where life was a thing of easy solutions and sunshine on the seashore and beauty that was cheap and available. He saw his arms swinging and his head thrown up. The road was a river of moonlight.)

Moving by the ditch-side, Leo's feet hardly travelled. He was shuddering within his loose black coat. The strain of his eyes to watch for the beam of a car's lights, a car that might pick him up and let him sleep to the rumbling rhythm of tires on a graded road, the feeble cracking of his fingers against his chest, the way he was turned and worried by the fall of the cold air on the mild wind, all these made him look like a scarecrow blown fitfully, an image of public humour and no significance.

No cars came and went. The high moon softened all objects with a silver pour. Leo's eyes watched the fence posts, his feet trembling after one another as he walked. It had taken him hours to get so little beyond town as he was now. He imagined that he could see strange things in the richly shadowed ditch above which he was walking. Thoughts of fear intruded among his sensations of speed and accomplishment. But he would bite his tongue and widen his eyes, remembering that he was from a good family, with a good background. He was an educated man. He had ideals. He was practical enough to go out after them, he told himself. Hence California.

Suddenly he found himself sitting on the edge of the ditch, retching emptily against his palms. He was tossed on his back by the strain of convulsion, and then he sat up again, feeling strangely more comfortable, and with a cleared sight. He looked around him and winced at the cold that fingered his skin through his clothes. He thought of lying down in the ditch to be out of the wind; and he crawled down into it, but it was capriciously filled with tumbleweeds by the wind of the afternoon, and he recoiled from the sharp burrs and thorns of the billowed, brittle bank. He pulled himself erect by a fence post. There was a dark shape in the field beyond the fence. He leaned on the post and focussed his eyes. What he saw was the body of an old Ford, a burned-out wreck that sat on the ground without wheels or top, no fenders or doors, only the rusty and dull black shape of the body, and the shapes, inside, of the front seat and the back seat. On the ground were scattered bits of débris from the wreck, old fenders, a lamp reflector, a shattered door, a broken wheel. In the pouring moonlight, these things shone clear.

"A car," said Leo to himself aloud. He raised himself to look better. He said that it would at least break the wind. He could lie down in the back seat and be out of the cold wind. There would be some protection under the curving back of the car's body, and there was no danger that he might be run over in that field, as there would be if he lay by the road to rest.

Feeling joyful, he decided to climb through the fence and go to the wreck. He lifted himself a little, raising his leg to climb over the barbed wire. He fell to the ground, astonished by his weakness. He could not pull himself up to climb the wires. He began to whimper, fearing that he would never reach the wrecked Ford, where he would spend the night. It had become the image of haven to him. He was too tired to change his plans. Bitterly setting his hands against the ground, he began to roll and crawl nearer the fence, and with a faint warmth of success, rolled under the lowest line of barbed wire and saw himself free in the field. He came to his hands and knees, and then arose, slowly, standing airily. He picked his way among the flung junk of the wreck, and reached the body. He rejoiced to discover that the rear seat cushion was there, left by the owner because it had been half burned up. There was still an old smell of fire about the wreck, and where Leo touched the metal and the charred upholstery, his hands came away black. Rust had followed fire. The wreck had sat in the field for weeks.

He clambered up into the tonneau. He lay down on the rear seat, and pulled his knees up to his belly. He heard the wind sing like a low gong as it stroked the charred fenders that lay beside the car. The wind passed over his head, and he gratefully lowered his chin to his shoulder, feeling a flow of self-comfort like a little child, while his hands kept on shaking and his touch on his own face was too chill and remote to be felt.

He had the idea that lying here, he was able to rest for the night, and still be headed right in the morning, for California. He was comforted by the fact that he was below the level of the wind. Nor could anyone see him, from the road. There was nothing to disturb him. He was half aware, later, of a car going by on the road, whistling against the cold with its speed, and touching roadside objects with vanishing light as it passed. (It made him think briefly that his own car, where he was lying, was moving swiftly down the road to the mountain. But he laughed at himself and repeated that he was not riding, he was walking.)

While his body, curled against itself and stiffening with cold and sleep, lay dark in the tonneau of the burned-out Ford, his dreams picked up from his thoughts and went on. He was walking toward a sky that was like sunrise and sunset. It was warmth to wrap himself in. (His face quivered and his eyes wept a little stream of liquid that glistened in the vast moonlight.) He dreamed that the sea was breaking at his feet on a shore of warm sand, and beautiful women crossed his dream, familiar in the black and white of the movies; American goddesses never before within his grasp. The dream's unreality was his only strength, but it was sufficient, against the night that grew colder as midnight passed and the still late hours followed. Sometime before dawn, Leo's dream ended. He died among its images, which came out of his deepest wants.

He lay in his car, in some way a responsibility of all the lives he had ever known; though when the farmer and his hand found him days afterward, it was with simple expressions of wonder and curiosity, deciding that he had died of exposure on the night the frost had cracked down on the valley.

Afterword

In my late youth or early middle age—where is the line?—I daily saw the places and persons of this novel, and I witnessed, though mercifully I was not hurt by it as they were, the central circumstance of their common life, which was the hardship caused by the economic depression of the 1930s. What they endured, how they tried to bend trouble to their wills, and find deliverance, and how their suffering found expression, I was able to feel by being there. Though my novel was written some time after its events, I contained these, it seemed, as though they were seeds which must burst their pods and assume new form in my work.

At the time of which I write, I was in the small city of Roswell, New Mexico. Now fast-growing, prosperous and diversified in its resources, Roswell was then feeling the depression. A county seat, it was also the home of the New Mexico Military Institute—"the Institute," as the townspeople always spoke of it. I was an officer of the school, which was then the city's chief ornament and source of business. For the rest, Roswell was a trade and marketing center for the cotton farmers of the Pecos Valley and the cattle and sheep ranchers on the plains farabout. When the depression settled over the land, the ranchers, farmers and small businessmen felt hardship grow steadily and fast.

I used to see them when they came to town on Saturdays to stand around on the corners of Second and Main or to gather on the Courthouse lawn, and I would make little wash drawings of some of them as I remembered them later. Their troubled thoughts wondered visibly in their faces. Presently I found that I was adding to their persons the characteristics of other people I knew and when my novel came to be written, it almost wrote itself, so ready was my design, so acute was the sense of need in life which anyone could feel among our citizens in that time, and so filled were my characters with the pity and urgency of universal human wants as these encountered qualifying difficulties from without. It is my recollection that I wrote *Far From Cibola* in twelve consecutive days of entire possession by its form and its echo of the passionate effect of human lives upon each other when all desires have a common object.

On those Saturdays when people gathered on the Courthouse lawn to take comfort from discussing their shared troubles, occasionally an orator arose among them. Inspired by the hunger of the family he was responsible for, he would lift his voice in the accents of the revivalist, and speak for all. Government relief was often mentioned, and in fact the New Deal was moving its machinery of mercy into action. But help was slow to come, and one day an electrifying report went through town.

There was a crowd forming, it was said, and the people were going to march to the Institute on North Hill. There they would break into the armory where the cadet regiment's rifles—"government property"—were locked in racks, seize the rifles, and at gun point demand food for the hungry, of whom, or what agency, none could say. The more prosperous citizens, looking grim, said that revolution was in the air. The military and civil authorities braced themselves for an assault, if it should come; but it never came. An extremity of meaning in the trouble of the times had exploded in rumor—and that was all. But perhaps it was useful. Government relief presently began to be effective.

This threat of violence in the human condition of the time was what suggested to me the beginning of riot in the courthouse scene of *Far From Cibola;* and when my sheriff fired his bullet into the cottonwood treetops to shock his fellow-citizens back to order, my young athlete's accidental death followed as a comment upon the sorrows of disorder and the witless tragedies inherent in power.

In its early seasons this book was appropriated by some critics as an example of the proletarian novel, which was then so drearily fashionable. I declined such classification then, and I formally repudiate it now. This book has nothing to do with masses, or classes, or crippling concepts of man as a being without soul. It is a poem with as many subjects as it has characters; but the subject underlying all others, though never stated, is human charity—"the greatest of these."

THE
COMMON
HEART

TO PEG AND BARRY DUFFIELD

Contents

Book IV   *THE EARTH'S HEART BEATING*

Book V   *THE TRIBUTARIES*

Book I • THE FAMILY STORY

I · PETER AND THE COUNTRY

I

One winter day, in the nineteen-twenties, the physician Peter Rush was driving carefully through a cold sandstorm that was blowing off the mountains, across the mesa, and down upon the town of Albuquerque. He could hardly see. His huge Packard touring car had the side curtains in place, but the sand whined through the cracks on the bitter wind and stung him in the eyes. The storm moved with rolling scrolls of yellow cloud that turned the sun blue and sent a pale chill light over everything. All his life he had known such days; even early chronicles of New Mexico had mentioned them. He knew how the change of light under the hurrying cloud of earth could make your heart sink. It was common enough for patients under his care to have "setbacks" on such an afternoon. They said they felt depressed, and that they could hardly catch their breaths. When they looked out the window, all they saw was that steel-blue light, and far off on the mesa, that sandy veil being dragged by the wind.

He rocked slowly along the dirt ranch road in the big car. Soon he would reach the highway, and then he could probably go a little faster. He was on his way back to town, where he would meet complaints on all sides about the weather. He could hear himself replying, as he had many times before, "You ought to've been out *in* it, as I was." He knew this wouldn't satisfy anyone, because they could all tell from the way he said it that he loved being out in the blowing cold sandy day. There wasn't anything that took place over that land which he did not enjoy.

But even a day like this? they would ask.

Yes, he would reply, even a day like this.

He had grown up in the town. His father had been a rancher, his mother a doctor's daughter who had come West to try a year of school teaching after a polite graduation from a young ladies' seminary in Washington, D. C. She had never gone back. But her only son's desire to become a doctor represented to her a triumph of her own heritage. The rancher father had accepted their son's vocation with a plains-born silence, and after the youth's college years were over, had sold his ranch and cattle, moved into town for good, and there died of inaction. In this his wife saw a landsman's willing bow to the cycle of life in its seasons, and found solace in helping with the struggles of her church in the raw little railroad town on the middle Rio Grande plains. She died out West during her son's internship in a New York hospital. When he came home for good to practice medicine, Peter Rush saw his boyhood country with the love of a man who knew what he came from, was able to respect it, and wanted to help make it good in his own time.

As the blowing curtain of sand thinned out momentarily, he saw the valley far below him, and he thought "There it is." He meant the town. It lay with its many facets of board and brick down toward the Rio Grande.

The river drew all things toward itself as tributaries. It drew whatever water lay in the sandhill furrows after storms; any green life of the wide valley; the line of the railroad that sought the water level; the cluster of houses; the thoughts of people, their very lives. It was one of four large facts of nature in that part of New Mexico. One was the mountain range to the east. One was the vast plain of the mesa just above the town. The third was the river itself, toward which these lands fell in grand steps. Lastly, across the river, there was a wilderness of white sand, from which arose three extinct volcanoes, sand-hued, and charred brown at their craters. Peter Rush remembered his mother always calling them the "Siamese cats" because that was what their color suggested. When he was old enough to think that it was an odd thing to call a dead fire-mountain, he was so used to the notion that it didn't strike him as strange at all.

His father loved and accepted the country without comment. His mother thought much about it and never got over the private feeling that she was there in exile. But the son had her speculative interest in the land as well as his father's native ease and sense of replenishment from it. His mother's letters to him while he was a student in the East inadvertently betrayed again and again her eagerness for the Eastern life he was living. When he came to realize it, to know what she had longed for all her married life, he promised himself to give it to her as soon as he could afford it. But she died first. He never again lost a sense of compassion for the private dreams, the inner dignities of people; anyone at all; and this was her legacy to his adult life.

As he came toward the town now, through the grainy air of that bitter afternoon, when it blew sand instead of snow, he bore toward what he saw an attitude that said,

"There it is, the whole stuff, and every grain of it has its own value. If I were a painter—and sometimes I feel sure that if I took up a brush and color, I could put down what I see exactly as I see it, I don't imagine it would be very much more delicate than some of my surgical tricks—I would paint everything about this town that I see every day. The trains coming in over the plains all day and all night, and red and yellow and green lights and steam and evening filtering down like blue dust. Paint the muddy river running sweet with sunshine. The long aisles of cottonwood trees on the streets. The yellow light of a day like this which sweeps all of it, the mountains, the mesa, the river, into one bitter blur. I would paint the viaduct over the tracks, and its rickety red wood burnt black with locomotive smoke. The saloon on the corner that is closed since Prohibition came last year, but I would get in my picture the sulphur color of the mistakes of men. The backside of the hospital with the rose brick and the silver smokestack and the feather-blue sky. The YMCA building of gray stucco there by the tracks, and I would get the comical virgin morality of little boys and earnest youths. I would set down what the American flag looked like on the front of the Commercial Club the day the Armistice was signed. My heart was in my mouth all day afterward, because it was over, and my little boy would have a chance to help work out Wilson's world, a job that will be worth some doing. If nobody has ever painted a picture of a small-town drugstore, and the country-colored men and women that come in off ranches to buy their needs, I would do it, and I would make it magical. If I got good enough, I would make a picture of my wife, and answer some questions in my heart with it. Is it possible to make a picture out of a memory? My boyhood? But my son is doing that every day of his life, right before me, and in a more precious medium. I have decided, anyway, that it is a very good thing for every man to have a great untried talent—like my painting—which will sustain him privately when his day's job doesn't go so well."

II

The Doctor always seemed to be so busy that nobody took him for a reflective man. Often, far beyond anyone's knowledge, he suffered for the troubles of his patients. They seemed so poor sometimes, in the face of the anonymous powers of disease. They all had the same fears, and what could dissipate these on the one hand but the feeling of health returning some sunny morning; or on the other the assurances that lay between the words of the priest when death was coming? The Doctor could say so little when they begged it of him to say. They touched him most when they were most courageous; for then he felt the continuity of spirit which really did take the present back into the past.

He kept a standing order with a bookseller in Boston to send him whatever he could find in the way of original editions of early-day writings by explorers, travelers, army engineers, who had come to New Mexico long ago. He had never seen the bookseller, but between them there had sprung up an alliance that, far beyond commercial concerns, served their passion for the history of the early West. If a particularly good item turned up that was very expensive, the bookseller wrote him first asking if he cared to spend that much. Sometimes the Doctor scribbled "Yes, of course" in the margin of the inquiry and sent it back. But sometimes he would ask his wife Noonie how much they had in the bank, and she would have a pang for what she considered his dreamy extravagance, and assure him that this month there wasn't a cent for any more of those dusty old books with the elaborate tarnished gilt and the ribbed cloth of the bindings ready to turn to powder. At such times he always grinned at her for what *she* read: huge piles of magazines which she read all afternoon in her upstairs porch, which was glassed in and dancing with light. The print traveled by under her eyes without making any impression at all, except that of a sort of visible passage of time. She read with fever. Her eyes sparkled, her cheeks turned rosy, and she seemed to hunger after the romances she pursued so hotly. Of what the words were about, and the people they described, she never retained any memory. That a word on a printed page ever could arrest something of life itself, and keep it alive as long as it could be read, she never knew. Seeking escape into love, she escaped those who really loved her.

What her husband "did" with his books would have given her genuine and admiring surprise, if he had ever told her. But loving her as he did, he was afraid to see just how wide the gap might be between his mind and hers. So he let her think the books simply kept coming in order to be lined up on a shelf upstairs, in his third-floor study, where he could look at them "between calls."

Some of the calls took him to the country (like this one today, out to a barren little ranch on the mesa, where the ranch hand had broken his arm in a fall off the windmill ladder). And when they didn't, he would go to the country anyway, bringing along his latest book, if it had a trace in it of activity hereabouts in the early days. He would search until he found the very place which the old words described; and then—alive to the past because he felt so keenly in the present— he would see again what had taken place long ago.

What he would see always made him conclude, even in that land-scape made of such durabilities as mountain and plain and river, that the one constant thing was man's spirit.

But though he did not know it, it was himself he was seeing in those terms.

He was coming down the hill through the cold wafts of the blow-ing sand. "The color of everything today is the color of the fur on the belly of a mountain lion. It is a cat-colored storm. The whole world has come into harmony with the volcanoes across the river. Thank God there's a little bit of green left here and there, even in winter."

He alluded to his own piece of public folly, which he nevertheless admired. Next door to his own three-story red-brick house he owned two vacant lots. There he had planted an evergreen nursery, with three varieties of pine trees, standing in strict ranks. As often as he could he tended them himself. There seemed to him a happy correla-tion between this matter of setting out trees in a barren country, and letting them grow just for the pleasure of it, and the pursuit of how this country looked to those who saw it new, generation after genera-tion. To the successive waves of travelers in the West, the land pre-sented a new meaning each time, for each was looking for something different from what his predecessors had sought. He remembered that to the end of her days, his mother had missed "the green" of the East.

Across town, from the hillside, where Central Avenue began to drop down to the river plain, he could see the green blur of his nursery.

When the sandstorm was over, the trees would glisten in the sun-light again, and he would look down on them from his third-floor windows at home.

III

He decided not to go by his office but to go home. If there had been any calls for him downtown, they would've been phoned out to the house. He drove through the streets many of which were not yet paved, and the blowing wind picked up the sand. He came home by streets far out on the edge of town. He always liked that point where the countryside and the town could be seen together. He didn't reflect about it, but what pleased him in the sight was the recollection of how it had been in his boyhood, when from almost anywhere in the town you could see the plains opening out at the ends of streets. The city was growing these days. He avoided the "metropolitan" look of its downtown as much as possible. He was unimpressed by what everyone else hailed as "progress." But he never felt it polite to say so. He allowed his fellow citizens their zeal and their ambition, which he described to himself as a kind of forgetfulness of man's real virtues.

At home he found a scribble on the tablet by the phone in the white-paneled closet under the front hall stairway. It told him to call the office. His downtown nurse answered and said that he had a call to go see a patient, a newcomer, who had been urged by Doctor Treddinger, of New York, to get in touch with him. The patient's name was Mrs. Foster. Her address was 1 Highland Parkway. She wanted to see Doctor Rush this afternoon, if possible.

He still had his hat and coat on, and when he hung up the receiver, he simply sat in the phone cubbyhole, as they called it in the family, and looked out at what he could see of his home from this narrow prospect. It was a spacious house, and everything about it was square and clean. But it sometimes seemed to him empty, in a curious way. The only place in it where he felt at home was his study on the top floor. He wondered if his wife Noonie was upstairs; if his son Donald was home from school; if Cora the cook and Leonard the houseboy (both Negroes) were out in the kitchen. He couldn't hear anything.

The living room had white painted pillars dividing it from the hall. The carpets were green. There was a brass and prism chandelier hanging in the hall, and another in the big front room. There was a lot of mahogany furniture. The stairway over him was of mahogany with a green carpet. The windows had loops of lace curtain and he could see the stern of the grand piano before the wide windows of the front room. He was hungry. But if he went out to get a glass of milk, he would have to listen to Cora complaining humorously about

Jacob her husband, who couldn't let other girls alone; or if Cora weren't there, he wouldn't be able to find anything. He considered having a small icebox of his own put into the study way upstairs; and then stood up, impatient at his general discontent in his own house, which made him feel guilty.

He went to the foot of the stairs, and called up:

"Noon? Are you there?"

There was a stir, first, and then an answer, from the big glassed-in sitting room where she did her mending, and loved to read, over the front porch.

"Hello? Yes?"

They both waited in silence a moment, considering each other out of sight and reach.

Then he said up the stairs, with his eyes shut,

"Are you all right, dearie?"

She paused again, long enough to let doubt into her reassuring words:

"*Perfectly* all right, dear.—Are you going out? Or coming up?"

"I'm running out for a few minutes, there was a call for me downtown. I have a million things to do. I'll be back for dinner."

"I should hope so," she said, bridling slightly in her tone.

He waited another moment, but if she was going to be habitually reproachful, there was nothing more he felt like saying. He went out to his car, climbed in and set off again, cruising through the bitter blowy day with the sand rattling on the isinglass of his side curtains. Mrs. Foster lived at 1 Highland Parkway. He knew the place, a large rambling house on two levels, built of logs against the hillside overlooking town. It was often taken by Easterners who came here for their health. If Doctor Treddinger had sent Mrs. Foster to him it was most likely a case of something respiratory. There would probably be a letter one of these days all about it. Willie Treddinger was always late with that sort of thing.

II · THE FAMILY STORY

I

After he went, Mrs. Rush sat still with her mending all about her, looking after him down the street. She was tired. She wished she had gone downstairs to see him. Every time he left her, she wished she had done more, said more, to give him comfort. Yet she could never explain to herself why she had been graceless with him. How much she loved him he did not know; and when he was patient with her, and forbore to rebuke her when she was remote from him, she had a positive passion of resentment in her heart which tasted bitterly to her thought.

How could it be that what had begun rapturously fourteen years ago was now, at times, so doubtful?

II

One week end in the winter of 1906, her cousin Willie Treddinger brought Peter Rush home to Rochester, New York, for a visit. They were both interns in a hospital in New York City, and shared the same small bedroom. They had been together in college, at Cornell, but their intimacy grew only after they had been graduated and sent to St. Luke's for their last two years of training. Peter was then very slim, with what everybody spoke of as a Western figure, with his flat wide shoulders and thin legs and narrow hips. He tried to look older than he was by wearing a heavy brown mustache. His hair was thick and formal above his merry face, which kept a dark tan from a boyhood on the plains. At a Saturday night dance he was introduced to Susan Larkin (whom everyone called Noonie from a childhood rhyme about "Susan-Noonan") and danced waltzes and two-steps with her all evening. There was said to be a half-understood arrangement between young Doctor Treddinger and his cousin Noonie Larkin, but nobody was surprised when the new young doctor from New Mexico seemed to take the inside track. Treddinger was a pink, round young man with infinite good nature. He watched his friend flirt with Noonie and even seemed to encourage him. Noonie was "furious" with him at first for giving up so easily, "froze" him with "looks" for a couple of week ends, and then as happiness began to steal into her heart, she could only remember that it was her cousin who had brought Peter Rush into her life in the first place; and she ended by kissing Willie on his fat cheek in front of everybody at a supper party in her house, and whispering to him that she would always be grateful to him, and would love him like a *cousin*.

She was the prettiest girl of the year, according to what everyone told her. Her eyes were dark and her hair was darker still. She often said she was as blind as a bat, and couldn't see anything ten feet away. But she refused to wear glasses, and her nearsightedness gave her a blurred and dreamy look about the eyes which (all her female friends told her) "broke" many a heart. She was as lively as a squirrel, and had many darling little tricks of gesture which made a man feel protective and hulking and a willing fool. She could sing adorably, played the piano at all the parties, and never missed a concert by either a visiting artist or any of the local musical societies, such as the German-American Saengerverein, which gave a choral concert every year with an expensive imported soloist, like Schumann-Heink, or Otto Goritz, or Reinhold von Warlich. (So much of that upstate culture reflected the "free" Germans who had fled the tyrannies of Prussia in the mid-century.)

Rochester's winters were gray and damp, and unless you were happy, or didn't notice things like that, you were likely to be chilled to the bone on more days than not. But Noonie seemed to give out light and warmth all that winter, for Peter came down every week end that he wasn't on duty at the big New York hospital. He even came the week end he had news of his mother's death way out in New Mexico. Noonie held his hand, and pressed his fingers, and her heart was in her mouth for what he was suffering, so far away, so lonesome in the name of the childhood which had just ended. He told her how he always meant to go home and get rich and give his mother everything she had always wanted, chief of which was an annual trip to the East. Now it was too late. They called off a party she had arranged for that Saturday night, and nobody was there with them but her brother Roderick, who turned the pages for her when she played and sang songs after dinner, to cheer Peter up. It was a quiet and almost tender evening, and it met his sorrow with another emotion almost as filling. He loved her. He saw a lifetime of such evenings with her. He could hardly wait to be in a position to offer to marry her. He went back to New York by the night train on Sunday. He hardly slept in his Pullman, for thinking about her, and all women, really. A few words spoken late at night in the creaking Pullman car by a woman who got on at Utica suffused him with sweet torments and sterling vows.

III

It wasn't long until he was acknowledged as Noonie's official beau, though they were not actually engaged. During a week end in spring, a friend of Noonie's came from Albany, N. Y., to visit. Her name was Elizabeth Kleitz. She was a hazel-eyed, bronze-haired girl who saw herself as a fascinating scamp, a troublemaker, and had earned a reputation for originality. Elizabeth set herself to break up the match which everyone took for granted. She wore dashing clothes with low-cut bosom, and put her face close to the men she talked to, and let her eyes rove up and down their faces; she had lace cuffs on her sleeves that came down to her knuckles, and she tangled her fingers in her radiant hair and let her eyes fail out of sight in what she believed to be the manner of Sarah Bernhardt. She was never quiet, saying "H-h'm, hm—him, 'm, 'm, 'm," all the while anyone was talking to her. Everyone was sure that she kissed everybody, but her vitality and assurance were so great that she was much admired. She asked everyone to call her Lisette.

She stated that she was scandalized at what she found Noonie up to, and promised everyone else that she would save the situation at no matter what cost to herself. Everyone had felt that Peter and Noonie made an attractive pair, up to now; but Lisette seemed to bring a new viewpoint with authority. Noonie's brother Roderick, especially, seemed to cast off his complacent acceptance of the love affair.

The night Lisette arrived from Albany, there was a concert by Eugène Ysaye. Lisette, Roderick, Noonie and Peter all dressed up in their grandest clothes and went. When the great violinist came out on the stage, the audience rose and clapped. He bowed. His dark golden hair, which reached to his shoulders, fell forward as he bowed. He went on bowing as he walked to the piano carrying his violin, which was the color of an oak leaf in winter. His accompanist followed him. The artists made a quiet moment of business about getting settled in their black and white clothes, under the yellow rain of the concert lights above them. Behind them was a painted stage curtain representing a woodland glade with a tiny marble temple in the blue and gold distance. The violinist took his violin aloft and settled it into his rolling chin, lifted his bow with his large white paw, closed his eyes and nodded faintly. The piano began to sing.

The bow came across in a deliberately beautiful arc, and began to woo the strings. Ysaye told the lovers all the things they thought no one else knew. Noonie was enraptured. Peter caught her enchantment, and did not even marvel at being elevated by music for the first time in his life.

Beside them, Lisette, like a superbly intelligent cat, spoke to Roderick about them with her hazel eyes. She had the property of seeming to keep up a running commentary even when she said nothing. But all her other means—hands, eyes, shrugs, breaths, sharp little teeth on lower lip, toe taps—were also articulate. No one was ever left in doubt as to what Lisette thought; or that she "thought" constantly. Her ambition was to have people turn, and look after her, and say, "Who is that fascinating foreigner?"

In the intermission, she seized Noonie's hands and said with a champagnelike glance from her yellow eyes,

"Ach, Noonchen, how could you ever give all this up?"

She often affected tender little Germanisms, having studied German at a fashionable convent-school on the banks of the Hudson River.

Noonie laughed.

"Give what up? I'm not giving anything up."

Lisette gasped softly and put her white-gloved finger tips on her lips.

"Na, what have I said! Am I not supposed to know *anything?*"

Even in her rages, she remembered to be "foreign."

She turned and rustled off down the hall in a fury. Noonie went after her. Roderick and Peter drifted together and lighted cigarettes, watching the girls in their elaborate costumes, with long white gloves, high-dressed hair, bare backs, long lacy gowns with loops and rosebuds and velvet ribbons and harsh silk petticoats and dragging trains.

Lisette let herself be caught up with, and her pale eyes blazed at Noonie.

"So: you will never confide in your oldest friend?—What do you give up if you marry that nice young rancher from out West? You give up evenings like this, and friends like me, and brothers like your darling Rod, he is so handsome and distinguished, and the best young lawyer in Rochester, how often do you suppose Ysaye plays out West, would he ever risk his beautiful blond hair with the Indians?"

Noonie blushed at this outburst, and took Lisette and kissed her lightly.

"Don't be such a goose, Lizzie, he hasn't even asked me yet!"

The gong rang to bring the audience back to the auditorium.

As they went back to their seats it was almost visible on Lisette's face (on which there was a hint of paint, which was meant to be daring) that it was an official relief that Noonie and Peter were not engaged. During the last half of the concert she ignored Roderick beside her and turned to Peter, leaning on his arm, enjoying the music exaggeratedly, brushing his cheek with tingles of her magnificent bronze hair, and losing her eyes upward in desperate emotions caused by his presence as well as by Eugène Ysaye's exquisite playing of the violin.

Peter maintained his composure as well as he could; but at times he had to bite his mustache to keep from laughing right out at her. But he knew Noonie was fond of her, and would be offended if he made fun of her.

They left the concert in a carriage, and the four of them being in the satin-padded interior, with the horse's hooves making a remote sound of progress on the pavement, gave them all a sense of privacy and grandeur. The young men held their silk hats on their knees because the carriage roof was too low. The street lamps as they passed fanned yellow light over their faces. The other three all found themselves watching for Elizabeth's face at every lamp. Its confined but expressive antics always rewarded them.

IV

Noonie's brother Roderick Larkin was black-haired and black-eyed. His gaze was black and white, and he had a mannerism of gazing intently at people, mostly women, without speaking, under the illusion that this made him irresistible. It would've made him unbearable, except that deep in his eyes there was always merriment, a kind of spiritual good health, which made people excuse his mischief. Noonie adored him, and he suffered her worship rather regally. It was he who had given her her nickname, long ago when they were both children. For years, he had to approve everything she did or wanted to do before she was satisfied. He worked in a rich law firm, and was always in love with a new girl, but the wise mothers of Rochester were already saying that he was an eternal bachelor, meaning by it that the most constant thing about him was his vanity; such as no girl would ever be likely to measure up to.

He was now amused to be Lisette's ally in the game over Peter Rush from New Mexico.

He had always treated Peter with a clubman's airs, using expressions like "old fellow," and "chappie," and in general contriving to make the young doctor from the West feel that he was dealing with a vividly presented character in a book by Richard Harding Davis rather than with a real man.

Noonie was quick to feel this difference between her brother and her suitor.

She resented the silent good manners of Peter's behavior toward her darling Roderick; and when she was alone, she felt like crying with disappointment at the courteous disdain which Roderick revealed by his exquisite attempts to conceal it, when he dealt with Peter. She tried all sorts of little tricks to bring them together, and Roderick behaved with almost creaking courtesy; the while his inner glance told her that it simply wouldn't do, the fellow was simply an outsider, and he would do all he could for him, but like him he simply could not.

Nothing was ever said openly about all this. It was plainly too dangerous. But in ways that were to reach far into the future it would have been better if brother and sister had come right out and quarreled bitterly, and cleared the air.

The fact was that neither knew the depth of feeling involved, and in some instinctive restraint, did not want to plumb it, for fear they might hurt each other too much.

All their lives they had been able to come laughing out of their little differences, and with a sense of being united against a stuffy world in which nobody else saw the colors, the jokes, or the beauties which they saw.

The Larkin house was an old square building of yellow sandstone, holding aloft a cupola, and trailing a carriage house at the foot of the gravel driveway in the deep garden. It was peaceful, comfortable, and thanks to the character of the parents, a house without "scenes."

It was only when Elizabeth Kleitz came to visit from Albany that there was an impish spirit in the old place. Her mother and Mrs. Larkin had been schoolgirl friends, who always referred in their letters to each other to what a comfort it would be when their daughters should grow up in their turn, in similar friendship.

But Lisette was far more bent on being fascinating than friendly, and this meant, first of all, for better or worse, unremitting liveliness.

v

All day Sunday she kept up her campaign against Peter. Roderick kept asking for certain songs, which he would turn for Noonie at the piano. Noonie watched herself drawn into a temper as the day advanced. She began to hate Lisette, and she was becoming annoyed at Peter's attempts at politeness and attentiveness to the visiting beauty. Finally, late in the afternoon, when Mr. and Mrs. Larkin returned from a series of Sunday calls, and they all sat before the fire at the marble fireplace, Lisette's restless duty had its assuagement.

She had a bunch of American Beauty roses at her waist. She broke one away from her satin sash, and put it by her mouth. It was startling and effective on her white cheek. They all looked at her. The elder Larkins smiled. They remembered a whole cycle of years of young children's parties at which Lisette Kleitz always had to be the leading lady. Lisette let a hazy smile drift across her face, faintly shadowing her lifted cheeks. There was never a greater image of innocence and charm than her face when she asked Peter,

"And when you finish at the New York hospital, Doctor Rush, where do you mean to live?"

He answered readily,

"Why, I shall go back to the West, of course, where I came from. I would never want to live anywhere else."

Mr. and Mrs. Larkin exchanged startled glances. They had often wondered what his future was to be, but they had never actually prepared themselves to hear that. They looked at Noonie, who seemed to be so in love with him. She smiled ardently at Peter, and said,

"I thought we had almost naturalized you."

He laughed.

Lisette sat back in her chair, and cupping her hands, held her rose as if it were a beloved face, to which she was confiding lovely mysteries. She had put into the spoken awareness of them all the things that she instinctively knew to be the sole difficulty facing the two young people, who were so sparkling and alive with love for each other.

Roderick bent his glossy head over a cigarette in his hands, to conceal his amusement over Lisette's wickedness. From that bent position, he glanced blackly and whitely at his sister. A pang hit him in the breast when he saw her eyes full of tears. His disloyalty to her was suddenly plain to him. He lost his airy feeling of indulgent superiority, and went over to Lisette. He took her wrist and brought her to standing.

"Come along, we'll go for a little walk in the park. The ice on the lake is breaking up. Sunset is very pretty over melting ice."

In a few minutes they were gone, Lisette bearing an ermine shako on her dazzling hair, and an ermine muff with black tails on her right arm. Her coat was of dark-green velvet. Noonie hated her out the front door. The elder Larkins went upstairs soon after, and Noonie faced Peter by the fireplace.

"How could you pay so much attention to her!" she said.

"I was only trying to be nice to your friend.—Actually, she made me nearly burst with inside laughter."

"Oh: she did!"

"Yes."

Over things they could hardly touch alive into clarity, their wills were at battle.

"You needn't make fun of my friends!"

"I won't, ordinarily.—Besides, she wants to make trouble.—What else do you suppose all that elaborate acting meant?"

"She is simply being loyal to me, in her way, which I admit is rather odd."

"Don't defend her, Noonie, dear."

She colored at the last word.

The strain of putting up with Lisette for the past twenty-four hours made her lightheaded now that her emotions need not be politely concealed.

"You don't mean that."

"Mean what?"

"What you called me."

"—You mean 'dear'? I do indeed. With all my heart, Noonie dear."

"If you did, you couldn't've said what you did before."

"When:"

"When she asked you where you meant to live."

"But I only said—"

"That's just it. You evidently don't mind going off and leaving— leaving *me* a thousand miles away."

"Oh: that hellcat of a redhead!" he said, laughing full of love, and reaching for Noonie's hand. Noonie put it behind her, longing for him to make her tremble and cry with the tenderness she saw in him.

"You are speaking of my house guest," said Noonie stiffly. She was making a fool of herself. She didn't know how to stop. What was in the way. Dignity? Pride? Hunger?

"Oh, nonsense. Look at me, Noonie."

She turned away.

He sighed.

"Well, then, *would* you come with me, when I have to go back out West?"

She turned and all of Lisette's most idle prattle now seemed full of wisdom and foreboding.

"You wouldn't *consider* staying here, I suppose, not even if you *loved* me?"

Her anger which was more than half love begot the same thing in him. He stiffened. He bit his teeth together. His jaw lumped.

"Turn the coin over," he said. "If you loved me, you wouldn't even *consider* coming with me?"

She stared at him. Tears rose and welled over to her cheeks. She was ravishingly pretty in the firelight. Her spirit danced with exasperation and baffled sweetness. The quarrel was as foolish as any of its kind, and while he saw her adorable desirability, he could see too the aching selfishness of love. He remained stubbornly silent and motionless. She wanted to bring his head down to her hot face, and tell him she was his, anywhere, forever, but instead, she bit her lips to be silent, and ran out of the high marbled room dim with Sunday afternoon quiet and twilight, and up the stairs.

When Lisette and Roderick returned, Peter was gone.

He sat in his hotel lobby all evening, staring out the window at the traffic. It had begun to rain. The carriage lamps and the few automobile headlights were like gold blooming flowers reflected in the wet pavements. The clerk called over to him once that someone wanted him on the phone, but he refused to stir, saying he was out. At eleven he got up and paid his bill, and went to the station to catch the Empire State Express. It was snowing by that time; a late winter storm; the ice on the lake in the park would be frozen again by morning. It would be, he thought bitterly, something for someone to take Miss Elizabeth Kleitz to see.

VI

There were a few weeks of official estrangement, during which Noonie was almost plainer to him in his misery than she had been during his week ends of good times in Rochester with her. For the only time in his life he was overtaken by a fit of laziness, or lack of will, or something that made him cloudy in the head when he was at work. He slept more than usual, and never seemed refreshed. He was haunted by her when he dreamed. He sometimes stared out the window over the telephone wires and roofs of 1906 New York, and looked at the pale sky where it was full of light over the invisible river. There to the West was his home. He longed for the sight of the plains, yellow in the winter, under the sky as blue as a bluebird's

wing, with those white feathery clouds that seemed to capture the sunlight. That was where he was born. That was where he belonged.
They were probably laughing at him up in Rochester for being
routed by a red-haired chatterbox from Albany.

And at the same time he knew that he would never be cured of this
slow poison, this weight of defeat in him, if he didn't see Noonie
again. He knew almost numbly that there would be an issue over
where they might live after they were married. One night he awoke
startled and sat up and stared at the dark room. Then he smiled
with a triumphant certainty. Once they were engaged, and married,
and everything, he would love her so much that she would *see* how
anywhere he went she must come with him. It was a surge of strength
and new resolve that flowed through him. He was suddenly full of
ideas again. Before he fell back to sleep, he had the most brilliant
idea of all, which he would execute the following evening.

The following evening he walked seven blocks to a drugstore far
enough off from the hospital so that he would probably be unob-
served by any of his cronies on the staff. There was a telephone booth
of heavily carved walnut with glass door panes etched in an ornate
design. He closed himself into the booth and asked the operator if a
long distance call to Rochester was possible on a commercial phone
like this. She said it was, but would probably take about forty-five
minutes if he cared to wait. He replied that he would wait all night,
if necessary, and gave her Noonie's number. The operator said not to
leave the vicinity of the booth. He went and sat down on a wire-
backed soda fountain chair and leaned his elbows on a marble-
topped soft-drink table. There was a copy of *McClure's Magazine*
lying before him, and he turned through its pages, carefully looking
at everything, and reading nothing, three times, before the phone
rang at last. He dashed to answer. It was his call. His heart was
pounding. Through the receiver came a steady roaring noise like
Niagara Falls, but he could also hear someone saying "Hello?" and
he recognized Roderick's voice.

"Rod? This is Pete Rush. I'm calling from New York. Is Noonie
there?"

"Yes. Do you want to speak to her?—You are talking from *New
York?*"

"Yes, it is what they call a long distance call.—Can you get Noonie
to the phone?"

"Wait a minute, old chap. Say, this is remarkable."

He waited, and at last here she was.

She marveled too, and then appeared to recall the reserve which had not yet been officially dispelled between them.

Peter asked her if she could hear him plainly. She said she could. He answered then that he was glad, because he had something enormously important to say to her. The roar of Niagara Falls could not drown out the falter in her voice when she said "What is it," and he said to her that he begged her to forgive him his temper, and to marry him in June, when he would be through at the hospital.

There was a long pause in which only the electric roar of the phone line kept up.

Then she said yes, but they had so very much to talk over first. He replied that there was nothing they could not settle between them. The important thing was to be together again, didn't she think so?

"Oh yes!" she cried into the phone. Her voice rang clarion over the wire, and turned his heart over.

He told her how much he loved her, and said he would be up the following week end. The operator cut in to announce that the time was up. Noonie delayed them a moment longer to ask if the expense was not simply frightful? making a call from New York? He laughed at her adding to it by asking about it, and they rang off.

VII

The following Sunday morning he was at her house as if nothing had happened. They were together in the drawing room about eleven o'clock when a messenger boy on a bicycle came up with a package and rang the doorbell. Noonie herself went to answer. She came back bearing a square basket of wicker, dyed purple, and tied with a purple satin ribbon.

"It is for me!" she said, reading the card as she came to sit down by Peter again.

"Open it," he said. He was blushing and there was a stinging in his eyes.

She opened the wicker lid. In the basket was a huge bunch of violets. Their damp, frosty fragrance seemed to fill the big old room. In the center of the mound of violets was a sparkling jewel. Noonie looked at him and then leaned over the violets and took the jewel up to see it. It was a ring, made of a large violet amethyst surrounded by a circle of diamonds. It sparked and spoke in the sunlight that poured through the windows upon them. She looked at him again. She saw his darkened cheeks and the fire in his eyes. She began to tremble and fell against him dizzy with happiness. He took the ring from her and put it on her engagement finger, and kissed it there. She threw her arms around his neck and hungered after him saying his name softly.

It was many minutes before they were composed enough to discuss the enchanting ingenuity of how the ring was delivered. All the rest of the day she told the story to everyone who came in. Her family's house was always full of people. The bleak ruin of love which had shown there for weeks was now replaced by the highest happiness.

VIII

When he next came back it was springtime. They went out for the afternoon in a hired rig which Peter drove. They went to the park and gave a boy half a dollar to watch their horse, and wandered over the grass among the fabulous lilac bushes which had come into bloom. Noonie said the city was very proud of the display. There were over seven hundred varieties of lilac represented. The air was cloudy with fragrance. Everything from pure white clusters to black purples was represented on the grand dome-shaped bushes. The afternoon sunlight was like gold embroidery on the grass. They walked hand in hand. She found a lilac whose color exactly matched her amethyst engagement ring. He looked at her sometimes and could not believe anyone could be as pretty as she was, so animated, so full of meaning when she looked at him. And yet there she was, and she was his. He felt ten years older than the year before, and grateful for the feeling. After he left her each time, he wondered how he could've been such a fool for years up to now. When things went well between them, he had the sensation of being wise and penetrating at his work, as if he came to know all sorts of *other* things simply through her; having her in his life; in his heart.

He told her this as they went back to the buggy from the lilac garden. She made him pause, and turned to him and set her hand on his arm.

"No, there is one trouble, Peter, dearest."

"What is that?"

"You are much cleverer than I am."

"Nonsense."

"Yes, you are deeper than I am."

"Nonsense, I simply had to learn a lot of things that you will never *need* to know. That isn't being deep. Merely wide. Or *wider,* anyway."

"I am really such a goose about a lot of things . . . Or I was, until I met you . . ."

He hotly defended her against her own depreciations.

She let him rave, as she called it, and then astonished him by saying,

"But after all, I don't think I want to be cleverer. I only want to be really a woman. I hate clever women.—Don't you?"

"Like Lisette?"

She was able to laugh with him about Lisette now. They had telegraphed Lisette their news, and received in reply a wire which read "Amazed thrilled heavenly news when wedding saw it coming always." Secure, they agreed that they could relent and let Lisette come to the wedding.

It was such a warm afternoon that they didn't want to turn homeward. They took the dusty, sunlit road that led to the lake. The fields were beginning to green and yield earthy scents. They saw Lake Ontario in the distance, sparkling soberly. They could see one or two sails leaning before the wind.

"Why don't we stop at the boat club," she said, "and perhaps we'll find someone who will take us out for a ride."

"It is rather late to start."

"Just for a little ride."

"A little one."

At the boat club they ran into Roderick Larkin and a girl he often took out. Her name was Evelyn Warner. She was called Evvie. She was a calm blonde who wore starched shirtwaists and held her beautiful head with a classical lift. She played the violin and was famous in local recital circles. Ysaye had heard her the afternoon before his concert in Rochester that winter and promised "great things" for her. She and Roderick were sitting on the pier, dangling their legs and squinting at the late sunlight on the water.

"Have you been out?" asked Noonie.

"No," said Roderick. "We just wanted to sit here."

"We wanted to go for a sail. Is anyone around?"

"I haven't seen anybody all day to go out with. I have the use of the Rogers's sloop, if you want to go."

It was agreed that they would all go. Roderick knew how to sail. They said they wouldn't be out long. The boathouse keeper helped to push them off. Their sloop was called the *Affinity*. It had a tiny cabin with cherrywood fittings and scarlet velvet cushions. But they all sat in the cockpit, with Roderick at the tiller. The wind was keener and brisker than they had thought. He kept the *Affinity* close-hauled and she leaned over considerably, and spanked a heavy spray off the very waves that had made the lake sparkle from a distance as they had approached the shore in the buggy. Evvie sat statuesquely lifting her Athenian blonde profile into the wind, and holding her flat straw hat on to her golden head with her hand. The shore grew smaller. Some white gulls flipped and sailed like chips of sunlight itself. They were all rather chilly on board, but also they were enchanted with the boat moving over the water, and the tickle of the spray, and the fact that when they wanted to say something, they more or less had to shout it, because of the wind and the thundering of their bows against the waves which came rolling, rolling "from Canada" which was way out of sight over the horizon.

They sailed parallel to the shore for a while. The sun was falling. They could see (far back it seemed) the birth of a few early lights in houses among the hills. Roderick said he would come about and they would return, before darkness fell. The twilight was the finest hour of all for sailing, he shouted. They enthusiastically agreed with him. The sloop came about and headed back. But the wind was not so favorable. The vast lake was glistening silver as the afternoon failed, and its depths began to seem black instead of deep blue. Roderick called out to them to be ready, he had to come about again, and make his distance by a course of short tacks, whereas they had come down the lake before on one long superb sweep. As he came about this time, he realized that the wind was riper, and the *Affinity* heeled sharply before he could steady her. As the boom swung over the cockpit, the others ducked and made for the high gunwale again. In their movement, they did not realize how far she had really tipped before she seemed steady again.

There was last daylight now on the very crest of the horizon, and the qualities of the shore became coolly blurred in shadow. The sun was just about to go down. It was making a magnificent tossing path of red gold in the water, and they were sailing more or less in it. As they looked back to the *Affinity's* wake, they could see the lake water tumbling and swirling blackly as if night were already there.

"Once again," called Roderick. "We'll be late getting home, even if we don't have to take a reef!"

He meant to test it again on this tack, and if the sloop was too nervous under all that canvas, he planned to come into the wind and drop sail, and put everyone to work taking a reef, or even two, so that if maneuvering would be slower, it would also be safer as darkness came and they worked back to the boathouse. He bore on the tiller, and the sail clapped and the pulleys sang. The wind seemed to disappear entirely for a tiny moment; then it took hold. It slammed the sail like a door, and the boom chattered. The *Affinity* kicked. She rose up and came back. She went over on her side. The boom shuddered and hit something and swung wildly. The sloop capsized. It was twilight. The sun was gone. The water was almost icy cold. For a few moments there was a frantic silence, and then Peter called out for Noonie. She answered him from the opposite side of the *Affinity,* which was sluggishly afloat on her beam ends, keel and spread sail holding her more or less steady. He called Roderick and he called Evvie and there was no answer. He swam around to Noonie. She was clinging to the tangle about the mast.

"Where are the others!" she asked. Her teeth were chattering.

"I don't know. Come on, darling. Let me help you on."

They struggled to the stern, and around to the other side where the keel made its elegant curve into the hull. He managed to hug her to the *Affinity's* side, and then lift her up so that she could crawl to safety on the elevated and rocking boat. The light was going fast.

"Evvie!—Rod!" he called.

Noonie suddenly cried to him from the boatside,

"Look! Peter!"

She was pointing. Astern the drifting wreck was a figure, barely floating. It was Roderick. He swam to him. There was blood on Roderick's forehead. He was unconscious and rolled slowly by the waves. Peter hauled him to the sloop and with Noonie got him up out of the water on the precarious refuge of the *Affinity's* speed-modelled flank.

"Hold on to him till I look for Evvie!"

He called and searched. There was no answer. The waves lifted and fell and the shore was merging with night. He saw what he had to do. His heart gave a wrench for Noonie's part in it. He swam back and told her there was no sign of Evvie. Roderick was evidently hurt by the last swing of the boom as they capsized.

"Can you hold on to him, Noonie, while I swim ashore to get help? Are you all right, dearest?"

She nodded, and said,

"You have to rest a minute first, you've been swimming everywhere—"

"I will. I'll hold on here for a second and get my breath. But it'll be too dark, soon, darling. I have to go soon. Noonie, no matter what you think, how long it seems, *hold on,* darling, *will* you? It will seem terribly cold and late and a long time once I am gone, but I will be as fast as I can. There's a launch at the club. I'll come right out. Rod couldn't manage alone."

"I know. Of course. Do go along when you're ready. I'll be here."

"Are you cold?"

"Yes."

"I know. Poor darling Noonie. What a thing for you."

"Poor Evvie.—The poor Warners!—I'll be all right, Peetsie.—Are you going now?"

He gave her a look she never forgot. It was like a kiss. His face was kind and anguished and determined. He pushed away and began to swim slowly toward the shore where the lights were innocent beams in a darkling world. She watched him as long as she could. Her heart was full of longing and prayer. She clutched Roderick by his coated shoulders. There was a moving equilibrium she discovered between his weight, the lift and fall of the hull, and the way she must counter the movement with her own weight and will. She could not see Peter. The wind dried her coldly. It came in a wide angle off the shore. The capsized sloop was drifting outward.

IX

Peter rolled slowly and almost lazily from side to side as he swam. He knew he would have to walk and search for help when he finally reached the shore. He was of course tempted to race, thinking of Noonie alone out there, holding on to Roderick, with the drowned Evvie somewhere near by gone forever. His heart felt warm with pity for the desolation he had had to leave her in. He prayed with his unformed words that she be saved; and by him.

It was pitch dark when he at last felt the sand under him. The waves were large, and trundled him in a grand swell on the beach. He lay breathing shallowly with his head on his arm for a moment. The cold struck him now that he was inactive. He had worked off his shoes and trousers and coat in the water. Now he stood up and took off his shirt and tied the arms around his waist and started up the dunes toward the road that ran parallel to the lake, inland. There were farms here and there. He could see lights. He began to run; and then he fell down in exhaustion. He became furiously angry at his own weakness. His heart was ripping away in his breast. But he forced himself to rest. He breathed gently and deeply. He was surprised to feel that his mouth and throat were dry. In a little while he felt that he could go on again; but this time he walked, and kept telling himself that the important thing was to get there. If he hurried too much, he might never make it, in time. All he could think of was the black water out there and Noonie alone saving Roderick.

She must be in terror. He often thought of her as like a kitten. She had that sort of exquisite animation, her small face was as touchingly pointed and set as a kitten's, and she seemed as fastidious and pretty in her movements and tastes.

He came over a hill and ran into a rail fence in the darkness. He hung on it a moment, and had a charge of relief, for there across the field was a lighted farmhouse. He climbed the fence and felt he could risk running now, and he ran to the back porch and beat upon the door, calling aloud.

There was a speculative silence within, and then cautious steps came across the kitchen and the door was swung open slowly. The farmer was there, with his head forward, his eyes shut down to peer carefully. When he saw the shivering, half-naked young man, he slammed the door and cried out, "Hallelujah, amen: The Lord deliver us!" Peter knocked again, and cried "Help!" The man opened the door again, and began to laugh, and said to come in, he was just startled at first, but it *was* a sight. He was all sympathy now, and he called his wife to come in with a blanket. They poked the fire in the range, and wrapped Peter in the blanket while he told them what was needed. The farmer went out to saddle his team to the buckboard. The woman heated the coffee in the big pot which stood never empty all day on the coal range. In a few minutes he felt desperate for action again. The kitchen was a cavern of comfort, its oil lamp smelled somehow dear, and the clinking bustle of the hotted-up range gave him new energy. The floor was covered with strips of tin nailed in a neat pattern and scrubbed until they looked like pewter. There was something heartening about the flavor of the place. The wife brought him a pair of trousers and a bulky old sweater of her husband's. They heard the team out back then, and the farmer call for Peter.

In the cold spring darkness they rattled and champed along the country road. There were a few stars showing and the trees as they went by seemed like shadows against the stars. They reached the boat club in half an hour. They turned out the keeper, and got the launch warmed up. They brought lanterns and blankets. The farmer said he would wait right there until the launch returned.

It took two hours of cruising to find the wreck. At last they bumped gently up to the overturned hull. They lifted their lanterns up. She was still there, and Peter could hardly recognize her. She was haggard and numb. She seemed to be paralyzed. She seemed to be asleep, with only one purpose alive in her: to hold on. She was holding on to Roderick and staring at the lanterns. They reached both of them and brought them into the launch. They were so far out that the boathouse light could not be seen. Peter went to work as a doctor, doing what he could, as the boatman put the launch about and headed them inshore.

He gave her some of the boatman's whisky. She was inert but awake in his arms. He held her like a doll wrapped in the blankets. Presently she felt a little warmer. She moved in his hold, and looked at him, and said,

"I am all right, darling."

Then she fell asleep on his breast.

She never said anything afterward about what she had suffered. Not a word of what she must have felt. She seemed resolved to dismiss the horror of the night from her memory. She exhibited fortitude that amazed everybody who knew her, that frivolous, pretty, delicate little bit of a thing?

Roderick recovered from his concussion.

Evelyn Warner's body was found two days later on the beach far west of the boathouse. They all went to the funeral, at which Evvie's violin teacher played Bach's Air for the G String.

x

Peter marveled at the—the: what did he want to call it?—the *quality?* fiber? valor? of the girl he was engaged to marry. It was evident that nobody else had ever suspected her great strength and character, under her famous gaiety, either. He felt that he knew Noonie's essential self, now, and that nothing in the world could ever make him forget it.

He regarded her as perfect.

It was a foolish and dangerous, even a disloyal thing to expect anybody to be:

She asked him sometime later if he wouldn't consider living here, and joining up with the eminent Doctor Donovan, who for years had been everybody's pet physician. He was an old man now, and must soon think of retiring. It would be a perfectly splendid arrangement. Her father, Mr. Larkin, had even had assurances from Doctor Donovan that he would be glad to see young Doctor Rush, anyhow; just for a talk; nothing binding. What harm could come of talking?

Peter's first impulse was to refuse.

He had a struggle with himself, when he made up his mind to go to see Doctor Donovan. It was one of those days in late spring when the softness, the trivial sadness, of pussy willows could be felt in the parks and gardens of that gray and green city. The sky was gray. It was raining lightly but steadily. The limit of the world seemed to be the next block *that* way, and the gates of the park the *other* way, and the sky was right there, heavy and forever gray, and outside the city were those beautiful but ever so close green hills. And yet the people he knew in Rochester were agreeable and nice. Doctors got rich in the East. It was just that he longed for a lifetime of vision that went out over the plains as far as the eye could see. Far mountains, and fabulous vistas of sky and cloud, and the reach of the Rio Grande from Colorado to the Gulf of Mexico . . .

He was in a state in which poetry and experience were the same thing.

XI

Doctor Donovan saw him at half-past five after office hours. He was an elderly Irishman, very tall, with silk-white hair and deep-blue eyes in a gaunt, pink face. He had a curiously soft voice, deep in his throat. His hands were slightly palsied, and he sometimes looked at them with a thin humorous set of his lips, as if to admonish them to cease of their idiot betrayal. He had a brother who was a priest. They had inner qualities in common.

"You are engaged to that Larkin child?"

"Yes."

"She has always been my kitten. I've taken care of them all for years."

"Yes sir."

"There seems to be some talk of your settling here."

"Some talk, yes sir."

"Do you think you would like general practice?"

"I think so, if I had some surgery too."

"I have always been happy, and very much occupied, with g.p. But I know: I know.—Well, I don't mind admitting that I've looked into you."

"Oh, really?"

"Yes, Ted Larkin and I are good friends. I've known all this for months."

"I see."

"Don't be stiff about it. Everybody acted fondly, whatever they did."

"Yes.—Thank you, sir."

"I believe, all things being equal, I'd like to have you."

There didn't seem anything to say, yet, so they both sat still. Then the old man said,

"However, do *you* think you can settle down here?"

Peter was startled. His misery was much deeper than he had himself admitted. He couldn't help smiling at how the old man had got right straight down to the one point that mattered.

"Why, I suppose I could live *any*where if I was happy in my work."

"Yes. And is there a reason for your wanting to come here to Rochester?"

"Oh, yes.—A very good one, I guess."

"Yes.—And is the reason yours, or hers?"

Peter laughed and shook his head as if in defeat.

"Hers."

The old doctor spread his shining pink fingers before him and gazed at their delicate trembling. He silently scolded the sight of them for a second, and then he said, looking at Peter with the craggy look of a blue-eyed eagle,

"Then you go and think it over again, Doctor. You can come back and tell me, if you like, whichever way you decide."

Peter got up and walked out, knowing that this had decided him.

He felt a surge of affectionate respect for the honesty of that old man who wasted no time with elaborate debate. He knew that he was going back to New Mexico; he hoped with all his heart that she was coming with him.

He need not have worried about that, even though she cried and doubted and rather elaborately "made the best of" how things were. He was like a virus in her blood. She knew that no matter where he went or what he did, she would follow him, for his very touch upon her had become a condition of life itself. Her reason, as she believed, told her what folly it was to leave everything she knew and was fond of, and go away, to an outlandish place, and she agreed with all her family's protests academically, and helplessly. When they said that if he really loved her, he would not take her away from her own country, the only thing she was certain of was that he did love her; but even if that had failed her, the last and most important truth was that *she* loved *him,* and that was what decided everything for her.

The wedding went forward as planned, in June. Doctor Willie Treddinger was best man. Elizabeth Kleitz came, with a somehow rapid effect, from Albany, and all through the quietest moments of the ceremony could be heard murmuring "H'm-h'm, 'm, 'm, 'm—sweet, exquisite—". They had an enormous party afterward, with champagne and toasts and an orchestra concealed but not silenced by palms.

Everyone expected Roderick to shine brilliantly when the time came to make the toasts, but suddenly they discovered that he was nowhere to be found. He had disappeared. It was the one cloud on the proceedings for Noonie, but she knew him so well that she hit upon the very reason for his disappearance: Lisette Kleitz had been industrious in her pursuit of him through the whole cycle of the wedding festivities, and it would've been just like her to *do something awful* right then and there, at the breakfast, as a consequence of which, Roderick might be maneuvered into the position of getting engaged to her. Her possessive and glittering antics of the past few days might well have scared off an even more adroit man than Roderick.

Just the same, his absence disappointed Noonie deeply, though nobody knew this. She buried some of her strongest emotions. Now she wanted her escape from her family to be granted to her by the brother she loved so well. She turned to her husband all the more ardently in her thoughts.

Great hilarity attended the moment when the photographer arrived and set up his box. He was like a ballet master, making little poses and steps, to cause the bride and groom and everyone else in the picture to make themselves attractive before the lens. He took one of Noonie alone, one of Noonie with Peter, and at Lisette's request, one of her with Noonie. Peter wore a Prince Albert coat and gray satin tie with his striped trousers. Noonie was in a cloud of white tulle and lace. They left for Watkins Glen. The carriage which took them down to the station was studded with bouquets of orange blossoms. "How awful!" cried Noonie when she saw it; but actually, she was pleased. She wanted her sweet news to be as public as possible. It was Peter who tried to act as if this were no extraordinary occasion at all. He held one eyebrow higher than the other and looked if anything almost bored. This gave her a pang of pity for him. She felt suddenly as if she had invaded his life and was now hung upon him forever. Would he hate her, when he found out that she would *always* be with him? She began to cry, and he thought it was just happiness and nerves, which was exactly right.

XII

By midsummer, they were in Albuquerque. It was one of the hot summers of local memory. There was hardly any water in the Rio

Grande, the streets were dried and cracked by the sun, and in the small house where they lived at first, there seemed to be no corner where they could be cool. But they didn't mind. He watched her to see if this was too different from the life she had known at home. She seemed wonderfully happy. He wondered, remembering how she had refused to refer to the tragic endurance of that night on the wrecked *Affinity*. He felt she had places to which he had no access. It was either that, or she was made happy by the smallest trifles. He worked hard, and his practice began to take hold from the minute he got home, for everyone knew him, his father and mother were well remembered, and Albuquerque was just beginning to be known as a haven for sufferers from tuberculosis, and all the doctors in town were busy.

Noonie didn't seem much interested in knowing anybody else. She wanted to be with him every possible moment, which suited him, too. Two years after they were married, a disaster befell them. It came from a quarter they could not have anticipated, and it was cruelly allied to the love they bore each other: Noonie gave birth to a son. The common ordeal, which she had awaited with excitement and devotion, nearly killed her. She was barely alive for weeks afterward, and when she began to take hold again, and climb almost consciously breath by breath back to life, she was not the same woman. It wasn't long before they secretly wished, as sinful as they felt in doing so, that their Donald had never been born.

It was as if their love story had already been told and finished. What it wanted in length, it had had in intensity for them both.

It was a calamity which Peter, as a doctor, could understand, however little that helped his suffering. The child was strong and grew well. As Noonie slowly recovered her physical semblance of health, just as slowly and as certainly they realized that she was afraid to think of having any more children. A fear so central filtered through everything else about her. She was afraid to be embraced. She was afraid she was ruining Peter's life. She adored her child, and was afraid that he did not really love her, as if the baby could perceive her inmost desolate unfaithfulness to the very springs of his being. Now for the first time, she felt as if she were in "exile," but it was an exile of the spirit, and it made life paradoxically more precious.

Instead of joy, there grew up habit between them.

Noonie was sometimes spoken of as "not very strong," though nobody knew how the illness of her fear seemed a new thing every day; as if the illness came and came.

They themselves wouldn't admit it except in tender, exasperated moments.

He tried to get her to go home for a visit. He knew it would help her. But she felt she "couldn't face them."

Above all, he kept reminding himself, he must never think of what had happened in terms of blame. It was not her fault. Whose fault was half the sorrow and trouble and illness in the world?

Feeling the love in her husband which had once made her breathlessly happy, she wrought misery for them both by her helpless refusal of the love she remembered and now would only let herself imagine.

An almost elfin kind of heartlessness grew within her, the more she lived in her imaginings. She presented to the world an appealing picture. Her face was still shaped like a kitten's, and under her little chin a great big silk bow would have looked appropriate. She often wore a spray of starched ruffle there in accordance with this style. Her cheeks had high color on some days, and on others they were pallid. Her eyes were dark. Her trim little figure looked best in little coats that matched tight skirts, and she was fastidious and extravagant about her clothes. The world might think the Rushes an ideally married pair.

Peter prospered. They built their big three-story red-brick house. The town stretched out over the plains between the mountains and the river. The boy Donald grew up properly. When the War came, Peter was accepted as a captain in the Army Medical Corps, and was stationed at the Walter Reed Hospital in Washington. Noonie stayed out West. It was her habit to live there now. She wrote him three times a week, full, attractive letters that made him believe she was recovering. But it was simply his absence which made her feel that she need not reproach herself so constantly. If they were separated, it was not her fault that she was a poor wife to him.

Her brother Roderick was an officer in the artillery during the War, and was killed in France. She was alone when the news reached her, and the letter she wrote to Peter telling him about it was brief but quiet in its tone. He knew she must have suffered a heavy blow, but with that same unexpected fortitude, she sustained it almost grimly, as if determined to bury the things that troubled her, deep, down, deep.

She worked hard at the Red Cross workshop. The ardent qualities which used to stand for something between her and Peter were admired by the other women she worked with. They said she seemed almost tireless. No drudgery was too great to ask her to do. When the War ended, and Peter came home, they found each other almost strangers.

Sometimes she would almost burst with desire to ask him if he had any idea how much she reproached herself for her compelling weakness.

He knew, well enough, and his eyes would cloud up with thoughts of the pain and the folly to which they were both locked; for to neither of them had the idea of divorce ever seriously occurred.

He picked up his practice again, and confessed that he was glad to be home.

She had no further need to work all day long down at the Red Cross, with the War over.

Life at home became a system of good manners for them all. They were astonished to realize now and then that you could get used to almost anything. And then they would discover that things continued to change, however smally.

III · THE NEWCOMER

I

"I feel sure it is really nothing," said Mrs. Foster. "Doctor Treddinger made me promise, though, that I would get in touch with you as soon as I arrived. I suppose he has written to you?"

"No, actually, he has not. But he will," replied Peter. "—I know Willie awfully well. He was my best man years ago. He barely got there in time for the wedding."

"I know men like him," said Mrs. Foster. "You're supposed to be annoyed with them, but I always find they're doing ever so much more important things than the things they're late *for*."

The day was settling outdoors, the wind was falling, and the sandstorm was keening far away down the valley toward Socorro.

Mrs. Foster had a little trouble in breathing. Peter watched her lift her shoulders now and then for a heavy breath. She looked down as if in apology for making such an exhibition of her asthma. The sandstorm had stirred it up. Everybody had said the high and dry air of Albuquerque would do her good for a few months this winter.

The second day she was settled in her house, here came the sand, which appeared to set her off right away.

When the professional part of the visit was over, Peter stood up to go. He was sorry. There was almost a holiday sort of feeling about sitting in this room talking to Mrs. Foster.

"You know this house?" she asked, looking around the long room dark with twilight.

"Yes, a number of people I know have leased it before now."

"I simply wrote my needs, and an agent found it for me. I must say I never expected to be living in a log cabin—a furnished one, at that."

"It is hardly what you ordinarily mean by that."

"I know.—It is very comfortable, and I love the views."

The house sat on a hill overlooking town. Each end of the long living room had a huge plate-glass window, one looking west to the river, the other east to the mesa. Downstairs the dining room had a big western window too. The rest of the house ambled along the curve of the hilltop among some young cottonwood trees.

"The house never looked this—this pretty before," said Peter.

"I brought a few 'things,'" she replied, making it sound slightly comic.

He smiled at her.

She was evidently impatient of convention, and yet lived with an almost exquisite observance of it. She was younger than he by about ten years, he guessed. Her hair was pale soft yellow, almost silvery. She had a very pale face, but her cornflower-blue eyes and her mouth rouged with pink carnation had plenty of color. She was slim and delicate. Her bones were small. She sat almost like a doll, so relaxed and "lost" she seemed in her corner of the huge Spanish red velvet couch which her landlords had set before the rough stone fireplace. In the rustic elegances of the house, which affected a combination of sturdiness with luxury, she seemed amusingly out of place. Peter was thinking all this and regarding her when a third person came in, a younger woman in a tweed suit and a green hat with a feather.

"Oh, hello Judy. This is Doctor Rush, who came to see about my wheezes.—Doctor, this is Miss Bridges, who is *with* me."

"Hello, everyone," said Miss Bridges. "I am frozen. Are we going to have some tea?"

"I hadn't thought to offer any to the Doctor, but if he has time to stay for a cup—?"

He nodded.

Mrs. Foster nodded to Miss Bridges. Miss Bridges said "Thank

God," and strode out to tell the kitchen. When she returned, she pulled the red velvet curtains, and a maid came in with a tray of tea-things. Miss Bridges put another log on the fire. It was suddenly warm and local and pleasant around the tea table. Mrs. Foster served the things and between her occasional careful long breaths, said that living in that house with all its red velvet and gold gesso'd candle-sticks and carved refectory tables and parchment light shades and heraldic andirons and white plaster and smoked wooden beams, she felt like someone in a Douglas Fairbanks movie. She said Holly-wood was in its scenic stage at the moment, and already she said you could find evidences all over the United States of what the movies were doing to public taste.

"I expect we'll be having garages with moats around them before long and crenellated battlements."

Miss Bridges went to the front door and opened it and whistled into the bluing twilight. In answer, a honey-colored spaniel came galloping floppily in, and climbed in an agony of pleasure up to Mrs. Foster on the red velvet couch.

"And this is my Brisky," she said, introducing the dog. She took the dog's head in her small white hands and made a comedy of gazing into the honey-colored face. "And did you cry your eyes out, Brisky? Spaniels always look to me as if they've been weeping."

The dog settled happily down with flutters of its silky fringes and upward glances of love from its lowered head, so that much eye-white showed.

"Do you often have times like today, Doctor?" asked Miss Bridges. She was a thin dark-haired girl with large violet eyes. She just missed being beautiful. Or perhaps, Peter thought, it was because Mrs. Foster was there. And yet she was so quiet, where Miss Bridges was rather muscularly active and vital. Miss Bridges made Mrs. Foster seem frail, and yet he would bet anything he knew about people that the stronger of the two was the smaller, the milder, the one who was ill.

II

But not very ill.

The tea seemed to've helped her shortness of breath. The wind was hardly moving.

"We have sand blows all winter and spring," answered Peter, "but they are usually brief, and they don't happen every day of the week.— You'll be sorry to hear that there is something about them I like."

"Appalled, if not sorry," murmured Miss Bridges. Mrs. Foster smiled at him.

"No," he said to her, in reply to her smile, "I really do. But then I love this whole country, and everything about it.—I grew up here."

"That is what does it," she said. "I find it, myself, and on only the shortest acquaintance, almost a *shocking* country."

"That's a funny word for it."

"So vast. So immediate, I think that's it. It is all right *there,* and yet the elements are so grand, I mean the mountains and the desert —you call it the mesa?—and the river, and heavens! those skies! I mean you have to be a sturdier creature than I to swallow it all so easily the first time you see it!"

Miss Bridges said, "I told Molly we should've driven out by car, and then we'd've gotten it all gradually. But we came by train, and woke up to find ourselves *here.*—Except that I hate motoring. I must say all this affected me the same way. Only I'd say it was a cockeyed combination of desolation and rather useless grandeur."

"Well," said Peter, wondering if he liked Miss Bridges at all, "people have made something out of that desolation for several centuries, now.—In small ways, of course, but somehow sufficient. And as for grandeur, the only kind I believe I could ever stomach would be the useless kind."

"Of course," said Miss Bridges, and her voice became almost deliberately musical and she smiled with a perfectly frank intention to be disagreeable, "there is a *cult* for the *West* which I simply cannot abide.—All that *pioneer* talk, and so forth. I get so *bored* with it. What's so damned *wonderful* about it?"

"It was quite a job in its day," said Peter. "The early West was no picnic."

"If there's one thing more tiresome than the *modern* West, it is the *early* West," she replied, smiling with a strange kind of high spirits which, he saw, was her version of anger.

Peter barked a little laugh. He was irritated, and yet he saw beyond her contentiousness into the vague hint of something desolate far, far within her.

"Well," he said, "maybe everyone has a kind of 'early West' within himself, which has to be discovered, and pioneered, and settled. We did it as a country once. I think plenty of people have done it for themselves as individuals."

"Of course there's a new snobbery for psychology, too, isn't there," declared Miss Bridges levelly.

"Lord, that's only a *word.* What it's *about* is as old as—as Sophocles; or Shakespeare," answered Peter. "Anyway, you'll find me hopelessly satisfied here."

Miss Bridges flashed a "keen" look at him, as if to say, "Is anyone? anywhere?" This disarmed him entirely, for he saw that her whole nature was wry and pessimistic, and he lifted his chin at her in a droll gesture used by the Mexicans, to mean anything speculative and insinuating.

"You see, Judy," said Mrs. Foster, leaning forward with a hint of dismissal in her attitude, and yet of great kindness too, "you've blundered into someone's house and been unpleasant about it.—I think I'm on your side, Doctor Rush. Or I will be if I ever catch my breath."

He stood up.

"You will.—I'll probably drop in next week unless you send for me sooner. I imagine the altitude and so on: everybody feels it: you'll be drowsy for a few days. That's all."

The spaniel rolled sideways and began to wave its flaggy tail.

"Brisky is saying good-by."

He leaned down to pat the dog. There was a faint drift of scent, a lilac, as he stood over Mrs. Foster. It made a thump of the dimmest reminder deep down inside him. Lilacs and rolling lawn with silver sunshine and an old happiness, the ghost of habit, and he was stirred as he had never hoped to be again, but ever so faintly.

Mrs. Foster smiled and gave him her hand. She had a surprising smile, for her teeth were not precisely regular. But their slight oddness—a trifling lift of one over its neighbor—added something witty, something special, to her expression.

"Tell me if that fat little Doctor Treddinger ever writes to you about me. And if I get into trouble I'll call you up."

"Good-by.—Good-by, Miss Bridges."

"Good-by, Doctor.—I'm sorry. I'm famous for being clumsy. I never *mean* it."

He laughed.

"No, I'm a victim of local patriotism, I suppose.—But I always got a tingle or a chill when the other children in school would sing the line about 'Land where my fathers died,'—*you* know."

Miss Bridges took him to the door.

"It's a wonderful thing," she said soberly, "to know you *belong* that much.—I'm one of those post-War females."

They shook hands. He thought he might like her. But it was Mrs. Foster he thought about all the way home. He couldn't help smiling at the unaccustomed airs of afternoon tea, here. He felt that Mrs.

Foster sought to seem anything but special or superior. You simply couldn't miss inflections of the world of fashion and all that went with it which she showed simply in the way she spoke. He was a little shocked that anybody should refer to Willie Treddinger, the most celebrated younger man in the country on respiratory diseases, as "that fat little doctor." But there was that about Willie, too, at the same time, if you stopped to think, regardless of Willie's offices on Fifth Avenue in New York. He found himself regarding Willie with her eyes.

He had a lift of spirits when he reflected that he could write to Willie that he found nothing much out of sorts with the Mrs. Foster he had sent out to the dry air and sunshine. He had noticed—but what an absurd thing to write to Willie!—that she seemed rueful, at moments; briefly; and that in her expression, her blue eyes, there was some energy in betrayal of consuming fires within.

He supposed everyone who knew her referred to all this as "charm."

He wondered who she was.

Book II · THE AGES OF MAN

IV · THE BOYS

I

Donald Rush, at twelve years of age, could not possibly say what was wrong at home.

He could forget it only when he was with his friend Wayne Shoemaker, who was in his room at school, and who lived eight blocks away at the other end of the same street as the Rushes.

They rode to school together on their bicycles, crossing the viaduct which went over the railroad tracks on that side of town. They never failed, at the top, to stop and gaze each way into the railroad yards below. The engines were as black as coal dust and as richly dull, and their white steam rose into the gold light of the blue sky. They could see where the tracks vanished far away into the earthen blur, and they had a sense of ownership over all they looked at. This viaduct was made of timbers painted and weathered to a dusty plum red, held together with long iron bolts capped with rusted nuts. They would speak of it as "ours," and crossing it on their wheels, they would simply regard it as their property, a fact which they often said to each other would surprise everybody very much if they only knew it.

On sunny Saturdays they would sit down and watch the tracks below, and the cars and wagons going over the viaduct, and one day they found a nut end of one of the iron bolts in the planked floor sticking up through the dust and dried manure and splinters that were packed along the sidewalk edge.

"Look here," said Wayne.

"That seems very careless," replied Donald.

"I think I ought to tighten it."

"I think so too."

He tried, and it seemed immovable.

"You can't tell, if this nut ever came off, what might happen."

"That's true."

Then they both sat back and looked at each other in glorified silence for a moment.

Then using the nickname he had evolved by spelling his friend's name backward, Wayne said,

"Say: Noddie:"

Don knew what he was thinking of, and he said,

"It would crash and go, the minute we unscrewed it."

"The whole thing, ka-froomb!"

They surged with power. The bridge which they owned had betrayed to their imaginations the vulnerable spot of its structure, of this they were certain, and they began to laugh, knowing with one half of their judgment that this was all nonsense; but with the other half, perfectly, exquisitely certain that if they chose, they could cause this whole bridge to creak and split and totter and fall, amid clouds of dust from wrenching timbers, to boy's music of crashing destruction.

"My changle-wrench will fit it," said Donald, pulling an imaginary tool from his pocket, and handling it in pantomime with a professional air.

"Then I believe," said Wayne with a certain sternness and righteousness that had them both convulsed inwardly with amusement at how grownups behaved, "I believe we should tighten it some, the trains rumbling underneath must jar it loose, and if we don't inspect it pretty often, no telling what:"

They set to work repairing the grave weakness in the viaduct, and as they were finishing, they heard a train whistling long to the east, and regarded each other and nodded, exchanging assurances that they had managed the job just in time; if the Limited had come through and had this faulty engineering not been corrected, at least temporarily, there would have been a disaster.

So they got on their bicycles and rode on down the other side, the masters of all they saw, and aware of their virtue. They had reached that degree of friendship at which things that would require hours and possibly days of explanation to make them plain and plausible to other boys were, between the two of them, instantly so. They were citizens of the world of the imagination.

II

In a way he could not describe, that world seemed to Donald to fill the rickety bungalow where the Shoemakers lived, out on the sandy edge of town, as it never seemed to him to exist in his own house eight blocks away, that high red-brick house with everything in it. He never wanted to hurry home when afternoon was falling. But if he was with Wayne, it was always exciting to come back to the Shoemakers' from the sandhills, or the mesa, or the river, side by side on their bicycles, through the darker dusk of town.

Ordinarily, their ways parted on the homewood outskirts of town, at a street corner where a single electric light hung high up. Donald and Wayne always debated whether they had time to "ride home with each other," an observance they kept whenever possible. Donald would ride halfway home from the corner with Wayne, and then Wayne would ride back halfway of *that* distance with Donald, and then they would separate, until next time, when whoever had the long ride tonight would have the short one then.

On this evening the winter twilight over the plains fell in waves of chill, and the boys rode faster the colder they got. Wayne called to Don,

"Come on all the way home with me."

"Why?—I can't."

"Come on and stay for supper, and we'll study."

"I'll catch the dickens."

"We'll call up your house from Mr. Daingerfield's."

"All right.—You call the number."

Their voices were like horn music in the quiet streets.

Cottonwood trees were overhead, bare and shapely for winter. The streets they approached going home were not paved, but instead were of packed red sand. On a corner two blocks from Wayne's house, was Daingerfield's neighborhood grocery store. They went in and asked if they could use the phone. Mrs. Daingerfield, who tended the store in the evenings while her husband went "out back" for his supper, said they could. Wayne called the Rushes' number, and when the connection began to ring at the other end, he handed the phone to Don.

They looked at each other soberly until the phone was answered. Then Donald looked into the phone.

"Hello, Cora?—Is my mother home?"

He waited a second.

"Hello, Mother? Can I stay at Wayne's for supper, and study with him afterward, if I get home by nine o'clock?"

They watched each other while Don listened.

Wayne began to laugh silently, which affected him like a pain in his belly. He felt so excruciatingly amused and enchanted by Donald's question because he knew that to ask to be out till nine was preposterous; he also knew that it was a *deliberately* unreasonable request, and that Mrs. Rush would agree to his staying for supper if he would promise to be home by eight. Ask more than you expect to get: this was a principle with them.

"Well, all right," said Donald waving Wayne to shut up and not choke with laughing that way, in case it could be heard. "I'll be there by eight, I *promise*. Good-by, Mother. And thanks. Thank you *ever* so much, I will do anything you want me to on Saturday morning."

He hung up.

"Goll, what did you get to laughing for? It might've spoiled everything."

"I couldn't help it. Can you stay till eight?"

"I have to *be home* by eight."

"Come on.—You won't believe it when you see Martha."

"Why? What's she got now?"

"She's got her hair funnied up now. I told her it looked very madamo-zell, meaning it as an insult. She took it as a compliment."

"My God."

They pedaled fast, their hams in the air. It was after six o'clock. The moon was out in the twilight blue sky. The boys felt happy in the cold early moonlight. They were full of ruthless energy. When they slid up to the front of Wayne's house in the sand lot where it stood, his mother could hear them inside. There was a citrous yellow light in the small window, from the pressure gasoline lamp that hung in the middle of the front room. In the late day-blue air outdoors with the sweet pallor of the moon in it, that yellow window was like a magic casement to the boys. The happiness in them seemed to gather suddenly, and knot up in the pits of their stomachs, and they crashed through the front door together, struggling shoulder to shoulder to see if they could go through at the same time.

"No, no! Wayne! Don!" cried Mrs. Shoemaker, turning fiercely on them and clapping her hands together rapidly. She was scowling and her hair was in strings down her cheeks, her face was flushed, and she was like a mother sparrow, gray, furious and whirring. But the two boys ran up to her and put their arms around her waist, and she hugged them back, still scowling, abating her fury, and saying

"Well!" with a snort and "Goodness!" with a breath, until she was smiling at them and smoothing her feathers back into order and calm.

"I brought him home for supper," said Wayne.

She looked at Don's dark small face, and a pang hit her under the breastbone. We haven't got much! she cried inwardly, and I have eleven cents in my purse and it's too late to go to Daingerfield's and buy some hamburger, these children will be my death yet, they never think of what it costs to live! All this went by in a streak, her habit of worry, at the same time that she smiled to Donald and said,

"I am so glad, Donnie, if you will eat all your crusts, which are good for your teeth, you are welcome to stay.—I'll tell Martha."

But Martha was only a few feet away, because the house was so small that her labors at getting supper in the tiny shallow kitchenette at one end of the room were not separated from the rest of the life of the house.

"I heard them," said Martha, not turning around.

"See!" whispered Wayne, poking Donald. "What did I tell you."

They looked at Martha, who held her back very stiff. She knew the two were in league against everybody else, including her. Her hair was a great cloud of small wiry ringlets, standing out from her head and neck.

"Oh, Madamo-zell," called Wayne gently and with exaggerated accent.

"Now, then, Brother," said his mother mildly, but with far more impact than her sparked fury of a few minutes ago. "We need some coal. Wait? I waited hours for you to come home and get me my coal. I'd've got it in myself but for the life of me I can't see why I should haul coal with a strong son like you in the house, only he's practically never *in* the house, where he spends his time the good Lord only knows, and at what, I am sure I never could say *on the witness stand,* if I was asked.—But to go back to *me,* I nearly had a *lank fit* today I's s'tired. And if you stand there and think I am going to haul coal in day in and day out, you are just ever so very much mistaken and you might's well know it this minute!"

III

All this while, she was setting the table, and the boys were gone long before she finished. She was very small, and every move she made seemed made in earnest. She had a worn, thin, but appealing little face; her hair was graying; her pale eyes always looked worried;

but she kept her prim mouth in a smile and she put a little rouge on it when she was working downtown at her job, just to brighten things up for the customers. She was a waitress in the Harvey House dining room down by the main line tracks of the Santa Fe railroad. Her energy and her pride made her the favorite waitress of half the people in town who went to the big gray stucco hotel that sprawled among patios and arcades by the tracks. She had one evening a week off, and this was it.

"Now Sistie," said Willa to Martha when the boys were gone, "don't start it again. He's just *getting there*."

"Very well, but it all seems one-sided. If he can treat me like that, I ought to be able to treat him *back*."

"No," said Willa, her eyes watering at the almost foolish glow of youthfulness and freshness about her eighteen-year old girl, "you're older. You simply must not laugh at him, just because he's young and your brother."

With everybody else, Martha was a young lady; but with her little brother, she was still a girl.

It was one of the details that made them a family, and gave their frugal and wind-trapped little house its climate of use and comfort.

Out in the back yard, there was a waist-high shed in which the coal was dumped . . . huge lumps of bituminous coal around which the sand had blown in miniature dunes. An ancient cottonwood tree stood in the back yard, so old that some of its branches were dead. But others held on to their bronze leaves all winter, and in spring, dropped them for a green skin over the silver-gray bark. Under this tree Wayne grew up. They could all see it from the one room that housed their kitchen, their dining room and their living room. A glance at the tree which filled so much of the small window would tell them inside how the time was outdoors. It was a venerable and beautiful possession to measure the outdoors by. It refreshed Willa Shoemaker simply to look at it. She was used to having "her boys" (by which she included Donald) live in the tree. The last time she could remember punishing her own son was for breaking off a little branch of the cottonwood while scrambling his way through its upper reaches.

Outdoors, the boys filled a scuttle with hunks of the coal. Some of the coal dust arose and when they breathed it it made their windpipes tickle.

"I have a word for you. After supper I'll get my dictionary. It's a word about the way to *be*."

"What is it?"

"I'd rather you *looked* at it, the first time."

They came back inside with the coal. In the center of the front room stood a big base burner. It was like a personage in the little room. In the winter when the sand cried against the walls on the cold wind off the mesa, they had to keep the stove positively dancing in its tracks with a roaring fire. The mother never failed to recognize with a pang how much each big lump of the black dusty coal was costing as it went into the bulging stomach of the stove, with its glowing little windows of layered mica.

"All right, throw in two of the middling ones," she ordered. The boys clanged and scraped at the stove.

One day that curved bellyfull of tiny windows had made Donald Rush think of the gorgeous gallery in the poop of a Spanish galleon, of which he had seen a picture in his pirate book. Ever since, they had called the stove the *Spirito Santo*.

They liked to name things when they found resemblances. The little kitchen was called the "diner" because Willa said it was like the narrow galley in the dining car which she remembered very well from the journey seventeen years ago when she had come out here with Mr. Shoemaker in the first place.

She promised to prove this to them "When we go home." By this she meant that someday, somehow, she was going to take her two children back to Michigan for a visit to her own old home.

"Now! That's just about it!" said Willa, looking over the table, her eyes snapping at the four places laid out, and the food partly on, and her hungry ones waiting. "Come on, Sistie, bring the rice and the stew from the diner, and we'll sit down."

IV

The greatest treat in young Donald Rush's life was to be asked to stay for supper with Wayne, on Mrs. Shoemaker's day off, when the sensation of festivity and happiness was so great in the little clattering house that he loved to help create it, and would wonder ruefully why, in his father's three-story brick house with two Negro servants and a lot of elegant truck like stained-glass lamp shades and thick green carpets on the mahogany and white stairways and a mahogany pianola in the living room that they didn't play any more because they were sick of it, why there was so rarely this feeling of the Shoemakers' that everything was simply *right*.

They waited while Willa bent her head and said Grace. The Shoemakers were Catholics. Donald sometimes went to Mass with Wayne.

He knew this prayer now and said it silently with them just as if he were a Catholic too. Then they raised their heads and Mrs. Shoemaker served them.

Martha resolved to be kindly, and offered Donald a piece of bread with such visible courtesy that he began to laugh, choked on his rice and turned a deep pink under his swarthy cheeks. They really thought he was choking to death (as they said later) and Wayne began to laugh too, knowing it was the ridiculous manners of his sister which had caused the whole thing anyway. They made an uproar, Willa helping and scolding, the boys gasping, and Martha making cool and miserable remarks full of scorn; for she knew what they were laughing at, they were laughing at her, and it broke her heart, which was both more and less than a heart. It was a vessel, a cup, and it was empty, and perishing to be filled.

When they recovered, they were so exhausted that the rest of the meal went off quietly, and the boys had to do their share by clearing the table and drying the dishes, which Martha washed. By then they were friends again and all three together did a popular song called "Taxi!" in which Martha sang the words—"Oh, taxi!"—and the boys whistled a response,—"Phwee-phwaa,"—and knocked the rhythm on the drainboard with their knuckles.

"Now get to work with your books," said Willa.

She had left the table cleared and brought them a kerosene lamp. She regarded herself as a well-educated woman, which, indeed, she was, but all she knew had come to her out of activity; not books. She was profoundly reverent of books. She often said if she ever caught either of her "two" mistreating a book, she'd take and spank the daylights out of him. She sent the two boys out to unstrap their schoolbooks from their bicycles, and set the dictionary on the table for them, and a jelly glass full of pencils of all lengths which she kept handy.

"Oh, yes, what is that word?" asked Donald when they came back and settled down.

"Oh, yes, I nearly forgot.—Here it is," said Wayne, finding it in the dictionary. Donald looked; it was the word inscrutable.

"H'm."

"Don't you see?—That is what *we* are."

"That's right. Nobody else knows a thing about what we think and work on."

"You see?"

Mrs. Shoemaker frowned. She didn't know what they were saying, but it certainly didn't have the perplexed energy she believed proper to the act of studying.

"If you're going to work, then *work*," she said to them. "And if you're going to play, then *play*. But if it's *play*, then off home marches Mister Donald Rush, one-two-three."

They closed the dictionary, and got their books of American history open and began to resemble, for her benefit, that image of studious children which, as they read, slowly became the truth about them, within and without.

Willa dwelled on them with her eyes for a moment.

v

Her son Wayne was light-haired, with a thin little face and a long neck. His cheeks were frosty with a sort of young lint, and under the skin were patches of dark color which made him look very intense. He had blue eyes, and his forehead was always ribbed with intention or belief or doubt, though he made a point of looking at ease. His mouth was sober and full-lipped.

He was the exact opposite of Donald, she reflected. Don was a little smaller than Wayne, but a little older, much solider in the body, and dark brown. He had black eyes which sparked and flashed with light, so intense were the whites. His head was round, and his hair was like blue-green-black cock's feathers, shiny curved spikes of elegance that fell across his forehead. He had dimples up under his eyes.

She knew the two boys were twins for energy, however different they looked, the one tall and rangy and wheat-haired, and the other a young black cat whose quick head swifted toward everything new. One was a rich boy, as wealth in the town went, the other as poor as "respectability" could possibly be there. Neither of the boys knew this; but Willa did, and so did her daughter Martha.

Martha went to business college during the day. She had graduated from high school the year before, and though she knew lots of young people, she worried her mother because she seemed so "alone." Night after night, Martha sat here, at home, doing her practice or sewing (she sewed beautifully) or simply lying back in her chair with her eyes closed, but not asleep. She was dismally unhappy, but could not tell anyone so. She was certain that she was hopelessly plain and unattractive; and her reveries were all concerned with hopes for beauty. The discontent of this was reflected in her face, and her own mother couldn't be sure whether Martha was pretty or not. Sometimes she seemed so, and then again—

Willa believed it sinful, almost, to imagine that you could *hurry* life. It was of God's disposing, and let there be an end to wicked rebelliousness in the heart!

She was a widow. The children's father had died when Wayne was a baby. All he left her was the remains of a chicken ranch out on the mesa five miles from town. He had died of tuberculosis, for whose cure they had moved here from Albion, Michigan, with just enough money to buy the mesa acres, and put up the long chicken house of adobe, with corrugated-iron roof, and front entirely built of small glass panes. Willa had thought for a while of returning to Albion; but nobody bought the ranch, and the very energy that drove her for the sake of her children also dictated loyalty to the vestiges of her husband's poor efforts; so she decided to keep the ranch, and get a job, and someday, Wayne should run it, and be his father's son. Already he was good about earning money when he could, doing odd jobs for Mr. Jensen, the Stationer, on Saturdays or after school. Sometimes when Willa came home Saturday nights aching from the extra crowd at the hotel, she found his money, some half dollars, quarters, nickels, pennies, and dimes, cleverly stacked into a tapering tower and surrounded with her silver spectacles, on the table by the base burner, by which, he knew, she liked to sit and rest for a few minutes while she read the Albion *Evening Recorder*. She indulged herself with this home-town paper, though the subscription price would have given the family a trifle of the luxury which they fiercely did without. But she was proud of her home country, and as the years went by, she read about boys and girls she knew back in Michigan and always saw them just like that, as they were when she'd left them; and she was her girlhood self as she wandered among the personal items and the revelatory little advertisements and the offices of life as recorded by the gray pages. What she always wanted most when she read about Albion again was to have Wayne and his sister Martha go back with her just for a visit. They had never seen that green country. And she would be so proud to show them off, her Western children, both so good and both so handsome.

One reason Willa was so positive about working for her life and her children's was that she knew that Eternal Life awaited them all; and to earn it by being faithful and busy on earth seemed to her, in conviction beyond thought, the very least anyone with a scrap of dignity could do.

She was never too tired after a hectic Saturday night at the Harvey House to get up early for Mass, and to see that Martha and Wayne got up too. They hurried to the autobus on the corner when the sun was barely fingering the top branches of the huge cottonwoods in their end of town; and were almost always on time for services in the big church on Sixth Street, with its embossed tin roof, its wooden towers with slats in the belfries, its painted plaster statuary, and the high mist of blue shadow that Wayne used to squint at in the ceiling, to make the distance up there seem farther and farther off.

Here abided the one reality that united all the others, and made them her servants, not her masters. Every act of her daily life was unconsciously released into energy, generosity, affirmativeness because she loved God and believed in his Son. People did not see her as an essentially religious person. She made few enough gestures and displays to prove it. But her furies, her worries, her determinations of will all reflected her belief. Her children knew it. Her will was righteous. They never would dream of trying to cross it, or cheat it; for long, at any rate.

She would work till she dropped to see that they got everything the other boys and girls in Albuquerque had. And the fact was, they missed nothing essential. That's what it was, to live in a small city, and know everybody, for everybody grew up together. Lately she had seen in Wayne little valorous furies which she believed were connected with his new rage for being big and strong. She found him several times in the sandy back yard "practicing not to be clumsy." Sometimes his voice sounded as if he were talking through a comb and tissue paper, with more breath than tone.

VI

The Shoemakers had a clock which was kept on a shelf in the diner. It always ticked loudly, and Donald suddenly heard it.

"Goll, I'd better see what time it is."

"It is five minutes to eight," said Willa, who could see the clock from where she sat reading her newspaper.

"Goll, then I'll have to *scratch*," said Don. "Thanks for the dinner, Mrs. Shoemaker.—I'll be *there*," he added to Wayne, meaning that the next morning he would be on his bicycle at the corner where the street light was, and they would ride to school as usual.

He got up to go out. The moonlight was like silvery blue air outdoors. The huge bare tree in the back yard seemed like a net set out to catch the moonlight. Donald saw it through the back window.

"I wish we had a tree," he said, perfectly seriously.

Willa gasped a little laugh at him, because Doctor Rush owned the lot next door to his house and there as a hobby cultivated dozens of evergreens, in nurserylike rows. But she knew what Donald meant, and was touched by the way he loved everything the *Shoemakers* had, and she said to him,

"Well, you may have ours, you know, Donald, so long as you don't take it *away*."

This struck the two boys as hilariously funny, and Willa, seeing what a funny thing she had said, burst into laughter too, and they all died laughing, until Martha abandoned her musing dignity and said, "Oh, for heaven's sake," and sassied her face at them all, Donald too, which delighted him as a mark of his membership in this family.

He went out the front way, got on his bicycle, slung his books by their strap over his shoulder, and rode off homeward.

V · FIRELIGHT

I

One of the advantages of living in a small town was that you could go home for lunch without losing much time.

Peter liked his house best at midday, when the sunshine seemed to come streaming in everywhere. He would have smiled at himself if he had ever recognized that he now followed a routine every day at noon when he came home. He had a huge red leather armchair in the bay of the front windows of the living room, and he had resisted all efforts of Noonie's to get him to give it up and let her place something a little more "in keeping" there by the lace curtains. As soon as he got home, he took the mail from the table in the front hall, unbuttoned his coat and vest, and went in to his big red chair, on which he always found the *New York Times* lying three days old, and whatever bundle of books might have arrived for him from the Boston dealer. There he settled himself in the sunlight, and glanced at the *Times*, yawning. He yawned tremendously, relaxing in great quaffs of easiness. The headlines swam in his comfortable tears, and he rarely found anything to interest him enough to read it through. He threw the *Times* down and shuffled the mail, making one pile for Noonie to handle, including bills, letters from mutual friends, appeals; and another for himself to take up to his third-floor desk to work on in the evening, when he did all his personal business at his private leisure. The best came last. Today, there was a package from Boston. He guessed it contained only one book. He always opened his packages last, during his noon ritual, using the little gold knife on his watch chain. He kept the blade surgically sharp, but always had to stretch and bend to make the knife reach on its chain. This was an inconvenience he was so used to that he no longer noticed it. He cut the strings and made a great scatter of wrappings on the floor. The book was a War Department report published in the '50s, describing an Indian skirmish of the previous decade. He flipped the pages, and came on a section of twenty-two lithographic plates, done by Messrs. Leuwenthal, of Philadelphia. The first picture was a portrait of an officer in full dress. His name was First Lieutenant Aubrey Worthing Barton, 6th U. S. Cavalry. He had thick hair like carved curls of black walnut, from which sideburns came down on his round, formal cheeks. His eyes were deeply shadowed. His nose was short and straight. His mouth might've been drawn by a child, so artless was it, with full scrolls of lip and shadow. His chin came in a positive curve down to the stiff white ruffles of his dickey, which cascaded over his gold-braided collar that stood up sharply on either side to his ears. His breast was broad, and made broader by the lithographed spread of gold braid that ended near his arms in gold buttons. He was looking at the artist; which meant that any later viewer would receive that same gaze, direct, light-plumbed, the record of a day and of a life. His left arm was bent, to cradle his sabre against his silk sash. Even within the conventions of its time, the lithograph was convincing. The young man was admirable and believable; women must have admired him; and nearly a hundred years later, what he had set down of what he had done was exciting to the Doctor because it had happened right here. He promised himself that after lunch he would go upstairs and read Lieutenant Barton's account of his Indian fight east of Albuquerque in 1850.

He folded his hands on his book over his belly and lay back and shut his eyes, to review what he had done that morning, and arrange what had to be done that afternoon. He could let down his tensions like an animal. His most lucid and at the same time recuperative moment of the day was this one before lunch. He had got everyone in the house to thinking that he always fell asleep for that fifteen minutes; he never dozed off, but it suited him to have them think he did, because they went softly, let him alone, detoured him discreetly until the bell for lunch was rung by Leonard, the colored houseboy, in the front hall. Three brass chimes hung in the high doorway between the hall and the dining room. Leonard enjoyed making variations within the limits of the three different tones.

Today, Peter heard him go to the hall and ring the chimes in this order: *high, low, middle, middle, low, high,* and then an elegantly final, *middle.*

II

In a moment, Noonie came downstairs, and he saw that she had been busy all morning, for her eyes danced, and her cheeks were flushed, and she had a sort of freed look. His heart rose a trifle as he got up to greet her. She looked up at him, to see, for today, if he was reproachful. He was not, and they went into the dining room. Donald was at school, and had taken his lunch with him, as usual.

They were served by Leonard, a light-yellow boy in his early twenties who had his own ideas of propriety. He set every plate down and took it away with a flourish. His elbows were elegantly sprung from his sides when he toured the dining room. He came through the pantry door as if on to a stage. His white coat crackled with starch. He was a smooth rounded creature whose hair looked like little wavy pencil lines on his skull, shining with oil. He had pale-gray eyes and an irrepressible smile.

When Leonard went out for a moment, Noonie made a reference after him with her eyes, and smiled at Peter.

"What is it now?" he asked.

"Leonard, again!"

"Anything wrong?"

"No, I am just amused, that's all.—I found him boxing in the hall upstairs again this morning."

"Boxing?"

"Alone. Dancing and waving his arms around and shuffling.—I heard him sort of *breathing,* so I came out of my room to see, and there he was, I thought I'd die."

"Shadowboxing, then.—I guess he still wants to be a boxer."

Noonie frowned in caution and then cleared her expression: Leonard was returning.

Peter looked at the young Negro and grinned. Leonard grinned back, and said,

"Yes *sir,* Mist' Doctoh," and set down his serving.

"You in training, Leonard?"

"Yes *sir,* always in trainin'."

"What for."

"How you know, sir?"

"Why, you look so in such good condition."

"Yes *sir*. Gon get me one 'em di'mon belts."

"Oh-ho. Prize fighter, eh?"

"Ess *sir!*"

"O.K., Leonard. Then Mrs. Rush and Donnie and I'll all live off your championship purses. We'll never have to go to the poorhouse."

"Hyuck!" said Leonard, vanishing through the swinging leather door with its brass studs. He felt immeasurably complimented and told Cora, the cook, so.

"Don't forget Don's birthday," said Noonie.

"No. Thirteen, isn't it: what shall I get him?"

"Yes, thirteen.—Do you think he's all right, dear?"

"All right?—Why, yes.—Why, I haven't noticed— —Have you seen anything wrong with him?"

"Oh no," she said, and he recognized her habit of worry, and crowded down a little flare of anger which it always gave him. "But he's growing so fast . . ."

"He looks fine. He *seems* fine. God knows I see little enough of him."

"I know. Neither do I."

"When I was a boy, some of my best times were spent with my father. I never see Don."

"If you would *talk* to him—"

He bit his jaws and considered saying that there was nothing he longed for more than to talk to Donald; but the boy seemed so unreachable; so *inscrutable,* he guessed he meant; and he knew it would never do to try to force anything. He knew too that if he said these things to Noonie, she would assume he was aiming them at her; she would meet his uncertainty with her guilt; and off they'd be on one of their exasperations; which always made them both sorry for hurting the other.

He shifted the tack.

"I think it would be awfully nice if you gave Don a birthday party."

"Oh, I couldn't," she said quickly.

"Why not?—Thirteen is sort of a milestone, I don't know why, it always seems to be, though."

"Yes, I know, but—"

He waited. Her first habit was to refuse. Often she brought herself to change her mind. This eternal negative!

"Still," she said, "I don't know."

Leonard came and went again.

"It might be fun.—He might adore it.—How we used to *do* things!" she sighed, but rather happily, he saw. "At home in Rochester our parties were famous. I'll never forget Roderick's best one, it must've been *his* thirteenth, Mamma spent days and days, she made me a costume out of white plumes and gilded palm leaves, it sounds awful, but it was adorable, and I was supposed to be Papagena out of *The Magic Flute.*"

"You needn't go to all *that:* but some boys and girls and games and God-awful rich food and jealousies and stomach-aches and fits of shyness and fits of love: it all belongs.—Let's do it. I'll come home early."

"All right, dear, if it would please you."

Her eyes sparkled.

"Not if it would please me, though it *would,* but it would make Don sort of *have a house* to bring his noisy and sticky friends to, as he ought."

"I'll have a staff meeting," she said with humor, "with Leonard and Cora. Don't give it a thought."

He beamed at her.

"What shall we give him?"

"I know," she said with animation, "why not ask Wayne Shoemaker? He'd know exactly what Don wants."

"Well, I will. He's a good little kid. I saw that girl of theirs the other day. She's a young peacherino."

"Peter!" she said in reproof, but she smiled.

"She is. All breasts and wet looks and corn silk hair and awkwardness. Made me feel like an *old fool,*" he added lecherously. "She come out sudden, as the farmer said."

When he talked that way, she couldn't help looking at herself mentally, always to her own disadvantage. She changed the subject.

"I've spent the morning going over your suits."

"Do I need anything?"

"Oh, you have them all made exactly alike.—And that beautiful Scotch homespun is always ruined by that dreadful tailor downtown."

"My Italian?—I hate suits to be different. He knows just what I want and gives it to me. He hasn't had to change a thing in ten years."

"*That's just it,*" she said laughing. "You're *so much* better looking than your clothes, darling."

"Everyone *ought* to be," he said, trying to sound gruff.

He had filled out since his intern days, when he had looked like a cowboy strayed East. There was an intent animal look in his black eyes, so that his whole head seemed concentrated toward his object. (When they were first married Noonie used to say, putting her hand over the thick hardy dark hair back of his ears, that she believed his *thinking* happened right *there*.) His brows came down over his look and shaded it with meaning. On his generous upper lip he wore a carelessly trimmed mustache.

When she faced his knowledge and directness, Noonie (like other people) asked herself, "What is it? What does he *draw* from?" In his buffed face she saw the plains, yes. But what else? He always seemed ready for what was next; the next thing; we'll do it; we'll manage; people have managed before, and even if they haven't, *we'll* manage.

It was the affirmative spirit that inhabited him.

She could see its likeness most clearly, perhaps, in his hands, which were powerfully veined, the color of sunny clay.

People often looked at his hands set to their tasks of divination and help, and then at his face, to see *what he knew,* and found out there that he loved life, and met it truly.

"What else did you do this morning?"

"I rested, then, and read a little—I read my magazines, that you hate so."

"I don't hate them at all."

"Yes you do, you said they were made up of either commercial or sentimental lies."

"Well, yes, but that doesn't mean I *hate* them, I don't *hate* morphine, or the people who need it sometimes."

"Oh. I see. I am like a drug addict."

"I didn't *say* that, either."

"I warned you once how really and truly stupid I am. You didn't believe me."

"I still don't. My mother was a schoolteacher, and my father never went to school at all, and they were both wise and successful people. They knew how to live where they lived."

"You do love this country, don't you."

"Past, present and future," he said.

"I think you're different, lately."

"I? Nonsense."

"Yes, I can't tell you *how,* but it's there."

He got up from the table and tossed his napkin down.

"Well, I am not aware of it, but I hope it is not unpleasant?" he said lightly, holding out his hand to help her up.

"Oh no, dear, I didn't mean it *was*—Happier, some way."

"Oh, good Lord:" he scoffed, and walked upstairs with his new book.

III

But it was true.

He marveled at the intuitions of womankind.

Every day for the past week, in his travels up and down the town, he caught sight at certain moments of the big window of the log house on the highland. Toward evening, the sun, going down behind the volcanoes across the river, would throw a glory of firelight on the big window and he would see it above the dusk which was filling the streets. The sight, the reminder, did make him happy.

VI · OTHER AMERICAS

I

Late one afternoon as Peter was about to leave the hospital, he phoned his downtown office to see if there were any calls.

The nurse reported two things to him from his memorandum tablet. One was to go to see old Don Hilario Ascarete, out in Old Town; the other (he knew it all the time for he had written it himself, but in an obscure search for whatever plausibility might later be comforting, he was calling now to be "reminded" of what he had been thinking of all day)—the other was to "check up" on Mrs. Carmichael Foster at Highland Park.

"Oh, yes. Thank you. Is that all?"

He hung up and went out to his big car waiting in back of the hospital on the circular gravel drive. There were two veins of thought running in him, and as surely as tributaries reach a river, they would come together, he knew.

He wanted to go to see Mrs. Foster, and he wanted to go to the sandhills to search out Lieutenant Barton's battle site.

He decided not to do the first. She was probably perfectly well.

Willie Treddinger would have written long ago if anything had been seriously the matter. She might feel obliged to bring out the tea table again if he dropped in. He had a sort of hanging discouragement in his breast at the thought of her, and there was no better cure for that sort of nonsense than a little action.

He went to the sandhills.

He had Barton's report with him in the car. Peter knew the town so well, with the images of both a boy's memory and a man's, that he bet he knew just the place to go to.

There was a road that led from one of the town streets across the main line railroad tracks, and up into the sandhills, ending at a gravel pit which hadn't been excavated for years. When his car got into the sandhills, and followed the winding road, Peter felt transported, as if he were lost in a desert whole continents away. This was because the hills rose sharply hiding the view of the town below, and alternated with one another so clearly, as if eroded blocks of earth had been set down in a maze pattern something like immense cog teeth. When the rain happened in torrents on the mesa, this winding place became a canyon boiling with pale-brown water that rushed upon the streets of the town and fanned out for blocks.

He could search months for another place like this one, but none other answered the description: "A zig-zag, almost road-like, course between sharply steep hills of gravel, in places forty feet high, and rarely less than twenty. As can be surmised from the nature of the engagement, cover in such a place was sure to be as hazardous to one side as to the other. We therefore, deeming it at least as advantageous, and possibly more so, proposed to keep to the tops of the miniature canyon, and were within a few moments of achieving this objective, when we were sighted again by the Navahoe, all of whom acted in concert to prevent our reaching an incline which would deliver us out of the sandy bottom."

That was what the book said: Lieutenant Aubrey Worthing Barton had written his diary in 1849 and 1850, describing his encounters and observations while a member of a preliminary survey party sponsored by the War Department. There was no mistaking the general locality, Peter knew. Albuquerque was clearly indicated on the maps in the old War Department report. Barton told how the land rose sharply some two and a half miles east of the Rio Grande; and that would be roughly just across the railroad tracks today. He told how the sandy course wound down from the much higher mesa. He said they had ridden parallel to the river, but inland, following the base of the sandhills in a generally straight line. They had camped for the night farther to the north, and leaving at dawn, had come six miles by the time the episode took place.

Peter left his car at the edge of the gravel pit, and walked around the huge crater made by the steam shovel, which still stood cold and rusty in the middle of the cavity. The gravel-haulers had taken away part of the nearest sandhill, but by squinting and leveling his sight about opposite to the top of the rise facing him, the Doctor could imagine the terrain as it had been, and though in Barton's account it had been earlier in the day than it was this afternoon, the time of year was pretty close, the mountains way beyond there hadn't changed any, and just such clouds could well have been going over the zigzag canyon.

The Lieutenant wrote with a bare factuality which made easy his movements to follow, places to identify, and (from their very absence) feelings to supply.

Peter could tell himself what had happened all over again, now looking for the first time at the place.

ii

They came along the edge of the hills, and once having been seen they didn't seem to care if they stayed in full view. They were off their ponies. In the same kind of sunlight they looked like little creatures made of baked clay, that earthen color, for they were all practically naked. They had lances and arrows, and Barton had seen sunshine on two rifle barrels, at least, as he turned his horse and backed his men up around one of those jutting cogs of sandhill. A bullet sang out from the Indian rifle. The soldiers wondered where in the hell an Indian had got hold of an army rifle, they could tell by the sound what it was, and the gravel just beyond them on the next turn of the canyon up which they were retreating puffed and fell, scratched by the bullet.

Some of the Navahoe were on the other side of the canyon, too. The soldiers went on up the sand course, riding fast as they could to get in and out of the light. Where the course ended there was a long incline of heavier gravel. They were going to go up it, because to be caught down in the shadow would be the end, they all knew, and Barton rode at the tail of the column to handle command and be the nearest to the enemy. He rode like a toy soldier, stiff in his stirrups, with his head bent around to keep an eye on the Indians. They had got their ponies again, and were coming along the rim like horsemen in a nightmare who rode and got nowhere. It was just because the soldiers below and the Indians above were going at pretty much the same rate of speed.

Barton called ahead to McIntyre, his second in command, to start right up the incline the minute they got there, and take the surveying party with him, five men with the instruments, the records, which they had on two packsaddled horses, and a squad of men. The rest would stand with Barton at the rear and cover the escape, it would mean seven cavalry soldiers and their lieutenant, and it was at the bump of the earth there on the right where the gravel showed in coarser strata that they made their stand.

Any sound in between the sandy walls was magnified.

McIntyre understood and signaled.

The civilian surveyors were willing as anybody else to stay and see it out; but McIntyre swore at them and charged up the slope.

Barton jerked his horse around and wheeled his squad. They hadn't time to dismount. They had no cover from which to obtain both protection and fire effectiveness. So they faced the crest above them on both sides and let go with their little short carbines.

Something happened to two of the Navahoe. Suddenly nothing sounded but the gong-ringing of the shots in the narrow place. Then as the white smoke drifted invisible and the clouds were far off again, and their ears subsided of their blood protest, they heard McIntyre's horses scrabbling on out of sight.

Barton knew what the Indians were doing, anybody would have done it, too, they were riding in a wide ring back from the canyon edge, and spreading out to head off McIntyre and the survey party when they should emerge from the sand on to the wire grass of the mesa.

Barton waited in the gravel for a moment, listening. Looking up, the sand walls framed the sky, which was china-blue with those light-gold clouds. McIntyre was pretty young, but he had been on the frontier longer than Barton, and Barton said to the soldiers with him that he'd bet McIntyre would come out of it, which meant that so would the survey.

It was the survey to which they were all detailed to afford military protection.

They had never been called upon for active fulfillment of their mission until this morning.

It seemed almost as if noon must be right upon them, but Barton's big silver watch with the hair-line Roman numerals and the scepter-like hands angled the hour at ten minutes before ten.

If the Navahoe left the canyon party to go after the surveyors and

McIntyre out on the mesa, there was only one thing to do, get up there and close in in another wide encirclement and make a battle diversion.

If the Navahoe on the other hand were still along the rim but out of sight, and coming like little brown animals to the edge of sight but not of visibility, then McIntyre would in due time come around and spare somebody for a counterattack on his own.

It was something that had to be found out.

Barton told the others about it, and gave his reins to his orderly. He said they were to watch closely, and if anything *happened,* they were to mount and ride on after McIntyre and join him, and in general, to get the party back to Albuquerque as soon as possible. A soldier volunteered to do the job but Barton said it was his to do, and left them there in the shadow which was creeping away from them as the sun went on over toward the zenith, so that they felt divested.

Barton went on all fours to the bellied gravel of the near hill, and started up. He went slowly, the ground was grainy and rolled under him in slides. He cocked his heavy pistol and set it down each time with much caution, because the trigger was beautifully ready. Ordinarily he liked nothing better than a nervous trigger; but now when he had to use his hand to help take him forward over the itchy gravel, he did wish his gun wasn't so trick.

But at the same time, he didn't know what might be awaiting him at the top, when he got there and had a look. The instant of cocking might be too long to wait, in some circumstances.

Below and behind him, the men watched.

Nobody could interpret the silence.

At one last forward take of the hillside, Barton paused and shut his eyes a moment. "Well, yes or no," was the sort of thought that hit him, but it meant things more elaborate than that in terms of what was going to happen immediately next.

Then he came on, one more crawl, and he looked over the edge, and he saw at the same moment he heard.

Ten yards away lay a dead pony and behind it was an Indian whose eyes were open and the livest motionless things anywhere. The lieutenant's pistol *did it* just as fast as he knew it would, and he ducked back again, listening. He heard a curious clipping sound, nothing an Indian might make, and presently he looked again, and saw a prairie dog four feet away using its teeth on something. The Indian was out of sight behind the dead horse's back.

Not another thing was visible on all the immense plain.

The wind seemed cooler up top here, and he shivered, for it just then registered against the sweat that was on him all over, and his clothes felt cold and heavy for a second.

He turned around to look opposite him on the other rim of the gravel canyon. There was nothing. He waved down to the troops in the half-shadow below to mount and hurry right up the incline, and he would run to meet them at the top. He heard the equipment squeak and clash as his men mounted, and a fine confusion of thump and scrabble from the hooves of the ready horses.

He went forward crouching to look beyond the dead horse. He had the pistol cocked, of course.

It is something to have it for the first time, he said to himself, this is the first combat I have known, and I sweat hard, and I was vaguely afraid of everything that might happen. But now we are safe for the moment. I believe I made the right decision, which is a notable relief, because many another hide than mine depended upon it, whatever it was to be.

That Indian is dead, behind the horse, I can see him now. His eyes are open, and perfectly dead.

An affectionate sense of the almost comic obedience of the horses made him grin with pride and relief when he and the men reached each other. He mounted his own animal. Standing in the stirrups he led them up the last mild rise to the mesa proper, and there they saw what looked at first like several of those dust devils which traveled whimsically over the flat plain, engendered by heat and the convection of air currents. But they did not whirl in a stately dance, they peppered and popped with speed, and the soldiers knew that galloping horses made the dust rise in so many small plumes.

"Here we go," cried the Lieutenant.

They rode at a charge. All they could hear was the wind of speed and the valiant fusillade of hooves on the spine-grassed earth. But they saw two white puffs ahead of them in the wide circling line of the dusty pursuit. Barton drew his own carbine from its leather scabbard, and signaled his men to copy him. He nodded them to fire after he did. The position in effect was that the Navahoe were sandwiched in between the retreating line of cavalry and a pursuing one. The diversion to save McIntyre was so far a tactical problem, executed with as much precision as if on the blackboard at West Point, under Major Thompson. Barton fired, and his squad followed. They were too far yet for the shots to take effect, even if accurate aim were possible while riding, but they were seen, and the widely scattered crescent of the dust trails ahead was suddenly broken.

The mountains were much too distant to offer any cover.

The mesa was as open as a great book, with a few shallow valleys such as a book made at the binding.

Down below, where the little adobe town of Albuquerque was among its cottonwoods along the Rio Grande, there were many deviosities which could make concealment.

The Navahoe turned into a racing single file and headed toward the wide valley.

At that, shouting like cowboys rounding up a herd, Barton and his men swung broadside. Far beyond the Indian column they could see McIntyre's squad do the same thing. Dappled by the sunshine and the little archipelagoes of cloud that drifted by in the oceanic blue, the three groups of furious figures raced toward the fall of the mesa. It all looked, to a detached recollection, like a rehearsed maneuver, except for the meaning of the white puffs of rifle and carbine fire that were exchanged all the way down the long mild slope toward the sandhills. All of the Indian shots went wild but one. That shot tucked itself with an energetic poke into Barton's left shoulder. He was out in front. He stayed there as the pursuit swung down the hill and the trees began. It was too heavily grown to allow a concerted escape. The Indians separated. Coming down, the cavalrymen could see that there were about a dozen Indians, and scattering like their quarry, scratched their way through the cottonwood thicket. In the cool damp shade the shots rang closer, and suddenly stopped, for they had come to the streets of the old town, and the Indians stayed by their horses, waiting. They were shining with golden sweat on their clay-colored breasts. When Barton came up he took the two Navahoe rifles, and found them empty. He asked for the spare ammunition, and they gave him empty pouches. They acted with neither defiance nor humility. It might have been a commercial transaction for all the feeling displayed on either side. Barton's blue flannel shirt was black at the sleeve where he was bleeding. When McIntyre appeared, they shook hands, smiling at each other, two youngsters professionally confirmed.

After a brief rest, they all rode into the town, and presented the renegade Indians to the civilian authorities in the Plaza, who received them with a certain reserve, the young officer thought, considering what capricious havoc the Indians might have turned against the town, or the trading wagons that came down the river road from Santa Fe every week during such fine summer weather as this.

At least, Lieutenant Barton hinted as much in his report.

III

The light was going.

Peter returned to the car and rocked slowly down the gravelly course until he was back on the street.

He came back into the present and found his half-mind, like a subterranean place, still coursing with its buried river. He heaved at the huge steering wheel of his car and headed for Highland Park.

He was admitted by the Swedish maid whom he'd seen before. She asked him to wait a moment in the hall. He heard tapping and clicking in the big room down the steps to his right, and concluded someone was using a typewriter. The girl returned and asked him to go in.

It was Miss Bridges at the typewriter, which was set on a cleared desk in the corner.

"Hello, Doctor Rush. I suppose you're expecting to see a patient? She's simply fine. I'll go call her. Sit down."

Miss Bridges made him feel that she would arrange any questions and answers that might be "indicated." With a kindly glance she left him.

I was right, he said to himself. I am a fool to come.

But he didn't let himself off any further than that. He knew that with the Miss Bridges sort of woman, he was worse than awkward. She—what was the new word?—she was sophisticated. She seemed to exist in a sort of slang of the emotions. Undoubtedly she'd "been" something in the War, and was the sort of girl forever stamped by mass association with males. "A bifurcated mind," he said to himself.

Mrs. Foster came back with Miss Bridges, and at once he felt sure of himself. She was smartly put together in a trim little suit with a sweater and a rope of huge Indian silver beads around her neck. She saw him looking at them as they shook hands, and she said,

"I've been the happy tourist since you were here last.—I begin to understand jewels and such ornaments as marks of bondage. These weigh a ton."

She seemed very well. Her blue eyes were free of the look he remembered, the humility and apology of suffering. She was pink from walking outdoors. Her pale hair was ever so slightly disarrayed.

"I've been out walking with Brisky all afternoon.—I saw you drive by a while ago."

"You did? Where:" he asked. There was a remote strike in his breast.

"I was walking out by the hospital, and over the sandhills beyond. It's a wonderful walk to make. It is rather rough country, and I am a frightful lazybones, as well as a fraidycat, and it is just exactly as rustic as I desire to be. And my wonderful galloping footstool, which is what Brisky looks like half the time, will assuredly protect me from rattlesnakes."

"This is rather good," he said. "I was out *in* the sandhills."

"What on earth for?"

Miss Bridges called across their conversation with a cool satisfaction at interrupting them,

"D'you think I'd bother you if I went on typing?"

"Oh: it might, Judy. Why don't you come over and sit with us and we'll have some tea, *now*."

Miss Bridges got up and made a sarcastically gallant gesture of resignation.

"No, I'll send it in, but I believe I'll go up and rip out all that I've knitted so far today."

She came over and shook hands sturdily with Peter, as if she belonged to his club.

Mrs. Foster watched her out.

"Judy's a dear, but nobody ever knows what will strike her how."

"Is she an old friend?"

"Yes.—She was simply heroic in the War. So were lots of others, too, of course. But you do see it sharper when it's someone near to you. She says she has the most fearful dreams, even still."

"What did she do?"

"She was in an ambulance unit. She married a boy from Boston who was killed in the Argonne, and it seems that the only way she could sort of surmount her grief was to take back her maiden name, and make herself a new life.—It's not everybody else's way, of course. But it *is* Judy."

"That's very interesting.—I'm glad you told me. I've been a little sharp, thinking about her."

"She's really a dear."

"—But she did interrupt us. I wanted to tell you about the sandhills."

"My sandhills," she murmured. The tea came and she got busy.

He told her he'd found the site of the first known Indian skirmish hereabouts between an American and the Navajos. He described Barton, and what he was doing out this way, and the diary he wrote for the War Department.

The maid drew the curtains and went out.

The room was dim and the fireplace was alive. When a log fell after a while, Peter, still talking, got up and went over and kicked it back, and came back and sat down, quite as if he were habituated to this, as if this was where he lived. He did it without thinking. Mrs. Foster watched him with amusement and with what else? She was disinclined to call it anything, and she knew how laughably wrong it was possible to be, and there was nothing worse, she could well remember, than to let something aspire within you which might have no counterpart where it desired one, and she wished she did not feel so animated in her heart. But the fact was, she did feel so, and she said to herself that, for a formal person, she certainly felt intimate with an unseemly earliness.

IV

As he talked, he watched her, and her responsiveness was something that fed him as wood fed the fire. Over her face there flickered that accompaniment of realization in another which anyone fond of talk is always seeking. He said that Lieutenant Barton was only a boy, really, when this thing happened three quarters of a century ago, more or less, and yet he had handled everything with the resourcefulness and courage of an experienced man. She smiled when he said it, and he paused to see why, and then he laughed, and said,

"I suppose you are amused by the male claim to triumph at any age."

"No, I was delighted by the way it all seems so real to you, just from looking at the sandhills.—And your boy Barton could walk right in the door in his epaulettes and his sidewhiskers and I would greet him like a long-lost brother.—Go on."

"Well, that's about all there is to tell, except that they saw the Indians safely delivered to the authorities."

"What became of Barton?"

"I looked him up at home after lunch after reading his diary. He was a Brigadier-General before he died in the Civil War. He was wounded at Chancellorsville."

"I always think there is something inexpressibly sad about soldiers' deaths. Soldiers and actors. They use *themselves* so to make their livings, I mean, their little own physical presences, and when it is finished and done for, the very *materials* of what they did are gone."

She filled their cups again, and then said,

"Do you know how this land of yours strikes me?—It strikes me as an almost wholly masculine land."

"Now Lieutenant Barton owes *you* a smile."

"No, I mean it. Do you see what I mean? I know dozens of places—in the East, the South, the Mississippi country—even California, the West Coast,—which don't strike me just that way. They're soft, close, narrow, compromisable lands. Any girl or woman is her own boss if she feels like it, in any town or city, generally. The sun shines, yes, but in such places, it doesn't enter everywhere. The *shadows* out here are burning with light. The country is so great and the jobs that keep us alive on it are so close to the first simplicities that it takes men to do them, all of them. It is Adam's own land. Isn't it?"

"I'd never thought— —Let me tell you something," he said, his eyes illuminated by memory. "When I was a boy, one day riding out on my pony by the river, on a Saturday morning, I met an old Indian, he seemed old to me at the time.—Have you seen the Indians?"

" 'm: they're so far from being really picturesque that I quite like them."

"He was, too. He was all faded and wrinkled and marked by work and had dried earth on him, in one form or another. He was watering his horse. I asked him where he was from. And what he answered I have never forgotten, and I think what you've said today may tie up with it, I mean that there may be several meanings coming together for me."

"What did he say:"

"I asked him where he lived, and he made signs and seemed to cover the whole space here, from the river to the mountains, East to West, and he said, 'I live in the house of the sun.' "

"How beautiful."

"Yes, but he didn't *mean* it to be *beautiful*."

"I'm sorry."

"No, all I mean is, that he was exactly describing where he lived and it had that real spaciousness for him.—And besides; this is what I didn't know then, as a boy: but the sun is the male source of life to the Indians. It is also the holder of fertility. The power of life itself. They use it in ceremonies and paintings and symbols to mean all these things.—I mean, you have arrived at the same answer as the Indians, if you see what I mean. I'm very clumsy."

"I'd hate for you to be as dry and as fluent as an archaeologist.— My uncle is one, so I can say that, can't I.—I do think that is a charming episode though. And I see exactly what you mean.—It is a man's country, and of course, I think any woman who is a *proper* woman, would be content there, for that very reason."

She saw a shadow fall over his face for a moment, and said nothing. Then he smiled and looked at her, and said,

"You might be describing my father and mother, by inference, as you talk about this country. He was a rancher. She was a schoolteacher from Washington, D. C. You might say that most of her life was spent at something she never had educated herself for. But she was a wonderful wife and a charming mother. After she moved into town, long, long, after I was a boy, she got in *her* licks for the church and the ladies' clubs and the first struggles of a public library. The only thing she ever missed was the green trees and fields of the country she came from."

"That early root is never really gone, is it."

"No, but some places it strikes deeper than others."

"I think the *place* is more in the heart than in the land."

"I guess so. I studied in the East, and would do it again, if I had to decide all over."

"But you came back here."

"I came back here."

"You know, I can't imagine that people of other countries have quite the same—what is it: the same *at-homeness* in so many different kinds of their own country as we have, in the United States? Do you?"

"I've never been in Europe. But I imagine life is very local and intense there, wherever it may be.—I think *we* are essentially *at home* in an idea, a climate of belief, maybe you could make a case for our being the most *philosophical* people in the world, with *all* our rawness and our movies and our habit of being raucously ashamed of our lack of foreign culture. I mean, if we are at home in the idea of being Americans, it is related much more to why this country was born than it is to where we live, actually.—This is odd, right on top of my passionate speeches about my own square of earth. But you know what I mean."

"Of course.—It has occurred to me before, that all our best works of literature have had the vitality of that idea in them, rather than strictly a local color."

"And we're always traveling all over our own country. How it looks and sounds and feels everywhere else. We all know that.—We all want to live in just one place, the best place for us, but we all know the other places too. I don't think a writer or an artist (or someone like that) can do us any good if he doesn't know more than his own little place. He can write about it all he likes, but he must have a sort of *versatility of the spirit* and bring home other Americas than his own. Then when he gives his own special America back, it will mean something widely."

The fire broke a log in two, and their thoughts broke with it.

He stood up.

"I've stayed much too long. I have a million things to do."

"But the time has simply flashed by.—I wonder what time it is?"

V

She went to the window and pulled aside the red Spanish velvet and looked out.

"It is nearly dark," she said. "You can see the barest daylight left on the river."

The house was on the hill. They looked down across town and out to the wooded valley where the river gleamed in opened turns of its course.

"You ought to drive along the river," he said. "In winter it is almost more magnificent than in summer.—The trees are made of beaten gold and silver. Groves and groves of cottonwoods with winter leaves still on the branches."

"I'll go. My car has arrived. Judy and I'll get around a good deal now. But she hates motoring."

He made a surprised face, and said,

"Yes, and we've forgotten entirely about your health! This is a professional call, after all, I was to check up on you."

"I'm glad we forgot it. I am perfectly fine. It was just something the sandstorm stirred up that time, and I must've been tired from the trip. Trains always exhaust me."

He told her she did seem perfectly well again. He said he was sorry, in one sense.

"But you will surely drop in again?" she said. "I'd like to read some of your old books about this part of the world, if you could ever bear to lend them."

"You would?"

They shook hands. He promised to bring some books. In an odd little way, they were now less than intimate. She said if she was out, just to leave them with Helga, who would take care of them. He said he hoped she would not be out, but in any case, this afternoon had been extremely pleasant. She thanked him and said it was awfully nice to know *someone* here, though she actually had come to rest, and didn't *want* to meet a lot of people. They parted with these valedictory trivialities; everything they had felt was still alive; but put down, deep, soft, spirited away.

VII · THE WIDOW

I

The sandy chill air made them all grateful for the warmth of the *Spirito Santo*. It was Willa's evening off, and (*for a wonder!*) both her children were home with her this evening. She was sewing. Wayne was supposed to be studying at the other side of the table. His sister Martha was at work on a letter to a friend of hers who had gone to school with her the year before, but was now living in Walsenburg, Colorado, and going to high school there. Martha's stationery was lilac colored, with a silver monogram that she had lately decided was much too elaborate; too childish; she would buy a "severely plain" paper next time.

But the conviviality of the family interrupted their separate tasks time and again, until Willa was ready to *admit* that there was nothing in life so sweet as having your children by you, harking to what you had to tell them.

It was all about Daddy, again, but they thought tonight she had a new power and animation in her remembrances that used to embarrass them slightly, and make them feel obscurely guilty. What had happened was that both Martha and Wayne had grown up enough to feel, at last, the truth and the depth of their mother's love for their father, and her fierce refusal to lose him even though he was dead so many years now. The children had a glimpse of far storms and glories in their mother's drab life for the first time; not from what she said so much as from the eagerness of the way she said it. She looked rosy and her eyes danced and there was a stab of girlish folly now and then in her gestures. In their two ways, the children were inspired and moved.

II

"—so the day he bought that chicken ranch out on the mesa, I hardly spoke to him all day. I said ·to myself my, he is such a fool, *imagine it, your daddy, how could I think that for a minute!* But he came home with the deeds in his pocket, and pulled them out and showed them to me, and he said, never mind Will, you may think me a visionary and a fool for doing this but someday you will bless the day. So of course I broke down and cried for thinking so meanly of him, and he hugged me, and he kissed me, and he fiddled his fingers behind my ear, this way, the way he always did when he wanted to please me, and nobody knows what that always meant to me, some day you kiddies will know what I mean. Your daddy was the kindest man that ever lived, I used to wake up at night and lie there and lie there, wondering what I had done to deserve such happiness.

"—and the thing he was always working for and thinking for was the future. When you were born, Waynie dear, I'll never forget how he came in as soon as they would let him see me, and he took my hand, and he rubbed his thumb across my fingers, he was trembling, and he said, Never mind, mother, no matter what happens to me, or anything, you have a fine strong son to protect you now, and he picked you up and held you for a second, and I remember, I thought it was the *strangest* thing I ever saw, he blushed when he held you that time, and the nurse laughed, too, because she noticed it.

"—and it *is* true, he *did* make money. He was just's clever's a barrel of monkeys, and if he'd kept his health, we'd all be *rolling* today. But he never let on, and *I* never knew, but after he died, the doctor told me he'd never had a chance from the minute he come here, but you think he'd let on? No siree. Not on your tintype. And when he was so weak he had to be in bed those last few months, he used to write down things for us all to do, and one day, Waynie, he watched you playing in the yard, the way you used to do? making your boats out of old planks and pushing them on the ground? he wrote down on his pad that perhaps you ought to be a midshipman at the United States Naval Academy? He told me how to get in touch with a Congressman if the time ever came. He said anybody at all had a perfect right to get in touch with a Congressman and get him to help to get their boy into the United States Naval Academy. He said the Government was the engine, all right, but he said the people, any old people, you and me, and your grocer and your banker and your doctor and your cripple that sells the papers by the bank on the corner and your druggist and your old nigger yardman, said the people *ran* the old engine, and never forget it.

"—I tell *you*."

She shook her head vigorously, but really had run out of things

to tell them, and what she meant was that the dead father from whom
their life had come was even larger in her thoughts than he had been
alive.

III

Wayne was hot-faced and packed with pride in her ramblings. He
could hardly remember his father, but his throat was full of a lump
of love and resolve. His eyes were glistening with wet light, and he
breathed with his lips open, staring at his mother until she returned
to the present and *saw* him. She leaned over and rubbed her knuckles
in his silken bristly hair.

"What dear?"

"Nothing, Momma. Only:"

He stopped, and she waited. How far could a boy go without
seeming foolish, he wondered. Would she laugh at him for what he
was performing in his mind? Or would she see that he was only
fulfilling his father's promise to the future?

She began to talk again, about the time the Rio Grande flooded
many years before, and how Daddy had put on hip boots of rubber
which he borrowed from the duck-hunting neighbor next door, and
gone out wading to help the rescuers in the west end of town who
were saving Mexican families by the light of oil lanterns. The sound
of the water was what he talked about most when he got back, for
in the dark, the rushing muddy waves seemed to roar and crash
louder and louder with every moment. He had such a cough when
he returned that she was furious with him. But from inside his shirt
he brought out and handed her two glasses of jelly that had been
rolled off their shelves by the water, and she reminded Wayne how
he always used to laugh every time she told him, when he was a
little boy, about the glasses of jelly rolling along in the flood, such a
strange thing for jelly glasses to do . . .

They were borne along by her voice, and by the remote cracking
and gasping of the fire behind the poopdeck windows of the earnest
iron galleon that stood on a tin matting decorated with a border of
stenciled vine leaves.

The children had escaped; Wayne, to the future, Martha, to love.

He almost lay on the table, with his pointed chin on his open
schoolbook, his sweatered arms curled about his face, and his eyes
shining above them like windows in a battlement. There were simply
no terms to describe the goodness and the power of the father whom
he had heard about. Such things as weakness, aimless imagination,

lack of vitality, all held together by a touching sweetness, played no part in his image of Mr. Shoemaker, yet these were true of him. Wayne was clothed with the grandeurs of executing a mission; a dedication laid upon him as sure as fate; and in his imagination he moved superbly out upon the bridge deck of a great battleship, that rode the waves without creating spray or a wake, but glided grandly like a wonderful plank of wood crossing a lawn of grass, toward a distance where a bank of clouds loomed in the late sunshine, revealing in silhouette the array of an enemy fleet, whose guns suddenly began to cough and charge the air with spurts of fire. He was fired in his heart by all the things which his vision tried to make clear to him, and he felt, but he did not know, how he was compounded of love.

IV

Martha's letter was abandoned.

She seemed to be listening to her mother, like her brother Wayne; but she too was lost. She was dreaming of her lover. She knew how they danced together, his arm around her, so; his body coming upon her with every step, and hers eluding his exquisitely; his whisperings while the orchestra seemed farther and farther away. She knew also how he sounded on the telephone, when he called her up to ask her for a date, or perhaps just to tell her something inexpressibly funny and at the same time perfectly darling that had just occurred to him; and how they would sometimes let the phone rest silent, and simply hear each other breathe—a thought which made her tongue tingle as if she tasted a flashlight battery, which she hadn't done for years. And she knew how it was when he came to call for her, riding his horse, and leading hers, and how they went to the wood where the sunlight struck through the shadows to a bank of moss and ferns, where they alighted and where they kissed. His hair felt like the cushion on the sofa in the corner, a golden plush, except that it was long and curly. What she could not make herself sure of were the things her lover said. Her heart was in her mouth at the breath-taking sweetness of how she felt and what she was *sure* of; but this lover of whom she knew so much was a youth she had never seen. She lived with him and longed for him, and knew nothing about him. But everything he meant, and everything she meant by inventing him in mind so urgently, was somehow already present in her mother's prattle of remembrance. And it was this that had sent Martha's thoughts where they went.

V

"—and all you have to do to see what a fine-looking fellow he was is look at my children. Wayne has his eyes, and Martha his mouth, and of course you have *my* hair, but he had, and you all have, beautiful foreheads, anybody'd know you anywhere for his children, if just only by that one little thing, so wide, and high, and such fine smooth bone at the temple. No wonder I'm just so happy, and willing to work, work, work, though I am sure he never expected me to *have* to. But he would've known how I'd've *done* it, if I'd had to, as it turns out I *did* have to, after all, and he couldn't but *approve.*"

The children were shining in wonder, though not at the same things. But their mother thought she knew why, and was content with them.

VIII · RIFLETIME

I

Wayne Shoemaker sometimes made a little money by working after school in Jensen's, the stationery shop and bookstore. He would drop in and ask Mr. Jensen if he needed anything, and Mr. Jensen would say the shelves all needed dusting today, and set him to work. Mr. Jensen had pale-blue eyes, which always seemed to be watering with some kindly weakness, as if he could never refuse anything that anybody asked of him. He carried an enormous stock of supplies, and was the rabbit transfixed by the snake eye of whatever salesman came along. He did a good business, but made very little money. Everybody in town knew him. The chances were, he liked that better than being rich. He felt sentimental about small boys of any kind, and in them, he saw the cartoon values of such symbols as the ole swimming hole, freckles, a can of worms to go fishing with, a loving cur dog, bare feet with a dirty bandage on the big toe, stolen watermelons and other comic attributes of small boys more rooted in folklore than in actual modern life. Wayne, with his sober blue eyes and his standing silky yellow hair, was sure of anything he wanted from Mr. Jensen.

Wayne liked his occasional job. He enjoyed handling the stationery supplies. There was a fabulous plenty about so many hundred dozen pencils, such ranks of ink bottles, such pyramids of paper. He dusted the piles of writing tablets with a dreamy pleasure in their spotless beauty. A bare page of paper always did something obscure to him, it made him want to set down something there; a drawing, a line of words; echo of life in some fashion or other.

II

He was working at the long center table in the store for some minutes before he glanced up and recognized Doctor Rush up front at the book counter. The Doctor was turning through a book. He seemed blurred with daylight all around his edges, as Wayne looked at him against the front windows of the store.

Wayne went on working.

Peter went on reading.

They were aware of each other.

Peter had seen him out of the corner of his eye. In a little bridge of truth and feeling between them, which had nothing to do with their relative ages, they felt shy of each other. Each denied it to himself, watching the other circumspectly. Each inhabited a world of Donald Rush's that the other knew little about.

Finally Peter put down his book and took up another, and in the act, "saw" Wayne, and nodded to him.

"Hello, Wayne. Are you working nowadays?"

"Just now and then.—H'lo."

"You're the feller I've been wanting to see."

"Well, sure," said Wayne.

"Can you slip out and have a drink with me next door?"

"I'd better ask Mr. Jensen."

"Well, you go ask him. I'll wait."

Peter watched the remote interview. Mr. Jensen appeared to meet Wayne's request with a toughness he did not really have. Wayne returned and said he could go. They went to the Mint Confectionery next door and sat in one of the booths and ordered. Peter had a Coca Cola, and Wayne took a marshmallow fudge sundae on chocolate ice cream, with ground nuts and a maraschino cherry on a dome of whipped cream, studded with slices of banana.

"You see a lot of my boy Don, don't you?"

"Why, sure."

"I know he is always making plans about doing things with you.—

You knew he was going to have a birthday pretty soon, didn't you?"

"Why, I guess so."

"Well, his mother and I are hard put to it to know what to give him for his birthday. Mrs. Rush said I was to find you, by hook or crook, and ask you for a suggestion. So here we are, meeting in a sort of folk gathering place, imbibing the fashionable indigestibles of the day, while I lay my problem before you."

"Well, I *see*."

"Can you think of anything he wants? Has he mentioned anything?"

"Well, goll, I don't know. Right off, that is."

Peter lighted a cigarette, sat back, and waited. Wayne went on with his sticky delight, spooning the sundae with a steady pace. They sat in silence for perhaps five minutes. He could see that Wayne was dying to say something but didn't know how to, and let him wait. Pretty soon the metal sundae dish was licked clean by the spoon, and Wayne sat back and stared out into the shop, whistling silently. Peter crushed out his cigarette.

"I won't offer to buy you another of those frightful confections. My professional integrity inhibits my natural generosity. It is not often that a general practitioner can intervene so effectively between a potential patient and the source of acute indigestion."

Wayne looked at him, and he saw that the Doctor's kidding was all really on his side, and the sparkle in his eye when he made those ridiculous sentences was rather youthful. He burst out laughing, and wondered why he had felt so tongue-tied. He wished he could talk that way. Maybe that was what the dictionary was for. He suddenly loved his dictionary fervidly.

"Well," said Peter, "I just thought I would *ask* you, anyway. We really want to give him something he really *wants*."

"I know," said Wayne, in the mildest and most natural voice in the world, "he wants a .22 rifle."

"I see. That's the sort of thing I wanted to know. Thanks, Wayne. We'd better get back to work, both of us.—A .22? Do you think he'd be careful with it? Would *you*?"

"Oh, sure. *Surely*. We would exercise extreme caution in operating the gun," replied Wayne, and blushed. Nevertheless, he felt a little flare of success in dealing the Doctor's conversation back at him. How excellent it was to be educated!

"Well, that sounds like *it*, then. I'll tell Mrs. Rush what you said. —I believe she is planning a party, but don't you say anything about it to Donnie."

"Oh, no, indeed."

Indeed was a good one, too.

They parted with a handshake. When Peter had disappeared around the corner, swinging in his energetic walk, Wayne felt older, taller, and more gifted than ever before. Doctor Rush made you *feel like somebody,* he reflected, and went back to his job furiously.

III

That afternoon, Peter left his office a shade earlier than usual, in order to reach the hardware store down the street before closing time. He just made it. They let him in the door, and then locked it after him, and drew down the striped awning shade over the plate glass of the door.

Ed, the clerk, was a man his own age with whom he had gone to school years ago here in Albuquerque. Doctor Rush wondered if *he* looked as old as that now. Good Lord, they used to go hunting together, way back then. The river on Saturdays, the mesa where the jack rabbits leaped up from behind unlikely bushes, the sandhills way over the river where quail speckled the memories of September . . .

Ed handed him one .22 rifle after another, now, and a host of simple joys returned to life in the Doctor as he handled the guns.

What a thing happened to a man when he took up a gun to hold! Atavism, he said to himself, but he couldn't dismiss the—the *basic* sense of rightness he felt at hefting a rifle in his hands. A gun made him want to be alone. How enormously simplified the terms of life were, if you thought along this line. Some sky, a wilderness, survival the first and last responsibility, mind bound to earth and earth's caprice its governor; how tempting, the lordship over the animal kingdom; what trials of innocence by the innocent; what wisdom in the impassive mountains, what justice in the fatigue of a body tired by the earth; to lie down when darkness fell by the chill mountain lake, and not stir until sunrise crept down the opposite peak . . .

He smiled and humorously gritted his teeth at the nonsense which welled up in grown men at times. Let the boy have the rifle. Rifletime was a season in any man's life. He laid his cheek on the stock and squinted along the sights. It was an expensive present, and a dangerous one, too, of course; but if he bought it for Donnie, he would also be buying the memory of his own boyhood, that he could put it from him, in the name of his son.

"This one's a beauty."

"Boy, sure is prettiest little rafle in the house."

"I think this's the one I'll take, Ed."

Ed didn't look *that old* any more. He was just a ruddy, skinny and familiar figure, who hadn't changed in any essential ways since high school. The streets were none of them paved, then, years ago, but *all* made of sand, and Peter remembered how Ed used to ride to school on an old mare who was tied all morning to the cottonwood tree out on the edge of the recess playground in back. It had seemed such an original thing to do when they were both boys in high school that he always expected Ed to be a famous and "successful" man.

"O.K., Doc.—Will you take 'er?"

"No, send 'er out Friday morning. It's Donald's birthday, and Mrs. Rush's planning a little party that evening at suppertime.—She'll hide it while the kids're at school. Thanks, Ed.—Glad to've seen you."

Ed winked at him, and let him out the door, and watched him a second, reflecting that this was a mighty lucky town to have a doctor like him, ol' Pete, and proudly he recollected going to high school with ol' Pete, who would ever've thought *back then* that ol' Pete'd amount to something? Just a litto biddy ol' *kid,* used to hunt *jack rabbits* with him, she-oot!

Ed dropped the canvas shade in its place and put the rifle into its flannel sock and tied a tag on to it marked for delivery. He expected that would be one happy ol' kid when he got aholt of this litto rafle.

IX · ANOTHER COUNTRY

I

Within the very fabric of the little family of Willa Shoemaker, something was going on which might have been whole countries away, for all it concerned them jointly. It was something like that that Martha herself felt about it; another country; another spirit; alien to her busy mother and laughably foreign to her little brother Wayne. But in her own heart, there were perceptions and vistas which were so new, so troublesome and so breath-taking that she concealed her state by an air of sullenness "not at all like her."

Martha wore her silky hair in a heavy fall beside her cheeks. Her eyes were very blue, and full of silver sparks. She rubbed her cheeks, whenever she could remember, to make them look highly colored; all the rubbing she could manage never added anything to their crab apple glow. Her mouth was rather large, but its lips were sweetly modeled and could hardly take the shape of anything but eagerness, a smile, the appetite of happiness. When a little younger, she had played a game with Wayne of being grown up, and severe, comically critical of everything; and then her mouth had pursed ridiculously, as if in a distasteful kiss, while Wayne had saved up his laughter until she too could drop her acting, and the two of them explode with mirth.

Now the expression of kisses, unspent, lingered over her mouth, and gave it a first ripeness that made people look after her when she passed. She said to herself often enough that she wasn't pretty; her fresh dresses and crisply laundered white collars that she wore to work at business college gave her a smart look, she knew that; her attempts to walk with grace and dignity instead of with the comic exaggerations that had convulsed Wayne so short a time ago as a year—this bearing she was learning by habit; and all her impulses to foolishness that had been part of her character in the family now seemed to sink deeper into her heart, and become part of the inner delight that she must keep the world from seeing, until she knew what it meant.

She supposed everyone would know, and speculate, and try to *influence,* soon enough.

She was suddenly in love with a boy she'd known in high school. He was a class behind her, so that now, a graduate and already ahead in business college, she was dating him even though he was still only a senior. He still had to ride his bicycle up the hill to the big red-brick and white-stone high school every morning at eight-twenty. His name was Richmond Summerfield, nicknamed "Bun." His father was a druggist, and the son worked in the family drugstore after school and on week ends. He was a year younger than Martha. She wondered sometimes whether this mattered. But when they were together, it never seemed important, and she forgot it as often as possible.

And it was an endless source of doubt and wonder to her that for years she had known Bun casually, simply as a boy with merry dark-blue eyes, and the face of a ripe peach, and dark hair combed in deep shining rakes that set off his handsomely shaped head, and the energetic harmonies in his body that made it seem powerful as well as young. She had never given him a second thought, any more than any other boy she knew. Instead, she had dreamed awake over her imaginary lover.

And then what: then like turning a page of a story, as cleanly
and sharply as that, and as easily, she had been smitten by his look,
across the counter in the drugstore, one day, while she was buying
some foot powder to take home to her mother who was on her feet
all day, as they'd heard her remark a thousand times, and the world
was a place in which one great secret existed, and it lay in Martha's
heart, driving out forever the foolish image which she now knew
had been so unreal and even shameful. For days she avoided Summerfield's Drug, as it was known in town.

What if he would "merely look" at her?

It would break her heart.

She crossed the street to the opposite side to avoid the chance of
encountering Bun, and of having him see her simply as some ol' girl.

When she was alone, she would shake her head as if to scatter the
thought of him apart.

But it did no good.

She wept at night and stormed herself to sleep with angry scold-
ings of her foolishness at allowing anything so implausible as the
hope that he might love her too to inhabit her days and hurry her
nights.

But the trouble became too great to deal with halfway. She resolved to go into Summerfield's and contrive to get any other clerk
to wait on her, and if Bun were there, she'd simply wave casually,
and complete her purchase, and walk out.

II

It went according to plan. There was a clerk named Rollie Glovers
who looked more like a drug clerk in his tan-colored linen jacket
than Bun did, and his pale face seemed vaguely medicinal. Down
the aisle behind the heaped counter she saw Bun, looking at her
with his dark eyebrows up in a surprised smile. He came toward
her. She nodded. He asked if Rollie was taking good care of her.
She answered him, Yes of course, but her voice croaked and itched
in a dry whisper and she coughed over it, and looked down, hating
her heart for beating so fast, and her cheeks for coloring so deep.

When she looked up again, she had what looked like tiny lights in
her eyes. Bun's face changed as he regarded her and he gave Rollie
a comedy poke in the ribs, to send him off down the aisle to wait on
someone else, and the two of them were left, looking at each other
across the pyramids of powder boxes on the perfume counter, until
the immediate betrayals they had both made began to embarrass

them, and they went confusedly back to the foolish excuse of purchase she had begun to make.

Her fresh, starched, frilly aspect and her long blonde hair and her lips pressed close together looked entirely new to him. His hands trembled when he snapped a rubber band around her little parcel and handed it to her. She looked at his hands and her throat began to beat, and she knew she could not say a word if her life depended on it.

He came around from behind the counter and took her to the door. He fancied he could smell the laundering of her clothes.

What the heck, he thought, at this extraordinary thought.

Then he asked her if he could have a date that night.

At once, an ease plumbed her deeply. Gone was the terrified, unhappy child within her who had made her days so heavy. She felt almost elaborately at ease, and with a curious kind of grandeur, she said "Let me see," and went through the parody of remembering whether she had an engagement or not. Then, to her appalled heart which only asked to say *yes,* urgently, and at once, she heard herself tell three lies, saying that she was engaged this evening, and tomorrow, and tomorrow, but the day after that, it would probably be all right.

She watched his face, to see if she had ruined forever the very terms on which her future life depended. But he smiled with what looked like humility, and his dark-blue eyes made little stars of thought deep inside which she said to herself later looked simply "gallant," he took his disappointment so dearly. He said if three nights off was the best she could do, it was still prob'ly better than he *rated,* and he asked her if he should come to get her at home. He said he had no car, and was never sure whether he could get his father's, anyway. She didn't want him to come to the little house so far out on the sand street where the street lights were so far apart on every other corner.

She said she had some books to return to the public library anyway. Why didn't they meet there? He said that would be fine, and took her hand to shake it, rather formally.

Their touch together was like a miniature jolt of electricity. Neither of them, as they said so often later on, felt that they could let go, *you know,* the way electricity does to you, when the current gets into you, they say sometimes you never *can* let go, and the shock keeps on going through you, and *going* through you, until at last somebody or something turns the power off, and there you are, weak as a cat, or dead, or something, never knowing what hit you . . . ?

That was how she felt, making her way up the street alone. Her mouth was dry, and her eyes felt as if they were shining and hot and stinging. There was a gulp in her throat. How tall was he? He was taller than she, and so deep in the breast and so broad in the back. She now felt her pulse racing, and she said to herself that it was the most awful risk she had ever taken in her life, what if he had simply raised his eyebrows and said, "O.K., I'll ask you some other time," which of course he would forget to do—why—and if he did, why, she would die. Her heart beat so she felt a little giddy and breathless. The only way she could feel what had really happened to her, was by suffering an imaginary tragedy. Tears for what might have happened came to her eyes, and drowned her happiness over what did happen.

Watching her disappear among the walkers of the sidewalks he felt ageless and very well, turning his big gold signet ring slowly on his knuckle. The ring had been his grandfather's, and was made to represent three ropes braided together, wound around a fancy capital S. His grandfather had been a medical officer in the Civil War. Bun meant to study medicine in college. The ring was an inheritance and a dedication.

He was a believer in the body, as an athlete. He was astonished at falling in love, and wondered where he'd gotten it—from her eyes, how she looked? Her voice, trying to speak? He went back into the store, came up behind Rollie Glovers at the counter, reached around his side and took the clipped pencil from the upper pocket of Rollie's starched jacket, passed it around his body and dropped it into the lower pocket on the other side, and chucked Rollie under the chin, and ended with a jazzy tattoo of drummed knuckles on Rollie's skull, saying, "O.K., babe," and passing down the counter to the back of the store and out of sight behind the swinging half-door to the prescription room, which smelled powdery.

III

Hovering up and down behind the counter, which had its masking battlements of merchandise, Rollie had enviously watched the two of them. He wished passionately that he would explain to himself why he never could seem to *win*. Every time he got into situations with other people, he never seemed able to make an impression. He knew perfectly well what was right and what was wrong; he was as sure of that sort of thing today as the day four years ago in Amarillo, Texas, when he had been converted during the revival meeting the spring of his graduation from high school. He was very careful in what he thought of as *personal habits,* too. He bathed twice a day and kept his clothes pressed and when a necktie he liked got shiny he would go down to the boiler room at the YMCA where he lived, and steam it and then flatten it overnight in the atlas he had bought two years ago for the purpose of memorizing five geographical names a day.

He loved his books, and often sent away more than once a month for a new one. He was *developing his memory* that way; and he was learning how to make *deft, ready conversation,* too. And—a shy, sensitive person, "like many thousand others"—he was also finding out how to be *never at a loss* when *thrown among strangers.* As for getting up and making a speech, nothing was further from his natural abilities; but he decided that the occasion might come up when he least expected it; and there was another book with diagrams and sample selections for him to study, so that people might one day say, "Listen to Glovers! We never *knew!*"

Was there anything simpler than training yourself to make a habit of having *one pleasant thing to say* every single day to every single person you met? And yet how startled people would look, at times, when he would try it. It was like the sort of thing he found out from those other books that came in plain wrappers, and which he approached in *scientific interest,* to have a well-rounded knowledge of the facts of life. There were chapters on *courtship* which told how to do, and yet when he had a date with a girl, and tried *how to do,* she mostly often would make sounds or gestures that meant, "Um-*hum,* but let's—let's just watch the movie," or "Why, Rollie!" and giggle.

And yet he was sure: the books all insisted, and so did the things he read more than anything else, the advertisements, he was *sure* that it was only a matter of *using spare time wisely* . . . there was actually a "boy" he knew in Fort Worth who learned to play the piano from the advertised thing, and was able at the same time to *avoid hours of tedious practice!*

And his health! How careful he was, and how regularly he took his various doses of medicine, so that *Nature's delicate balance* would not get out of whack! That last book, *Adding Ten Years to Your Life,* had a series of charts of the human body, with things to check every day that had to be done to *keep vigor.* He checked them carefully, and looked at himself for traces of the *perfect, radiant health* that was sure to result.

Sometimes he thought he found them, and at other times he was miserably discouraged.

Because what it all came back to was that *people* didn't seem any different toward him; and there were actually moments when he faintly thought that trying harder might not be of any use.

And yet if that were going to be true, why, what about the things that *everybody* believed? You couldn't tell *him!* that all that millions and millions of dollars spent on advertising was spent for nothing, why, everybody knew that wasn't so. Everybody *did* what they read about, and bought, and that was how everything helpful got discovered, after all.

So he would fiercely clench his thoughts and (though he never admitted it to himself) actually he would pray that his faith be sustained.

Oh forsake me not, for that I am *thy* child.

Oh, I want everybody here tonight to *know,* I want them to know that I have *been* weary and sick *at* heart, *oh,* I want to *say,* I want everybody to hear me *say* that I have been trying to find the way to the Vineyard, I have searched among the *de*vious paths, I have humbled myself before the gods *of* offering, *oh,* grant unto me that *I* find the *way,* in six easy lessons. *Oh* how to keep regular, do *you* need the answer to the secret of how to make an impression? Oh there *is* a way, for every smile on your face there is another smile waiting somewhere in the world to be smiled right back at you, did you know that, *Oh* Lord? Oh, *a*men, *a*men, I say unto you, why did she turn and snicker? *He* didn't know, but all the rest of them did! *Oh* hear me. Ha-ha is what they said behind their hands, what makes our friend look so listless, no pep, Oh, did't you know, he is not *regular?* Where is the Pretty Girl who will give the word of advice about This New Way?

How do they get to smile in the pictures of After? Oh I know all the pictures of Before. What has not been vouchsafed unto me are the sweetnesses, the powers, the winnings, of After.

Do you want to be attractive?

Check the answer yes or no.

Someday the coupon, the *right* coupon, will come along, guide me to the paths of the righteous that I may know it when it appears, and I may enter into my kingdom by mail, in six easy lessons, in plain wrapper, Amen.

IV

And yet Bun and that Shoemaker girl had gotten together just as easy as falling off a log.

Rollie was passionately envious, and vowed he would watch them, and "be in on" what they did, by whatever means he could command.

X · THE BIRTHDAY

I

A kind of sweet fury took hold of Noonie. She had decided to astonish and enchant her child and his father with a revival of the delights of the old days in Rochester, when all birthdays had been festivals lasting weeks. The family would start out weeks before the actual *day,* and prepare. There were forbidden areas in the house where the celebrant could not go. There were sweeps and whisperings of tissue paper. The sewing machine whirred and sang all day. At night there were unexplained rustlings while packages were taken up the back way. Everybody sustained an elaborate pretense that there was nothing unusual going on. But Noonie could remember how Roderick would be looking at her with his black-eyed smile, his head down, his mouth parted in hot-breathed speculation. The family connotations of such intense labors came back to her here, now, and she was tireless in her preparations.

To have her small mystery was wonderfully good for her. She had rosy cheeks, her eyes sparkled, and her conversation was arch and endless, since she had to keep them thinking about everything except the thing that was going on in the house.

Donald would surprise her in intent conference with Cora, the cook, and be whisked out of the kitchen with his glass of milk and plate of sandwiches before he could even ask for anything. He found large piles of department store boxes out in the alley refuse cans. He saw names and telephone numbers written on the hall pad, and heavily scratched out so as to be illegible. One afternoon he deliberately tested the atmosphere of secret and ecstatic labor by going up

to his mother's bedroom and sitting down and fiddling with everything on her dressing table, while she worked hard, over by the sunny
windows, in front, to seem idle and patient. He could tell that she
was bursting with something. He had one of his rare desires to go
and put his arms around her and hug her. She didn't even seem tired.
He saw the lid off the sewing machine in a corner of the room, and he
recognized snips of crepe paper of bright colors on the floor, where
Leonard had not really swept up.

"What are you doing with my things?" she asked idly, threading a
needle. He noticed that there was no completed darning anywhere
on the sewing table. She was just pretending while he was there.

"Nothing."

"Look out for my rings."

"Where are they?"

"In that little Dresden china box with the three cats on it."

"Oh. Can I look?"

"You've seen them a million times.—Yes, go ahead. What a funny
boy. You always loved sparkles."

He took the lid off the box. It was lined with mauve velvet. There
lay three rings, with big diamonds in them and one with a large
amethyst circled with diamonds. He picked them up and walked to
the sunshine of the window, and held them up and squinted at them,
and was needled by their fiery stabs, and he saw magic in the jewels.

"Why don't you ever wear them, Mother?"

"Oh, I don't know: I don't *feel* much like diamonds, nowadays."

"Why not, Mother?"

"Oh, I don't know.—You wouldn't understand."

"I would too!"

"Darling Donnie!"

She reached for him, and now that she wanted to kiss him, his
desire to hug her disappeared.

"What's the matter?"

"You do know I love you, don't you, Donnie, I am such a poor
mother to you!"

"No you're not!" he said. *"No you're not!"* he cried again, and refused the obscure doubt that he had known for so long.

She kissed him on the cheek, and sat back again, and let him go,
and he turned the rings in the light.

"Will you wear them if—if we ever *do* something?" he asked.

"What do you mean: *do* something."

"I mean, like a party, or anything."

"Party?" she said, with an airy laugh. This was exquisitely the kind of close shave that made the secret preparations ever so worth while. "Who said anything about a party: don't be such a silly-billy boy."

But there was the most cunning laughter in her voice, it came from her heart, so full of devoted and clever plans, half of which were already carried out. Wait till he saw the enormous drum, made of crepe paper, cardboard and gold cord, which she and Cora had slaved over, and which was filled like a huge pie with presents for everybody. It would be brought in and set on the dining-room table and then the sliding doors would be shut, and locked, till the party. Then each child would be given a golden cord to pull, and out would pop the most adorable presents for everybody . . . And the paper hats: none of your cracker kind: she was making every single one of them. Paste, scissors, sewing machine, colored papers, fringe, tassels, seals . . . out of them all came the most beautiful shakos and fezzes and helmets and tiaras and busbies and "Merry Widows" and "Toscas" and "Gainsboroughs," which the children would never have seen the like of. And Cora was going to decorate the cake with three colors, and it was coming in on a large new wooden palette because Donald loved to paint and someday might be a great artist, and use a thing like this instead of that battered box of water colors. And she had got a number of games together, which the children would all play, and even planning the order of the games was something of a job in itself. Nobody would ever expect such elaborate and ingenious things as were in the making besides.

"Party?" she repeated. "Why should there be a party?"

"Oh, I don't know. It just occurred to me, as a remote possibility."

"—Where on earth did you learn to talk like that.—Honestly, growing boys are like magpies, they hear something and pick it up."

She was certain that she had handled it just right. He didn't suspect a thing. She said,

"Aren't you going out this afternoon? Or do you want to sit downstairs and read.—You ought to rest more, darling. Drink your milk and take a little rest. You never know when you will need your reserve of strength! Look at me!"

This was in her habitual style of worry. Sometimes she felt Donald's strenuous life was a burden to her; a rebuke to her own weariness; proud of his furies of ingenuity and activity, she was unnerved by them, too, and was always advising him to rest, be more quiet, drink more milk, stop *racing* so, as if she could store up in her child what she lacked herself.

He could not bear these advices. He could remember, if he could not explain, how divided they often felt, in that house. They all really loved each other; and their exchanges ranged widely from overly thoughtful attentions to bursts of black-eyed anger and scorn, which were never patched up by apology, but allowed to be dissipated through two or three days of slowly thawing silence among them. Noonie would make some remark that if taken up tactfully could weld them together again. "How are the trees doing, Peter?" or "What are you and Wayne doing this Saturday, Donnie dear?"— and they could then talk about the lot next door with the evergreen nursery which was the neighborhood's smiling folly, or about how the boys would take a pack of lunch, and maybe ride out on the mesa for the day, and see what they could see, perhaps at Wayne's old abandoned chicken ranch where the adobe walls were weathering under the wind into rounded edges, and the mountains seemed so near, and there was supposed to be a snake pit full of rattlers which they had never yet found but would surely find someday.

Donald went back and put the diamond rings away, and stood in the middle of the room, looking at her, smiling with a frown, with his head a little on one side, like his father.

She laughed fondly, and said,

"All right, go on, do anything you like, only don't stand there and *diagnose* me."

"Are you trying to get rid of me?"

"What in the world *for?*" she asked, lyrically, and once again, the charm and excitement of a surprise in preparation was implicit between them.

"Then I'll go," he said, and she remembered how her brother Roderick always used to do the same thing; publish for his own the reason for anything he did.

II

The Doctor got home a little after six the evening of the party, and found his wife in the green-carpeted hallway of their large, comfortable and ugly house, watching the birthday party in progress. There were a dozen boys and girls in the living room. The player piano was going. The light was harsh and bland, falling through the crystal prisms that hung from the brass discs set near the white ceiling. The children were flushed and unconscious of themselves. A game of pinning the cloth tail on the printed donkey was under way. Some of the boys had lost their tissue-paper hats. Some of the girls wore theirs with conscious style. Noonie's eyes were dancing, and her breath came in little hot wafts through her lips. He thought she looked pretty, and he hugged her with his hat and overcoat on, standing spread-legged around her and laughing privately on her cheek.

"Don't, Peter, look out, do you think they're having a good time?"

"They're O.K.," said the Doctor, ignoring the roomful of busy children.—"You look's'if it was your own party yourself, Noonie, look at me."

"I'll be dead when it's over, I've worked all day. But I do think he's loving it.—I've saved your present till you got here."

The Doctor was suddenly shy. He dropped his arms away from her, and took off his hat and coat. He wanted to say that he wished he didn't have to give Donald the rifle in front of all those children. They never looked really aware of anything as it really *was,* and he dreaded their jumping staring acceptance of a present that it had given him such delight to buy and bestow with his imagination and his love upon his boy.

He walked to the white-pillared doorway between the hall and the living room. Donald and Wayne sat side by side on the piano bench, watching the Truman boy from the other side of town stagger in blindfold toward the sheeted donkey tacked on the closed mahogany sliding doors of the dining room. The Doctor's heart sank. If he had ever seen an image of boredom it was his own son, with those big, staring eyes in that brown face with its excited color but blank expression. The other youngsters were full of noise, and seemed oddly so much younger than those two on the piano bench. The player piano was puffing and clanking out its tune. Nobody listened. Edward Truman pinned the tail on the donkey's very middle, and pulled off his blindfold, while they all screamed at him, and he made an idiot face, crossing his eyes, hanging out his tongue, and wabbling his fingers under his chin, to make his own point of how gloriously he had failed. Then they all fell silent, looking at the Doctor. He smiled at them all. Donald looked up at him with his face lowered and smiled back. Nobody did anything. The Doctor felt suddenly angry. After all her work, he thought, and these little devils won't help to make it a party, it's dying on her hands. Valorously loyal to his wife's helplessness and her hope, he turned and took her hand and pulled her into the living room with him. He didn't realize it, but it was his arrival that had changed everything. They were now all self-conscious, it was the Doctor, when you were sick they sent for him, he gave castor oil, he smelled like the hospital, let's get out of here, there wasn't enough ice cream anyway, "h'lo Doctor Rush" —for he had greeted them all. He went to the corner bookcase which had glass doors behind which were curtains of stretched pongee silk. He unlocked it. There stood the long package. He got it out, walked over to Donald, and handed it to him, saying, "Happy birthday, Don."

It was such a big package that they couldn't get close enough to see, while Don unwrapped it. He knew by the weight what it was, the balance of it, and when he got to the gray flannel sock in which the rifle was finally protected, he was dumbly reluctant to open it further. He looked up at his father.

"Goll, Dad, thanks."

The others cried for him to go ahead, and open it up, what was it, was it a gun, gosh.

Doctor Rush noticed that Don looked as if he might suddenly cry, and his own heart melted in him at that, and he leaned down and took the gun off his son's lap, and knelt there and gently opened the flannel sock, bending down to hide his own face. He got the gun out and handed it back to Donnie now, and stood up rushing air out through his mustache.

"There you are, son.—D'you like it?"

"Goll, Daddie:" but he simply could not talk any further, struggling to preserve his calm and powerful interior. He lost his battle when the gun had to be handed around to the other boys. He charged like a football player into his father's middle, and butted and hid his head against the Doctor's vest, hugging him around the pockets frantically, not caring who might be looking, all those kids, and girls, what of it. Somehow foolishly, the gun ended up in Noonie's hands, where it looked like a large spoon, the way she held it. But her face was what they all were drawn by, and in the midst of this heartless and noisy young public, the Rushes had one of their united moments.

III

Shortly after that the children went home, leaving Wayne and Donald and the .22, in the middle of the green carpet on the living-room floor. The gun had a rock-gray barrel, shining along the myriad rings of its tooled surface. The stock was a beautiful leathery brown, which felt smooth and cool under the palm. The bolt sounded simply beautiful when it was clicked open and closed, riding its element of oil, which smelled sharp and almost sweet. They both knew that Donald would sleep with it tonight on his sleeping porch upstairs. They all knew that his thirteenth birthday, and the party, and the present, were all points of history for them in the family . . . even to what happened just before the Doctor and his wife sat down to dinner. Don came and said Wayne had to go home, now, and he would like to ride home with him; which broke the harmony so lovingly born among the family half an hour before. Peter said he might at least stay home this one evening, on his birthday, and Noonie was exhausted enough to murmur that he never took time to sit down and *talk* to them, after all the work she'd gone to, but if that was how he felt about—why let—and if it meant no more than— still, the boys *had* had their supper, the party supper was at five- thirty . . .

Wayne was there, and said it was just so he could give Don his present, it wasn't much, so he hadn't brought it here to the house.

Don told him never mind, to go on home, he'd see him tomorrow. Wayne thanked Mrs. Rush for the party, went out, got on his bike, and rode as far as the nursery, and paused there, sitting his saddle, and hating the change over everything in the big house.

In a few minutes, Donald came out the back door with his new rifle, got on his bike, and rode along the sidewalk past the evergreen nursery. Wayne wheeled around to join him, calling in a loud whisper.

"Can you come?"

"Y'p."

"Is it all right?"

"I guess so."

"Gee, I'm sorry."

"We simply have to be superior to disturbances of that kind."

Then they both laughed with pride at this statement, and were at once together in their private world of authority and power. They charged on their bicycles, riding like the wind down the sandy dark street where the intersection lamps showed the way far ahead like diminishing stages of a tunnel.

"I can hardly wait to see the gun."

"I'll let you have it the minute we get there."

Their tires spurned the loose gravel, and sang.

Presently they were there, coming to rest under the big cottonwood out in back of the Shoemakers' house. Wayne got off his saddle, but Donald didn't, so he waited. But Donald said nothing. What he wanted to do was apologize for the trying episode at his own house. He was so happy to be away from it that he felt guilty, and thought he could fix it up if he said something to Wayne. But that was not possible after all, for it would seem disloyal.

The evening was chilly, they shivered, turned and saw the moon beginning its ride up from behind the mountains to the east, on the mesa. It would be fully spring before long. This was simply such a moment as they would remember forever; the pungent cold night smelling deeply of new leaves on a wind from the loamy river; the heavy rise of the thick old cottonwood trunk from the swept bare clay of the back yard; the bower of leaves and stars overhead as the branches opened and grew so slender and airy; the wonderful, common moon which they had known for so long in thoughtless mystery; the sense of home in the yard, the street, the town, the plains, and each other.

"I sneaked out," said Donald, finally. "I'll go back soon. I had to see what you had for me."

"Come on in, it isn't much.—But it *belongs*."

They went into the back door of the canvas house. There was another surprise waiting for Donald. It was Willa Shoemaker, who had taken this evening off instead of her regular Wednesday, to be there when Wayne brought Donald for the second birthday celebration. She had heard them ride into the yard, and had lighted the candles on the cake she'd made. The *Spirito Santo* was hotting with a windy fire and trembling on its cast iron claws like a tremendous amiable dog. She hugged Donald and wished him a happy birthday, and he blushed with unbearable guilt and delight at this party. They were all excited, she most of all, and proud of the event and her family's contribution to it. Wayne went to the sewing machine in the corner and from the top drawer he took a small package which he thrust at Donald.

"Here it is, and happy birthday, Noddie."

It was two boxes of .22 ammunition.

They talked about it then for some time, while they ate the cake and the ice cream Mrs. Shoemaker had ready for them. The rifle lay on the table between them, shining in the kerosene lamplight. They both spoke animatedly but often without making sense, Mrs. Shoemaker thought, smiling over them behind her newspaper in the corner. She almost wished now that she had invited Doctor and Mrs. Rush to the party, too, there was certainly enough food for them all in ordinary portions. She reflected that she had little enough chance to *entertain*, working as she did all day and, seemed, all night.

Her thoughts took flight comfortably.

She saw them come, what charming people, she had always liked the Rushes, our children are such friends, do come in, Martha, here're the Rushes, come say hello to them, my, what is that that smells so delicious, why that is my famous fricasseed chicken which I know you'll enjoy, my mother back in Michigan taught me the recipe, you add just a pinch of curry powder, how handsome Doctor Rush is, some people wouldn't think so, but I do, shall we sit down? Doctor, you here on my right, it does seem such a long time since we've had a chance to *talk*, everybody is so busy . . . The daydream was a mixture of the facts of this little house and the enormous resources of the Harvey House dining room, and her vision tickled her with its outlandishness as much as it comforted her with its wishes.

"And yet, I'll bet, if I asked them, they'd come," she thought, coming back with a humorous frown to the present.

When the ice cream and cake were gone, the boys insisted that she pull up to the table with them to play the card game of Authors; and all three of them took pleasure in the succession of faces on the cards, famous to them out of their schoolbooks. At the end of the game, Donald said,

"Here's Washington Irving," and made a face.

"Here's Emerson!" cried Wayne.

"Bryant!"

"Who's this!"—with a scowl and a mustache made from a curled-up lip.

"Mark Twain!"

The stove was quieter. The mica in the poop-deck panes nicked with a little sound of cooling. It began to feel late. The party was over. Wayne rode halfway home with Donald, and then added an extra block because of the birthday.

IV

After the birthday party, late at night, Peter awoke to hear Noonie weeping, and when he asked her what was the matter, she answered that it was one of her headaches, the pain was unbearable, and made her feel so dreadfully sad in addition to hurting her head so.

He got up and turned on a shaded light in the far corner of the bedroom, and she winced at the faint glow that dawned on the white wallpaper with the silver stripe in it. He went to their bathroom and mixed her a powder and brought it back. They could hear the clock downstairs in the hall, and it sounded as if it were walking slowly, rocking from heel to heel, up and down the polished hardwood floor, all night long.

"Here, drink this. You'll fall asleep."

She wanly shook her head.

"It'd only make me more nervous."

"Nonsense.—Come on, Noonie."

She turned away.

She put her fingers over her eyes.

She was exhausted looking, and the petulant suffering in her face reached out and touched him. He had a thrust of desire at her white and fainting prettiness, with such shadows around the eyes, and at the same time, he wanted to strike her.

He loathed the weakness that fed upon itself which he had gradually come to admit in her.

He bitterly conjugated "to love" in his thoughts, and he wanted to shake her by her white, lovely shoulders until she should cast away the headache and the futility which had produced it, and begin to live on being a woman again, instead of on the dreams of fear and disdain which had seemed to be her growing substitute for feeling and thought.

But he simply stood by her bed, looking down at her, scowling almost professionally, and controlling himself with his habit of lumping the muscles of his jaws.

It would do no good, he reflected, if he added his anger to a situation already without much sense.

In a moment his perverse hatred left him, and he took her hand, and squeezed it, and she let him do so without looking at him.

"Look at me, Noonie," he murmured, and she came around at him with her eyes which were dark and mysterious to gaze upon. She saw him ruddy, his hair tangled and his eyes dancing brightly, his nightclothes outlandishly youthful with broad stripes, heavily wrinkled from sleeping in them, and he was a warm presence beside her, and his dearness smote her out of the years in which she had failed him, and her guilt, her intolerable burden of refusing him his children, made her want to take him in her arms and forgive herself over and over through his love.

But her head throbbed and her mouth was rueful, and she believed he was full, and justly so, of silent reproach. So now out of unworthiness, she lost once again, between them both, the thing they both desired.

"I must remember," he said to himself, watching her eyes kindle with these thoughts, and then stream with tears again, "I must remember that weakness can visit anyone. What if I judged here, at home, the very thing I try not to judge anywhere else?"

He patted her arm, and tucked the satin covering up to her ears, and went to turn off the light. She was proud of the bedroom, its crystal lamps on her dressing table, the silvery elegance of the wallpaper, the soft white fur rugs thrown over the morning-glory blue carpet, the long mirrored doors, the clouds of filmy curtains at the bay window that looked over the street.

As soon as the light was off, he knew that he was wide awake. He didn't need much sleep anyway, and was used to being called during the night. He rubbed his head and stood in the darkness of the room a second, and she listened for what he was doing.

"What?" she said, apprehensively, as he didn't move.

"Nothing. I think I'll go out on your porch and read a little while. I'm not sleepy."

"Now I've kept you from going back to sleep."

"No-no. It doesn't matter.—Get to sleep yourself, Noonie. I'll be quiet coming in."

He put on his bathrobe, a richly habitual garment that she often said was a disgrace, it was so old and rubbed, and went to her sunporch and closed the door and then switched on the lamp. He found heaps of magazines on little glass tables, and piles of mail, circulars and advertisements and booklets which she had sent for by clipping and filling out coupons from her women's magazines. He smiled at such evidence, and sat down on her gray satin long chair, and took up one of the magazines she had left there. It was long after midnight, by the way he felt, if that was any way to tell, and he began to turn the large colorful pages quizzically. What a world of health it was! How everybody smiled in the illustrations! What pretty girls, all of them exactly alike, what modest and muscular men, all of them brothers! Here his wife sat day after day, living, with such innocent companions, the risks of rivalry, the penalties of misunderstanding, the rewards of virtue. He began to read one of the stories, it was well enough written, it moved easily, he knew every moment what was coming; but as he read, he seemed to perceive Noonie between the lines, and his heart began to burn at the pity of her life, and its search for answers here, in the lifeless conventions of these pages.

Poor Noon, he mused, closing his eyes, the happy ending can't be handed to you, I'd do it if I could. It's worth more than half-a-dollar, anyway. *Anyway,* you can't buy it.

XI · PERSONAGES

I

The next time he went to see Mrs. Foster, he had a pile of books, some of the Spanish letters of old days, reports from early American venturers, and a volume called *The Western Attorney,* written by a young Missourian of the 1850's, Elias Gray, who had come over the Santa Fe Trail to serve the Territory of New Mexico as assistant to the United States Attorney.

"Now you can begin to get some sense of the past, because the settled life of our time has made hardly a scratch on the spaces here. You can have the sense of how things really were, for those older struggles."

"I was saying to Judy only yesterday that you do really get the most extraordinary sensation, sometimes, of stepping from one time into another, when you go poking around the country."

"I know. I have felt it for years. The land itself keeps telling us."

"Yet I could not say how."

"Nor could I. I only know that when I find evidences of how other men, older men, in forgotten times, loved the land and worked here, I am confirmed in what I feel now, in my own time."

She then said something which startled him.

"Are you anything of an artist? I mean, do you draw, or paint, or try to write down how you see things?"

"Why, no.—But this will possibly amuse you, and it may even make you think I am pretty conceited. But I have always had the feeling that I *could* paint, I mean that I have always *seen* things exactly as I could *fix* them, for good. Some days it seems to me that everything has a crystal clarity, and that I have too. And I say to myself that if I had time, I would make pictures of everything that appealed to me. I don't see how the job could be much more difficult or skillful than what I do up at the hospital in the operating room."

"Provided you *see,*" said she, "I don't see why you couldn't either."

"Why? Why did you ask?" he said.

"Why, simply that I get the impression that you *do* see as an artist. You have the kind of respect for things that an artist has. A sort of mixture of goodness and yet a sort of detachment from formal morality. And I think you see, and get so much from, the past, that it makes you full of all kinds of little head starts on understanding the present."

"Well! this is all news to me. But if you get that impression, I am of course flattered and glad.—How do you get it: are *you* an artist?"

They both looked a little surprisedly at each other. They had never made plain between them how little they knew of each other; and yet they felt intimate. They both knew what it meant; they both told the truth with their eyes, if not their lips.

"Oh, yes," she said, offhandedly, "I write, now and then, there is no virtue in it, but then one has nothing to say as to whether or no. —I sound like something in Mother Goose."

He had to go. He left her the books, and said they would talk them over when she'd had time to read them. He thought she looked "hard" when she spoke of writing, and he wondered why.

II

It was Noonie who told him really who Mrs. Foster was.

She said that here for weeks they'd had a celebrity in town, and nobody knew it, and he asked who. She said the novelist Mary Carmichael was here, was staying in that large rambling log house on the hill, and the public library was having a run on her books. Noonie went to the library one day and the librarian told her that Miss Carmichael was in town, was writing a new book, had come to find high air, sunshine, and peace, and would undoubtedly produce another best seller right here and everybody in some splendid if unknown way would share in the virtue of that local act.

Peter was dumfounded.

He felt sold out.

He had heard—who had not?—of Mary Carmichael, but he never had connected "Mrs. Carmichael Foster" with her.

Noonie said that Mrs. Foster was a "divorced" name. Carmichael was her maiden name, and when a woman was divorced, she kept her husband's last name, and used her own maiden name, that is, if she was fashionable. She was delighted and eager about Mrs. Foster's fashionableness. She had found out that Mrs. Foster lived with little accents of style and circumstance quite unusual in the town as it then was. She kept a small car and had a chauffeur who had brought it from New York. Her cook had come with her, and a housemaid. She had a secretary along, too, who typed her manuscripts every day.

This explained Miss Bridges.

Peter felt an unreasonable want to hear no more. He hated hearing anything about Mrs. Foster from Noonie. It posed them too closely side by side in his thoughts. But Noonie was fascinated and went on.

She said they said Mrs. Foster was seeing no one. The librarian had tried to call, when the news got around, as it *would,* but Mrs. Foster, or Miss Carmichael, as you liked, had sent word that she was "seeing no one," having come to take a rest cure, but sent an inscribed copy of one of her books to the library, and in general tried to indicate that she was grateful for interest, if unable to meet it with gestures on her own part.

The librarian said Mrs. Foster saw no one but her doctor.

"Yes," said Peter, "Willie Treddinger sent her to me."

"What! to you!" cried Noonie. "You never told me."

"Well, Noon, (a), I didn't know who she was, and (b), as you know, I never say anything about my cases, even here at home."

"That's true. Well: anyway:"

She said they lived with great style in the log house. Mary Carmichael was worth mints of money, from the way her books sold, and the gossip around town was that she disliked the way the house was, and the dishes, and all the *things,* so much, that at incredible expense, she had had the whole place done over, and had barrels and barrels of china and boxes of silver sent out, and kept a whole flock of expensive and delicate dogs, and in general lived like an actress or an opera singer, with fresh flowers by the dozens, every day, and long distance calls and heaps of telegrams, and so forth and so on.

"Don't you think it would be nice if I called," said Noonie, "inasmuch as you're her doctor, and we all know Willie?"

"Do as you like, but I don't believe I would, if she really wants privacy. She never said anything about it to me."

"Isn't she *well* enough?"

"She's well enough to do what she likes, but if she wants to be left alone, I think that's that."

"Of course. I certainly wouldn't *throw* myself at her.—You'd die if you could hear the kind of thing everyone is saying about her. —They say she is simply exquisite, a blonde, and that she could make a fortune in the movies if she wanted to, and that Douglas Fairbanks offered her the leading part in one of his pictures, and she refused. Imagine."

"She's very pretty," he said, with a heavy heart, because something was expected of him. "I don't see why the town should lose its head over her, to quite this extent."

But he saw the animation in Noonie's face which everyone else would have, who made of Mrs. Foster's fame and presence a really pleasurable event.

III

He went out presently, feeling cheated, somehow, and yet he laughed at himself for feeling that way. He had always felt she was a very special person, and to find out why he had felt it, in its common terms, from the legitimately interested prattle of his wife, made him conclude that he was a graceless clod. He had asked her if she were an artist. She had probably thought he knew all along who she was. She might consider him the worst of all snobs, the snob who makes a point of ignoring in any relationship with an eminent or gifted person the very gift and the eminence it yielded. He blushed at the idea. He hated any distortion of honest interest. He felt that Noonie was far more natural now in her cheerful outpourings about Mrs. Foster than he was in his suddenly readjusted view of her.

Well, anyway, it revealed to him the true nature of the attraction she had for him.

He said to himself that if she was a famous novelist, and a public figure, and a local tradition already, then he would excuse himself from her orbit in the future. He had enough to do without pursuing her. There was a kind of bitter peacefulness in deciding that. He was spared a harder decision later on, he felt, by making this one now.

He turned his car toward Old Town, where he wanted to go to see old Don Hilario Ascarete, who in his late eighties had reached a kind of tentative survival that could afford to deal only with concerns in life which had connotations of eternity.

IV

Old Town lay down by the river bottoms. Its streets wandered like the ditches that fed the cool green fields. Peter often wondered whether the original lanes had not indeed followed the ditches, which all year long needed to be traveled to supervise repairs, and see that robber farmers had not broken the ditch banks to conduct water wrongfully to fields that were not allotted irrigation. It was very possible that a hundred years ago, and more, when there were no streets, but only the Plaza, the town network was made up of the scattered houses, and the paths which connected them came less from design than from habit. So a pastoral town never had the grid pattern of a railroad town, where everything was laid out at right angles to the tracks.

The Old Town was made of the very same substance upon which it stood: the river earth, adobe. Walls, streets, barriers, were all of the pale dried mud which even in the sunshine always seemed to have the palest lilac shadow of color over it.

Some of the buildings were older than the oldest giant cottonwoods that crowded the low roofs and the wandering walls. They were so old, Peter thought, that they seemed eroded rather than just worn by human occupancy. A corner of a house would look like an old man's shoulder, bent and drooping from carrying the weight of years; but still vital with duty's residue. The ever-renewing process of plastering with mud after hard rains gave those houses a sort of organic life, in which they put forth new parts when old ones wore away. Nothing delighted Peter more than to see, in the early summer after a violent rainy spring, a little colony of weeds and grass growing out of the tops of adobe walls or earthen roofs. It seemed to him like a compassionate arching over of the earth's life, to cover as well as support the life of man. It was not a gloomy parable to him, a living grave; it was evidence of the vitality on which all living creatures drew mindlessly, most of the time; but which, he was certain without knowing just how or why, could be explored and used in conscious self-renewal by men if they would only look for their own true natures and find peace within them.

But of the complexity of those natures, he had of course seen plenty of evidence in his professional life.

Peter brought his big car along the dried ruts of the road running past the Old Town church. On his right was a long wall of a house that looked like the road itself lifted on edge and rising and falling in roadside wavers with the contour of the ground. It had deep boxed windows. There was a double door of aged paneled wood from which all paint had long since peeled. It must be one of the oldest houses around here. Don Hilario would know.

He turned into a lane across a field, and came to the Ascarete house, which was set on the broomed packed earth of a courtyard. The house made a right angle. One side cast a long triangle of shadow on the other side. Where the triangle hit the ground, old Don Hilario was sitting with his back to the warmed wall. Crouched over his stick, his knees brought up by his middle because he was sitting on a low bench, he resembled a votive clay figure in a funerary deposit such as were brought out of the pyramids of Mexico. But when he saw his visitor, he pulled his hat off across his face and half arose from his bench. Incomplete and crippled as it was, the gesture had the politeness of real pleasure in it. His voice was like a broken old tune-pipe, a country flute. He spoke in Spanish, and Peter answered in Spanish.

"Why, how delightful, my young friend the Doctor. Come in, come in, sit down, sit down."

"You're looking fine this morning. What a pretty place to sit and look out over the meadows to the river over there and the sandhills way beyond."

"I've been following some blackbirds that sat up there in our tree. They went over the field and tried another tree. Since then they've never made up their minds. Back and forth, back and forth. Like my grandchildren."

This was a joke. His tiny black eyes and the folds of wrinkled face around them were always squinting, as if to see and estimate shrewdly. His name suited him in a fascinating inner harmony. He always struck Peter as being a highly humorous man, and a very good man, essentially.

He had many children and grandchildren, and a galaxy of great-grandchildren.

"They are strangers, to me, you know?" he said to Peter, squinting.

"Who?"

"My relations.—Oh, in and out, in and out, I see them, they have no idea at all of what I know, how much I know, they come to speak to me respectfully, and I can look at the youngest ones, the boys and girls just growing up, and I can see right straight inside of them. No wonder they blush when they look into my eyes. There is nothing they do and want to do which I don't know. To forgive: this is half of life. To do: this is the other half.—Such pretty children, they come and look at me."

"I suppose they just belong to their own times, and they hurry ahead in the present."

Peter knew how the cheerful young Spanish-Americans lived with enthusiastic observance of current styles. Their repainted Fords, their soft drinks, their Saturday movies, their United States slang, exiled old Don Hilario in a fixity of the past.

"Let them go," he said, as if he were a fixed point in life, and they but wanderers. "They all have to find out that everything I have told them is true. When they are old enough to know that, they are ready to tell their own children. I have seen many things; but all you have to know are a few things."

"I want to ask you about something."

"Something to remember?"

"Possibly."

"It takes me a long time to remember, but if you will do me the favor, I'll try."

"Of course. Take as long as you like."

Don Hilario reared back and made a noiseless laugh, a little round black cave of mouth in which the joke of his having all the time in the world, with one foot in the grave, was relished by his tongue, curved up like a chicken's. This was not morbid. Going to die was like going to a party, for anybody so old and so full of what might be called death's health: peace and readiness and completion, on earth. Peter resumed.

"I would like to know all you can remember about that long house, coming down the lane, this way. That is a fine old doorway, and such deep windows.—There's a grocery store at the front end of it. You know. The Sanchez's place.—Was the house standing when you were a boy?"

Don Hilario shut his eyes. Two streams of liquid, not tears, but little runnels of sunshine strain from his weak old eyes, coursed down beside his nose.

"I will have to meditate," he said. "The next time you come back I will have it all ready for you. When I sit down to remember something, I like to have it in order. Give me some time."

He glanced up at the Doctor, an arch old look of pure nonsense. They both knew he was being contrary. But it was as if the old man had a comic propriety which meant much to him. Peter sighed with satisfaction, as if over a curing patient, and took his leave. Years ago, half a lifetime, Don Hilario had been a lawyer, a man of cultivation with a voice in affairs. He had been wealthy and had lived like a grandee. His two oldest sons, now long since dead before him, had been educated in Paris and in Spain. He had known everybody of consequence in this part of the country, and had had a voice in Territorial matters of any importance. Not many people remembered such things about him now. He didn't seem to mind. Neither did he seem bored or discontented. Only those who had never given everything at their disposal to give away, such as ideas, talent or power, ended up by being bored in their declining days, Peter decided. Anyway, the courteous privilege of past grandeur could be allowed

Don Hilario now. Out of what his imagination could dig up that would be true to the past, Don Hilario would spend weeks in making a tale for his young friend the physician. Peter thought that it was worth while from everybody's point of view. Few enough people found living value in the old man nowadays.

Book III · ADAM'S OWN LAND

XII · WANDERING BARKS

I

They did meet at the library that evening. Martha brought her books back, and left them at the loan desk, exchanging a word with the librarian who was a good friend of hers. Then she turned around and surveyed the reading room with a deliberately hard look, standing something like a fashion figure in *Vogue,* a shoulder up, her legs elongated by a feeling of elegance, her mouth faintly disdainful with expression and brilliant rouge, which she had put on after leaving home. She wore short white gloves which made her bare arms look brown. She was trying to look much older, and independent, and private. Her second self was alive within her again, that smaller girl who seemed to tremble within all her limbs, and make her heart seem low and heavy, until he should come. Like a lady of great fashion, indifferent to onlookers, she drew out her heavy bone-rimmed glasses and put them on, looking around the room for him.

He came up to her from behind.

He had been standing among the bookstacks watching her. His face was furiously red, which made his eyes flash with blue and white light. He imagined everyone in the reading room was watching them. He took her elbow with two fingers, which she disliked for its tentative, clumsy possession, and without a word, steered her to a table in the far corner where nobody else was, and sat down with her at a yellow oak table.

He was dry in the mouth. All his street-corner lore left him. She could neither look at him boldly with her rouged mouth ready, nor greet him idly. Their constraint made their hearts sink. It was a mess, a mistake, he was a year younger, she was an impostor, made up like that, trying to be older than she was, when they both knew that inside, she was a child yet, and he was only a thickening cub with dreams in his eyes that were merely embarrassing and had best be lived through as quickly as possible.

What would save them?

He put his hand out on the table, and she looked at it; the look of it restored her; she took off her glove and put her own hand beside his; it was a fragmentary portrait of their two selves; and in a moment, he covered her hand, hiding the neat, small, clever, white hand with his large mild hand, which felt warm over hers, as if the sunshine which had tanned the relief map of his veined fingers and hand-back were still in his flesh.

She remembered that looking at his fingers had first made her feel so much.

Now she began to blush, and he smiled, losing his extra color.

"Now I am glad I came," she said.

"So am I."

"I nearly didn't."

"I's afraid of that."

"But I couldn't go back on my word like that."

"I knew you couldn't."

"We'd better not hold hands here."

"Let them look."

"No, someone might know us."

"O.K."

So they separated, and searched for things to say.

It was possible for them to smile knowingly, because they knew that boys and girls on dates always went somewhere where it was dark, a patch of grass in the park where the bandstand was, or someone's automobile, to make love. They had kissed other people at dances.

They knew what to do.

But it wasn't what they wanted to do now; not that same way; they felt in their bones that if they went out now, one of two things might happen; either too little would come of it, or too much. It was too soon. They had some hovering wisdom that respected what they were feeling more than *that*.

And yet they knew too, that until they felt each other, and drank from one another's words, and heard one another's lost breath, they would be miserable.

Tomorrow night, maybe; the next night, perhaps; perhaps he could get the car from his father; they would then be free in a private world. Meantime, let them simply look.

II

Talking was discouraged in the reading room. One or two older people had apprehensively stared at them as if to frown on their first attempts at conversation. They whispered a couple of commonplaces. Martha looked around. There was a bookshelf with casual volumes in it, selected for browsing by the library staff. She nudged Bun, and he went over to the case, and got several books. They spent the first evening of their passion leafing through books, sitting side by side, commenting in croaking half-voice on whatever struck them as interesting. They were picture books . . . one of them contained colored photographs of scenery in the Southwest; another held plates of art masterpieces from the museums of Europe, where they met their counterparts in painted lovers by the grand masters, and found no reality at all in arrested attitudes of passion or in the elaborate nudities of heroic bodies; and another volume was an edition of Shakespeare's Sonnets, with illustration for each poem, in black and white lines, which made no sense to them. But when they came to this book, Bun took charge with some vitality, turned the pages until he came to something, and then put his finger down on certain lines, and looked at her direct.

She looked back, never caring if she ever saw the printed words, for the look on his face, which was all the poem she cared to read. But he insisted with a nod, and when she bent her head down, he saw in her look what she had seen in his; and a rush of something in his blood made him swallow, he widened his thighs apart, and put his hand over his hair, and bent down with her to look at the printed words which for some reason he had never forgotten when his grandfather's books had first been unpacked, years ago. He must have been only eleven or twelve at the time. The big wooden boxes had come from Kansas City, after the old man's death. The day the boxes were opened, Bun had watched everything as it was unpacked, and the one book it had been his fortune to clutch for a few minutes, right away, was a much pencil-marked copy of Shakespeare's works.

"It is the star to every wandering bark."

That one line was all he retained, but he suddenly knew what it meant, after a childhood of confused, attractive images established within him by the words.

III

So their first evening together was prim: leaving the library shortly before closing time at nine-thirty, they walked down the hill toward the tracks, and passed the YMCA, and stopped at the Mint Confectionery for some ice cream. Then he put her on a bus that would take her to the corner near her house, far out on the edge of town, and after watching the bus turn the corner, out of sight, with a sort of a *lump,* he guessed it was, in his throat, he put his hands in his pants pockets and walked down the street to the White Elephant where the click of billiard balls sounded past the open door, and went in to see what he could see. But it looked curiously sordid to him, the same scene where he had often breathed the smoky air with delight, and he felt now older than those boys and men bending over the green tables which were islands of light in a general gloom. Smiling absently at the proprietor, he turned around and started home.

He sighed deeply, as if something within him had awakened to make demands which he could not recognize, or appease.

Then a memory of his married sister's baby appeared to him for no reason that he could pin down, and how he'd held the child, and seen its nodding face so near his own, and how, holding the baby under its arms, he had let it trundle and dance on his lap, and at the memory of that gleeful striving without aim, Bun turned hot with what felt like joy and shame both, and entirely bemused at intimations of his next time of life, he began to run easily along the dark sidewalk, observing beautiful form, and once again becoming a power at the muscular art he knew better than anything else, so far.

XIII · THE DESTROYERS

I

Around ten o'clock Saturday morning, Wayne and Donald set out for the mesa on their bicycles. It was a warm spring day, like summer itself, and they had summertime in their veins, so that they had no idea of what they wanted to do, but had to go and do something. They spoke very little as they rode across town and approached the viaduct. Don carried his rifle across his legs. As they crossed Silver Avenue, they began to feel invisible, and squinted relentlessly at the sights of the streets. They could hear the trains working on the tracks over to the left two blocks away. They suddenly had a surge of delight in anything at all. They bent double and began to pump hard; their threadlike spokes made a silvery music and twirled with the blaze of sunshine.

A couple of blocks away they could see the old red sooty viaduct begin to rise between the buildings on the corners. One of the buildings was a bottling works. Its bricks were painted tan. Over the windows were carved cornices of blue stone. Built long ago, the edifice had an antique dignity. The boys always thought of it as a château, from a resemblance it had to a picture in their geography book. Only châteaux really had towers like the one that rose from the corner of the bottling works, a tin dome with a wrought-steel lightning rod and miniature dormer windows, where pigeons lived in irrelevant splendor. The second-story windows were blind with boards behind their dusty glass. The boys vaguely believed that suites of rooms elegantly furnished were hidden there, where crimes of passion, as they declared unknowingly, had been committed, by Monsieur le Vicomte, a generally useful character whom they had distilled out of the novels of Alexandre Dumas. Actually, years before, the building had been put up by a Missourian "from back East" to house himself and his family on the second floor; while below, he set out a line of general merchandise. He was a rich man for his time, and of polite tastes. What the château tower stood for, in him, cost him his fortune. As a little railroad town years ago, Albuquerque was not ripe for grandiose investments. Business moved along other streets. The Missourian sold his building and went back home. What he did and who he was Donald and Wayne had never heard of. "History" had nothing to do with *their* lives.

They charged around the corner past the château and began the ascent of the viaduct. It rose across the tracks. At one point of the climb, the mountains far across the mesa seemed, if you squinted, to be exactly on top of the viaduct's highest level. It was another of those days when the engine steam was golden with sunlight, and the sun was hot and comfortable on the bare head and the leather-jacketed back. The shadows of all the things they looked at were sweeps of rich black, and the lights of the day were sparkling with color in everything. Up on the mesa they could see the sand devils spinning in miniature whirlwinds before the pale-violet screen of the rock-crumpled mountains. Sweeping their sight from left to right, or north to south, they encompassed the immense plain and longed to be on it, lost and secret masters of such land.

They gained the summit of the viaduct, and saw there again the bolt which they had declared to be the one indispensable in its structure. They slowed down. The warm wind blew through their hair. Donald turned his hot black and white gaze on Wayne.

"There it is."

"I see it."

"I believe it is time to make an end of this wretched viaduct."

"Perhaps you are right. Certainly they could not follow us if it went."

"We would be miles away by the time they repaired it, or found another pass."

"It will take perfect timing."

"I have a perfect sense of timing. I know exactly how much time to allow between the last turn of the nut and the escape."

"They could see us from the château."

"Ha-ha. Much good that would do them. The tower stairs are steep, and we should be gone before they reached the courtyard. I should be willing to notify them first, even, and challenge them to prevent us."

"You recall that it was my calculations which betrayed this weak central point in the structure?"

"Indeed I do, mon cher confrère. You shall be decorated for your discovery.—Well?"

"Let us dismount."

They left their bicycles and bent down over the bolt.

"Seventy thousand pounds of frugal pressure, as I estimate it."

"Correct. I calculate that twelve turns will bring the last thread of the nut to the top. I believe that the adjustment will be so delicate that the least vibration to follow will release the nut and the bridge will fall."

"In other words, the very attempt of anyone to follow will bring it down?"

"Precisely, my dear Doctor."

"Ah, Monsieur le Vicomte, allow me to congratulate you."

"And now?"

"To work."

They pantomimed the reversal of the nut.

Their eyes were scowling and glowing, and their whole belief in their drama depended upon the intentness and the technique of their actions. They never mistook the imaginary for the real; they interchanged them deliberately.

"There!—Quick: careful!"

"Mount!"

They flew down the other side of the viaduct with the wind in their mouths, and as they reached the street, they paused and turned, and making with their mouths the sounds of wrench and crash and crack and splinter, they completed their imaginary destruction of the viaduct by agreeing that it was falling, it was breaking up, clouds of coal dust and slivers and drifted dirt were bellying up into the lovely hot sky.

And then for a moment they were abstracted and they gazed idly at the street, the occasional car going past, people down the block, without seeing them.

II

Then they started awake again, and turned their wheels around and headed up the long hill before them at whose summit they would find the mesa. They were hungry but did not know what for, and perhaps would never know. Long assuaged by play and dream, like the affair of the viaduct, they owned powers that were rousing toward acts.

They gained the crest; rose through the scattered streets of the town way out there where the wind blew so close and the tumbleweeds danced so free, and they paused to look back. Below them in the golden clarity lay the town of Albuquerque; far at the end of its streets went the river. They could see the silvery skeins of the water that took up so little of the wide sandy river bed, which was edged with the fragrant boskage of the *algodones*, the cottonwoods, so fresh and green in the baking forenoon.

"I wisht we had gone to the river instead. It is warm enough to go swimming."

"We'll go next Saturday."

"The current has changed the bank where we always go, did you know that? It moved right in under old man Rhodes's fence and took the ground away. There are the posts and the wires just hanging there."

"So much for old man Rhodes."

Above the river rose the sandy cliffs of the other side, and then the sand plains, and then the three volcanoes with their blackened cones that powerfully suggested the fires that had flowed there so long ago, and had died into rocky ash and turned to sand.

"Where shall we go now?"

"Let's ride out to the ranch."

"It's too far."

"No it isn't. We can eat our lunch there. We can look for snakes. You've got your .22."

"O.K."

They rode out the highway that reached through the mountains. Halfway there, they took a straggle of sand toward the left that made a lane through the dusty sweet-smelling desert bushes. Once on the mesa, which looked so flat from below in the town, they found all sorts of variations in the levels of the plain; riding up and down long hills, now buried in cool drifts of blue shadow, now emerging into sunlight where the rancher's road wound along the easiest slopes of the shallow hills.

III

Before long they could see the abandoned ranch. It consisted of a single-room dwelling of adobe and the long chicken house out in back, with its face made of dozens and dozens of little square panes of glass set in wood. The buildings stood on a raised table of wind-swept ground. Long easy slopes fell away to the common level of the plain in all directions. It was like an open stage, standing under the sunlight in the fragrance of noon on the mesa. Tumbleweeds were blown to the house and the long shed. Miniature dunes of sand swept up to the adobe walls. It was a forlorn place, yet to the boys it represented a rich property of which they had the control. Neither of them could remember it as it had been when Wayne's father was alive. If they could have recalled how it was then, they'd have been obliged to admit that it was a foolish venture, this chicken ranch, way out here away from everything and everybody, and no wonder the widow had been unable to sell or lease it when her husband died. She hadn't been out to inspect her property for years. She always thought of it as a valuable resource, and felt earnestly secure in the hope that if there were ever a costly calamity in the family, why, they could "realize" something on the ranch to tide them over. In time, she came to view the worthless investment as a piece of far-sightedness on her husband's part, and would reflect devotedly that "Daddy was a very very clever man when he bought that place out on the mesa, never know when it'll come in handy." Meantime, it was left to the wind that blew away its adobe edges until they were rounded and flaked off in the drying heat.

But here the boys had a sense of property. Here they were alone in the midst of the teeming plain. The humble shed and the house could be a palace or a fortress to them; and after toiling so infinitesimally over the baking distance, they would have all the pleasures of reaching haven when they came to Mr. Shoemaker's investment.

They always watched for rattlesnakes, having heard years ago that there was a snake pit on the property somewhere. How far their land went nobody could say, because there were no fences. The boys were free to own as far as they could see.

Today, they set their wheels in the shadow of the house. The door was of solid boarding, and was padlocked.

"I didn't get the key from Mother."

"We won't want to go in, anyway."

They looked in through the window at the shadowed end of the house. It was all there, safe, a table with an oilcloth top, a broken rocker, a rusty stove. The other window was covered with tacked burlap on the inside.

"Shall we lunch yet?"

"Let's find some snakes first."

They put their bicycle padlocks on their wheels, and set out, walking to the east. Ahead of them the mesa was furrowed with lines of blue shadows from the high clouds, which made the ground look like a series of parallel valleys. They would imagine that in the next few minutes they would reach the nearest band of shadow; but they never did. The bright sun was on them all day.

They kicked up a little dust as they went, and they crushed the plants they walked over; they breathed the dusty fragrance of bruised desert grass, it smelled warm, part of the day, reminding them of what they had always known and owned of the country. They felt hollow with pleasure at the unconscious reminders of their freedom, their triumph of existence this near the earth.

They longed for a sight of the snake that was their superb foe.

"I believe we are coming into snake country now."

"Come on, we'll go more slowly."

They bent double, and went ahead peering at the roots of all the grassy clumps where in the noontime shadow they *might* see the clay itself begin to move and flow across their path, emerging from the cool blue into their dazzled vision as the clay-colored diamondback.

They were full of hope and yet of dread. Today for the first time they were armed for such a hunt.

"You'd better load 'er up."

"She is."

"Then cock 'er."

Click.

"May I try one, if we see anything?"

"S'sure."

Their teeth were almost chattering in the baking day.

"There's one!"

They went to their knees, staring, with their mouths open. But it was only a prairie dog's movement which they had seen, as the little thing scampered down into his hole. But their hearts beat and their spit dried as if they had seen the great snake itself; and how they viewed it in their thoughts came forward out of a long darkness of inherited fear and desire, so that each was a young Adam, hunting for the symbol he was at the mercy of in Eden.

Presently they came up to their crouching walk again and went ahead through the hard-caked dust of the ground.

"Listen!"

They froze and cocked their heads; but what had sounded like the first flicker of the rattles was the beginning of the upward grind of a locust, saluting the hot zenith with its song.

They grinned at each other and nodded, and went on. They felt superbly fit. The very agony of their caution made them sure of their prowess and their hunger for danger and destruction.

"There is a hollow place, look at the shadow on the side of the rise. I'll bet that's it."

"We'll come down on it from above. We could shoot right into it and beat a retreat back over the hill."

"If we had to."

They hurried in a wide circle to the top of the low rise where the silvery heat wavered in the air and made the deep-blue sky seem to glisten slowly. They had a bowel-hollowing excitement and were perfectly sure they had found the pit. They came down on their bellies very slowly and silently, looking on all sides for the enemy, for this was just such a hillside as tempted him to lie in the speckled shade of a hot sweet-smelling tuft of dusty grass. They must not dislodge any of the white alkali clay that was caked into little clods like chalky stones, for they might then roll down the shallow slope into the mouth of the snake pit, and stir up that terrible music which at one of its stages did sound so much like the shelled song of the locust.

IV

Now they were so close that they had the flaking crust of the ground in their nostrils as they breathed. Right there below them was the pit. They could see its downward rim, and the bushes that grew there. There seemed even an old pathlike place which led down into the pit from the other side. The shadow hung immediately under them in the stand of noon. Tumbleweeds had blown into the pit, and the sand was modeled by the wind into body-looking shapes.

"Listen:" whispered Wayne.

They laid their cheeks down on the ground and closed their eyes to hear. There was a slight stir down below them, a whisper of movement, they could feel a faint hot breeze wander over their faces and wrists, and could not decide between sound and movement as to what they heard and felt.

There was that little faint hushed whisper or slide or scratch of something moving down there, and now they were terrified. They opened their eyes and looked at each other, and knew it. Donald's brown jaw was shaking his whole head because he had his teeth clenched. Wayne knew exactly how he was feeling, and why, and that they both agreed on what to do, regardless of how they felt.

"Let's go," he whispered.

They had one more pause for the savor of courage, and then more scared than they had ever been in their lives, they nevertheless scrambled around the edge of the pit until they could look straight down to behold what it held. When they saw, their eyes began to smart, and they felt their hearts beating for the first time, in big, slowing thumps. Tangled at the bottom of the sand pit was an old flag of newspaper which the hot quiet wind was moving against the weeds. There was nothing else there but the rounded sandy beds made by the sheltering rim, and the shadow of the miniature cliff lay there coolly.

Wayne slid down into the pit and took a box of matches from his pocket. He lighted the paper and danced back to the edge. The fire caught the tumbleweeds, and blew upward with hollow fury making black oily smoke in which the silvery heat and the orange flames spiraled together. It was like the relief they both felt, and it also burned away their disappointment.

"I bet they can see this smoke from the city!" said Wayne.

V

"I haven't shot my rifle yet."

"Save it for something good."

They started back. A vagrant noon wind was whipping up around them. They were nearer now to the sand whirlwinds which danced at freedom on the plain.

"I'm hungry."

"So am I.—Let's get our lunch."

The long shed of the chicken house concealed their bicycles from them, to which their lunch boxes were strapped. They hoped everything was all right, and still there, and began to trot toward the two buildings which from a distance were like little blocks of hot blue shadow set up on a disc of pouring light. In a moment, by silent agreement, they fell into a run, and raced across the undulating plain. They got hotter and hotter, and when they came around the chicken house, they were panting. The bicycles were there, safe, the boys stood in the enormous quiet grinning, and the wind gusted at their feet. One of the sand devils of which they had seen many all morning as they had toiled over the mesa came shooting dust ahead of itself and while they stood transfixed to see how close the thing would come, it came between them with a miniature blast. It funneled the dust high into the air and went shocking across the separated clumps of grass, and faced into the chicken house. There it changed its course and went rattling down the length of the shed, banging the loose panes in their faded white wooden frames. It was like a scale in music. The glass was all loose. One of the panes at the other end of the shed fell out and broke. In a second, the wind was gone. The sand devil left the earth and its funnel cloud simply drifted into the blue as a fading lift of dust.

The boys laughed at the wind, and spat the dirt out of their mouths, and rubbed their heads to free their hair of sand. They were charged, as if the whirling cone of sand had charged them electrically. Their eyes were blank and a little wild. It was the way ponies acted in funny weather, all stirred up when the wind pranked viciously down on the ground near them and screamed around in circles that would strike they never knew where.

They could smell the sweet hot ground, and they felt the sweat tickle and run inside their clothes.

"I'm going to shoot!"

"What at?"

"Anything!"

"There's a can."

"Here, you try it."

"No, it's yours."

"What'll I aim at?"

"There's a board sticking up on the chicken house."

"Hey!"

It was a command to watch. Donald set his rifle and laid his cheek down on the nut-smelling wood of the stock. He aimed at one of the panes of glass in the face of the chicken house and shot. The glass cracked and went.

"Hey!" said Wayne, but at the same time he did not know whether this was an objection. He put his hand out for the gun, and Donald gave it to him. Then he too took aim and fired and another pane of glass crashed to bits in the most instant reward. They fell on the ground on their bellies and rubbed themselves into the hot earth until they had comfortable hollows made and they set out to destroy the glass front of the empty and sand-blown shed where the glass was so loose that it rattled when the breeze blew.

An intoxicant wave of destruction swept over them. The gun cracked and the smell of the powder was like something that could make them drunk. Their faces got hot and their eyes glistened. They licked their lips and held the .22 shells in their teeth until they were ready each time. They traded the gun back and forth after each shot. It was a single-loader, the oily music of the bolt was a delight to hear, and they felt happier than they could ever remember. The glass began to lie all along the base of the shed, pale, water-colored splinters shining in the sun. They could hardly wait for their turns at the rifle. As long as they had any shells they must continue to break the glass. Their sense of power was a seasonal force; it had so long been latent; it was now so free.

VI

They knew all the time that what they were doing was wrong. Their eyes told each other that when they looked to exchange the rifle. It was clear to them that they were destroying something that cost plenty of money, and that did not belong to them, and whose loss would trouble someone very much.

They fired and the glass crashed. The recoil of the gun was like a blow in return for what they did.

But they knew exquisite freedom in the act, and they went down the rows and rows of the little square panes until in a surfeit of wreckage, they were finished, and ready to think again, and not a whole piece of glass remained in the faded wooden squares of the chicken house.

They rolled over on their backs and stared at the sky. They still had the electric taste of the copper shell cases and the oily feeling of the lead bullets in their mouths.

"We're out of shells, about."

"Y'p."

"Do you like the little ol' gun?"

"She's a beauty."

"I wish we had something else to shoot at."

But this was not true, they both knew it, and said no more. They tasted folly now. They were shy about looking at each other, or the wreckage they had produced. How would they ever face Mrs. Shoemaker now; and where might they ever get enough money to replace the glass; what was such fun about breaking all those panes, now that it was done? Why did they have to go and do something so stupid for? Why had it seemed so different while the gun was shooting and the smoke was drifting so blue and so sharp-smelling in the hot day on the mesa?

"Are you h-hungry?"

"Are you?"

"Oh, sort of.—Not very much."

"Neither am I."

They went over to their bicycles in the shade of the house, got on, headed back toward the highway, and returned to town. Neither of them had ever thought much before about being good or bad, they had simply behaved one way now, another then. Now they were filled with and committed to knowledge of their own acts. They spoke very little; but they were dimly tried with recognitions of how people *were,* that they had always heard about, and neither of them knew what to do about it, and each searched for himself in the criminal foolishness of the mesa, and knew obscurely that something had happened *to* him rather than that he had *done* something.

When they got near home, they slowed down to separate, and before they parted, they impulsively shook hands, to preserve their league, after disaster.

XIV · THE EMPEROR'S NEW CLOTHES

I

What was guessed about life as it went past in the streets of a small town was often wrong, and hurtfully so; but sometimes it was true, and no less hurtfully.

Noonie heard that her husband was "seeing" Mrs. Foster. The gossip was as usual rather late; for by the time it had currency, Peter had given up going to call on Mrs. Foster. But it was almost as if there were a kind of collective intuition in the people, and as if they had become aware of something almost by waking up to it. Nobody really told them. Noonie got it by hints and solicitous comments and moments of false charm in which one woman would say to another how fortunate it was for such an interesting person to be in town, and to have met the one person who could probably speak her language here.

But it was all so vague that Noonie couldn't be sure. And even if she were sure, she said to herself, how had she the right to rebuke him?

What had she given to him which she had promised so long ago in Rochester, when everything had been so gay, and even a clever and outrageous creature like Lisette Kleitz from Albany could not swerve him an inch from his path? No, no, no, stormed Noonie to her heart. She wept when she was alone. She knew that the worst was true. She would castigate herself for daring to expect him to be more true than any other man could have been, and in a humility which exhausted her by its self-punishment, she would find a certain peace at last. But it was always coming back to the realization that things were "not the same" that made her head throb with pain, and her heart rise into her mouth, and her whole life seem a shocking waste. One shred of determination she did cling to, and that was that she would never let him see that she "knew." If he ever found out that she "knew," then he would surely hate her for having no more spirit than to suffer what was going on without proclaiming her rights.

The curious mixture of truth and nonsense; suffering and illness; something sweetly staunch and at the same time feebly hateful;

brought to the situation a focus of everything about Noonie as she was at that time.

II

Peter hadn't seen Mrs. Foster for weeks. He was absorbed in forgetting all about her; the consequence was that everything reminded him of her. He had no idea of the gossip that was going around. It had gone around before about him, as it would about any other personable man who was also a physician, much in the public awareness, his car recognized everywhere, his comings and goings at all times of day and night both explainable and debatable. He was attentive to Noonie, and was surprised to see how sometimes this seemed to grieve her. (She was certain that he was concealing things by being especially sweet to her.) He was working hard. Vaguely troubled, he knew that every year had some times in it when a man didn't feel his best, or up to himself, or confident and powerful. Times like that passed. Nobody saw the effects of them. He had no patience with a human temperament he often ran up against professionally—that which demands as some sort of obscure but tyrannical right the optimum of happiness, health, or achievement, day in and day out. Many invalids crippled themselves further by their rage against fate when many of them could have accomplished a life's plenty by demanding less of life. Nobody had a *right* to happiness, he believed. Everybody had a right to try to *earn* it. He wished, if there were to be happy endings for him and his, that they be granted as the results of their own decisions. Decisions as to what to give and what to keep; what to value and what to sacrifice, the one compelling the other. Such a frame of mind reflected the position of his life now. The letter from Mrs. Foster brought back something he had given up.

III

"Dear Peter Rush,

I am now out of reading matter. You brought me the most extraordinary things, and I am hungry for more, if you have the time and the inclination to lend them. I've been working very hard, and I am sure you have too, but if you can drop in any afternoon, I'd love to take on over a passage in one of the books you left with me . . . *The Western Attorney,* by that master-prig of all time, Elias Gray. I have been hugely amused at his airs and his judgments. He came out here nearly a hundred years ago and saw everything with the sniff of a Missouri intellectual. I'd like to know whatever became of him! He is detestable, and yet he is so sure of himself that he writes quite fully and frankly of himself and the result is, I feel I know him *well*. And knowing him *well*, I cannot help liking various little bits of him. Do you ever have this odd sensation? From reading, I mean?

"I had the most casual note in the world from Dr. Treddinger, who wonders if I am prospering under your care. I do think you ought to come and tell me how I am feeling, so I can answer him properly.

"Yours sincerely,
Molly Foster."

When he folded the letter up he laughed at the fragility of certain resolves. She was vividly before him. He was still angry at her for never telling him who she was. But that meant he was cross at not having known on his own, and was just blaming *her*. He saw her repose, the white, faintly pinked cheeks, and her little mouth which she kept rouged, and which sometimes looked sad, he thought, when she was not speaking. She was so small, he remembered, when she put herself on the couch in front of her fireplace. But all this sounded very pink and white and frail and colorless if you left out her eyes. What blue fire he saw in them, deep down, the jeweled energy of thought and feeling, speaking to him, he was certain, of the same thing he had carried concealed since the very first day he'd seen her. Her eyes were large in her small face.

How on earth could he believe he knew so much about her when they'd met so little, and then spoken of everything but themselves?

He made up a package of books from his shelves way upstairs, and the day after getting her letter, he took them to her. There was every legitimate excuse for such a course; and the fact that he told that over to himself made it clear again that he was a shyster, dwelling on the plausible aspect of everything but truth.

He did make one concession to his resolve; his pique, actually. She'd said to come in any afternoon. He stopped at her house about eleven in the morning. If she were working, he would simply put the books in the hands of the Swedish maid, and leave them with a message. It was a hot morning, the light stood golden everywhere. Above the town, he could see the roofs glisten. Approaching the front door, he was stopped when Molly called to him from the shadow made by the living-room wing of the house. She was sitting in a deck chair, wearing black glasses, and she was holding a sheaf of typed pages on a lap board.

"Hel*lo*."

He turned.

They both knew instantly that they were cross with each other. She hated being interrupted at work. He hated being caught violating her conditions.

"Oh. You're there. I brought some books, but I thought I could simply leave them with Helga."

"Do come over. I'd be glad to take them.—I look frightful and I am furious with you for catching me this way."

"I'll run along. A million things to do."

"Million?"

"Dozen, then."

"What have you brought?"

She reached for the books.

"Some more diaries and so on. I don't imagine any of them will amuse you like Elias Gray."

"That man!" she said, setting her papers down on the grass next to her, and putting the books on top of them. "Will you stop for a cigarette?"

"I'm bothering you."

She slowly took off her glasses and set her small mouth in a speculative line. It was very deliberate, she looked prettier than he had ever seen her, this way, with her hair breezed about her face, and her cheeks reddened by the temper she saw in him and felt in herself. She got out her own cigarette and lighted it before she answered him. Then she said,

"There's something the matter."

"No there isn't."

He smiled grandly upon her.

"We've been frightfully polite before this, but today we're as polite as cats getting ready to fight.—I wish I knew what to say. It is true I hate to be disturbed when I'm trying to work. Maybe *I've* been rude."

He scoffed at this in a brief laugh.

He squeezed his eyes almost shut, looking at her. He wondered where the doctor and his patient had disappeared to. This was a new atmosphere today. He decided to be honest with her, and at once, he felt easy and unconcerned about what might happen.

"Well!" he said, nodding his big head slowly at her, and settling down on the warm grass, "I am furious with you."

"There! at last.—Why!"

"I suppose I feel duped."

"Duped?"

"Yes, duped. Here you let me come here and fumble along, talking to you about things that you probably see instantly, or know by intuition, and parade myself as a special soul who enjoys looking around *in back* of life, and one day I am told quite casually who you are, and what you do and how famous you are, and I suddenly feel like a schoolboy caught making up his recitation as he goes along."

"My *dear,*" she said softly, leaning forward, her face waved over with blushes and misery. He was amazed at this reaction. "How frightful for you! I know how *vulgar* you must consider it. I couldn't very well hand you a brief autobiography, on arriving. It never occurred to me that:"

She broke off, and looked slyly at him. It was an urchin's face she made.

"—This will make it even worse," she said, mocking herself. "It never occurred to me that you *didn't* know all that, whatever it's good for. I thought you were being well-bred with me, and sparing me any direct reference to my sordid livelihood."

"I see. Well. Anyway, I didn't. And I suppose I felt clumsy and foolish when I found out."

"How?"

"My wife mentioned it. She was all of a dither."

"Oh."

"The whole town is."

"No, really?"

Her cool detachment irritated him again.

"And I feel with them that they have a right to be.—I certainly wouldn't begrudge them a little flurry of excitement if someone distinguished and beautiful and mysterious comes to town."

She threw her cigarette inexpertly on to the driveway. He said to himself that women should never throw anything. Then she leaned down toward him.

"Now please pay attention," she said. "Once and for all, let me say what it is *really* like, this trying to write books. I know, simply because I've had a share of popular success, what people think, and how they have a strange, almost silly awe, of anyone who, as they say, is a 'creator.' I had it myself when I was a child, going to sleep with my first scrawled notebooks under my pillow, and imagining how it would be to meet Marie Corelli. I've since found out. Actually, it is an arduous business, which makes hags of females, and short-tempered blusterers out of males. They are always having to question life in themselves. They often fear they haven't the answers which contain both truth and beauty. They beg their works to reveal likenesses to those of great masters who have gone before them, not remembering that a good book is first of all like no other by anybody else. They measure their successes by their own doubts, and their failures by their own certainties. They are wretched away from their works and plans, and they are ruthless and selfish and wretched *at* them. There is no more glamor or distinction about it in their own view than a plumber has, whom they envy because he can forget his plumbing when he's off the job. Their enchantment, and their rewards, come from something about their work which nobody else ever mentions, if they ever see it, and that is an occasionally granted sense of the universal in both beauty and evil. To sing a song, or to tell a tale, and so somehow tap that universal thing in the response of other people—this is about as close to giving thanks as an artist can ever come; for all great works of art are thanksgivings, in one way or another, for life itself. If you knew, too, how often people like me felt like swindlers when receiving applause and admiration from good people who have made a mystery out of the things we do! They have made it for their own delight, I know that, and often I have tried to believe what they have expressed so kindly and with such radiant virtue of association! How *moral* they have made me feel, at the very moments when they have enjoyed seeing me and my kind as escapes from morality, the morality of habit and duty and father and mother and children and kitchen and hope!—So if all of this seems to you anything to have been impressed by, so that you had to be sulky over its discovery in my own hard-worked person, then I hope I have changed your mind.—Do you see, Peter?"

She sat back and looked at him.

He reached for her hand and squeezed it and began to laugh. He spread his legs out on the grass and rubbed his hair and sat up. He had diamond lights in his eyes from the tears of amusement over which he squinted in the sunshine that had moved over them shallowing the shadow of a while ago.

"Well, I'll call you Molly, too.—I am black and blue. If I'd never made you mad at me, I don't believe you'd ever've stopped being fragile and refined and exquisite with me. You're a fake. There's nothing delicate about your health. You're as strong as a horse. All writers are swindlers, then."

"They all invent ill health from time to time, so they'll have an excuse not to work today. The good ones never get away with it, to themselves."

He stood up.

"Well, I'll never ruin your morning again, but I'm very glad to've done it today."

"You might as well stay to lunch, now. I'll never get anything more done before noon.—Or do you have 'a million things to do,'" she added, smiling.

"I can't. I'm expected at home."

"Of course."

She looked at him quietly. She never mentioned his wife, in any way, inquiry, reference, anything. He vowed that next time they met he would deliberately talk about Noonie. He didn't like the idea of having one door leading to Noonie, in his mind: or heart: and one to Molly. Just as certainly, though, he knew Molly would prefer the two doors.

"Come in. I'll give you back the other books."

IV

They went into the cool, dim house. She found the books on the long table behind the red velvet couch. He stood next to her. How cool. How gentle the air here, after the blaze of sun outdoors. He looked down at her. He was moved to her. His heart gave a thump. A cool, sweet lightness came into his arms. Oh, Molly, he thought. She turned and held the books to him, and looking into his eyes, she said,

"I never showed you the photograph of my Betsy, did I!"

She took up a silver frame from the table. The picture showed a serious child of fourteen, with straight silky light hair, standing in sunlight before a big tree, dressed in riding clothes, with a big collie in front of her slim boots.

"Your daughter?"

"Yes."

"Where is she?"

"At school in the East.—She's a darling. She writes me every day."

"I suppose her name is Foster?"

"Yes. She sees my husband's family in New York a certain number of times a year. I—Dickenson Foster and I were divorced four years ago."

"Isn't he terribly rich?"

She laughed.

"Westerners!" she cried. "I'll never get used to them. It's what so many want to know, but nobody else ever asks, right off.—Yes, he is. But it doesn't have anything to do with *my* life. Or Betsy's."

She said,

"Oh, there was one place in Elias Gray I wanted to point out to you: where is it: about the time he went to Chihuahua, and was taken to the *salon* of a famous female gambler. What a prig! My heart went out to her, after the way he spoke of her."

She ruffled the pages until she found the right one, and then she began to read aloud with a superior tone to suggest the character of the author of *The Western Attorney:*

" 'I had not been long in Chihuahua City, whither I had traveled from Albuquerque in the company of an American trader in a train of six wagons, when I was informed that one of the sights of the place—otherwise a pretentious dust-heap—was a certain Doña Catalina Anonciación de Gutierrez. This female functionary, who would elsewhere have been notorious, was the chatelaine of a famous and elaborate house of ill repute, and was in the flower of her gifts as a gambling proprietress. With a certain temerity I will confess in the face of my reader's judgment that I agreed to go one evening in the company of my trading friend to observe the laws of social life as exhibited under the guiding genius of Doña Catalina, a confession I make thus boldly since her establishment housed, in addition to its other blandishments, the seat of such simple social commerce as one might otherwise find in the home of a leader of society.

" 'Madame Gutierrez, because of her rumored proficiency many years before as a music hall singer, was given the soubriquet of "La Voz." This has the touch of the underworld, even in the States, where low characters are often said to be designated by nicknames illustrating capacities, traits or physical peculiarities. "La Voz," then, was a small female of uncertain age, fantastically painted as to face, and outlandishly garbed as to person. She was a past-mistress of those arts of insincere cajolery whereby wretched men are flattered into risking their money at gaming, and their souls at immoral traffic. She moved about her premises with a self-possession which I must confess impressed me at first as suggesting a certain grace. But her hands which I chanced to notice as they operated at one of the gaming tables were those of a greedy bird of prey; and any sympathy, or more properly, should I say pity, which I may have felt start up in me, at her self-condemned plight, lasted only so long as her pretensions to ladyship. She was evidently most popular with her visitors, who attended her *salon* in great numbers. I caught glimpses of her all evening, now (detestable habit which even respectable females share in here) smoking a cigarette with this man, or again, imbibing a potion of brandy with another. Our acquaintances of the evening all spoke of her with admiration, and seemed to base their regard on the oft-reiterated assurance that "La Voz" lived a life of the strictest propriety herself, and was never even known to look at a man save as an adversary at the gaming tables. When we were preparing to depart, we were given our *congé* by "La Voz" herself, quite as if we had been guests in a home of the most irreproachable *ton*. I am told that because of her wealth and general style of living, which is lavish, though hardly tasteful, she is one of the most influential and respected figures in the local society. The perception of such social differences as this, between our own fabric of decorum in the United States, and the essentially looser, less moral-minded scheme of society in the Western provinces and Mexico, has, in itself, repellent as some would find it, been of sufficient interest to justify my foray into so inconvenient and unenlightened a region.' "

Molly slapped the book shut.

"The self-righteous fool!" she said, "doesn't he make you furious?"

"I remember that book.—La Voz was a famous lady. She was here, you know, for a while."

"In this town?"

"So they say.—Nobody knows where, or exactly all about it, but when the American Army came here in the forties, she was supposed to've been here. I've wondered about her. Elias Gray certainly allows her very little, doesn't he."

"Well, the proper fate has overtaken him.—Anybody who sets out to raise himself at someone else's expense, even by complacent contrast, like Gray with Madame Gutierrez, ends up by looking very cheap in the end.—When you write novels, you have to be so careful about taking sides with your characters. They have the oddest way of confessing what your vanity would conceal.—Children sometimes fail to see our happy disguises, too. They don't see the Emperor's new clothes at all. My Betsy was like that when she was younger."

Peter took up the frame from the table and looked at the young girl again.

"I have only one son," he said.

Because of the sound of his voice, she was moved to put her hand on his arm, briefly. She said to him, in her mind, You will never be able to conceal anything, will you? This made her heart tumble, for the betrayal, the honesty, the innocence it carried about him to her. She saw herself acting "forwardly," and she began to color again, in her cheeks, and she took her hand off his arm. Her hand was trembling. She was powerfully moved. She felt a little sick and dismal, to be so at the mercy of—of him, or anyone. He looked gravely down at her. He knew he had given away more than he'd meant to.

He said silently, What a mess.

Out of nowhere, it occurred to him to fend off this moment by saying,

"Have you ever driven up to the cliff ruins of Hano?"

"No.—It was one of the places to which Judy Bridges and I had planned to go after my car arrived from the East. But we never've done it. Judy hates motoring, ever since her ambulance days in France, in spite of everything I can say to her about setting out to *tour away* her dislike of it.—For the wrong reasons, you know, she keeps all sorts of troubling things alive. But she won't go."

He watched himself think it up, and savor it in imagination, and conceive how she would do about it, and say to her then,

"Would you go with me, someday, pretty soon, when I get sort of a gap in my schedule? We could leave in the morning and be back by dark, or even a little before.—It is a fascinating drive, by back roads, mostly, but when you get there!—I couldn't possibly describe it. I haven't been myself for years and years. I'm about ripe to go again."

Yes, he thought, perhaps doing things, and having something to show off, and lecture about, would be the way. He meant that it might be the way to skirt the sweet peril he was sure of now.

"I will go," she said. "Even if Judy won't. Yes. It will be fascinating."

They were then at some sort of delicate peace, agreeing to be together again, and having made no avowals concerning that which they both felt sure of, that it existed; but which they were unsure of, as to what they must or must not do.

He nodded and said he would let her know. Arming his books, he went out and drove off downtown. The hot noon wind rippled the pages of her manuscript on the grass outside. She suddenly remembered it, ran out to gather it up, and was smitten in her breast by the way she spent hours inventing what happened to people. She made almost a prayer that her inventions might come close to the truth of such things as she was feeling now, and that they have the courage to betray her very self, if need be.

XV · THE KISS

I

The young lovers met again at night, under a street lamp on the library corner, with its globe up among tree branches, lighting the leaves with the freshest green, and sending down to the grass and asphalt ground a ring of pale light in which they stood, waiting for the bus that ran up the hill toward the mesa. All around the tree, and themselves, was nighttime; and in the very center of that vague dark world were the ring of light, the emerald canopy of leaves, and their two figures.

They said they would not go into the library this evening; rather, ride out to the end of the bus line, and take a walk.

The bus ground its way up the hill, past the hospitals, the tuberculars' bungalows with canvas curtains inside screens, past the buildings of the university at the crest of the hill, and out a way on the graveled highway that led to the mountains.

At the end of the line, they got out. In silence, they began to walk down a street toward the darkness. There were a few houses scattered around on the mesa. If they turned to look toward town, the lovers could see the skillet of light that lay down on the plain that led to the river. But they did not turn. They saw a street lamp, a single globe of light hanging from a wire strung between diagonally opposite poles, at a far corner. This was their objective, by common agreement. The night was warm. Far beside them as they walked lay the rocky shadow of the mountains. Over them were the stars. A car went by now and then. The silence in their heads was about to break of their desire and their desperation. Martha knew that the higher courage had to be his, when the time came; and so she spoke now, and it cost her a heavy beat at the heart, to hear herself making trivial words, clothing passion, as it were, with propriety.

"—I spent the afternoon writing letters."

"You *did?*" he asked in disproportionate surprise.

"I certainly did. I must've written half a dozen."

"I think that's *perfectly remarkable.*"

"Oh, no it isn't, not at *all,* I often write eight or ten a day. For *that* matter."

"You *do!*"

His tongue almost cleaved to his mouth.

"And I typed them all, without looking at the keys."

"Not at *all?*" he asked with ghastly roguery.

She felt her jaw tremble as if she were icy cold.

"Well, just enough to be *sure,* when I was *doubtful.*"

"Oh, I *see.*"

Bunny laughed uproariously. She pinched his arm.

"Sshh! people will *wonder* what—"

But she herself began to laugh, and took his arm, bending over as if she were choking.

Nobody was around.

They had walked into the influence of the single street lamp, and looking around them, they saw no houses. It was a new real-estate development laid out in hope rather than in cash.

In the light, he looked at her.

She looked off into the darkness.

The street ended where they stood.

As if pushed by the idle little wind on the mesa playing in the evening, they went on past the end of the street, where the country faded in, and the sandhills were undisturbed, and the starlight began to make its faint show.

II

Neither of them ever forgot the place. Years later, when the streets were paved out there on the mesa, and families lived in the houses set so near to one another, and radio music drifted from one window to the window of the house next door, and the big planes heading for the airport came beating their way over the houses leaving a wake of tumbling sound, and children of tonight were citizens then, years later the edge of the sandhills in the starlight would come back to them in dreams or reminders in their experienced lives.

He first of all did a delicate thing, which made her heart beat, but not from fear. He took her fingers and one by one set their tips on his lips, as if to acquaint her with him. He could not have said why he did this. He hardly knew he was doing it, in the sense that he would know his own more prosaic acts. It was a poetic animality that moved him.

Then he knew in the pulse that they remembered how they looked, he and Martha Shoemaker, whom he had seen for years in perfect indifference; and he set his legs and put his arms around her sloping back, and bent down and kissed her on the mouth, and took what he gave.

She seemed to faint in his arms; and as if to bring her back against him, he pursued her with his lips, and she returned, never able to tell him or anybody else how far she had fled, and how swiftly she came back again.

In the whole evening they hardly said fifty words.

When he let her go, they were shaking, and she took his hand and pressing it urgently, and keeping it by her in the darkness, by her side at her breast, under her arm, she hurried them along, walking back to the highway, where the busses ran, which they must find, and on which they must ride home at once, coming into the area of electric light and peopled streets and cars going around corners making their tires whine.

He wanted to know if she was sorry, and she could do no more than squeeze his hand in anguished tenderness and look at him and then look away again.

He wanted to hold her again, and kiss her no matter where they were; her puzzling behavior was entirely unlike anything he had ever known before. He worshiped her for being so agitated; he sorrowed to know if he had hurt her; and from her hand on his, he knew how much she loved him. Her maidenliness tormented him as no practiced loving ever had with some of the girls he knew.

They rode to her corner, and he got out with her; but she wouldn't let him come to the house. She kissed him on the cheek and whispered that she would be at the library tomorrow night, and left him. He was dizzy from what she gave him. It was actually less than many another encounter he had known; but the feeling she conveyed—this was something entirely new.

He was longing and content in the same breath. He shook his head and said to himself with comic sobriety that he sure had it bad. He wanted to take her head in his hands and stroke her hair softly and vow that he would take care of her. At the idea, tears came to his eyes, and a plunge of rage in his breast made him suffer for what he would do to anybody who knowingly or unknowingly should ever hurt her.

III

When Martha got home, Wayne was in his bed, and called to her, but she ignored him, which was nothing new. She went to her room, and pulled the curtain which was all the privacy she had in her own little doorway, and lighted the kerosene lamp by her mirror. She had framed the mirror in pleats of white cloth with large green satin bows at the top corners. She was still trembling. She looked at herself. She said to herself that she was almost *sickened,* she could taste it yet, she could feel it now, the wetness of his mouth, the *other*ness of it, the invasion it made of her strictest self. On her breast she could touch the depth to which she had been stabbed by her heart when he had kissed her.

She went to her washstand and took a glass of water and some mouthwash and rinsed her mouth out and sought to recover herself from what she had done in the darkness on the mesa, saying to herself that it was only a kiss, dozens of kisses, and nothing like this, they had meant nothing, why should this one?

Unable to answer, she sat down on her bed which also had white pleats and green satin bowknots, for which she had saved up all she could afford for seven months last winter, and asked herself what he had seen of her in that moment; for it seemed to her that she had given herself wholly, and shown herself entirely to him; to a man; and that the Martha Shoemaker who had ridden in miserable eagerness up the hill on the bus was a child, and indeed, not even related to the Martha Shoemaker who had come home with his hand in hers, and his flavor and essence on her lips and on her fate.

Whatever he had seen, in the knowing blindness of lovers, it was his, now.

Was it only last month that she had spoken to him in Summerfield's?

How much can happen in so short a time! she mused. She felt wise, womanly and passionately dedicated to a privacy that was almost the same thing as virtue; and would defend what she now knew against anyone's *wondering.*

And then she was ashamed of washing her mouth out, and decided that it was the final act of the girl she had once been . . . She would never, never tell him, or anyone else, about it; of that she was sure.

I

Willa Shoemaker saw little enough of her son Wayne, and had to
come to her late knowledge of him by flights of intuition, at moments
when she was home from the Harvey House dining room. Every time
there was something troubling him, he took the most elaborate pains
to conceal it, and usually resorted to carrying on his puckered brow
a series of bored wrinkles, and to whistling a little tune without making anything but a musical whisper. These measures gave him away.
Willa had come to know them as signals of distress in her boy's inner
life. But the time had long since passed, she knew, when she could
take him on her aching legs as she sat before the *Spirito Santo,* which
in lieu of a hearth was the family center, and rock him on her thin
breast, and enfold him in protection from whatever it might be that
troubled him.

One night she came home late, as usual, and found her house
asleep. The children had left the lamp turned low in the living room,
where they also cooked and ate, and she settled down to the Albion
Evening Recorder with her glasses and a box of crackers and a mug
of milk, preferring these things to eat at home over the "menu" food
she could have had free at the Harvey House. It was a fine night out,
glistening with moonlight in early spring. She had caught the last bus
home. She was tired but richly and virtuously so, and let her weariness hang on her limbs like a rug. She thought she must have dozed
over her week-old news from "home," the Yeager place had burned
down on the edge of town, Martin Yeager was away at the time, and
Grace and the three children were alone in the house, the paper said,
when the flames cracking awakened Tommy, the youngest, and he
aroused the rest of them, and they all got away safely, but the house
was gone. She remembered——red brick and a white square tower full
of cobwebs, they used to go up into it in the summertimes, Martin
Yeager was at school with them all, and the rich man's son of the
bunch, and now without a house, but's not's if he couldn't build four
more just like it and *never miss it,* still he was a good boy, she remembered exactly how he looked twenty years ago, and saw him in her

musings as he would return home from his trip and find his red-brick house blackened to the ground which was so green all around, a stocky and merry-faced boy, Martin, with black hair, and something in his eyes which even now made her stir and imagine she was blushing, for the way she used to think of him and the things he would say, and *mean:*

But of course long ago, when she was a girl, she had never had any doubt about who it was she loved. It was Freddy Shoemaker, from the very first. Martin was Freddy's best friend. He was like an old pillow somebody kept around, a comfortable boy, always merry, and watching everyone cleverly to see what they would like to do. And when he knew, why, then he was ready to go and do it too. When Willa and Fred were married, Martin Yeager thought up all the jokes and the hectic things for everyone to do, and she had always been certain that Martin had kept Freddy from getting drunk ("spiflicated") the night before the wedding, for which she had always been grateful. How could she ever explain some things? When she and Freddy ran away to the buckboard, the last thing she did was hug Martin and she never forgot how the tears came to her eyes, and she laughed, and the tears ran down her face, and she cried out that she was so happy! Then she and Freddy drove away to everything that had happened because it was meant to be . . .

An odd thing! she would sometimes think busily, with no pangs, how much she thought about Martin Yeager later on! She never felt disloyal to Freddy's memory in doing so. She never felt *that* way about Martin. He was simply a very old friend who was now married, and had his own family, and was keeping right on being rich and taking care of the money his father left him back in Albion and being a good Catholic citizen. She sometimes imagined how it would be if they were ever together again, and she freely felt critical of Grace, the woman Martin had married, and all her doings, though she hadn't seen Grace *since* then. . . .

And yet, at the very same time when she would be living with animation an inner kind of life over Martin Yeager,—and yet whenever she thought of happiness or hunger, worthwhileness or doubt, it was always her poor dead Freddy she thought of; for it was he from whom she'd learned the meanings of these words. His flesh had taught her so, and his notions, too.

But she could not help dreaming of what might have been, or might someday still be, through her daughter Martha and one of the Yeager sons.

It was, this double life of memory and desire, the compact in herself of the timeless and the placeless: half was learned and half was divined, and the whole was a dear possession.

II

The paper slid from her lap with a hard whisper, and she came out of dozing to hear something else. It was Wayne, muttering in his sleep, and she tiptoed to look at him on the sleeping porch, where the moonlight bounteously lay upon him through the screens. He was moving obscurely under his blankets, and his face was ghostly with distress, his mouth open, his fingers walking under his chin. He made no words, and she was frightened, yet as she stood there, she calmed her heart and said to herself that he was Wayne her baby, and not to be afraid of this visitation that made him seem so far from her as she stood and watched him; and her eyes swept his length on the bed, and she could hardly believe he had grown so big, and she asked God to let him sleep in peace. It was simply an answer to what she held of him in her heart that, hardly had she made the prayer, than Wayne seemed serene again, and cheeked heavily down on his bed in long exhausted breathing.

She watched him for another moment, then left him, and said to herself that she had seen for days how disturbed and warningly indifferent he had seemed at home. The little incident had exhausted her, too; and she made her way to her bed in the built-on lean-to at the street end of the house, and without lighting her lamp, she laid herself down, and fell asleep.

A dialogue of dream selves asked her for Wayne. One said,

"Never change, you are my baby, you must never leave me. What would I do without my baby? Everything you need I am here to give you, do not betray me, do not change the look in your blue eyes, do not hold your little hands away from my breast, I know each one of those ten little fingers, and they have hurt me but they have needed me."

And the other said,

"*Let him go.*"

"No, no, he is my baby, he will suffer so if he grows up and goes away to life."

"*It is the only way to let him know anything. He must pull out his roots and take them along with him, and that will hurt. But his legs grow long and his jaw gets square and his fingers are big and tender; not little and ruthless any longer.*"

The one cried on in her dream,

"I did not bear him to have him grow and leave me."

Replied the other,

"He has already left you."

"No, no."

"Yes, he is already a discoverer, and kicks in his dreams against what he now knows. Standing to watch him as he slept you already knew this too."

The one within her seemed to sigh, and say,

"So it was. I sorrowed to see him weep in his sleep, and I could not reach him to comfort him."

The other within her said in a victorious and easing power,

"You will give him to joy as well as to trouble, when you let him go. Remember that. It is a worthy thought to awaken on."

She awoke, the moonlight was white outside, and lay like snow on all it touched. She had a dim memory of what had possessed her before she awoke, and she felt her face where she had wept silently asleep. But she couldn't imagine why she had wept, and concluded that she had yawned, for a deep peacefulness lay over her and she felt no longer tired. Listening for Wayne again, she heard nothing, and she smiled and meant to herself that he would run into troubles soon enough, but he would have to learn to handle them himself, and besides, think of all the joys of growing up and being a man and knowing life and having a family himself some day, they would all be pretty children, and *he* would know then what it meant to lie awake nights and worry, and *worry* over your children, bad enough to have to work hard all day, back and forth, back and forth, still, worth it, when you would fall asleep like this, and be oh so happy, with everything secure about you, *how Martin Yeager used to laugh without making a sound, like to bust, Grace always was crazy about him.*

She slept again.

III

By morning, there was no memory left of what had possessed her during the night; and she was brisk, a little breathless, comically sharp with her children, getting them both started for the day.

XVII · AN OLD ENDURANCE

I

The hospital of which Peter was senior surgeon had been established long ago in the eighties by an order of nuns who still ran it. It was a faded, rose-brick building of three stories with a white pillared portico. On its hillside above town, just below the mesa, the sisters had coaxed green grass and shady trees out of the sand. It had walnut window casings, many of them rounded at the tops, and its rooms were old-fashioned with plaster moldings and high ceilings. The public reception halls and rooms were caverned with shade, and were now furnished with a sort of itchy elegance of the period of 1910. Every ten years the rooms were done over completely. It was about time for another refurbishing. The objects that would not change were the enormously enlarged photographs of the Archbishops of Santa Fe, in full canonicals, which hung in the reception room, and the framed illuminated parchments with papal blessings from the successive pontiffs, sent all the way from Rome.

The nuns were efficient. Their hospital made money. A fund was lying by which would soon be large enough to build a completely modern annex to the institution. Meantime, they did with what they had. Doctor Rush was given anything he asked for for the operating room. He got on famously with the sisters, and they felt they owned him, and often spoke of him as "such a *boy,* to be so *able,"* which had been true of him say fifteen years ago. But the sisters were always long on traditional matters, anyway, and he would be considered boyish as long as he worked under their auspices. He was not of their religion, which they forgave often in arch little pokes of humor in his direction, a wistful recognition that God's goodness extended everywhere. For his part, he often said that if he *had* a religion it would be that of the hospital where he spent so much time. He understood well enough what a priest said to him once: "You have a religion, all right, Doctor. I doubt if you and I would quibble over anything much more than vocabulary." They laughed heartily, and meant to each other that all services to the proper affirmation of life eventually met in a philosophical perspective.

The sisters were proud of Doctor Rush. He had been identified for so long with Saint Joseph's that they always assumed as a matter of course that he would be a part of any great occasion, such as the silver jubilee of the Sister Superior, which was held this year.

A whole day was set aside for the celebration, which was made august by the presence of the Archbishop of Santa Fe, who came down in his black limousine the night before, spent the night in the rooms always reserved for him at Saint Joseph's, and pontificated at a solemn high Mass early the next morning. The Sister Superior was crowned with a silver wreath, which she wore all day. Presents and telegrams arrived all day long. Her married sister from Des Moines was there, and was much made over by all the other nuns. An atmosphere rarefied by the simplest joy and charity filled the staff all day. Irritations were forgiven, and favoritisms erased. If Sister Superior sometimes did seem cold and distant it was today understood to have been simply the nature of her position which made such an attitude inevitable, at times. Twenty-five years! Think of it! And the long distance calls from the Mother House in Chicago, and the purse sent by the school children of the parishes, and the rosary from Rome, and the morocco leather album of testimonials from classmates at the convent so long ago, and the moving picture camera to take pictures with *yourself,* and the machine to show them with, and the set of altar linens made by the children at the orphanage and presented to Saint Joseph's chapel in Sister Superior's name, and the garland of Masses promised by Sister Superior's brother who was a Jesuit missionary in Alaska, and most exciting of all, the banquet in the evening at which the Archbishop presided, with "Sister" on one side of him, and Doctor Peter Rush on the other . . .

The patients' dinner hour was set ahead thirty minutes so that the big room with the white pillars and the opalescent glass bay window with the ferns banked in it could be made ready for the celebration dinner, which was ready at seven-thirty.

The nuns outdid themselves in the arrangements. The table was one continuous plateau, making a large m-shape with square corners. It was lighted by candles dipped in silver paint, and held by silver sticks. A mound of roses made a bank down all the table, which glittered with silver dishes, icelike crystals, gnarled silver knives and forks and spoons, all the treasure which the nuns reserved for only the highest occasions. There were heaps of candies and nuts and there were place cards hand-painted in water colors. At "Sister's" place a silver basket held all the telegrams of congratulation which had been coming all day. Selected ones were to be read aloud later by the Archbishop himself.

At his place there was a throne chair upholstered in red velvet, and topped with the arms of the archdiocese. A velvet footstool was waiting for him under the table. His napkin was tied with three yellow roses. Everyone else had pink ones. The papal colors were yellow and white, and everyone, except the Doctor, understood and commented upon it. The tone of the occasion reminded Peter of a cross between a children's birthday party and a wedding jubilee. He was a little embarrassed at first by the innocent exuberance of all the sisters, and amazed at the labors they had expended. The ceiling was tented with streamers of white and yellow satin ribbon. The walls were hung with sacred sodality banners glittering with silver-gilt embroidery and fringe. The air was full of little cries of simple joy from the nuns, whom he knew better in their other selves, quick, determined women who did their best to lessen suffering among the living.

II

But if he was embarrassed at first, at what seemed to him in a pang of pity an overorganized expression of joy, he lost that feeling when he saw the look on the Archbishop's face. The prelate was a tall, heavy man with a big face and a big nose and a big mouth, and light-blue eyes. His hair was graying, but he looked only middle-aged. He wore glasses. This evening he had on his purple moiré mantelletta and white lace surplice, and his magenta skullcap. It was a full dress affair. Peter was in his squarely cut tail coat which he had not worn since 1915 when he had read a paper on thoracic surgery in St. Louis to the American Medical Association. What Peter saw in the Archbishop's big amiable face was an amused and yet gratified look of agreement with how everybody felt. It was as if he, too, was touched by the enthusiasm of the occasion, and yet wise enough not to despise anything that innocently made anyone happy. His eyes were shrewd enough, Peter decided; and yet they were also full of liveliness and tolerance. And he had the friendly knack of taking homage at its true value, and that was, according to the pleasure it gave the giver; not the receiver.

After a little while of an official grace by the Archbishop, and flurried exclamations with table neighbors about the "exquisite" appointments, and exchanges of clever place cards, the party settled down. The speeches were to follow the dinner. Peter had a sinking of the stomach when he thought of his, and what he would manage to say.

"Do you ever get over feeling awful before you have to make a speech?" he asked the Archbishop.

"Nev-er?" said the Archbishop, turning on him with light-blue recognition. He spoke with the flattest and slowest of accents, Middle Western and somehow disarming, in a man of power. His words rose and fell in a sort of arch simplicity. "Now I have made? myself a the-ory aboutt-it."

"What is that:"

"I belieeve my stage-fright is *always?* use-ful. It makes me give a better speech? to the exact de-gree of how? frightened I am, be-fore."

"That could certainly be. Maybe I can kid myself into that, too."

"I often kid myself, Doctor,? but I al?-ways admit it to myself when I? do so."

"Sister, did you hear that? The Archbishop admits that he kids himself, at times."

"Oh, Doctor, how can you say that!"

"He'ss right, Sister? but I ad-mit it privately? first."

They laughed politely with each other.

The Archbishop then said,

"I love slang. It is a relief? to use it, the Americans are won-derful with it."

This had a faintly foreign timbre to it. Peter smiled at him, and said,

"Did you have foreign parents?"

"Yes, I did. I was born in Chi-cawgo. Bohemian stock. How did you know?"

"Just a little hint, in your speech, somehow."

"Is that your hobby? Most interesting."

"No."

"What *is?*"

Well, what was. He hadn't thought of it as such. Probably it was his collection of books and—and *places,* in the history of his home town.

He told the Archbishop that.

"Places? Yess. History is always? alive, isn't it."

"I grew up in this town, went to school here, and when I came home from interning in New York, I was so glad to be back that I said to myself there must be something behind all the way I felt. So when I began to have a little time, and a little extra cash now and then, I began to get books. I mean the old ones, as many as I could find, and afford, by the old fellows who wrote what they did themselves, when they first came to this country."

"Wouldn't it be? fine," said the Archbishop, "if everybody loved his homeland as? much as you do. My! What citizens we would have! wouldn't we."

"Oh, I don't know.—Yes, I imagine so.—But in the places where I was a boy, somebody long ago was a man, working to use the wilderness."

"M'm."

The two men, both powers, in their way, were a little shy, for a moment, at the almost poetic terms their thought was taking. Then the prelate went on:

"You know? We are gathering all the parochial records in all? the little churches of the archdiocese."

He added that he was having a vault built for such precious records in Santa Fe. It was a work that should have been done long ago. But there was still time to save a lot. And who knew what they would reveal of the intimate life of the Spanish generations when scholarship was able to study them?

There was one little scrap of brownish paper, the Archbishop declared, that was to him the most remarkable and touching document in the whole lot so far catalogued. It was a letter, written in the winter of 1598, in Spanish, of course, from an encampment somewhere near here: somewhere in the vicinity of Albuquerque itself, as a matter of fact: written on Christmas Day in 1598, by the father of a child born the night before. The letter went to the Captain-General de Oñate at the pueblo and capital city of San Juan, telling of the birth, and the quality of omen it had, Christmas Eve, mind you, the anniversary of the birth of Our Lord Jesus Christ, and so far as anybody knew, it was the birth of the first child among the new settlers who colonized New Mexico that year.

"I have often? wondered ex-*actly* where the place was!"

Peter was stirred by this discovery. His eyes sparkled and he illustrated by his enthusiasm what the sisters always meant when they called him "boyish." He asked if he might see the letter some time. The Archbishop answered that if he came to Santa Fe, he could see it any time. Or better still, meantime, a copy could be sent down by the first post after the Archbishop's return to his office.

He said it would interest the Doctor especially, from a medical standpoint, too; because the letter reminded the Captain-General that the writer and his wife, their servant, and a soldier, had been left behind to camp because the woman, in a difficult pregnancy, could not travel any farther for fear of dying. She was not strong, and they all preferred to risk the strangeness of the country than continue the racking journey by oxcart, with its day-long discomforts. So they had stayed behind for several months, and the child had been safely delivered, and as soon as they could travel again, they would overtake the colony at San Juan, where the baby could be baptized, and the Captain-General himself could be its godfather, which the writer prayed he would agree to do.

"If you will send me the letter, I'll go and find the place, if there is any description at all in it of where they were."

"There might be a hint?"

"I'll find it. It must've been somewhere on the road to the north, there are only a couple of ways the old road could've gone."

"You find it for me. I will be much? moved to know where the first soul was born not a stranger to this land."

III

A rustle in the banquet room brought them both back to the occasion. Something was coming. The nuns knew it, and stirred at their places. They were like pupils in school, sharing a charming joke which excluded the teacher. They bent their hooded faces to each other, and the sibilants of their speech made a little flight of bees through the room, as they cautioned each other to "watch S'st' S'perior" when the doors opened and the cake came in.

This proved to be an enormous dome of pastry, borne by four orphan girls on a huge breadboard wreathed in smilax. Twenty-five silver candles blazed away on the iced dome, which was garlanded and studded with sugar sculptures, and the date, and the name of the recipient. Everybody stood up and clapped, and began to sing in fervent stridency:

"Holy Day, with joy we rise,
And sing our praise to thee.
Let our song reach to thy skies,
And let us happy be."

After that there was small chance for further conversation. Speeches followed, the reading of the telegrams, the playing of jokes, and finally the staff's gift to their head, a sumptuous silver crucifix mounted on an ebony base, and draped with a little rope of fresh violets. This reduced Sister Superior to happy tears. The woman before whom they all trembled in official life, in tears, like anybody else! It was almost too much, as a spectacle, and the emotions of sympathy changed the tone of the party. The Archbishop turned it all to laughter again when he rode over them with his rich voice, saying that they must watch out, or they would have him weeping too.

Peter, when it was all over, said to himself that he was glad he came; not only for the conversation with the Archbishop, but also because if he had sent regrets, which he had considered doing, he would have put a blight over the party by not realizing how important it was to the fifty or so women in the room, all of whom seemed so full of joy. He preferred not to think of his own part in the programme, the speech he had given through six foolish minutes, as he recalled. But they had applauded him fondly, and he supposed it could not have made much difference what he said, they just wanted him to *take part,* they were all tipsy by then, anyway, with excitement, and food, and candy; candlelight; the break in the discipline of hospital routine.

IV

Two days later, the letter came from Santa Fe. The Archbishop sent a translation into English of the original letter, and also included a fairly clear photostatic copy of the old document.

To the Captain-General and Governor,
Sr. Dn. Juan de Oñate, at San Juan.
Excellency:
In the name of the Father and of the Son and of the Holy Ghost, Amen.
On the Feast of the Nativity of Our Lord, in the valley of the River of Our Lady, near the black mesa which you will recall, we have all stayed since our company left us to pass onward to the North, owing to the feeble condition of my wife who has now been happily delivered of a son, last evening, with much trouble, but eventual safety. My servant will bring you this news by his hand. I will keep the soldier Ruy Martinez de Quevedo whom you so well ordered to our protection. We have had no worries from the inhabitants. We are almost at home here; having set up walls of earth against the weather, which comes off the black mesa above us. But the fall of rocks where we all encamped together provides natural protection. There are many trees which we can use for fuel. My wife is weak but safe. My son is your first native colonizer, surely. I pray you with my wife to act as godfather when we are able to set out to join you and the rest. We are in a fine place for a city, details of which I will report. When I am able I intend to return here

and set up a shrine to the Holy Nativity on this spot where our fears have come safely to such blessed issue. Nearby there is a protrusion of yellow soft rock from which blocks could easily be cut. Our horse and our burro forage freely, but suffer from the cold which has been extreme for two days, with snow falling above us on the mesa, and at times blowing down over our shelter. But I have kept the fire alive for weeks, and have traded for extra bedding with some Indians nearby, who have let us alone otherwise, though I believe we are watched from a distance. They are good people, and I have the idea that they have been waiting for us to come, with the word of God. It was snowing at dawn this morning when we awoke. I, my servant and the sergeant all knelt together by the bed and recited prayers to celebrate the Nativity. When we looked out it was but a curtain of white that we saw. But we were never prey to the terror of solitude, for truly we were not alone, but in the company of God, who mercifully blessed the life we all attended here since November. I am restless to join you and resume my duties. I hope my steward is attentive to my wagons and possessions, upon which at your will you must surely and freely draw as suits the need of the colony. We will come to you in about a week, unless reverses visit us, which God forbid. My oxcart is now in good repair and excellent comfort for wife and infant. We have made a covering of skins. There are many beavers on the river to the west of us, about two miles. Given in homage, this 25th day of December, 1598, in the kingdom of New Mexico, at his camp, by

> José Diego de Nájera,
> Captain of the Governor's Army,
> and Commissioner of Deeds and Titles,
> by Patent of His Majesty the King.
> (Flourish.)

They must have marched north along the river road, passing right through the site of Albuquerque and continuing by the riverside as far as possible. But there came that point where the river cut through volcanic terraces, and any road would have to abandon it, and strike inland, holding due north as far as possible. Peter believed that the little family must have gone about twenty miles beyond where the city was today. He reviewed the country where the black mesa was, and where the rocks cropped out in yellow ocher, and where there was a heavy forestation of cottonwoods. There were many places that he thought of. But while making a call in the country village of Atrisco, which was on the highway to Santa Fe, he had an impulse of recognition.

V

They had telephoned him from the grocery-and-filling station store on the highway to come at once to see Señora Aguirre, who was very painfully sick and was believed by all who saw her to be dying. They gave him directions, you come out the main highway to the gas pump, turn right on the dirt road that crosses the big ditch, follow the fence and the trees to the first turn, and go right on past it, until you come to the second turn, which you take, to the left, and there are four houses, of which the third is where the sick woman is. There is a Ford touring car in the yard, and a row of hollyhocks. He should bring medicine with him, to give right away, since she is extremely ill, and cries out momentarily, with the sweat pouring down her face. Her whole family are with her, except her second son, who is "working for the State" (that is to say, a prisoner in the penitentiary). All others are at hand, and much grieved. This is a neighbor speaking. Please hurry.

It took him about forty minutes. He wasted no time, nor yet did he break his neck to get there, knowing the temperamental liking of those people for the social opportunities of crisis, which led them to interpret every megrim as a last illness, and celebrate it with enthusiastic grief. When he reached the shady lane from which the sounds and smells of summer were baking upward in sweet drowsiness, he certainly could not miss the house of pain. The yard was animated by chatting neighbors. Babies played on the packed earthen floor about the house. Two wagons and the Ford touring car illustrated the focus of importance in the village. The sunshine dwelled whitely over the pale lilac mud color of the house, the dark-green alfalfa field out back with lacy black shadows under the plants, and the colors of the hollyhocks which cupped the light in silky shades. When his huge car was sighted coming down the dirt lane, rocking magnificently like a landship, Peter heard a chorus of pleasure, relief, anticipation come up, and he arrived in a triumph.

As soon as his eyes were used to the darkness of the house, he began to examine Señora Aguirre. She was fat and had a sort of grand doleful prettiness about her face. His first guess was acute indigestion; but he made a very careful examination before he came back and confirmed it. When he was able to risk it, he gave her some medicine, and explained the tortures of flatulence to those by the bedside who held positions there by family precedence. It was true that *Mamá* already seemed better, able to lean up on one elbow, and

command the middle daughter to bring the Doctor a piece of chocolate cake from the table there. He nibbled at it enthusiastically, but
sparingly, as if to make it last. Weak with reassurance, Señora
Aguirre guessed that it was the orange fizzes she had drunk on top
of the *frijoles, atoles, enchiladas, tamales* and cherry ice cream last
night at the party she had gone to in Los Griegos, that might have
brought on this infirmity today.

She next commanded the same daughter to bring her the rose-
painted china teapot from the shelf above the stove in the other room.
With a gesture of the greatest propriety and charm, she lifted the
lid off and drew forth a thin clutch of dollar bills, asking the Doctor
what his fee was for restoring her (already!) so much to that peaceful
health she was accustomed to enjoy. He replied with instant good
manners that his fee was one dollar, but she need not pay it now if
she cared to wait; he would have his office send her a bill. This
caused her to hesitate a moment; it would be possibly more refined
to receive a bill, through the mail, stamped, addressed, delivered to
Atrisco. But she was first of all a woman of great good sense, and
she shrugged, and selected the cleanest paper dollar from her supply,
and handed it to him forthwith, to save him further trouble.

He closed his bag and stood up and shook hands around the room,
and was almost carried to his car by the friends who were now planning to stay on for lunch, since they were here, and Lolita was feeling
already so much better, they would all have a bite together, a few
beans, some coffee, somebody would make a pan of cornbread.

He asked if he could eventually get back to the highway by continuing on the lane in the direction he had come from. They said
yes, but he must watch the little wooden bridges over the ditches,
with that heavy car of his. The place to turn to the right the last time
was at the yellow stone slab, which he would see to the left of the
lane. Four squares of yellow rock, so, that stuck up a couple of feet.
The road couldn't go much farther, anyway, because the cliff was
there, so it turned south again. They used to say there had been a
shrine there, long ago, but that was unlikely, since there was no reason for it; no highway, no house, no church.

VI

When he was by himself, driving along in low gear and rocking
on the rutty dried mud of the path, he shook his head again over
that experience he had known so many times in his country; of taking one single step from the golden present and knowing so sharply

the feeling of the golden past; the focus of thought or vision didn't even change; simply a step into that other time, where he—or anyone who made it—could see the edifices of the imagination.

He had to leave his car presently by a bend in the ditch which fed the alfalfa field to the right. The road crossed the ditch at a sharp angle, such as mules and a wagon could negotiate, but not his enormous car. His certainty began to fade a little. Nothing really looked like *the place*. But he wandered ahead on foot, through the shade of the big green trees with their softly clattering leaves, the applause of summer in the river valley. Now he could see no houses. The field of alfalfa was behind him. Somewhere ahead, he knew, were the main line tracks of the Santa Fe railroad; but they were hidden by the wild grass and the cottonwood bosques.

He knew how this place must be in winter.

And that was his clue.

Now he could begin to see.

The trees would stand silvery thin to the washed pale sky. There, ahead, what now looked like a shadow in the distance, was the face of the black mesa, and through winter's trees, it would be very plain and near. He began to walk faster. The weather often arose in the mountains which were way back out of sight across the upper mesa, from where he was now, and it swept forward and down over the black cliff on the wind. If there was shelter to be had, it was to be had right near the mesa fall; that black volcanic rock that looked like velvet from even the littlest distance.

The road was full of grass.

In winter, the snow would blow along and lodge in the ruts. But long ago, there were no ruts. There was supposed to be a tumble of rocks protruding from the ground; he knew how they would look; squares of yellow stone like magnified clusters of crystal shapes.

All about him were the three stages of river forest. He saw dead trees, which looked as if they'd been polished by wind until they had the sheen of old silver. Mostly he counted the mature trees crowned loftily with domes of green shadow. And scattered everywhere were saplings of the heroic line of descent, tender whiplike stands which in their turn would make the river groves endure.

The family of José Diego de Nájera saw very much the same aspect. What they had experienced near here, somewhere, was familiar enough to Doctor Rush.

He saw the wild grass rising ahead of him, losing the lane. The lane turned to the right, heading south. No doubt in time it found a straggling way to the main road. He came out into a little clearing of sunlight. He saw something he believed he almost remembered, as if he had seen it before. There was a body of rocks grown up with grass, and the stone was yellow. The black fall of the mesa was almost misty with blue shadow. In the tall grass where he stood he saw a small platform of the yellow stone, four squares laid together. Whatever their purpose, they had been so laid by men, how long ago nobody could prove. Peter had no doubt at all that in 1598 the son of José Diego de Nájera had been born on this spot; and that the father, keeping his promise to himself, had come back when he was able and had built a shrine to give thanks for the happy issue of his worries. But the Royal Highway didn't come by this way. The motor road of today was a couple of miles to the west, across grove and field and water ditch.

With the aid of three men, and a fire they'd kept going for weeks, and with woven pieces bought from the Indians, Señora de Nájera bided her time. Her husband was a man of education. It was possible that she was a well-born lady, and it was known that she was not robust. Her education would not of course match his. She had no particular need of learning off the page something that her body would know by inheritance. What they all learned most usefully, probably, was what they heard in church. Time and again the factor of survival was spiritual. Any doctor had seen plenty of evidence of that. The weather could drive like a bird through the air, and enter everywhere. Three men could make a go of it, ordinarily, one a servant, another a soldier, another a civil administrator. It was hardest to wait for what was going to happen. As Christmas Eve drew nearer, it occurred to them all that there might be a true and exalting purpose in the trial they were enduring together. But perhaps they did not think it a trial? There was no hint of such an attitude in the letter the father wrote when it was over. Life, then, was never a burden? It was a mission to be executed, no matter what the conditions of the moment.

The day before Christmas, probably in the early morning, for the Señora, a frail and suffering woman, the intimations of pain had begun. Nobody could do anything helpful at such a time but keep the place warm; it was snowing, remember, and the smoke blew along the ground. The gray light would fly with the clouds over the empty reach of the trees. Risk, of course there was risk, the men would be more aware of it than the woman. Pain and forgetfulness and resolve drifted in and out of the woman's mind all day long, one purpose alone inhabiting her. The men would smile at her and promise her safety when she was able to see again after a bad time. It wouldn't matter to her where her baby was born. At home in Mexico City, in a stone room hung with curtains and woven pictures, and busy with women, and scented with medicines, there would have been essentially the same thing to suffer and complete. It might have been a lucky thing that Señora de Nájera had no real picture of how far they were from everywhere, the four of them, with their oxcart and the two oxen out in the grass.

But the husband knew, and he knew too that if she should die, and her baby with her, he must leave them there. She was not a strong woman, they had always felt. But she was stronger than the wilderness, and the distance, and the cold, and the anxious fellows there, and the tradition of poor health, and the crippling modesties that attended so much of life.

It must have been over before midnight, and the firelight wavered over the five of them.

No wonder they had the instinct of commemoration, and vowed, after this prosaic prodigy, a thankful stone. An honor, the rebirth of man which was the first chapter of the life of Jesus, had visited the family in the river wilderness. That they should be simply one with the Holy Family was clearly the intention behind the fall of the birth upon Christmas Eve. A devout man could hardly conclude anything else.

For the rest, the Spanish letter was full of worldly responsibility. Captain de Nájera was a busy man, by temperament, and the land, the resources, the *chances,* all preoccupied him, once the hazard was past. A place for a city; the kind of rock; the animals; things to do as soon as he could get at them, when they rejoined the main colony.

It was entirely likely that in a week or so, they had gathered up their things, and started on again.

But Nájera evidently meant what he said, as a general rule.

VII

Peter stood up on the yellow stone platform and glanced around. The land was generally level, and the oxcart might have gone right on north from here, for a little distance. But the black mesa jutted out sharply about half a mile up, he could see the dark profile through the trees. He could see too, standing on this small elevation, a silver pole with a painted signal arm and red and amber and green glass, and he said of course, it was the railroad.

As he went back to his car, he heard the whistle of an engine far down the line.

It spoke to him as it always did to Americans. It told of distance and speed and of going somewhere. It unerringly found the boy within him, as in every man. He did not feel obvious or banal when he contrasted it in his mind with what the little Spanish family had endured and brought to triumph so long ago, in a wilderness. The oncoming train was a symbol for all the complexities, the ease, the accustomed powers of comfort in his own day.

He next said to himself that in re-enacting the events of the Spanish letter here in this sun-latticed grove, the birth of a child in hazard and love, he had answered out of the past the longing for more children which the trouble in his family had denied him.

He wished for Noonie something of the wilderness challenge of survival or death; to give life to others rather than harbor it for yourself; and he knew that if she was ever to become whole again, it would have to be at the risk of crisis; of just what kind, he could not say.

Things changed.

The spirit endured. Find it, recognize it, respect it, share it. He scowled and nodded, alone, and vigorously, as if to justify himself for such meditations; how embarrassed the people he knew would be if ever called upon to hear this sort of thing spoken by one of themselves! "The happy materialists," he murmured, recalling what bad form it was, among the Americans of his time and position, to acknowledge the soul and to question the laws of the speak-easy and the country club.

The train now came charging upon the embankment in a triumphant harmony, like some creature of tremendous music. It was the California Limited, demonstrating the beautiful curve of the land at the base of the black mesa, and its shine and sing, its plume of smoke capturing the sun in gorgeous turbulence, its roar and glisten, its length and passage and clickety elegance, swept over and past him, and on through the sandy distance toward town, and back to today.

VIII

He wrote to the Archbishop in the evening, upstairs in his attic library, announcing his discovery, and arguing circumstantially for its recognition.

To this the Archbishop replied that it was gratifying that he had possibly identified the spot where the first native-born child of the colonists had seen the light, and added that he for one was not astonished to learn that the evidence of such a lonely birth had been a moving experience, since after all "it was a beginning. Any birth, any time, is the greatest of all beginnings, for it is the life of a new soul, the confirmation and the hope of all the immaterial knowledges which men have always been certain of, in the face of demands for proof from the more material-minded of our diverse and fascinating fellow mortals."

XVIII · HEAR ABOUT LOVE

I

One afternoon Peter came home unexpectedly to pick up his black looseleaf pocket notebook in which he jotted memoranda about his cases. He ran upstairs to his third-floor retreat, found the book on his desk, with his lump of cleanly sheared obsidian on top of it, and hurried down the stairs again. Down the hall, the door from Noonie's sunporch was closed, but the afternoon sunlight was caught in a film of curtain behind the glass, and he wondered if she were there. He went to the door, and tapped, and opened it.

There she was.

He was pleased at the picture he saw. She was reclining in her gray satin chaise longue, doing Don's mending. The light came in and flooded her with a golden diffuse pour. She was smiling like a child full of mischief. She had deliberately kept silent to see if he would come to find her. Her cheeks were flushed with pleasure at the little game, the little echo of courtship they made. The glass of the many windows was dazzling. The scent in the room was leafy, from her boxes of plants that lined the front wall. He had a glimpse of the girl she had once been, and he was lifted by it.

He came in and sat down on the end of her long chair and she dropped her sewing and leaned toward him and kissed him. She seemed full of gaiety. Her eyes danced and her lips were hot and shining.

"Darling, what are you doing?" she asked.

"I ran in to get my famous black book, I've been without it all day, and I've needed it a dozen times, so I decided to take a moment and really get it.—What are *you* doing?"

"—These shirts of Donnie's. He is pushing right through everything he owns."

"You look very sweet, sitting here like a little puss in the sunshine."

"Do you know I have never gotten used to the way your coats always smell? Medicine."

She shuddered with comic fastidiousness.

"Do you mind?"

"Of course not.—It's *you:* isn't it?"

"Come here."

He kissed her, and asked her silently, by his eyes upon hers, whether she had come back to him. He never tired of asking this question, in whatever way the moment dictated.

She clung to his shoulders, and said,

"Don't go now."

"I have to, dear. I'll be home as soon as I can."

"Come back at five, then, and take me riding in the car. It is so long since we took a drive together."

The whole town had the habit of riding around, just to look at things, the streets, the river, the mesa, the mountains, in the late afternoon. The country roads weren't very good, but nobody had the habit of driving very fast. The automobile was just ending its age of innocence.

"Well, I have to operate at five. But I'll come as soon as I can, after that."

She sank back on her satin tufting.

"I knew it."

"Knew what?"

"That you wouldn't."

"Couldn't."

"Couldn't, then.—Oh, I *blame* nothing," she said airily.

He could see that she was being elaborately "reasonable." It was lost, that fond gaiety of a moment before. He saw her forehead cloud with the expression that always meant "one of her headaches."

"Really, Noonie:" he said soberly, to indicate his desire to keep the air clear.

"Oh, never mind," she replied, putting her fingers to her temples. "It simply *is,* that's all. You'd better go. A nagging wife is certainly no asset to any man's career. One finds one's place, I am sure."

He had an ironic twist of thought, and wondered what she had been reading lately. This wasn't her native style. His hope sank. How could he've expected it to last? He went out and down the stairs and got into his big Packard and drove off. What: what: what: will help her? His heart came into his mouth when he asked himself that. He was afraid of what it would need: what finality: what ordeal: to help her.

II

After he had left her, she began to cry, telling herself she was a fool. But it did not help her to feel any better. As usual, when she gave way to a troubling emotion, it was as if a sluice gate had been lifted, through which other emotions were free to pour, so that at times she ended up in misery over something far afield from what had set her off.

This is what happened to her now, in the sunny upstairs porch where her magazines were stacked high on the mahogany table, in two neat bastions flanking the silver lamp.

Out of some story or other she had read, in some one of the radiantly printed magazines by her elbow, an idea, a phrase came back to her. What was happening to her? Here she was nearly in middle age; possibly someone would consider her *actually* middle-aged, and what did she *have?* Her tears flowed and her breath blew hotly over her lips. It was true, wasn't it: "love itself was passing her by." No, no, time could never be recalled. No, no, whatever could make the heart feel, seize upon it! Why, love was a birthright, what else did a woman need in her life? Imagine, being "passed by by love itself!" Not Noonie? That attractive little Mrs. Rush?

She stood up and rushed into her bedroom and turned on the crystal lights on her dressing table.

Her mirror had pretty colors and sunlit spaces to show her. She looked into her own eyes, and looked away despising the imaginary creature she saw.

She stopped her weeping, and powdered her face, and smoothed her hair. Her hands were trembling, and she thought it would make her seem more in command of herself and what she was going to do if she put on her rings. She opened the Dresden china box before her mirror and took out her three big rings, diamonds, all of them, and put them on.

She went to the hall. At the head of the stairs, she stopped and listened. Far below, in the basement, there drifted the sound of Cora ironing, the dim thump of the heavy iron when she set it down, and the wisp of monotonous singing which the Negress always gave out when she was content at her work.

Yes, she was there.

Yes, she was another woman. It didn't matter who she was, or of

what color. She was a middling-young colored woman who had been
with the Rushes for six years. She was married to a black man who
was a porter at the Harvey House downtown. Every year or so she
left him declaring that she was th'oo with his cuttinups. But pretty
soon, without any more said about it, she would return to their union,
and her big smile would be like a lamp in the kitchen. The other
servant, Leonard, who served in the dining room, and kept the house
clean, the lawn cut, the car washed, and the table waited upon, was
her vassal, whom she required to address her by her married name,
with "Mrs." and everything.

She saw Mrs. Rush come into the basement laundry, holding a
scrap of paper which she knew at once was a "list," and she wondered a little gloomily "now what." If there was anything she loved,
it was being let alone, and the laundry down here was a nice room,
sunny, for a cellar room, that is, and off by itself, and the laundry
smelled so nice? and felt so smooth when she ironed a piece? and
her voice sounded so pr'tty?

But Cora saw then that Mrs. Rush was *looking that way,* and
became fascinated at once. She thought Mrs. Rush looked mighty
pr'tty, but sure did seem upset. Sure did seem *frail?* Cora, like an
animal that knows when a human is afraid, knew that Mrs. Rush
was the weaker of the two of them. She set down her iron, and said
"Yes, Maaam?", and believed that Mrs. Rush had just been crying.
The Negress was naturally warmhearted. She wondered if she should
go and put her arms around her mistress, just for no reason at all,
but she figgered maybe not, all them diamon *rings.*

So she waited to discuss the "list."

But Mrs. Rush said,

"Go right on with your ironing, Cora.—Go on."

Cora resumed, wondering.

"I just—You don't mind if I ask you? Are you living with Jacob,
again, now? Cora?"

Cora made a musical sound, laughter and scandal all in one, and
said, yes, she was, she sure was, that *ma*-yan! he never let her be, no
matter what he *did,* no good but to go right straight *back* to him.
Shoo! My oh *my.*

Yes, there it was, Noonie said to herself, there was a woman full
of love, there it was, what was it like? Cora, how ample, how true,
how sure. She licked her lips and put her hands together, her rings
trembling with light.

Noonie's cheeks burned with shame.

"Do you love him?" she asked.

Cora laughed weakly and flopped her hands loosely from her wrists and let them hang there while she comically wagged her head from side to side, and said,

"I *guess* 'azz what you call it, I cain't *hep noth*in when he wants me to!"

"He—he wants you all the time?"

"Shoo! He's a buuull? that ma-yan!—I c'd kill him when he trifles on me, but he *need* more woman 'n jus' one? I honesly figger so, but I won't *tell* him so."

Noonie began to fold her "list" carefully into little even squares. She gazed at it as if it were a very important task, and made her hands stop trembling as well as she could. She cleared her throat and meant to sound perfectly serene and mistresslike with Cora, and asked Cora to tell her more; all about it; Jacob; what it was like; loving like that; did it really exist; could she stand it; getting loved that way.

Cora was a little shocked, not at the question, any woman might ask that who was a close friend, shoLord, she talked enough and she heard enough when 'm ol yellow gals got together 'thout their black boys aroun to hear what they said and git all swelled up and conceited, hearin thataway. But this was her employer, and a white woman, and don' know; summin funny about it. But there was something pleading in Mrs. Rush's attitude, standing there folding that slip of paper with her little white hands. Lord, honey, thought Cora, if you wan' hear 'bout *love* that much I'll sho tell you.

She resumed her ironing and told her. Her talking voice was silken and gentle, and deeply full of animal music and possession.

Noonie began to tear the little piece of paper into exact little squares and drop them to the floor while she listened to Cora.

Cora was good. She honestly owned what she celebrated. She had no shame. Her pride was happy. She knew her sorrows because she couldn't help being jealous sometimes. Thing is, he never did fail to come back to her, even if he went off cattin sometimes. It seemed to her that there wasn't anything you did that you couldn't talk about, if you saw it where it belonged. When she looked up at Mrs. Rush again, she felt compassionate at what she saw in that composed face, with its downcast eyes, desire and fear both showing through.

The torn bits of paper drifted to the floor.

"You'll be all right, Mrs. Rush, honey? I make you a cup tea?"

She tactfully put them back to where they belonged in relation to each other.

Mrs. Rush shook her head, and said with a smile that she had forgotten *what* it was she had come down to *speak* to Cora about, and pale with her thoughts of what she had heard, she turned and went upstairs.

III

Cora sighed, when she was alone again. She had never understood, and she didn't understand now, how come so many white folks get like that, over *that*. Live in a house with white folks, couldn't hep knowin some things. White folks sure got unhappy lot time when ain't no *sense* to it.

XIX · THE POETS

I

The lovers, separated by going to their homes at night, sometimes knew formless poems of passion within themselves even greater than those to which they tried to give form in their kisses together.

Late at night when the whole house was asleep below, Bun would awaken in his attic den, where his narrow iron bed was. The dormer windows were swung open. The starlight looked cool far out there, and the nights when the moon was swollen with pure light during the early hours before midnight were a third and strange time of day in his room, that light on the floor, on the books tumbled before the bookcase, on his clothes like fallen clowns by the chair, on the single sheet which was all he could bear to cover him, on the long legs he flung free of bedclothes for the need of the cool breath of night and the wash of moonlight on his hard flesh.

It seemed to him sometimes that he raged all night in his bed, with love.

He hated his room then. It was a boy's room. It had those models of locomotives on the neat, narrow shelves that he and his father together had built to carry that miniature display. This bed was wide enough for nobody else; and so it was too often peopled by phantoms of love. The roof sloped to a peak above him, and it was as if a man could stand only in the middle of the room with his head up. There were possessions too trivial and too dear for his present freedom.

They reminded him of too much that he wanted to forget, in order to be free with his passion. He blushed to remember the little boy he had been, because he wanted now to outgrow the little boy with acts of creation. Sleep came down upon him only like a wing that was lifted again in the flight of his desires before his thoughts.

Let the moonlight go away.

When the cool air wafts in through the windows I can smell the river sometimes. It is cool, and I smell roots and leaves and the silky dragging of the muddy water. If I squinch my eyes shut maybe I can see the place again where I used to go swimming and all the other boys I knew and we knew everything and we didn't care and we were naked in the mud and pure in the heart because nothing bothered us the way things bother us now.

He would get up from his bed and go to the window and look out to the west to see if he could see the river in the moonlight, way across town there below the highlands. If the moon was perfectly right, distant water caught a gleam and shone there, a tiny wedge of silver among the banks of trees on the far edge of town, which he could look down upon.

It cooled him. It freed him for a moment. It made him forget himself, and the flow of shame that followed the waves of power released by his desirous thoughts.

Now I will go to sleep in her name, he would think, and return to his cot, purified. Across the room in the darkness he passed the mirror on his bureau and he made a silvery shadow in it, going through the moonlight. He ground his jaws at the shadowy mirror.

II

Martha lay awake and could see out through the screens how the moonlight poured on the dark varnished leaves of the huge cottonwood in the swept back yard. The tree was alive with tiny points of moonlight on its dark shiny leaves, moving in the wind which (fantastically) could have been but a veil of air localized to the tree itself, since no stir seemed or sounded in anything else hereabout. Beyond the tree, in the limitless silvery blue of the night sky, there was an immense cloud, miles and miles away. It was so disposed that it seemed to echo the very shape of the tree crown in its imaginable domes and caverns; mighty, towering, fabulous in the pour of white moonlight upon its white cliffs. Regarding it, she was its owner. Nobody else saw it, she felt, just as she did. Traveling hugely and in tremendous airiness, the cloud was some sort of signal for her; a confirmation of the senses just before sleep. So her heart traveled, and so her thoughts arose. So her eyes saw, when far lightning pierced the interior of the vast cloud, and showed her vistas of silver like the very future, in the highly echoing galleries of the thunderhead muttering dimly above horizons too far to see. To the north, even farther than the moonlighted palisade of heaven, she saw a star, troubled by distance so that now and then it lost its beam; but still it shone, when she searched for it; and she owned it as poetry. Purely she loved, so that her whole self was alive to love. She whispered to herself with her eyes closed, seeing the words as remembered shapes upon Bun's own mouth,

"It is the star to every wandering bark,"

and by this she meant the love they held together; and if there had ever been anything mean, or funny, about their two heads over the printed page in the yellow table lamplight of the public library where they had come upon Shakespeare's words, such connotation was gone, and justly so.

The lightning walked vastly in the cloud galleries; the thunder crowned far mountains that were out of sight; the star's beam was dandled by the altering depths of the earth's atmosphere; all faithful to themselves as she was to herself, and true.

XX · THE CLEANSING RIVER

I

"——And now they telephone," said Noonie to herself Saturday morning. She was standing in the hall calling upstairs to Donald to come and talk to Wayne, who was waiting at the other end of the wire. She had forgotten that when she was a child, the telephone was known; but saw it now as an astounding modern invention with which even children could make sense.

In a moment Don came down and she watched him. As he neared her, she wanted to put out her arms and stop him with an embrace; but she knew he hated such demonstrations, and she smiled remotely at him, feeling that same odd, lost feeling that her son gave her now and then, and she half-decided for the thousandth time that she had given all her own strength and health to him, and that he was uncomfortable with her as if he dimly knew how much he owed her, and chafed in the debt.

He went to the phone cupboard under the stairs where there were a light, a mirror and a little shelf with the Doctor's memorandum pad.

"Hello Way."

(What's the matter, Mrs. Rush wondered, he doesn't sound like himself.)

Then Donald swung the door of the cupboard shut, and she could hear no more.

In a few minutes he came out, closing the door carefully after him, and started upstairs again. Noonie came out of the living room with her magazine and asked him if Wayne was coming over, and if they were going out for the day, did he want a lunch put up, if they were? Or would Wayne stay to lunch here, it was such a lovely day, she said she was so glad he had such a good time with Wayne, she said she never had a minute's worry about them. But he hardly stopped going up the stairs to tell her no, Wayne was not coming over, and about the lunch, no thank you, he was going out by himself, and wouldn't need any.

"—Need any!" she echoed, "You most certainly shall have some, I'll have Cora fix a box, you most certainly shall not go hungry!— What's the matter. Is anything the matter, darling?"

"No, of course not," he said, and disappeared in the upstairs hall to his room.

She said to herself that he *said* there was nothing the matter, and so she was probably worrying needlessly. But he looked very peculiar, boys *were,* they just *were.*

Upstairs Don knelt down by the window and put his fists and chin on the sill and stared out over the side lot where the evergreen nursery grew. He did not know how he would eventually make it up with Wayne. He would have to find a way to do it. He all but had to hang *up* on Wayne who had begun to insist that they go to the river together for a swim. Donald said this, and that, giving excuses; but Wayne had a ready answer for each one, and didn't believe him. Donald couldn't tell him exactly what he wanted to do, and where, because it wasn't exactly clear to himself, even; but he knew by how he felt that he had to be alone this morning; and it was the first Saturday morning since he could remember that he and Wayne hadn't gone out together, or at least explained what prevented their meeting. Wayne finally didn't say any more on the phone but just stayed there in silence. Both boys held the phone and said nothing. The wire sounded alive and connected, with a little far sound like gas escaping somewhere. Neither wanted to be the first to hang up, or start talking all over again. Finally Donald said,

"Well, I'll call you later on, Way."

"Oh, *very* well. Good-by."

"Good-by."

Click.

He certainly sounded put out.

Don got up from the window and went to his closet where he found the rifle. He put on his blue corduroy cap and got a sweater whose arms he tied around his neck; and he began to tiptoe to the front stairs, listening. He didn't want to get caught and be handed a box of lunch. He didn't *want* anything to eat. He could hear sounds in the kitchen, his mother and Cora; they were rattling waxed paper and fixing him something. Deciding on a dash, he flew on tiptoe down three steps at a time and was out the front door before anybody saw him. His bicycle was out in front. In a second he was riding down the street toward the meadows that lay off to the south through which the great river crawled shallow and sandy in the spring sunshine.

He found the dried mud road that ran along beside the *acequia madre,* the big irrigation ditch from which the little ditches of the meadows got their water. In a very short while he had left the town behind him, and was free in the country-smelling, hot river land. He had his rifle under his arm. People who saw him would think he was on his way to shoot birds. The river was edged with deep stands of cottonwoods and willows. How fresh their green was at this time of year! They gave such a sweet-smelling shade that he loved just to go and lie down in such a clump and shut his eyes and love the trees by not thinking or caring or wanting or doing anything. Maybe if he went today:

So he hurried his riding, and presently came to the place where the great ditch between its high banks turned and ran parallel to the river. A footpath went up the ditch bank and led across the brown run on a clayed plank. He dismounted and struggled up with his bicycle, for to leave it on this side of the ditch was to risk robbery; and there were always plenty of others around on Saturday—the Martinez gang from Old Town, who ranged the meadows like a revolutionary army, would steal from you and take your clothes and chase you, if they ever outnumbered you enough. He got the bicycle across the plank with exciting difficulty, because a vagrant swing of the front wheel might plop it off into the ditch below; and down over the other bank of the ditch, where the heavy greenery began. He found a clump of young willows that made a perfect blind, and there he laid down his bicycle, locking the rear wheel with his special padlock. He stood listening. He believed that he could actually hear the river, not that it made a rushing sound as it went, for it went too slowly and shallowly on the wide bed. But he could hear the wet life of the banks, and he shut his eyes the better to receive those tiny sounds of suck, and seep, and he knew from what he remembered how the mud was glistening where the river wet it, and how the banks under the trees might be wet from high water that came from melting snow in the mountains to the north. There were insects singing in the radiant green air of the riverside glades. The sandhills across the river were white golden in the sunlight. Far to his left would be the bridge that crossed the river in Barelas, where Borelli's saloon stood on this side, and where all the tin cans were dumped down on the river edge. The cans, when the sun was just right, glittered magnificently from this distance, like a huge pile of enormous diamonds.

II

He wished he could stand like this with his eyes shut remembering everything else until he forgot how he felt.

But he opened his eyes, and pushed on through the green tangle of willow and cottonwood saplings walking in wet ground until he saw the flat bank and then the river and then the other side, and the high blue above it.

A great heron heard him coming and claimed a lift with its wings and sailed inland over his head out of sight above the trees.

He did not bring his rifle to the aim.

He had no bullets.

He went to the edge of the bank and began walking south, as close as possible to the river. Now he could see the whole open riverscape, the bridge, the black structures of the edge of town, one white steam plume from the Santa Fe shops, and behind, the blue mountains.

He kept out a wary eye for other walkers along the bank; but he saw none. Perhaps he could just make out what that little glisten of light might be by the bridge, down by Borelli's; he looked again; it was boys in the river. When they stood up he could just recognize their flesh. He must be done at the river today long before he got that far.

What he was watching out for was quicksand.

Many was the time he had come to swim here with Wayne, and the two of them had recognized what they were sure was quicksand . . .

an extra movement of the shallow current, the little particles of sand rolling and boiling ever so gently, the way a stone would fall there as they threw it, and then begin slowly to shine with the sand climbing around it, and then the polishing work of the water as it closed over the top and went on down stream dragging a little sandy trail for a few minutes and then again nothing at all but the cool pale muddy color of the whole river.

Walking down the edge, he could kick off a clump now and then and by so little change the course of that always changing river.

Ahead of him there was a point of new territory, as he thought of it; the end of old man Rhodes's pasture, which the river had cut into during the last flow of melted snow in the north. Now a fence line hung unsupported between point and point, where the river had cut away a new miniature bay. The uprooted poles and the wire stretching from terminals on still solid ground were collecting driftage. Branches made a barrier there. Donald went inland and climbed through the solid fence and came back out to the bank beyond.

As he thought; the water was shallower here because of the new spread of the river into old man Rhodes's pasture. Here he would be able to go into the river and get across to the dry bank in the middle, and he would cross that, and come to the other vein of the river near the opposite shore. That great land spit was like a miniature desert lying between two independent streams. The quicksand was well known to be more treacherous and rapid over there on the other side.

He sat down and listened again, this time for voices; but heard none. The eleven o'clock whistle from the sawmill way across town blew its steamy music into the air, and he heard it with pleasure. It was a cheerful sound, mellowed by distance. When it died out, he looked around and decided he was alone. The meadows stretched inland, the trees were still, the far bathers at the bridge seemed hardly nearer for all his walk. He untied his shoes and kicked them off, and then his stockings, and then he stood up and yanked off all his clothes. The air felt sweet on his warm skin. He began to feel dread for the certainty of what he must do. He made a bundle of his clothes, climbed a cottonwood that had a lot of low leaves, and stowed his things in a hidden Y of the tree.

He debated a moment whether to take off his waterproof wrist watch; but he decided not to bother. Then taking his rifle, he went to the river and stepped in. The current was warm and pushy as it rose on his legs. Underfoot he felt sliding mud; not quicksand that drank you up steadily. Suddenly he was up to his waist, but the water was still idling, so he held up his arms with his watch and rifle and pretty soon he was coming shallower, and stepping into flowing mud, and then the mud came up to the emerging flat, and lay there, a plain of still wet but baking warm river earth that felt delicious to walk on. Beyond that was the long spit of smooth dried mud, so rich that it was pale purple, and cracked by drying into edible-looking little cakes. On to this he now emerged, and both banks seemed far away. He was happily lost in a wilderness of sunlight, separated from his world by a river on each side of him. Upstream or down, he was alone, and now he wished for Wayne, but he still knew that what he wanted to do he had to do alone.

III

He had gone alone the day before to see the man at the paint store, where they sold glass. The store was crowded, but he waited, whistling silently. Pretty soon, that little skinny fellow with a face like a smiling rat, a rat who was friendly and didn't see anything funny about looking like one, came up and asked if he had been waited upon.

Donald replied that he was interested in buying a pane of glass.

"What size?"

Don frowned, feeling that he must look deliberate, and held out his hands as far apart as the size of the panes of glass in the chicken house up at the Shoemaker ranch.

The clerk nodded.

"Bout eight by eight?—I'd have to cut it for you."

"Could I watch?"

"Sure."

"How much would it cost?"

"Bout twenty cents."

"Apiece?"

"Why, sure.—You want more'n one?"

"Oh, no, I was just figgerin."

"Well, come on back. I'll do you a pane that size."

They went to the workshop out in back of the paint store. There were picture frame molding and frames and stacks of paint in cans and sheets of glass in excelsior; and two old rocking chairs hoisted against the ceiling by ropes, evidently just to get them out of the way.

Don watched while the agreeable young man "took and scratched" the right size on the corner of a large pane of window glass. The diamond cutting tool bit the glass with a grind that made him shudder comically. Then the great moment came, of tapping the big pane to make it crack the little one off, clean and astonishing.

"There she is."

"Well, thanks.—Here, I'll pay for it."

"Twenty cents."

"Here it is."

"Sure do thank you. Come back and see us."

"Sure will."

He went out and rode off. He knew what he wanted to know. Twenty cents apiece, and they must have wrecked about—how many? —about three hundred, with the .22 rifle. His heart sank at a new thought. The glass would cost something to *put in*, too. He turned around, rode back to the paint store, and asked what it cost to *put in* a pane of glass that size.

"Just the one? In a window?"

"Well, yes, in a window."

The clerk took a pad and pencil and as he spoke, he read out the figuring he was doing.

"Eight b' eight, twenty cents, time and labor, twenty cents, materials, that is putty and depreciation, ten cents, it'd cost you right around fifty cents?"

"Thanks."

"O.K.—Hurry back."

"Sure will."

He rode off again. His face was hotly flushing. When he reached the park on the way home, he rode up on the lawn and lay down on the grass. He had a scrap of paper in his pocket and a fine pencil which wrote red at one end and blue at the other. He multiplied three hundred panes by fifty cents and it came out one hundred and fifty dollars.

He was ruined.

It was a fortune.

The most money he had ever earned in one week was a dollar and five cents, helping Wayne down at the stationery shop when they were rushed during textbook season, and all the school children came to get their books and pencils, and things.

He rolled over and buried his face in the grass.

It was the first time he had ever realized that the Shoemakers were poor. A hundred and fifty dollars meant the world and all to Mrs. Shoemaker. He had practically robbed her of it. He had never believed sums like that before. It had been easier to imagine seventy million dollars in pearls and radium, the rare treasures of M. le

Vicomte, than it had been to know what a hundred and fifty dollars meant in actual value, of time, labor and pride.

They are so poor! he cried inwardly, in the agony of discovery. That's what that little house meant, and Willa Shoemaker working so hard and jerking so thinly when she walked so fast, and the way Wayne's clothes were always darned and patched and the way Martha cut his hair sometimes, instead of his going to the barbershop . . .

He hated his big ugly brick house and the servants they gave money to wait on them and the jewels his mother had upstairs in a china box.

He knew of no way to discharge the debt he owed.

But a way of expiation by sacrifice did occur to him. That it would cost him so much gave him a stoic's resolve and strength.

IV

He went on walking over the dried river middle toward that other side which brought the desert of the sandhills down to the very water's edge. The dried mud was hot to his feet. Over his skin the sun laid a garment of feeling; when he turned toward it, he was clothed by its touch. He fancied himself turning browner, looking down his breast. He was proud of the muscled plates developing on his body. If Wayne were here, he would run him a race. They could race for as far as you could see, upstream or down, on this wide dry river between the two waters.

The ribbons of sunlight on the other half of the river were beginning to be blinding as he walked nearer. There no trees grew, everything was lifted flat and empty to the sun. There was a miniature cliff of crusty earth a foot high which marked where the river ran. He came to it, and it caved in under him, so he moved back. This was the treacherous side. He began to walk downstream, watching intently for the kind of current, the sort of shallow glisten of the quicksands. He picked up a clod of dried mud in his free hand, to be ready with it. His stomach felt hollow with suspense, and he had his belly muscles sucked in so he looked hard and lean, the color of the dried river land he was trudging on alone and small.

"There it is!" he exclaimed, and leaned down to see. The water was washing almost idly over a glistening lift of river sand. The channel had moved gradually away from him, and was taking the swifter water downstream by the opposite shore.

"I wish" he said, but he had no idea how to say what he wished.

He heaved the big clod of dirt into the sand, and it began to turn dark with water, like a lump of sugar held edgily in a cup of coffee. The sand seemed loose and fat and hungry, and into it the hunk of mud began to sink steadily. In a moment the water was sheeting along over it. Whatever fell in there would vanish that same way. He sat down to look at it. He lay down and crossed his arms over his eyes, leaving his rifle athwart his middle, but it burned him from being in the sun, and he got up again. He had read about people feeling that their hearts were in their mouths; and that was how he felt now.

Now it must be something like an accident, or people would never be able to think well of him again. Perhaps if he began to see how close to the edge he could walk, without breaking down the cut-out edge of the bank, along the place where the quicksand was, he would have to be careful about keeping his balance to avoid falling in.

He began to tiptoe as near as he could. He held his arms out to balance himself. Over the water he held his rifle.

In the sunlight he was sweating and shining.

"Now another step," he thought, "This is a game after all, to see how close I can come without actually falling in and getting caught, there is nothing I would not lose to keep from being caught in the quicksand, *not even my new rifle.*"

He stepped, and the crust of mud gave way under him and he lurched. His right leg went into the water and he felt the cold, fluid, terrifyingly easy slide of the sand up around his leg. He threw himself sideways to solid ground and he called out, and let go of his rifle which flew through the air and landed flat in the shallow water. He rolled himself to safety, far back from the bank, and felt his heart pounding at the narrow escape he had had. His wet leg itched where the sun began to dry it. Heaving, he got up to look for the rifle. It was gone. The water was as idle and unruffled as if nothing had ever fallen in there, and been buried from sight and out of guilt, on that jelly of wet sand.

He sighed deeply.

That was exactly what had happened, and it was what he could tell everybody.

Now he turned and began racing back across the land spit toward the green side of the river. When he came to the other water, he left the run in a long sailing dive and buried his head in the muddy flow and drifted downstream in warm oblivion as long as he could hold his breath. Then he caught at the other bank and lodged himself against some roots and let the current run over him and eddy him gently and with its earthen power, wash him clean of his fears, his remorse, and his actions.

He felt better.

Punishment was done.

Whether the instrument deserved it or not, he did not consider.

Drowsing there, he soon seemed an accustomed part of the life of the riverbank; and all the little things he had scared away now returned and were part of the noontide drone . . . the water spiders skating near the bank, the mocking birds that had taken a circle in the air before returning to the leaves, the beaver up the way who was examining old man Rhodes's ruined fence where the drifting cottonwood branches were piling up. The air shifted this way from the south; not actually a wind, rather a medium for sound. The boys swimming down by the bridge appeared here by their voices, tiny sounds of Saturday music that reminded him of where they were and how they looked in the sunlight, gold toilers in the golden river distance.

He wondered who they were.

It was enough to get him up.

He climbed from the water and ran upstream to his tree, and by the time he got there he was dried off. He dressed quickly, and started back. When he came to the place where he turned inland toward his willow brake, he aroused the same heron, which bandied its way once again into the air. Through the grove ahead he thought he could see someone, and he stopped to peer, wondering if he would have to fight for his own bicycle, or even to retain the key of the padlock. He came ahead carefully, and then in a plunge of high spirits he recognized Wayne, sitting on the ground beside his own wheel, waiting. Donald ran through the saplings, crashing and eager.

"Where's your rifle?" asked Wayne.

"How long've you been here?—It's gone."

"Gone?"

"Yes. Let's go. Let's ride back by Borelli's."

"Where's it gone?"

"I'll tell you."

They got their bicycles up and over the plank across the great ditch, and down on the meadow path which they would leave for the road running inland from the river, but more or less following its course.

"I had it with me out on the river, on the other side, in case I saw anything, and when I got over there, I was going along the edge watching the quicksand, and she caved in with me, and I just barely fell back myself. The rifle flew out of my hand tzing! it was gone in the quicksand."

They rode in silence.

Then Donald said,

"Don't you believe me?"

"Sure."

Wayne added to himself that if he'd been along it probably wouldn't have happened.

Aloud, he said,

"Are you going to tell your Dad?"

"—I don't know. Sooner or later, I guess."

"I haven't said anything to Mom yet."

"Neither have I."

"Let's speed."

They rose on their pedals and charged down the fragrant dirt road. Pretty soon they came on open land by the river and saw how near the bridge was, and Borelli's saloon. They could hear the boys swimming, and to see them, and who they were, they rode through the dirt street up onto the bridge and came to rest on their saddles, looking down on the bathers who were far enough off to be naked and unrecognizable except that they looked like Mexican boys.

"It must be Joe Martinez and his gang."

"I guess so. They come every Saturday."

"What do you suppose they do down there?"

"They'd show us quick enough if we got anywhere near.—Remember the day Neddie Truman went by there? They practically skinned him alive.—They busted his wheel up. You remember that."

"That's right."

V

A sudden concert of noon whistles began to ascend from all over the town. Their sound somehow made the day seem hotter still. The old bridge rattled its planks under the traffic . . . an old wood wagon or two, intermittent cars.

Wayne suddenly turned to Don, and said, with an air of coming at last to what was unspoken between them,

"I don't know what got into us that day."

"It was a week ago today."

"Is that why you lost your rifle?"

"It flew out of my hand, I tell you, or I would have fallen in, I would rather let my old gun fall in than get caught myself."

They felt sober.

How childish the pretending of all their past seemed now! That

play about destroying the viaduct! It was a sort of anguish to sit here
on the sunny old bridge and remember such things.

"Let's go?"

"Where:"

They turned their wheels and glided down the ramp toward Borelli's saloon. It was washed with the tremendous deep cool shade of the
cottonwoods that stood around it and above it, and out in back, near
the bank, there were some willows. In summertime, Borelli had an
open-air beer garden there, with lattices whose paint was faded. The
front door was open. The place looked cool inside. The nickel piano
was fumbling through a remote tune in the back room. The street in
front was of clay, and so were the walls of the house. The boys rode
slowly down to the door, and sat, looking in. From the front room
there issued a cool draft of air with a beery fragrance that made them
blench wondrously, for all it suggested.

They felt lost.

This shabby and comfortable old saloon was like a symbol of a
world where the lost retreated.

They longed to enter, in woeful excitement.

Borelli was a blue-faced Italian with a ceremonial belly and a
sentimental indignation about the morals of the young. His sixteen-
year-old son Nick spent his spare time hanging around the place.
Nick Borelli was as slow as anybody they knew in school, to understand what they talked about and liked to think of; and yet on the
other hand, Nick was at home in a whole world of which they knew
only the scrappiest references. Nick was sixteen, and privy to what the
talk about women and what they *did* really was about; he used to
tell the younger boys, some of whom did not believe a word he said.
Nick's voice sounded as if it were full of crumbs, husky and satisfied.
Nobody ever forgot the day Nick had a bottle of beer with him at
school. It passed around the tender little mouths still without character and they all swallowed some. He assured them all that down at
the "Place," by the river, there under the willows and cottonwoods,
he could get them anything they wanted, at any time. His old man
was an easy one to fool, and never really knew how much beer, and
cigarettes, and stuff he ever really had on hand, so he would never
miss a thing.

Nick had brown, softly shining skin. He was always smiling under
his curved nose. His heavy black hair grew down to his temples and
almost to his eyebrows and under his sweater his shoulders bulked
big and round. Everybody liked him because he was so friendly, besides the things he had to tell. He never understood a thing of any

importance in the classroom, but was encouraged in such activities as penmanship, at which he would spend hours, making expert and decorative pages full of capital S's, with heavy downstrokes, and light, birdy upstrokes. He was often allowed to decorate the blackboards, which he did publicly and proudly, turning to the class for silent applause from time to time. The boys all liked him; but the girls knew he was just better than a simpleton, and let him alone. He didn't seem to mind. He liked the women in the other house by the river, who worked for his father, and who treated him like a mascot.

The world of the imagination, where Donald and Wayne were so busy, would never be revealed to him.

From the cool vista of the back room, Nick saw the two boys out in the sunshine, peering into the door. He got up from the oilcloth table back there and came forward through the several doors and the boys greeted him.

"Looking for something, kids?" he asked with his father's ministerial cordiality.

"Nope."

Nick had a face full of innocent friendliness, because that was just how he felt.

"Come on around back, if you want to do a little business.—The old man is in town. Come on."

He jerked them toward the back yard with his shiny black head. He seemed infinitely older than they. It was intolerable not to know as much as that about everything.

They walked their bikes along after him on the hard swept adobe ground.

It was hot and quiet in the yard and they could see glimpses of the river through the long-hanging willows with their new green fingers.

Nick treated them like esteemed customers of no particular age, and sold them two bottles of beer and a package of Egyptian Deity cigarettes. He wrapped it all up for them in a couple of funny papers, and thoughtfully provided a bottle opener.

Nick told them they could go sit down in the back room, if they liked. But they suddenly hated him. They wanted to get away from his oozy good nature. They also dimly thought of cops and raids, for they'd heard of Prohibition. No, they said, and went back to their bicycles and rode across the bridge to the far side of the river. At the end of the bridge, they wheeled down on to the sand, and went around under the bridge, where the old planks above them made alternate bars of shadow and blades of sunshine. The sand was cool. Little ranks of river grass grew there. They sat down and felt private in the midst of life. Overhead the planks rattled and thundered musically whenever a car or a wagon went across. Low down to the ground, the two boys saw a flat world—the river stretching widely afar; little water; much light; land fading into the distance, finally rubbed out by the heat.

With the same question in their eyes, which neither could translate, but which asked if there were no end to folly, they opened their beer, and lighted up their smokes; confirmed by their dismal trophies of indulgence.

XXI · THE PROGRAM

I

There was a rising and falling, and as they spoke of it, eternal flow of their rapture that made Martha and Bun want to keep a secret for some time yet. They would meet evenings at the library, as usual; only now, with a sense of design come into their lives where before they had only known and been vaguely dissatisfied with a succession of things to do, they embarked upon a program of what they called "self-improvement." They were sober and inwardly excited about it. They pulled long faces over their intellects, and this very attitude gave them an almost unbearable, delicious inner reminder of their desire, which was now so channeled and controlled that it became a kind of engine source for their very lives.

If it was worth while to be together, then it was worth while to make the most serious plans for the future. The most serious plans for the future meant looking at themselves to see what they needed to realize their hopes. To realize their hopes meant knowing what Bun was going to do. What Bun was going to do was become a doctor.

"The only doctor I know is Doctor Rush. My brother Wayne is a great friend of little Donald Rush."

"My father says Doctor Rush is the best one in this town.—He knows them all as only a prescription druggist can. Says Rush is a deep one, too. He *studies* a lot."

"What about?"

"Oh, I don't know.—Just *studies*."

"Mrs. Rush is not very well."

"I'll bet she has never been in love, then," said Bun.

Martha looked at him in delighted amazement.

"There. That's what I mean," she said.

"About what?" he asked.

"About you.—Two weeks ago you would never've made a remark like that."

"Like what?"

"As intelligent as that, about Mrs. Rush, and love."

"Oh." He laughed airily. She wanted to eat him up, she said to herself, when he looked as charming as that, with his eyes almost smiled out of sight by his smooth and glowing cheeks. "I believe love is health," he added, crowning his first effort with one even more delectable.

"You will be the greatest physician in the Southwest. You already have what very few of them have."

"What is that?"

"Intuitive genius," she said soberly.

"I believe perhaps you're right. Of course, it is a gift for which I can hardly accept credit. My mother always said that my grandfather Summerfield, *her* father-in-law, that is, was a very superior man.—This was his ring."

They regarded it together. In silence he took it off his finger that was like a young branch in spring, with sun-pinked bark, and put it on her thumb. For several moments they did not speak. And then with the dramatic inspiration of their state, she gently took them from the beating impulses of desire and wooed them back to their intellectual league, and they bent again over the book on the table before them—a history of medicine which they were absorbing together, page by page, reading in silence, and nodding when they were one by one ready to turn the next page.

They had a program of further study all mapped out.

One page of German grammar every evening. One page of French essay writing, "because the French were so good at clear argument." This was a sentiment Bun had found in his sophomore notebook in his attic den at home, where Grandfather Summerfield's books had been put. Five pages of *Pickwick Papers* every evening. One § of the medical history, though sometimes they were unable to finish that assignment before closing time because some of the §'s were longer than others. And finally, a book on the care of babies—a subject which they approached with a sort of stern modesty, declaring that there was too much prudery in the world about so wonderful a fact as birth and so delightful a birthright as rearing children.

II

One evening she suddenly faced him during their study, and asked him why he was called Bunny. He said that an aunt came to see him, Susan Leighton, from Kansas City, when he was a little boy five years old, and he remembered vividly that it was Auntie Susan who had first called him Bunny, and that they had all been photographed on the lawn of the house out on South Walter Street, and Auntie Susan had held his hand, and got him to laughing by asking him *whose* bunny he was, he was *her* little bunny, so that when the Kodak clicked in the hands of his father, he was laughing in glee, and on the print when it came back from the developer's in its yellow paper envelope was the record of the moment when they had all started to call him Bunny, which later years and older friends had changed to Bun.

"Bring it to show me tomorrow night, darling!"

"I will if I can find it."

He was suddenly shy. He knew perfectly well where the picture was, it was cornered into the black-sheeted photograph album that lay on the under shelf of the mission-style library table at home. Nobody looked at it any more. Auntie Susan was dead, too, but what fun she had been, how clever she was with her humor and her devotion to him as a little boy. She died an old maid, but if her life had never been full to the brim, she had certainly helped to give others a lot for their own lives; he frowned and tried to remember if this might not in itself have been a fulfilled mission for Auntie Susan.

Anyway, he did bring the picture the next evening, and Martha pored over it, and he thought she looked almost greedy.

She felt like his mother, possessing the little boy in the snapshot with her eyes. She had a sentimental film on her vision which she turned away from him so he wouldn't think her a fool. It was so exactly like him now, twelve years later, by her side, in his always fresh clothes, his pressed trousers, his spotless sweaters, his bulky-shouldered coats. He was the cleanest boy she ever knew, and the strongest-looking, not with bulging knots of muscle, that bored her, but with a harmonious look of flowing arch and staying tension; bone and flesh. And in the snapshot, there was the gleeful little boy, laughing with all his heart, and over him, the bending figure of Auntie Susan, whose face was hidden; all that showed of her was the anonymous attitude of love and protection. To one side, patiently fond, was her sister Mrs. Summerfield clasping her own elbows, as if resigned to awkward usefulness.

"You do. You look exactly like a bunny," said Martha finally, "with such a big-toothed smile.—May I keep the snapshot?"

"It's Mother's," he said.

"Can't you get another?"

"The negative is lost, I guess."

"Then I guess you want it back:"

"—It's Mother's."

"Oh: very well."

"She'd miss it, darling."

"Oh, very *well*, take it."

He was calm, because he was right, and never believed in apologizing for being right. He put the snapshot back into his wallet, and reminded her that after all, she had his Grandfather Summerfield's braided gold ring.

She knew what it was that had irritated her. Not the snapshot, which turned her heart to water, but the feeling of having put herself into his mother's place for a moment; this was guilty; poor Mrs. Summerfield; how total love was; some day she would find some way to have Mrs. Summerfield forgive her without knowing exactly what for.

"I am a fool, but I don't care," she said, turning them back to their book again.

They were serene and sure in working this way together. It made the future seem a clever little arrangement of their own devising. They had a sense of movement and direction which seemed to them unique. All other people—such as also came to use the common riches of the public library—seemed to them "little people." A sense of pity suffused Martha and Bun when they looked around them at others. They never knew it, but they were arrogant in their love.

XXII · FORGIVEN

I

When Peter came downstairs from his office and went out to his car late in the afternoon, he was astonished to see his son Donald sitting there waiting for him. Now what on earth: he thought. But the Rushes were so rarely articulate with each other that he simply smiled at the boy, and got in and drove off.

Something was up.

But he would never get at it by asking. He drove in easy silence for several blocks, and said to himself that maybe Don just wanted to ride around with him, and if he did, why, he was more than welcome. It had never happened before. It might never happen again. But if there was anything beyond sense it was what a boy that age might take a notion into his head to do, or want.

Don pursed his lips to whistle, but made no sound. Peter could see a dark shadow along the boy's deeply curved lip. You couldn't call it a mustache, but it was a hint of where a mustache would be, one day. Good lord, already, what do I remember of my own adolescence? Hardly any details. But it all turned up very sharply in the memory of feeling a couple of years back when I was reading that book on rites of primitive peoples. No wonder they mark every stage with a duty or an act of suffering or an ordeal by shock. They make life a series of stages, and simplify what is expected of everyone by making it all cut and dried, perfectly plain. What do we do? We just let our children slide from phase to phase, and nobody can be expected to develop with the same harmonies as everybody else, if there are no clearly marked lines to cross, obligations to undertake, and phenomena to recognize. Our obscenities (and some of them, willy-nilly, are acts of discovery) are all secret. That's where the savage has it over us. His are exposed and even ceremonial, and their purpose made plain and impersonal.

I believe I'd've been abysmally unhappy myself as a boy if I'd had rich parents, or been born in a city, but as 'twas, all this land to charge around in; my horse to ride; my share of work to do to keep the house warm in winter or the field plowed and tended in summer; my Bible lines to learn every week; the cycles of animal life on our

ranch; nobody much to be with, even after we came in town so I'd
go to school; you wouldn't believe the difference of the two worlds,
my boyhood's, and my son's. I may be wrong.

II

He drove to the edge of town on the south, where he had a call
to make in a veritable shack, the home of a tubercular patient. He
took his bag and left Don in the car and went into the house. Don
sat looking out at the plain into which the street opened and vanished, as if it were a river reaching the illimitable sea. The sun was
going down and the light was long and golden. There were some
towering cumulus clouds far off beginning to look like pink marble
in the softening light. Donald wondered if he might someday be a
great artist, noted for sunset effects, and have his name printed in
books with two dates, in brackets, showing when he was born, and
when he died, like *Sir* Anthony Van Dyck (1599–1641). This troubled him only for a second. Should he tell Daddy about the rifle?
Or, rather, *would* he tell him?—For that he *ought* to do so, he knew.
He knew well enough that the Doctor would never ask anything
about the rifle. A lifetime of presents, and his father had never once
checked up on what was done with them. His father never came
around butting in, he would say that.

The door of the house opened, and Peter came out, followed for a
couple of steps by a young woman who was smiling sociably with a
white, drawn mouth that would break the other way when she was
alone again. He was always reached by the social courage that people
tried to maintain when he had to leave bad news behind him.

"Now let's see, where next," he said, turning the big car around
and heading back to town. "I'll run by the hospital the last thing.
Let's go by old MacClellan's house and see what's wrong with the
government today.—He's been a lot spryer since I told him to quit
reading the *Literary Digest*. Just did it to make him *start* reading it.
Now he gets in a fit over the nation, and forgets to snarl about his
liver. Liver's all right, or it'd be a scandal if it *were* any better in a
man his age."

They stopped at a miniature copper-roofed castle of red brick and
white stone down by the park in town. While the Doctor was within,
Donald squinted his eyes dreamily at the deep windows, the towers,
and stained-glass jewels in the upper halves of the front windows, and
made a king's palace out of it.

A golden twilight was at large in the streets when they drove on again.

After a couple of other calls, they parked up at the hospital, on the graveled circle of driveway in back.

III

The hospital stood on a knoll, and Peter sat at the wheel of his car for a moment, gazing abstractedly out across the sandhills below them. Under the yellow sky, all things on the earth were graying to a dusky black, the roofs of little houses, the lines of fences, the bulk of sheds and anything built. Twilight brushed across these mean structures and their silhouettes came together in one long earthbound line, rising and falling like a melody. What fixed Peter's eye and penetrated his spirits like a song, clear and sweet, was, commonly enough, a single electric light bulb hanging from a right-angled pole at the intersection of the dirt streets of the sandhills. The light globe hung against the yellow heaven and burned and burned like a clear yellow star. This sharp clarity of the lamp against the grander general clarity of the light-poured sky over the shadowed earth was a sight on the outskirts of Albuquerque that never failed to visit a brief enchantment upon him. It always made him think of the ingenuities of people, bold and clear, against the impassive beauties of the earth's nature. It turned his heart over with affection for the one, and with humility before the other.

He thought of speaking of it to Don, but changed his mind, and got out of the car.

One of the nuns met the Doctor as he came up the steps.

"Good efening, Doctor, who is that in the car vit you?"

"Hello Sister, that's my boy."

"Your cude liddle boy? How sveet!"

"Oh, yes, he and I are great buddies. He rides around with me on my calls all the time."

"Na!" cried the sister softly, at this pleasant marvel of family life, as the Doctor went to the elevator.

Now that's odd, he said to himself, what on earth made me tell such a ridiculous lie?

But he admitted that he knew, all right, and when he came down half an hour later, he felt a little shy of Donald, as if the boy knew the hopeful sentimental imposture his father had made.

So they rode again in silence, but this silent being together was enough for them both, they both being Rushes, as the father mused humorously, and he was deeply happy, and he thought Don seemed at peace, too. At dusk they got home, sure of each other, just because they could ride around together for two hours and not have to explain anything.

Anyway, though he couldn't say why, Donnie felt forgiven.

XXIII · ON THE MOONLIT MESA

I

Bun had managed to get the family car from his father, and was waiting at the library corner when Martha got off the bus. He was smiling like a Chessy cat, she told him, not realizing at first whose car he was standing by. When he told her that he had the car for the evening, she was suddenly embarrassed, and disappointed him by her meager response to his achievement. She got in, blushing furiously, and sat down, hating herself for being so unreasonable; but what stormed within her was pity for them both that they weren't married and independent, with their *own* car. How long would they have to meet this way like naughty children, and suffer the infrequent charity of the druggist who let his son use the car for the evening?

Bun was stiffened with irritation too. He had performed miracles of "logic" to argue his father into letting him take the car, and now she didn't seem pleased. How could you ever know what women would think! His pride in being at the wheel was punctured. He felt like driving her right home and letting her out at her corner, and turning around, and driving back to town, and getting drunk in the back room of the White Elephant, where he had heard liquor was sometimes sold to minors.

He drove out to the mesa, waiting for her to speak. He kept looking out the left side, his side, of the car because he didn't care to look at her.

By the time they reached the open plain he was really angry, and she was frightened. Her heart skipped along in a rapid race with her thoughts. How could she forgive herself, through him? Was it gone? Their carefully built edifice of security? What about the program of self-improvement; the care and feeding of babies; the pledges of their lips and hands?

She thought of kissing him wittily as if to make him realize that she had only been fooling. But he was monolithic beside her, and there had been too long a silence.

"Our ranch is out here somewhere," she said at last, but her conversational sound mocked sincerity.

"Oh, is it?"

She felt committed to a policy of hollow lightness, and with her heart in a squeeze of dread, she went on.

"Do let's drive over to see it, there's enough moonlight, I haven't been up here in ages.—Poor Mumma! She thinks it is a gold mine, or something. My father used to have it to raise chickens on, but his health got worse and worse, and finally when he died the ranch was just abandoned. But we still own it. My little brother comes out here with Donald Rush sometimes on picnics.—I'll watch for the road. It goes off to the left, somewhere, here.—There it is!—No, wait. That's the neighboring place. Ours is just a tiny place, a couple of acres or something. But it has some cute little houses on it."

He drove on, simply looking at the left lane of the highway. Before them were the mountains, lifted as if the surface of the plain had been raised from below, a cosmic tablecloth beneath which unseen hands created a row of mountains.

II

Now a thought began to burn in her head. Why shouldn't she and Bunny take the little adobe one-room house at the ranch and fix it up and live there when they got married, and got started on their own?

She took his arm and with her touch, begged him to forgive her. Her animation reached him. He turned and looked at her.

"All right, we'll go see the place," he said, and she thought it almost as if he answered her excited thought. "But I'm not going to be any more impressed with it than you were with my dad's car."

"I'm sorry, honestly, I am, darling, I am such a fool, Bunny, all my life when people have got me nice things I have been so happy that right away something *else* seemed to happen inside of me, and I acted as if I was *ashamed* of what they gave me.—Poor Mumma has worked her fingers off for me and Wayne, and when I think of it, I want to *die,* but I can no more hug her and thank her than I can *fly!* —About *something else,* I can make her see how much I love her.—I must be an ungrateful and terrible woman. I don't know why you ever looked at me. They say a mean spirit shows in your face first of all. I must have a *hideous* face."

Her humility was so much greater than he expected or wanted that he thought what a bum he had been to say a thing like that to her. He put his arm around her and laid his head down on hers for a moment, still driving.

"Hush yo' mouf," he said. It melted her heart to hear him assume another character for her amusement; he was usually so forthright and always seemed to her as unchangeable as the mountain rocks ahead of them.

"Wait," she said, and sat up. "There's the road."

He turned off into the sandy lane, and they drove, lost and found among the shadows of the moonlighted foothills, until they came to the little ranch with its two blocks of adobe.

"Here we are.—Doesn't it look *tiny!* I remembered it as a little more like something than *this!"*

"A ranch!" he said, laughing.

"Well, that was the chicken house, there, and—The glass is all broken. Look. It is like snow on the ground, in the moonlight."

"—Not a whole piece left.—Roving kids. What could you expect?"

"Mumma will be *killed* when she sees this . . ."

Her voice wailed. She was like a forlorn child, feeling what her mother would feel.

"Is that the house?"

"Yes. It has one room. Shall we peek in?"

They looked in, and could see nothing but the pale squares of the window across the room from them at the other end of the hut. The darkness between this wall and the opposite one seemed rich with excitements and suggestions to her.

III

Calling his name softly, she turned and took herself to his arms, shutting her eyes to see them together in such a little house, by themselves, as if night could last forever and this kiss, too.

It was such a pure and beautiful triumph, to erase their little misery over the car in each other's striving embrace.

They denied the vast thoughtlessness of the land around them with their burning thoughts and aching selves. They were possessed. They could not let each other go. No, no, no, she said to herself, and even to him, half-aloud, when she could, her breath skipping in a suffering laugh; but neither would he let her be, nor she him.

She loved him wildly, at the same time trying to call to the rescue such things as "a page of German grammar every evening." It availed nothing.

He rode his passion as if it were a horse of which he was master, yet which he let run where it would.

The night was perfectly still; but a cloud came over the moon and gave everything a chill sense for a moment.

Trembling, they broke apart.

"*Gosh,* darling," she said. She sounded sore-throated with emotion. No poetry if she had spoken it could have tumbled his heart more in her name.

She fell against the adobe wall and put her fingers to her temples. "We'd better go."

He put his hands on the wall up above her and fell to her and took her mouth again with his. Holding him with her lips, she began to press him away with her hands on his hard belly, which yet caved in at her touch, and this time when he desisted, she ran to the car and waited for him in silence, wringing her hands and shaking her head slowly, as if saying, Oh my, oh my, oh my, and wondering not with mind but with blind ages-old memories of woman, what she had done . . .

He came back presently.

He was composed.

He was silent. But she knew he was not angry. He was dizzied by how narrowly they had walked, and how willingly. If he had spoken, he could have asked only one thing. He knew how a maiden heart could beat now.

IV

Halfway down the hill, when the lights of the city were well spread before them, and the cars ran ahead of them and people were in the streets, he sighed and it sounded humorous, and he reached and took her hand and squeezed it, meaning that they were safe again, and how could it be that it was true that everything passed, except their love itself.

XXIV · THE STRONG TIDE

I

Willa Shoemaker saw evidences of something stormy in her daughter. She saw Martha rarely during the day, and in the recent evenings, attempts to talk to her had been unsuccessful; really *talk*, that is. Martha was "charming," and "considerate," hurrying to help if she was needed, and once she had thrown her arms around her little bony mother with an ecstatic hug, but had instantly withdrawn herself as if sorry to have betrayed something.

"What is it, Mar, dearie, what *are* you doing?"

"Nothing, Mother, I am in a *silly* fit."

"You haven't had a *silly* fit for years, nor Wayne, either, my children are growing up so fast," said Willa, looking at her daughter earnestly, which made Martha sharply angry for its penetration. "I remember," Willa continued, "you and your little brother used to hang out your tongues, and dangle your hands from your wrists, and run around in circles, and when I would ask you *what*, you'd both say you were having a *silly* fit.—I wonder if other families are like ours!"

Martha looked at her direct; with hard, pretty eyes, and with the blazing vitality of anyone young which made anyone older look dowdy and used-up, and said the cruelest thing she could think of, as a protection for what she cherished in secret:

"I suppose all families are pretty much the same, except that ours isn't as *happy* as most, I guess."

Willa looked at her with an animal's eyes, flooded with misery, but she was too well-bred, the mother, who waited tables all day for a living, to reveal her deeply hurt pride and security, and left the selfish girl to go and consider what made her so selfish.

Willa had a pretty good idea.

II

It was part of the texture of talk in such a town that *who went with whom* was sure to be common property sooner or later. Willa had heard about Bunny and Martha from one of her working friends down at the Harvey House, whose younger sister worked at the public library. Willa knew Bun Summerfield, and his whole family, but to refresh herself as to what *kind* of boy he was, she took some time off on an afternoon and went to Summerfield's Drug to make a purchase and see him. He was there. He didn't wait on her, Rollie Glovers did that, with his pale and rather ghastly politeness; but Bun bowed to her, and she smiled back, not without feeling a pang at how much of a threat he represented. She said to herself that he was a sweet-looking boy, with such an open, frank countenance, and he smiled the most honest smile sh'ever saw, he had such beautiful teeth. He was so well-groomed. He seemed to take to people in a lively eagerness that was very likable. Why did he look so beautifully dressed in his tan linen jacket with "Summerfield's" embroidered above the pocket, when Rollie looked like a pillowcase held up at the corners? She took her parcel . . . more foot powder, for it seemed to her she could never have enough in the house, she got so tired these days . . . and as she went out the Central Avenue door, she looked again at Bun, and was startled to see that he was just as avidly looking at her. Her heart sank. *She* knew, even if he was not old enough to know, how much people could communicate without words. She went back downtown to the Harvey House grieving for Martha, and yet stirred by a reverie of Martha's time of life.

Who was she, the mother, to deny what her child would reach?

There was a lump in her throat when she remembered the meadows of her own girlhood. It was such a green picture, the land flowed with silver brooks, and the trees hooded over young people in the evenings in summertime, and where love first of all came alive was forever the picture of the country where her heart would dwell. How different from this desert country where her husband had brought her! How sweet to plan and scheme and hope for a return to Albion, with her grown children, where they too might find their start in life, as she had!—This boy Bunny Summerfield was like any boy anywhere. —Martha would forget him.—When could she afford to make the trip?

This thought returned her to the present, for she knew they had no money for such an undertaking as the three of them going home to Albion for that long-dreamed-of visit.

As she always did when there was something troublesome to be got through with, she squarely looked at it, and said to herself, We can't go, and that's the end to it, don't be a fool, Willa Johnson—using her maiden name. In many ways she was, to herself, a maiden still. People saw one aspect of this when they remarked on her energy, her eagerness that seemed so friendly.

III

For the next several days she watched Martha and her suspicions stayed alive.

Martha was so funny lately, trying so hard to be her old self. Willa didn't know how much to believe, or what to say, and when her thoughts raced along as they could not help doing, with images of Bun and Martha, both so sure of their beauties, so strong and proud and indifferent to anyone else, she would almost lose her breath to *think* that they *might*—what they *might* blunder into, in spite of their righteous upbringing.

She didn't know whether she should give up all chances for temporary peace in the family, and come right out with it, and *talk* to Martha, or not.

What if she did that, and what if she was wrong, and Martha and Bunny had nothing to—to be ashamed of?

How would she feel then? How would Martha feel? Wouldn't it kill Martha's love for her mother, forever, not to be trusted any more than that? It certainly would. She shivered at the narrow escape she had had (in thought) of losing her daughter's trust and love.

Yes but.

Would she *ever* forgive herself.

To think of what might happen for want of a sympathetic word, *in time*.

What if it'd've been possible before it was too late—? If for the want of what a mother could tell and save, her daughter should've gone and . . . ?

She worried and worried, and watched. She consoled herself by thinking of Bun, and of how "clean-cut" he was, and of what innocent happiness danced in his eyes. He would never be the one to:

And yet in her heart, in little stirrings, there were likewise starts of obscure wish that love should visit the two youngsters and declare them one. After such hardly recognized seedlings of feeling, she would be doubly anguished, even jealous, at the romance that worried her, and she would scold to herself that no-matter-what, Martha had to be talked to.

But Martha: the *dimmedest* thing (as Willa thought, using her nearest approximation to a curse word), was unapproachable in the most subtle and final way. She couldn't say *why* she couldn't talk to Martha. There was simply something in the way. Martha was like a little *woman*, whose rights would not be infringed, not by anybody, not even her own mother. It was all very plain and un-touchable.

IV

Oh-sigh-oh-my, 'll watch and 'll *watch,* and there's that *boy,* that Bunny, still you never could know, if she'd only come and tell me, just anything, a *scrap,* just say she's *meeting* him, and who he *is,* of course I *know,* but still: what a goose I am to worry-worry-worry, tears in m'eyes, lump in m'throat, has to come to everybody, look at how happy *I* was, do you suppose I made my poor mother Sarah Johnson as miserable as this, yes, I suppose so, we used to get the surrey in the evenings, and four of us go buggy riding, taking a long road around to get to the Yeagers' big brick farmhouse, where all the parties were, where Martin Yeager was, too, *what did Martin have in his eyes,* he had lights that danced, poor Martha, my poor little girl, I hope God keeps you as He kept me, for it is a strong tide that runs in the strict course of love . . .

XXV · THE TRIP TO HANO

I

It was a day in early May. Little white clouds like flags were whipped out in the scented wind which played warmth over the land. Peter went in his car to get Molly. She was ready and waiting. Miss Bridges was with her in the big dark front room.

"For goodness' sake, don't come back till late," she said. "I can get the most enormous amount of work done if you will keep Molly out of the house all day.—We've promised the typescript by next Wednesday, and I'm having my hands full."

"You're sure you wouldn't like to come along?" asked Peter.

He saw Miss Bridges's eyes flash and her mouth rake downward in an ironical denial which confessed far more than it should've, about how much she really wanted to come, and how much she punished herself for reasons that were obscure to her and everyone else.

"I loathe motoring," she replied.

"I told you that, Peter," said Molly.

"Yes, I asked Mrs. Foster if you wouldn't come, and she said you hated driving."

Judy Bridges shrugged and pursed her mouth looking at Peter with angry humor.

"You should call her Molly, you sound very stuffy being formal with her when she is first-naming you all over the place."

"Ju-dy, hush," said Molly softly, and lightly kissed her on the cheek. Then she turned and nodded to Peter that they might leave now.

Judy had made enough of a comment to make them feel a trifle constrained as they headed out to the country in the big car. He had always liked the way Molly would simply sit and say nothing when a silence fell of its own weight. So many people he knew couldn't bear to let minutes pass without making or hearing talk. But he felt right now as if he would give anything to break the silence which Judy's ironical farewell had led to. It was as if Judy had challenged them to say, to reveal, what was plain to her, that they were in love, that they were escaping together for this day all the just dues of habit, and that to anyone with even half the brains and experience of Judy Bridges, the whole thing had been perfectly plain from the first moment they set eyes on each other.

But for a while he could not invent anything that would let him down easily, out loud, and so he looked at Molly beside him, and believed that for the first time since he'd known her she seemed moody. She was glancing out the right side of the car, her head tilted in its shadowing hat, as if to "see" the country better.

They were driving down the river road, now coming under airy tunnels of arching cottonwoods, and now crossing golden sandy spaces of sunshine. The river was to their left. The road curved near and far from it as it went down the valley. Beyond they saw the mountains, or if the near ground rose to hide the mountains, they saw their effect in the cloud clusters in the sky, faint with golden heat.

Molly suddenly sat up and turned her attention back to him with decision, as if she had sharply finished feeling a certain way, or thinking a certain thing, and was saying "There!" to it. She smiled and stretched her arms before her.

"This is heavenly."

"It's going to be a hot day."

"I shall simply love it. I want to bake like a lizard and simply confess the power of the sun.—You don't *feel* it anywhere else. Whoever really *sees* sunlight back East? You take it for granted. You don't get struck by the flat of it as if it were a sword when you step outdoors there. You don't say to yourself, *My, there it is again, the source of life,* when you step into East Sixty-Seventh Street in the middle of the morning. I could write a whole mythology, with pretty little temples and clever ceremonies and some symbolical but harmless sacrifices, about the New Mexico sun. I suppose this has all been done, but ever so much more seriously than I would do it.—I never feel any charm, I mean cunning, little, daily *sweetness* in the mythologies which professors record in their tall narrow books. Do you?"

"I don't know. I never read any."

"Well, anyway, I would make mine a sort of *darling* system of gods and goddesses and powers and attributes and sins and penalties."

Peter laughed with a sudden idea of what her books must be like, from the way she invented this happy nonsense.

"Is that what your novels are like?"

"Oh."

"Oh *what.*"

"Oh, then you have never read any of them?"

"Why, no.—I thought you knew that."

"No, I just thought you didn't know who-I-was in relation to all those books."

"No, I didn't know anything about any of it."

She smiled ruefully.

"I suppose only women read what I write. What a horrid thought."

She was being lighthearted, he saw, but also there showed in her face a suddenly hectored look, and he thought it made her look the way a child does when you get a sudden hint of what the child will look like in old age. It was a flying shadow of the future. He was moved. Whenever he was touched his face became absolutely fixed. It was a stern expression. He was articulate only when his heart was easy. He thought now of anybody's frailty, but it came clear to him in her likeness. He sounded almost harsh when he said,

"Why is that horrid? What's the matter with women reading your books?"

She had no idea of what notions her remark had brought up, either about her, or about his wife, and her habitual sleight-of-spirit which substituted romancing for living.

"Oh, women are so *avid,*" she said. "They keep looking for themselves in books. I imagine a man who loves to read is always seeing other people in them, people he knows, and admires, and hates, but rarely himself. He is so sort of *decent* about it that when an author *pinks* him with something he didn't know anybody else ever knew, or thought, or imagined, he is amazed, and says to himself, *Why, how in the world did that fellow know that about it, why, that's the way* I *am.* But a woman would be reading everything, all along, as if it were all about her, and she would coldly condemn anything that the author had his characters do if it wasn't what she herself did or would do.—This is so silly, all I mean is that if my books have only what women like in them, then I am in a rage."

"I don't think you can make such a reckless accusation about all women. I have known some perfectly selfless women."

"I know it, so have I, I'm just *talking,* of course.—But I do think women in general would admit the *kind* of thing I meant."

"You do:"

"Certainly I do.—Women don't ever shrink from facing and admitting the worst about themselves. I suppose it's their most really clever weapon.—And if anything happens to their children, they're so much better about *managing* than men."

He kept thinking that if she had a chart of what was wrong at home, in his house, she could not've been treading more close to everything that troubled him. He refused to carry it any closer. He pointed to a road they could see rising and fading in the sandhills to their distant right.

"See that road? That's where we turn off on to get to Hano."

The earth and sky met in an almost yellow blur of heat in the faraway.

It was late in the morning.

They felt like runaways.

In a moment they reached the place to turn off from the river road. A rolling desert of sandy hills lay before them, and they had the sensation of being lost in it when they left the green mercy of the river side. Once again there was that sense of going beyond time which Peter had when he came direct to the country. The air was hot and the sandy dust off the road came up after the car in a cloud so dense that it now and then overtook them. They literally tasted the earth. It was oddly bittersweet.

"What is it like, where we are going?" asked Molly. And then a double sense of her words made her turn to look at Peter, and she put her hands to her cheeks and wondered while a throb felt in her breast. Used to using her emotions for what she wrote, she was subject to the power of words, and the question she had asked seemed to her full of the doubt, the possible sweetness, the hurtful guesses which any future held. If Peter too felt the second-thought in what she'd said, he didn't show it. He was squinting slightly as he drove through the desert glare, and she saw his face, brown, a faint glisten on his weathered skin, a shaft of light in his eye, a boyish lift to the tip of his nose, a browner red to his rough mouth, and the round cut of his solid chin, fixed against the background of the sandhills which moved past beyond him.

He ignored her question.

"As for what happens to children," he said, after about two miles of silence and road-eating, "which you mentioned a while back, nothing can happen to them which could possibly be as serious as the things they don't actually see or touch."

She was now sure he was deliberately evading her question; why, she didn't know.

"How? in what way."

"I mean the first important thing for a child is a certainty of being safe. As the child grows, this security from without can be allowed to lessen as the child learns what hazards are and how to meet them from within, until its own security is woven part and parcel into its character."

"Yes."

"But the thing that makes or unmakes this kind of safety for a child is the thing the child feels at home, unspoken, alive in the air, a food for the heart. A psychological security. It has nothing to do with money, or good food, or careful upbringing, or what school you choose, or who your children play with. I have seen families with the shabbiest kind of surroundings and the most careless treatment of all the things the Public Health office would have fits over, and the craziest diet, and the riskiest kind of life for their kids; and the kids've been wonders of health, happiness, proper toughness, and even beauty. Why. Because the father and the mother were in love and truly mated and loved being with each other and seemed to belong together and the children felt it, could know it without seeing it, and the security which the parents felt in each other simply became a climate for the little ones to grow up in."

He was frowning as he drove. She suddenly felt that she must not intrude into his thought with any questions. She decided to be academic with him.

"That sounds awfully arbitrary. I feel that the first thing is decency in the physical life of the child, good food, and proper hours and care, and enough baths and fresh clothes, and you may say all you wish about the charm of love in a hovel, but I'd prefer to have my daughter able to cope with germs if they beset her, which has happened and will again."

"Risks, yes. Preventive medicine and such are grand, and I not only practice but I preach the same. But if I had one thing to rule as a sacrifice, in a given situation, it would be the very things you regard as the more important. I believe that nothing else matters *as much* as that a child shall feel from his first to his last day in his father's house that all is well there, for him, and those in it, between each other. If there is a failure there, the child will know it, even if there's nothing of it outwardly visible. The more I work with—with ailing people, the more I am convinced that the first factor of life on this earth is spiritual, as it is in the next. Any doctor has seen miracles of recovery which could only be traced to health in the spirit."

"You do convince me, nearly."

"That's the sort of health I'd like my child to have forever. I'd never worry about him, no matter what befell him. I've seen plenty of what does befall people now and then."

What is it, she asked him silently. You are telling me something out of your heart, and I am ready to hear it. She became oddly agitated within her outer composure. She wanted to put her fingers to her temples, and for a moment be out of the sunlit wilderness of those baking sandhills. But she knew from how he sounded that he was telling her of how things were in his house, and her heart beat when she believed that he was coming upon discoveries for himself about what he might do in the future for his son. All she knew was that he had an only son. The boy stood before her in imagination now, clearly, and so did the mother, called up in her thoughts by the way he had spoken, as if such bitterness were distasteful to him, yet had to be said by his own lips.

She rode with him in silence, until he said, some time later,

"The country where we are going gets into foothills pretty soon, look, you can see a faint and cooling line of blue beyond the farthest sandhills. Those are mountains, but long before we get to them this sandy country is gone, and we are in winding hills of rock and scrub pine, and once or twice in a dark forest. We get pretty high, and at last we come to a place that winds up to a tremendous mesa, at the foot of which there is a river. Often there is no water in the river, which has cut a deep canyon in the floor of the plain below the mesa. One side of the canyon is much higher than the other. Its face looks out over what seems like a world. Up toward the top of the canyonside, there is a cliff that stands clear and open like a brow of earth. The closer you get, you will see that there are little places in it, they are windows, and doors, and they are walls of mud-cemented stones, and that is the empty cliff city of Hano, where people lived a long time ago."

"Is there no one there now?"

"A Park Service guide, probably, but probably no one else."

They came into a huge island of cloud shadow which cooled them for a few miles.

He was withdrawn into thought. He felt that there could be no better proof of the intimacy he felt with her than this, that he feel easy about such a withdrawal from casual talk. After a while, as if with a decision in his mind, he said,

"My own boy, for instance. My wife is very dear to us, to both of us, but when he was born, something happened to her, it's hard to explain, and commoner than people know. Anyway, she feels she cannot have another child. It is without sense, and an illness of course, and it has meant a good deal of patience and sympathy. But those are not the same things as happiness. I don't believe grownups have a right to demand happiness. But I think children ought to have it. The kind I was talking about back there.—That's what that was all about, I suppose you gathered that by yourself. I don't mean to be heartless talking about Noonie to anyone else, and I never have before in my life.—It is some sort of relief. If you're embarrassed, perhaps that would help excuse it all."

"Oh, no!" she said. She cursed herself for the readiness of her emotions. They came up and choked her. She said to herself that she loved him, and pitied him, and must not say so to him.

"Anyway, what I've felt for some time is that something big and maybe awful will have to happen before anything can be better with us."

"Oh, I do hope not!"

"So do I."

He turned and looked at her, for the first time on the long drive. He thought she was almost unbearably pretty and that she looked different from when they'd started. He scowled at her which gave a dark band of intensity to his brow, and he ground his jaw forward a trifle, nodded once, with vigor, and then looked back to the road.

It was as if he had said that never before had he allowed to be so plain to anyone else what had been clear to him for so long. He seemed to confess to great tenderness and at the same time to great strength, if these two things should have to be at cross purposes in his life. He had the air of someone who's made a resolve, and would fight forever if allowed to, to keep it. If anything should happen to break it beyond his power, he might become a different person, and meantime, the hardest thing in the world for him to do was to admit to anyone else the weaknesses which he had seen in others, but never before in himself.

She had a habit of irony which appeared more in her books than in her relations with people. It now repeated to her, without any answer, the answer, the question she had asked him before. What is it like where we are going? A rueful look accompanied that sort of thought over her face. Her life had been tranquil for some years, and lonely, and for the most part she was grateful for it, after her marriage to a rich drinking man, and after her divorce, she welcomed what seemed almost an inability to feel things much at all. Now she felt a pain at her heart, and she shut her eyes for a second, as if in dismay at the power to feel.

"We are coming to the foothills," he said, "look, there is the first scatter of the piñon trees."

II

The road curved and all they could see were the noonday glooms of the pines which made forest on both sides. The air was cooler. The road climbed up and turned back upon itself, crossing a mountain ridge. It dropped down the other side, they crossed a green plain, and entered a wide valley, which turned slowly to the west. As the car came about this grand turn, they were in full sunlight again. The valley became a river bed to the west, full of pinkish sand. Above the river hung the cliff. Peter let the car roll to a stop, and they both stared at the upper face of the cliff, where the empty dwellings were, with windows and doorways shadowed by the bright sun. It was quiet. The dust of the road settled back to the ruts.

"We're about two miles away still."

"—Do we want to go closer?" she asked, turning to him with a sudden reluctance to see this ghost of life which stretched along the upper cliff for a mile. She was uncertain of her feelings; but it seemed to her that these were almost like open graves, these dark little caverns in the clifftop.

"Why, of course. It doesn't *mean* anything till you get right up into it."

He drove on.

They came along the valley until they were at the foot of the city. They left the car in a clump of piñon trees, and by a weathered silver cottonwood bridge they crossed the river bed, which was dry. A board shack stood at the other end of the bridge, bearing a sign which read "Custodian." But it was closed, no one was to be seen, and

Peter led the way up the path which began to climb from the river's edge. It was a sandy trail. The sun was like a hot iron on their backs. The trail was steep. They had to stop for breath many times. When they paused, they turned their heads in the silence. They were almost pressed by the silence, which made the blood beating in their ears seem like little thunders.

"We'll have to climb the ladders, the last stage of the way," said Peter.

"I get dizzy."

"It looks harder than it is."

"Do we want to go on top?"

"Oh yes, you won't get the lift it must have been to live here, long ago, if you don't see the world as they saw it."

His eyes were sparkling. He was open to yesterday, she saw. His imagination was kindled by the memory of this long-empty town in the cliff. She had a little current of misery and irritation at finding herself so moved by the empty cliff houses still far above them. They began to climb again. They could not talk. It took all their breath to proceed.

The trail finally brought them to a sort of shelf, where weeds grew in the rocky crevices, and the first of the houses stood in the dust of rock and time. The walls of the house were made of flat rocks mortared together long ago by mud plaster, of which none now remained. Yet the walls were worthy, and the windows and the doorway, with its high stone threshold, and its rock-colored wooden beam, were shapely. The room within looked as deep as a well and as cool. The floor rose in rounded sweeps to the inside walls. Opposite the door was another doorway, half-high, leading to an inner room.

"Here is where they lived."

"Who were they?"

"The Hanos, the sun children, you notice that their city faces east. Turn around."

She turned and looked over the valley. Far away at the horizon the midday made a white blur, but the hills between were blue, and the valley floor, so sharply below them, was golden pink, from the sand.

"When did they go away?"

"They think about seven hundred years ago. Nobody knows how or why. There is a palace up on the next level where things were found that told of occupancy right up to the moment of abandonment, evidently."

"What things?"

"Oh, furniture, pots, dishes, toys, and even the exposed body of a dead man. His skeleton was found surrounded by little bits of life, like a clay kettle, a bone awl, and some fabrics. Things of that sort."

She looked up at the upper cliff.

He nodded, and led to the weathered wooden ladder that leaned against the next ledge. He told her not to look down, and asked if he should go first. She nodded. He started up. At the ledge, he leaned down and helped her up, and now they were on a ledge which was in effect a one-sided street. Hundreds of rooms looked out over the valley. They were cunningly carved out of the sandstone itself, or as cunningly built into the natural contours of the cliff. Their security, their wisdom, their shelled design for human life, were profoundly moving.

"It is the most extraordinary place I ever saw.—The most extraordinary *feeling* I ever had . . ." she said.

"I know. You cannot put your finger on it. It asks such an eternal question. It is a question we can answer in the heart, but never in words."

"There must've been hundreds of people."

"Oh, yes. Easily. Maybe thousands."

She shook her head.

"I feel almost *unwanted* here. Don't you know what I mean? As if *they* would not want anyone here?"

He laughed.

"They were peaceful people. I think. One school of thought says they lived up here because they were afraid of roving warriors down in the valley. Another tries to suggest that these people were themselves warriors, who sallied down from this fortress, robbed and killed, and came back to security here. I don't think either of these is enough the truth."

"What is?"

"Can you climb again?"

She nodded.

They went to another upward ladder, and scaled a long blank face of stone, until they came to a u-shaped landing at the ladder's top. Here they found a trail worn smooth in the rock, curving out of sight like a slow spiral stairway, which brought them around a tower of boulders until they were on the very top of the valley wall, on a high mesa where long silvery grass grew, stretching away to the west in the blinding white sunlight like shimmering water.

Another city stood there, built up from the ground of adobe and stone. It was in ruins. No roofs were left, hardly a whole wall. It was like a comb of honey, cut and emptied and dried brown by the sun.

"Now look all around," said Peter. "Imagine morning up here."

Facing the east was a long redoubt of grass-grown earth. It curved like a half-moon. It was a sort of ramp, or walk, and it was the easternmost thing of the mesa city.

"Good people came there in the first hour of daylight to make their devotions and learn the day. I think they lived here not because they were scared or were bandits, but because this is a noble place for a city, at one with the sky, the plain and the river.—Doesn't that sound as plausible as anything to you?"

"Yes, of course.—It is a heavenly spot.—Somehow, I am more comfortable with these ruined houses on top than I am down below, where the walls are perfect, and the doors, and windows, and stone benches, and where it simply seems like the noon hour, and everybody will be back at one.—You know?"

"Yes, sure. Any kind of a mummy is disturbing. That is a mummified city down there.—Man has never been satisfied with physical attempts at eternity, or survival. We know more about it with our souls, which never need more proof of anything than their own conviction. —But it is so easy to look at the cliff, and see them all again, under the sun."

"Were they happy?"

He smiled fondly into her eyes.

"Yes, I think so. The men had much work to do. Look at that much rock to be carved. And the farms up here on the meadow. And the women—This is a country of the man.—Remember? The sun, there, he was the begetter.—You asked a woman's question, didn't you."

"I only hoped they were happy.—Shouldn't we start down?"

He looked at her searchingly.

"You don't much like it here, do you:"

She shook her head. She didn't know what was responsible, the climb, the poignant emptiness of the city, or the solitude with him, but she was shaken. Her face was white, in the shadow of the broad-brimmed hat she wore.

"I don't think I like Indians," she said, trying to sound light-hearted. But it sounded petulant, and she was sorry to have said it. He shrugged, and led her back to the ladder.

"Even dead and vanished Indians," he murmured. She saw that he was nettled at the failure of his expedition. They went down the ladder to the next level, where all the houses stood throwing back the heat of the sun.

"Please," she said, "I'm sorry, if I seem so miserable about every-thing.—I am just very much moved by this whole place."

"Of course. I know.—Shall we rest a moment?"

They leaned and sat on some large boulders by the foot of the lad-der, and gazed out over the valley. The blood was thudding in their ears. The littlest exertion at this altitude was noticeable.

He longed to speak to her with his arms.

In the silence, they rested. The heat! The clarity! The empty rooms! thought Molly, closing her eyes.

III

And then suddenly, at their level, and near to them, a brown and white bird flew past, the only thing alive which they'd seen. Molly didn't see it, but Peter watched it. It brought the sky to earth, and the valley floor right up to them. As it passed, the bird called suddenly out. The sound was like a flash of lightning made hearable. Terribly loud, it echoed and struck from the cliff over the silent valley. Molly looked, and the bird cried again, farther down the cliff, and she felt her heart turn over within her.

How could a single bird so fill the deathly city that its cry sounded from end to end of the riddled cliff?

It was like something out of time, that cry and passage, a shearing scream of abstract melody, and it pierced them. It seemed to tell of people gone, and of life surviving.

"It unselfs me!" said Molly, "that poor, amazing bird!—In this silence and heat and emptiness!"

Peter nodded. He too was reached by the bird's cry, a spirit's whis-tle in the windowed street.

His hand was trembling as he put it forth to her. The bird's cry echoed in their ears. He bent down slightly, looking into her shad-owed face, and he smiled sweetly and shook his head a trifle, as if to deplore for them both what he would do. He kissed her enfoldingly.

She was lost, and he was too. They shut out the dazzling day, the silence, the solitude, in each other.

Overhead, flying back from the far end of the cliff, the bird re-turned. His piercing cry echoed again, and they blinded themselves to it, shutting their eyes and hungering and easing through their kisses, which said no, and again no, no, to the dry caves of death above them in the cliff wall.

XXVI · MARTHA AND NOONIE

I

Martha knew little enough with her head about what had taken her heart whole. Ever since the night on the mesa, she had been full of a bewildered, sweet guilt that turned her cheeks pink whenever she remembered it. Heaven only knew! if they hadn't left when they did! what might!

How can I tell anyone what it is like? And why do I feel that I must tell someone? And who is pure enough, who *knows enough,* to listen to me without smiling, or being sickened at what I *feel,* not at what I have *done,* for I have "done" nothing . . . ?

How ashamed I am for washing out the taste of his kiss the first time he kissed me!

Is it the very same thing he gives me that I give him?

Does he think of me like this all the rest of the time as I do think of him?

What if: but it is ridiculous, I know: yes, but *what* if I had his baby, *now?*

What do women talk about when they are together? Has it ever happened? Does anybody know in her heart if a baby ever came to life from just *loving?* The way *we* love? *Enough* love—this would give life to a babe, without sin. For people do talk about sin. Do I know for the first time what miraculous beauty lay at the root of the birth of the Infant Jesus?

I pray: I do not mean to blaspheme to compare myself with the Virgin Mary. I pray and I argue that all love *starts* as purely as Hers. This is what it means, oh surely, this is what it means!

Nobody who looked at Martha in such moments could fail to have a pang for her possession by life; her eyes were so full of light, her skin so fresh, her breath so deeply drawn and so rueful, somehow, with what bothered her. But for many whom this aspect delighted, without their knowing quite why, there were others whom it distressed.

II

In the afternoon of the same day when Peter took Molly to the empty city in the cliff, Martha went to see Mrs. Rush, at an hour when she was pretty sure the Doctor was out. She knew that Donald was with Wayne, somewhere, they had gone on their bicycles. In her exquisite confusions, Martha was thinking that Mrs. Rush always looked so gentle, and smiled so kindly upon everyone and everything, that she wanted to—what did she mean?—sort of to *test* her love for Bun on somebody else, and perhaps see how it would strike an older woman. After all, she was going to spend the rest of her life with him, wasn't she. How proud she would be to hear someone say that it was a most suitable plan. Martha couldn't tell herself clearly why she didn't want to say anything to her mother Willa. But the whirr and the clatter, the worry and the looking at the problem from every angle that would ensue, she simply could not face.

But she did long to share her news, and see it sanctioned by what must follow: exclamations, questions; promises; perhaps a trifle of envy that would be flattering, and then some tender advice? It would be like seeing her love in a mirror, from another angle, and seeing it as if she were somebody else, and knowing what they would think.

Noonie had just come home in her car. She was still wearing her street clothes, and the little foray into town she had made gave her excitement and a sense of achievement. She wore a hat with a veil. She had brushed her hair very particularly and her little head looked smart. Her eyes had a dimmish look that was vague and appealing. Her suit was neatly made. Her white gloves were crisp and clean. She had been reluctant to get out of these clothes, and caught glimpses of herself in the hall mirrors with satisfaction. If people saw her as she really looked, that day, she mused, then she must have made a charming impression. Her thought leaped up as if to say to her that every day of life brought new hope with it; what if she had been, for so long, so tired, so listless, so unresponsive to the thing she wanted most, and that was her husband's love? She wished now that she had gone to call on him at his office; but she realized too that with patients waiting to see him, he would never have been able to greet her intimately.

When Martha rang the bell, and was taken by Cora into the green velvet and white enameled sitting room, where the pianola was, Mrs. Rush was delighted. She decided to come downstairs in her hat, veil, and gloves, and receive this caller with what would surely be described as charming formality.

When she saw that it was just that little Shoemaker girl, Wayne's sister, but so grown, really, she laughed at herself, and began to take off her gloves, her veil and her hat, and explained that she had just this minute come in from shopping.

"I think it's very cunning of you to come see me," she added. "—We do so love Wayne in this house . . ."

"He is a darling, and of course Donnie is an absolute member of the *family* with us, Mrs. Rush."

"My, you look sweet, Martha, you are so—so grown-up, suddenly, it seems ages since I've seen you."

At that Martha blushed.

"I know it, I go to school, every day, of course, I am working really very hard."

"Oh, I didn't mean to reproach you.—You've become so pretty! That's all I meant."

Noonie stared at her. She could feel herself growing tired, a creeping sense of heaviness in her own limbs that she knew so well, and dreaded almost daily. What was in the girl? Why did she blaze with such beauty? Her eyes melting at their own messages? Her lips like petals, her body poised as if unable to take an ungraceful shape? Why had she come? In the face of any such likeness of life, how heavy and empty anybody else seemed, anybody like herself, Noonie thought miserably. Had she herself ever looked like that? Surely all girls didn't look like that. Only those to whom something wonderful was happening. What was happening to Martha?

"Mrs. Rush, you'll have to forgive me, I am really an awful fool, but I—"

"Oh, no *I* am," interrupted Noonie in an unbearable burlesque of her own misery at feeling so poorly in the face of such vitality as the child's.

"Mrs. Rush, honestly, I don't know why I wanted to talk to you, but I had to, and my poor darling Mumma works so hard and is away all day, I couldn't ever get her to listen . . ."

"Your Mother is—Doctor Rush and I both admire her ever so much, you and Wayne must be very proud of her!"

Her eyes looked teary.

"We do, how can we ever show her—But—but I never know *what* she'll think . . ."

"About what? You'll make me nervous, if you beat around the bush much more."

Martha looked at her with pleading.

"I hope you won't mind, I really have no right to talk to you, but Donald and Wayne are so close, and I always think of you and the Doctor as *part* of us, Mrs. Rush, I am simply terribly in love!"

She showed all the polite signs of regret at making such an intimate confession and possibly embarrassing someone; but it was only a show; and behind her words was such a total sense of, yes, glory, that to Noonie, it sounded boastful.

There was a silence for a moment. Then Noonie with a great effort said,

"How charming, how happy for you, who is it, anybody I know?"

"Yes, at least, Doctor knows his father, it is Richmond Summerfield."

"Oh.—Yes, of course.—Yes, I remember him, but he's so *young*, Martha."

"I know. Can't help."

"I know.—But you're both just *school* children, my dear. Does Mother know? Shouldn't she?"

But Noonie needed no stormy proofs that it mattered none at all if they were just school children. She could see how Martha was wholly given and taken in love. Her heart sank. She was full of pity for the young people, sorry for what would come to them, and miserable over herself. When had *she* ever been so consumed by anything outside herself? How could *she* ever hope to feel herself again in the great pull of life toward creation, as these infants were? Well enough she knew why Martha would have to tell *someone*. She was touched that Martha had come to her; but it plunged her into the deepest sorrow for her own frailty, her own division from the most thoughtless and profound experience of everyone else. She came to Martha and embraced her, and Martha had the curious idea, with revulsion barely concealed in her movements, that Mrs. Rush was feebly appealing to *her* for—for something, instead of the other way round.

"I hope you will be very happy, then, Martha." She returned to her chair.

"Yes, we will, of course we can't be married for simply ages, yet, he has to go on to medical school, and so on.—Sometimes—Maybe you have never been *uncertain* of anything, Mrs. Rush? It is a terrible feeling!"

How bitterly Noonie felt those words. When had she ever been certain of anything? She wished this exquisite girl would go away and leave her to her own ashen self-awareness. She had a sense of crisis gathering in her breast. She said to herself dimly that she was looking straight at the thing she had lost in her own life, through nobody's fault, and she spoke with utmost effort to Martha.

"Uncertain? What about: what do you mean?"

"We have made love, oh, *terribly,* Mrs. Rush, I am simply crazy with love when we are together, and I sometimes hardly can tear myself away from him before we—But I know, I know," she added, at the alarming expression on the older woman's face.

Martha was anguished with modesty and foolishness, and she sounded almost patronizing with her next remarks.

"I have thought it all over, we might get married right away—I've been looking around, in the shops, and there's a china pattern down at Rosenwald's which I like. And then for silver, I've selected that Dickenson 'Regent,' you know, it is so severe, with just that primrose pattern at the top?—But I suppose we *can't,* for ages. Of course, I'll leave everything to Richmond, I always feel that family decisions must be made by the husband, don't you? Marriage always seems to me a sacred trust, I don't believe enough people remember that, do you, Mrs. Rush? It has to be a partnership, I have always said that, it has many problems to iron out *together,* and we believe in talking things *through.*"

Then she looked at Noonie, and blushed at how her words had sounded, but she shrugged energetically, as if to say that in terms of what was in her heart, she didn't care how she appeared to anyone else.

Noonie could not laugh at the child. Martha's glow and boundless depth of the commonest possession in the world shone through even the bumptious prattle she indulged in. In the girl's preoccupation with all the hardware and the platitudes of marriage there was a tender sort of betrayal of the world of desire, and dream, and the mundane prices of love.

"You are such a goose, Martha dear," said Noonie, standing up and taking her by the hands, and clasping her in her arms. Martha hugged her and shook her head.

"I know it, but somebody had to tell me so, or I would've died," she said, meaning she wanted to live beyond anybody's power to say.

"Now kiss me and go along and be as sweet with your Richmond as he wants you to be, and if he is as fine a youngster as I am sure he is, you are both safe."

"Oh: Mrs. Rush:" said Martha, "you've been darling to me.— Don't you ever tell anybody what a really big damned fool I am!"

"Hush, such words."

"You look tired, I hope I didn't tire you out," said Martha, with solicitude which wounded the older woman inexpressibly. "I'll run along now."

She kissed Noonie swiftly on the cheek again, and left, seeing nothing of what she left behind her.

III

With her hands on her cheeks, Noonie went upstairs to her bedroom. She found a little bottle of tablets in the lilac-scented handkerchief drawer of her dressing table, and went to her bed, rolling a little mound of the tablets out into her trembling palm. She put them into her mouth and tried to swallow, but had to take some water from the Thermos carafe on the bed table first. Then with tears streaming down her face and making no further sound, she lay down to die.

XXVII · THE RETURN OF NOONIE

I

Once across the river again, and in the cool if meager shadow of the piñon trees, Peter and Molly felt that they had come back to their own time and place. They had the cool sweetness of the pine boughs in their feelings. Their spirits were almost hilarious, and they talked like children, of anything that entered their heads. He thought he had never seen her look happy before. He thought he saw why she paid so much attention to the idea of being happy. They agreed that they both knew this was coming, sooner or later, from the first day they'd met. They reminded each other of the various ways they'd used to conceal from each other what they'd felt all along.

He had a picnic lunch in the car, packed for him by the Harvey House dining room. They ate it there among the scrubby trees.

One half of him spoke with caution, in his thought, and said that he was now stripped of everything he knew and had put on with his years. He felt like a boy again, and even at the moment, could smile at how often he'd heard other men say that, and of the joke it made, when you saw their jowls, their pendulous bellies, the blur of leg where once had been a hard line of thigh like a curved blade. He said to himself that he must not be a fool. But he knew he was ready to be, if that meant what he felt now, with her. She was voracious and exquisite. Her animation was like the most perfect extension of good manners. He thought her pretty before, but now she seemed grace itself. He believed he had only half known her till now. She took his thought from him, and said,

"I feel truly myself for the first time in years.—Not that it has any originality, most truths are maddening about that, they're so *same,* as we used to say when I was a child, but I do really think a woman without love is only half herself. The trouble is, sometimes, fitting it in where it belongs in—in the *scheme.*"

"Scheme? What scheme."

"Why, the scheme of how things *are*. That's all that has ever given anybody any trouble about love.—I'd like to call my next book that. *Trouble About Love,* by Mary Carmichael. Adam and Blaine, New York and London.—Darling, what'll we *do!* We can never talk shop together."

"You *mean* this scheme thing, don't you."

"Of course I do.—What are *we* going to do, for instance?"

The shadow of a big cloud often came over the open land and made an island of dark blue, drifting on the serene face of the plain. It brought cool, too, and a somehow different day. Something like that happened across their faces now. He shook his head at her, as if he had no answer, but this one, and leaned to her and kissed her again.

She went into nothing in his arms, as if she had turned into fire, or water, another element. And when that happened, he became firmer being than ever, power in flesh.

Presently, he looked at her again, and shook his head, meaning that she was right.

"You know something?"

"No."

"Well, when this can happen to us, to me, grown-up, and full of beliefs about the way to *be,* and so on, then how in the world can young people, even little boys, like my son and his confederate the Shoemaker boy, how can *they* know what to do?"

"When?"

"When they want to raise hell."

"Are we raising hell?"

"That's what would be *said,* you know."

"D'you mind?" she said, looking cool.

"Yes."

"For whose sake?"

"All ours."

"I know."

"Just the same:" he said, but stopped.

"Yes?"

He ground his jaw a trifle, smiling at her, with almost a comic tenderness, and she laughed in a little gasp.

"That look!—You look like one of those painted fauns, or satyrs, if you ever look at me that way in front of anyone else, my reputation won't be worth a shred.—If you weren't so sweet at the same time, I'd say you were leering."

"I am leering."

"—'Said he, meaningfully.'"

He nodded.

"Well, you asked what were we going to do, and I wish I knew. —I know what I'd *like*."

"What?"

"We'll get in the car and start back. I'll tell you as we go."

They gathered their things.

"Do you notice all sorts of things about me?" asked Molly. "Because I do, about you."

She sounded so like a complacent little girl, laying down "tactfully" the rules of a new game that he burst out laughing and told her just that.

She sobered for a second, and said,

"You'll know pretty soon about me that I'm an awful lot a child, still, and one thing about it, is, I suppose it is what *makes* my work. I mean, to see things like a child, and think about them as a woman would.—I have a frightful temper, too, darling, the awful kind that doesn't throw things, but smolders and plans campaigns of hurtful things to say, and lets them out one sting at a time, all in a cloud of perfect composure. That's why I look so ridiculously young at times. —You look out. A passionate child inside a woman is *something*."

"You sound like Carmen."

"What do you know about Carmen?" she asked in surprise.

"I used to go to the opera in New York years ago when I was an intern. One of the other fellows was a brother of one of the singers, and he had tickets now and then. I heard *Carmen*. I loved it."

They crossed the plain again in the car. The afternoon was hotter than midday, and full of the herblike scent of the baking desert.

Presently she asked him what he was going to say.

"You always answer questions five remarks later, don't you," she said.

"Do I?—I hope it doesn't sound shrewd. I don't like shrewdness."

He drove silently a little while. Did he want to say it? He thought about it for a mile or two, and then to his own helpless amazement, he said,

"I wish we might go off to California together.—California is the Nirvana of everybody else in this country."

She was silent. He looked at her.

"Would *you?*" he asked, looking at the road again.

"You mean, simply run away? for a while? or forever? In due time?—All *that*."

Again he was astonished and pained, when he said,

"Forever. Another life."

She took a deep breath.

"Yes. But I probably think it is harder to do than you do.—I probably want it more, and see the troubles more than you do."

"I doubt that. It—a lot of sorry suffering would be involved."

"But there would be so much else!" she said, perversely, thinking of the way her heart tumbled with excitement when she saw his car coming, or heard anyone mention his name.

"This is an *enchanted* day," she said. "I will tell you how we shall be, whenever everything is arranged. No, not *arranged,* that is like an undertaker's word. I mean, when we have bolted and run."

All through her gaiety, the comedy she made out of feelings so true and yet so chanceful that she seemed hardly able yet to grant them their future, he was full of revolt. He asked himself why he should not seize the joy which was within his grasp. Betrayal? Well, but if people knew: and yet a shred of light somewhere in him shone clear, and meant that every betrayal ultimately would come back to himself; it would be himself he betrayed most of all in betraying anyone else. He frowned such ideas down. He wiped out all the years of his manhood with delight in the impatient longings alive in him now. He kept saying to himself that if it were someone else, a commonplace creature, a dull, promiscuous girl from God knew what kind of life, all his qualms might have power. But not with Molly. She was truly delicate, passionate beyond her frailty.

As the miles went by in the blazing dust of the afternoon, and they crossed the sand again, and saw the river vein of green in the glaring desert, and the mountains take shape and change and elongate and veer, like grand squadrons on a horizon of sea, he hardly listened to Molly, but sought and found what he called his formula. He said to himself that Noonie certainly wasn't happy *now*. It was likely that "the other way" she would probably not be happy either, but prob-

ably not much unhappier, if at all. Perhaps she could go home, back
to Rochester, and find her old life again. She had plenty of money
from her father's estate. Wouldn't it be a relief, anyway, to have
something settled, one way or the other?

He searched all such notions for the frame which would justify
the surge of sweetness he felt; the breath of desire he breathed.

Molly was at ease when he was silent. Once or twice she glanced
away from him, looking at the glare of the land. She felt that rather
gulpy fullness in the heart which people have at a stroke of preposterous good luck. Things will work out, she said to herself. They've got
to, if this much is true.

"We shall become a legend in town," she said. He smiled, and she
didn't really need him to listen closely, but let him alone with his
thoughts, while she went on with her parody. "Of course everybody
knows everybody else, and we'll hardly be gone to California until
the telephones begin. I think like this: I'll go back to Kansas City in
the most public of all possible departures, and then take the next
train back to the Coast, and when I get to town here, you will get on
the same train, to attend a medical consultation in Los Angeles, and
I shall sit in a drawing room with the shades drawn and the fan going. As you stagger by my door laden with luggage, the train will
start, and you will stumble having lost your balance, and fall against
my door. The door will fly open, and you will lurch into my drawing
room, and out of surprise, you will give such a start that you will fall
upon the seat opposite me, and your shoulder will brush the window
shade, which will fly up, exposing us to the gaze of three professional
gossips who are paid by the railroad to watch the California Limited
go through every day. They will gasp and say, Isn't that that attractive
Doctor Rush, in the private compartment with that Foster woman?
Yes, it is he, this can mean only one thing. And as the train pulls
westward, word is already abroad in the streets.—Do you wish to hear
what comes next?—Well, the Associated Press inquires where I am.
My publisher denies everything. Mr. Hearst's Sunday scandal-sheet
(I have met Mr. Hearst, who thought I was a picture actress, which
enchanted me), will have a full page about it, with a pen drawing of
me showing my blonde hair in wavy lines, and an old photograph of
William Farnum, with a mustache added, which will be you, saying
you were the stroke of the Cornell crew. The point of the story (designed to please Mr. Hearst) will be that you have found a new cure
for old age, and that my new novel will tell about it, and that the
cure was what undermined your family life, and what we went away
about.

"—Then, in California, we will be asked to go into the movies, having become national figures as a result of all the unsavory publicity, and both of us being very natty looking. I will be tempted to accept, but you will never understand why, and the Los Angeles papers will say that while you and Douglas Fairbanks have left together for an unknown destination, I am the guest of Miss Pickford who is trying to reach you by long distance to patch up the quarrel. Miss Pickford will succeed, especially since you and Mr. Fairbanks have only been out on the golf links for a quiet game.

"Finally, I decide that a small brownstone house in San Francisco near the Pacific Union Club will be suitable, and we go there to live, where we have rather 'fast' parties on Saturday evenings, and all the 'Bohemian set' will come, and I will appear to be both tragic, and deliriously happy, as befits a notorious woman of great talent, in whom many things can be pardoned . . ."

But such nonsense was only another delicacy on her part, for she could not really weigh her happiness yet, in terms of decisions; and wished to leave them for him to make. The teasing sort of irony in her novelette of their future was almost like a guard, should it turn out that she needed one.

He drove into town and before they came to her house, he laid his hand upon hers, resting it in affirmation on today's happenings. She got out of the car in great content.

II

It was not quite six o'clock that evening when Peter came home and went upstairs, wondering what he would say. In the big front bedroom, he found Noonie, as he thought, taking a nap. She was lying on her bed. On her face was a smile of such dazzling sweetness that he was spellbound by it for a moment. However long had it been since she had looked like that! He remembered it well. His heart came up into his mouth, and he shook his head for the difference in her. But in a second, her breathing alarmed him, and he bent over her. Then he saw the bottle on the glass table by the bed, and knew what she had done. Then he had a rise of rage in him that anybody should throw life away, and he set to work to recover her.

With the first hint of success, his heart turned over, and was weak with gratitude. He made her sit up, and shaking her back to awareness, he kept saying aloud to her, "Poor Noonie, poor Noonie."

Her face looked pathetically young, and flushed, and the first moment she opened her eyes, he felt a little unearthly about it. He was looking through her eyes at the return to earth, of one who had tried to leave it behind forever. He could not see the images in the pool of her unconsciousness, but she had made that journey toward Lethe, and had looked upon the face of her fear. She saw again while dreaming toward death what had happened one day, years back, when she was a child at home. Her brother Roderick, that tall, dark-haired, black-eyed governor of her childhood, whom she had adored, said to her one day in the garden of the house in Rochester when they were playing a favorite game of making rival kingdoms out of the flower beds, and conducting wars between them,

"How little you know."

"I do too."

"No, you really do not understand anything."

"What, for instance?"

"You only *think* you love us all, here, at home."

"I do too! I love all of you!" and she had begun to cry.

"No, you will forget us all some day."

"I will not! I never, never will!"

"Yes, you will go far away, leave us all, marry, and have children, and we'll never see you any more!"

"No, no, no, I'll never!" she had cried, storming and weeping, imploring him to "Take it back." But he was obdurate, he condemned her to a future faithless to this childhood hour, and it was more than she could bear. She cried as if her heart would break, and as if he had cast her off, with his smiling clever face, his authority, his piercing black and white eyes, his whim of elegance so impressive to an adoring younger sister. She begged him to say that she would be forever faithful and secure at home, and he smiled and shook his head, and said,

"Well, after all, that's life."

But she was so hideously distressed, her suffering was so appalling, that he had created more of a sensation than he had bargained for. At last, touched by her protests of love for her father and mother and himself, and her vows of eternal devotion, he sighed, and said that perhaps he was wrong, and she really meant what she said. He smiled, and the garden seemed a fair world again, with its high screen of trees, and the flower beds like continents in a green sea of lawn, and like a gracious monarch granting the most binding of favors, he extended his hand to her, and permitted her to kiss it respectfully. It was many minutes before her sobs retreated entirely, but she came back to content at last, and had she only known it, had bought the present at the expense of much of her future.

This scene was so vivid, so enchanting, to Noonie, that afternoon years later, that she was smiling at it when she was discovered by Peter. He was bringing her back, he was arousing her, and it was like the movements of waves, like coming back from a drowning lake, and she saw again the wreck of the yacht *Affinity,* and the terror, and the faithfulness, of how she had saved her brother Roderick from the black water that night on the lake. She saw again the glow of the white sail fallen on the water, and barely showing pale in the starlight. She prayed again the words she had said that night, to ask God for strength to save Roderick until Peter should return with help. It had been so pitiful and so earnest that it had bound her like a vow of fidelity. She smiled exquisitely at the safety they had all found at last, during that night.

Peter slapped her to restore her. It was a stimulant of pain. She yielded to it, and she began to come back to consciousness, and with the other memories there now merged one of childbirth, and when the three memories had all come together their fears were seen lingering on the edge of daylight, as she awoke. When her eyes first saw Peter now, they looked back at life in perfect serenity.

He thought it was because she did not yet realize "where she was."

But it was the look of someone exorcised of terrors confronted and banished.

Still smiling, she wept for shame and gratitude, at peace with him. He looked upon himself bitterly, and stroked her hair, and stayed by her.

XXVIII · FAREWELL TO MOLLY

I

None of this was ever known around.

Like many mortal decisions, those in this case were made in private, with the persons involved looking the truth in the eye, alone, and, in terms of their natures, admitting its power. Romance would have dictated neater solutions, grander fulfillments of the moment; but given how things were, what prevailed was the formal outline of "morality," which was an unfashionable term, but which carried a timeless authority.

II

Peter telephoned Molly and said he wanted to see her alone as soon as she could manage it. She said to come the next afternoon about three. Miss Bridges would be out with Brisky, the spaniel, and she herself would be supposed to be taking her siesta, to which she always retired with a column of books and a lap-desk for the writing of notes. She wrote dozens of notes a week, five- and six-line greetings to people all over the world. It was one of her pet vanities to keep in touch with everyone, and she enjoyed it when everyone asked plaintively how she managed to find time to do so many things.

He went about his work as usual the day after the awful discovery at home, but he had waves of remembrance now and then during his busy hours, and he would ask himself how could he ever have thought that anything else would ever have done, than what he had been so powerfully shown was his duty? However much it may have lacked freedom and glamour? Nobody suspected what he was thinking about, or that there was within him a recognition of the depths of his own fault. How long he had hoped that Noonie could be spared a crisis; how certain he had been that it was coming; how much, now that it had happened, he himself had learned from it!

In the afternoon, at three, he drove up to the big log house, and was met by Molly. She was cool looking and exquisite. The awnings were down outside. The big room was dark. She was so glad to see him that he began to frown, and barely took her hand. She saw at once that nothing was as they had left it between them yesterday. She moved away from him and lighted a cigarette, and sat down opposite him by the cold fireplace. He saw her bring her head up and regard him with a sober little face. The childlike sweetness in her eyes, at seeing him a moment ago, was gone. She was expressionless; and when she was like that, there were little signs of strain, of—of *experience,* that showed about her eyes and her mouth. She was still very pretty; but it was a sceptical prettiness, that had looked on so many things in rueful discovery, that she seemed like another person.

She was dying to ask him what the trouble was. But she so dreaded to hear what she saw in his face that she stayed silent, and held her cigarette up before her and watched him. He was burned darker by the day's outing yesterday, and he was scowling. He licked his lips, and kept looking into the charred cold fireplace. It was only a moment or two, but he looked for that time like a youth, appalled by the world. Then he lifted his head and looked at her, and his eyes were so full of compassion for things beyond them both that she felt the breath forced out of her breast as if his hand had pressed her over the heart, and she said at last,

"Peter: what is it:"

and he told her what he had come upon at home last evening. She listened to him quietly but her heart turned cold. She felt abominably chastened by the terrible news he had, and she saw immediately what it meant for the two of them. Not until now had her feelings of all this time seemed anything but blessed. Now they seemed mean, and vulgar, and cheapened; and she could tell herself even while she listened to him that this violent revulsion of her heart was simply proof of how deeply she'd longed for what she had found. What a coward desire was, how it shriveled up and vanished, when other claims opposed it tragically! When he finished his little history, which he made as matter of fact as possible, she saw in his eyes the loving look she had come to know in him, and she also saw that he had made his decision, and that it was final.

She wanted to go to him and shake his shoulders, and say to him that everything was just as real as it ever was, time would help, there were always ways to heal wounds, nothing could change what they had discovered under the time-silenced city of the day before.

But she saw that for everything she could say, and believe, he had something that was even truer for him. And so she held her tongue, and looked at him until he looked away again. She began to cry in silence. As if she were a creature in one of her own stories, she saw herself stop the crying with a handkerchief and a hold of her breath, so that when he looked around again, he wouldn't have to face the added difficulty of a weepy female. Her mind heated with bitter comedy when she saw herself rapidly review a series of codes which would be useful, and select the one that became her most at "a time like this," and she smartened her shoulders, and assumed a wistful half-smile, and she knew she was pretty that way, and she believed that this might trouble him, but it was the least she owed herself until she could be alone. She got up and went over to him, and said, aching with insincerity,

"There is only one thing for you to do, and that is, to stay home.— And only one thing for me, and that is, to go away. I am so sorry, dearest Peter."

He jumped up. His awkwardness, no, his brutality, almost, she thought, was a cleansing thing. He had no repertoire of emotional notes to strike, as she had. He was awry and disordered and he expressed it in every movement and every word. He was rough and miserable. He put his hands on her shoulders and leaned to her and kissed her hardly, and her heart sank. It was so unlike a last farewell of storied lovers, so little declaration, so little expressed nobility, that she felt the poor truth of everything all over again.

"Yes, yes," he said, "Molly, I have been in torture all night and all day.—You see that. This is where I must stay with everything. After *now,* I must. I don't know how much she knew, or if she knew anything. But nothing like that is ever any sole person's responsibility or job. We're going to stay with it. I had to tell you as soon as I could. You see it. I knew you would see it. I'll never forget—"

"Oh, shut up!" she said, losing her exterior. She dropped her face into her hands, and she sobbed, and he saw her true self come before him, and it was somehow a relief, after the poised creature he had seen here today. It was just as bad as he had expected it to be. But he said to himself bitterly that he had earned this, too, just as much as all the rest of it, the delight, the promises, the prophecies.

She clutched him with her hand, and then with her other hand on her sobbing mouth, she let him go, and went out of the room.

He reached to the silver urn on the table and took a cigarette, lighted it, and went out to his car and drove to the hospital, saying to himself that it couldn't be worse, and that nothing of it must appear to anyone else, who might need him for help or comfort in any way.

He knew he would never see her again.

Not even then could he hate the order of the world, which had cost him so much. He followed Molly in his thoughts as he drove, and if to have a heart full of demands for the safety of someone is to pray, then he prayed for her as he rounded the gravel driveway of the hospital and came up to the white-pillared entrance out in back where the staff always entered. He rode upstairs in the automatic elevator to the fourth floor. Walking down the corridor to the operating room at the end, he passed the chapel. The doors were open. He stopped and looked in. Four nuns were kneeling far from one another. Their backs were to him, as they faced the altar anonymously. It was an image of prayer in the abstract. He felt his heart thump at their certainty that man's lot could be alleviated and understood through their faith in the power of prayer.

"Yes," he said to himself, going on down the hall. He meant a great deal by it.

III

He was surprised, a few days later, to bump into Judith Bridges down at the railroad tracks, where he was seeing a favorite patient off to the East. The patient had recovered from tuberculosis, and was heading home to try a few months of his old life, to see if he could stand it. After the train left, Peter dawdled for a few minutes, watching the elegance of the observation car diminish into the desert perspective. Miss Bridges came up behind him, and said,

"That's us, tomorrow, but going the other way."

"Oh: hello: to California?"

"Yes. I thought you probably knew."

"No.—I haven't seen Molly."

"Yes," said Miss Bridges, looking at him with perfect frankness, and much interested in what she might see in his face, "we feel we have exhausted this environment. I've just been getting tickets and things. It would be difficult to stay, now.—You know what I mean. She told me all about it."

"Oh."

"Good Lord, don't look at me like that, I'm her oldest friend in the world, and anyway there'll be a book about it some day, there's no use fooling anybody.—I needn't beat around the bush. I'm glad it all busted up in time."

"Look here, Miss Bridges, I—"

"Don't run off, yet, Peter. You hate me for meddling like this. But what *I* think about it is just as much part of the truth of the situation as what anybody *else* thinks, who *knows*. And *I* think it's a damned good thing."

"You're a strange sort of friend."

"I adore Molly, and she's practically saved me from a bad crack-up after the War. But that doesn't mean I can't *see* her."

"See her?"

"She's Lady George Gordon Noel Byron."

"What does that mean?"

"She's an artist first of all. And anybody like you could never be second-of-all to anyone. And you would've had to try."

He looked cross and outraged, and she insisted on her point by nodding.

"Yes, she was. She *is.*—*That's* what she's married to, and just how good or how bad she is at it, time will tell. I think she's pretty important, in at least three books, anyway. But once it got her, the power of the word, it kept her. And everything tends to nourish that, as if she were a pretty blonde lady spider with cornflower-blue eyes.— That's what went wrong with her first marriage. Dick Foster never really got to know her, and nobody else ever could, *that way*. So he, being a weak character, got sorry for himself in a bottle of whisky, which was the end of him, finally.—But it'd be ridiculous to pretend that anything could ever come of it if she tried it again.—Poor darling, she keeps *thinking* and *hoping,* herself.—She doesn't know all this about *herself.*"

"But you do, eh, is that it?"

Miss Bridges leaned down to stroke Brisky, the pale-yellow spaniel who was panting in her shadow.

"I certainly do.—Can't you *allow* it in her, Peter? Or did you see her as anything at all but a darling little blonde with twirling blue eyes?—I sometimes think no man ever saw a woman as a live human being, as full of holes and flaws as himself. If any man ever did, and admitted it, and loved even the flaws, what a lover he would be!"

He looked down at her, with a frowning smile. You busy, hard, intellectual virgin you, he thought, even if you've slept with a hundred people, you're still virginal, because you've never yielded up your self-image, have you. But he didn't say anything, and as she stood up, she held out her hand, and gave him a hearty handclasp, and he then believed that she meant to wish him well, almost hungrily, and he had an echo of sense in what she'd been saying, when he saw how sincere she was. He watched her stride off up the brick platform with the brushy dog frolicking along at her heels. He guessed she said all that sort of thing with difficulty, but out of a conscience born of much trouble in her own life.

Then came a confirmation from Molly herself. It was a letter, written to him from town the night before she took the train westward. Without salutation, the letter read:

> I still have a few of your books which Judy is going to mail back to you, to your office address. I have much enjoyed them. It touches me to know how much they mean to you. It is one of the things I feel I really and truly know about you, the actual aliveness in your thoughts, of all this country, and your hunger for what it used to be like here. I have long since concluded that you really do find things in the life of the past which help to illuminate for you how people are today, and I dimly feel that you've learned more from such reflection than I ever could. It saddens me for myself; but it gladdens me for you.
>
> Whatever will remain of what you now think about me?

But that is a question which it is unfair to ask you. As for me, I am humiliated, now, and in time, I may be grateful. What you see by my writing here is how my habits are forever formed, and whatever happens to me is material to be analysed and stricken off into images. If the world ever knew all this, they would say that I have been saved from a folly by your goodness. How cruel goodness sometimes is!

If I close my eyes, I can see again that terrible sunlighted cliff of empty houses, and I can hear again the scream of that single bird, which struck some strange kind of life from our intentions. Were you moved by this? I never felt that you were moved by it in just the way I was. I have none of the mystic in me, ordinarily, but I must admit that on that day, I felt all those vanished lives all about. Pity, pity! How much of it is love?

I have been hurt, but that is of no consequence. I pray that you have not been. I love you. I cannot worry about you. There is the most immovable strength in you. I could see that when you came to tell me good-bye. I was jealous of it. You wouldn't really like me, at my utmost. I hope you can admire me, and so I shall say that I hope your troubles will truly be over, and that health and peace will come back to you all. Perhaps you yourself can be the source of that for those you love; for that you do love them is what your faithfulness finally means, doesn't it? I think it does, and I hope it is so. I can bow my head to that with real humility.

We leave tomorrow.

As Lady Caroline scribbled to Byron, "Remember me!" She was ardent and addled, and I am behaving very coolly. But oh how I mean it. Good-bye.

Mary.

When he was done reading it, his cheeks were hot with a flush that rose to darken his whole head. He tore the letter into tiny pieces and snowed them into the wastebasket by his office desk. His heart was beating rapidly. The faint flavor of irony in her letter troubled him almost more than the frankness of its feeling. Oh my, oh my, he thought, recognizing that this was just one of those things you have to wait for to be over.

Book IV · THE EARTH'S HEART BEATING

XXIX · GROWING UP

I

Wayne came home a few days later at suppertime and told Martha that Mrs. Rush was very ill. Donald hadn't been allowed to see her for several days. She was going to be all right; she was terribly weak, they said, and Doctor Rush was pretty worried. Don didn't know what the trouble was. But he wrote her little notes and sent them in, and the nurse brought back the answers. It was something sudden, one day she had been perfectly well, and the next, bang, sick as a dog.

Martha was getting supper for the two of them. She paid small attention to his gossip. She was curiously interested in looking at him. It was too bad about Mrs. Rush, she had looked so pretty that day, perhaps she had taken ill that same night. You never knew, did you. Anyway, it was Wayne she was regarding with a new sense of his person.

He is simply amazing, he has changed overnight, too, isn't it strange how I never saw it coming? Or is it me; do I see everything differently, even my young brother? He is ranging out, taller, he has that hair like a field of long yellow grass, it trembles as if it had a wind playing in it gently, all the time. I used to pull his hair when we were both younger and he would not let me alone. I had to do *something*, he was a fiend, maybe he still is, it doesn't show anymore.

He looks as if he knew a lot, now.

I'll bet he doesn't.

But why should he look so?

I always used to think he was a cute little boy, with his dark lashes and pale hair, and I used to pretend to everybody else that he was an angel, but that was to hide what a devil he was, and just because he was my brother.

But he isn't cute any more.

Sometimes he looks very sad, like a puppy dog that is hungry, and doesn't know where to turn for something to eat.

And sometimes he looks powerful.

Look at him curled up in the chair there with the evening paper, staring at the page as if it were resisting him. His face is brown from the sun, and his arms are more than long nervous bones now, and his legs are shapely. Does he know it?

What has happened to him without our seeing?

But I am a fool.

It is just that I never knew before what growing up meant. I never knew that you grew toward everything all at the same time. I thought you just grew bigger and stayed the same little girl you always were and that eventually you seemed to be grown-up and could never remember anything about children.

She was setting the table.

They hadn't needed the *Spirito Santo's* fire for some time, and Wayne stared at it critically. In summer, the base burner was something yet again. They kept flowers on it, and yarn waiting to be wound into balls, and the mother's purse often hung on the knob of the handle of the poop-deck door with its mica panes. The stove was the central object in the room, and they often propped notes for each other up on its top when there was no fire in its deep belly.

"What?" said Martha, in the family habit to share in the other's thoughts.

"Nothing.—The *Spirito Santo.*"

"Oh. What about it?—I always said it has such *personality,* don't you think so?"

He made his face severe and weighed her statement so long that she turned to look at him, which was what he wanted.

"I do not," he replied finally. "If it has anything, I would agree to say that it had *stovality.*"

She felt obliged to lift her eyebrows at this preciousness, but she was touched by pride in his ruthless intelligence. She felt dimly how he really saw the *Spirito Santo,* its short powerful little legs, its bulging shell like dull old black silk, the glistening window with the light of opals in its tiny panes, the royal headdress of the nickel urn on top with the florid handles, and the smoke pipe, rising so powerfully to the roof. It was not too much to say that Wayne's whole life would be educated and affected by pangs of comfort and well-being related to the old stove.

He suddenly wrenched himself out of his chair, went to his room, rummaged in a box he kept under his cot, and came back with a piece of red tissue paper which he had saved off a Christmas package. He next went out to his bicycle under the great tree in the back yard and detached his dry-cell flashlight from the handlebars. He returned to the house and opening the main door of the *Spirito Santo* he set the flashlight on the cold grate which smelled so sweet of cold ashes, and slid the switch turning on the miniature electric bulb behind the flashlight lens. Over this he then laid the red tissue paper, and closed the mica'd door, and backed away to see the effect.

Martha watched him.

He paid no attention to her until he decided to remove the things inside. When this was done, he acknowledged her witness by saying, "Just something to try."

He put his things away and settled down again in the big chair with the evening paper.

II

Yes, she thought, he too.

She began to blush and turned away to hide it in case he looked up suddenly.

He'll be like Bun someday, doing to some other girl what Bun does to me, *that little male,* and nobody else'll ever know what he'll feel. Of course, I am the happiest creature in the world; but will *he* be? Can I save him, in any way? I should hate for him to be hurt. He should be so careful! I wonder if I could talk to him.

But this idea was ridiculous when she glanced back at him. He was so secure, so complete in his own person, so cool in his attitude, the way he kept his eyebrows up and his mouth pursed in a silent whistling, that she realized how far apart they were, and ever would be.

She called him to come to supper, and he came, a miniature lord, and sat down, and cocked his eye at her, and asked her if she'd had a busy day, without really being concerned for the answer. She could've laughed outright with joy at his imposture that was yet more of a prediction; and could not resist leaning over and chubbing his cheek, as they used to call it in the family, taking his smooth cheek in her thumb and finger and giving it a pinch and a shake. He flared, and sparred her hand away, and all but hissfully spat at her. His wheat field of hair swept back and forth over his tall smooth bony forehead. He instructed her coldly to be her age, and keep her cute little tricks for her boy friend, and when he saw how this had scratched her, he inquired with an elegant burlesque of charm, whether she hadn't better get wise to herself? and cease from robbing the cradle?

He was the first worldly rub which her passion met up with.

They ate their supper in silence.

Of the two, he was already the stronger, and they both knew it.

III

After supper, Wayne went off on his wheel to meet Donald, and Martha did the dishes, and then met Bun later on. When he asked her why she was so silent, she tried to tell him about Wayne; but had no way to make him, and herself, see clearly her discovery that life reposed for donation in all creatures, even in her little brother Wayne.

That year an airplane came to Albuquerque to stay. A barnstorming pilot had put up a shack of a hangar out on the mesa, and took people up for rides, at three dollars for ten minutes.

"I went up this afternoon," said Bun, sensibly getting her off her funny ideas, which sounded almost as if she was *sorry* for everything.

"You didn't."

"I certainly did. It was wonderful."

"I'd've been scared to death, if I'd known."

"—Why I didn't tell you. But what you can see! Next time I get three dollars, you're going up with my compliments."

"Oh never!"

"Sure, you'll love it."

"What can you see?"

"To hell and gone.—The mountains look entirely different. The river never starts and never ends, it's all the way you can look, north and south. The funniest thing is the *green*."

"How do you mean?"

"Well, there's this straggling path of green by the river, and that's all. You think here, in town, on the ground, you think the trees go on just because you're among them all the time. Even if you drive up to the mesa, you don't really feel the trees stop, they're right back there, in town, heck, you can go back. But from the air, you see the other part, the plains, the desert, it's all like rock, full of light.—And the houses, at first you can't tell which is the house and which is the shadow. They both look flat."

"Flat?"

"Yes. It's wonderful.—We looped the loop."

"No, oh Bunny, how could you take such a risk, think of *me . . .*"

He squirmed a little, because if there was anything about love he didn't quite care for, it was how they always tied everything up to *themselves,* everything a man did, whether he did it for himself pure and simple made no difference. But that was a small enough disadvantage, and he thought the wise way to handle it was to ignore it kindly.

"There's nothing to the loop. It is a tail spin you want to look out for.—I was deaf for twenty minutes when we got down, too. Open cockpit. The motor sprayed a little oil, not enough to mean anything. I got some on my shirt."

She was jealous.

Would she always be discovering things in him that derived not from her, but from other things he liked, and had to do?

The difference was, she loved herself through him, and he loved the world through her.

Later on, under a tree in shadow around the corner from the library building, and in between the passing of cars with their sweeps of light, they resolved that difference for a little time of kisses.

XXX · HIGH FEELINGS FROM LONG AGO

I

As soon as he could find time, Peter went out to Old Town to see Don Hilario Ascarete. It was another Sunday morning, there was nothing to do at the office, and things were quiet at the hospital. He found the old man moving along the ditch that ran past the adobe house of the Ascaretes, and out through the alfalfa field in back. Don Hilario made every step as though it were a separate event, to be considered, decided upon, and taken. The water idling down the ditch moved ever so much faster than the old man. Peter marveled that he was living every time he saw him. He ate hardly anything at all, they said, in his family. And as for sleeping, if anybody ever looked in upon him at night, he was always awake. He was up before anybody else in the morning. Some days he could hardly move, though he never seemed to be in pain from anything. He would doze all day, but if anything "went on," they would find that he was aware of whatever it was. Some of the younger great-grandchildren said he gave them the creeps, and coldly wished he would stay out of the way, or die, or something, because he upset them with his knowing indifference to what seemed of the utmost importance to them. He was an uneasy reminder of large, simple, eternal things, in the midst of the selfish excitements of their young world.

Peter came up to him, and walked around to face the old man, and greeted him in the special cordialities of Spanish.

Don Hilario stood with his mouth open, regarding him, nodding, leaning on his apple bough, and though the sunshine was bright, staring at Peter's face with unblinking eyes, a long moment, before he answered.

"Yes, yes, yes, good morning, my young doctor friend. You've been a long time coming. Shall we retire to the patio and sit down? I have much to tell you."

"About the old house?"

Again Don Hilario looked keenly at Peter, and appeared to be reading him with attention and ease.

"Well, the house, and possibly about many other things.—We'll go back along the ditch. Today is the first day our ditch has run this year. Look at it."

The water was muddy and lazy, and smelled rich and sweet. They made an infinitely slow progress along the bank, to the L of the house where Don Hilario liked to sit, and which he referred to as the patio. Peter studied him as they went. The old man was tiny and frail. Peter supposed he hadn't been bathed in years and years. He was neither dirty nor clean. He was like a patch of ground, baked by the sun, and dried by years, and clothed in his own element. Presently they were sitting by the wall, feeling the heat through their backs.

"Everybody has gone to Mass," said the old man. "I would go, but it takes them too much time to get me ready, and into the car, and off to the Plaza. I walk over there by myself now and then, when the Church is empty, and at such times, I explain everything."

"To the priest?"

Don Hilario made his silent laugh, that rounding of his open mouth.

"No. To Our Father in Heaven."

"Oh."

Peter was delighted at a man who was on explaining terms with God.

"Well," said Don Hilario, looking at him, "everything is not always as simple as that, is it."

"No.—What do you mean?"

"Nothing. You are like my grandchildren, when I know too much. They shy away like a horse that does not want to be caught."

Peter had the feeling that simply by looking at him, old Don Hilario could read the depths of his heart, and see its trouble, its suffering, and the faithless impulses it had held. He began to blush like a schoolboy. What curious perception lived in the aged! he thought, leaning down to pick up a pebble to hide his confusion.

Don Hilario said,

"The worst pride is that which considers itself above trouble, and it always falls the farthest."

Peter looked at him and burst out laughing.

"You old devil," he cried fondly, "what are you getting at?"

A ghost of coquetry, of slyness, appeared in the old face, as Don Hilario replied with a marionette's surprise,

"Nothing, why, nothing at all, except the things I have to tell you about the house down the street which you asked me about.—Why. What else is there to get at? Have I touched you?"

This was an elaborate courtesy. Peter knew that somehow the old man had seen in his face or felt in his presence the echoes of the last weeks of what he had been through. But he replied,

"No, what else could there possibly be. Well. Tell about the house."

"Well, I thought and remembered, and I thought and remembered."

He shook his head as if in wonder and compassion for what people had suffered in their far lost energy of life. Then he went on to say that the house down there on the corner, where the Sanchez family had that grocery store, was once the property and the establishment of "La Voz," as she was called, though more properly known as Doña Catalina Anonciación de Gutierrez, the celebrated female gambler and singer, who had also made a fortune out of professional love.

Don Hilario said he had seen her as a very small boy. Everything he knew about her, and which had taken some time to recall in its proper relation and order, as befitted a legally trained mind, he had remembered from other people's accounts, and what a stir of gossip there once had been.

"High feelings from long ago," he said, with a sort of dusty humor in his dim voice. But he looked at Peter, to show that he meant to be more than funny.

II

When Don Hilario was a young man, the house had already long been built, and now that he was an old man, it was still standing, though it had changed hands and become respectable, since now what was left of it was a combination grocery store and dwelling for the family named Sanchez.

It was on a narrow street leading away from the Plaza toward the north. The Church of San Felipe de Neri was only a few yards away, with its twin white towers that had white-shuttered belfries and black wrought-iron crosses. The cloister and garden of the priests was on the far side of the church. Doña Catalina's house was on the near side, and of course, rather more removed, but still in a curious juxtaposition to the house of good. People remarked it always, meaning to be sly or horrified, according to their temperaments. The house of Doña Catalina was a celebrated brothel and gambling place.

It ran for a hundred feet along the road, where the walls were always well plastered, and turned the corner by the irrigation ditch, and made an L for one half of the patio. The base of the L was sixty feet long, and was met at right angles by a high wall which wavered in its course to enclose several big trees. The fourth side of the patio was a long outdoor sitting place, a *portal,* where in the evenings you could see the watermelon pink of the sunset mountains, and drink your wine, and smoke your cigarette at ease. There was a well in the middle, plastered and tiled in bright colors. Doña Catalina kept a flock of parrots, and their lively conversation, which scandalized passers-by and educated small boys who listened outside the forbidden walls, made a wicked kind of music in the still clear air.

There was a heavy lawn in the patio. The interior of the house was whitewashed, and the walls in daytime reflected a green light. At night, the shutters were fastened to, and no light escaped, or eye looked in. The shutters were supposed to be armored, because Doña Catalina made more money than anybody in Albuquerque, and was subject to banditry. However, she had been molested only once, by a repentant young *rico* who had thrown away all his money gambling and had drunkenly returned one night with three companions, all masked, and had tried to break in and commit robbery. The loyal patrons of Doña Catalina had resisted the assault bravely.

The proprietress herself had come from El Paso at the age of thirty, already a woman of authority and charm. She was wealthy from a career in Mexico City, where she had been a theater singer, and mistress to a high government official. When he was overturned by a moderate revolution, she had left both his protection (which had simply ceased to exist) and the theater (where she felt the work was too hard for meager returns). But he had taught her to gamble, and she announced on arrival in Albuquerque that she intended to run a gambling palace, and invited all the gentlemen from the garrison, the ranches, and the town itself, to inspect her house at a grand opening.

She was an exciting addition to the life of the shady river town, almost a hundred years ago.

She was far from beautiful. Don Hilario said her face was really almost that of a toad, with bulging eyes, and a flat nose, and a wide mouth. But he said she was clever, her eyes were always dancing (he showed how with his own old blinkers) and she painted her face which gave her, he said, a very "imported" look, and fascinated everybody. She was a little bit of a thing, lively as a wasp, and nothing could put her down. She often slapped the face of a drunken patron who was angry and troublesome at losing all his money at the tables. The priests thundered execrations at her from the pulpit, and she was always there at Mass when they did so, with her black *rebozo* modestly pulled over her face, and sometimes she seemed to nod in agreement with what the scathing sermon was saying about her kind of woman.

Out of church, she was generous and friendly with the priests, sent them fine foods across the Plaza, and curtsied and crossed herself when she met them in open air; and they bowed to her, blessing her and thanking her for the offerings she made, and in general recognizing her humanity without condoning her expression of its failures. When asked why they didn't simply take their Franciscan cords and whip her out of town, they replied that the chances of sin resided in us all; let us all conquer them within ourselves. They knew that to persecute Doña Catalina would not ultimately solve anything.

Life was so lived then that the women were resigned to what befell them.

The men though made a sort of club out of Doña Catalina's establishment. In time, it was recognized as a legitimate social feature of the old town, and there were many men who went there simply for companionship with each other, to gamble, to gossip, to drink, to make brown-paper cigarettes and talk.

When a boy began to talk like a raven, and pull at his lip with fingers that believed they had found a mustache starting, and pass in and out of alternate clouds of modesty and desire, it was the commonest thing in the world for his father to bring him one evening to Doña Catalina's, introduce him to her with an air of ceremony and occasion, and yield him over for initiation. A personable boy would cause a great commotion, be exclaimed over, petted, praised, and in general embarrassed out of his wits by the approval of Doña Catalina's women. And of course there were men in numbers who came as regular patrons to the row of small rooms that flanked the *acequia* at the far end of the patio. Each of the rooms was named after a different flower, and was plastered and frescoed and furnished to suggest its quality. The lady occupant was known by the name of her particular room.

This was all about the time the American occupation happened.

Don Hilario had been a boy then, but as he grew up, he came to know the tradition of Doña Catalina's and was able to report details he may not actually have observed himself.

None of the respectable women ever spoke to Doña Catalina. When they would go to the markets or the bazaars or hurry to inspect the contents of a wagon just arrived from Mexico City, the respectable women couldn't help bumping into her, for she was an ardent shopper too, and had more money to buy the first luxuries with.

The house had splendor, in terms of the taste and the difficulties of the time. The main social room was fifty feet long, with heavy beams crossing the ceiling, and immensely deep window niches curtained with olive-green velvet and shuttered with iron. The furniture looked religious, with carved crosses and enormous silver candlesticks with what looked like fists of silver knotted in decoration in frequent stages of their upward way. There were heavy paintings of ladies and gentlemen nobody ever recognized. But Doña Catalina enjoyed traditions above all else, and gave herself dynastic airs and satisfactions with her pictures. There were benches that resembled choir stalls along the walls, and decorum was encouraged, and even rendered inevitable by the uncomfortable magnificence of the furnishings of this main room. Here concerts were held, and the Señora herself was sometimes induced to sing, which she did in an inexpressibly bright and unmusical voice which reminded everybody of one of her own parrots. But when she sang, the eye, if not the ear, was moved, for her animation surpassed anything they had ever seen in Albuquerque. She was full of references to the cosmopolitan world of Mexico City, and its own faint echoes of the great world of Europe. In a society as remote as that of the old river *villa* in the mid-nineteenth century, this was more important than might at first seem plausible.

The gambling went on in rather smaller rooms, opening off the main *sala*. There were richly shadowed, candlelighted groups around the heavy tables, and little sacks of silver on the board, and gold pieces like autumn leaves piled up, and a general air of insincere good manners behind which greed flickered like fire through a grate. The gambling rooms were as plain as a barracks.

Beyond that were the living rooms of Doña Catalina and her staff; and they were as casual as you please, disordered, capricious and without the rigidly maintained style of the rest of the house. The kitchen was an enormous room with an open range and a huge copper hood that led to a hole in the roof.

Nobody was fooled, of course, by the accents of grandeur and propriety that were to be seen in various qualities of the house. It was just as wicked as such a place could be. There were no vices that were not enthroned there, and plenty of lost souls could be seen failing to find themselves in Doña Catalina's care. She had a great capacity for sympathy, and in her etchy voice she used to make little scenes of pity and concern over her most drunken or vicious customers.

But in herself she was a scrupulous and remote woman. She never took a lover, from among her friends in town. She made an edifice of her personal virtue, and it really seemed to be a citadel in which her spirit could lurk, as if in remote purity, to supervise the sins of others, of which she was innocent herself. This gave her an authority which infuriated others at times, such as her employees, and to them she would show a side of her nature rarely displayed to the town; a fantastically sardonic and icy face, uttering the most cutting of execrations, reciting the depraved accomplishments of the miserable inmates to their faces, and whipping them back to submission at last, weeping and conscience-torn.

All told, she was a successful and interesting figure for several years. She had amassed a fortune, nobody knew how much, but she kept buying jewels and furniture and dresses and silver services and sending sums to the church and having painted carriages brought from Mexico and pictures from Italy until everyone assumed that her wealth was far greater than it actually was. She had reached an age when she would make a whole evening of mellow comedy out of picturing in words the time when she would leave the active life, retire, buy a place "in the country" (what a citified expression! this whole town was practically "in the country") and by a few adroit gestures, win her way into respectable society and become a great agent for style and goodness in Albuquerque itself.

III

But before this could happen, the United States Army marched down the river from Santa Fe under command of General Kearny in 1846. It was a cavalry force, and it had peacefully annexed the whole territory of New Mexico, proclaiming amnesty and bringing a beginning of civil stability to the little towns and pueblos. There had been trading parties through here before, and legendary trappers who one by one as single human beings conquered the wilderness of mountain and prairie. But there had never before been so many Americans anywhere in New Mexico at one time. These troops were the most exciting thing to happen in generations; in fact, since the extraordinary visit of the Bishop of Durango and his suite in huge carriages with leather curtains in the previous century. The province was overwhelmed with the importance of the expedition, and very shortly after that, enchanted with its conduct. Troops were going on to the West coast of the continent if they could get through. What was this: a printing press which they had brought along? There had never been such a thing here before, the American General's proclamations were set up and printed right here, and handed around before the ink was dry. Society had more to do than it could manage. There were balls, and suppers, and reviews, drills in the Plaza, and during the few days while the Army halted in Albuquerque, the house of Doña Catalina was "like a blacksmith shop," (according to what she was said to have said) ringing with bottles and glasses, and the sound of coins on the tables.

The local gentlemen took the visiting officers to Doña Catalina's as to a club. No other establishment in the town had the resources, the richness, the profusion of foods, of drinks, of simple room, space itself, to entertain the Americans in, and enough women.

To explain what then transpired, Don Hilario reminded Peter how the women of the Latin race sometimes reacted to the *gringos*. A heat came on them suddenly, he said, when they saw blue eyes, or yellow hair, or pink skin, and only the most rigidly instructed girls preserved their ordinary reserve during the American Army's occupation. The soldiers were on the average much bigger than the men of New Mexico. They had laughing humors and in comparison with the dark-skinned New Mexicans, they seemed very open-faced and innocent. They were, in brief, like a lot of huge boys. Mexican men matured early, and there was little difference between a boy of eighteen and a man of thirty. But these Americans had pink color showing under their tan, and they played like big puppies all the time. They seemed never to be serious. They bought like princes, and had the most refreshing manners, without guile, which the women expected in their own men, and without ceremony, which generations of Latin tradition had made habitual in the New Mexicans. They were gay without getting drunk, and as conquerors, they were more like guests at a party, charmed with the arrangements, wide-eyed at the social novelties they beheld, and certain that everyone was as nice as could be.

There was an officer named Captain Henry Houghton Somers in command of one of the troops. He was a well-bred young man of thirty from the little town of Batavia, New York, and had been in the Army for twelve years. He was able to remember echoes of the War on the Great Lakes, and the triumphs of Commodore Perry. He believed that service in the armed forces of his country was the most honorable of professions. His wife and two babies lived in Batavia. He wrote to them last from Saint Louis, but a package of mail was going back from Albuquerque, and he was getting a bundle of pages ready for the bag all during his visit here. He was over six feet tall, he had hair the color of autumn corn shucks, and long sideburns, and his head was richly framed by the high gates of his full-dress collar with all the gold lace on it. His eyes were blue. He hardly ever sat down, but had a way of lounging in muscular ease against the furniture or the walls or a doorway. He smiled frequently, and tried earnestly to speak Spanish. He was like the biggest and most awkward and most willing pupil in a class of schoolboys who pretended he might be stupid out of some kind of good manners, because he was really very smart. The new country and the strange people he was seeing stimulated him highly.

What was a sparkle of interest and intelligent appraisal in his fond eyes looked like something else to Doña Catalina.

Turning false to all her shrewd principles of professional detachment, she fell publicly in love with him, which is to say, her infatuation racked her and betrayed her to everyone.

He went to her house as a matter of course, with all the other soldiers, and met and talked with the local gentlemen. He would take a drink, and ring a coin or two on the table in the inner room, and bow charmingly to the ladies of the flowery rooms when they made their formal gestures of blandishment for his benefit. He was made to realize that an extraordinary honor was paid him when

Doña Catalina herself took his arm for a whole evening, and went with him through the rooms, and sat with him in one of the misplaced choir stalls, and explained all her extravagant treasures to him. She even drank with him, which she had never been known to do before with a visitor. She wore every one of her jewels one time when she expected he would be in attendance. She powdered her face to a dazzling white and painted her mouth with red paste, and dug fascinating caverns of shadow about her eyes with black paint so that there would be flashes and sparks riding on her glance. She used a fan with theatrical archness. She smoked and blew the smoke over his face and hid her mouth with her silver lace mantilla. She said her heart was a girl, and that was all that mattered. Captain Somers was gay and cordial; he would laugh uproariously as if this was the heartiest joke on earth. He escaped her by his simple enthusiasm, you might say. Everything delighted him, equally.

The inhabitants and visitors watched the desperate romance being played before them by Doña Catalina during the stay of the American soldiers.

Another evening she would appear in a new role, her face uncolored, her eyes subdued, a black mantilla over her head, her gown of black, black lace mitts on her hands, no jewels, but an onyx crucifix hanging on her lace-covered bosom. The Captain spent the evening admiring the crucifix.

IV

With her heart sinking as the day approached for the Army to march west, Doña Catalina decided to give a party for the officers at which all her gifts would be most flatteringly and convincingly displayed. She commanded extra musicians in from Atrisco, Bernalillo, and even a harpist from Santa Fe. She had the main *sala* cleared for dancing. Supper was laid in the patio on newly built tables. It was midsummer. The moon was like a lantern among the tops of the immense cottonwood trees. The fragrance of the river mud and the faint bitter smell of the cottonwood leaves and the drift of cicada music out of doors and the bump and pulse of the orchestra in the big house, guitars of all sizes, the harp, four violins, and a zither, and a hint of summer off the mesa in the grand drift of cool air . . . it was such a night as they would always remember of Albuquerque. The officers were in full dress with swords and white gloves. Doña Catalina and her court were in spreading skirts of silk and satin over which their long mantillas cascaded to the floor in back. For fields away, the people outside could hear the bass guitars gulping the music like bullfrogs, and see the lights reflecting upward on the big trees that stood within and atop the house. They could hear the laughing and the singing. The soldiers sang a chorus, a bawdy song in English, and smashed one of the improvised tables by banging on it so strenuously in rhythm. Outside the house a whole string of horses waited for their masters. Mexican servants and Army orderlies waited too, and they felt giddy under the moonlight, just listening to the party within.

Doña Catalina gave a toast to the visitors, calling in it for a drink and a kiss, and since every man had a girl on his arm, and some of them two, they drank, and kissed their girls. Captain Somers was the guardian of Doña Catalina herself, and at the end of her toast, she turned up her vivid, ugly face and he kissed her out of sheer good manners. When he heard the high cheer go up from everybody else, he realized that they were being watched. He blushed like a student and bent over and shook hands heartily with the proprietress, strode out to the front hall holding his great sabre off the floor, went out, called his man, and rode off to the encampment which was glowing with white tents in the moonlight and the remains of the cook's fire in a field north of the Plaza. Once there in his tent, he wrote for a few minutes, the sentry could see his shadow on the tent, and then went to bed.

The party was ruined.

Doña Catalina was in a rage at everyone for commenting so openly upon her love, which had driven him off. And that he had gone, "just-like-that," was an insult to her. She hated him as much as she loved him, both at the same time. She drove her guests away, retired to her cluttered bedroom, and raged all night. By morning, her sense of injury was full-grown. She sent for a friend who had often patronized her place, and said he must do her the favor of challenging Captain Somers to avenge the insult.

The second chosen by Doña Catalina's champion waited upon Captain Henry Houghton Somers the next morning after the party, and was received with a perfectly charming burst of unaffected laughter. It was inconceivable to the happily married officer that he should risk his future in a ridiculous brawl thousands of miles from home, here in this outlandish river town, and all because of a clever but miserable woman who kept a bawdy house. He assured the second that he failed to see that any insult had attended his departure from the party the night before. He was tired, he had returned to add a few pages to his letter which was going to his wife by the next bag, and he begged the Señor to understand that the valor of arms were better reserved for a serious need, such as the United States cavalry might well encounter when they marched tomorrow for the Indian country to the west.

It was an unheard-of refusal.

The second returned to his principal, who flew in fury to Doña Catalina, who in her turn thought she would die of the rage and misery in her breast. To be repudiated *this* way also was too much.

By evening, the whole town knew what was up, and there were factions, mainly three, divided between those who believed in respectability and considered the Captain right; those who sided with Doña Catalina out of sympathy; and those who—entertaining no views as to the merits of the complaint—still considered honor an abstraction whose formalities must always be observed, and thus felt the Captain should accept the challenge. But it took the energy and originality of Doña Catalina herself to focus all the conflicts of opinion with one supreme act. She dressed herself like a rich widow, sent for her carriage, drove to the headquarters of the American General, and demanded an interview.

General Stephen Watts Kearny was a model of tact in his dealing with the inhabitants of the province he had taken for his government.

He had met the lady before, and now caused her to be brought into his office.

He treated her with much courtesy, and listened to her florid complaints with composure. She claimed that the only thing that mattered to her *now* was that Captain Somers had refused the challenge of her protector. This was an intolerable affront. She demanded of the commanding General that he *order* Captain Somers to accept the challenge, and by fighting for his own honor, *prove that she had some, too.* Otherwise he was a coward and not fit to be an officer in any army, much less that of the United States. There was still time for the duel, the troops were not leaving till morning. It could be fought by firelight in the field beyond her own patio. She would have her personal physician there, and the Army surgeon could attend also. She would be content with a superficial wound. She had never in her life been so humiliated, and only considerations of the highest propriety made her come, this way, to humble herself before the friendly and talented General of the United States forces.

He watched her with great interest as he listened to her passionate demands, in which vanity vied with desire.

She was impressive though anything but handsome. Her eyes smoked and flared with the inner lights of her emotion. Her bosom, which was pretty, became a dramatic organ in its own right. She wrung her hands and her jewels danced in the air.

But the issue was plain to them both, a ruinously commanding issue. It was good sense against fantastic frustration; respectability against outlawry, really, the moment at last when Doña Catalina challenged the other world in its own terms. She knew she could not afford to be beaten.

The General let her rave, and when she was breathless and silent, he took her hand and pressed it ardently, like a grand-uncle. He said that if Captain Somers accepted the challenge, he would be dismissed from the Army. There was a very strict code about such matters, in *gringo* life; just as strict in its way as the dueling code was among the Latins. He would have to admit that many duels were fought unofficially, and all of them were deplorable. But this case was now a matter of official record, alas, *through her own statement of it to the Commanding General;* and he might actually have to consider *placing a guard* upon Captain Somers until the departure of the troops, to insure that he *did not weaken,* and enter upon the engagement at arms *after all.* Somers was one of his best officers, he said; let nobody think him a coward for returning the challenge. It simply would not do, that was all.

But if she desired, he would send for Captain Somers, to afford him the opportunity of making an apology.

She sprang to her feet. Her silks whistled as she whirled to the door in a fury, and in a fire of Spanish invective of which, everyone agreed, she was a formidable mistress, she burned the General's ears, and left him.

The town was waiting for the duel.

Nothing happened.

The encampment went to sleep, with all preparations completed for the morning's march.

Doña Catalina's house was dark for the first night in years.

v

The bugles called the soldiers in the morning. The town awoke with them. An August morning, with white sunlight rising over the mountains. The troops were going to march on the river road as far south as Socorro, and then turn west. The New Mexicans turned out to see the assembly. In the preparations, they could see Captain Somers moving about his duties like everybody else. He seemed earnest, at ease and in fine humor. It was a little after eight when the troops mounted. The wagons were drawn up in formation. The guidons fluttered in the air. There was that pause, waiting for the General, when everything was ready but himself in his own saddle. But at last he came out of the house where he had held his headquarters, and this was the signal for the bells of the Church of San Felipe de Neri to start ringing. They clamored and tangled their stinging sweet discords in the white-shuttered belfries.

General Kearny nodded to his adjutant, who turned in his saddle and saluted the commanding officer of the first squadron, who raised his arm, and signaled *At a walk, forward march.*

The General let them ride for a few paces at attention; then another command was passed "through channels" and the men were at ease. They waved, they called out, and traded the last, most insincere and charming of promises with the people, largely the women, of Albuquerque. Going under the big cottonwood trees, they were showered with coins of sunlight through the leaves.

In a little while, the dust was down on the road again. The saddle creaking was part of the morning farther down the river. The hot day was under way in Albuquerque. Shutters were closed against the heat. After the troops forded the river, they went up that little rise on the other side, and then down again, and were out of sight.

But the quiet of summer in the dirt plaza was hardly drowsing again when the door of Doña Catalina's house flew open, and she came out to meet her carriage which came richly braking its own speed around the patio corner. There were four little mules in the harness, trotting rapidly. She entered the coach which had its leather curtains closed, and set off to overtake the Army. She forded the river, came up the rise on the other side, and looked her last on the little town where she had been so successful for so many years.

But she would never have been so, if she had not had a most realistic stripe in her character.

She now summoned it to her final aid.

A carriage alone can travel much faster than a body of troops. Overtaking the Army on the road to Socorro, Doña Catalina's carriage jingled and rang. The driver and the servant on the box cried out for passage. The troops closed in to the edge of the road. With its painted and paneled body rocking on its leather springs, and its leather curtains flapping in the speed, it carried Doña Catalina rapidly and disdainfully past the slowtrotting soldiers on the road to the south, in a cloud of white dust that rose like the breath of summer in the wilderness, and settled back again in country silence.

If they expected to find her at Socorro when they got there late the third day, the soldiers were wrong. She had gone through on the way to El Paso, they heard, and that was the last of her in these parts.

A few months later her grand furnishings were packed and shipped to her in the city of Chihuahua, where later travelers saw her queening it over local society and getting richer by the minute.

VI

"Yes," said Peter, "I've read about her life in Chihuahua City. I've got a book by a man who went down there in the fifties, and saw her. He was pretty hard in his opinion of her."

He remembered Molly as she read aloud to him the description of "La Voz" by Elias Gray, in *The Western Attorney*. Had there been a prophetic irony in the act? He remembered her voice, its cool, cultivated sound, along with which there always sounded an involuntary catch of breath now and then. He wondered how long such details would have the power to turn his heart over.

"No," said Don Hilario, "it is not necessary to be hard in one's opinion of Doña Catalina. She was simply one of those women, and I have seen many of them in my day, one of those women who think love is an end in itself, and can be bought and sold, without paying for it with life. That is what children think, too, isn't it?"

He looked at Peter again, as if from across the grave.

Peter stood up. He knew he was no match for the old man in a duel of proverbs or epigrams. Don Hilario had the facility of his race at polishing off a situation with proper saws.

"Would you like to read the book I mentioned?"

"I haven't read a book for twenty-five years, since I retired from the Supreme Court of New Mexico. Sometimes I sit and hold one, because I like the shape of a book. All my books were sold when I moved here. I had one of the finest libraries in the Territory of New Mexico, and I could quote more law in Spanish and Voltaire in French and Gibbon in English than anybody in these parts. Sometime I will tell you about my trip to Paris, and the time I met Count Cavour in Rome, and discussed the freedom of Italy with him."

"I'd love to hear it."

"You will have to give me time to remember it."

"Indeed I will, and thank you very much.—Perhaps I might just listen to you now, before I go."

He meant that he would use his stethoscope on the old man's heart. Don Hilario shut his eyes and appeared to remove himself from any part in the examination. Peter listened to the heartbeats. Widely spaced, they were remote and delicate, and made him think of steps walking deliberately along which one day, and not very far off, would simply cease walking as if to end a journey in good order. He straightened up and nodded, and Don Hilario nodded back, with his round silent laugh, as if to say that such witchcraft was nonsensical, an unnecessary refinement, at his time of life.

He accompanied Peter to the front of the house. Down the lane they could see the Sanchez grocery store on the Plaza corner. It was stuccoed gray, and the plaster had caked off here and there. There was no sign of the old patio. The ditch still went by the rear of the place, but was now fenced off by a neighbor. The huge cottonwood trees Don Hilario remembered of the old patio were gone. He said you could see a stump of one of them left, and when Peter passed it a few moments later, sure enough, there it was, covered with a vine of sky-blue morning glories. At the corner, he saw the windows of the Sanchez grocery store, full of cardboard cigarette displays and merchandise and spider webs. There was only one detail left which might recall the house of a hundred years ago, and this was the style of the windows, and of one door, down on the alley side of the house. The face of the house wavered and sagged, betraying the neglect of a century. But in it were set that doorway, and those windows, deep and severe, with classical pediments of carved wood, long softened by repeated paintings, and as grand in their dilapidation as they must have been in their heyday; for their design was pure to start with, and always would be.

XXXI · BUSINESS: A SKIRMISH

I

Just before the Harvey House dining-room doors closed for "late," Willa saw the man come in for breakfast, treading heavily on the sunlit floor of the restaurant. He was enormously fat, and walked with his weight poised so that he leaned a little backwards. He was spanked for the morning, with powdery pink jowls, cheeks that dewlapped over one another in tingling splendor. Beautifully groomed, too, a fat man who cherished every inch of his great surface. His eyes were still liquid and blurred from sleep; but so enclosed by the flesh which he put forth that they seemed remote little vials of intelligent blue, lost in that Chinese profusion of curved surface. His movements had something of that spacious and impressive quality to be found in a larger reproduction of something ordinarily familiar on a modest scale. He was captain of an incidental majesty, and moved to his table like the essential half, the completive force, of any whole.

When he sat down, he opened wide his legs, so that his southern hemisphere could depend in space. He set his left hand elegantly tented with spread fingers on his serge thigh, and gazed upon the menu. There was a very special melon announced. He conversed about its promise with Willa and she gave it a fine character. He ordered it.

In the little pause, he looked around, and yearned for newspapers on a near-by table, but let them lie. His neck rolled like a rubber bag full of water over his tight and beautifully pressed collar. His hair was brushed shining flat on his Roman pate.

Then Willa started across the room with the melon, and he watched her.

He watched the melon coming toward him, the cool succulent, taste-thrilling sight of it, that pale sparkling heart of fruit, with the chilled lime lying on it to be squeezed. He settled a little nearer the table, and his great pink head moved to follow her as she curved around him to set his fruit down.

And now the morning became spangled and tingling with delight.

He sat so close to the table that he had to look straight down his rolling cheeks to see his plate. This would have buried his little avid eyes in their sacs if he had not raised his eyebrows to stretch his upper lids open so that he had drawn mandarin folds of skin there. His mouth worked slightly open, and appeared to pretaste what he readied.

His whole immense bulking body was intimate and tender with anticipated pleasure. His clean, packed fingers turned the melon and sparkled the lime juice on its every facet, and his lips worked, his cheeks shrunk with tart excitement away from his lips, and his hands were delicate, so fond, in their touch. His tongue was the agent of his hope and want. The taste buds electrified him with the messages he liked best of all in this world to receive. He moved in little pressures against the table, toward his dear melon, that cold and glorious experience at the start of day.

He had the confidence of the blessed. If after all this it were not a good melon! But he salted it, and the sparkle of the salt and the fragrance it induced from the melon meat could mean only one thing.

He set the plate a trifle away, then, the better to see, and like a pianist serene with arrogant technique let his right paw fall to the silverware where it ever so lightly and surely took up the large spoon.

He moistened his lips.

He opened his mouth, while he spooned out a large and inspiring morsel of the melon, and because his bosom was so vast, his arm had to travel not across it but around it, and the elegance of this arc was like a consummation.

The delicious, dripping moment arrived, and he expressed appreciation in every fine and happy pound of his being.

He took the bite in his mouth, and from his little eyes so genial and so fattened over, there came a tiny stream of appreciation, the fat man's ichor, his thanks for this Thy bounty, and his right thigh trotted ever so slightly on the edge of the chair seat, and the spoon descended for yet another and another scoop of chilled fibrous fruit.

When he had filled his cheeks several times with the luscious grainy meat, so that he was assuaged for a moment, he took a deep breath and turned his attention to Willa, believing that he was doing so without her noticing. He wanted to size her up. Clever thing to do, come here for breakfast first, get 'n impression, make plan, not enough men in bizness took trouble, look ahead, find out class of client got deal with, that was all. He was almost panged by the "pushover" before him. She was little, and gray, and pathetically eager, he felt. A word from whom? from a majestically dissatisfied patron of this dining room, and what? What: out she goes. Power. Big man, Treadwell. Everybody said Treadwell was a shrewd bizness head. Otis L. Treadwell. Name's on m'card, here, in m'inside pocket. —and conversely, a kind word, flattery, and likely the deal was done.

Willa saw him, all right. A salesman type. She knew enough about them. No more morals than an alley cat. *Look out,* she always said, look out for a man who spends so much time on *how he looks,* fat or lean, don't matter, all they want is feed theirself, at somebody else's expense.

She served his breakfast silently and neatly, and when he strode away with the gentle ponderousness of his weight, his arms swinging out from his body because they couldn't hang down, she snipped her nose in the air with her opinion of him, but said again that the public was made up of all kinds, never forget that, she was before the public, and she always felt almost more like an actress than a waitress when she remembered that; a charming dare.

II

That same day, Willa was sitting down for a moment, just a *moment,* for a glance at the morning paper (it was the middle of the afternoon, at that) (first moment she'd had all day) (who could begrudge her?) when Margaret, the headwaitress, came to the pantry and said there was a man out in the dining room who wanted to see her. It was a chilling announcement, as Margaret made it, bringing Willa all the little rises of worry that a life of expectations instead of achievements could make. She got up and started through the swinging doors, and paused a second behind the leather screen to shut her eyes and squeeze her fingers in a prayer. Then she went down the long room with her quick steps and a birdlike alertness in the set of her little head. There *was* a man waiting, by the far doors. He had a heavy, red face and was holding his hat and a cigar. She began to feel easier as soon as she saw him; for he seemed to be making various small attitudes of ingratiation, such as a policeman, or an undertaker, or any bearer of threat or bad news would never make. Then she saw that it was the fat man of this morning's breakfast. She added dignity to her carriage.

As soon as she came within range, so to speak, they commenced instinctively a little ritual of approach and parry; almost a miniature social ballet, in which he advanced and retreated, with male waggery, florid, confident and artfully chaste; while she impersonated a grand lady, choosing to miss his suggestive flattery which she had seen so often from men of his type, who made a male-female pattern out of the idlest contact, such as that between a waitress and her gentleman customer. She nodded grandly to him, and indicated that he might sit, in a dining-room chair, while she stood to hear him. He begged her to be seated, sweeping his fat red hand with its nugget of a ring toward the chair for her, herself. They ended by both standing. She privately guessed that he was a heavy drinker, and worse, and she was cautious because he seemed so cordial.

"This's Mrs. Shoemaker, I believe?"

She bowed.

"I am Mr. Treadwell, representing the Diamond Realty Company. —I have a card here," he added, fumbling in a shiny wallet and selecting a fairly clean card from a little sheaf under one of the leather flaps. He gave it to her as if in his fat, sober gesture there lay a sacred donation of his person; his quality; asking it to be honored as he would be honored. The scrap of soiled paper was full of dear excellence to him.

"Thank you."

She looked at it and bent it with gentility against her thumb nail, waiting for him to proceed. Neither of them referred in any way to their encounter of the morning, the patron-waitress relation.

What on earth could he want.

He seems to *want* something, it sticks out all over him. I've seen *him* before. Well, he'll get nowhere *making himself* at me. I have no time for his type.

"Mrs. Shoemaker, I believe you own some property out on the mesa?—A former chicken ranch, I believe?"

That riddled her with apprehensions.

Swindle/tax foreclosure/my babies/last thing own.

"Yes, I do."

"Mrs. Shoemaker? Would you be i'rested in selling?"

"Oh."

He entered upon his still-dance of ingratiation again, his fat elbows up, his head forward, his knees springing ever so slightly.

"I represent a party who is prepared to pay well for your land. Like to say he is making a very-very generous offer.—Had you any thought of selling?"

She looked at his card again to prove that she was no fool, and could be as shrewd as the next one, and was not one to be swept off her feet by the first red-faced, barbered and powdered fat man that came along. He relished the details of the transaction. He glanced with his wet-shining eyes at the cigar wreck in his hand, and asked if he might smoke? She nodded, and, somehow making it seem a tribute to her presence, he put down the cold butt on an ash tray, and drew out an entirely fresh cigar, which he clipped, rolled, licked, and lighted without once removing his white-lashed eyes from her face.

Her heart was beating so that she felt it.

It may be m'chance, she said to herself, the two buildings on the place should be worth so-much, and the road, we helped make that road, there, fifteen years ago, there's that fence, and the land itself, and the chicken house is a *model* chicken house, the glass alone is worth a small fortune, I'll sell, and *we'll go*. I'll have Martha's clothes all done over before we go, she'll be the prettiest thing to hit Albion in years, since *I* left it, for that matter, and Wayne'll be in seventh heaven with the train, it'll *take* two and a half days, I'm not getting any younger, *why not?*

"I *have* thought of it, off and on," she said, lifting her head. But he saw her hands going, the card trembling. Her hands were little gathers of bone and vein; hardly any flesh on them at all; he "spat" mentally at how easy it was going to be, if he just remained genteel, because he felt sure that his subtle fleshy hints of flirtation were what fetched the poor little thing right off.

He took a deep breath and it made him wheeze, and he coughed, and the cough turned into a laugh, an explosion of great sociability in the huge empty dining room. He was like a bullfrog enchanted at good fortune, and when he got his voice back, suggested that they just get in his car, out front, and run up to the mesa, and look at the property, while he relayed the offer he was privileged to make as agent.

"I believe I can arrange to get off for half an hour," she said, and went to ask Margaret. If Margaret refused permission, then: then she would *resign*. This was a matter of business. Fortunately, Margaret understood that, but wished to know what it was about. When she heard that it was about some property, she was briefly haggard at the really impressive note of this.

III

All the way up the hill, Mr. Treadwell made conversation. It was all calculated to arouse sympathy and pity for him, so that *she* would feel almost responsible for *his* welfare at the moment of closing the deal. He said that she was very lucky to have such a nice piece of property, and he only wished he could be sure of leaving anything as suitable to *Miz* Treadwell. Or at least: he *would*'ve, except that lately things didn't seem quite the same between Miz Treadwell and himself. He naturally had to be away a good deal on business, and last time he'd come back, she's gone. Slick's a whistle, gone to Abilene, where *her* mother lived, and the old lady was *sure* a hellcat, if she would pardon him. Lonely? Nothing's lonely's a house where the *lady's* away. Like to say it was an attractive house, too. One letter since she'd gone, not a word about returning, not *mad,* mind, not *final,* or anything, just up and lit out, and he guessed she wanted him to get in the car and come after her, and bring her back, had had to do it before, and guessed go' have to do it again. He sighed, and pressed his lips together around his cigar, and glanced elaborately out of the car as if to conceal feelings which struggled to betray themselves.

Willa hardly heard him. She was calculating the future in exact terms. They'd have enough money (she was sure) to go to the Hotel, and stay there as long as the Albion visit lasted. They'd take a suite with a living room, and keep it full of fresh flowers, and Martha could meet her little friends there, and all the *old* friends could come in, what good times they would have remembering everything together, and bridging the gap of years that had lasted as long as— as it took to rear a lovely daughter like that one, there. Dennison Yeager probably would have a car of his own by now. Summer in Albion was terribly warm, but oh! so sweet with the smell of the green hills and the vines and the roses that grew almost in tufts, they were so thick. Those country roads would be just the same, long tunnels of shadow in the starlight, and if it was hot in the evening after dinner, there would be drives. And a whole summer of it, there would be parties at the Yeagers' place, the paper said they were rebuilding already, the old burned brick farmhouse had been torn down, and Grace was putting up a Norman-French château-type of new house, according to the *Recorder,* out of Indiana limestone and asbestos shingles. It sounded wonderful. Martha would take her place easily among such surroundings. Perhaps Lawrence wasn't yet too old to play with Wayne. Somehow a bicycle for Wayne would have to be managed so he could get around, too. Wayne would see where his father had come from, that white clapboard farmhouse which had long ago been sold to the Mastersons, but still, if she went with him, and pointed it all out, as she remembered it, and took him by the Kalamazoo River and showed him the dam where they used to have picnics, and then that pool where the fireflies were really *reflected,* because they flew so low and the water was so still, why, then, he would see *what-she-meant,* and about his father, who had started out there, even if he didn't end up there, and it was *home,* and that was probably what she meant, by *all this,* anyway.

Grace Yeager was always clever. She could look right through me. She always thought I wanted to get Martin, and she got him instead, and of course she is the rich lady of the town, and I don't think she ever loved Martin as much as she loved his horses and rigs and the old brick house, it burned down, didn't it, she used to take on so over the *antiques* in it, and she never *heard* of an antique until she became Mrs. Martin Yeager.

They have those boys.

And I always thought: and now Martha and that Bunny: and *Sacred Heart of Jesus, have it not too late already,* think of it, if Martha married Dennison Yeager, he is twenty-one this year, 'll be out of college in June, I saw his picture in the *Recorder,* blond,

Grace's eyes, sweet-looking boy, and with Martha's honey-look, what a couple they would make, and all that money, say what you like, money counts, *I know,* when has Grace Yeager ever worked on her feet all day, running trays in and out of this dining room and pantry, how I hate the smell of wet drain boards, it is the only *clean* smell I hate.

Or if not Dennison, then the younger one, Lawrence, they say he's rather fat, but he'd be good-natured, and Grace's spoiled him, she always was a fool, still, a Yeager, Martha would go home and assume her *rightful position,* after all, we left when I was just a girl myself, but I couldn't even take her home to *visit* if:

She had no idea her longing to get back was really as profound as it was until the chance to go really seemed to have arrived. She had a misty shine in her eyes, and Mr. Treadwell thought it was in tribute to his virtuosity. His own eyes flooded in sympathy with hers.

They came to the ranch lane, and turned off the highway. She leaned forward, and saw it before he did. Years since she had come up here. Was that all it amounted to? She must conceal what she felt. How far did twenty-five acres stretch? But the buildings're bigger than that, they always have been, she thought in panic.

I do want Martha to marry "East," she thought as they drove up, Wayne and I'll return here, that won't matter, but I'd love to have a daughter in the East, it is where *I* was born, and raised, and fell in love, and married. She was holding dearly to her own past by these wishes, with small regard for Martha's.

"Here we are," declared Mr. Treadwell. He flourished her out of the front seat of his car, and they stood, looking around. The afternoon light was sweeping in long rays from over the river, and the whole mesa was golden. The mountains were cast with a pale silvery light over their rocky gray.

"Now you may wonder," he said, "why anybody should want to buy this property, Mrs. Shoemaker."

"Indeed I don't, it's a very fine piece!"

"Oh, no, I didn't mean *that,* I assure you, a very fine piece, for what it *is,* if you know what I mean. No, but the point is, like to say my client is a fair-minded man, and willing to go the limit. Point is, he has just bought all the adjoining property from the former owners, and lacks this piece here to complete his section. Like to say he feels he'd like to complete his section, and so wishes to buy your property. Not that he needs it. Run all the stock he wants on what he's already got, for that matter.—Now your fence runs—"

He pointed over the land, but she was again not paying any attention to him. She had found the ruined front of the chicken house.

She exclaimed, and searched for a single whole pane in the framed front, and found none. She bent down and gingerly touched the glass dust on the ground. The place was wrecked. It would destroy the price. She was sick with rage and couldn't say a word. Her plans—which always turned into realities for her—crumbled in ruins. Mr. Treadwell tried to get her to stand up again. He couldn't understand why she was so concerned.

He said that as a matter of fact, his client was going to clear away the little buildings right off, anyway, when he got possession. The buildings had never entered into the consideration, one way or the other, he said. All *he* wanted to do was to straighten out the fences, and close the sandy road that led in from the highway, and keep everybody out from then on.

But Willa was honestly outraged at the destruction of what she had always thought of as tangible assets. She said she wished she could get her hands on whoever did a thing like that. He answered that why look, there're car tracks all around, he said lots of people must use the place, and come on out here, and *park,* the wonder is the whole walls ain't down and hauled off.

She searched the ground miserably for answers to her indignation. In a moment she found one.

There was a scatter of empty copper cartridge cases for a .22 rifle, hundreds of them. Somebody had shot the glass to bits.

"Well," said Mr. Treadwell, "now that we've looked it over, you'll see that my client is making a very fine offer. Like to say you won't do better anywhere else."

Willa could always do it when she had to, she reminded herself. She looked right at him, and her small sober face dared him to cheat her.

"Well?"

He proposed paying her five hundred dollars for the whole property, but his white-lashed look was indirect, and she attacked him like a furious martin. She said they'd put thousands into the place, and she'd paid taxes on it for years, he could look up the assessor's record and see what the county thought it was worth, and everybody knew the tax assessments were half or less of the actual *business* value, and she said she never would've come up here with him if she'd even thought he was going to make such a ridiculous proposal. If that was all there was to it, she would turn around and *walk* back to the Harvey House, before she'd deal with him on any such terms.

Her disappointment lived in images, not dollars. They couldn't *go,* on five hundred dollars, the three of them, not the *way* she intended for them to go. She was in a passion of fear and loss. The future was gone. She started back to the car, too addled by misery to recognize in Mr. Treadwell the idiomatic dodges of trading. He was appalled at her reaction. He had orders to buy the place, and a top limit of two thousand had been placed on it, that was all, whatever he could get it down to, why he could "sidetrack" the difference between the actual sale price and the limit which his client was willing to go, that was all, probably it was better judgment to say it'd gone for eighteen hundred, good-by to the other two hundred, too bad, but better to be safe, and not be greedy, that was all, the papers could be fixed, and anybody else'd be's shrewd as that, given the chance, that was all.

He started after her, taking the air with each hand before him in an energetic heave, being so fat and wanting to be in motion so quickly. He patted her shoulder, and said he hated to see a lady so upset, and after all, there was such a thing as an opener, that was all, and he'd like to say he was ready to hear her asking price, the thing wasn't settled, yet, anyway.

It was with a deeply fleshed sense of exasperation and shame that he ended by agreeing to pay her twelve hundred and fifty dollars for the property as it stood. She was either an outrageous fool, or else the meanest little woman he'd met in a long, long time. Without seeming to make an effort, or resorting to any of the dodges he was used to handling in business deals with men, she had taken him for something of a ride, and he seemed to've been *watching* himself going down the chute, without knowing how to stop it. She was so bent on *something.*

He was a huge and sore man, baffled once again by what a woman *had,* there was simply no dealing with them, if one of them ever made up her mind she wanted something a man could get her, then God help the poor son of a bitch, was all *he* could say, wow!

The papers were in order, and the next day, he mailed her a cashier's check for the full amount.

IV

Like to burst she was so happy, she said to herself, when she reached home at night with Mr. Treadwell's check in her purse. The house was still. She listened holding her breath to "see" if the children were in. She always did this, and rarely was able to detect her answer without actually going to look. As she was about to cross the tiny front room to look out on the sleeping porch, she saw a square of paper, an envelope, leaning on the top of the *Spirito Santo*. On it was written "Mother" in Wayne's writing, in pencil, heavily pressed into the paper, and made largely, as he always wrote, with a certain strength to the formation of the letters, as if he were building a fence out of the words he made.

Now what/good Lord/let me see, she fluttered, taking it up and scratching the envelope open. Inside was a sheet of paper from his school notebook, ruled in blue. She could read it without her glasses.

Dear Mother,
    I am not worthy to be your son. I have worried for weeks and I cannot any longer defer my statement that I must make to you. This is my statement. I went to the ranch that Saturday with D. and broke all the glass in the chicken house shooting at it with D.'s new birthday twenty-2 rifle. We used the boxes of twenty-2 bullets I got him for his birthday. Ever since it happened I have suffered the tortures of the damned and now it will be hard for you to forgive me. But I will earn the money somehow to give back to you. All I ask is that you only give me the chance, after the ruin I have inflicted. I did not stop to think. I promise you hereafter I will always stop to think. After the way you work and slave all day long for us, I feel awful. I could not desist from telling you any longer. No matter what you will think of me, I am

Your loving son,
Wayne Shoemaker.

P.S. Of course I have been to Confession about this.
W.S.

Rascal/darling/precious boy/how could he/what a nicely written letter/where does he get such words/that's *right* the cartridges!

She listened for him, now, and tiptoed to the porch. Her heart beat longingly. Wait till he heard *her* news! He was asleep. She was a trifle disappointed. But what could make her feel more reassured about him, more secure in what she had given him (of herself, her hope, her goodness) than that letter? She went to the icebox and found an apple, cold and hard, and went back and laid it on the wide mattress next to his pillow. If he awoke and found it, he would know right off who had put it there. Here: she slipped his envelope under it so he'd know she'd read it. She wouldn't be surprised if they neither of them ever mentioned the thing again. But she held on to his letter, and would keep it forever among her few treasures.

I

Noonie thought for many days about something she wanted to say to Peter. But she didn't want to risk in words the hope she now knew. She felt obscurely that if she spoke it aloud, it might disappear. What she meant was that now that she could *see* that she had been ill, she could get well again. What had happened to her? She had been delivered from a spell. It was like something out of untold time, the stories of folk experience and need in the common heart, a parable of the lover who broke through an enchantment, and saved, freed, the beloved.

What was character but the world's own material of magic?

II

Peter had to admit to himself that it had not surprised him; though he had kept on hoping that Noonie in some way might never have to face the tragic issues of her own weakness. The days after his discovery of her at the brink of dying were oddly peaceful for them both. He had a nurse with her all day, and so felt safe to leave her for his work. He saw Noonie growing more relaxed and he began to wonder if he saw something in her eyes that had not been there for years. But he was patient, and he had also a tactful allowance for the secrets that gave trouble to other people; even to his wife. And so it was not until she was recovering from the shock of the terrible afternoon that what he hoped in his heart could be risked in words between them.

One night in the darkness he said to her, "When you've nearly lost something, it becomes perfectly clear how much you want to keep it."

She was suddenly terrified.

She clutched his arm and he could feel her trembling. Now she saw what she had tried to die out of.

"What is it, Noon?"

She could barely speak. Her tongue clove to her mouth, and she had to free it desperately. Waves and floods of feeling poured through her. She was taken and trundled by such feeling as she had not known for years. It was like waking up from a paralysis. She had never thought she would ever feel anything again. She was borne upon a wave of belief and realization, and it flowed to her from him. If there was a moment upon which they could later have fixed for the return of her health, this was it. She began to weep, but it was not with pity for herself; it was with gratitude for being again alive to the reach that came to her from her husband, the vessel of duty and debt in life.

He knew the relief that followed the delivery of a patient from a state of shock. He saw it happen to her that night. But that it should come in response to something he had said to her, the thing he had shown her, was in its way quite as curative for him as for her. Whatever had developed those years of increasing remoteness in her, pity, apathy and doubt, he could never determine; but he believed now that it didn't matter; for this was a strong tide beginning to flow in the other direction. It gave him passion; and this he gave to her, too. They felt that they were solving not only this moment but also an unsaid, unsayable, problem out of the past.

He thought much, alone in wakefulness long after she had gone to sleep.

After all, it was pretty desperate, wasn't it. This is the only direction in which things *could* turn, there wasn't any more room to travel in the other direction, was there.

Even now; what a narrow escape; if I hadn't just happened to feel it was the right time to say anything to her tonight—but it was right. Lord! Lord! Lord! I hope it does keep up, I hope I am right in what I *feel* about it.

It must be a lock, locking us together, so that when there are any other threats, the aftermath of despair which is now so sweet will not fall away as suddenly as it came up.

So for days there was one half of him that was almost judicial in a terrible, impersonal way. He knew what might happen most clearly, if Noonie's almost-fate threatened her again. He was on the watch for it, like a captain at sea, riding the unknown forces which may produce the known disaster all over again. And he was ready for it if it should come; fighting against it with all his power, which was revealed prosaically in the response they were able to make to each other in daily trivialities. If they both held on long enough, almost like children holding their breaths for fear something wonderful would vanish as soon as they *let* go, then: then maybe in peace they could keep each other all the rest of their lives. What would finally tell them? Something would tell them. Health, if nothing else, would tell them. He felt *yes* about it. *Yes* he would save Noonie. *Yes* things could be found out in time. *Yes* a man has powers to use. What else was his life dedicated to, after all? What else had it shown him?

III

No one had a really true picture of himself. Peter didn't know just how inevitably like himself he had acted in renouncing the future that had tempted him. He thought a lot about what might have brought Noonie to the edge of the abyss, and he said he wished it was possible to put your finger on the one moment, long ago, the series of moments, which had precipitated a consequent chain of weaknesses. If you could do that, how easy it would be to understand, to help!

This suggested the obverse of the situation to him. He suddenly recalled an episode of his own youth when, if he had turned another way, and yielded to something that he was scared of, he too might have carried the obscure scars of it all his life. Pictures from his boyhood came back to him with a sort of simple clarity, and he saw again one of the things in his whole life that he could put his finger on and know as an achievement.

IV

He went up to Colorado during the summer twenty-eight years ago, when he was fifteen, to visit his cousin Jack Winterhood. He didn't know Jack very well, but Jack's mother was the sister of Peter's father. She was a widow who taught the rural district school in the country of the South Fork of the Rio Grande. She had a large schoolhouse built of logs stained brown, and it seemed to Peter then the only desirable school he ever saw. He stayed with her and her son, who was a year older than himself, in their white-painted farmhouse, set in the greenest field he could remember. The big river ran past their place two hundred yards away.

What a river! It came rushing grandly down through the open tunnel of rock, and the water was the color of smoke-colored obsidian, but perfectly clear: the color of daylight reflected in a dark mirror. He used to lie for hours and watch the water go by, swept in thought by the mystery of its movement, and the eternity of its source from the mountain groins in the rocky peaks that lay back against the northern sky.

One branch of the river came from the west and the north. The

other came off Wolf Creek Pass to the south. Where they came together, going mightily out toward the plains, there was a point of
land that narrowed as the division between the streams until it was
gone. But off the tip of this point there was an island, it lay in a
tangle of willows and cottonwoods and it seemed to be removed from
all the life around it as completely as if it were another world. It was
a long spit of land, not very wide across. The river was deep and full
of silvery rapids on both sides of it, and below. But above it, by a
curious roil in the meeting of the two mountain flows, there was a
deep black pool which turned slowly and mysteriously like a magic
lake, lapping delicately at the island's upper end, as if independent of
the powerful quick river forks that met so urgently at the island's
other end.

Cousin Jack Winterhood was a calm active boy with brown eyes
and a pale freckled face, and short-cut brown hair. He had flecks of
yellow light in his eyes, and when he was thinking something over,
he would simply regard Peter, and those flecks would seem to kindle
with deliberation and justice, and when he decided what he thought,
or would do, he spoke crisply and Peter could never do other than
his will, for it seemed to have been so inevitably arrived at. Peter was
at the age when it was instructive to imitate someone, and it was
his cousin Jack whom he most wished to resemble, though oddly
enough, he made Peter see virtues in his father which even he had
never before recognized, the rancher in New Mexico. Jack admired
Mr. Rush very much, whom he used to see passing through on the
D. & R. G. railroad on his way to buy cattle in Western Colorado.

This railroad ran through that valley, along the river course, in and
out of canyons. It fed the gold and silver mining camps up in the
mountains to the west, and it hauled cows back to the plains and
connected at junctions for reshipping on broad gauge railroads to the
markets of Texas and Kansas. One of the main delights of that summer was to play along the right of way where the miniature engines
and cars went trolling by. In that green canyon country, where bare
rock looked so silvery in the sunshine, it was music to hear the
whistles of the D. & R. G. engines come beating ahead against the
Rocky Mountains and to hold your breath and listen again for
the echo that would follow sometimes when the wind was right, and
to hear mixed with the whistle the sound of the river slipping fast,
fast, through the green and clear-cut channel, with the hushing
sound of silk.

The station was painted ocher yellow with a dark-red shingled
roof. It stood in a miniature park of grass and flower beds filled with

cannas that drank the sunshine and turned scarlet among the coal-black shadows of the station house. Jack introduced Peter to the agent's son, a boy their own age named Ted Barksdale. Ted regarded Peter as a native of another country when he heard he came from New Mexico. He thought Peter should speak nothing but Spanish and ride a burro and eat chili peppers. When Peter protested that he was an American just like him, and that New Mexico was only a hundred miles away, Ted would laugh and say that he would understand him if he'd say it in Spanish.

Ted and Jack were in a sort of implicit league against Peter as the outlander in their land. It was a humorous attitude, and merely a convention of hazing the newcomer, and if Peter had had another stranger along, to back him up, or if he had been older, their superiority would have disappeared.

It was in vain that Peter poked fun at Ted Barksdale for having to spend time on some days working at the canna beds or cutting the lawn at the freight house, when the other two could be off fishing in the meadows below the house where the grass ran right down to the great river. Nothing ever upset Ted. He was the best hunter of his age anywhere around there, Jack said. He said Ted could go out in the winter with his father's rifle, when the snow was high up along the trunks of the pines, and disappear for two or three days at a time, alone. He always came back safely and with game, as much as he could carry, and caches made of what he couldn't carry, to which he and his father would return to collect what he had shot . . . turkey, deer, mountain cat, and once even a bear. Ted was the cleanest-looking human being Peter ever saw. It was a quality of his skin, which was smooth and the color of the softest brown buckskin, only with a warm rose in it somewhere. His eyes were pale blue and below them were rolls of flesh in a perpetual expression of merriment. His hair was buckskin colored too, but on the yellow side. He seemed all of a piece in his coloring. And he was this too in his character. Peter decided that he was near to what an Indian of the great prairie days must have been like. A fellow of the animals and the plains and the weather, cleaned by them within and without.

V

Peter was only there two weeks that summer, with his aunt Winterhood and those two friends. Ted got his father to let all three of them ride up to Creede on a freight train one time, and they faithfully stayed in the caboose because that was their agreement. Every time the train crossed the river they could feel the trestle trembling with not only the weight of the cars but the black hurry of the river itself. They all felt bigger than usual in the tiny caboose of the narrow gauge. They sat and listened to Tode Chedester the brakeman, who was the most evil-mouthed man Peter ever heard. He told them stories and rhymes and vicious chronicles, all with a hesitant zest which was deceptively modest. It was just the manner to make them think they were hearing about "life." He went on until Mr. Richards, the freight conductor, came into the caboose. The conductor was a family man who carried around in his pocket a volume of the sermons of Henry Ward Beecher, in which he marked passages that struck his stern fancy. He read this one aloud to them:

"By fire, by anvil-strokes, by the hammer that breaks the flinty rock, God played miner, and blasted you out of the rock, and then He played stamper, and crushed you, and then He played smelter and smelted you, and now you are gold, free from the rock, by the grace of God's severity to you."

In this sentence, the conductor found himself.

Peter's aunt often made them packages of food and sent them off for a day's tramp, following the river. One day they climbed so far that they caught sight of the falls of Wolf Creek Pass long before the wagon road showed it to them.

Cousin Jack was planning to be a lawyer, and to live in Denver, which was grander in his dreams than London or Paris or New York. He used to ask the other boys if there was any capitol dome in any of *those* cities covered with genuine gold? It was hard to understand now how much the sound of the name Denver could bring alive in the West of Peter's boyhood, but he remembered how Jack Winterhood sounded when he used to speak it. Jack was a worldly boy even then, in a sense that Peter never thought of being, and that Ted Barksdale never even heard of.

VI

One day Peter asked Jack about the island at the confluence of the two rivers that ran together like liquid obsidian. (It was this Peter recalled with the piece of obsidian on his desk upstairs in his room at home. He loved to pick it up and look into it against the light, and see again the heavy stunning flow of the river.)

"There's nothing on it."

"Have you ever been on it?"

"Lots of times."

"Has Ted?"

"Sure. He took me the first time."

"Is it hard to get there?"

"It's hard or easy, depending."

"How do you mean?"

Jack explained.

You could go to the west end of the island and swim across the backwater there, which was no trick at all. You had to cross the South Fork of the river to do it, and the most convenient way was to walk over the railroad trestle on the open ties, with the water running beneath.

That was the easy way, if the longest.

"What is the other way?"

"The other way is to go about a mile and a half west along the main river past our house, and when you get opposite *this* end of the island, why, to try and swim it, there. Do you remember how it looks there?"

"Yes," said Peter, coming to mind of the willow-laced banks and the fall of the meadow to a pebbly shelf of shallows where the trout played in and out of rays of sunlight on the polished stones. He thought of the freshest and thickest of green and the clearest and coldest of water, and a few yards from the near bank, the plumy rise and boil of the river where its doubled stream hit the drowned sierras of the rapids. It was deep there, where the river went free; where it was impeded by the stone, there was a clash of force and firmness. Outstream, the water even seemed to run more swiftly than here by the near bank. Looking up the river Peter could see the endless lifts of the current coming toward him. How often he gazed and marveled at the anonymous power in the river's flow. How thoughtless it turned him, and how river-taken he had been in his desires. With that strength and certainty, he would so obediently move in his course, too, if he could . . .

"I remember how it looks there," he told his cousin Jack Winterhood. "Have you ever swum it? Has Ted Barksdale?"

"You can't get to the island unless you swim."

"Yes, but did you ever swim the rapids at the east end?"

"We always went by the west end."

"Where the pool is?"

"Yes, by the pool."

"Has anybody ever gone the east way?"

Jack gazed at Peter with his lawyer look, keen and yet absent-seeming, the yellow pips of light in his eyes dancing with thought. His nickname was "Judge," even as a boy.

"Well, not exactly. There was a fellow here named Hound-dog Cooley who tried it."

"Did he make it?"

"Nope."

"Why? Did he turn back?"

"Nope."

"Well, *what* did he:"

"We fished him dead out of the Rio Grande eleven miles farther down the next morning. He was cut up pretty bad. Lot of rocks in that water."

"Oh."

"It can be done, though, I believe. Hound-dog was drunk and he took it on a dare."

"Oh."

"I've always meant to try it. I'll tell Ted you want to try swimming the east way to the island."

"I didn't exactly say that."

"You sounded pretty interested."

The simplest thing is often the hardest for a boy to say. His cousin Jack Winterhood had it in his mind, at first out of orneriness, and then out of conviction, that Peter was dying to swim the Rio Grande at the confluence there, and the next time they were together with Ted, he said,

"The Mexican wants to go to the island by the east way."

"You don't say," exclaimed Ted. "Has he ever so much as glanced at it?"

"I have, of course I have," Peter said, "but I never said I actually wanted to swim it. I just wanted to see what was on the island."

"Why don't we?" asked Ted, with a rise of his brow.

"Well, we've meant to, often enough, haven't we," said Jack. "All right. Since my cousin from Mexico really wants to," he added, "I feel it only meet and fitting that we do our best to entertain him. I believe we ought to go tomorrow and swim the east way, and spend the afternoon on the island. There'll be nobody around to bother us. We can leave a note under a stone, and then of course on returning we can always pick up our own note, and tear it up and nobody'll ever have to bother with it."

"A note?" Peter asked, but he knew Jack meant that in case they never came back, somebody would find the note and discover what they had tried and at what they had failed.

He couldn't tell whether they were nervous about it, and he searched their faces. So far as he could see, they were unconcerned.

Later that same day Jack was hunched down in a book in the front room of the Winterhood house, and Peter said to his aunt that he thought he would go for a walk by himself. She looked at him and asked if anything was troubling him, and in her eyes he saw his father's look, whose sister she was. He had a lump in his throat, but he assured her that everything was fine, and that he was having the best summer of his life, visiting her and Jack and Ted Barksdale this way.

He went out and drifted to the river. He watched the willow shadows creep across the glassy flow as the sun fell, and when it was chilling to dusk, he came to the point on this bank opposite the east way to the island. How black the rapids were. What white ruffles they made. How stony the roar of the waters when he held his breath and turned his head to listen. A mocking bird was somewhere about, and his powerful pipe was doubled and made into song by the echo off the river. The hazard they were committed to for the following day seemed to Peter unbearable. He stared at the shining depth as it hurried past. Evening arose in misty breaths off the island opposite. He thought of his home in New Mexico, and the plains, where the sky was yellow at sundown, and the mountains were distant and rosy, and the river—the very same river as this one—was an idle, shallow, warm muddy stream going lazily past the town of Albuquerque. Here he was surrounded by the rocky dark of mountain and canyon. We will never make it, he thought. I must persuade them that it cannot be done. Remember Hound-dog Cooley, I will say, and what happened to him, how would you like to be found eleven miles downstream gashed by the rocks?

Late that night he awoke and lay hearing the river. If he lay on one ear it could seem as if the sound of the river was inside his head. But if he rolled over on his back and looked up into the dark, he could hear it plainly and actually, and it sounded dark and cold. Jack and he slept on the back porch of the white house. Jack's cot was across the doorway from Peter's. He didn't stir. Peter wished that he owned a legal mind. He was sure he knew what Hound-dog Cooley looked like, and the only thing that permitted him to go to sleep again was that he vowed he would speak to Jack the first thing when they woke up.

VII

Yet all the next morning he could not. They were going to meet before noon, take a lunch from Mrs. Winterhood, and their swimming trunks, and set forth. Ted was in high spirits, and Jack was solemn, as befitted one who would enter wholly but not lightly into a pact with death. Peter thought that they were deliberately not looking at him, and he believed that he must have showed his misery.

It was a bright summer day. The air in those mountains was like a mirror for the sun, so clear, so golden. They walked the same way Peter had gone the evening before.

About noon they were there, and Jack said they would eat their lunch first, then lie down for forty-five minutes to take a nap and digest their food, and then they would try it.

Still Peter could not say anything. He ate his sandwiches and beat his mind wondering why he could not bring forth the anguished protests, the certainty of folly, that he had within him. They seemed sure of themselves, and talked of this and of that, and for the first time he heard Ted's ambition: somehow to get passes on all the railroads leading to the Northwest, and to ride on these passes until he found himself in the Canadian Rockies. Once there, he would hunt the biggest game in North America, and explore the most echoing wilds. He believed that a man could spend years in such a grand wilderness without beginning to exhaust all that it held in the way of challenge and reward. When he talked about it, his stone-blue eyes flashed and glittered. He scaled mountains and glaciers in his mind, and lovingly brought down the most dangerous of animals. Peter's heart ached because he knew that Ted would be drowned long before he could find another frontier.

Jack asked Ted if he never wanted to go to college, and learn something.

Ted replied that he knew enough to last him all his life, right now, for what he wanted to do.

Jack laughed and said he had a life-sized picture of anyone getting rich by concentrating his mind on new ways to get off to some forest or other.

Ted said he didn't want to be rich, especially, once he had all the railroad passes he could gather. He said it was much better to ride on passes, even if you could afford to buy all the tickets you wanted. Passes were harder to get.

They kindly turned to Peter and asked what he wanted to do, and he replied that he was supposed to be a rancher, for his Dad's sake, but that he really wanted to be a doctor. Jack nodded with approval, and said that some of the biggest men in the medical profession made as high as twenty thousand dollars a year, and were pretty important men in their communities. The hauling river tore itself in long sliding shreds not a hundred feet from where they sat munching and talking. Jack Winterhood had the look of someone who knows exactly how things are, and when you know that, Peter felt, then you could not help getting what you wanted out of life, in the way of material returns. Peter suddenly loved his cousin for his serene unawareness of his destiny.

Jack now said they must all lie down, for they would need all their strength for the coming struggle. Peter asked what they would do with their clothes. Jack said they would leave them here in the willows with a couple of stones on them, where they could find them when they returned. As he lay down he took out an envelope from his pocket and handed it to Ted, and nodded him to read the page within it. Ted glanced at the paper, and with perfect indifference returned it to Jack. Peter could imagine what it said. The sunshine cleaved the broken river with swords.

They lay down to their naps.

Once during that awful restfulness, Ted drowsily asked Jack if he thought their things would still be on the island from the last time they'd gone there—over the west pool, of course. Jack replied that he imagined so. A few minutes later, with sudden energy, Jack raised his head and said,

"You can *swim,* can't you, Pete?"

Peter said he could.

Jack sighed with elaborate relaxation, and went back to his nap.

Peter was so tired from anxiety and from choking on his own words that he fell asleep. The next thing he knew, Jack and Ted shook him, and danced off down the narrow shelf of sand and pebbles to the water's edge, calling to him to hurry and come on. It was time to start.

They had put their clothes under the flat stones back of the willows a little bit up the bank. He put his there too, and saw the envelope, the "note," on which Jack had written "To Friends of Judge Winterhood, Ted Barksdale and Peter Rush, July 27, 1892." He was suddenly overwhelmed with gratitude and pity for being included with their names on this mortuary document. But they were calling him, standing in the sunshine and shivering by the river's edge. The light hit their cheeks, their shoulders, their flanks with dazzling brightness, and blazed without color as if on metal. He ran to join them.

Like man in his ultimate contests with Nature, they were naked and without weapons as they waded into the Rio Grande.

The water was icy cold. The boys skirled at the touch of it, and waded upstream gingerly until they were opposite the deepest and yet most powerful channel. Jack's purpose was to launch into the current and fight diagonally across it, until by perfect timing they would be deposited on the very last tip of the island, and of safety.

There was still time; but Peter could say nothing.

The river flashed in their ears and eyes.

Jack began to run with the clumsy gait of tugging water. It was like gathering himself for the final plunge. The sun was hot on their backs. The island had a thick screen of willows and scrub cottonwoods facing them. Beyond that lay what they were seeking. Peter didn't know what it was. He caught his breath when Jack plunged, and then Ted, into the black glassy run of the current. They swam powerfully and with valor, and were taken away it seemed so fast that he thought they were lost from the very first. In obedience to something they left in the air, in his mind, behind them, Peter came to the same place and plunged in, and he too was lost, for the bearing motion of the river swept everything else out of him. He beat with his arms and kicked and hugely drank in air when he could, and felt the mindless flow of the water; of the earth; of Nature, and it seemed to him the very essence of death.

"No!" something cried in him.

But there were two ways to make that answer.

He turned and buried his head in the current, and given might by the fear in his breast, he kicked and beat his way back to the shallows behind him, and sobbed with the water in his mouth, and felt fiery with determination even in that icy race, and sure enough, in a few minutes he was back and safe and hanging on all fours like an exhausted dog over the little stones and the idle back eddies of the river at the shore he had started from.

For a time he could not do anything but hunger for breath, and try to hold his joints together against the weakness of fear and relief. The river roared in his ears, and he shook his head. And then he thought he heard something, a shout, above the river sound that filled the whole day.

He turned around sickened with what he must see, and at what he saw, his heart sank, but not the way he had expected it to.

On the edge of the island, dancing in front of the rustling green,

were Jack and Ted, yelping like Indians, and motioning him to come,
why did he not come, what was he doing there, look where they
were! Come on!

"Come on!" they shouted, and swept the water from their bodies
with their palms.

It took them a few minutes to realize that he was afraid.

When they knew that, they produced themselves as triumphant
proofs that the east way could be swum. Come on! We can't wait here
all day!

He nodded and shook his head.

He had tried it, they knew that, why did they keep making him
have to try it again?

They were laughing and playing in the highest of spirits. They
had earned the right to play. They boxed together and danced apart,
and turned to Peter and exhorted. He could hear hardly a word. But
he knew everything they were saying and meaning. Come on! We'll
help you, see? They crouched down at the island's edge and held out
their hands to show how they would grasp his when he came to them.
Jack shook hands with himself at him in the air. Ted put his hands
together pantomiming the act of swimming and gravely indicated
that that was how it was done. Jack trotted up the island and motioned Peter to parallel him on the other bank, and when he stopped,
Peter stopped, and there, he showed, was where he should start again.
It would be just the right angle to bring him to the island's lower tip.
Go on! he waved, start now, and I'll run down to the tip, and meet
you!

Peter was shaken with the most crippling of agues. It was one
within. He wrung his hands and said no with his whole body. Two
were strong and successful, and one was afraid.

They finally looked at each other, shrugged, and shook hands, as
if in witness. Then, their bodies, dripping with sunlight, broke against
the willow screen on the island, fought the green fantasy of the
boughs for a moment, and were gone into the interior. They had
done all they could. Peter was alone with the river.

VIII

Then he knew that he must join them. He must be of them. To
belong was the strongest of all forces at times. That was why Peter
couldn't speak last night, or this morning, when the folly of the
scheme seemed to him so final.

He had his breath back now, and his doubt was gone, and instead of fear of something that might happen, he had a perfect certainty that he would go out into the river, and that he would drown, but that they would know later that he had tried to fulfill what they had all agreed upon; and this seemed to him the most powerful reason on earth for going.

It was worse, alone.

He cheated a moment or two longer, catching the cold water and splashing it over his breast. But that couldn't go on very long, he could think of no excuses. He went out again, and fell on his belly and began to fight.

He didn't know whether his hunger was going to be greater than the river's.

He tried to swim with long, powerful strokes. He tried to remember to be intelligent about not holding his breath, but to drink deeply of the air when he could, and expel it as deliberately. The first time he looked up toward his goal, it seemed like a vision drowned, all wavery and slowly moving. But he knew in a moment that a wind was bearing against the willow screen on the island, and he saw sharply that he was going downstream past it. No, he said, and squeezed his eyes shut, and rolled from side to side in the current, as if to bore his way through it like an auger.

It could not take forever, he knew, until the results would be clear.

But when he saw himself more than halfway across, and the island still tapering a little way below him, the conviction turned around, and he shouted in his heart that he could make it, and that he must make it, now, and that if he stroked and kicked twice as hard he would not feel so cold, the warmth would come back, and warm him in his small displacement of the river. Come on! they had cried, over and over. He dug a tunnel with his buried head and beat the slipping, pulling water, and his breast felt like breaking open, like the bottom of a wooden ship whose ribs are beating upon rocks while the waves drove after life within.

His breast was stabbed with pain, and he coughed for air, and shook, and looked up, and was himself like the ship on the rocks, lying on a jagged stone, and he could stand up, and wade the rest of it, to the wild grass that lay like the shadow of the willows along the island edge. In his breast there was a deep cut from the rock and the blood was washing down. He touched it with his fingers and in some ceremony forgotten and remembered from what primal impulse, he put his bloody fingers to his tongue, and tasted the cost and the proof of triumph. Dear river, I have beaten you, and I love you, he said in his blood.

He washed off the blood, and recovered from his gasping. How eager he was to find the others! And yet he was not ready to go and look. He fell down on his back and lay cruciform, gasping his way back to ease. He wanted to be alone for just a moment longer, to appreciate what he had done. He stared at the golden-blue sky and what he felt was thanksgiving not that he was alive but that he had dared to die.

IX

The island was very narrow, a sandy spit made by the river itself, in which the young trees would stand only until the next year of flood. He was suddenly recovered and eager to find the others. It would not take very long to search the island. He leaped up and began to arm his way through the tender thickets of willow branch which cut the sunshine into showers of gold light.

The island was boat-shaped.

He tried to walk as well as he could down the center. The sand was white and deep and hot under foot. He started a bird or two. He turned his head to listen. Everything was washed out of silence by the slide of the river on each side of the island. So he did not hear them and they did not hear him when he came upon them, at what would be amidships of the island.

Jack and Ted were sitting on the sand, playing blackjack with a withered old deck of cards. They were smoking cigars, and the smoke was pale blue in the sunlight. They had the air of being perfectly at home, sure of seclusion, like members of a club. Half buried in the sand to keep it standing upright was a pint bottle partly full of whisky. For poker chips they had piles of tin disks used with nails to tack tar paper over pine boarding. They had a perfectly settled look, as if their present comforts and refreshments were the most natural thing in the world in that small wilderness. Peter was shy for a second about intruding; they seemed to have forgotten his existence, but he then thought Why shouldn't they have forgotten my existence? and this was enough to make him sail forward out of the thicket with a yell, and sit down before them.

They jumped up, and yelled back. Their delight was great and genuine. They slapped their legs and capered, and tugged at his hands and pulled him up, and shook hands with him over and over. They asked about his wounded breast. They took him back among them. He belonged again. They began to fall all over themselves telling him about "their" island, and how often they came, and what they had, see: the wooden box which they kept buried when they were not here, but which they could always find, it contained their things, their cigars, matches, the playing cards, the whisky: (come: he had to have a pull at the bottle:) the tin poker chips, a rather sandy hank of licorice, some reading matter, and an old leather case made like a cylinder.

They gave him a cigar and lighted it, and they all sat down again. They taught him to play blackjack, generously handing him a lavish pile of tin chips. He won for a little while, which seemed to delight them all over again. There seemed to be nothing of theirs of which he had not rightfully now earned his due. When they were tired of playing poker, Ted said to Jack, that since Peter belonged on the island now,

"How about the telescope? Why don't we show that to him?"

Out of the box, they got the old leather case and unstrapped the cuplike top, and drew out an old brass telescope tipped with rusty black leather. Peter's eyes swam and his mouth watered at the sight of such a treasure. It was evidently the choicest thing they owned, too, and they handled it lovingly, passing it back and forth.

"Sometimes we spend whole Saturdays here on the island," said Jack, "looking through this glass at everything around here. Try it."

He handed it over. Peter went to the edge of the island and they followed. He put the glass between the branches and looked out over the fields across the river. What a world bloomed alive in the silver-gray light of the lens, a curious and beautiful halo of blue and yellow around all objects. The signal arms by the railroad embankment which unaided he could barely see as a pole standing against the distant bank of green hill was, through the glass, a brightly painted toy set near enough to touch. They let him sweep up and down the valley with the glass, smiling at his exclamations. But at last Ted took it away from him and said that was fun, and all that, but what was really interesting was to set the glass on a spot—any given spot—and lie down on your belly and watch. Just watch. Any spot. He'd bet ten dollars if you watched long enough that something very interesting would come to pass right there, no matter where you plopped your eye. He said that was the way they used the glass. It was a serious scientific instrument and should be respected as such.

They settled down with the glass. They made a carriage for it out of heaped sand. Jack trained the lens on a miniature bay in the opposite bank of the river . . . the side they had come from. Leaves hung over it, and shallow water idly backed up into it. Shadows on the grassy bank made it look cool and damp and remote. You could barely notice the little bay with your naked eye. In the glass it was like another country made visible.

Nothing moved in vision.

"Just leave it there and keep looking. Chances are you'll catch something," said Ted.

Jack yawned. But he had good manners, and he knew that the telescope experiment wouldn't be as much fun if he went to sleep and could not be reached with reports if something interesting did come into the lens. So he sat hugging his knees and chewing his cigar, and seemed to be thinking, as Ted Barksdale never seemed to do.

X

After a while, Jack said,

"Do you remember the way Tode talked that day we all rode up to Creede in the caboose?"

Ted nodded.

"Well," said Jack, "I have decided that if I ever hear him talking like that again, I will stop his mouth."

This was a striking promise. Peter turned away from the glass, and stared at his cousin. Jack was frowning splendidly, his eyes with their yellow flecks flashed with sober spirit. Ted looked happy, like a fawn-colored puppy, lean and big pawed.

"Why, Judge? I thought you were enjoying all the dirty stories as much as we were," said Ted.

"I was," said Jack. "I laughed as loud as the rest of you."

"He sure could tell'm," Peter said. Tode was able to suspect and seek out and touch the most secret susceptibilities of other men. Though he would seem to be telling his depraved histories in a sort of musing comfort, as if for his pleasure alone, his little eyes in his scrubbily bearded face had looked sideways at the boys in sly estimate time and again. Until he saw them het up by his talk, he was not successful.

"Yes," said Jack sternly, "I suppose I would laugh as loud as anybody if he started some time again; but I think now that I would have to tell him to shut up."

"Why?" asked Ted lazily, rolling over on the sand.

Jack hesitated, looking around with his light-kindled eyes. His face was always pale, with faint golden freckles. His body was as white. He never tanned under the sun. He was muscular and spare.

"Well," he said at last, "it wasn't only that Mr. Richards came in and began spouting sermons to us. Though of course that was proper.

I just have decided that it is within our power to choose our characters. I just don't think Tode is a very admirable individual. I don't think he would do as my Mexican cousin just did, just to prove to himself that he could do it."

Ted looked at Peter with the impersonal eyes of a forest animal, a deer, perhaps.

"And besides," said Jack, "I like the kind of talk that Mr. Richards can do better than Tode's. I am going to study law, and when I stand up, and open my mouth, you will be stunned at the magnificent things that will roll out."

He got to his feet.

"Did you ever read the Webster-Hayne debate?" he asked.

Ted Barksdale laughed.

"You needn't laugh. We have a set of books at home of the best speeches of all time, and I have been reading them. Yesterday afternoon I memorized something. Listen."

He turned and walked a few steps off, and then faced the other two boys in an attitude, and began to declaim in a loud voice, but with great deliberateness,

"But, sir, the coalition! The coalition! Aye, 'the murdered coalition'! The gentleman asks if I were led or frightened into this debate by the specter of the coalition,—'Was it the ghost of the murdered coalition,' he exclaims, 'which haunted the Member from Massachusetts, and which like the ghost of Banquo, would never down'?"

Jack's voice rolled sarcastically forth, and he scowled, revealing his belief that great oratory and anger were indivisible. These words of Daniel Webster were like meat and drink to him then.

Ted and Peter sat up, and stared.

It was such a scene as one boy could make for other boys only if they were removed for the moment from the world; where no value persisted to embarrass them but their own; where intimacy was a matter of being together in a fellowship of hazard and idleness. He tried his powers and the other two were enthralled. Denver! How could Denver one day fail to bow before him, with its pure-gold dome, the famous men and women posed by the iron balconies of the ten-story court of the new Brown Palace Hotel, the cavernous mirrors of the old Windsor Hotel, the superb teams pulling flashing carriages down the mud-and-cobble streets!

" 'The murdered coalition!' Sir, this charge of a coalition, in reference to the late administration, is not original with the honorable Member. It did not spring up in the Senate. Whether as a fact, or as an argument, or as an embellishment, it is all borrowed. He adopts it, indeed, from a very low origin and a still lower present condition." Jack showed, with his hand, as well as with his growling voice, how low. "It is one of the thousand calumnies with which the press teemed during an excited political canvass. It was a charge of which there was not only no proof or probability, but which was, in itself, wholly impossible to be true. No man of common information ever believed a syllable of it. Yet it was—"

Here he forgot. He held his command with lifted arm, while his eyes roved back and forth, searching for what came next. He snapped his fingers for it to come to him out of the void. But not wasting too much time on a mere lapse, he shook his head impatiently, and returned to what he believed the character of Webster to have been like, and jumped ahead to his tremendous conclusion, speaking slowly and with a fine-grained irony that held them transfixed.

"—It is the very cast-off slough of a polluted and shameless press. Incapable of further mischief, it lies in the sewer, lifeless and despised. It is not now, sir," (he glanced at the imaginary president of the Senate, a lightning dart) "in the power of the honorable Member to give it dignity or decency by attempting to elevate it, or introduce it into the Senate. He cannot change it from what it is, an object of general disgust and scor-r-n. On the contrary, the contact, if he choose to touch it, is more likely to drag him down, down, to the place where it lies itself."

Ted and Peter were spellbound when Jack finished, and could only look at him with open mouths. He rubbed his short-cut hair and in his modest, everyday voice, he tactfully brought them back to the present. He said,

"I just don't think I have room in myself to entertain *both* Tode and Daniel Webster in my studies."

Ted was too excited by the performance to sit still. He got up and ran off a way, yelling and slapping his hips, bounding like a dog. It was, in its way, a real tribute to an eloquent communication. Jack laughed in delight at him.

"I can't make hide nor hair out of what you recited," said Ted when he settled down again, "but it certainly was pretty the way you did it, Judge.—What about our books, in the box, over there?"

"That *is* true," said Jack. "I had forgotten them."

"What books?" Peter asked.

"Just some dirty books we've got.—You haven't looked in that glass for a long time. You might be missing something."

XI

Peter turned back and set his eye, and called out at what he saw. In the field of the telescope, a round picture cut forward out of another world, he saw a big striped snake trying to swallow a fat frog. The snake had the frog's left leg in his gullet, and was struggling to enwrap the other one. The frog was struggling slowly. Slowly the snake was working. The mortal combat went on with slow intensity and the blades of grass in which they moved showed up clear and bright and stiff in the lens. It was immensely exciting, and Peter told them about it, and they came and looked, and they all hated the snake. They pulled for the frog, watching the sun-fixed struggle as helpless partisans.

"You should have watched," shouted Jack, "maybe we could have thrown stones and scared him off if we'd seen it start!"

The lens was so faithful and so powerful that they could see the snake's eyes like drops of dew, black with a pin of light in them. As he worked and swallowed, his eyes would roll from sight and then as he relaxed they would show again. The frog's eyes seemed to look nowhere and everywhere. The snake coiled himself elegantly about the frog's body to reduce it if he could into a palatable shape. The river ruffled past in the miniature bay, and at one point in his sliding of efforts, the snake's tail wove in and out of the laplets of water behind them. Now the battle seemed halted. They rested a moment, perfectly still, locked in their parable of life and death. Peter could not take his eye off them, and the others let him keep the glass.

"What was that!" he cried suddenly.

"Where?"

"Something came across the glass, a shadow.—There it is again!"

Jack looked along the telescope as if to see with his own eye what Peter was seeing in the brass tube. But it was Ted who saw it first.

"Look up!" he whispered loudly. "It is a hawk, he's sailing around to make a dive. You must have seen his shadow when he came down before."

They looked up and there in the white sunlight was the superb bird. He was sailing down in a narrowing ring and Peter had seen his shadow waft over the tiny meadow where the snake strove and the frog strove so silently.

"Watch!" said Ted. Even before the hawk dropped, he knew when it would; many the hawk he had had in his days outdoors.

"Use the glass!" whispered Jack to Peter.

Peter looked.

The clash of claw and beak and feather was tremendous in the lens—the black beating shadow with the golden flecks of feather, the white breast, the green whip of the snake. He saw the sharp elegant talons make their clutch, and the cloudy wings batter the ground for a second before the heavy rise into the sky. The hawk's scowl in the powerful head flashed once into vision. The snake curled and relaxed, curled and relaxed, but was taken away, and the frog fell free on the grass and remained panting. Its white throat vibrated like a little drum.

He moved away from the glass and told them to look.

The hawk climbed and climbed.

Jack used the glass on the frog, and said,

"He's trying if he can move.—There he went. He jumped into the water. I'll bet he's glad!"

So were they.

Ted was true to himself when he said,

"Golly, I wish I'd had my rifle with me, I'd sure potted that hawk on his way up.—I could do it easy from this distance."

Jack was too, when he said,

"Well, that is the law of wild creatures. They take what they are. But *we* may say for ourselves what we shall be."

He went over to the box.

"What're you doing?" asked Ted.

Jack nodded but did not answer. He picked up the gray-looking paper books in the box, and with exaggerated ceremoniousness, he carried them to the edge of the island and threw them into the river. They floated rapidly off downstream.

Ted shrugged.

"Well, I had read them all, anyway," he said.

"Let's all have another drink," said Jack.

There wasn't much whisky in the pint bottle. They passed it around. They all choked on it, and swallowed it, and felt important and secure in their island league.

XII

The sun was going over. Dusk came early even in summer because the mountains over there were so high and met the sun so soon in its decline. They sat around and talked a while longer, and Jack advised them to memorize a passage every day from the debate between

Webster and Hayne. Ted said he believed they all ought to practice marksmanship at least once a week; said it was the one thing a man could rely on for himself. Peter wanted to contribute to this symposium, and could only offer his belief that the first thing a fellow ought to learn was how to swim, because you never knew when it would come in handy.

They showed him how things were stowed away in the box, and how the box was fastened, and how the box was buried. They told him that he was now privileged to come here and use the box at any time. They said they had built the box, using Mr. Barksdale's tools at the freight house.

It was turning chill with the lessening light. The water already looked dark, like shining mineral, and Jack said, when they were ready, that they would go back by the west pool, where there was hardly any current to speak of.

"We have earned the easy way," he stated, like a judge handing down a decision.

They ran through the little trees to the other end of the island. The sky was still white, but the ground was bluing with shadow. The pool was black and calm, its surface turning majestically in a slow wide wheel. They dived in and crashed across to the other bank and climbed up on a cool green field.

That was where the river made a Y, and they had landed across the right arm, and still had to cross the leftmost arm of the Y, to reach their clothes, and be on the home side of the river forks. It was now twilight, and no life stirred. The fields were quiet. They skulked along the edge of the bank. A few hundred yards off was the D. & R. G. trestle. They were going to walk across that to the other side. Just before they reached it, they heard an engine whistle. It came from behind them, up the canyon. They might not be able to beat it across. They crouched below the cindery embankment and waited till it came. It was a combination freight and passenger train, and it was on them before they knew it, trembling the earth as it went by above, clouding them with steam, and adding to the fall of night with its heavy soft coal smoke. It sailed on the slow grand curve the tracks made approaching South Fork. The boys stood up when it had passed, and saw the red and green caboose lights drifting evenly through the dusky distance. Peter thought of Tode and the freight conductor within, and of their two wills.

They hopped on the ties across the trestle, came down to the branchy cover of the other bank, following it to their flat stones. Jack said "H'm," when he lifted the stone and found the envelope he had left there. With a kindly sort of indulgence of themselves as they had been a few hours ago, he tore it up, and they dressed.

They started back toward the houses across the fields.

There were a few lights showing.

They suddenly felt hungry and cold and were ready to go separate ways.

When they reached the freight house where there was no trace of the important little train that had just passed through, they paused and said good-by to Ted Barksdale.

"Well, Judge, one thing more," said Ted to Jack. He said that there would be no further point in speaking of Peter as a Mexican, since he was no longer a foreigner. They shook hands on that point.

XXXIII · "HUSH!"

I

During his office hours one day Peter had a telephone call from Old Town. Don Hilario Ascarete had died an hour or two ago, and the family intended to hold open house that evening, if he would care to come. Everyone knew how much the old man liked his young doctor friend. The funeral would be tomorrow. After lunch, Don Hilario had retired for his usual siesta and when Catherine, the sixteen-year-old great-granddaughter, had gone in to say a word to him on her return from school, she had found him "gone." Everyone couldn't be there tonight, of course, you couldn't assemble such a huge family just-like-that, but there would be plenty of them, and if the Doctor would come, it would gratify everyone immensely.

After nine that evening, he drove out to the party. The doors and windows were all open. Orange-colored light spilled out on the cleanly swept yard. The air was full of bittersweetness from the rustling cottonwoods. The fields out that way were cool the minute the sun was gone beyond the river. There were cars parked for a block and a half. In the Plaza, light streamed forth from the open doors of the church, where preparations were being made for tomorrow's funeral. Peter could hear loud talking and laughter floating in the air as he came down the street on foot, having left his car in the Plaza. He could see candles burning in the front room, beyond the animated heads of the crowd. The whole house seemed to be full of people. They were laughing, eating, drinking, without boisterousness, but with good cheer. He came into the front room, and when he was recognized, a gay clamor arose to greet him. Way was made for him, he was received with respect, and taken at once to gaze upon the bier.

Don Hilario lay in an open coffin, dressed in an ancient suit of evening clothes which was far too large for him. But it was of stiff, rich material, and its faded grandeur covered him with almost hilarious distinction. His face was tiny, and his mouth was suddenly prominent, for the cheeks had fallen in and left the lips protruding. It was as if he were uttering an eternal "Hush!", but not chidingly, rather in a polite invitation to listen, and hear what went on behind the clamor of the world. In his expression lingered some odd ghost of his lifetime's humor and resignation. Peter never expected to feel so moved as he stood there looking down at the ancient body in the midst of the social noise of the room. He supposed he was the only man in the room who had any actual notion of the scope of the old man's experience, and he smiled ruefully at the thought that now he would never hear about the interview with Count Cavour, and the freedom of Italy.

Presently he turned around, and was spoken to in turn by each member of the surviving family, and he saw that many of them were proud of their ancestor, and that the very size and bounty of the party they were giving was proof of the importance he held in their family tradition. They were proud too of the worldly aspects of their kin, and all the Ascaretes who were, or were married to, figures in politics and the professions were introduced by title, Judge This, Professor That, Assistant-County-Superintendent of Schools So-and-So, the Reverend Father Et Cetera. This house belonged to one of the poorest of the clan, with whom the old man had elected to live out his days. Now it housed enough dignity and propriety to make anyone at all feel welcome, to pay homage to the little old man who had suddenly, after twenty-five years of retirement, assumed the most final of importances.

II

All evening the cars rolled up, visitors came and went, toasts were drunk, little eulogies were delivered. Someone had to stay up all night with the corpse anyway. It was such a beautiful night outdoors. The moon was nearly full. The young people drifted outside, and walked along the ditches where the moonlight shimmered upside down. The women gathered in groups, some in the bedrooms, some in the front room, some in the kitchen, and exchanged news. Some of the political cousins went off in a corner and accomplished several things toward the fall elections. A handful of children, unimaginably remote in their relationship to the figure in the coffin, played out in the alley, and presently began to shriek with fury and attack each other with mud and stones, making a scandal of the moonlight night. A cow was tethered out in back in the alfalfa field, and often she lifted her heavy head and groaned through the cool air in response to the disturbing activity of the house. The mocking birds stayed up, too, and whistled and mimicked across the low roofs of Old Town. The smell of the slow, muddy river came across now and then, the smell of wet earth, and it was like a pleasant shiver in the other elements of the scene.

Lying there in the middle of all this, old Don Hilario was finally ignored by the gathering.

Peter said good-by to them all and drove home through the ravishing night, in which the very qualities of the moonlight, the song of the mocking birds, the scent of the cool river, seemed to be interchanged, so that you could not say whether the moonlight made such silvery sound, or the river gave such sweet glow, or the mocking birds brought the river airs with them. He thought the old man was like a cottonwood tree, at the end, with the gray of its bark on his skin, in a very harmony with the earthen, grass-sprung, river-turned place of his life; arrived at death as if at a completion, rather than at an interruption. "That's what I mean," Peter said to himself.

XXXIV · THE FAREWELL

I

Willa's joy was the most tragic thing in life to her daughter Martha. There was no resisting so powerful and innocent a force as her mother's delight in the dream that was coming true, bag and baggage, off to Albion for the summer, to show everybody back there who's who and what's what, you could just bet your bottom dollar!

Martha's first intention was to refuse flatly to go along on the trip. It was as if her love were a creature living independently inside her, which flared into savage defense of itself when threatened from without. She was sick with the impact of the news; she felt hollow, her head ached with an insistent banging pain, and all she wanted at first was to be alone somewhere so she could sob extravagantly without anyone around to hear her and ask her what was the matter.

Never before had the whole little family's life-long dream of going "home" seemed a menace to her. Her mother was so confident of everybody's delight in the news of how at last they could go, that she never watched how Martha would take it; and with great control, Martha managed to exclaim, and give Willa a hurried hug as if she were too delighted to say more. But the minute she was able to, she left the house, and walked toward the country at the end of the street, leaving Willa busy with lists at the table in the front room.

How could she tell Bun?

Would he regard her as a traitor to their passion, if she ran off from it now?

She knew well enough what the plans were in the back of Willa's head.

School was out. Wayne was free to leave town now. The business college closed about the same time, and she had completed her course, and could get any job she liked, if the college was to be believed. She made a dozen schemes a day, and they consisted largely of variations on the plan that she would get a job and work, here at home, until Bun was through all his "premedical," and then, and then, they would get married, and with all the money she would have saved, they would be able to keep a little apartment while he interned in some big hospital somewhere. If the hospital had rules against interns marrying, then she would pretend to be his girl friend, and they would go on having "dates."

How easily she could slide into such visions of the future! How impossible, when she was so happy, to remember the dismal facts that had to be faced, and sooner every day!

What lay in store for her?

She was to be taken back to Albion and thrown at the head of that boy she had never seen, Dennison Yeager. He was a rich boy. She *hated* rich boys. He would be a stuck-up prissy boy with his own automobile, and probably treated all girls as if they would fall down and *worship* him the minute he smiled at them. She wished she had a million dollars so she could *buy* the Yeagers out of their house and home, and then disdainfully turn the place over to—to a cat and *dog* hospital or something worthy. Nobody on earth, no one's cheek, or hand, or voice, or blue eye, or combed hair, or shoulder blade under coat, or dancing confidence, or musing grin, or cool ears, or beliefs, could ever possibly mean what these things of Bun's meant to her. Nobody ever loved anybody as hard as she did him. If it would *help* any, in any *way,* she would go and die, like Juliet, more sorrowful, and prettier than ever. She sat down on a bank of sand grass, and hugged herself and wept.

One thing she knew. She would have to go. You can't wreck the twenty-year hope of anybody else, for *any* reason. She hated her mother, she now believed; but she couldn't make anybody as unhappy as her refusal to go would make her mother. Besides, to be honest, her mother still had the more power and strength of the two: Willa would grow hoarse, and seem thinner than ever, and command her to stop being a silly, and get ready, 'cause she was *going*. That was the truth of the matter.

But beside that, if Martha knew she had to go, in her heart which served as a temple to the solemnity and purity of her feeling, she vowed that she would let nothing turn her from the love of her life, and that Dennison Yeager or no Dennison Yeager, she would come back in the fall. Her heart beat even now at the picture of how they would meet again after being separated so long . . .

But how should they say good-by?

II

For the next several times she saw him, she was afraid to tell him what was ahead for them both. He was as animated, as gentle, as amusing as ever. Now he was excited by something that made her jealous. In the store the other day, who should come in but Doctor Peter Rush himself, to get a prescription filled to carry in his medicine case. Bun took the written application to the pharmacist in the back room, behind the swinging doors, and then came back to talk to the Doctor. The Doctor asked him what he was going to do all summer. He said he was not sure, he supposed he would work in the drugstore, though some fellows were going fishing in August up the Pecos, and he might go too. The Doctor said that was fun. He added that what he really meant to know was whether Bun really was going on to study medicine eventually. He said sure, he always meant to. Doctor Rush said that was the spirit, and asked him if he'd like to watch an operation occasionally? Now and then there would be cases from which a youngster could get something, by watching. It used to be a good system, when an old doctor would take an apprentice, and teach him through association and example. Not that anything should ever take the place of a good schooling and first-rate interning. How about it? Well, Bun was so surprised he could barely answer, but he made the Doctor understand that nothing would delight him more, than to actually see an operation, and get the *feeling* of it so early in his career.

So Doctor Rush said he'd call him up sometime, and they'd "see." This was all Bun could talk of.

While her heart was cracking and washing away and floating down the *river,* he was alternately telling her about how it would be, and staring silently and smilingly ahead of him at the future.

He never even noticed that something was *wrong* with her.

She began to think he was making her as unhappy as Willa was. Everything was wrong.

She dreaded quarreling with him. She knew that if she didn't tell him soon, his innocent failure to console her would make her do something or say something she would be sorry for.

Their evening dates were curiously settled, as if they were married. She wondered why they didn't go ahead, *and* marry, and then the fact that this seriously should occur to her made her miserable at how *sane* the world was, and how impossible it would be to be married now, with college ahead of him, and medical school, too, and the interning years.

III

Finally, she wrote him a letter, explaining what was ahead for them. She mailed it so he would get it the day before they were leaving. That night would be their last. In all honesty the tears rolled up into her eyes and fell down on the letter. She dratted it, and said she would have to copy it over now, because the ink ran. But a second wave of justice overwhelmed her, and she said, Why not, why shouldn't he *see* what it's doing to me? He will know I am crying, as I write to him, I *want* him to know, I don't *care* if this looks like an old movie with Viola Dana in it . . . She mailed it as it was. Now when they met, as usual, after supper, he would already know what was about to befall them, which she had actually been afraid to tell him for the past days.

And sure enough, when he got to the library, and found her waiting in the vestibule, where it was fairly dark, he took her arm, and said,

"Hey, *what's* this:"

He sounded half-furious at having his life upset that way, and instead of bursting into tears, as she fully expected to, she felt herself *freeze* with dignity and self-possession.

Love.

You simply never knew.

"You know perfectly well, I wrote you all about it."

"Why'n't you tell me?"

"How can you *speak* to me that way, especially now!"

"What way, I'm not speaking to you in a *way!*"

"You are too, you sound so—so critical!"

"Oh, *bilgewater,* you don't—"

"Don't you say *oh bilgewater* to me, Richmond Summerfield!"

"I'm sorry; but this goofy idea you wrote me about, about going on a *trip—*"

"I daresay if my poor backbreaking hard-working mother wants to take a little trip and have her family along, then I daresay she has a simple right to do it."

Her elevated social tone stung him and he entered upon the same irony.

"I daresay."

He was mocking her. She hated herself for defending the very thing that made her so unhappy. Why are we *doing* this? she wondered.

They were divided in silence, looking at each other. Then he melted her by blinking both eyes slowly at her, and sticking out his lower jaw in a calculating grin, a reminder of the expression he always assumed when he felt like loving. It raised them both out of the hostility of their meeting. He had made the overture with his eyes. She must respond. She licked her lips and said,

"Well, where'sh'we go?"

"I didn't get the car. I couldn't have it tonight.—Let's walk down to the river."

"All right.—Let's walk over the viaduct. Let's keep out of sight. *This is our last night.* Darling, I'll *die!*"

They crossed the main street and walked down in the darkness of South Edith Street, their arms locked together, their woes uniting them as closely as a moment before they had been widely apart.

She explained what had happened, to their family fortunes, and how it had always been her mother's desire to go back to Michigan someday and show everybody. They would be away all summer. But in September, she would return; and think of all the things they would have to tell each other!

He asked what was it like, back there in Michigan. She said she didn't know, couldn't remember a thing, she had been a baby when they left there to come here for her father's health. He sternly told her she'd better come back, he was speaking medically now, for her own good, and if her father had died of t.b., then she must take no risks of breaking down with the same thing.

He pointed out that the disease was not necessarily hereditary; but the *tendency* to it was considered so. She shivered at his authority and charm, in discussing things as a youth which later on as a man he would be paid for saying to grateful patients.

The streets were dark. They turned the corner and saw the viaduct with its old lamps blooming in the night air over the railroad tracks, where a powdery glisten of drifting steam from below caught the light. They walked across, looking down at the tracks and the engines. There was a train standing by the Harvey House, headed East.

"Look!" she cried, grasping him and pointing.

He saw what she meant, she meant that tomorrow she herself would be on the same train, it was going East, and he would be left here. He would be a fixed point for her to come back to. He had the sensation of something wrapping his arched breast in tightening bands, and squeezing until he could hardly breathe. He seized her and kissed her with hunger.

Her mouth talked to him in devouring silence, even while her hands tried to hold him off, and when again they were desperately apart, she shook her head as if she had been hit, and said no, no, not here, this is too public, the cars going by now and then, and let them walk on. But she knew of pride and security. He wanted her that much. She loved him to the exact same degree. Time and distance would be trivial foes.

They walked out First Street, dark and dingy. They were deliciously startled now and then by dark creatures revealed in alleys by the sound of dim talking. The tall windows of the Santa Fe shops were so high and empty of everything but a sort of blue industrial light that they felt like lost children in another planet. It was a night of such darkness as happened between the shows of the moon, there, and even the high heavy cottonwoods were invisible along the streets, except where light spilled faintly forth from a nightlight in a store window, or gleamed in back of somebody's house in a yard where bootleg liquor could probably be bought.

It gave them anonymity to be wandering in this unsavory part of town. He knew well enough about the town's underworld from school rumor and boastful gossip. He would have welcomed a threat against her just because he could have defended her so mightily against anybody, the Joe Martinez gang, for instance.

They came around a half bend in the street, the pavement ended, and they saw a glow two blocks away, green tree, yellow doorway, and heard what: was it music? a nickel's worth of gaiety from an electric pianola?

"There's Borelli's, by the bridge," said Bun.

"Oh: I've heard of it. They say he is a bootlegger."

"Why, it's a saloon, and also a—I mean, you can just buy any drink you order there. He doesn't trouble to hide it, even."

"What else is his place?"

"*What* else, what do you mean?"

"You started to say it was something besides a saloon."

"No I didn't."

"Yes, you did."

"No, really, I just meant—"

"You were *going* to say it, don't you deny it!"

He wouldn't answer.

They were walking.

The bridge was ahead, they could just see its old iron basketry in the air, and hear the planks rumbling under a car coming this way.

They both knew they were skating perilously near to suggestions and words and ideas and guesses that lived under their words.

He wished she wouldn't talk like that, all around the point, and try to get him to say right at her what he was having a hard enough time with as it was.

She was wholly aware of her two selves, one acting serene and innocent, the other in a turmoil of longing.

They glanced into Borelli's doorway. It was a panel of light, with people sitting at the tables. The piano was raking its own entrails and the felted hammers could be seen through a glass pane wincing and striking under the impact of ghostly hands. The back yard and the vacant lot next door and the adobe house by the river edge were dark. They imagined they could hear the river. Their knees were weak. What was there about this place?

They went on up to the bridge and went out across nearly halfway and leaned on the rickety handrail.

IV

After a while, he said,

"I guess this's where we have to say our good-byes, hon."

"Oh, I don't know," she said, but her voice was just simply lifted in half so she talked high and breathy.

"I won't have a chance to, at the train."

"I suppose not."

"I was sore, back there, at the library, when we met, just because I hated the idea of you going off."

"I know. I knew it all the time."

"You *did?*"

"Why, *sure.*"

"You didn't sound like it . . ."

"*Cer*tainly."

They were clutching at any social pretenses to save them from the tides that were ready to run.

"O.K.—Just the same, I didn't mean to be cross."

"You're *never* cross, *darling.*"

He swallowed.

"Don't *sound* like that!"

"Like what?" she asked, as if she were a little girl five years old.

"Oh God," he said in a whisper, hanging his head down and shaking it and staring at the shallow drift of the slow river which looked fathomless in the starlight.

She could not desist. She put her hand on the back of his neck.

"Like a Teddy bear," she said, feeling him there.

He bristled under her fingers, she felt it, the little hairs on his skull rose up.

They were pierced now by the frenzy that had gone around and around in him.

Everything they felt told them formlessly of death and the passage of all fair things, and the very ingredient of beauty itself which was mortal.

They heard the clank of indulgence from Borelli's piano across the river water, and they smelled the bitter flavor of the cottonwood trees which the night air bore.

There lived a suggestion in the very atmosphere. It was no accident, nor even a decision, but a fatal pursuit in his half-dream-mind that had led them there together.

He turned upon her, and she said,

"Tomorrow night I'll be gone."

and he groaned and hurried her to him in a misdirected kiss that hurt them both. But they modulated themselves and flowed into each other through their embrace.

Presently in a voice like the night itself he whispered to her and ground his jaw upon her cheek, and told her where they could go, down the embankment at the end of the bridge, and along the shore, all the boys used to play there, he knew every inch of the river, and there were little groves of saplings where no paths went, and it was a warm night, and the river flowed past, and the moon was under, and tomorrow and tomorrow and love and tonight and God oh God how I love you *sure* I've thought of everything before a million times and never forget and that is you and this is me and that is me and this is you, were you ever anything but sure yourself?

She turned up her lips and stopped his words and wouldn't budge otherwise.

Then long afterward, she tried to see his eyes in the darkness, and couldn't, really, but between them alive and waiting for an answer was simply the ? and the poetry that raged alive in their hearts must be delivered in flesh or fade away.

Of the two, he was, the man, the poet, delivered to the instant. She set her hands to his face and accomplished that miracle which kept both his love and her inviolability.

She whispered to him that she was his for whatever he wanted of her, that was how she felt *now;* but she couldn't help thinking for just a tiny second of how they might feel later. She said this with a rueful sweetness that simply turned his heart over and he was a changed man. He groaned with tenderness, and everything urgent fell away in a chastened kind of strength that made him want to protect her forever.

Pretty soon, peaceful and dedicated, they came back off the bridge, and strolled with linked fingers across town toward her street.

V

Like a deep breath, that lifted her heart, and her head, a new notion sprang alive in Martha. She felt twenty years older, *at least,* and smiled privately at the so-recent storms of feeling that had troubled her. She now had once again, and more dearly than ever, proof of their love. Secure in that, should they not think, and feel, and do, for others?

"We must be very understanding, darling," she said to him gently, beginning a sober comedy of virtue.

"How do you mean?"

"We must not be selfish. I mean: after all, you know and I know what we mean to each other.—I think we should say to each other, when we part, Good-by, I love you with all my heart, now don't be lonely, but go and have a *good time,* until we come together again. —Don't you?"

"No. I don't."

"Darling."

She hugged his arm.

"But what I really mean," she continued, "is about Mother. I mean: think what this means to her? I don't want to *go* any more than you *want* me to go. But if you knew how she's dreamed, and skimped, and planned why you'd see it as I do.—I under*stand* Mother, of course, it'd be hard for you to see what I mean. But I mean: all that Mother wants, or has ever wanted, is something *real.*—I'm not like that."

"How d'you mean?"

"I'm such a fool."

"No you aren't."

"Yes I am, I'mean: I cry my eyes out over wanting something im*pos*sible.—I did, that is, until *you.*"

"Until *me?*"

"Yes."

"Silly."

"Yes, but I'm not *afraid* to be silly now. I used to be so afraid to be silly or that I'd do something *ungracious.*"

"You couldn't possibly. You're the most gracious person I've ever known."

"Oh, I *want* to be, for *you* . . ."

These exchanges seemed to them somehow profound and full of the future. They would have died laughing if they'd overheard another couple saying the same things. The power that held them gave them the gift of illusion, too, as well as that of desire.

"But Mumma—the wonderful thing about Mother is how she *makes* her dreams come true. I'mean: don't you think that is a wonderful ability?"

"It's a miracle, if true."

"Of course it's true.—And you know why?"

"No."

"She never really wants *hard* for anything that isn't perfectly *possible.*"

"Oh."

"No, it's more than just '*Oh.*' You don't *see,* darling.—It goes way back to her girlhood. She only wants to finish the story she began then, when she fell in love with my father, and married him. All she wants to do is go back home to Albion, and see it all again, and have all her old friends (I'll bet they're a bundle of *frights*) rave and moon over me and my little brother Waynie, and then come back here. That's all she has ever dreamed of. And now she's going to get it! I'mean: it'll make her the happiest person on this *planet.*—She's going to buy me the most gorgeous clothes at Marshall Field's on the way through Chicago. She's been making lists for days. You won't know me when I come back. I'll be so *modish.*"

"Do you suppose I could *talk* to your Mom at the train tomorrow night?"

"Talk to her? How:"

"About *us?*"

"Oh no. Oh *no.* It'd just upset her and I do think we must give her just this one perfect summer, don't you, darling, and then afterward, we can:"

He laughed.

"You mean afterward, we can raise as much hell as we feel obliged to, is that it?"

"I think you're mean to laugh.—And I wouldn't put it that way."

"But it's the truth, isn't it:"

"I suppose so."

"You're awfully clever, you must *think* all the time," he said in loving mockery.

"I do.—But you're *brilliant.* You have genius. You don't *have* to think. Things are just *there.*—Aren't they:"

"Oh, I don't know."

"*Aren't* they?" she insisted, defending him against his seemly modesty.

"I—I suppose so, after all."

"Sweet," she said, ever so proud of him.

"What does Wayne think about going?"

"I wish I knew! Sometimes I don't think that boy ever *does* think. —He always looks as if he were too superior to bother with a little thing like stopping and thinking."

"He's a funny kid."

"He's a darling, and don't you think anything else.—But sometimes I worry so over him."

"Worry? Why."

"Oh, he's getting so *big,* and you never know just how a boy is going to *mature, you* know what I mean."

"No I don't.—He's all right."

"I mean, in a few years, he'll be as old as *you* are, and then—"

"Then what:"

"—He'll get some *girl,* and God only knows what they'll— —Richmond Summerfield, don't be so dense, all of a sudden, honestly, sometimes you can act just like a stone wall."

"Oh, I *see.* Well, more power to him."

"What do you *mean:*"

"*Now* who's a stone wall."

"I think you've got a horrid view of things."

"Just because it's your baby brother.—And what's more, I was just wishing him as much luck as *I* have got. That's all.—You mustn't *imagine* things, dear."

"Bunny, how darling of you.—You have as many facets as a rare jewel."

"Yaa."

"No, I mean it."

On the second proffer, he always accepted her tributes.

They walked in silence for a long time, resting in union through their fingers.

Then she added with a sigh, embracing life as she knew it,

"Momma is just true to her own heart, and I suppose that means, to everybody else's. It is the strongest thing in the world, you can't fight it. I'm resigned to everything, now, because I see it is right."

This was too much for him. He stopped and took her face in his palms and kissed her devoutly. How much! they thought, how much they drew from life through each other! Just being with each other! How much opened up, thing after thing, like the petals of a flower! What children they used to be, only a snap of the fingers ago!

She put her hands on his neck and held him there, under his ears, which were cool, as always, and said softly,

"Every night when I go to bed I will lie down facing the west, and every night when you go to bed, you lie down facing east, and we will fall asleep that way, darling, until we meet again."

They were drowned in inner music, the bare jazz of their period, and they heard it again and they beautified what it said; the pick-up orchestra that used to play for the dances for the high school crowd, sometimes at the Woman's Club, sometimes at Colombo Hall, a cornet, a piano, a saxophone, and the traps, of course; an acrid combination, through which, nevertheless, they heard what was coming to them; and it sufficed.

XXXV · "INSCRUTABLE"

I

Summer was coming down the river.

It was the last chance Wayne and Donald had to go swimming before Wayne left for the East.

They had found a willowy room by the water's edge. The sunshine came in through the leafy lace like a school of little silver fish swimming in the warm blue. The boys were so silent that all sounds about them lived distinct. The very sound of the river seep glistening into the sandy bank could be heard, tiny, remote, like little lips meeting and parting. There was a hazy song of flying bugs in the air. Far, far down the way, it seemed, though it was hardly a mile, the boards of the Barelas bridge were trundled by cars and wagons crossing the river, and made an agreeable miniature thunder. The boys lay face down on the ground. Under him, each felt the earth's heart beating; how deep and personal it was, as if it beat only for him, and yet for all other lives too! Unimaginably far down and deep, and true, and supporting, that heartbeat went profoundly on. It felt as if the earth were shaken ever so slightly at each beat. Drowsily, thoughtfully, they felt it. Neither one reflected that it was his own heart that was thumping against the earth where they lay, and that it was they, not the earth, that shook with the beat. But whichever it was did not matter. They were upon their element, and contentedly were part of it.

II

But there were things to say, as well as to feel.

"I finally told my mother about the glass."

"What did she do?"

"Nothing, it is all right. But I had to tell her."

"Did you tell her I did it too?"

"I mentioned it."

"I thought you would."

"I am sure you feel as I do about it."

"Certainly."

"Have you said anything to your Dad?"

"No not *said* anything. But—but it is all *right*, anyhow."

"How do you mean?"

"I can't explain. But I think we understand each other now."

"That's good."

"I sometimes think it takes something funny to bring people together."

"What if you could always know what people would *do!*"

"I know, wouldn't that be wonderful."

"As it is, I believe you and I can conceal the slightest hint of what our intentions are from anybody else, don't you think so?"

"Yes. We are both absolutely inscrutable."

"If anything, I would say you were a little more inscrutable than I."

"Oh, I don't know."

"Yes, it is my blue eyes. People with blue eyes are never able to be as inscrutable as people with brown eyes. There's something about it."

"Well, maybe. But the ordinary person would never in the world regard you as any less inscrutable than I am. In fact, the fact is, *you* thought of being inscrutable first."

"Yes, that's so. I must say it has stood us in good stead, in school, for instance, and with Nick."

"He never knows what we are thinking."

"It's a good thing to be able to be. Any fool can *show* what he's thinking."

"Are you going to try it when you get East?"

"I imagine so. I will write you how it works out.—I don't really want to go, you know, all we could do here all summer, on the river, and the mesa, and everywhere. But my mother has no idea I *feel* that way."

"That was inscrutable."

"Utterly."

"I'll sure miss having you around. I think I'll put in my time till you get back, writing a novel. You can read it when you return."

"Why not let's write it together? I will send you ideas from Albion. Monsieur le Vicomte could be the leading character."

"All right. Think up things for him to do. I'll put them in."

"I'm hot again."

"Beat you:"

They leaped up and crashed through the willows at the riverside and dived into the warm muddy stream, making a blinding explosion of water and sunlight when they hit it, summer's denizens.

XXXVI · THE TRAIN

I

At the station the next evening, Bun stayed out of sight, but she met him by the mailbox, and they were drawn in the face and excited and forlorn. All the nobility and resignation of the night before were gone. They kissed hurriedly and made what references they could to their understandings and pledges. Then he brought out something from his pocket, and handed it to her, and when she saw what it was, the mother he had betrayed for her, and what he had given of his symbolical past, Martha burst into tears and ran off from him and stood waiting for the train to go, while he watched her through the evening distance.

He had brought her the snapshot of himself taken by his aunt Susan on the front lawn, years ago, the day they had first given him the nickname of "Bunny."

II

Wayne and Donald stood looking up and down the tracks at the engines and cars. They had nothing to say. Presently Willa Shoemaker came hurrying from the baggage room where she had checked the family trunks. She was exhausted looking, and had bright spots of color flaring on her cheekbones. She was telling herself aloud the things that had been accomplished, which made their departure a safe and orderly one. "—water in the house turned off, gas company notified, my ferns taken down to Daingerfield's on the corner, to look after till I come back, oh yes, I nearly forgot—"

She turned and seized Donald Rush.

"You will remember, won't you, Donnie? About watering my petunias? Just tie that piece of gunnysack around the end of the hose, and let it run slowly, about an hour every other day? I'll just *die* if I come home and find them shriveled to a crisp!"

He promised.

He thought it was going to be a bore, with the Shoemakers away. Still he couldn't see why such a fuss was always kicked up when people saw people off, for now there came a hurry of female figures out of the Harvey House dining room, it was Margaret, the head-waitress, and some of her girls, come to say good-by to Willa. They were just in time. The engine bell began to roll, and the engine let off steam. It made a loud noise, but through it the high enchanted voice of Mrs. Shoemaker could be heard crying, "Good-by, good-by . . ."

XXXVII · MAIL FROM ALBION

I

Bun got a letter from Martha, written on the train, on the railroad stationery. He could imagine her sitting in the observation car and writing at the little desk with the pierced brass lamp, probably putting on the airs of one who did this five times a year, though it was her first trip since she had come West as a baby. Her writing was neat and clear. Even the lurches and impulses of the train couldn't make her page look like anything but a well-kept ledger. How remote she seemed, in this medium! But as he read, his heart kindled, and he warmed with longing.

> The picture! Oh, my darling Bunny, the picture! I did not expect such a parting gift from you. It is not much as a parting gift according to the way other girls would look at it, just a Kodak print. But to me it spoke volumes. I shall always treasure it. I have looked at it six times this morning, already. It is much more interesting than the Godforsaken country we are passing through. Last night I could not help crying as I fell asleep, just a little, because the train kept going the way away from where you are. But I must not let myself think of anything but when I come back. Otherwise Mother's whole trip will be spoiled. So I shall just act educated and attempt to be pleasing, which will only be a pose, because how will they know what is inside of my brain? Only I will know, and you will know.

He had a postcard from Chicago, where they changed trains, which said,

> Nearly there. Gorgeous trip. We will do it together some day.

Then for a week he heard nothing, and worried. On one of those days he got possessed by something, he didn't know what, which nearly drove him wild. He went to the post-office box five times in that one day, and on finding nothing, even the last time, after dark, he went around to the cement deck behind the post office and knocked on the door, peering through the wired-glass window, until a clerk came to see what he wanted. He blushed and said he was sorry to make a bother, but could it be that a letter for Richmond Summerfield, Box 446, might have fallen back on the floor inside the wall of boxes? He was almost sure that there was a letter, and yet he had not received it. If the clerk would look? The clerk told him to wait, and stared at him a second out of tired buglike eyes under a green eyeshade. It was a look that chilled the young man's heart, for it seemed to say, from a point twice Bun's age, "What could possibly be that important? More important than my aching bones, which hurt the more with every step I take?" But he finally went to look, and Bun watched him across the big open room with its hanging lamps and their golden dusty cones of light in the dark air. The clerk came back and shook his head. Bun smiled energetically to hide his trouble, and went off with his head in a whirl. He couldn't imagine what was wrong. He hardly slept that night.

II

But when he awoke the next morning, it was in a sort of restored peace that was something like indifference; or so he thought, until he got to the store and found a letter for him which had been collected in the early mail at Box 446. At the sight of her careful and clever writing, a weight fell in his breast, as if he would never catch it, and he retired to the farthest corner of the stock room, among cardboard pyramids and wooden cases, and read her letter by the light of a window high up near the ceiling. Here he was uninterrupted, except once by Rollie, who seemed to be looking for something.

"Go, go, go," she wrote, sounding something like her mother Willa. "You must think me an awful pill for taking so long to tell you everything. But honestly, we have never been given a *moment*. I never saw such hospitable people in my life, though they say themselves that if a person's a stranger here they might just as well resign themselves to the cold shoulder. But when you *belong* here, why it is entirely different. You would never know Mamma. She looks ten years younger, we got the prettiest clothes in Chicago, you won't know me, and we are living here at this hotel, and I never would have believed it. The way Mamma is somebody here. All her old freinds, the ones who are left, take her right in, you would think she is a girl again. I guess it must just be fine to come home that way, and find out that Willa Johnson is still very much loved by all who knew her. Mamma's family really were somebody around here, evidently. I can hardly remember Daddy, but we drove out and saw the house where he was born, it was sold some years back, but it is a lovely old white clapboard farm house, which is now a tea room and antique shop.

"But honestly, I'll never understand Momma. Here after all the talk and the planning and the breaking all our necks to *get* here, she says nothing is the same, and she worries about things back home, and the petunias at the house, and have I heard from you, she's suddenly gone crazy over you, and I'll never understand her as long as I live. She hasn't said so right out, but I honestly think that if either Waynie or I suggested it, she'd run for the first train home. Except that so many *affairs* have been arranged for her that she *couldn't* leave now. But you ought to hear her talk about her responsible position at home, with the Harvey System, and so on and so on. I simply *die* at her! She was telling everybody what a *'good'* boy you are, though not a Catholic, and the *best-looking thing,* she said. (Guess who else thinks so!) But Momma does have an air, and loves to spend money as if she never heard of it and as if it don't matter one way or the other if you have it or if you don't.

"Well, where to begin. There have been parties every single night. I never see Wayne at all any more. He has found himself a lot of little freinds." (He smiled fondly over her misspelling.) "We see a great deal of some dear old freinds of Mamma's, the Martin Yeagers, they all grew up together, and we take dinner there, or we drop in for tea, or we sit on the lawn in the evenings when it is so hot and watch the fireflies. They have three boys, the oldest one Dennison just graduated from college. He is really an old pill, but he is trying to be nice, and as I told Mamma, the least you can do is act appreciative, and I don't see anything wrong with making freinds easily, do you. Don't be jealous you have no cause. He is very good looking in a different sort of a way. Blond and brown-eyed, you see not a bit like my own dear blue-eyed Bunny, at all. (Jealous?) He has a Stutz Bearcat runabout and we all pile in I mean some of the younger crowd and go off swimming. You ought to see him in his straw hat, the first time I saw him in it I nearly burst out laughing right in his face and I never could even imagine you waering a thing as awful as that hat. He said everybody at Ann Arbor wore the same kind of a hat so I could kindly keep my *millinery opinions* to myself. I didn't even address a single remark to him after that until we got back for supper.

"The Yeagers live in a new house they have just moved into, after their old one burned to the ground. It is a stunning new Norman-French style country house, and all the old Yeager family heirlooms look lovely in the rooms. Mrs. Yeager has outstanding taste. Mr. Yeager jollies her and says there's no place in the house for poor old Pop, meaning himself. He is an awfully nice old man, and seems to have taken quite a shine to yours truly. He told me he was once madly in love with Mamma, and I nearly died laughing right in his face, until I saw that he meant it perfectly seriously.

"Well, what else. We're going to Detroit one day next week to go through the Ford factory, near there, Mr. Yeager has a freind" (he promised to teach her to spell that word) "who is high up in the company. Wayne can hardly wait. Why haven't I heard from you? Forgive me I will write more often now. Are you remembering to do what I promised we would both do, go to sleep every night facing toward each other? I have kept my vow faithfully. See that you do. Sometimes when I am with these other people and suddenly think of you I can hardly stand it, but what can you do."

He was vaguely disquieted by the letter, and read its final endearments with his heart in his mouth. He thought of his agony at the post office the night before, and he wondered if he was being foolish in resenting her activity, her new interests, the rich college boy she was tearing around the country with in a Stutz Bearcat. He had a wave of hot thought, it seemed to sweep over him, and turn him scarlet, and he rushed out the back door of the drugstore, and went down the street to the Western Union office. He wrote her a telegram:

"I LOVE YOU I LOVE YOU I LOVE YOU DARLING,"

making the even ten words, and not looking at the clerk, paid for it and walked slowly back to the corner to go back to work. He wondered now that it was done whether she would think the telegram both as passionate and as clever as he did. He felt deeply depressed.

III

Though he conducted himself as a relentlessly Christian young man, Rollie Glovers was actually a pagan, adoring physical beauty with a passion and an envy which the illiterate energies of his preachers never aroused in him on Wednesday evenings, or Sunday mornings, or during those week-long revivals which he attended in zealous communion with other excited people.

He desired above everything else in the world to be strong and shapely. He believed that as soon as his muscles bulged and his chest expansion was increased to six inches, he would only have to look at a girl with a meaningful glance to have her fall into his arms. He hated Bun, and was elaborately courteous to him. He watched him to see how he made such a grateful impression on people, mostly girls and women who came into the store, and he knew Bun was "soft on" Martha Shoemaker. He saw Bun read Martha's long letter, and was tempted to sneak it out of Bun's jacket pocket and read it. But he sternly told himself that this would never do. But the idea aroused a passion of jealousy in him, and he wished there were some way in the world for him to declare himself as Bun's rival, and then simply "take her away" from him. But he supposed he had to content himself with his courses of self-improvement, first.

He exercised regularly and hunted through the morning papers for columns on health to winnow of their self-improvement diets. He sunbathed, and swam, and used the rowing machine downstairs in the YMCA and never turned off his light to go to sleep until lying on the floor he had raised and lowered himself ten times, "keeping the legs stiff and the back well arched."

Then he would look into the mirror, and weigh himself, seeking evidence of what he so truly desired.

He had come, lately, to an expression of his ideal which gave him such pleasure as he could afford. On the newsstand down the street in front of the pool hall, he got used to buying a magazine called *Body Harmony,* which came every month and contained articles on hopeful philosophy; advice as to exercise; many advertisements for physical culture systems which guaranteed to "make a man" of anybody who felt the need, and within ten days, at that; and best of all, a section of photographs, elegantly reproduced in a sort of powdery brown ink, showing "art poses" by amateurs of the cult of the body.

Many of these pictures were highly encouraging. Against board fences beyond which the despairing clutter of city alleys could be seen, they showed skinny youths standing in puny nakedness wearing loincloths that sagged about their hipbones. And then if you turned the page eagerly, there were other pictures of the same youths showing them six months later, displaying the fruits of their self-love in richly lighted poses made in photographers' studios . . . impersonations of the Discobolus, the Doryphorus, the Dying Gaul, as well as improvised positions in which the young men fiercely yet softly grasped at their own wrists to make their biceps bulge, their breasts stand out, and their abdominal muscles turn into high-lighted knots of strength.

To Rollie, these photographs of living bodies were the classics. He longed for such splendor for himself.

He cut out the pictures and tipped them onto cardboards out of his laundered shirts, and tacked them to the wall until he had a gallery. Some of the figures, which looked as if they had been oiled before displaying themselves almost amorously before the lens of the photographer, wore loincloths of leopardskin, and stirred the darkest and most empowering of atavisms in Rollie as he looked at them. That was what it was to be strong! To do battle with a jungle cat and win his pelt for your own clothing! Or, barring that, to have the privilege of ordering a pair of such leopardskin trunks from the Hercules Physical Culture Studio, along with a set of bar bells, which could be paid for at the rate of a dollar-fifty-five a month until the bargain price was fulfilled.

He promised himself that someday he would have a pair of leopardskin trunks, even if he had to wear them in his bedroom, where nobody could see him.

So he contented himself with worrying about living cleanly, and taking wholesome exercise, and saving his God-given body for the girl who was waiting for him, sometime, somewhere; and doing all he could to improve it, like this fellow in the last issue of *Body Harmony,* on page 43—a picture decidedly worth cutting out and putting up:

> Herman Otto Janowski, 433 Pearl Street, Buffalo, N. Y., age twenty-two, who spends his spare time from his job as a linotype operator on the Buffalo *Volksfreund,* developing his superb physique, by doing bar bell work in the family backyard (Herman is unmarried—look out girls!) and meeting his friends three evenings a week for contests of strength in a neighborhood gymnasium. A fine example for those who believe their case is hopeless: just turn the page and see a month-by-month record of "Ski's" (as his friends call him) body development.

IV

A few days later, Donald Rush received a letter from Wayne Shoemaker. It occupied three pages with a suggested synopsis for the novel to be written about Monsieur le Vicomte, which Don could use or not, as he chose. There were two postscripts. The first one said,

P.S. This country would get on your nerves. It is too hot, too crowded, too wet and nobody does anything. What I really liked was the great city of Chicago, with its handsome hotels and museums and perfectly groomed men and expensively garbed women. I'll tell you all about it.

The second one:

P.S. 2. My sister Martha ran off and got married to Dennison Yeager, a guy she met here, yesterday. (Married yesterday, not *met*. She's been sweet on him all summer.) Everybody said it was love at first sight but I do not believe in the being of any such thing. If you ask me I think she did it out of spite for Mrs. Yeager who did not favor the match but Mr. Yeager was all for it. Mother don't know whether to laugh or cry. They drove to Ann Arbor another town near here and got married there. The next thing anybody knew was a telegram from Toledo, Ohio. Boy oh boy. Quick work.

In the evening paper the same day, the town of Albuquerque read of the elopement. Many who read the account thought it sounded rather like Willa herself, and concluded that she had mailed it to the paper direct.

Friends of Mrs. Frederick Shoemaker who has lived in this city for some years will learn with pleasure of the marriage in Ann Arbor, Michigan, at the rectory of St. Rose of Hungary's Church, on August 3, of her daughter Martha Elizabeth, to Mr. Dennison Yeager, of Albion, Michigan. Mrs. Shoemaker was an Albion girl, and the Yeager family are old friends. The honeymoon couple are motoring to Eastern points, including Niagara Falls, and Atlantic City, and will return to make their home in Albion. Mrs. Shoemaker and her son Wayne, after completing their visit with friends in Albion, will return to the city late this month, where she is connected with the Fred Harvey system. Many affairs are being given for Mrs. Shoemaker by old friends in her girlhood home city.

It was this paragraph which told Bun the news. He found the evening paper lying on the cash register counter, folded open at the society page, with a ring of red pencil marking the item, and a large red question mark carefully written beside it. It was Rollie Glover's way of being in on something. Bun picked it up and read it during a lull of business in the store. He did not know he was being watched by Rollie, from behind a castle of Listerine bottles on the opposite counter. But he instinctively concealed his feelings, and folded the paper back together, and put it back on the counter and went off up the aisle whistling gently.

But his mouth was dry, and he wanted to go somewhere but he did not know anywhere in the whole city where he could be alone enough with his news. He stood in the doorway on Fourth Street, looking out at the hot summer evening as it settled like a fine cloud over the people, the store windows, the streets. Something like that settling happened over his spirit, and he did not think it could ever lift.

—Then even while she wrote to him that way, she no longer belonged to him? Still rehearsing the gestures of the love she had declared with him, there was another love alive within her, and gathering force that would at last prevail? Then she had just *practiced* on him, as it were? What about my own poor excellence: this very quality that *I am,* and which I wanted to give to her? What about that? Did it mean so little after all? Was it altogether a lie when I held her little face in my big hands and looked deeply into it? Is anything in the world as empty as my two hands now?

—And why couldn't she've told me herself, if this was the way it was going to have to be!

I'll never understand it.

The phone rang in the store. He ignored it because Rollie could answer it. But it rang and rang, and at last he had to go and answer it. He wrote down the order that came over the wire, politely thanked the customer, and hung up, bitter at the way things went on, even at a time like this. His own voice rang in his ears with saddening normality. And then he knew a wave of comfort in the distinction, the aristocracy of a grief that should be utterly private. It should be revealed to no one. If it was supposed to be a blow to his pride, as well as to his love, then let them see how many of them could make anything out of his reaction!

Rollie came back from delivering a package across the street. He had a pale and careful smile on his face, and he came up to Bun, and said,

"Sorry, Richmond, I really am."

"What about?"

"You don't have to be conventional with me.—I've seen the paper. I know what this will mean to you."

"I don't know what you're talking about."

"—I don't mean to intrude. But I have *known,* for weeks."

"Known? What?"

Rollie smiled patiently and lowered his eyes and a veil of *great understanding* went over his expression.

"Honestly, Richmond, you'd feel better if you'd just talk with someone—anyone, even *me*. You're going to be all right. It's just hard to realize it *right now*."

"Why, I *am* all right."

Rollie closed his eyes delicately and said,

"Oh no, you're not.—She was everything to you, wasn't she?"

Bun put his hands in his pants pockets and tightened his fists there. "Oh, now I think I see," he said. "You mean the Shoemaker gal? —Who just got married?—Why, just because I had a few dates with her, you thought—?"

Rollie sighed, and made a face of patient compassion, full of allowances for *how people felt at such moments.*

"Nuts," said Bun, and grinned at him, and frowned too, and was rewarded by a flick of doubt on Rollie's cream-colored face. "And I see now," he added, "who put a red ring and a question mark around the article in the paper! Well I'll be— —Just a pal, aren't you, if that's what you thought, all along. Come here."

Bun took Rollie by the arm, and held him while he hooked Rollie's necktie with a finger and yanked it out over his tan starched linen jacket. He pulled the points of his neat collar up and left them sticking out. Lastly he brushed Rollie's shining, particular hair forward over his face. Then he patted him loftily on the head, and gave him a little push, having momentarily wrecked the most valuable thing in life to Rollie, which was neatness.

v

But if he won this petty skirmish, he still had the load of a defeat deep in his heart, and it stayed there for days, and actually got worse when he received a little package postmarked Atlantic City. It was a cardboard box, containing his grandfather's braided gold ring, and the same snapshot over which, he thought, so much war and love had been waged in their intimate terms. There was a little note scribbled and folded down into the box with these objects, but it told only one thing which they did not silently make plain.

Dearest Bun, by now you must have heard, and all I can do is send these back, and hope with all my heart that you will continue to be my freind. I can never in the world explain what happened to me but all I can say is that it happened like lightning. I want you to know Dennison some day. You two would like each other. *I am so happy* and 1 hope you wish me well and can forgive me and count me always a devoted freind. I respect you more than ever now that things have turned out the way they have. If you ever come East, please know that we want our home to be yours.—Martha Yeager. (Mrs. Dennison)

He had the afternoon off, and he went strolling to the river. Maybe a swim would make him feel a little livelier. When he got there, through the sandy shore full of willows, he saw the river bed, so wide, so shallow, perfectly dry. The sun beat upon the dry sand and the pale cracked shells of mud, which blazed back at the sky. In August it was time for rains, but so far there were no signs of any, except the grand façades of cloud that hung in gold shadow on the remote horizon.

But he was alone, and that was a mercy, and he could still dimly obey a desire to tell his trouble to the river, if not in her waters, then on her great dry channel. He walked out on the sands into the light, and trudged among his sand-heavy thoughts down the river. When he got as far as he felt like going, he could double back to the river road, and pick up a ride with someone who was headed toward town.

The one thing that stuck in his craw the more he thought about it was the way she took the first opportunity that presented itself to sign her married name at him.

Book V · THE TRIBUTARIES

XXXVIII · DR. M^CGINNIS

I

In the main hall of Saint Joseph's hospital, Bun Summerfield waited alone. He was thinking of running away. It was shortly after two o'clock in the afternoon. The outdoor heat was muffled in this shining, dark corridor to an atmosphere in which clock-tick, the smell of polished woodwork, and a soft gasping sound far away that was made by a window curtain moving, got mixed up together. But before he could obey his racing heart, and turn and run down the steps to the street, one of the nuns appeared from a distant door and came toward him. Her glasses winked at him with unexpected hilarity, and when she stood before him, he saw that she was a little old woman quite capable of gaiety.

"Are you vaiting?" she asked.

"Where is Doctor Rush?"

"Ach, ja. He has gone upstairs to the o-*per*-ating room."

He licked his lips dryly.

"Where is that?"

"The elevator vill take you to the fourt' floor. And ven is the fourt' floor, turn to the left and go all the vay. You vill see."

"Thank you, Sister."

She was like a closed door behind him. He went to the elevator, got in, and pressed the button marked "4," and was conducted laboriously and slowly upward. He watched the bricks of the elevator shaft pass downward. He wondered if he was about to faint. He put out his hands and looked at them. They were not trembling. This did not reassure him. Perhaps he could tell Doctor Rush he had an errand to do for the store, but would be glad to see an operation some other time. The elevator stopped. He hesitated a moment, and then in rage at his panic, he hauled the heavy door aside and stepped out on the fourth floor. Far down the hall to his left he saw a partition of frosted glass, lighted goldenly from the other side. He saw two nurses pass across the hall from opposite doors, hurrying. He walked toward the end of the hall, and a sound in his own ears began to turn real and he heard steam hissing somewhere. There at last was an open door. He turned to it.

Doctor Rush was in the room, bare to his waist, scrubbing his hands and arms in a stream of running water over a deep stone basin.

"Hi, Bunny, I began to give you up. You'll have to hurry."

The Doctor saw an old image of fright in the boy's face, but he admired also the attempts at concealment which he saw there too. He believed it would be easier for Bun if he gave him little chance to say anything.

"Take off your shirt and use some of that soap. You have to scrub yourself raw.—Go ahead. Now. They've brought the patient up. I'm going to introduce you as a visiting doctor when we get you all hooded up and masked so your own mother wouldn't know you. I've had the orderly lay out a gown for you, gloves, everything. You might as well play the part right.—Scrub hard. You know why we do this, of course?"

Bun nodded.

His cheeks were dark red.

"It is a simple case of appendicitis, and I don't look for any trouble. We ought to be in there about twenty minutes."

The door to the operating room was behind them. Bun looked around. He could see vague golden shadows passing on golden frosted glass. The steam kept hissing somewhere.

"I was pretty excited my first time," said the Doctor, watching the boy. "Everybody always expects to faint, but hardly anybody ever does. You probably have thought of it. Well, you won't. As long as you're thinking *of* it, you can think *against* it. Keep your knees loose. —How old are you?"

"Nearly eighteen."

"I'd call you older, from your build. You look ready for medical college right now. Or, at least, you look more like twenty. How old do you *feel?*"

"I feel about nine and a half, right now."

"Nervous?"

"Yes."

"Stage fright is useful. I imagine a race horse always has stage fright. I bet a steam roller never does."

Bun laughed exaggeratedly, but he felt better.

He straightened up and faced the Doctor.

Peter saw his pulse beating below his breastbone; how powerful, how even, how rapid, how scared.

"Now we're reasonably free from infection. Put on your gown, there."

They got into their unpressed muslin operating dresses, tied the strings at the back of neck and waist, capped themselves and tied the gauze masks across their faces.

"You look like the Dean of the Medical Faculty himself," said Peter. "Let's go."

He walked to the swinging door of the operating room, and turned and kicked it open with his heel, and ducked through without touching it otherwise. When it swung this way, Bun caught it with his elbow and went through himself, into a new climate that smote him and choked him. The room blazed with white light, and yet it seemed misty with steam. He smelled the steam through his cloth mask, and it turned his stomach over. On the air was a heavy cloud of ether. He was not prepared for what he saw. The patient was already on the operating table. Nurses stood beside it. The anesthetist at the end of the table was dripping ether on to a cloth cone over the patient's face. The steam hissed loudly in here. He saw the nickel sterilizers in triple cylinders and the little flags of steam escaping from their cocks.

"Now, Doctor," said Peter Rush, turning to him. "Sister, this is my old friend Doctor McGinnis, from Detroit, just dropped by to see me, brought him along. Doctor, this is Sister Mary St. Francis, our head operating nurse.—How is everything?"

"Oh, yes, Doctor, splendid."

"Good.—Doctor McGinnis, will you just sit there, on that stool at the foot of the table? I believe you can get a good view there."

The steam and the ether and the sound of the steam were smothering him. He saw a nurse offer him a pair of rubber gloves on a towel, and he took them and turned away to put them on. He squeezed his eyes shut and bit his tongue. He was ready to die of sickness at his stomach, he thought. Then he heard somebody starting to whistle a tune, and he turned around, distracted and startled by such an odd thing at a time like this. It was Doctor Rush who came over to him as if to share a private joke. He leaned near and whispered,

"Don't you let me down, now, they all think you're Somebody.

—So do I. Don't try to hold your breath. Now go sit down. You'll be fascinated in about two minutes.—And that's what I *mean*, Doctor," he finished in a jovial tone which everybody could hear.

Whistling again, the waltz from *The Merry Widow*, Doctor Rush took his station.

The anesthetist nodded.

There was a brief pause.

The steam seemed the only thing alive in the room.

"Um-h'm, Sister," said the Doctor, and the cloths were laid back, the patient's belly was exposed, now rapidly with never a second's space between one action and the next, the operating nurse swabbed the skin with iodine, and the fiery yellow stain spread so fast and so widely that no resemblance to flesh remained.

From his station at the foot of the table, Bun saw the skin tightened by rubber-gloved fingers that spread it smooth, and the knife in the other hand tossed once to feel the weight, the balance, and then the fingers taking a delicate grip of it, brought the blade down, and he wanted to look away, then, for this was the moment that he had thought to run away from downstairs in the hall, and the course from which there was only one direction to take, and that was ahead:

The Doctor turned his head slightly and looked at Bun. Bun caught the look. Something happened behind the Doctor's mask: an expression: it spoke clearly through his eyes, the little flickers of meaning which pass a disguise: they said, Hold on, now.

And so Bun did not look away, and the knife went, and went, and went, in short steps, and the incision was done.

He sat back a little, and then leaned forward again.

He forgot himself.

II

The sponges went in, and the lips of the layered incision were held back by the weighted nickel retractors. He saw veins and cords of white and of scarlet and faintly of blue. The hands kept weaving the fabric of the routine over and within the wound. The waltz from *The Merry Widow* kept up, with a perfectly even rhythm; it was even more serene than the cheerful melody of the steam in the white-tiled corner.

There was no tenseness among any of the workers at the table. They understood each other perfectly. Every gesture was answered with another. There was no drama visible.

The patient gasped softly.

The anesthetist leaned over and lifted an eyelid. Satisfied, he resumed the dripping of the ether, but with drops more widely spaced than before.

"Yes, Doctor, there it is," said Sister Mary St. Francis with almost a tender sense of congratulation. The appendix had been found, and the Doctor was now tying it off. His fingers were like a shuttle, not moving very fast, but with an evenness of pace that seemed the height of technical accomplishment.

The Sister handed over the forceps. The appendix was cut, and dropped into a standing basin. It stained the solution there pink. A few drops of blood appeared and were blotted with a patch of gauze.

For the first time Bun wondered if this were a man or a woman on the table. He knew they were nearly done. He wanted to speak but he couldn't think of how to say what he felt. He was filled with worship for the surgeon. He knew he had no way to mention it.

The basins were floating the cloth sponges now. The whole operation assumed a bloody aspect as the doctor made the retreat from the focal point. The steam hissed louder and the room turned hotter and the boy wished suddenly that it was not nearly finished. He was flushed, and in his belly was a burden of such deep joy, such a grasp of his bowels by the most hungry fulfillment, as he had not felt since he was a small child, lost among his toys on the floor of his room at home and surrounded by protection on all sides.

But the sutures were being made, and the retractors lifted away, and the ether cone was off the face at the other end of the table.

It was a woman; her face was white and her hair was bound within a muslin cap. Her eyes were caved with blue shadows, and her mouth was partly open, hungry for plain air. Her cheeks in their drugged relaxation sagged softly back toward her ears, and drew the expression of her face wide and helpless.

Now the surgical machine was humanly separated again, and at the sight of the woman's face, Bun came back to why this unearthly efficiency had been developed, and he believed that if he had seen her first, he could never have watched the operation upon her.

How can he do it, he wondered, watching the Doctor, and then he thought, Yes, but that's what you have to do, and now that it was over, he began to tremble. Nobody could see that he was trembling, it was inside him, along his bones, overwhelming him with significance now that all danger was past.

"There!" cried Peter, stepping back and hauling off his gloves which he dropped on the floor. He raised his arms and stretched, and yawned deeply behind his mask, and they all laughed when he did, and saw the yawny tears gather in his eyes which they could see, and they were relieved of the burdens they had carried so accustomedly.

"Come along Doctor," he added, and turned Bun with his hand and led him with his arm back to the dressing room, leaving the nurses to remove the patient and clean up the room.

When they were alone again, he said,

"Good boy! I was very proud of you. You gave me a rough moment there, you looked sort of green, just once, but I knew you'd make it.—How are you?"

"Fine," said Bun, but his teeth chattered a little.

"H'ho! You worked so hard you've got a tiny bit of shock! Never mind. Next time that won't happen.—Did it interest you?"

Peter realized that his friend couldn't say very fully what he wanted to say, and so he offered him a cigarette. They both lighted up, and with the cigarettes in their mouths so they squinted out the smoke, they scrubbed their hands again, and made another date for a gall bladder operation two days later.

In a moment Peter was dressed and off downstairs to see the patient. Bun wondered if his interior trembling would stop soon. He stepped into the corridor and walked toward the elevator. He pressed the button and brought it up to the fourth floor. When it arrived, a nun in white uniform came out. It was Sister Mary St. Francis. He stepped aside for her.

"Oh, how do you do, *Doctor McGinnis*," she said, ironically lowering her eyes as she passed him, and for a moment he was dazzled by the possibility that he really *looked:*—and then he flushed at her comedy, and rode downstairs.

But he refused to let himself feel foolish. He knew he had found where he belonged.

III

He was supposed to work in the store the rest of the afternoon. It was hard for him to go back there right away, he wanted to go somewhere, maybe down to the river, and be alone and savor what he knew. But without saying why he had to be away for an hour or so he had promised Rollie Glovers that he would return as soon as he could. He wondered if Rollie would notice anything. The trembling kept up, remotely. Perhaps it was not so much that he was trembling, actually, as that he felt a little weak when he stopped moving.

The drugstore was crowded when he got back. He had a glance of righteous reproach from Rollie who was gliding swiftly back of the

counter to the prescription door. Rollie, like many pale, efficient people had the unearthly talent of making others feel gross and guilty.
Bun hurried to the back room to put on his starched linen jacket with
"Summerfield's" written over the pocket in green thread. Rollie was
there explaining his order to the prescription clerk, and with no
greeting, said to Bun,

"Large woman in straw hat by the cosmetics, first, and next, the
young gentleman by the phone booth, we've had the rush of our
lives."

"O.K.," said Bun, "I'm sorry. Is Dad here?"

"He went out half an hour ago. He asked where you were."

"*Oh*-oh," said Bun, meaning *Now I'm in for it,* and went out to
wait on the customers.

He did his duty until half-past five, which was half an hour longer
than he was supposed to work, since he was on again from eight
o'clock until closing time today. Rollie noticed how he stayed over,
and coming as close to an apology as anyone of his temperament
could, he laid his hand on Bun and said,

"We would surely have been up the creek if you hadn't stayed a
little extra, this evening."

"I'll be back a little before eight."

"Don't hurry. We can manage."

"I don't want for you have to *manage*," said Bun, in revolt against
the world of half-meanings and unspoken reproaches.

He needed more than ever to be alone, and it was getting toward
twilight, the high yellow light of the sky would soon be a pale china
gray, and then evening would sift in a vast draw of powdery darkness
across from the mountains, over the mesa, down the lowlands of the
town, across the river, and finally to the western profile of the last-lit
sandhills beyond.

IV

Suddenly he turned toward Borelli's.

He wanted a glass of beer.

He wanted to feel his body kindle as his spirits were kindled.

He walked out along Fourth Street, swinging energetically, because
that way he did not notice the excited weakness of his limbs. As he
walked, his thirst grew positive. He tantalized himself with how good
the cold beer would taste, stinging his mouth with its golden shafts.
A week ago, it would have been almost an adventure for him to go
to Borelli's and hang around outside for a few moments, debating

about going in or not, and wondering if there'd be any trouble about a high school senior getting an illegal drink of beer. It would have been something to tell about the next day when he saw any of the fellows.

But tonight this seemed a regular course to take. He felt years older. The Doctor himself said he looked twenty. Do you grow up in jumps, like this? he wondered.

He walked right in the door, and sat down at one of the round black tables, and waited. He heard a door open in the far side of the second room. Borelli himself came through.

"Hello, Mr. Borelli. I'd like a glass of beer, please."

Borelli gazed at him quietly.

He expected a boy's confusion after such a bland announcement, during Prohibition, and under age at that. But there was none. Bun simply smiled at him with a blue-eyed eagerness.

Borelli shrugged his shoulders at himself, and said,

"Why not?"

In a moment he was back with a tremendous mug crowned with live foam. As he set it down, he said, with the accents of one who is still no fool,

"Thirty cents, that'll be thirty cents."

"What're you doing," said Bun, fishing in his pockets for the money, "building yourself a poorhouse with hot and cold running water?"

He tossed the money out for Borelli, who took it away with him, lamenting what a man would swallow for a few cents. The only thing in life that wasn't disappointing was the money he had in the bank, which would never lie to him, or cheat him, or speak so sassy to him, or run off to El Paso without a word like that girl last week, or make him feel guilty about anything, when he was trying to go to sleep. All he had to do to sleep like a brown baby was to think of the money in the bank, and his eyes would water without yawning, and his huge belly would rest like a fine melon on the mattress as if warmed and ripened by the sun.

The place was empty.

Bun took a drink.

It stung him exactly as he had expected, and tears came to his eyes at the tingle of his taste. He was suddenly and deeply at ease. He leaned back, spread his long legs out in front of him, and felt strength return. He drank about half the glass of beer, and the mild stimulus of it cured him of what had actually been a slight case of shock. He came back to himself, and felt like a full man. The marvel of what he had witnessed and survived in the operating room was something he wanted to consider, almost without thinking about it. Tomorrow, or sometime, he would tell somebody about it. If Martha were here tonight, he could have told her. He swallowed at the thought of her.

The room was important to him. In this room he celebrated his coming of age. The stained apricot-colored plaster of the walls, the ancient calendars, several of them with diamond dust flittered over their embossed welts, the naked electric globe, the bare boards of the floor, the warm evening outdoors over the river and the sound of traffic on the bridge out of sight; yes, his town was wonderful.

But (as in a parable of how briefly all things endure), Nick Borelli came in from the back room, smiling with secret purpose in his thick lips drawn down. He came around to Bun, following the outer tables, as if he approached with flattering fearfulness.

"Hi Bunny," he said.

"Hi, Nick."

"Glassa beer, eh?"

"Ye'."

"Purr' good beer."

"O.K."

"Like beer?"

"Sure."

"Atsa boy."

God, why can't I be *alone,* thought Bun. Why did he have to come in here fat/smooth/oily/mean.

Nick came and stood before him, seeking him with that same thick smile, and moving his hands in his pants pockets.

"Want some'n else?" asked Nick, finally, making a hint of a sideshow hoochie-coochie movement with his thick, graceful legs and fat belly.

Bun frowned.

"Whatdya mean: I don't want anything."

Nick closed his eyes and rolled his eyeballs behind his lids, and smoothed his own belly with his short hands that were impersonating snakes' heads.

Bun turned hot, and stood up.

"Come on, I show you," said Nick, looking again. "Over 't the other house. Hot mamas just waitin' for *you.*"

Bun choked on the smoke of an invisible fire. He braced himself on his sprung legs and hit Nick in the belly with his fist. Nick melted with comic swiftness. His face turned gray and he dropped to the floor, rueful and bewildered. He was like a child whose make-believe has turned pitiful and real. He was not angry; simply betrayed. He sobbed a couple of times and sat there. Bun strode out the door and walked back toward town.

It was much darker out.

The street lights going up to the mesa were coming to power against the dusk.

Why did I do that, Bun wondered.

He knew why, vaguely. Bun didn't consider himself a prig. But he had learned that afternoon a hard and triumphant lesson in what a man could do and he was dazzled by the things that lay waiting for him. It was the very glow in his face as he thought of these things that had attracted Nick to him first of all.

Walking up the long slope to the Highlands, Bun was sorry for what he had done to Nick. He remembered Nick's sleepy, confident face, and now it did not seem monstrous to him; only, before the astonishment of pain had flabbed down over it, full of some want.

It was a human claim, such as Bun was learning in all its forms. Some of them, like Nick's, were puzzling, and, unanswered, could only produce rage.

He reached the public library, and went in. He was full of splendid intimation. He recalled Martha almost sternly. Here he had met her almost for the first time. They had sat at the battered oaken tables and through each other discovered how people really were. Their minds had joined in thought and taken flight together. Imagine, he thought, how powerful their union was when it could actually produce a thirst for knowledge and a sense of pity! He was full of sharp longing for her when he looked around the reading room, with its silent readers bending over their books under the hanging green lamp shades. What clever things she had said to him here, and how grandly his mind had worked in response to her stimulus. Had anybody ever fallen in love before in a library? This large, brown, battered room, which had once been a schoolroom when the eighth-grade pupils had used the building? Never mind, it was almost like a temple to him. Too restless remembering her here with him, he could not sit down anywhere. He felt dammed up, ready to pour out his beliefs, his knowledges, his loves. He drifted to the bookstacks which were wooden ranges with long tunnels of black shadow between them. The librarian at the desk told him politely to turn on any lights he might need, and he nodded abruptly at her, remembering that she was Martha's friend, and afraid that she might ask him about her. He went down the aisle as far as he could get from the desk and the readers in the room, and pulled the string turning on an overhead light with a green glass shade.

He looked along at the book titles.

They were scientific books.

It was an astonishing coincidence.

Here was a book on physiology, and here was a large stout worn volume with a binding of rubbed calf and an old morocco label dyed red, with gold stamping that was still rich and clear. It said *Anatomy of the Human Body, by Gray.* He took it down. The binding was like an old door whose hinges were loose. He opened it and seemed to walk in.

In the brittle flyleaves there was much writing in rapid, sloping letters that had turned a faded brown. He looked for a name. On the title page he found it: "Edward W. Drew, M. D., Albuquerque, New Mexico, 1889." Why, he remembered old Doctor Drew. He was dead now. A funny old man, always driving a disgraceful ruin of a car with a canvas top and leather straps holding the top to the front mudguards. He was regarded as an "eccentric." In the growing town he had gradually been forgotten, until his practice consisted of fifty-cent consultations for poor Mexicans and desperate tuberculars living on the edges of town and of hope.

Bun turned the leaves.

His heart began to pound, though he didn't notice it, as such; he simply felt excited, and he knew why. Here was the science of the actuality of the afternoon. He leaned against the bookstack and turned page after page, staring at the engraved diagrams of *Gray's Anatomy.* His face turned dark red. His head swam. A lump came into his throat at the desire the pages aroused in him. He could hardly wait to *have* them, to know all that they held. The light from the overhead lamp poured hot and yellow down on him, his hair shone with light as he turned his head, his brows cast depthless shadows down his burning cheeks, he was carved out of the darkness by the empowering light over and within him, in the aisle of the old converted brick schoolhouse that served the town as library.

He was in a fury of creation, for he was inventing the future, with vows of himself, and it was a pledge of greatness which consumed him entirely, heart and all; he had forgotten Martha, for his true love now lay quietly before him in the scratched-up pages of old Doctor Drew's copy of *Gray's Anatomy.*

V

It seemed a long time afterward when he remembered that he had to return to work at eight o'clock. He took the book to the desk and checked it out, impassively discouraging conversation with the librarian, who could not possibly understand what it held within its rubbed leather boards. Old Doctor Drew! How wrong everybody had been. He really hadn't been a walking cartoon at all, a sort of comic spider who crawled along the streets in his rickety old car. Bun walked downhill fast, apologizing in his thoughts to the long-dead owner of the old book.

He would be a few minutes late again, but if Rollie so much as looked anything about it, he would be forgiven tonight.

There ahead of him on the corner was the drugstore.

Hurrying toward it, he was smitten with a sense of recognition which made him smile and lift his brows. All his life he had been looking at "Summerfield's" and it was now as if he were seeing it for the first time. The sight had a dazzling trueness about it which seemed beautiful to him. In the darkness, the drugstore flashed and shone with lights of many colors. The long sign over the door spelled out the name in electric lights, and glimmered within a border of running green and yellow globes. The immense windows were like caverns exposing heaps of treasure. Huge jewels hung inside the panes, globes of peacock blue, and emerald green, and diamond yellow, and ruby red, the apothecary's signs. A high street lamp on the corner threw a general glow over the white brick of the store front. Over the front door a silver-bladed fan made the light spin in midair. Beyond the windows in the lighted depths of the store he could see the rows and rows of merchandise, the glass plates of the show cases, the counters full of shining boxes, displays with miniature electric signs, a profusion of fresh and gleaming wares that sparkled with vitality and excellence. From a distance, the magazine rack inside the front door was like an oriental rug. He loved the slick ink and the varnished colors of the covers. Behind the soda fountain, these profusions and these lamps were doubled and redoubled in the immense mirror which he had polished so many times after school, earning his allowance, and as Mr. Summerfield said so often, learning the value of a dollar. And far in the great mirror were depths of gleaming darkness, the image of the night outside, from which he was returning in such energy and prosaic splendor.

XXXIX · THE TRIBUTARY

I

It was now full summer. The days were laden with the teeming scent of the cottonwood trees, whose shade made great pools of coolness, the only refuge from the heat. The nights lately were breathless. Everyone spoke of it. They said the one thing they always had been able to say up to now was that no matter how hot it got during the day, the nights were always cool. Vast panes of glassy air waved over the mesa and obscured the mountains. The river was bone-dry, and its sandy bed was the color of bone in the light. The trouble was, it didn't rain. Fields dried up, and the leaves hung down on the trees, and tempers grew short, and hardly a cloud came up over the mountains. At evening, the streets of town and the roads in the country were fuller than ever of cars whose owners were out after a breath of air. Yet as always, when people felt the same way about a thing, in this case the hot weather, it was like a revelation of the town's character; and people found their fellows to be patient and resourceful, keeping humor alive in trying moments. They all knew it was only a matter of waiting long enough. The cloud would come.

One afternoon it began to form.

They could all feel the light change, no matter where they were, indoors or out. In the north, a black and blue sky began to gather. The dusty green of the trees suddenly looked like bright new paint, in the false twilight of the distant storm which made an immense shadow all the way from the mountains at Santa Fe down the river to Albuquerque, and below. People came into the streets and looked to the north. The dark banks seemed to keep their distance, like armies massing before a battle. The air was still, and still hot. The storm seemed to be holding its breath, way off in the darkened north; and so did the people; as if the release of the one would effect that of the other.

II

Peter came home a little past five in the car, and picked up Noonie and Donald to go for a ride.

"There is a perfect beaut of a storm coming up. I thought we'd all ride out the river road and see what we could see."

They got in with him in his great, open Packard, and he headed them out along the Rio Grande road where they were in the greenest of valleys. They could see the river bed, pale and dry beyond the ranks of trees at the bank. They passed houses of adobe whose walls looked almost violet under this slate-blue darkness. The sun was hidden. The warm air blew into their faces. The town lay to their right. As they drove, Don watched the silver water tank and the tall black stacks of the sawmill changing against the face of the mountains way back on the mesa. He saw a white blow of steam rising from the roof of the laundry against the day-black sky. It made him think of the inky satins and white ruffles in a picture by Anthony Van Dyck which he had looked at many times at home, in one of the books of culture kept behind the pongee silk curtains of the parlor bookcases.

"It is evidently not coming any nearer," said Peter.

"Peter," said Noonie, turning half toward him and putting both her hands on his sleeve.

He looked down, delighted by the impulsive and tender gesture. "*Yes,* Noon:"

But she looked at him with her mouth a little bit open, and shook her head. She looked back at Donald in the tonneau, a swift glance of reference, which her husband understood from long family habit of silent meanings before the child.

"Not now?" he said.

She nodded.

"I'll remind you," he promised.

It was a very little thing, this instance of a league of intimacy, even against his son, but it warmed his heart. He never let her know when he was observing her, but he saw with stubborn faith the slowly unveiling marks, week by week, of her returning self.

They were now in the land of ditches that were made for irrigation; but the ditches were empty, like abandoned roads on a half-scale map of an old battle, and the dried fields had the complexion of ruin over them. The big car rocked on the dried ruts of the road. He delighted in following every lane, every scratch that led to the remotest house. Everywhere was the hush before the storm. They saw Mexicans in doorways, watching the black north, and in their faces hope was again allied with patience.

At last a lane took the car where it could no longer go.

Noonie glanced at Don, and with a meaning which the father understood, she said to the boy,

"Darling, don't you want to get out and play around a few minutes?"

Donald assumed the look which always made her think of Wayne Shoemaker. It was the way the two of them looked when they were planning something together; an impersonal, unreachable look. She always felt "nervous" at it.

"I think not, thank you," he said, understanding clearly that a move had been made to get him out of the way for some exchange from which he was to be excluded.

She made a fleeting little shadowed smile at Peter, and it was like a sigh of resignation.

"Let's go back," she said.

He started the motor and began to back the big land-boat around. And then a marvel occurred.

III

The sun came down below a hanging curtain of black cloud across the river, and shone with almost a wet gold light against the western face of everything in the valley. The trees and the houses were gilded in fire. Way to the north, where the sky had been blackening in tremendous shadow ever since midafternoon, the lowering sun now struck upon the bodies of the thunderheads and gave them glorious form out of the general dark. They climbed and bellied and towered, the fiery light, that would last so briefly, describing their cheeks and cheeks of curve and curve. It was appalling and wonderful. It was the golden promise made plain by the vanishing sun. Everyone who saw it could only stare at the magnificence of the apparition, and believe that no night could erase the memory, as well as the sight, of it.

They turned around and headed back to town as the sun went down behind the sandhills over the river. Darkness came like a hood after it. The lights of town were comforting as they came closer.

In the streets, between people, in the air, hung the suspense of weeks.

As the Rushes came into their house, the phone was ringing, and Peter hurried to answer it. It was a call. He had to go right on to the hospital. He kissed Noonie and said not to hold up dinner. It might take him half the night; an old man's case that had turned the way he had fought off, and yet expected. She clung to him a moment and shook his shoulders as if to say, Oh, why, why, why. And then let him go.

As soon as he was gone, she was ashamed of herself. Why do I always show him my worst self, she wondered, and then a wave of warmth swept over her, at what she believed for the future now, and she turned to find Donald. He was in the front room, reading with his book laid on the piano keys, and his elbows comfortably propped on the mahogany edge of the keyboard. She bent down and kissed him on the cheek, and left him forthwith. He watched her out of the room, astonished and charmed by something in her appearance. She looked so lighthearted, a new way for her to look. She was as pretty as he had always *wished* her to be. Knocking his book aside in a confusion of energy and sweetness, he ran after her and caught her, and hugged her, blushing furiously.

"Why Donnie!"—but she wisely said no more, and when he was ready let him go back to his book, after this burst of feeling, lately so unfamiliar.

As the Doctor had advised they did not hold up dinner. But the boy and his mother had it together almost as if it were a party. They didn't say very much to each other, but they behaved "something extra," as Donald said to himself. He was extremely courtly, he felt, and she was a dazzling beauty, quite like a lady in a book, and he was delighted to see that she had put on all her rings for him.

"Mother, isn't it almost too hot for all your diamonds?" he asked, meaning to be clever and very funny.

She waved them in the air with a theatrical gesture.

"My dear Lord Rendall," she replied, "I never notice them, I am so used to being crushed with jewels."

It was proper to the game that he should nearly die laughing at the very thing they were both pretending.

After dinner they decided to do their work together. She had her sewing box; he, his pad and pencil, and his water-color box too.

All evening she watched him on the floor, seeing the gray line of his writing on the pearl-gray paper with the blue lines on it as it spun some fantastic small life out of his imagination. He was at work on his novel, and though he did not speak of that, he did show her the drawing he made of Monsieur le Vicomte, when he had it done. A smiling and elegant creature, with mustaches and pointed goatee, a top hat, an "opera cloak" thrown back over one shoulder, and a slim long pistol held in one gloved hand. She admired it, wondering privately where on earth he had picked up whatever allusions to style there were in the picture—the hat, the cloak, the whiskers. But she had not gone to see the film of *Arsène Lupin* when it had been shown two years before at the old Crystal Theatre. Monsieur le Vicomte was a stylized transcription of a character in the movie.

The evening was deep and hot.

Where was the cloud?

Once or twice she went to the window and looked at the sky, but could see only darkness. No leaf flickered in any air. She put her fingers to her temples, and wondered why she didn't have one of her headaches. Her hair was damp upon her brow. She remarked aloud that she must look frightful. Donald replied that on the contrary, she looked prettier than he ever saw her. It was true. How ridiculous, she thought, but her heart made a beat that she felt in pleasure and gratitude.

Oh, yes, thanks, thanks, it said, not for her little boy's loyal compliment, but for everything large that it stood for.

It was too soon time for him to go to bed. For the first time in years, he let her come up with him, and when he was in bed, he wheedled permission to read for ten more minutes. She handed him the books he wanted; he asked for five, and made a bulwark of them alongside his covered legs. Five books! she scoffed, how could he read them all. He answered that he couldn't, but while holding one, he liked to know that the others were by him. She saw that they were, for him, alive. She left him to himself. She meant to go downstairs again and wait up until her husband came home; but suddenly she was overwhelmed with sleepiness, and she stood a second in the upstairs hall, listening for Cora and Leonard; but they must have gone, everything was quiet in the back part of the house. It was as quiet outdoors too, the darkness was a vast box in which nothing was happening under the heat. If nothing happened soon, she felt, she would almost have to clap her hands to make an event.

No, she could not stay up any longer. She went to the big front bedroom. The windows were open, but the filmy curtains hung listless. She didn't even turn on a light, but went to bed as quickly as she could, and with the feelings and comedies of Donald's evening still fresh in her like comfort itself, she fell asleep.

She was still sleeping when Peter came home, late and exhausted. He had worked for hours at the hospital. The old man was still living, but God only knew which way things would turn by morning. He had done everything possible. He kept very quiet when he found Noonie asleep, and got to bed without disturbing her.

IV

He must just have fallen asleep himself when the crash came. The box of air over the town was shattered by lightning and thunder. It was a clap of thunder that must have taken the whole piled life of that thunderhead of the afternoon. "That first clap," it was later called by everyone who spoke of being awakened when the storm broke. Noonie sat up, and called out. He answered her.

"Oh," she said, and sank back again on her pillow, now that he was home beside her.

Then came the torrent, and the wind. The house was trundled by the storm. There came sky after sky of lightning, and whole avenues of the thunder's bombards. And in a trice, everything was drenched. Everything drank and was slaked. The powers of the heavens slit their hanging bellies and the rain fell in lakes. Its roar upon the roof, the streets, the ground, was tremendous. It made as much fear as it did joy. Now that delivery was come, save us, save us from the deluge!—this whisper of racial memory coursed in the hurried blood. But to be grasped all such natural forces had to come into scale with human beings, with a single one.

"Peter," she cried, and turned toward him. She was trembling. She sought him in the darkness, in that first moment of the storm's release. He comforted her, and they waited for the next crash together. When it came, he hugged her tightly, and when its echo caverned off up the street, he said,

"Just listen to it rain! We've waited a long time for this!"

She whispered that it made her afraid.

"There is nothing to be afraid of. I only hope it will rain all night. The lightning will spend itself soon. Then it will pour and pour."

They listened and waited tensely for the thunder, in the darkness, in which the cooled air moved over them.

But no thunder came yet, and she laid her hand on his cheek, and told him that what she had tried to say that afternoon, when Don would not leave them alone for a moment, was that after so many years, and all that fear, and helpless sorrow, now she had conceived a child again.

He laid his head heavily into the hollow of her shoulder and then they were both shaken again by a bout of thunder, and it seemed like their storm, come to tell them something, for the way all things took the meaning of their own lives once again.

His heart bounded back at the thunder like an answer. He exulted and felt confirmed. He told her everything she desired to hear from him, though with no new words to do it in. It didn't matter. She heard him truly. They lay listening to the rain in the darkness. The flashes were moving away now, and the thunder was rumbling farther away, over against the mountains. The downpour had turned steady, after the swiping gusts of the first wind.

A moment later the phone rang, and he said he had to answer it. She called to him as he went, to look in on Donnie, and see if he was all right. The call was from the hospital. A number of the patients were disturbed by the storm, but especially the old man he had been with all evening. The crashes frightened him. He was fighting the storm. What could they do? The Doctor authorized a weak dose of morphine. Let the old man sleep. Let him cheat the terrors of the storm that was walking tremendously back to the mountains. The nurse herself sounded grateful for a word of order, of decision, from the Doctor.

All over town there were minds awake with gratitude and alarm. Lights turned on for a little while as householders checked their property in the downpour. The earthen streets ran with little rivers. The night sounds of the city were engulfed by the washing of the rain. Nobody heard the switch engines plying the tracks . . . that sound which for generations had been woven into the texture of sleep in the wide valley. Was that a fire engine bamming and sirening its way up some street in the other part of town? The lightning had set something afire. Or did the rain ring with such portents upon the streets that all imaginations came alive to its power and promise?

Peter hung up the receiver and went down the hall to the sleeping porch where his son Donald slept. He cautiously opened the door from the hall, and let the light spill past him. The rain was misting in through the screens, but no stream blew upon the bed where the boy was sound asleep. He hadn't even stirred, not even the first clap had stirred him. He was sleeping almost energetically, his father thought, applying his whole self to it, as if to be suckled by dreams, to take huge restoration into his soul with his deep breaths. The bedcovers were like a relief map, a small mountain range made of the living hills and valleys of the young body. Like buildings built on that scrap of earth, five books lay scattered all about it. The whole sight was eloquent of a separate life. To see that it was safe was what the father went to do. He retreated softly back into the hall, and went back to the big front bedroom manned by love and thankfulness that his house was secure. It rained almost all night.

V

In the morning, he said he had a million things to do but even so, he stole a few minutes and drove out to the Barelas bridge to see if the river was running. Sure enough, when he got there, he saw the second life of the storm, coming down the river from all the tributaries of the hills, flowing under the bridge, bending superbly to the curve and the sand islands—a long run of water from the mountains brown with earth and bright with sunlight.

Afterword

This novel celebrates affirmations in life appropriate to different levels of age, and it speaks also of two backgrounds which correspond to those of my own life—the green country of my early memories of New York state, and the bare desert and blue mountain rock of New Mexico. The thread which weaves in and out of all these materials is the love of Peter Rush, the central character, for his native earth and its human history. How he sees these and feels about them provides the sustaining emotion of the book, with its several intertwined stories.

The contrasts between the life which I left in the East and that which I found in the Southwest were great. I have ever since belonged to both East and West, for different interests, which is primarily why I do not consider myself a "regional" writer.

I was born in Buffalo, New York (not Buffalo, Texas, as a German publisher reported on a book jacket). My father, of Irish parentage, and my mother, of German, made through intelligence and industry on his part and spirited charm on hers a pleasant place for our family. Talent ran through both sides, with aunts and uncles and cousins who could draw or paint or sing or act or write. Life had comforts and graces, in all the accepted values of those days.

Buffalo, like other provincial cities then, had a lively culture—many concerts by the great musicians of the time, a theatrical season sustained by touring companies of the greatest actors, a first-rate resident stock company, several good libraries, admirable museums, like the Albright,—a general texture of cultivated social forms. As children we went to school at Miss Nardin's Academy, and swam at the Buffalo Club, and ice-skated at the Park Lake, and were sent weekly to Mr. Van Arnum's dancing school in the Twentieth Century Club ballroom where the boys wore patent leather pumps and the girls enormous satin sashes and hair ribbons and both wore white kid gloves. I was a violin student. Family tradition calmly holds that I got as far as the Tschaikovsky concerto, which I may doubt. Buffalo winters were fierce with blizzard or heavy with months of still gray light, summers were wilting with heat, and everybody went away—we, to a little island in an Adirondack lake. It was a sort of Scott Fitzgerald world for children—and in fact he had lived it in Buffalo only a few years before us.

The family destiny was suddenly changed when my father fell ill with tuberculosis. Doctors then ordered tubercular patients to high, dry climates. We came to Albuquerque, where we found very few of the flourishes which decorated the routine of life "back East." There was not even a violin teacher to carry me further into Tschaikovsky. In more serious wants, there was, for our family, no longer that sense of confident, ever-expanding achievement in the world's values which my father had worked so hard to obtain—so hard, in fact, that his effort cost him his health, and, too soon, his life. Other values must be found.

After a year or so of getting used to the swift and amazing change in the conditions of my boyhood environment, the values I began to absorb had to do with the vast land and its great river nearby, the mountains off there, and the golden sunlight that seemed to hold the past as well as the present in its power of revelation. Because the land was so vacant, and its forms so huge and abiding, it seemed that what men and women had enacted there long ago could still be seen if you looked hard enough with eyes closed, as it were. And if history did not tell enough about what people did in that land, then what they did must instead be invented. Among other of my fictions, *The Common Heart* illustrates this notion.

A novelist often imagines that persons whose likeness he draws from life are sure to be immune from recognition. I felt so about Mary Carmichael, my novelist in this story, who comes to stay in Albuquerque long enough for her and Peter Rush to fall in love. I did her portrait from an actual lady I knew slightly and respected fully as one of the best novelists of my time. None of the things told about Molly Carmichael in the book happened just so in real life to the lady I had in mind. Since I tried only to suggest her presence and her character in circumstances which I invented, I was comfortably certain nobody would recognize her. This lasted until the agreeable day when I first met the poet and critic Winfield Townley Scott in Santa Fe.

"Tell me," he said very soon after our introduction over lunch, "isn't Molly Carmichael really a portrait of —————— ?"—naming the lady I meant.

I have never known whether to be uneasy over his penetration or pleased at my success in catching someone to the life.